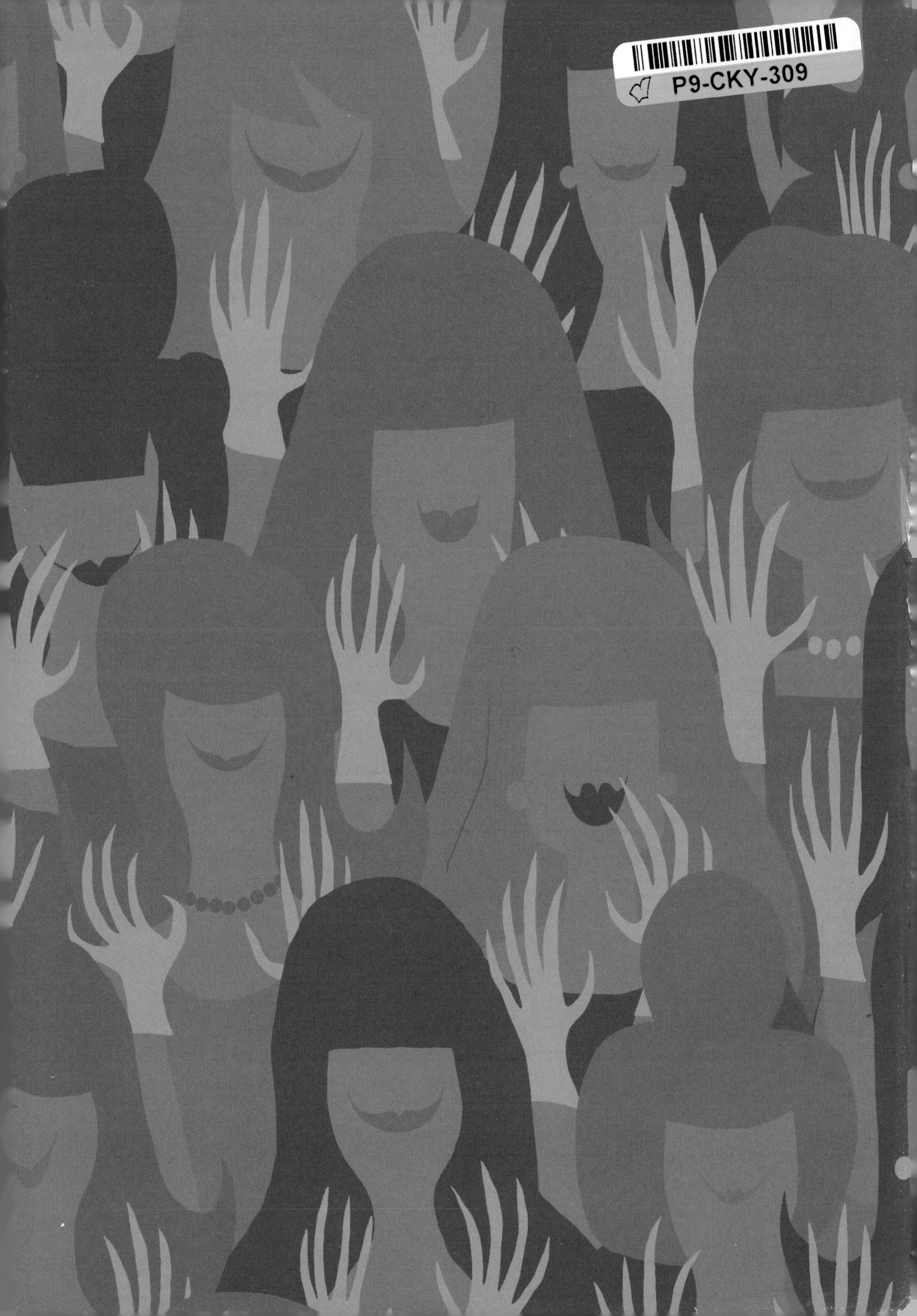

LAS BRUJAS

Papel certificado por el Forest Stewardship Council®

MIXTO
Papel procedente de fuentes responsables
FSC® C117695

Primera edición: abril de 2020
Título original: *Sacrées Sorcières*

Printed in Spain – Impreso en España

ISBN: 978-84-204-4024-8
Depósito legal: B-1.718-2020

Maquetado en Punktokomo S. L.
Impreso en Gráficas 94, S.L.
Sant Quirze del Vallès (Barcelona)

AL40248

Penguin
Random House
Grupo Editorial

ROALD DAHL
LAS BRUJAS
PÉNÉLOPE BAGIEU

Traducción de Mariola Cortés

ALFAGUARA

A mi queridísima abuela.

P. B.

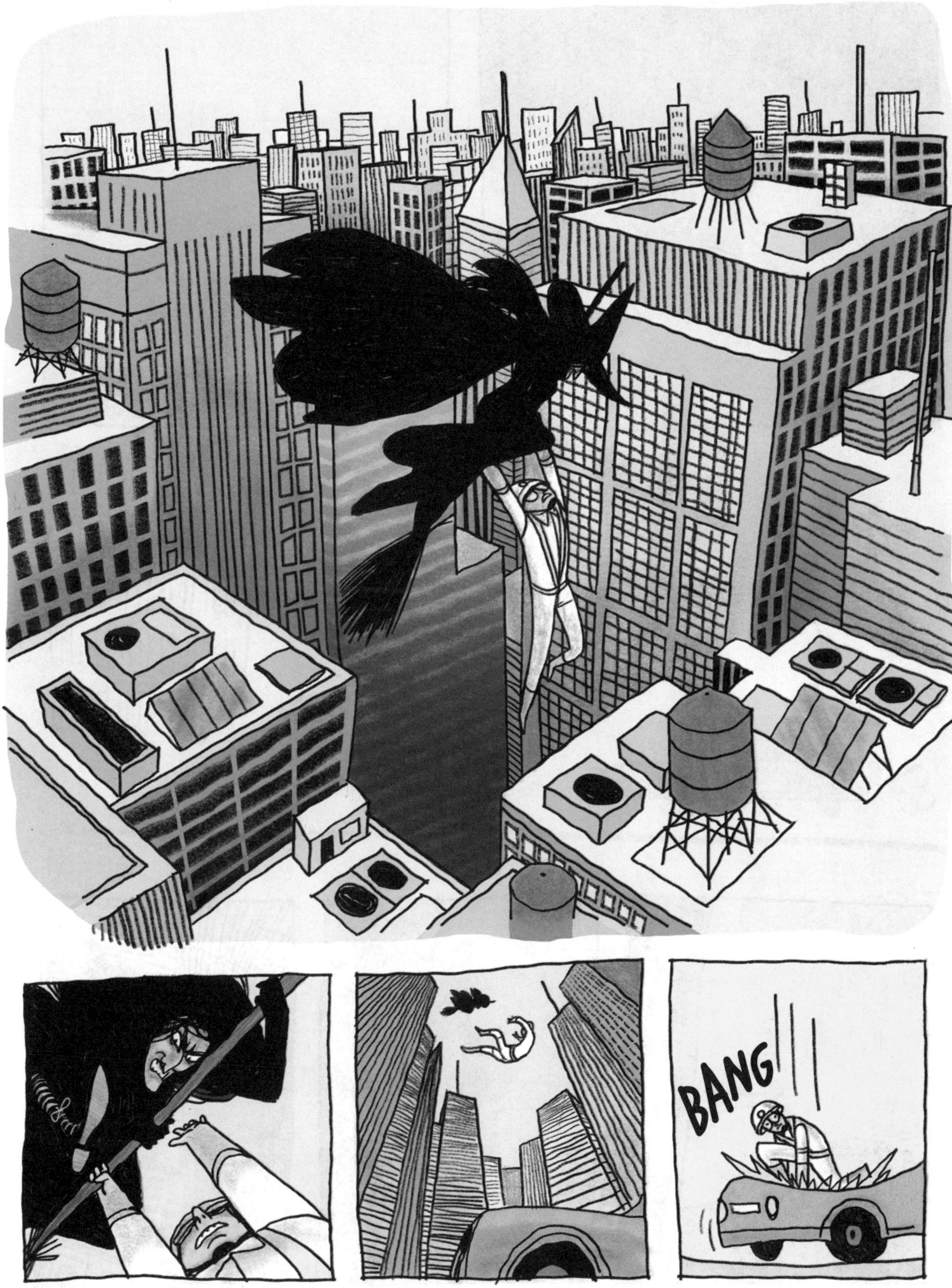
BANG

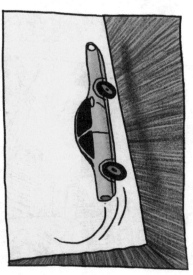

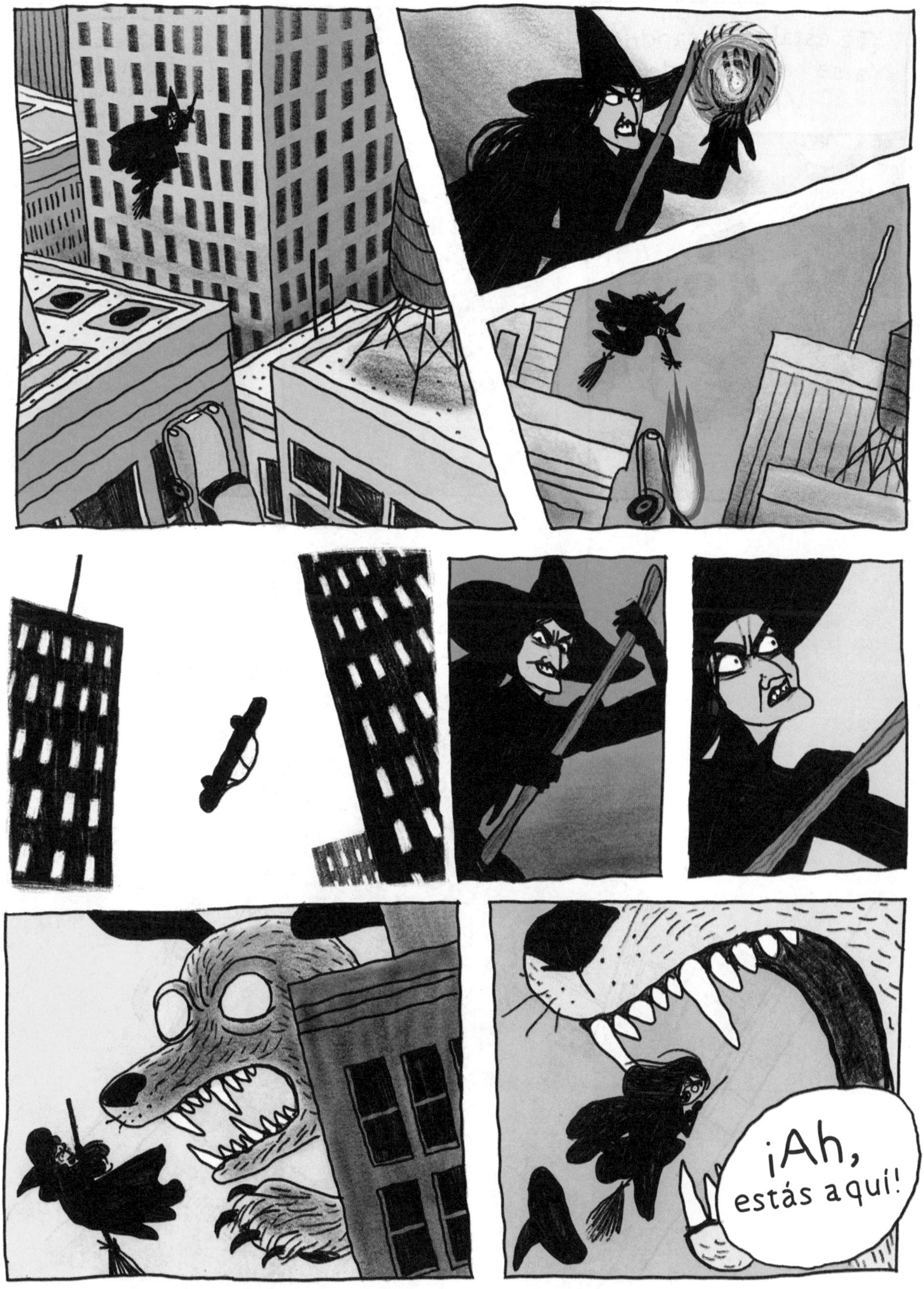
¡Ah, estás aquí!

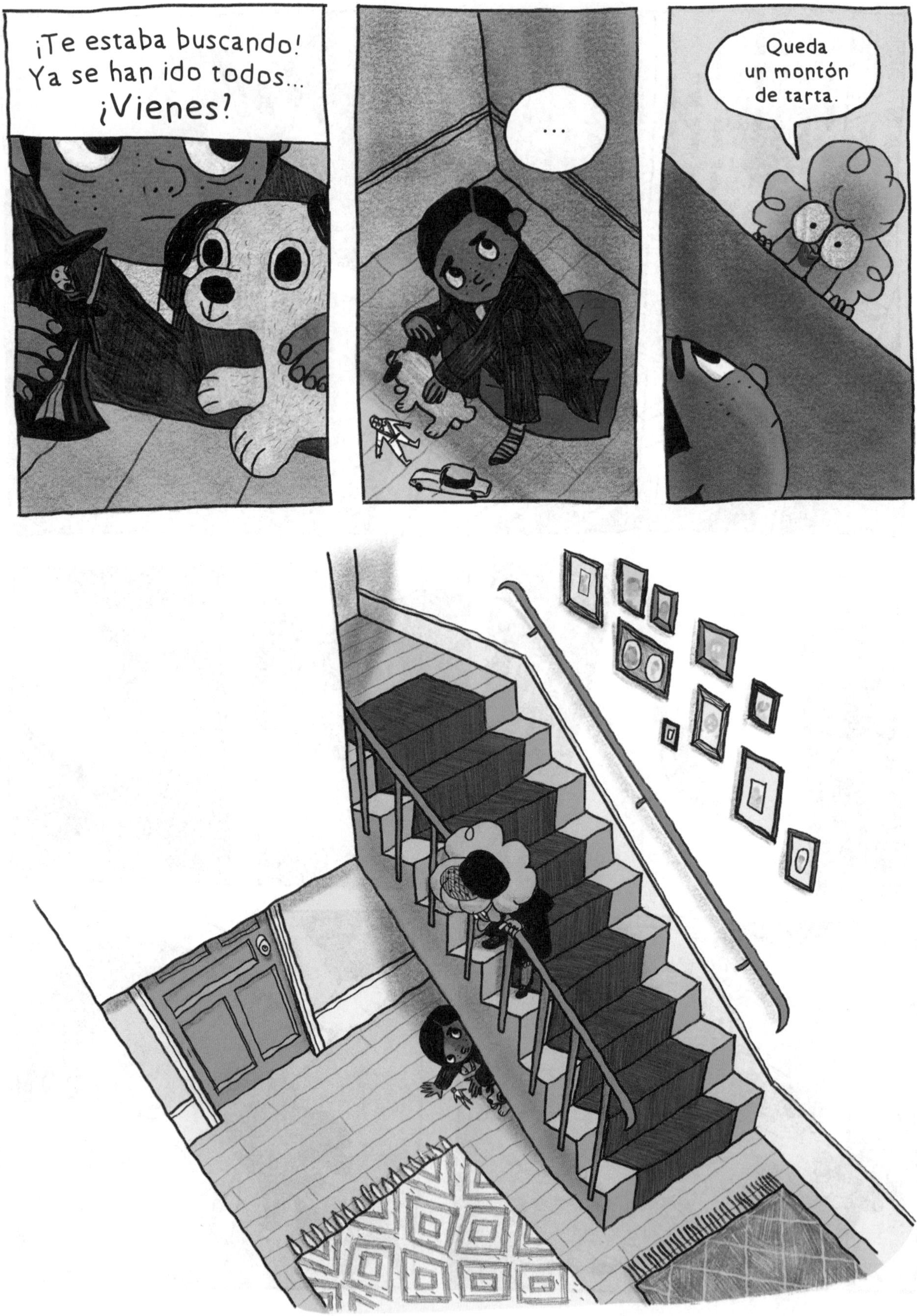
¡Te estaba buscando! Ya se han ido todos... ¡Vienes?
...
Queda un montón de tarta.

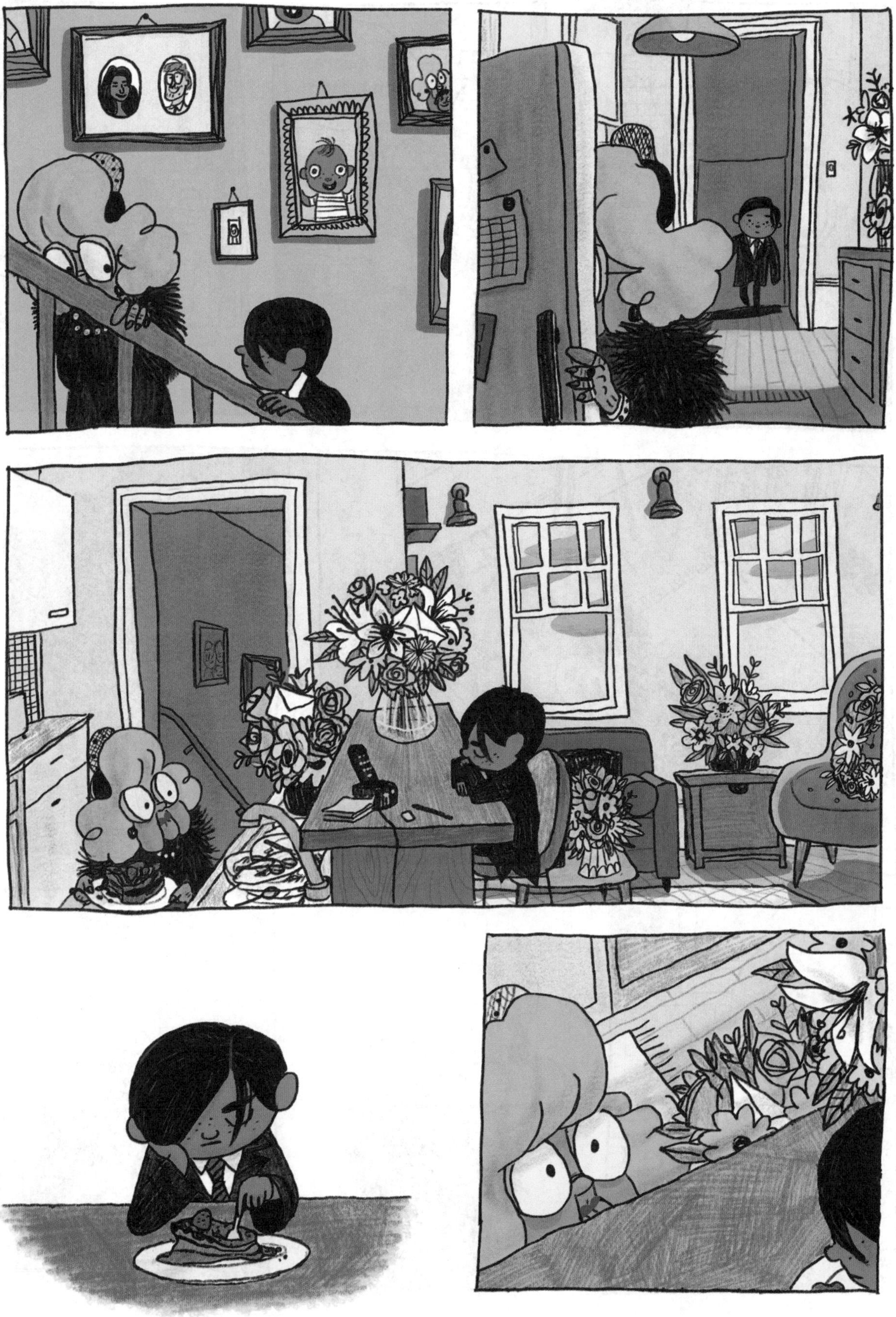

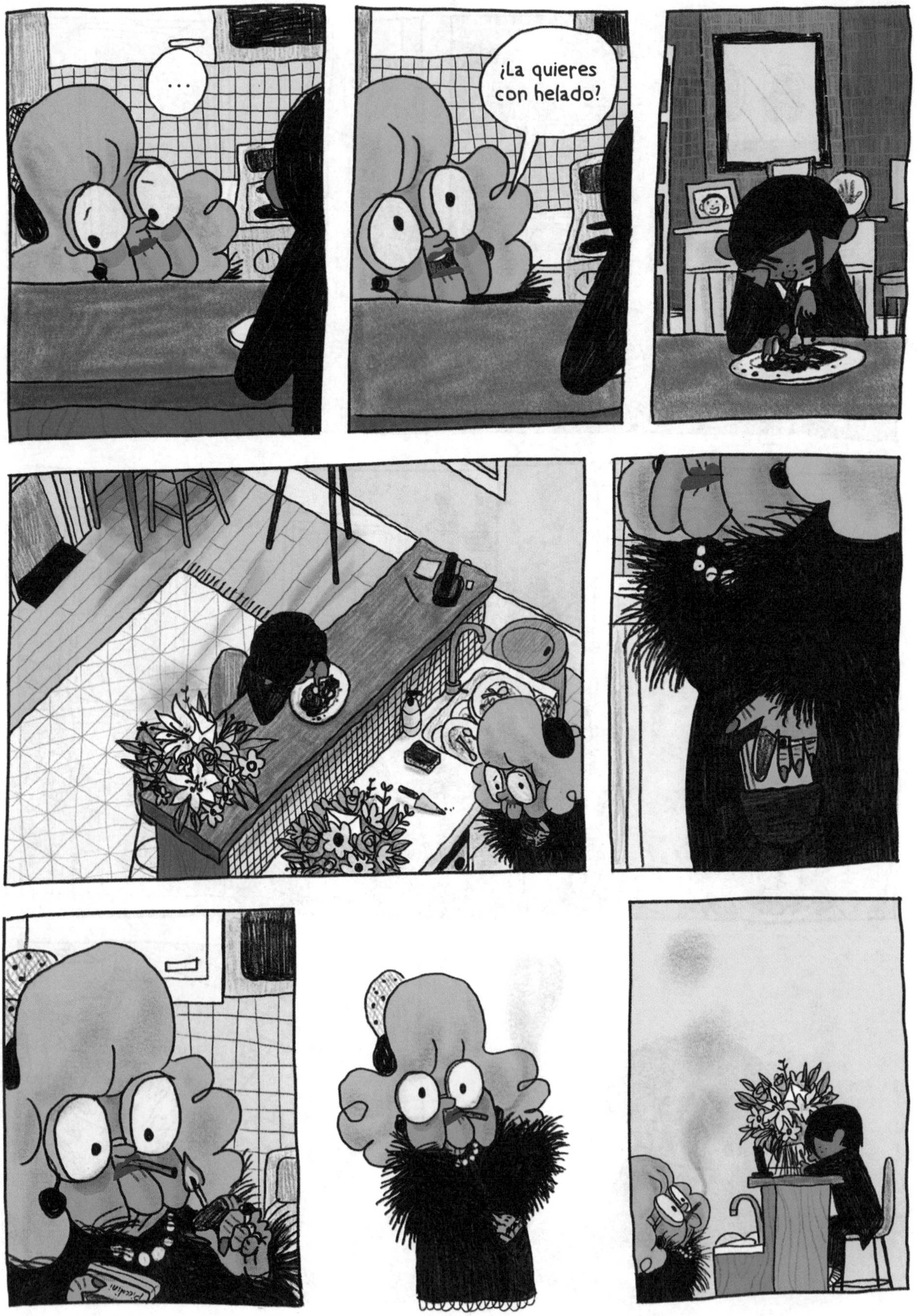
...
¿La quieres con helado?

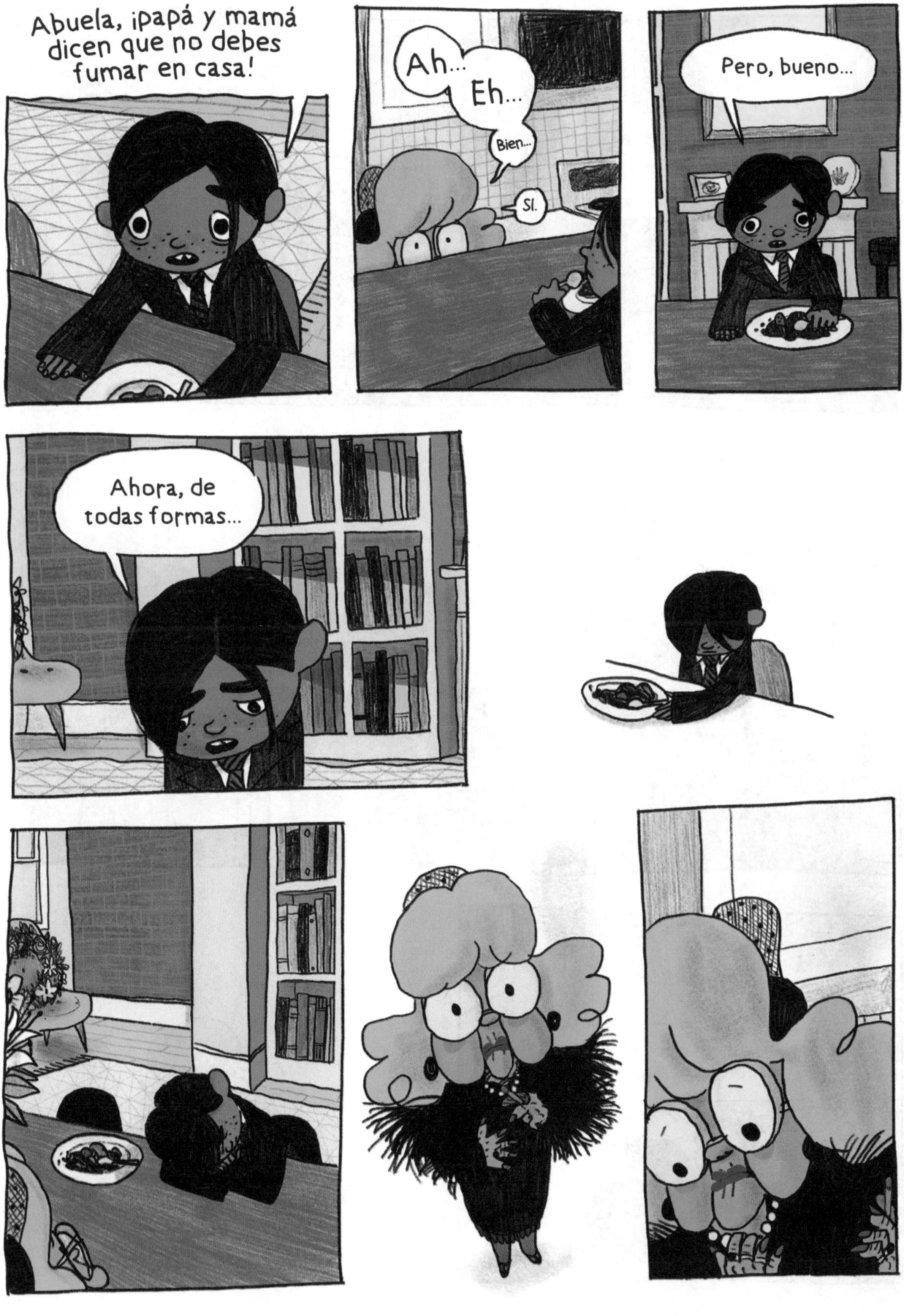

Abuela, ¡papá y mamá dicen que no debes fumar en casa!
Ah...
Eh...
Bien...
Sí.
Pero, bueno...
Ahora, de todas formas...

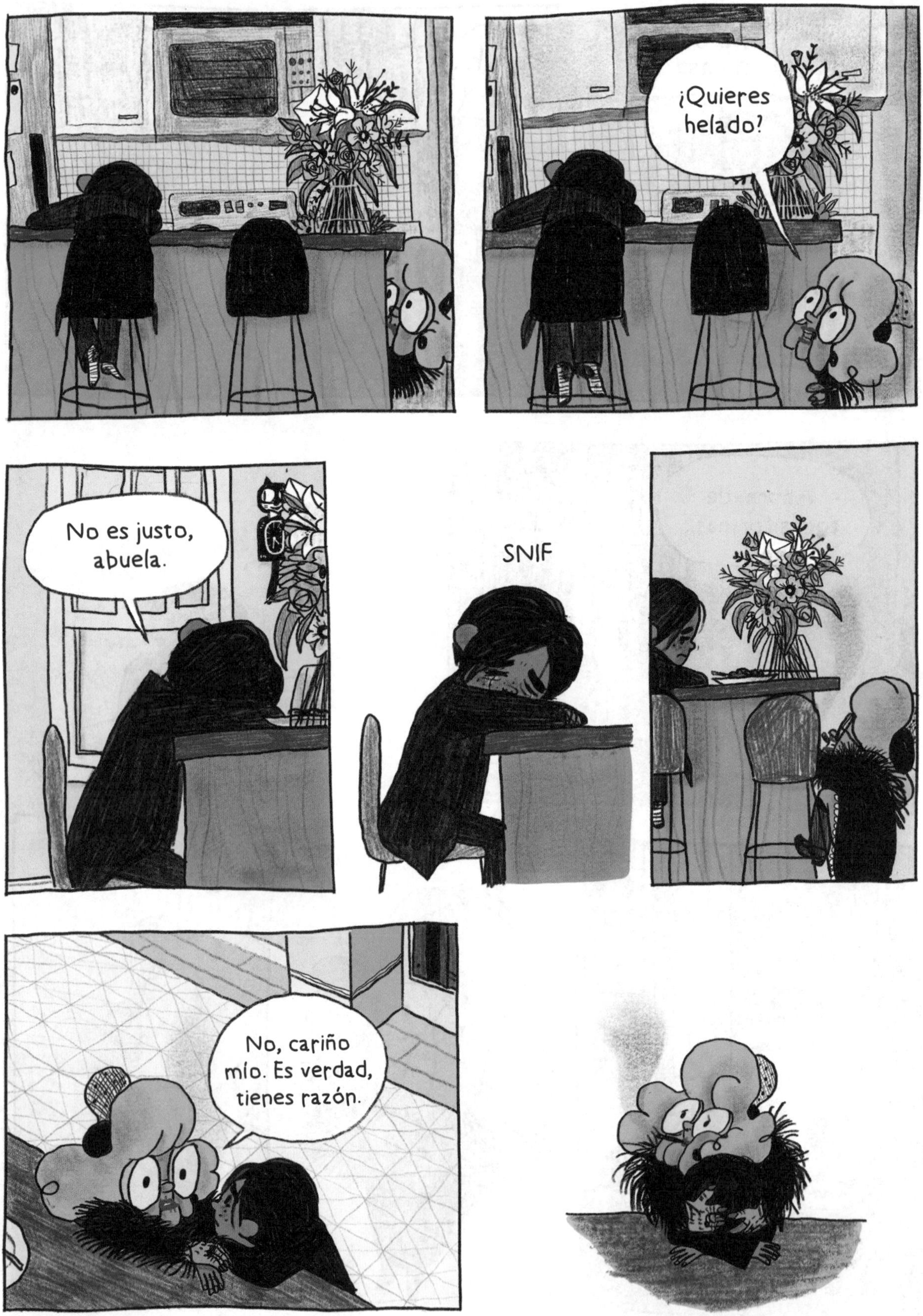

¡Quieres helado?
No es justo, abuela.
SNIF
No, cariño mío. Es verdad, tienes razón.

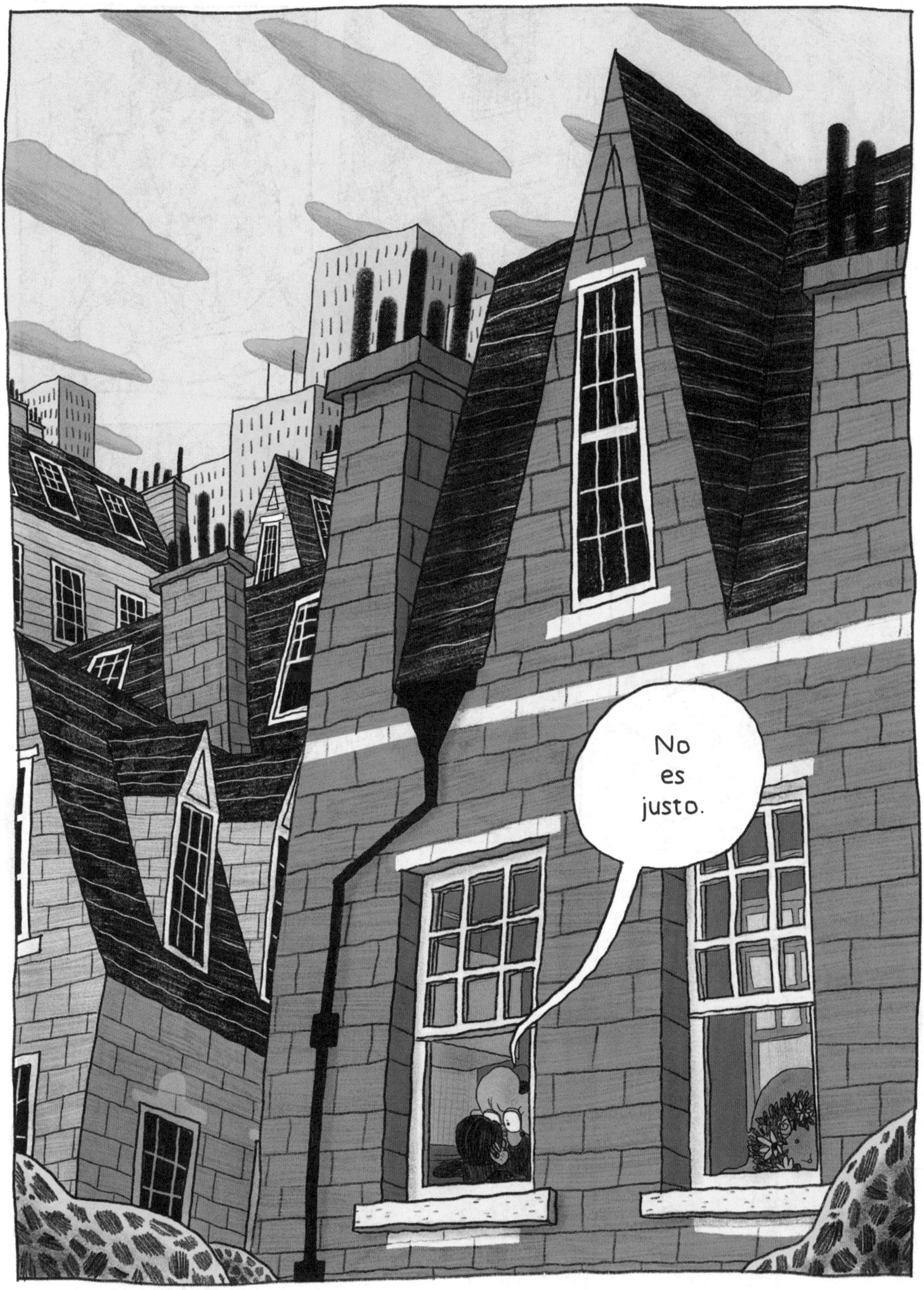
No es justo.

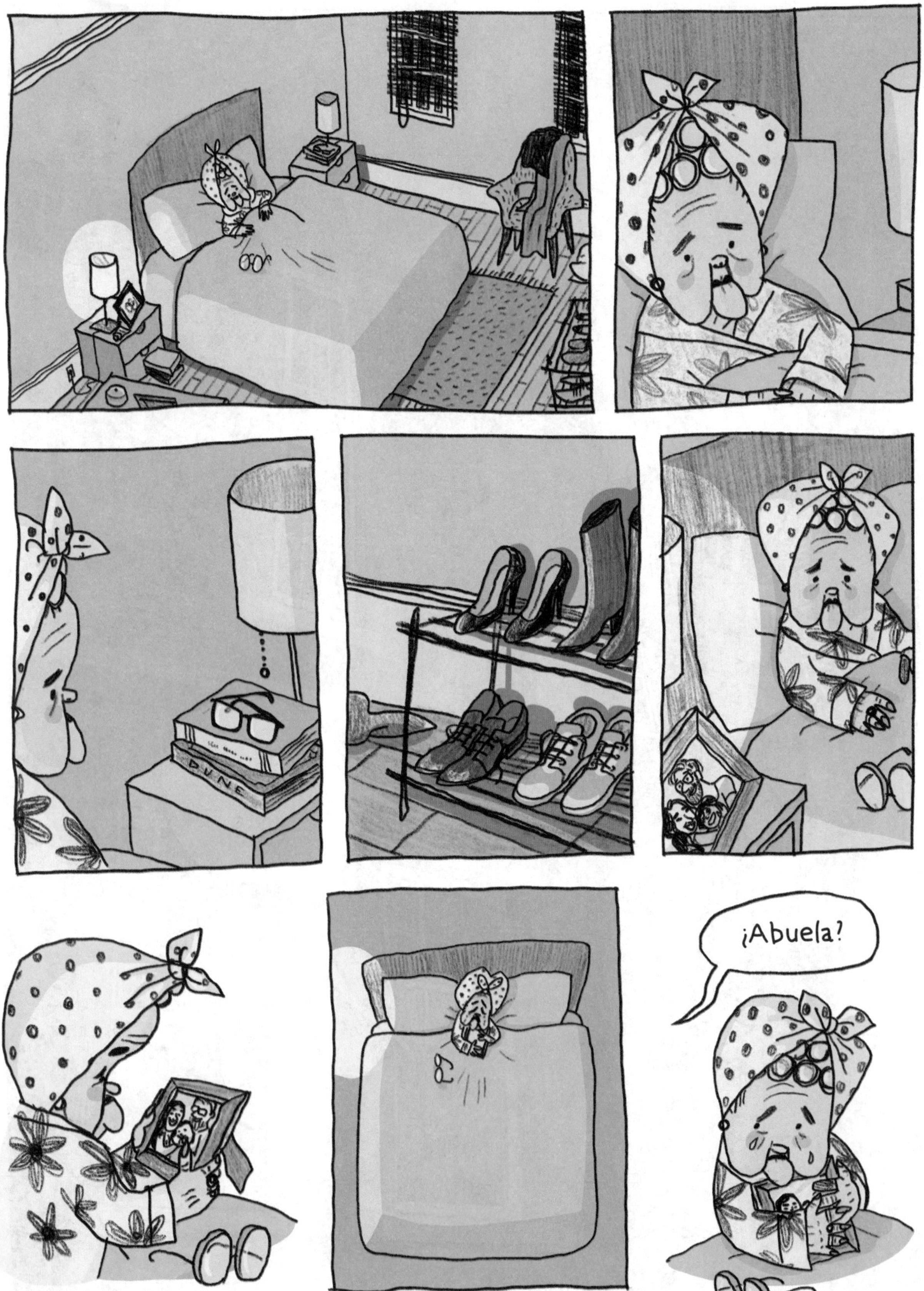
DUNE
¡Abuela?

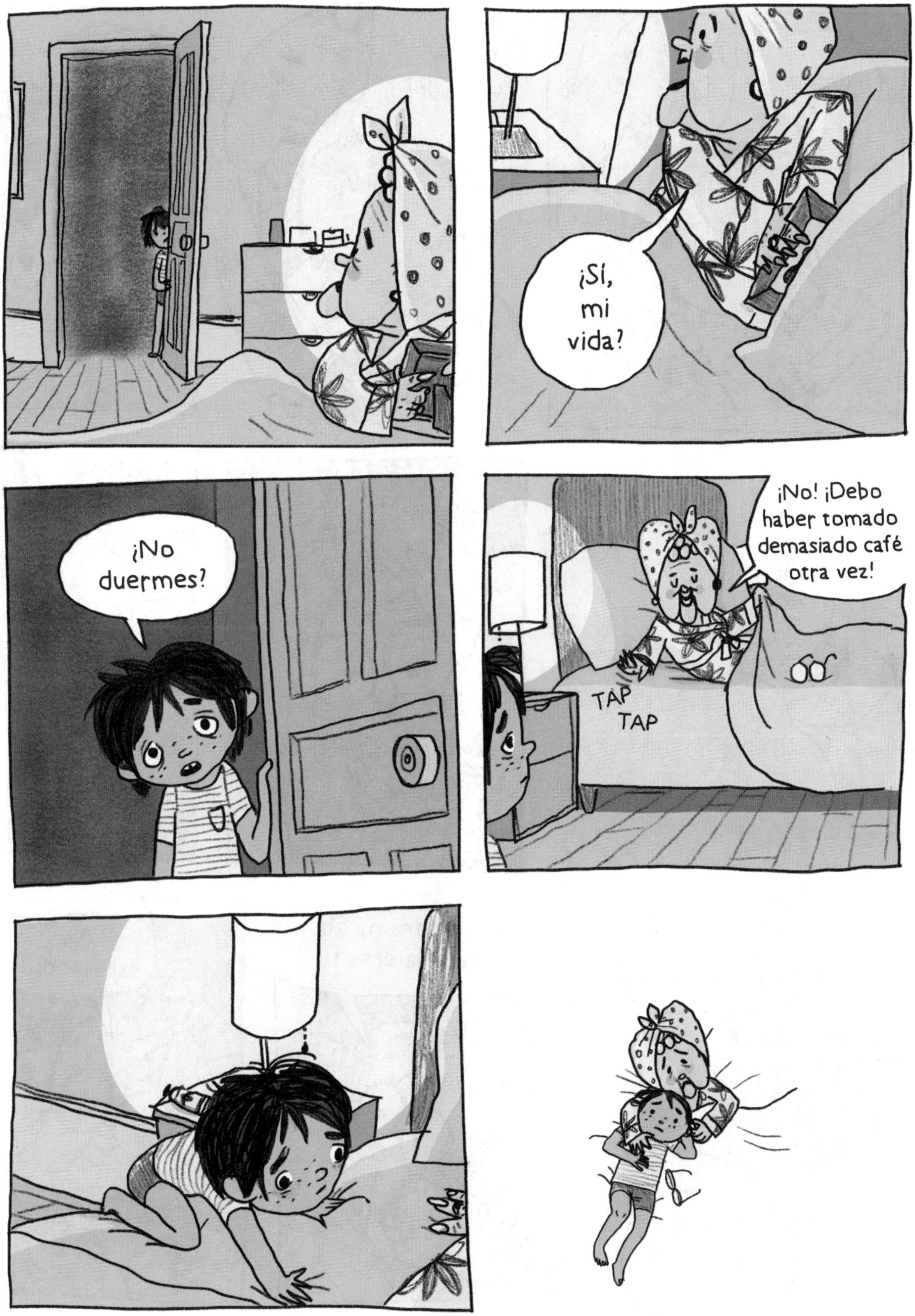
¡Sí, mi vida?
¡No duermes?
¡No! ¡Debo haber tomado demasiado café otra vez!
TAP TAP

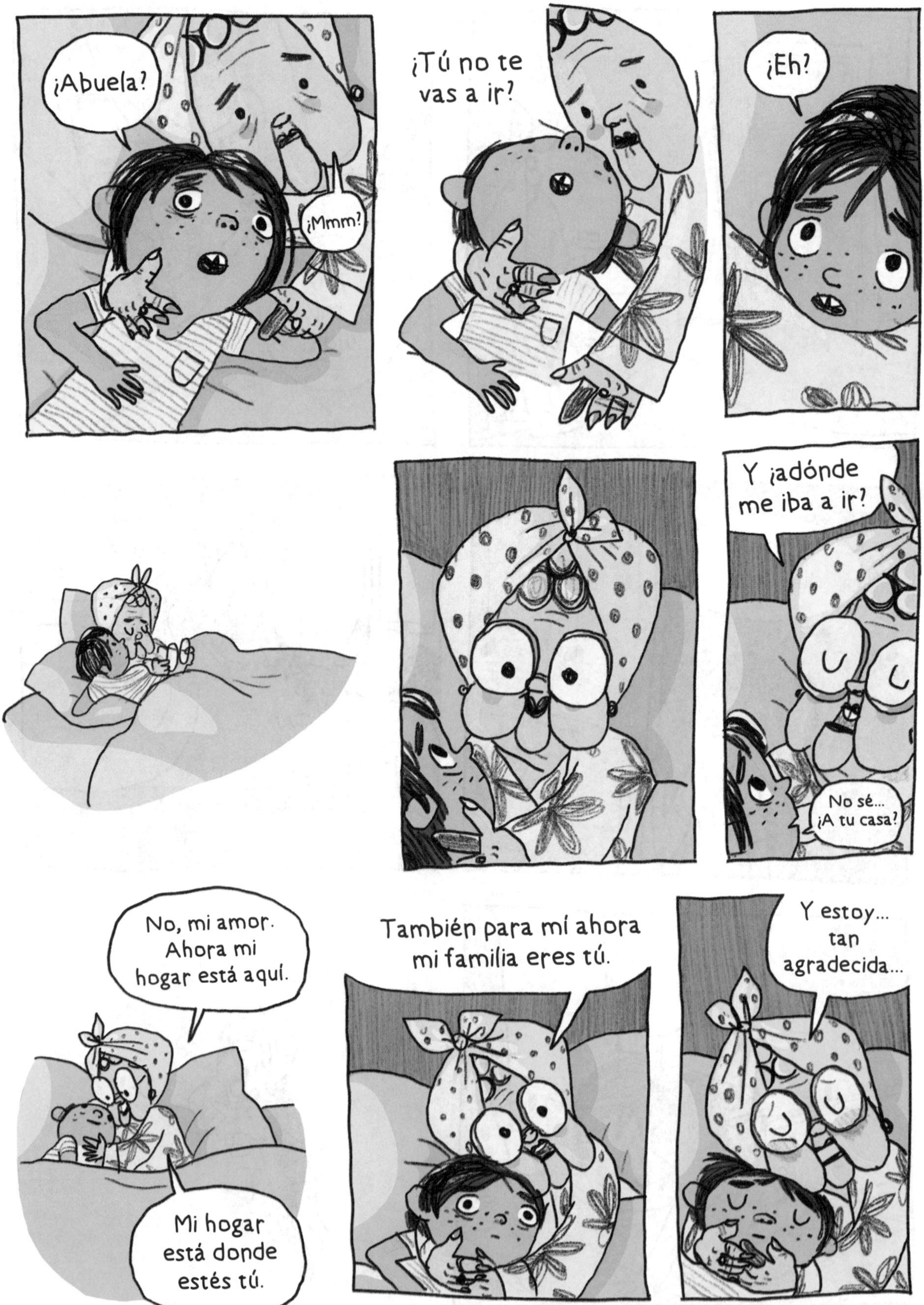
¡Abuela?
¡Mmm?
¡Tú no te vas a ir?
¡Eh?
Y ¡adónde me iba a ir?
No sé... ¡A tu casa?
No, mi amor. Ahora mi hogar está aquí.
Mi hogar está donde estés tú.
También para mí ahora mi familia eres tú.
Y estoy... tan agradecida...

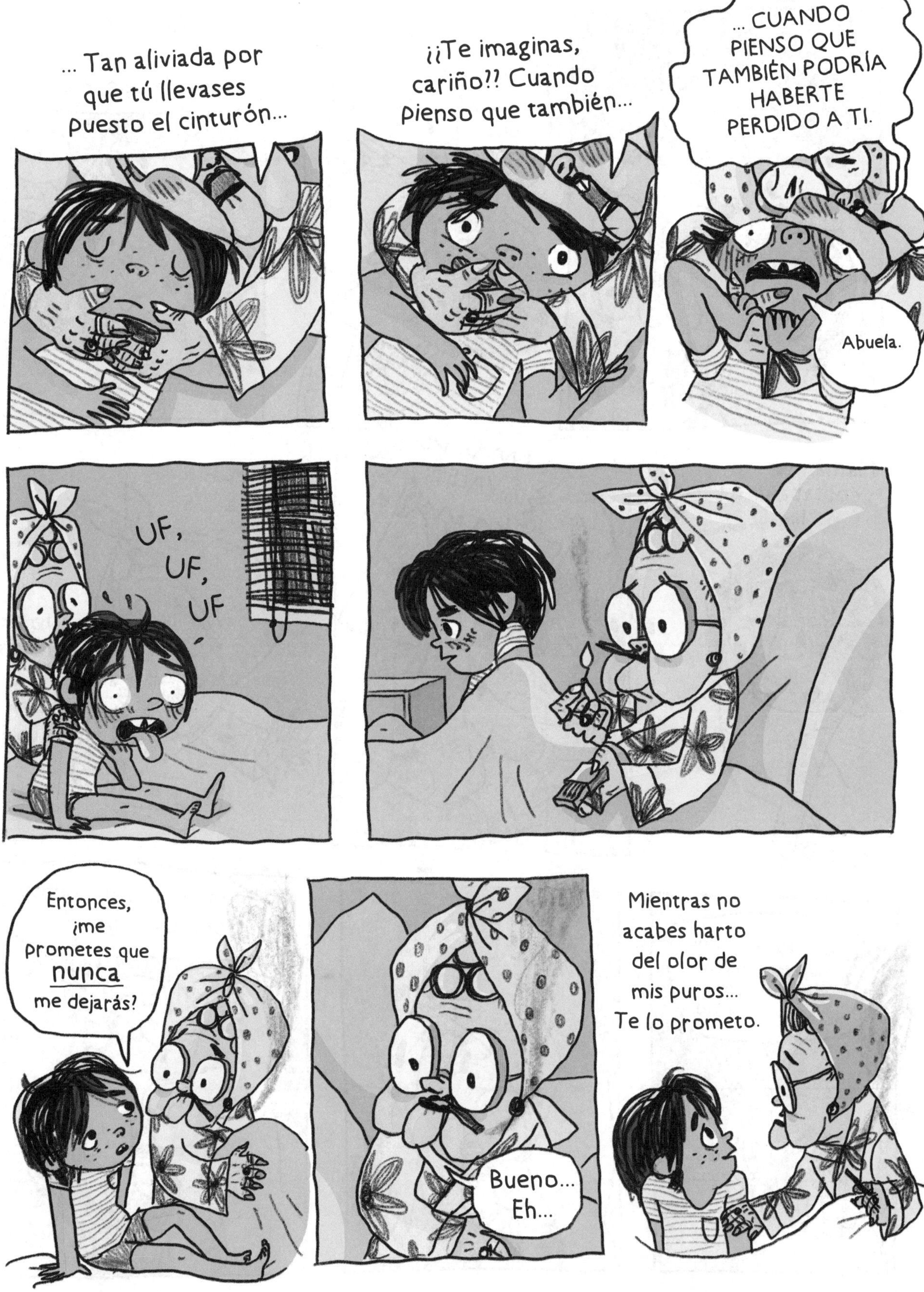
... Tan aliviada por que tú llevases puesto el cinturón...
¡¡Te imaginas, cariño?? Cuando pienso que también...
... CUANDO PIENSO QUE TAMBIÉN PODRÍA HABERTE PERDIDO A TI.
Abuela.
UF, UF, UF
Entonces, ¿me prometes que nunca me dejarás?
Bueno... Eh...
Mientras no acabes harto del olor de mis puros... Te lo prometo.

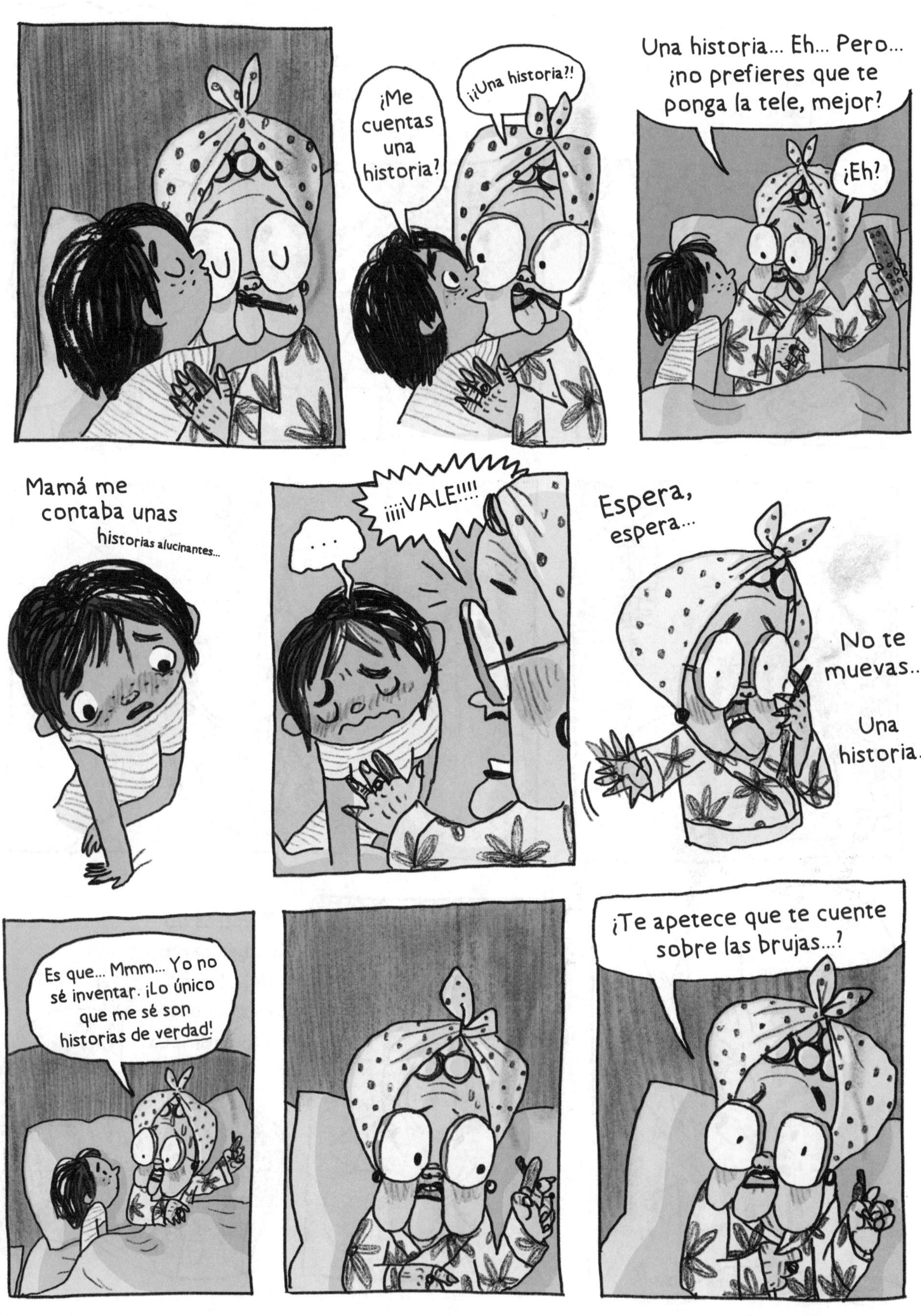

¿Me cuentas una historia?
¡¿Una historia?!
Una historia... Eh... Pero... ¿no prefieres que te ponga la tele, mejor?
¿Eh?
Mamá me contaba unas historias alucinantes...
...
¡¡¡¡VALE!!!!
Espera, espera...
No te muevas...
Una historia.
Es que... Mmm... Yo no sé inventar. ¡Lo único que me sé son historias de verdad!
¿Te apetece que te cuente sobre las brujas...?

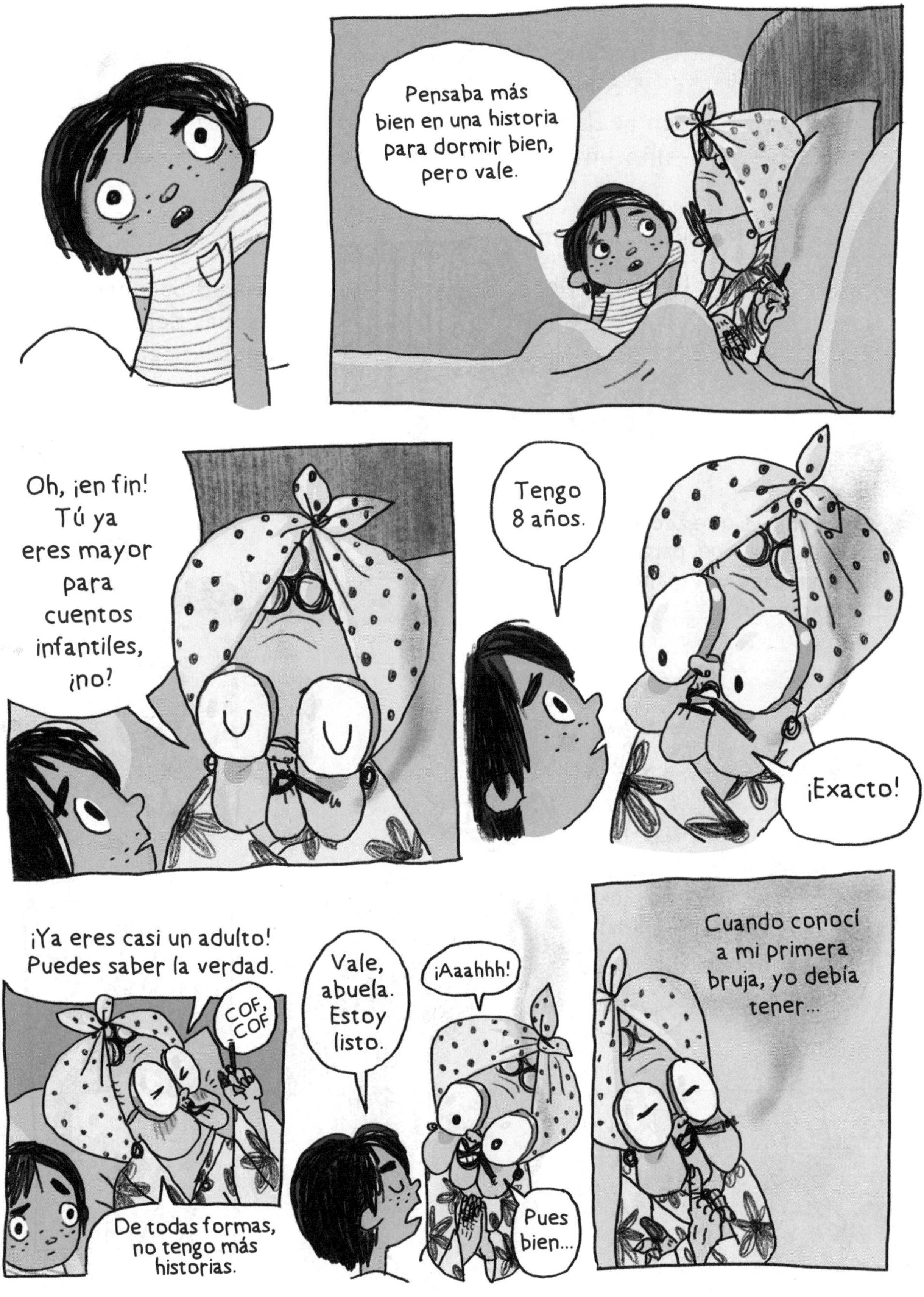

Pensaba más bien en una historia para dormir bien, pero vale.
Oh, ¡en fin! Tú ya eres mayor para cuentos infantiles, ¿no?
Tengo 8 años.
¡Exacto!
¡Ya eres casi un adulto! Puedes saber la verdad.
COF, COF
De todas formas, no tengo más historias.
Vale, abuela. Estoy listo.
¡Aaahhh!
Pues bien...
Cuando conocí a mi primera bruja, yo debía tener...

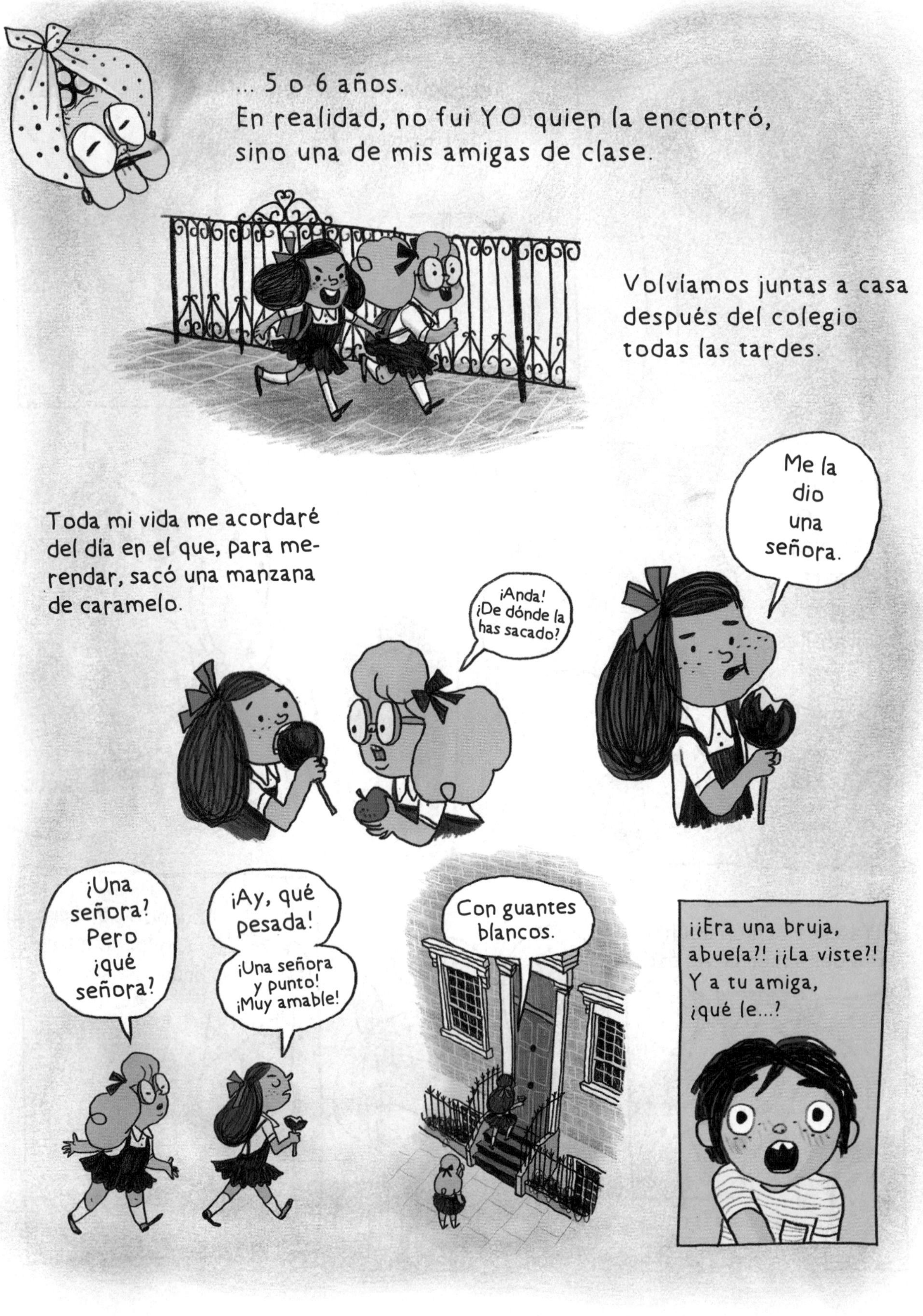
... 5 o 6 años.
En realidad, no fui YO quien la encontró, sino una de mis amigas de clase.
Volvíamos juntas a casa después del colegio todas las tardes.
Toda mi vida me acordaré del día en el que, para merendar, sacó una manzana de caramelo.
¡Anda! ¡De dónde la has sacado?
Me la dio una señora.
¡Una señora? Pero ¿qué señora?
¡Ay, qué pesada!
¡Una señora y punto! ¡Muy amable!
Con guantes blancos.
¡¿Era una bruja, abuela?! ¡¿La viste?! Y a tu amiga, ¿qué le...?

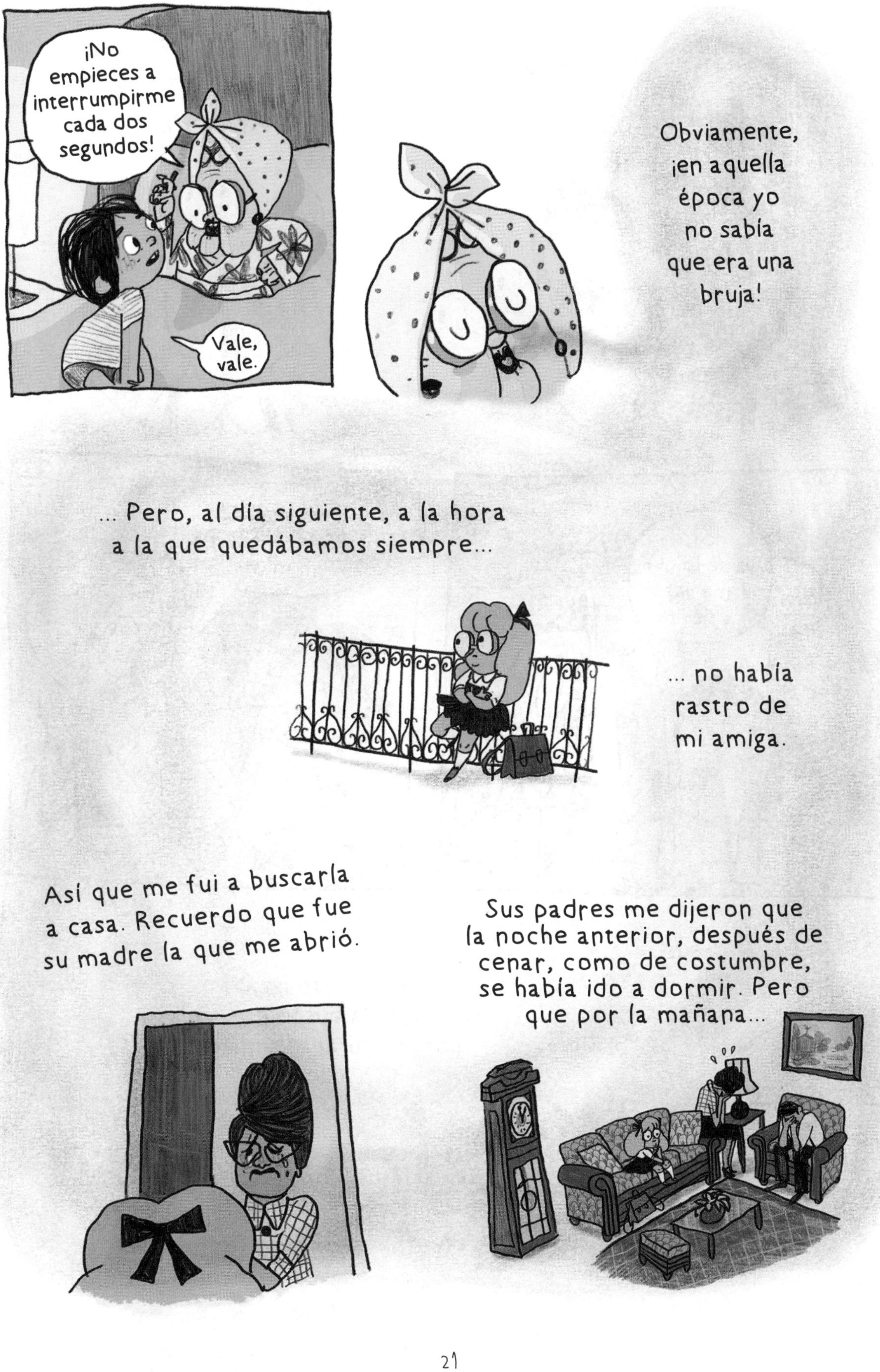

¡No empieces a interrumpirme cada dos segundos!
Vale, vale.
Obviamente, ¡en aquella época yo no sabía que era una bruja!
... Pero, al día siguiente, a la hora a la que quedábamos siempre...
... no había rastro de mi amiga.
Así que me fui a buscarla a casa. Recuerdo que fue su madre la que me abrió.
Sus padres me dijeron que la noche anterior, después de cenar, como de costumbre, se había ido a dormir. Pero que por la mañana...

... No estaba en su cama...

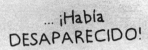

... ¡Había DESAPARECIDO!

Pero...

Sí, ya sé lo que me vas a decir:

«¡No se puede DESAPARECER sin más!».

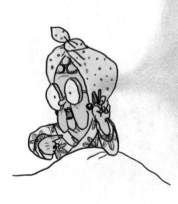

Pero mi amiga SÍ. La policía la buscó por todas partes, durante semanas.

Se había **volatilizado.**

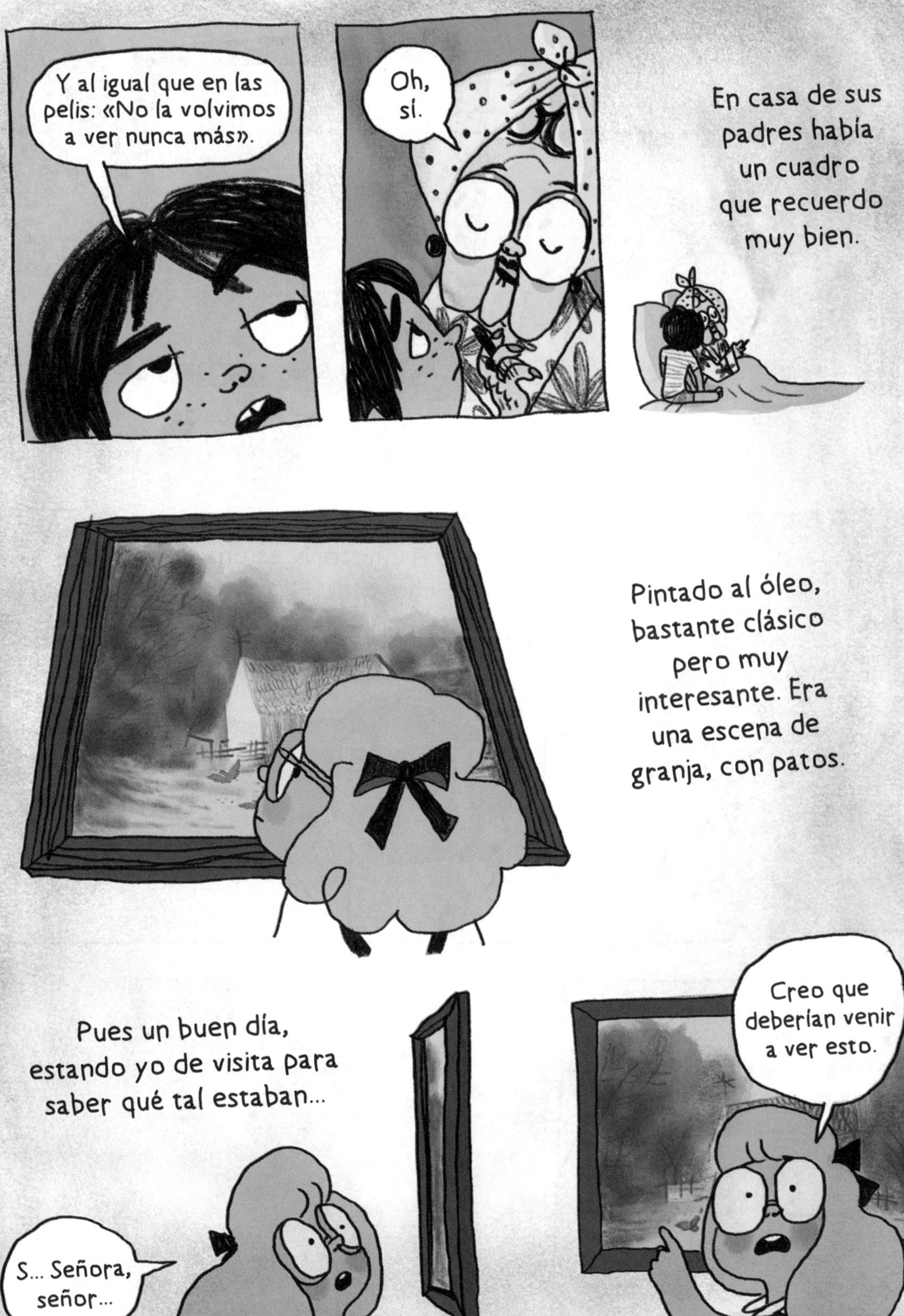
Y al igual que en las pelis: «No la volvimos a ver nunca más».
Oh, sí.
En casa de sus padres había un cuadro que recuerdo muy bien.
Pintado al óleo, bastante clásico pero muy interesante. Era una escena de granja, con patos.
Pues un buen día, estando yo de visita para saber qué tal estaban...
S... Señora, señor...
Creo que deberían venir a ver esto.

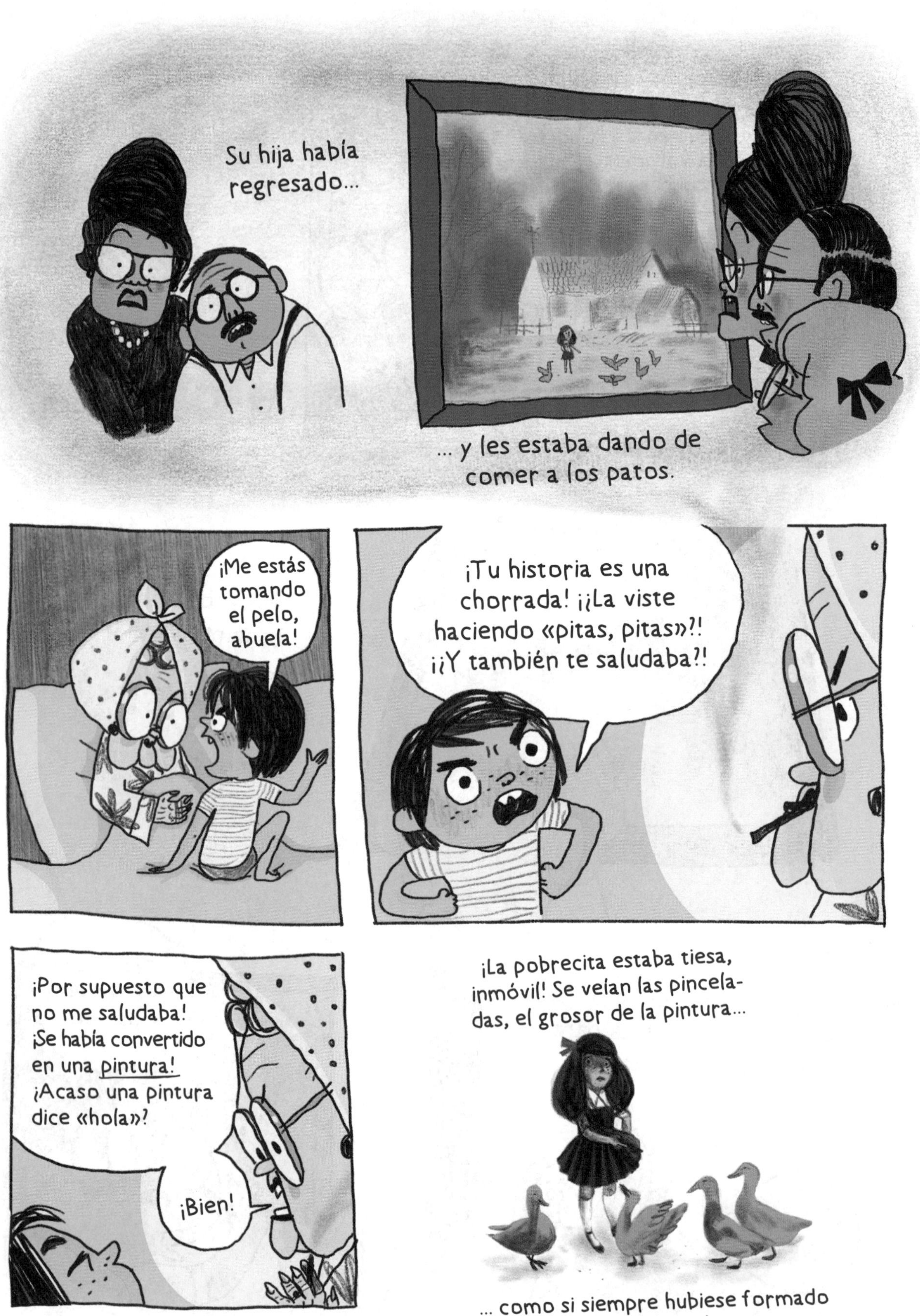
Su hija había regresado...
... y les estaba dando de comer a los patos.
¡Me estás tomando el pelo, abuela!
¡Tu historia es una chorrada! ¡¿La viste haciendo «pitas, pitas»?! ¡¿Y también te saludaba?!
¡Por supuesto que no me saludaba! ¡Se había convertido en una pintura! ¿Acaso una pintura dice «hola»?
¡Bien!
¡La pobrecita estaba tiesa, inmóvil! Se veían las pincela-das, el grosor de la pintura...
... como si siempre hubiese formado parte del cuadro.

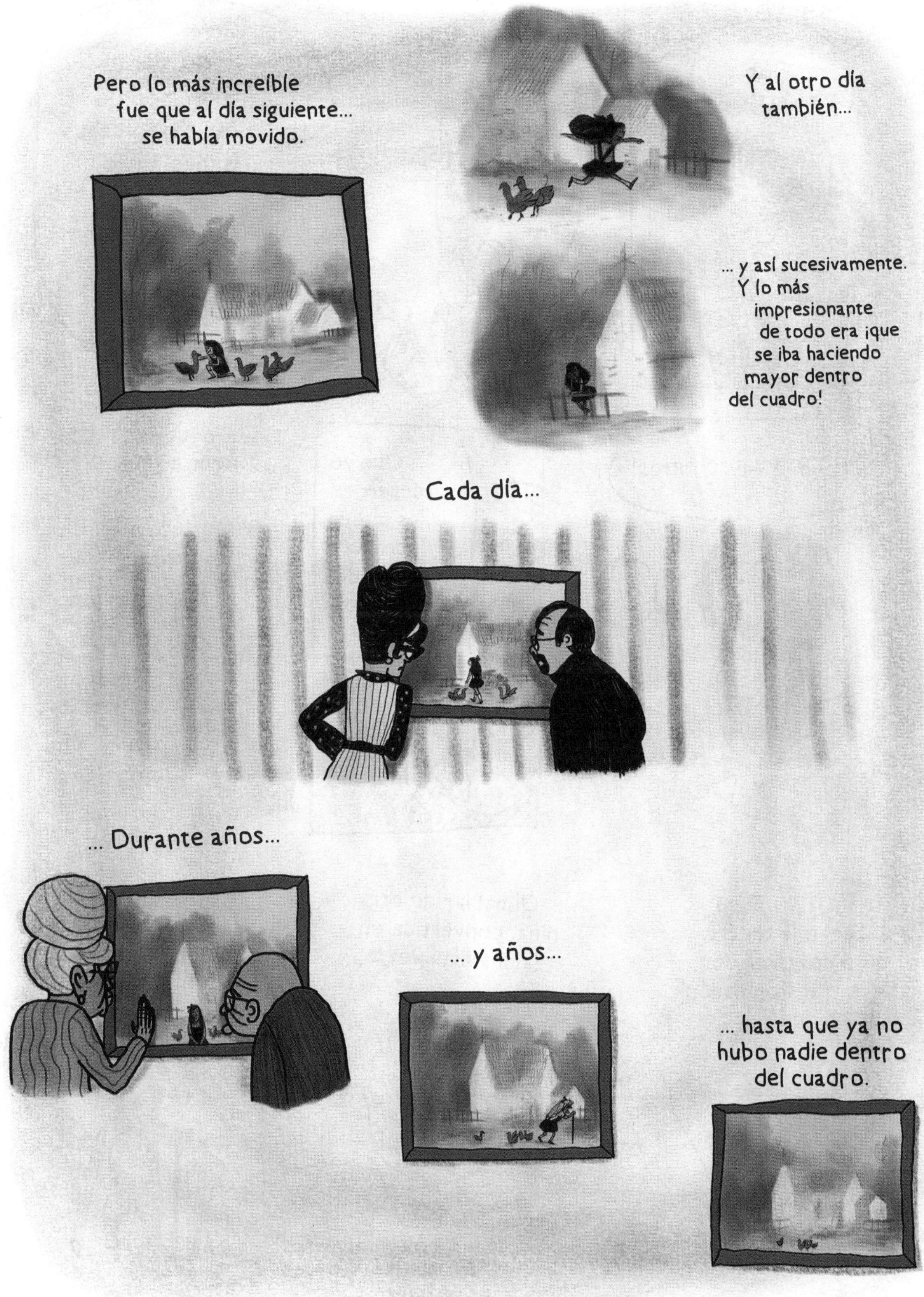

Pero lo más increíble fue que al día siguiente... se había movido.
Y al otro día también...
... y así sucesivamente. Y lo más impresionante de todo era ¡que se iba haciendo mayor dentro del cuadro!
Cada día...
... Durante años...
... y años...
... hasta que ya no hubo nadie dentro del cuadro.

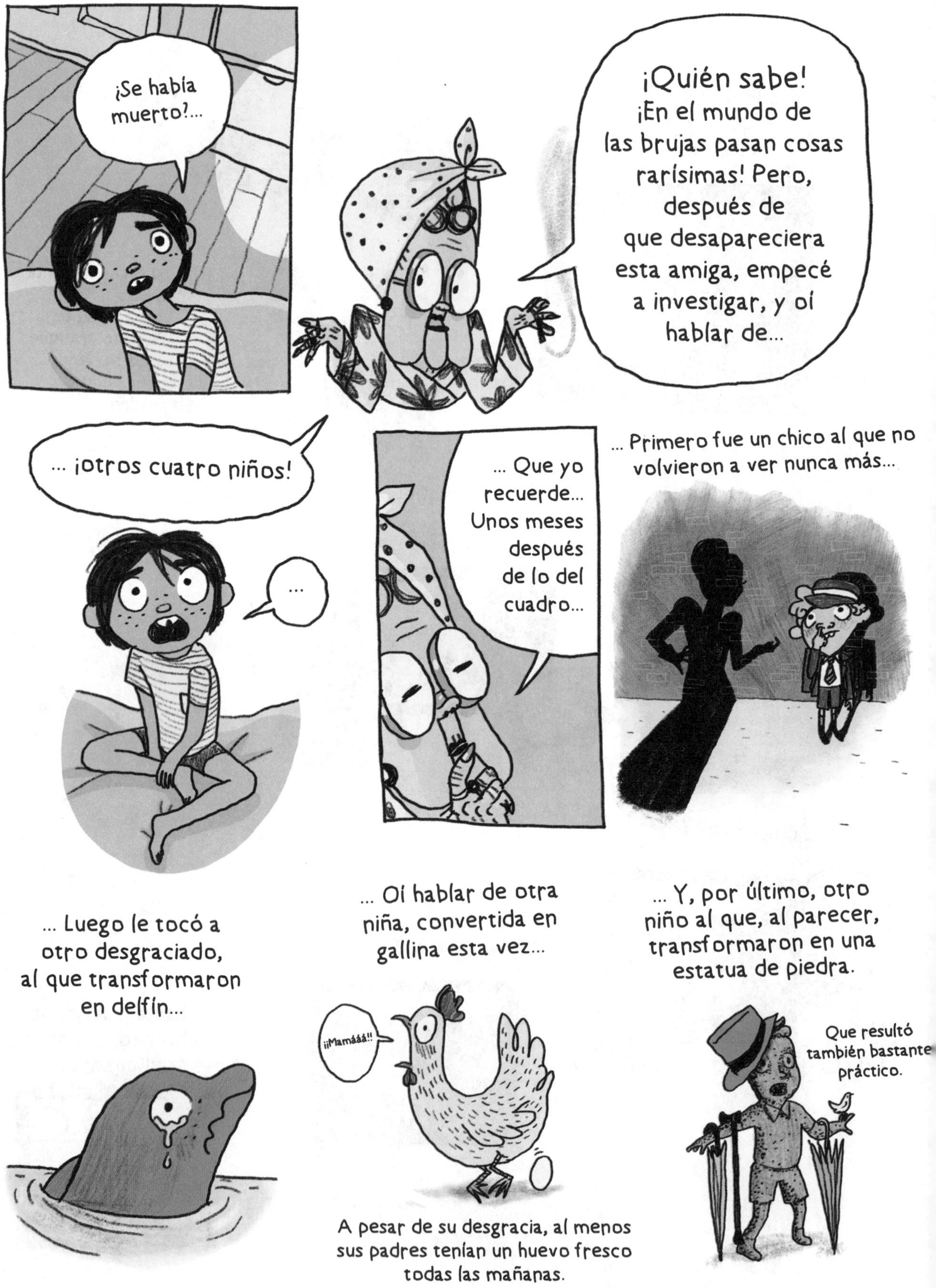

¿Se había muerto?...
¡Quién sabe! ¡En el mundo de las brujas pasan cosas rarísimas! Pero, después de que desapareciera esta amiga, empecé a investigar, y oí hablar de...
... ¡otros cuatro niños!
...
... Que yo recuerde... Unos meses después de lo del cuadro...
... Primero fue un chico al que no volvieron a ver nunca más...
... Luego le tocó a otro desgraciado, al que transformaron en delfín...
... Oí hablar de otra niña, convertida en gallina esta vez...
¡¡Mamááá!!
A pesar de su desgracia, al menos sus padres tenían un huevo fresco todas las mañanas.
... Y, por último, otro niño al que, al parecer, transformaron en una estatua de piedra.
Que resultó también bastante práctico.

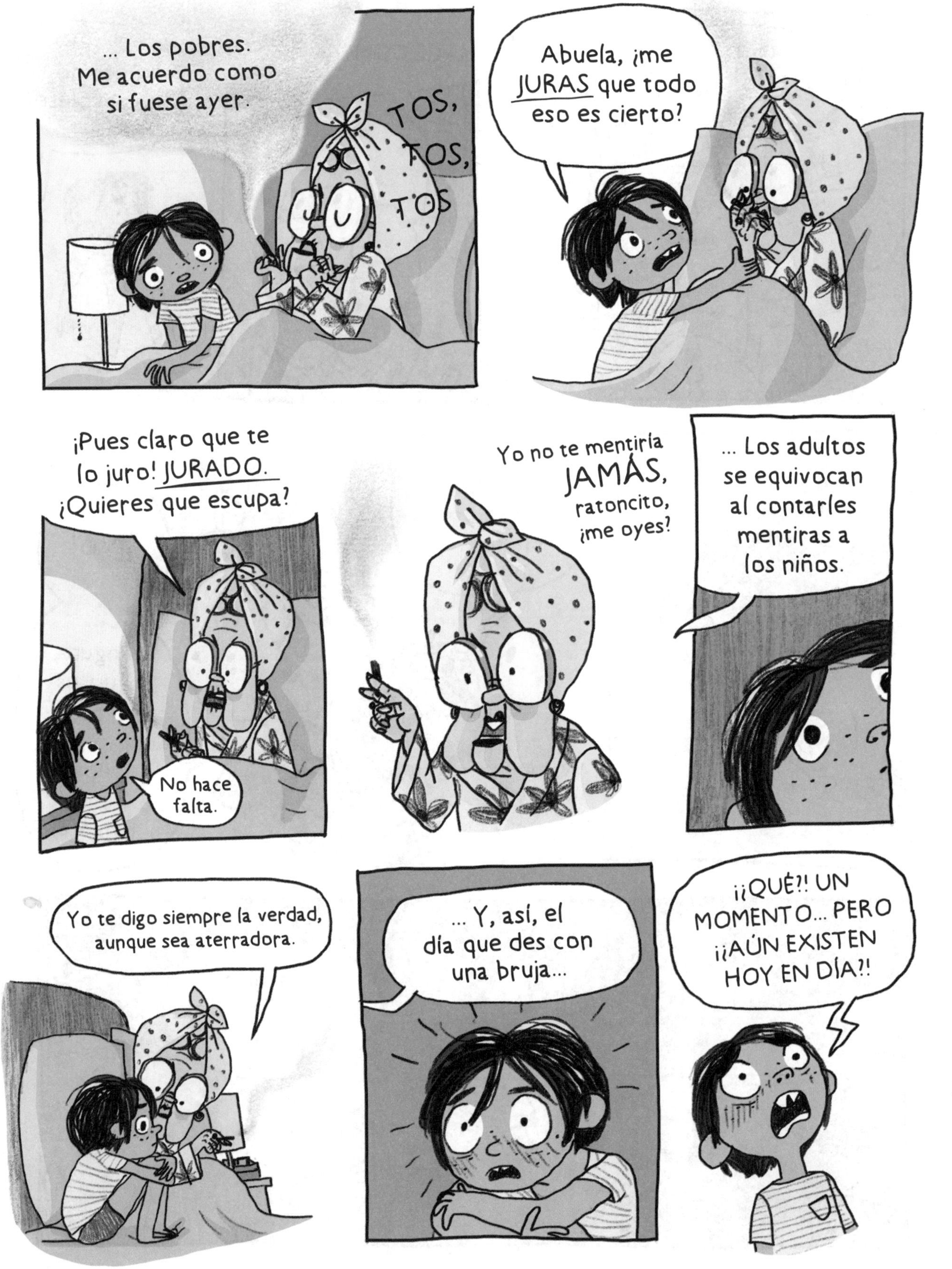
... Los pobres. Me acuerdo como si fuese ayer.
TOS, TOS, TOS
Abuela, ¡me JURAS que todo eso es cierto?
¡Pues claro que te lo juro! JURADO. ¿Quieres que escupa?
No hace falta.
Yo no te mentiría JAMÁS, ratoncito, ¡me oyes?
... Los adultos se equivocan al contarles mentiras a los niños.
Yo te digo siempre la verdad, aunque sea aterradora.
... Y, así, el día que des con una bruja...
¡¿QUÉ?! UN MOMENTO... PERO ¡¿AÚN EXISTEN HOY EN DÍA?!

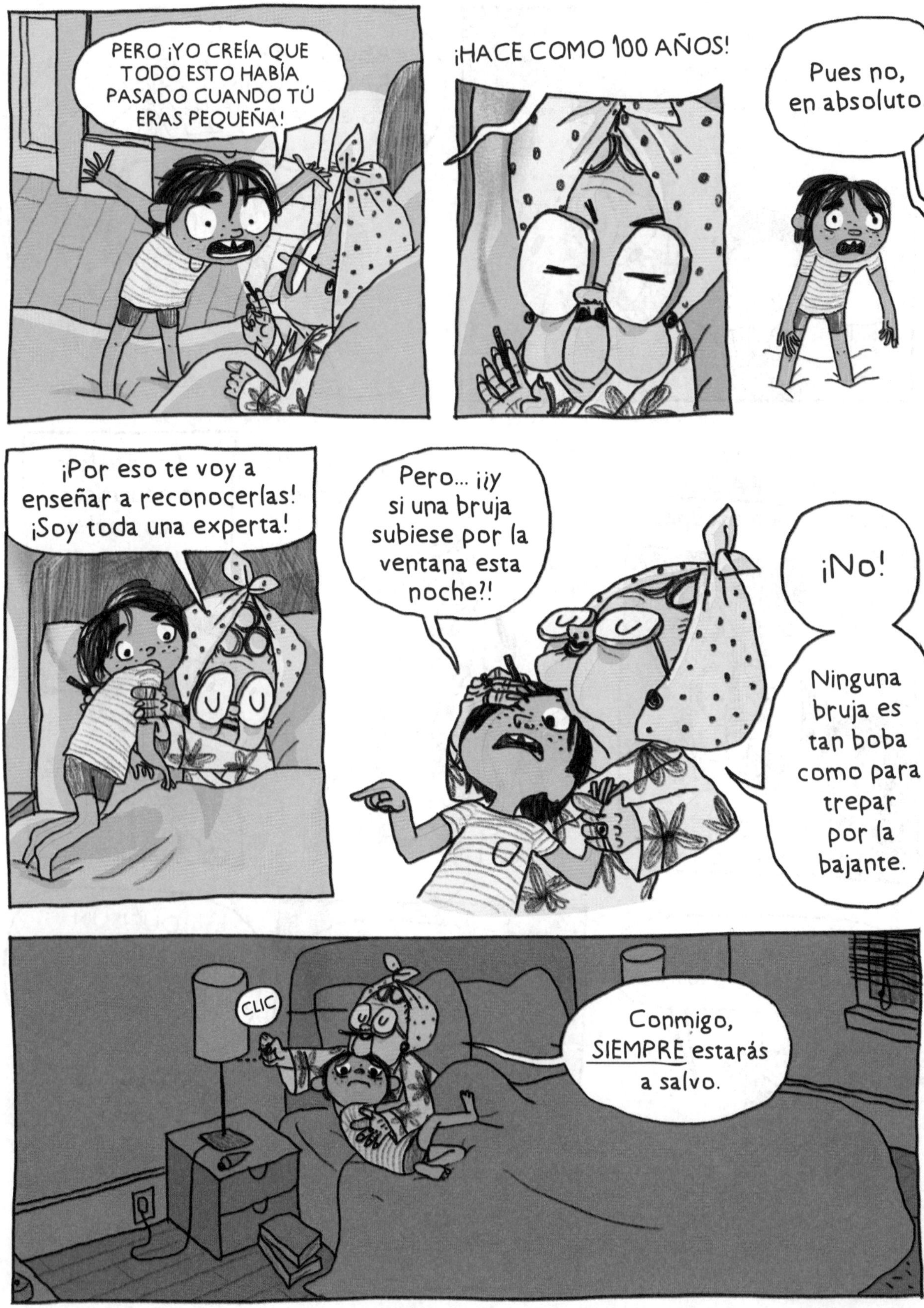

PERO ¡YO CREÍA QUE TODO ESTO HABÍA PASADO CUANDO TÚ ERAS PEQUEÑA!
¡HACE COMO 100 AÑOS!
Pues no, en absoluto.
¡Por eso te voy a enseñar a reconocerlas! ¡Soy toda una experta!
Pero... ¡¿y si una bruja subiese por la ventana esta noche?!
¡No!
Ninguna bruja es tan boba como para trepar por la bajante.
CLIC
Conmigo, SIEMPRE estarás a salvo.

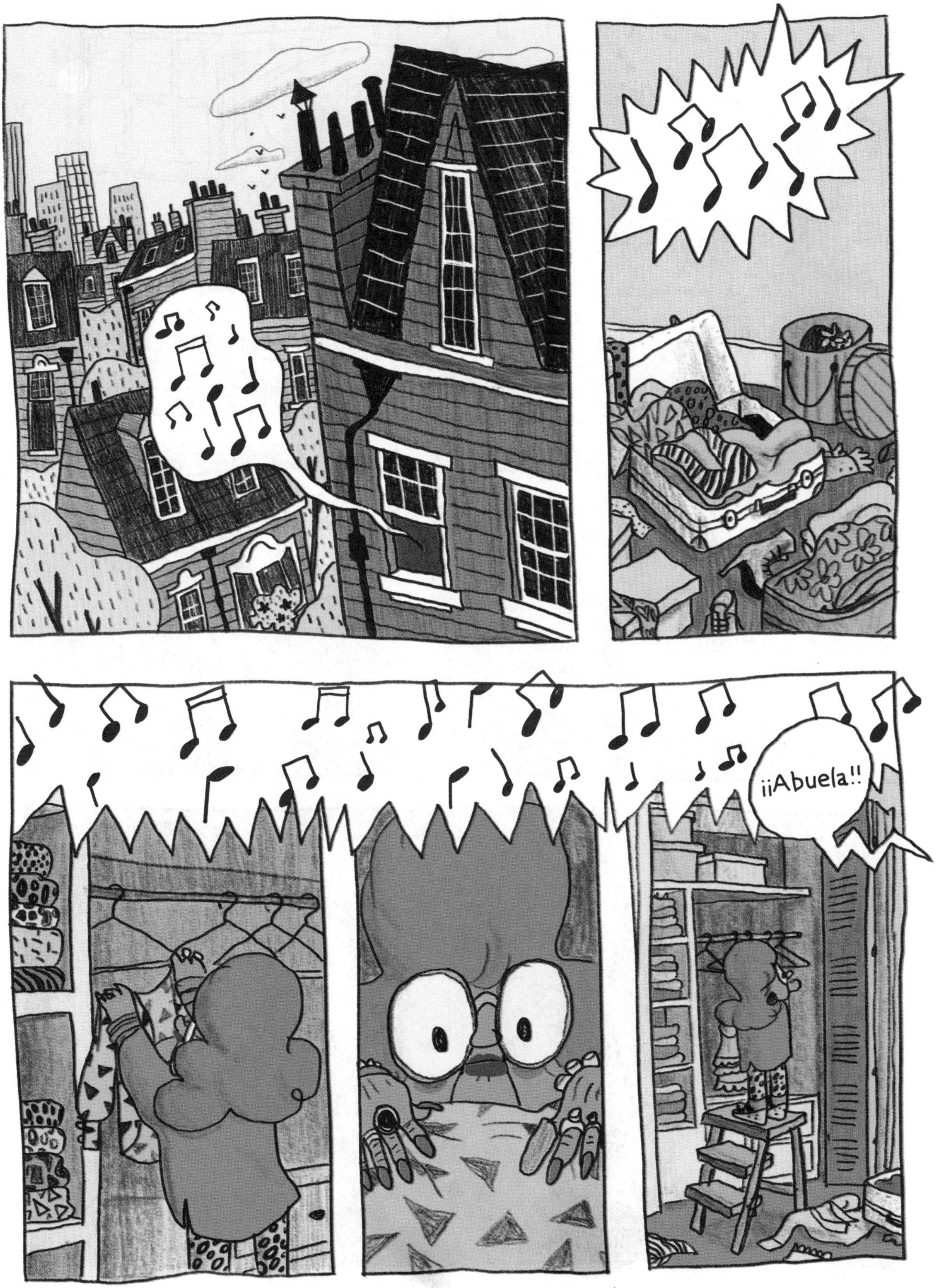
¡¡Abuela!!

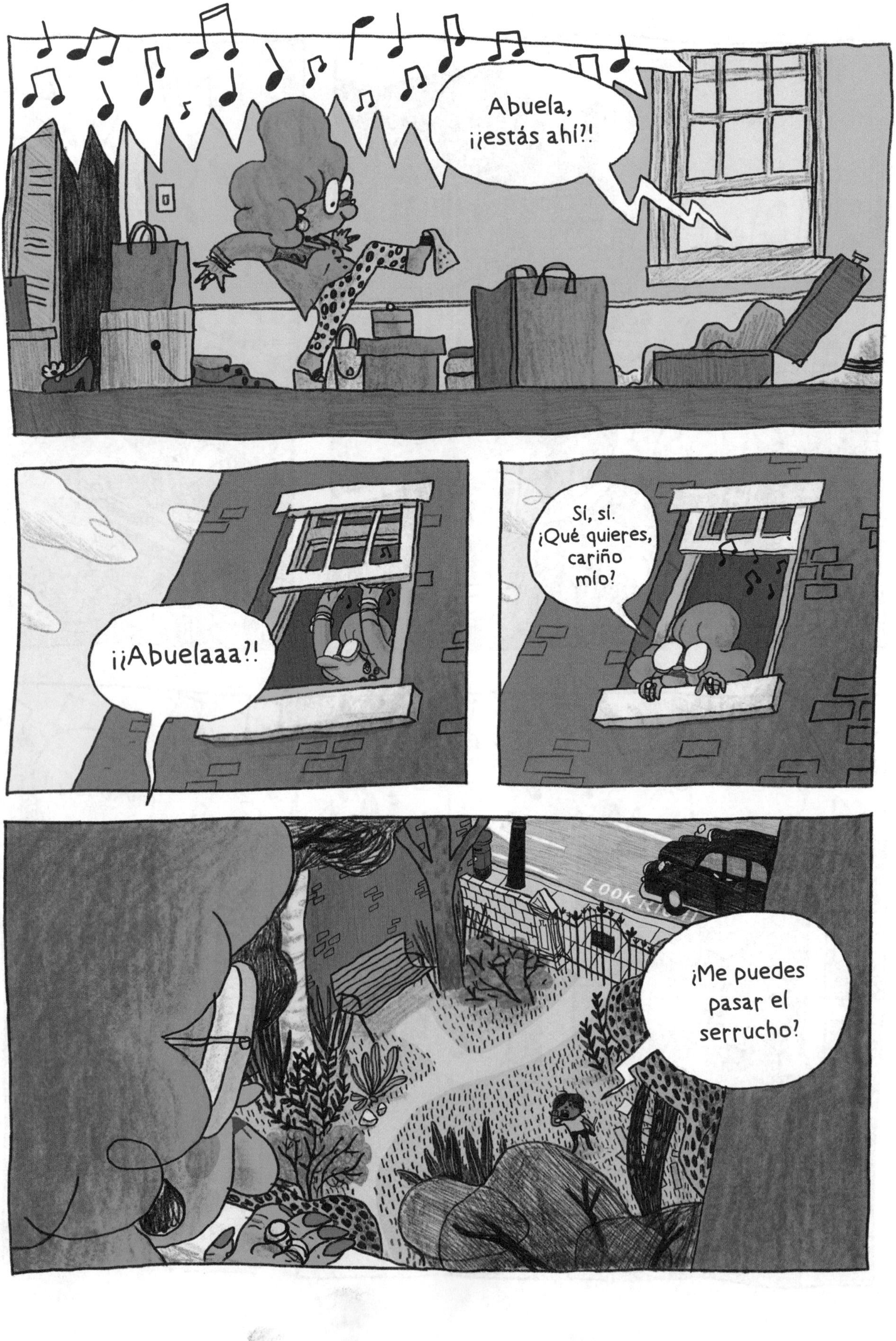
Abuela, ¡¿estás ahí?!
¡¿Abuelaaa?!
Sí, sí. ¿Qué quieres, cariño mío?
¡Me puedes pasar el serrucho?
LOOK RIGHT

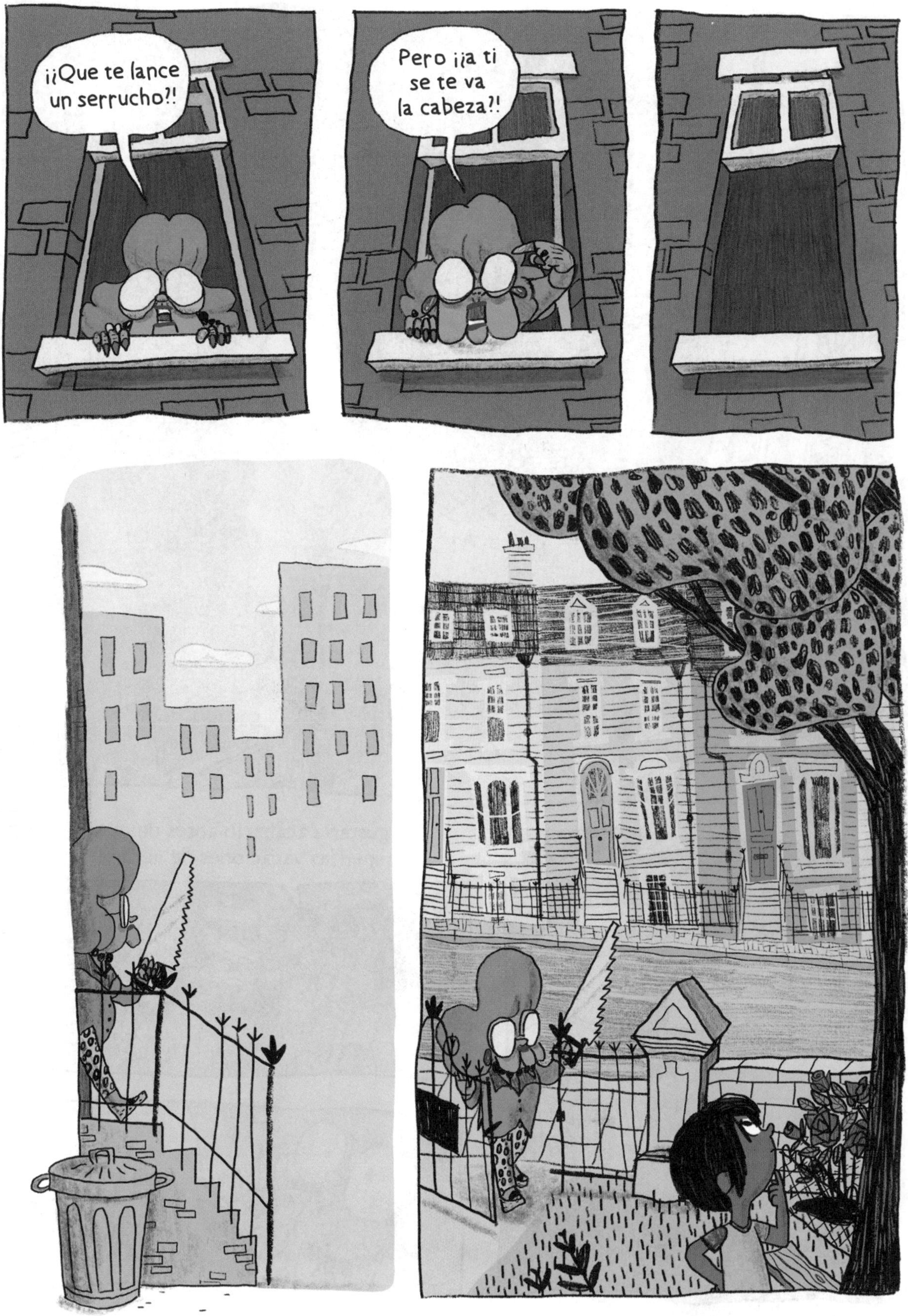
¡¿Que te lance un serrucho?!
Pero ¡¿a ti se te va la cabeza?!

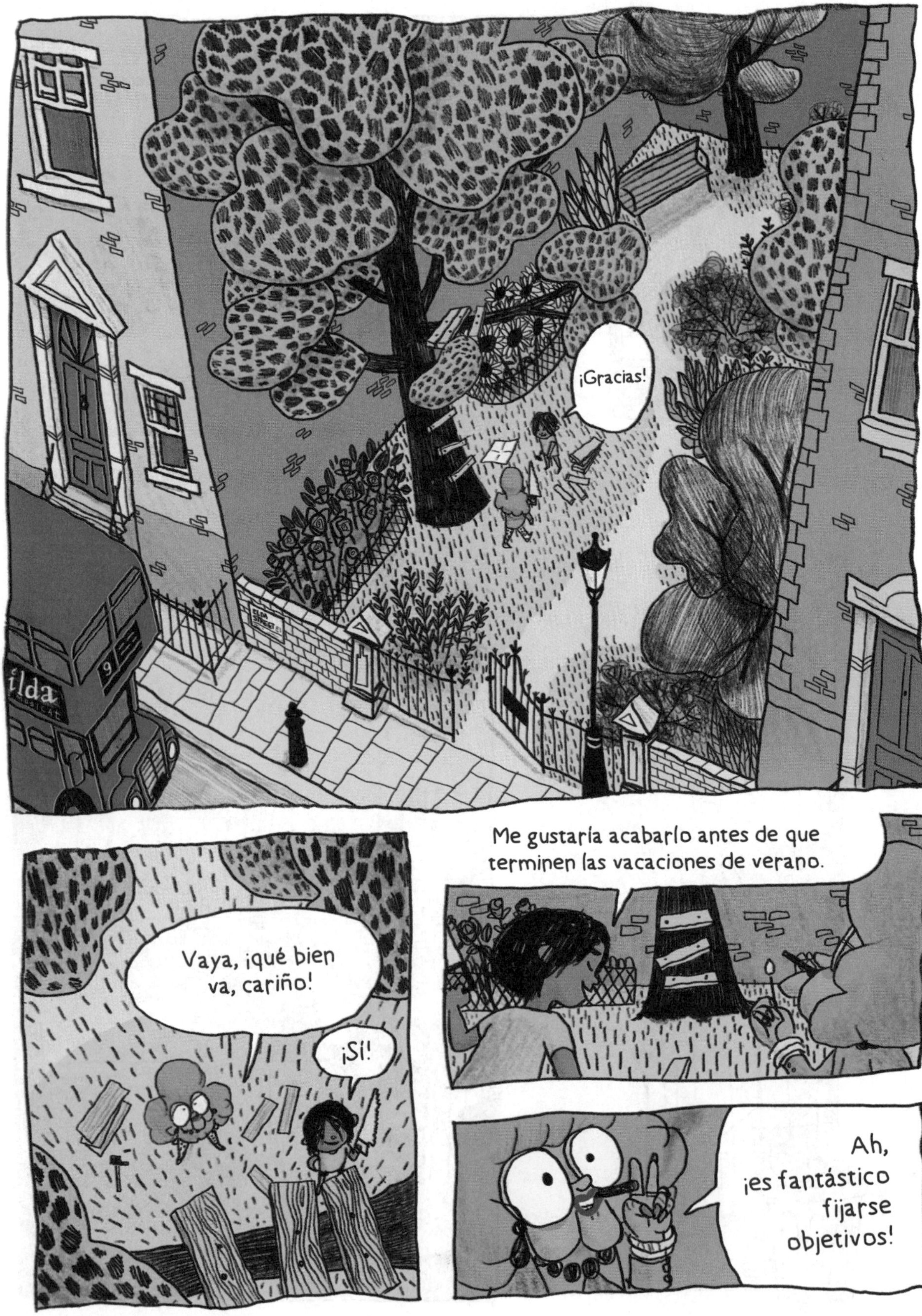
¡Gracias!
Vaya, ¡qué bien va, cariño!
¡Sí!
Me gustaría acabarlo antes de que terminen las vacaciones de verano.
Ah, ¡es fantástico fijarse objetivos!

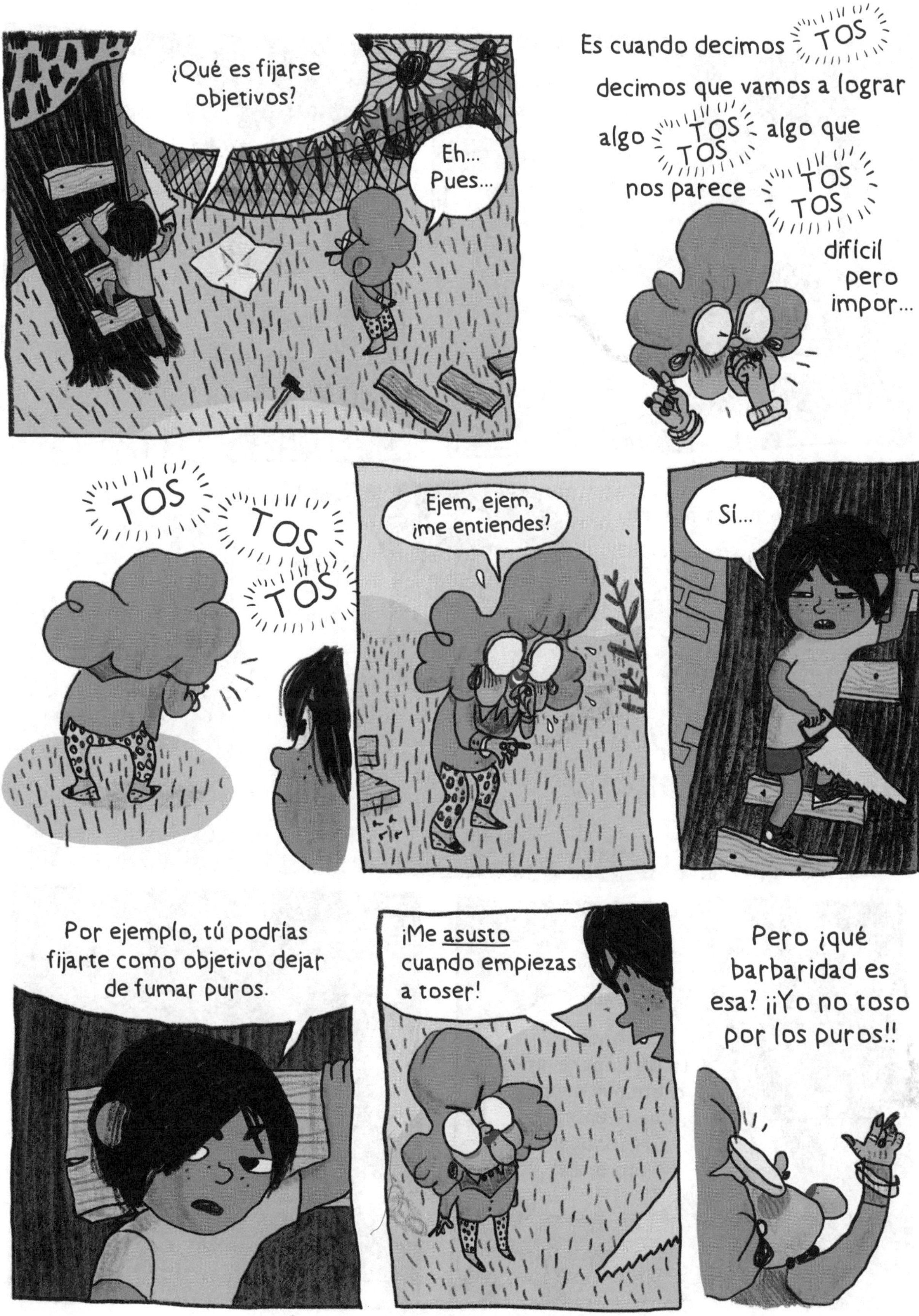
¡Qué es fijarse objetivos?
Eh... Pues...
Es cuando decimos TOS
decimos que vamos a lograr
algo TOS TOS algo que
nos parece TOS TOS
difícil pero impor...
TOS TOS TOS
Ejem, ejem, ¡me entiendes?
Sí...
Por ejemplo, tú podrías fijarte como objetivo dejar de fumar puros.
¡Me asusto cuando empiezas a toser!
Pero ¡qué barbaridad es esa? ¡¡Yo no toso por los puros!!

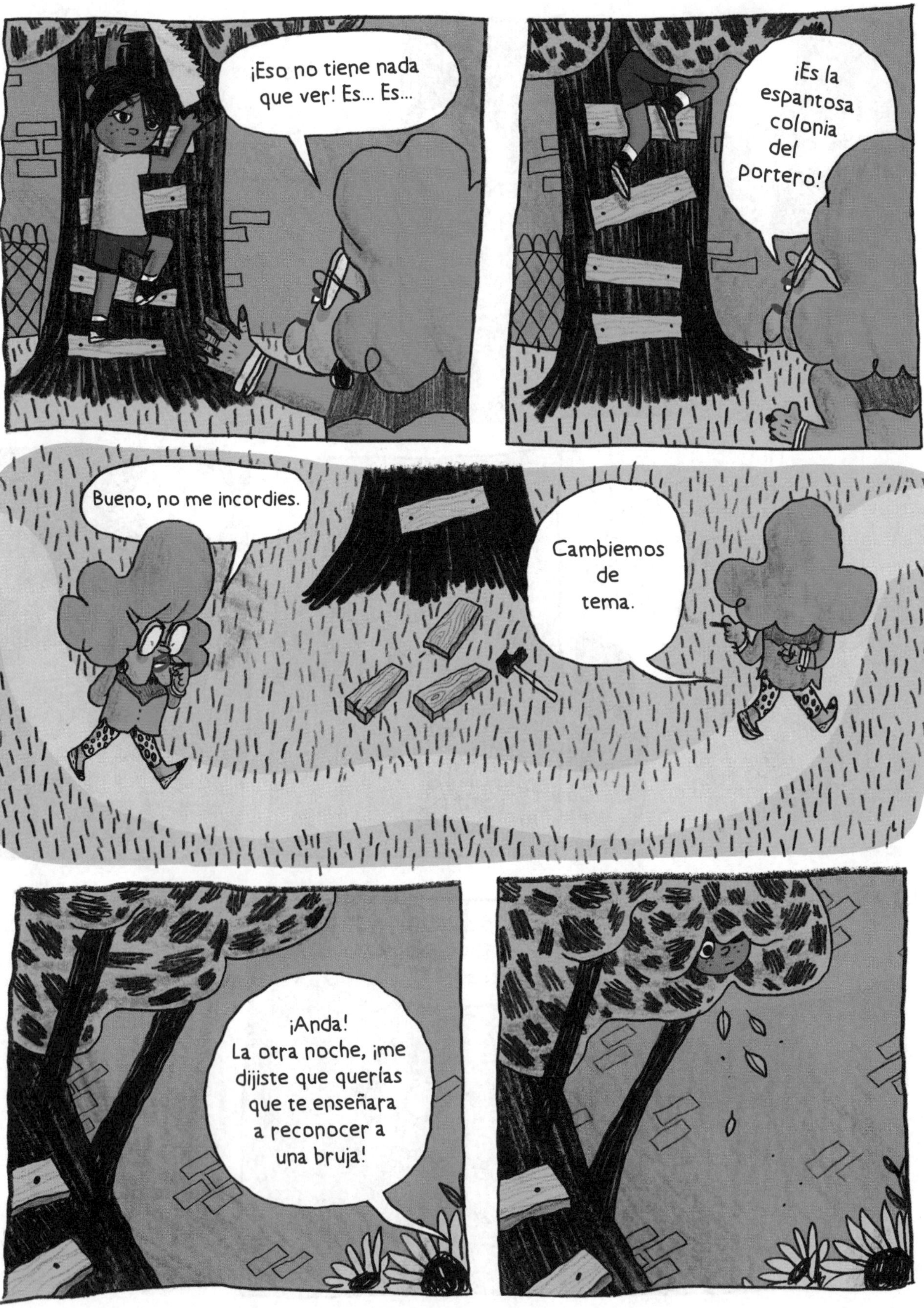
¡Eso no tiene nada que ver! Es... Es...
¡Es la espantosa colonia del portero!
Bueno, no me incordies.
Cambiemos de tema.
¡Anda! La otra noche, ¡me dijiste que querías que te enseñara a reconocer a una bruja!

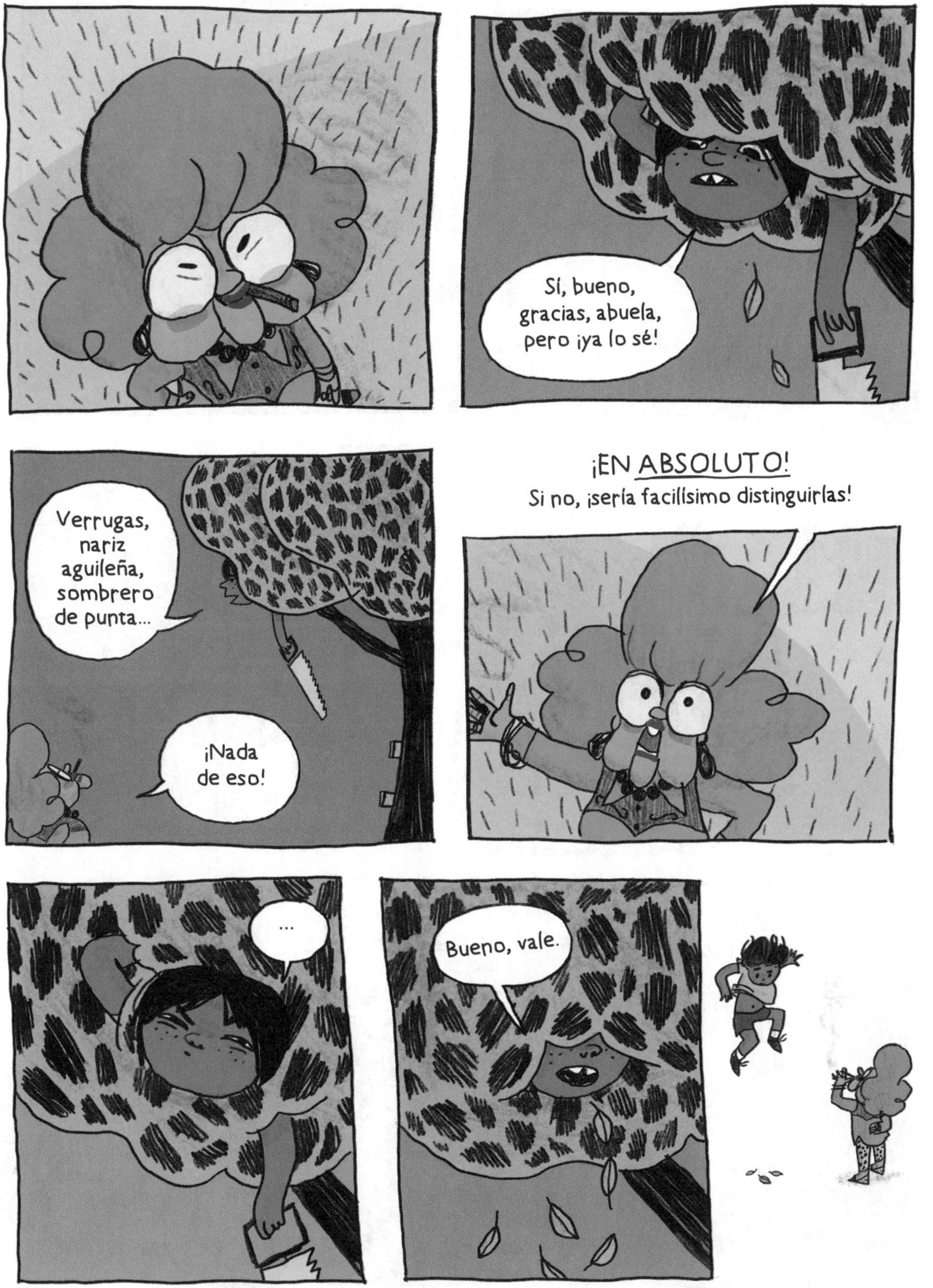
Sí, bueno, gracias, abuela, pero ¡ya lo sé!
Verrugas, nariz aguileña, sombrero de punta...
¡Nada de eso!
¡EN ABSOLUTO!
Si no, ¡sería facilísimo distinguirlas!
...
Bueno, vale.

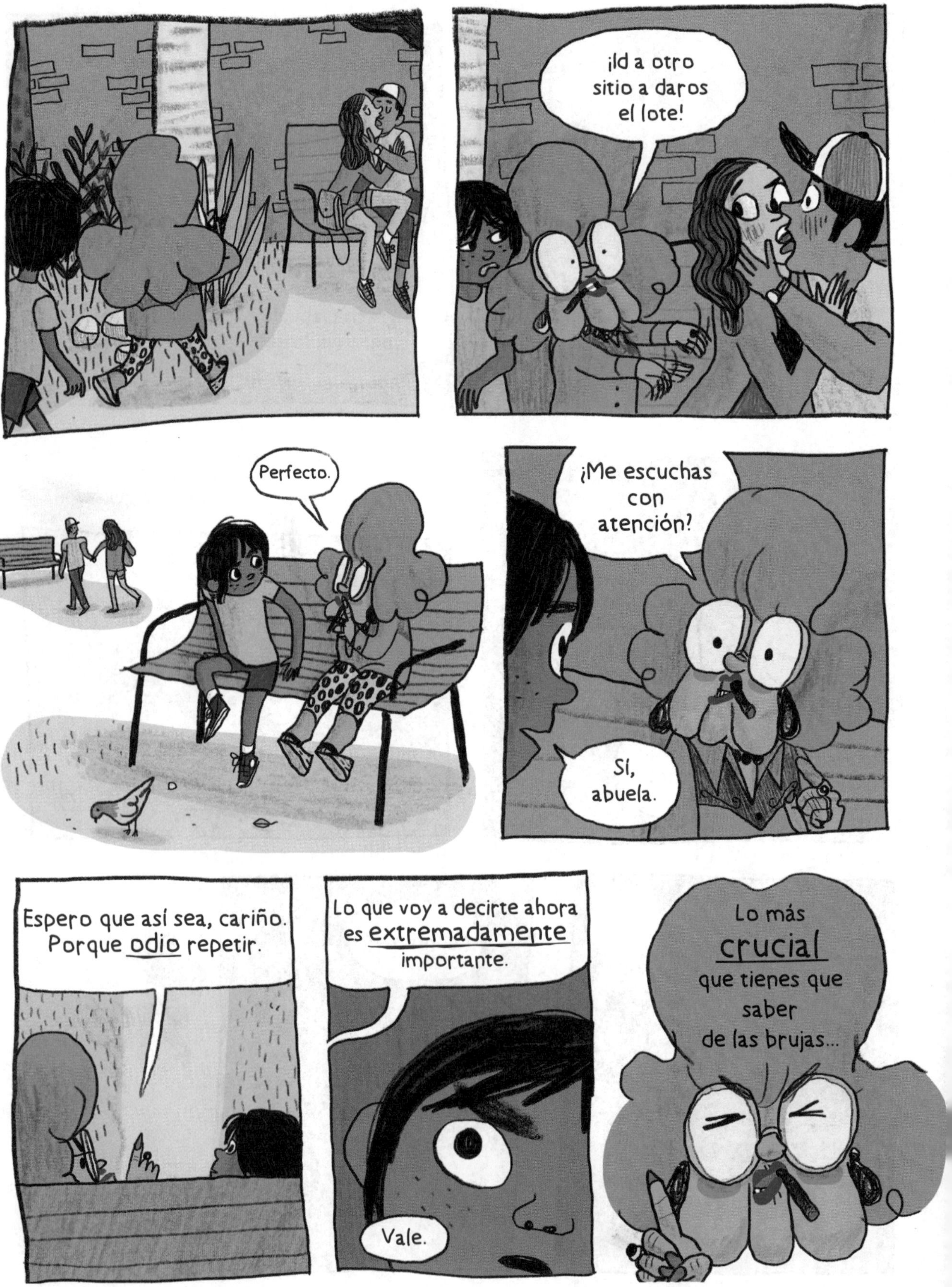
¡Id a otro sitio a daros el lote!
Perfecto.
¿Me escuchas con atención?
Sí, abuela.
Espero que así sea, cariño. Porque odio repetir.
Lo que voy a decirte ahora es extremadamente importante.
Vale.
Lo más crucial que tienes que saber de las brujas...

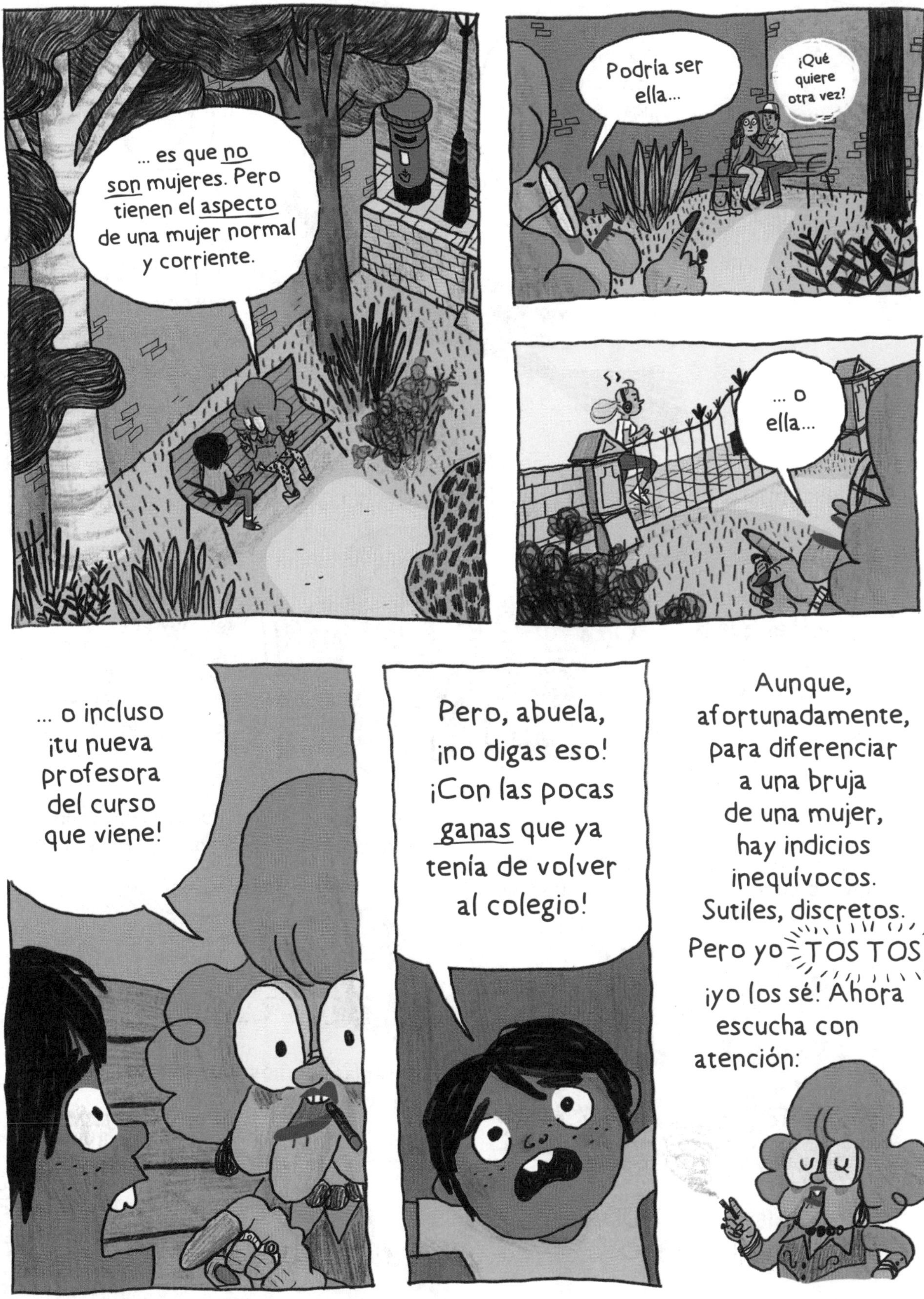
... es que no son mujeres. Pero tienen el aspecto de una mujer normal y corriente.
Podría ser ella...
¿Qué quiere otra vez?
... o ella...
... o incluso ¡tu nueva profesora del curso que viene!
Pero, abuela, ¡no digas eso! ¡Con las pocas ganas que ya tenía de volver al colegio!
Aunque, afortunadamente, para diferenciar a una bruja de una mujer, hay indicios inequívocos. Sutiles, discretos. Pero yo TOS TOS ¡yo los sé! Ahora escucha con atención:

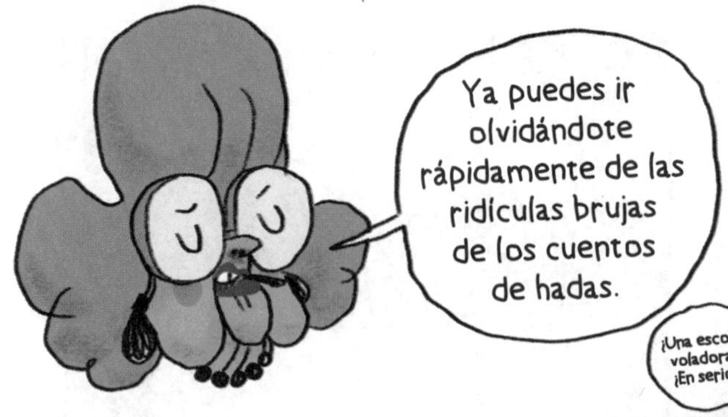
Ya puedes ir olvidándote rápidamente de las ridículas brujas de los cuentos de hadas.

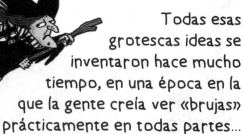

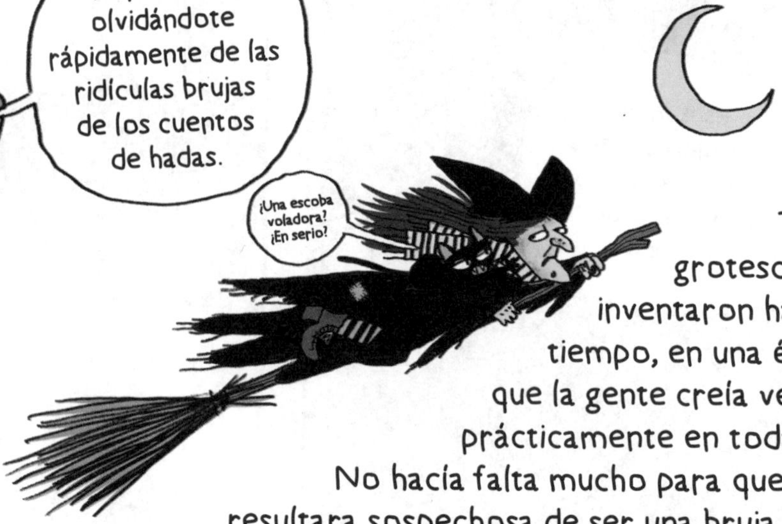
¡Una escoba voladora? ¡En serio?

Todas esas grotescas ideas se inventaron hace mucho tiempo, en una época en la que la gente creía ver «brujas» prácticamente en todas partes...
No hacía falta mucho para que una mujer resultara sospechosa de ser una bruja de verdad.
Se desconfiaba de las ancianas rebeldes, ¡y decían que tenían poderes maléficos!

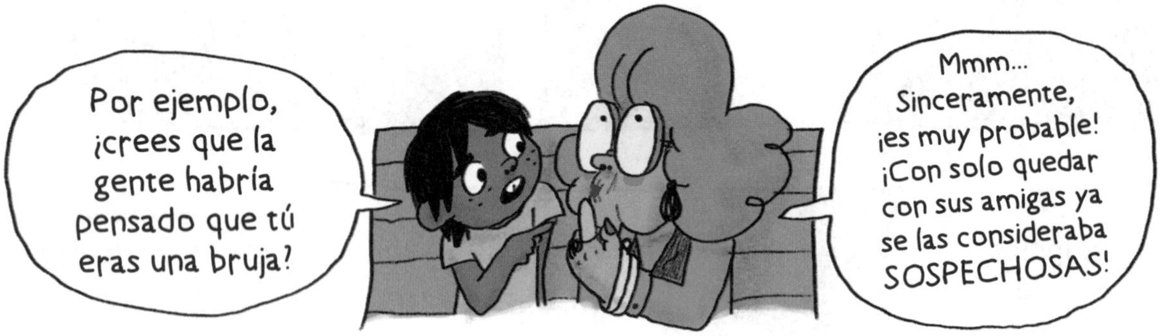
Por ejemplo, ¿crees que la gente habría pensado que tú eras una bruja?
Mmm... Sinceramente, ¡es muy probable! ¡Con solo quedar con sus amigas ya se las consideraba SOSPECHOSAS!

Solo hacía falta que no estuvieses casada, o que te curaras el resfriado con unas hierbas para que te acusaran...

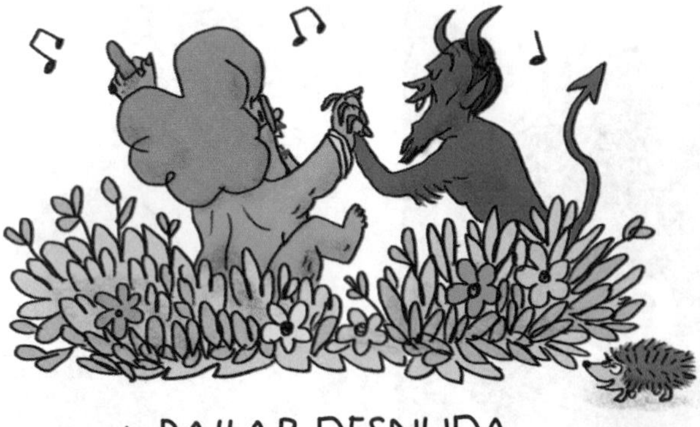

... de BAILAR DESNUDA CON EL DIABLO.

Para «demostrar» que eras una bruja de verdad, te tiraban al agua para ver si flotabas.

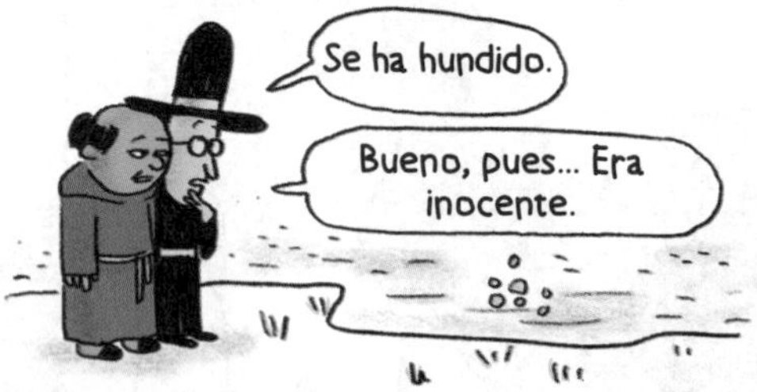
Se ha hundido.
Bueno, pues... Era inocente.

Y tenían medios muy persuasivos para hacerte confesar.

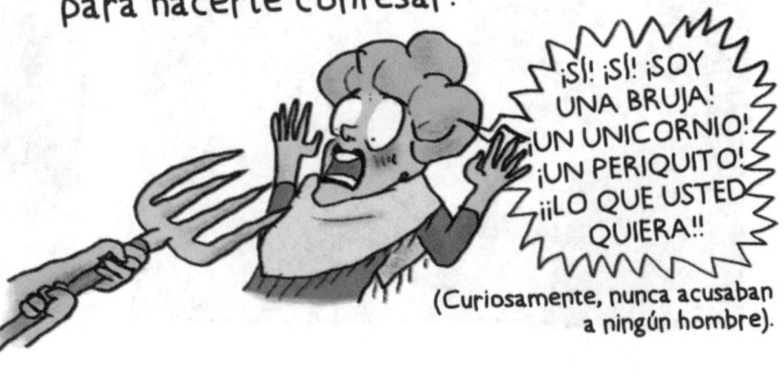
¡SÍ! ¡SÍ! ¡SOY UNA BRUJA! ¡UN UNICORNIO! ¡UN PERIQUITO! ¡¡LO QUE USTED QUIERA!!

(Curiosamente, nunca acusaban a ningún hombre).

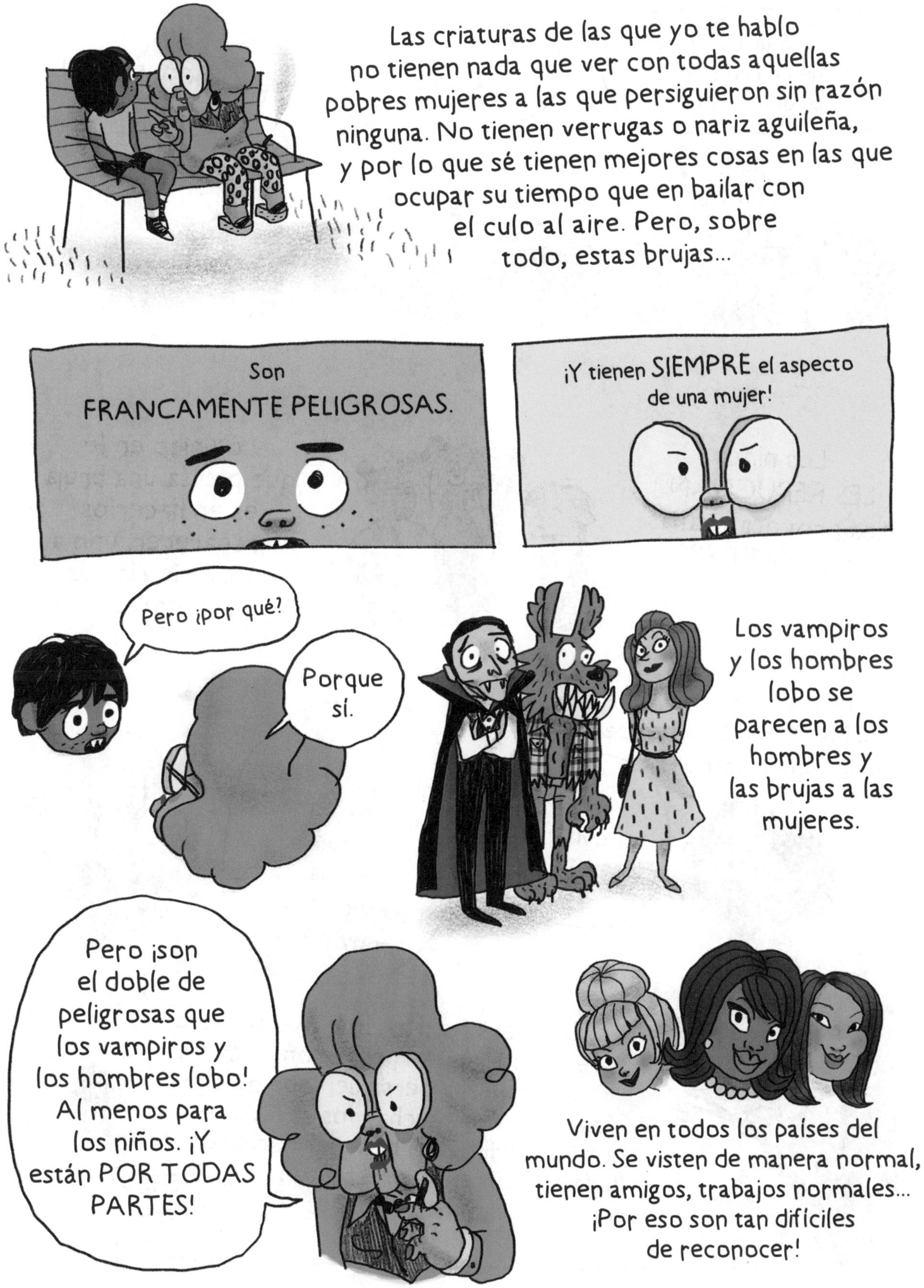

Las criaturas de las que yo te hablo no tienen nada que ver con todas aquellas pobres mujeres a las que persiguieron sin razón ninguna. No tienen verrugas o nariz aguileña, y por lo que sé tienen mejores cosas en las que ocupar su tiempo que en bailar con el culo al aire. Pero, sobre todo, estas brujas...
Son FRANCAMENTE PELIGROSAS.
¡Y tienen SIEMPRE el aspecto de una mujer!
Pero ¿por qué?
Porque sí.
Los vampiros y los hombres lobo se parecen a los hombres y las brujas a las mujeres.
Pero ¡son el doble de peligrosas que los vampiros y los hombres lobo! Al menos para los niños. ¡Y están POR TODAS PARTES!
Viven en todos los países del mundo. Se visten de manera normal, tienen amigos, trabajos normales... ¡Por eso son tan difíciles de reconocer!

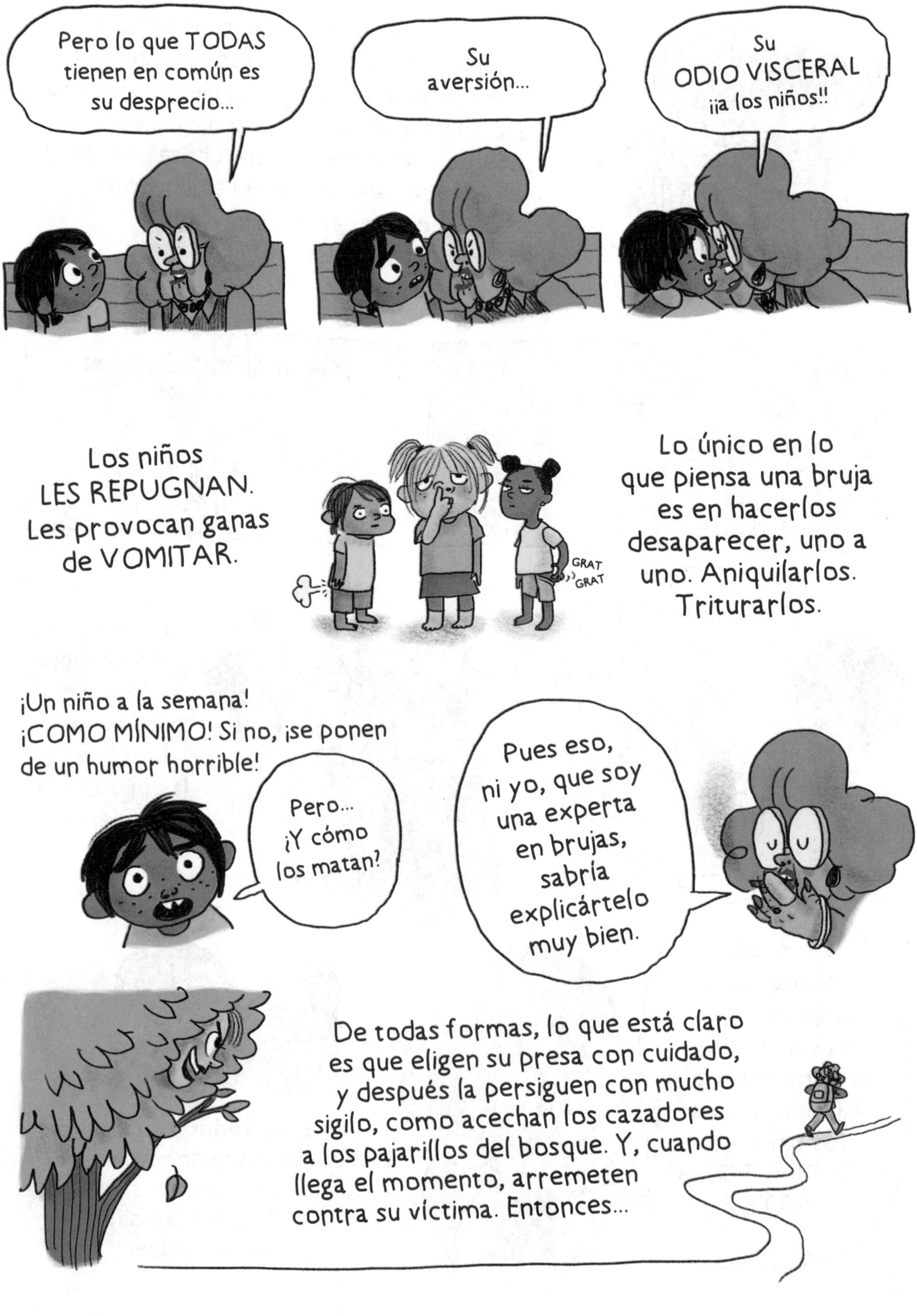
Pero lo que TODAS tienen en común es su desprecio...
Su aversión...
Su ODIO VISCERAL ¡¡a los niños!!
Los niños LES REPUGNAN. Les provocan ganas de VOMITAR.
GRAT GRAT
Lo único en lo que piensa una bruja es en hacerlos desaparecer, uno a uno. Aniquilarlos. Triturarlos.
¡Un niño a la semana! ¡COMO MÍNIMO! Si no, ¡se ponen de un humor horrible!
Pero... ¿Y cómo los matan?
Pues eso, ni yo, que soy una experta en brujas, sabría explicártelo muy bien.
De todas formas, lo que está claro es que eligen su presa con cuidado, y después la persiguen con mucho sigilo, como acechan los cazadores a los pajarillos del bosque. Y, cuando llega el momento, arremeten contra su víctima. Entonces...

¡El niño desaparece!

Pero... ¡¡CÓMO??

Ni la menor idea. En cualquier caso, la policía no ha detenido nunca a ninguna.

Y ninguna va jamás a la cárcel.

Afortunadamente, no hay muchas brujas hoy en día.

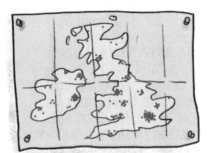

En Inglaterra debe haber unas cien.

Están en TODOS los países del mundo. Pero obedecen solo a una misma reina. La más poderosa y terrible de todas:

¡LA GRAN BRUJA!

Es extremadamente misteriosa y no aparece más que en contadísimas ocasiones. Igualmente, también podría pasar, a ojos de un humano, por una mujer perfectamente normal.

Bueno, y entonces ¡cómo se las reconoce?

Bien, como te he dicho, son criaturas que tienen que estar siempre disfrazadas para poder pasar por mujeres normales.

Pero ¡no es tan sencillo para ellas! A pesar de todo, ¡hay cosas que las traicionan! ¡Y eso es lo que permite desenmascararlas!

Desgraciadamente, no es seguro al cien por cien. Sin embargo, después de mis pesquisas, estos son los detallitos que podrían ayudarte:

LAS BRUJAS

LAS MANOS

Figura 1
Con guantes

Figura 2
Sin guantes

Tanto en invierno como en verano, la bruja lleva guantes para ocultar sus garras y dedos encorvados.

EL CRÁNEO

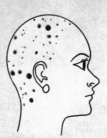 

Figura 1   *Figura 2*

La bruja está totalmente calva (Fig. 1)
La bruja lleva peluca (Fig. 2)
Pero el roce constante y rugoso los 365 días del año en su cuero cabelludo le provoca picores horribles a los que llaman «erupción de la peluca».

Bruja aquejada de erupción

LOS PIES

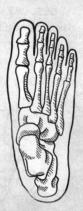 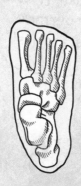

Mujer   *Bruja*

La bruja no tiene dedos de los pies. Tiene el pie cuadrado. Lo esconde, en cualquier época del año, en zapatos cerrados de punta fina, que le resultan incomodísimos.

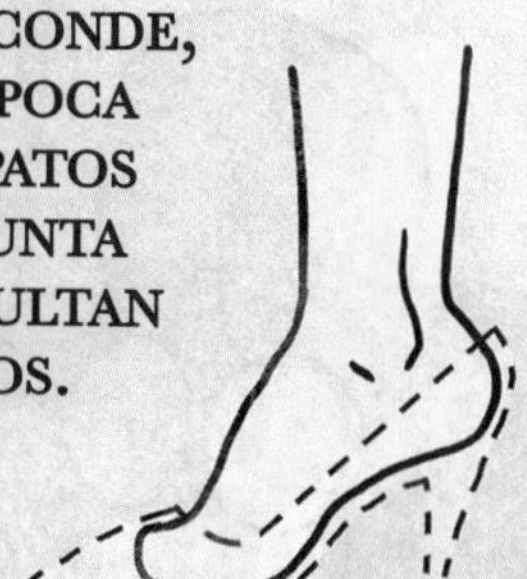

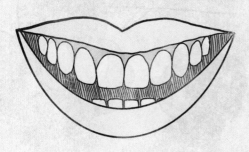

LA SONRISA

LA BRUJA TIENE LA SALIVA SUTILMENTE TEÑIDA (DE AZUL ARÁNDANO), LO QUE LE DA UN TONO DE COLOR A SUS DIENTES.

LOS OJOS

Figura 1

AL CONTRARIO QUE EN LA PUPILA HUMANA (FIG. 1), EN LA DE UNA BRUJA SE APRECIAN CRISTALITOS DE HIELO Y LLAMAS QUE BAILAN (FIG. 2).

Figura 2

LA NARIZ

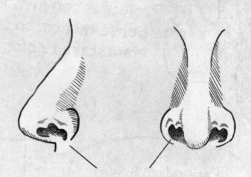

Fosas nasales de bruja

LA BRUJA TIENE LOS AGUJEROS DE LA NARIZ RETORCIDOS Y ONDULADOS PARA OLER MEJOR A LOS NIÑOS.

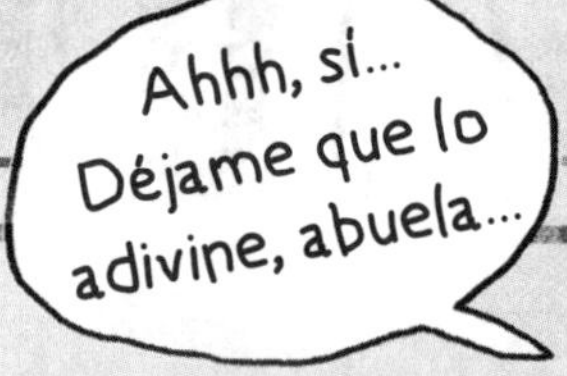

Ahhh, sí... Déjame que lo adivine, abuela...

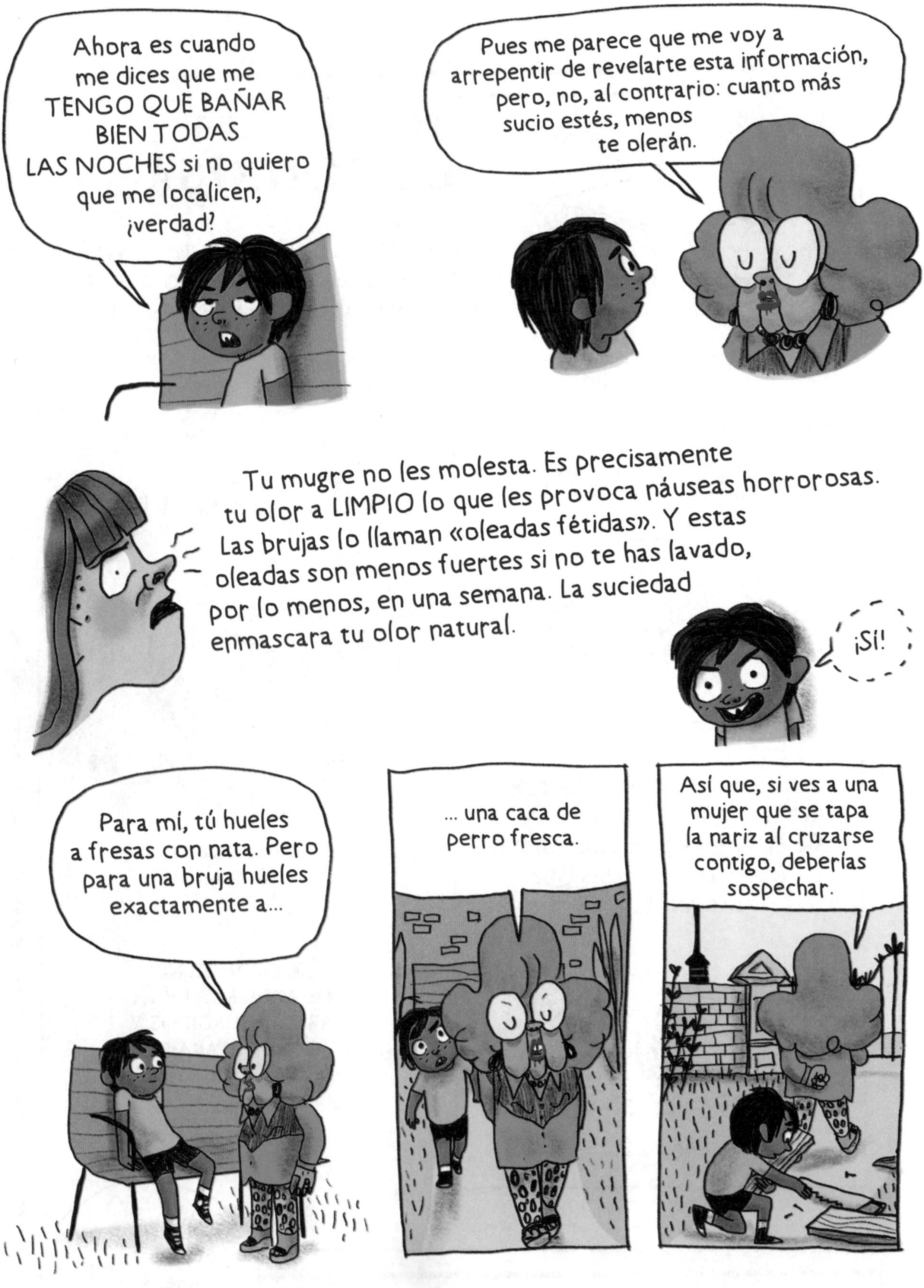
Ahora es cuando me dices que me TENGO QUE BAÑAR BIEN TODAS LAS NOCHES si no quiero que me localicen, ¿verdad?
Pues me parece que me voy a arrepentir de revelarte esta información, pero, no, al contrario: cuanto más sucio estés, menos te olerán.
Tu mugre no les molesta. Es precisamente tu olor a LIMPIO lo que les provoca náuseas horrorosas. Las brujas lo llaman «oleadas fétidas». Y estas oleadas son menos fuertes si no te has lavado, por lo menos, en una semana. La suciedad enmascara tu olor natural.
¡Sí!
Para mí, tú hueles a fresas con nata. Pero para una bruja hueles exactamente a...
... una caca de perro fresca.
Así que, si ves a una mujer que se tapa la nariz al cruzarse contigo, deberías sospechar.

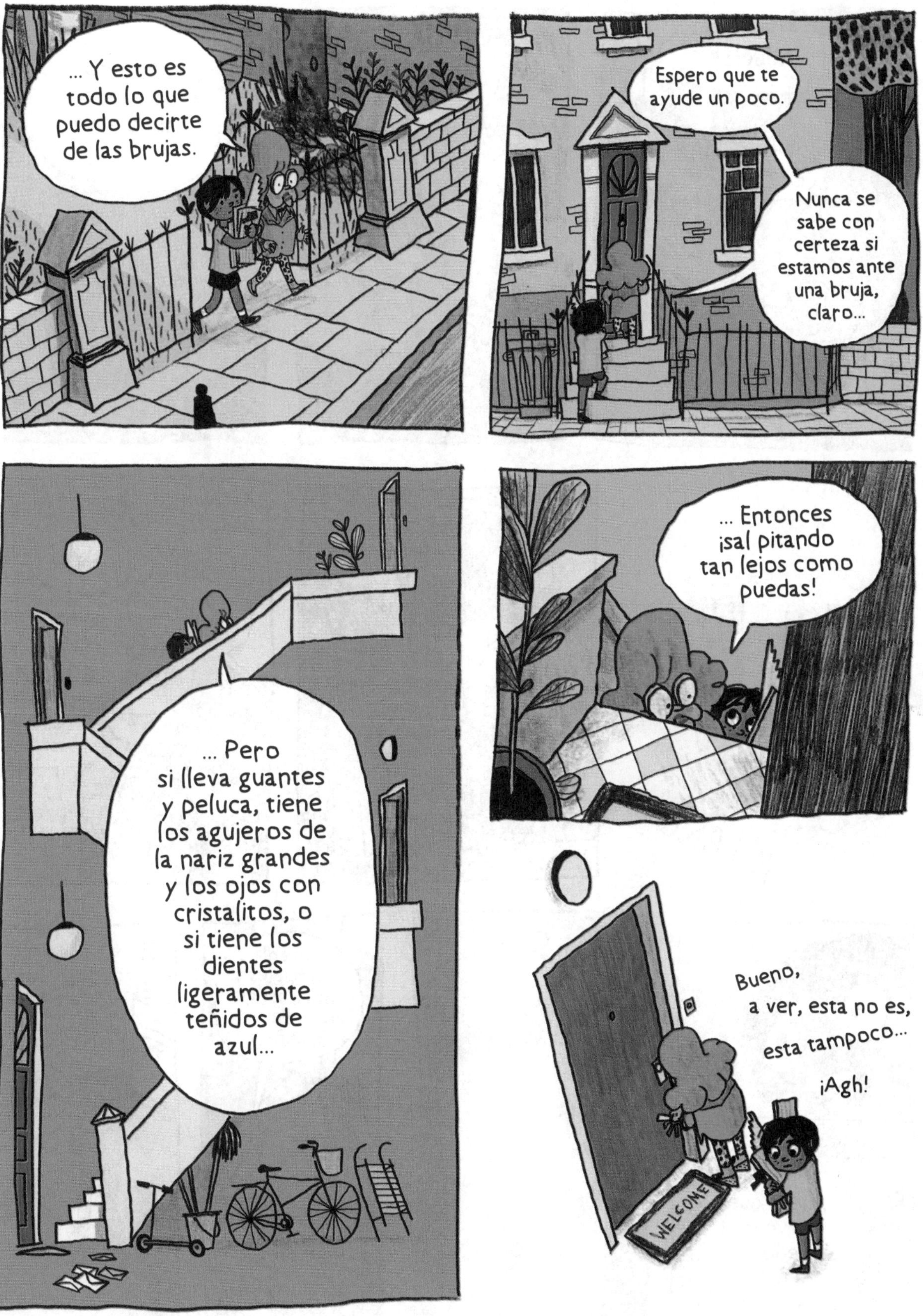
... Y esto es todo lo que puedo decirte de las brujas.
Espero que te ayude un poco.
Nunca se sabe con certeza si estamos ante una bruja, claro...
... Pero si lleva guantes y peluca, tiene los agujeros de la nariz grandes y los ojos con cristalitos, o si tiene los dientes ligeramente teñidos de azul...
... Entonces ¡sal pitando tan lejos como puedas!
Bueno, a ver, esta no es, esta tampoco...
¡Agh!
WELCOME

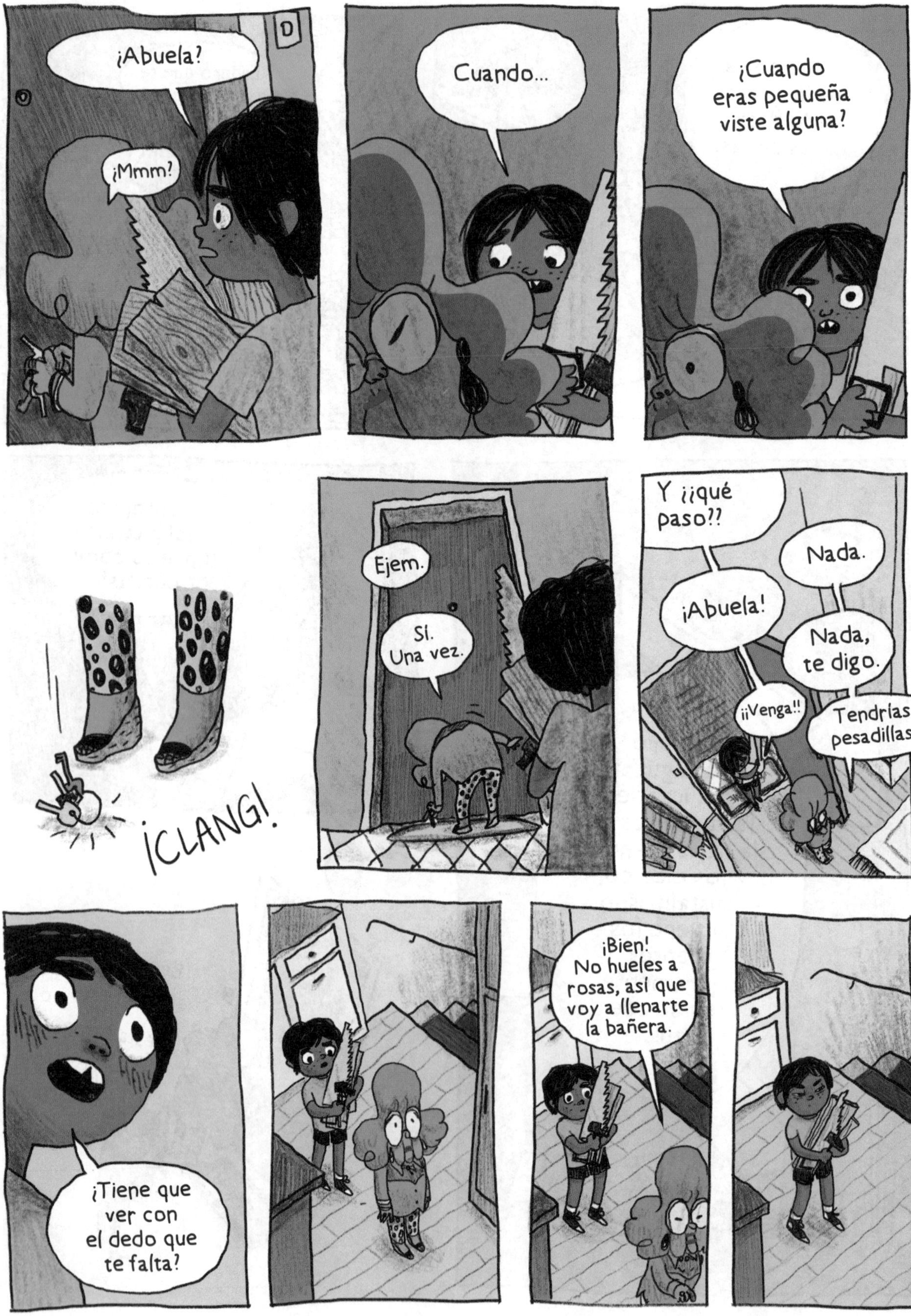
¡Abuela?
¡Mmm?
Cuando...
¡Cuando eras pequeña viste alguna?
¡CLANG!
Ejem.
Sí. Una vez.
Y ¡¡qué paso??
¡Abuela!
Nada.
Nada, te digo.
¡¡Venga!!
Tendrías pesadillas.
¡Tiene que ver con el dedo que te falta?
¡Bien! No hueles a rosas, así que voy a llenarte la bañera.

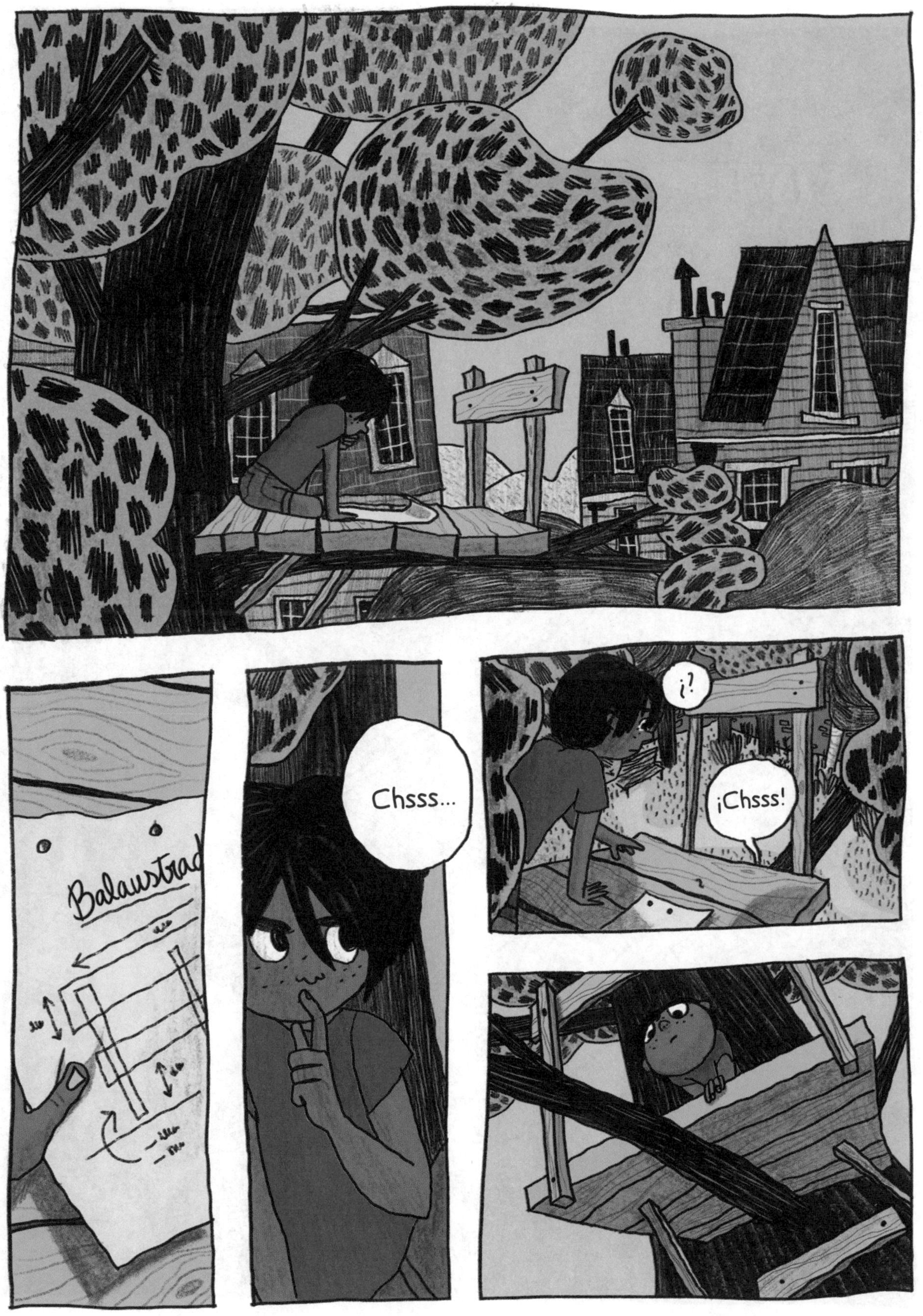
Balaustrad
Chsss...
¡?
¡Chsss!

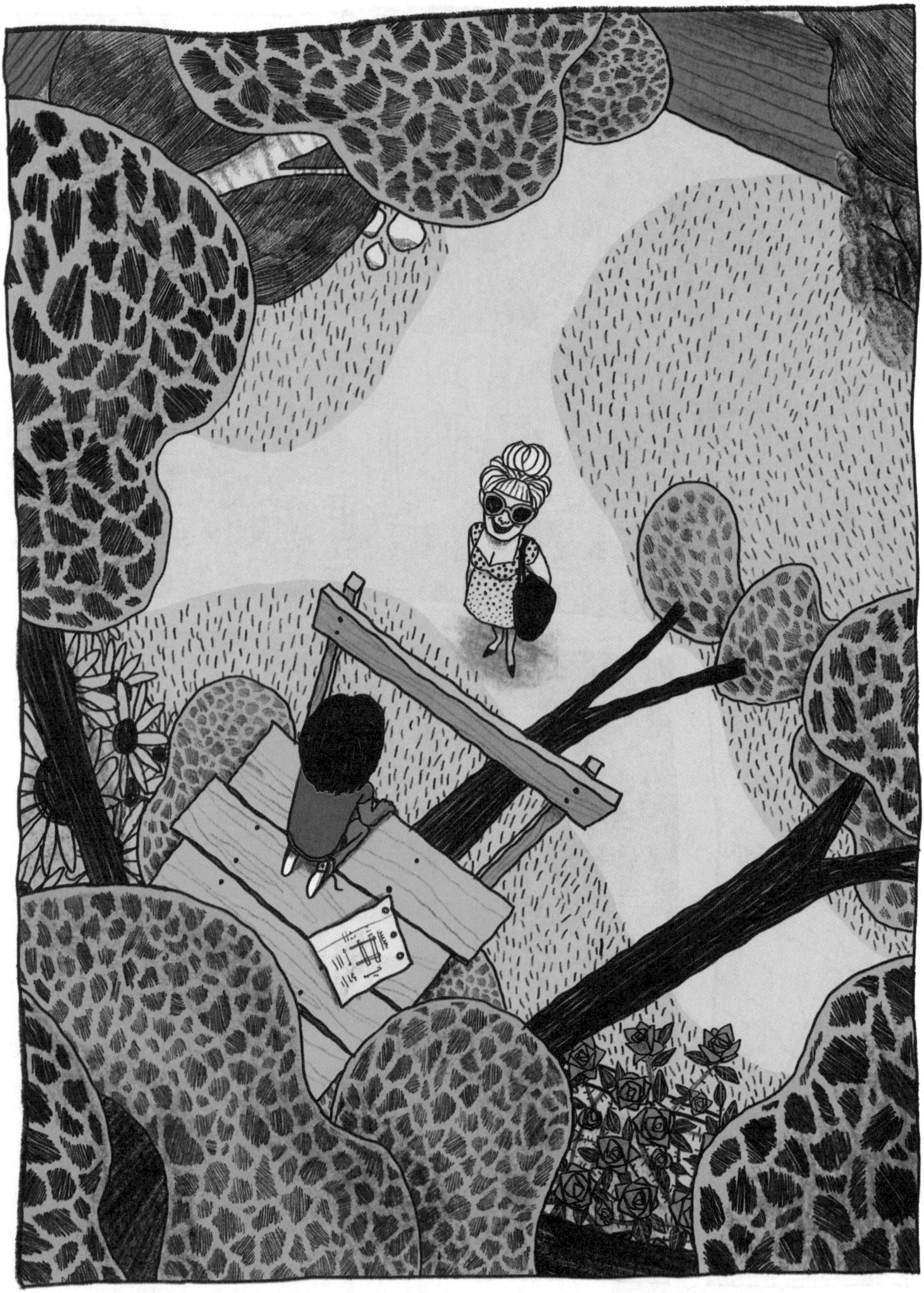

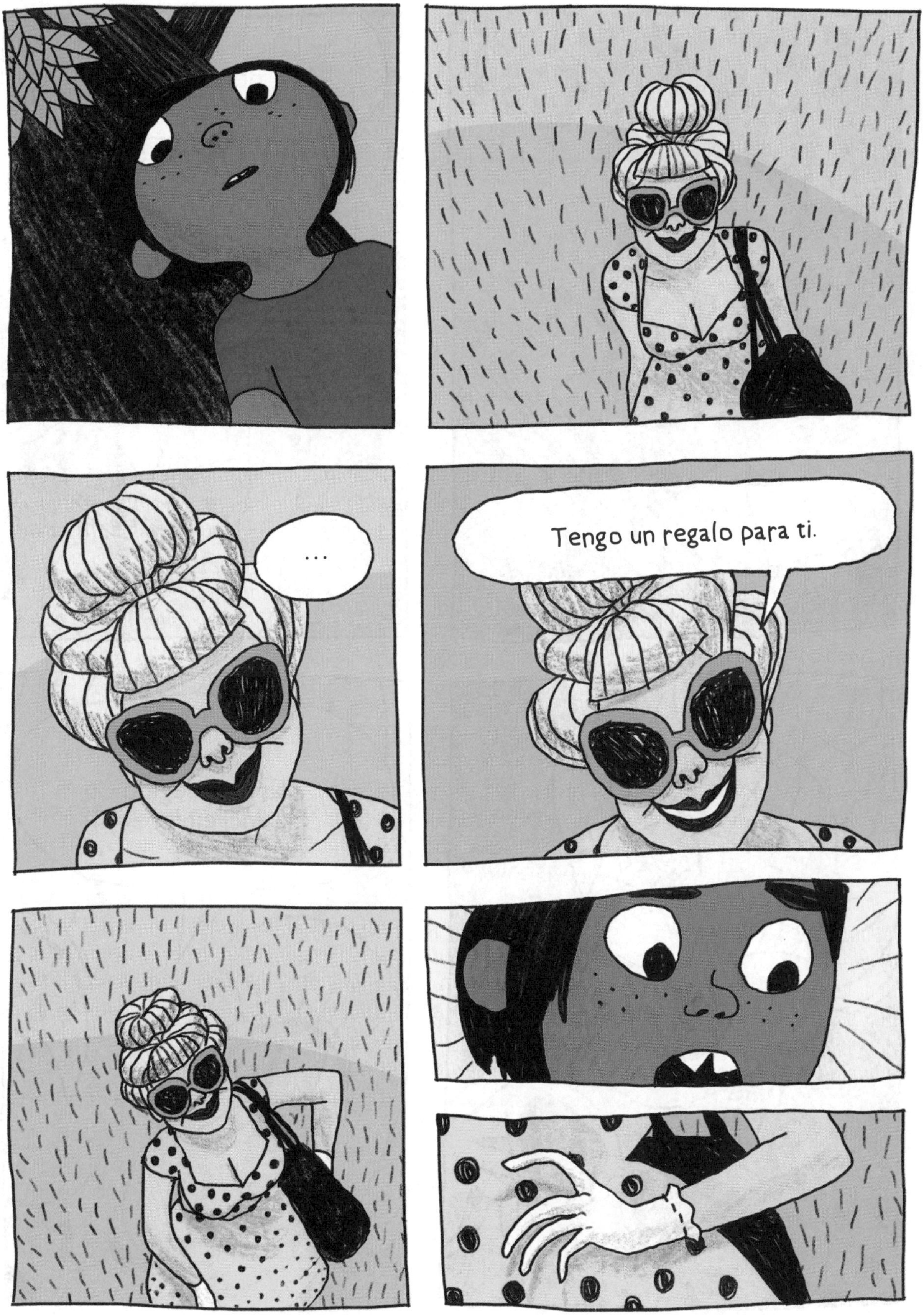
...
Tengo un regalo para ti.

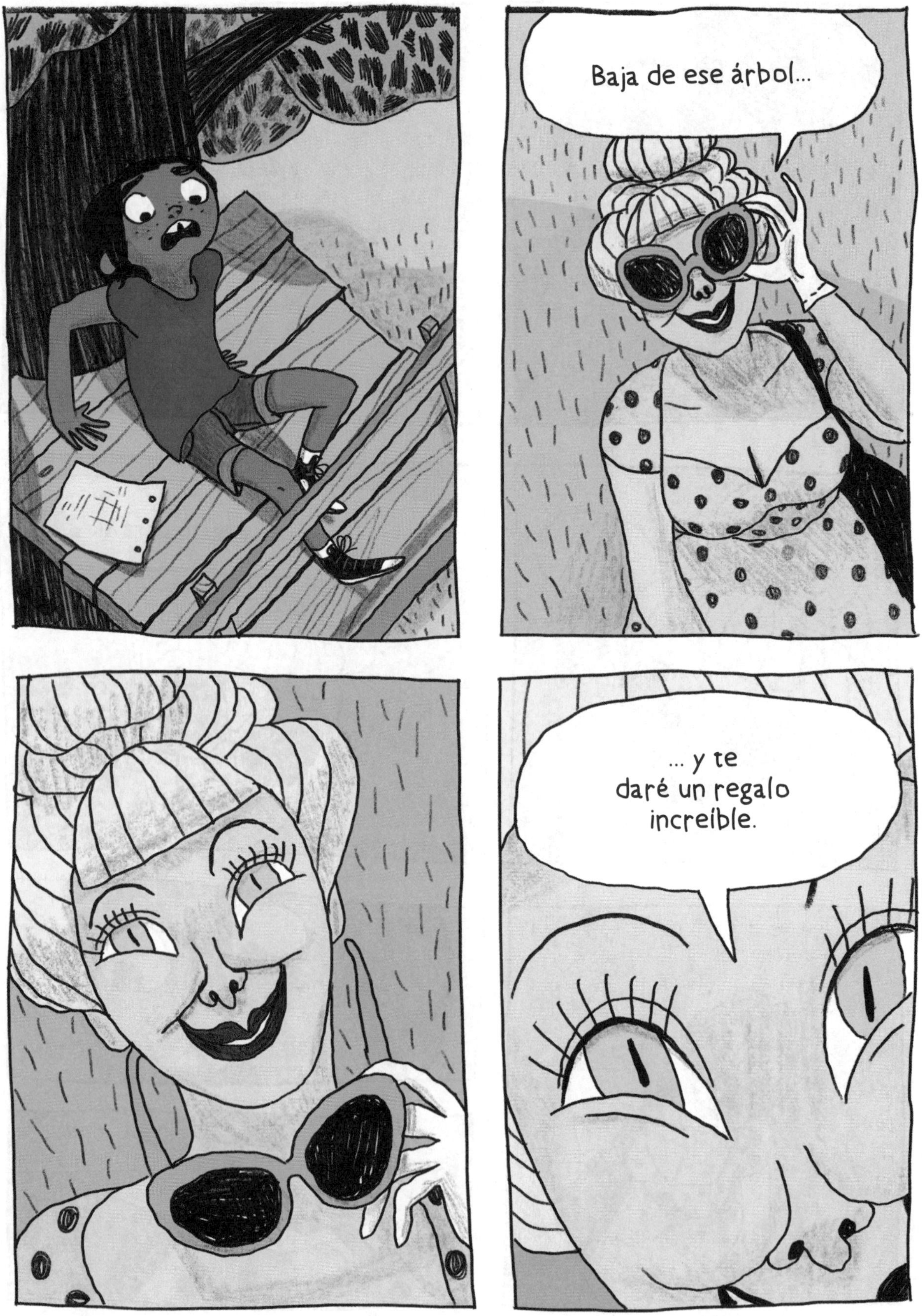
Baja de ese árbol...
... y te
daré un regalo
increíble.

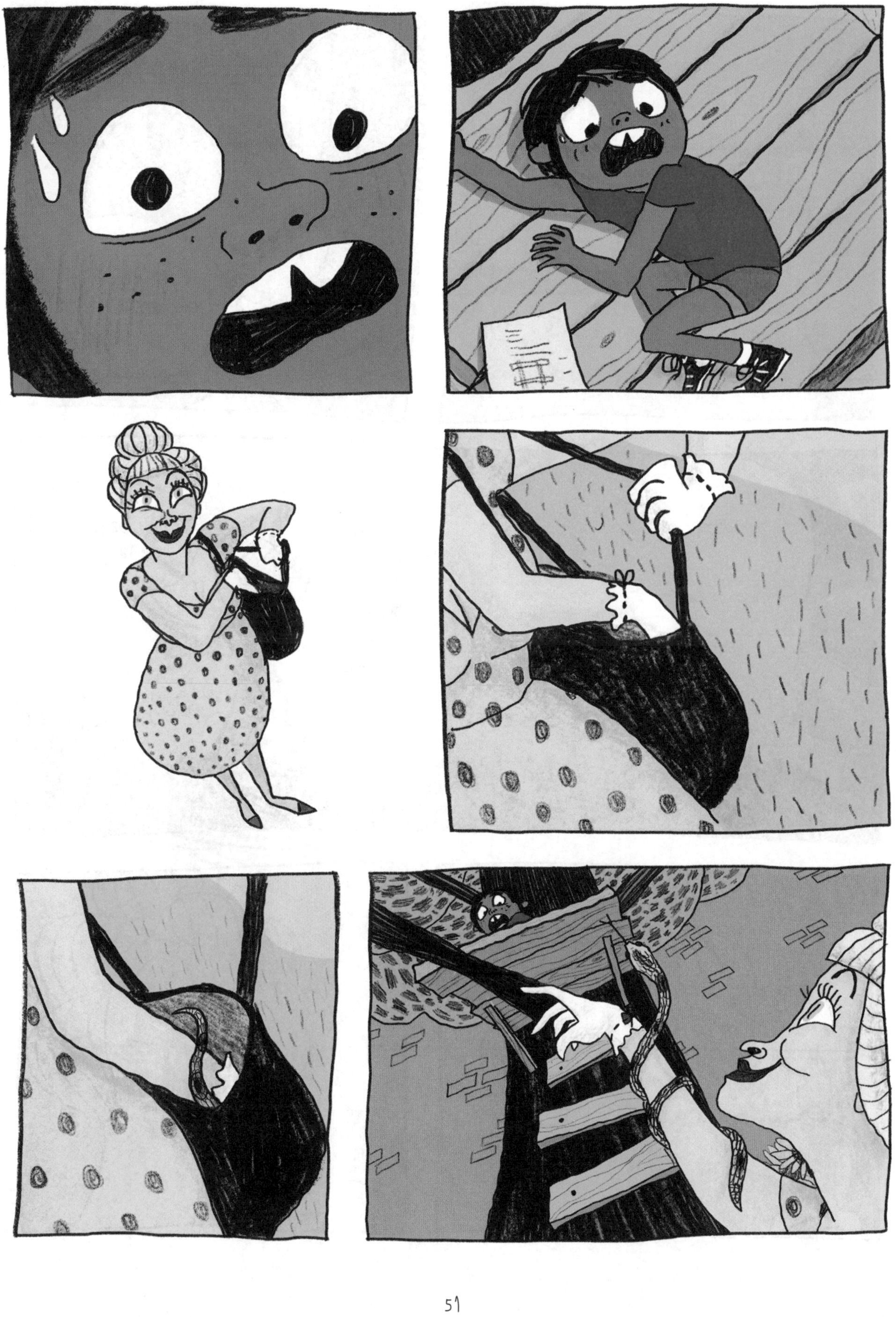

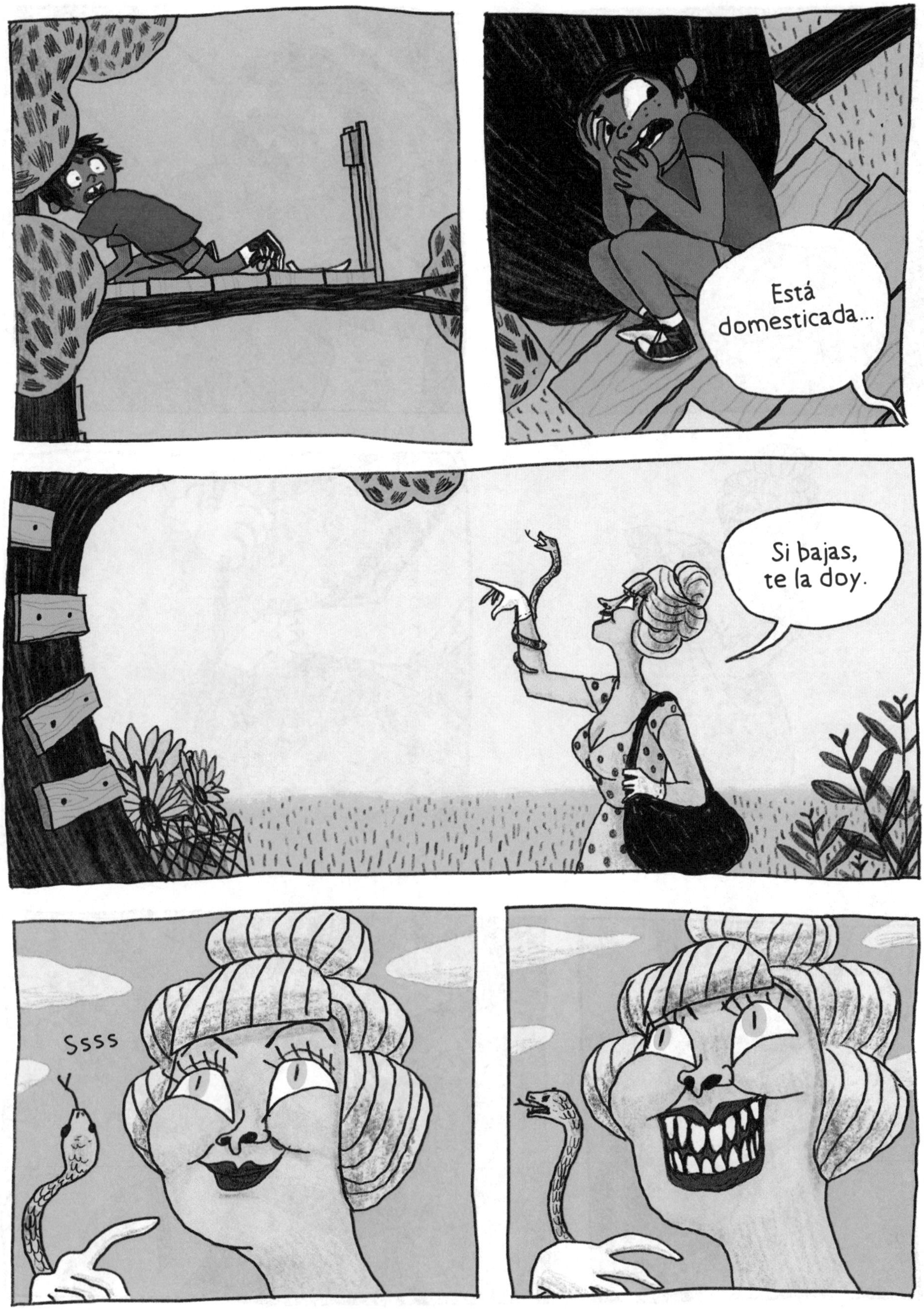
Está domesticada...
Si bajas, te la doy.
Ssss

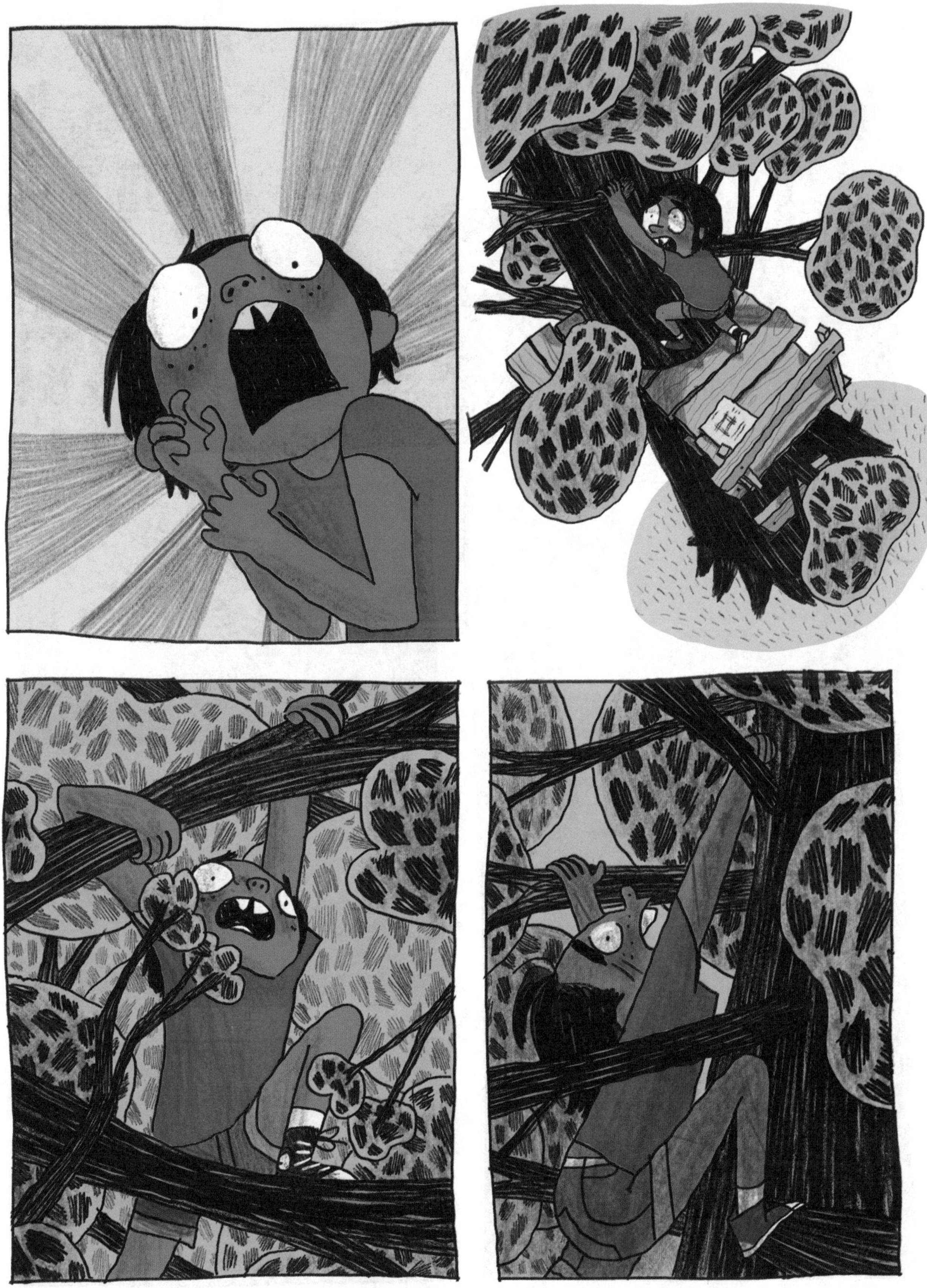

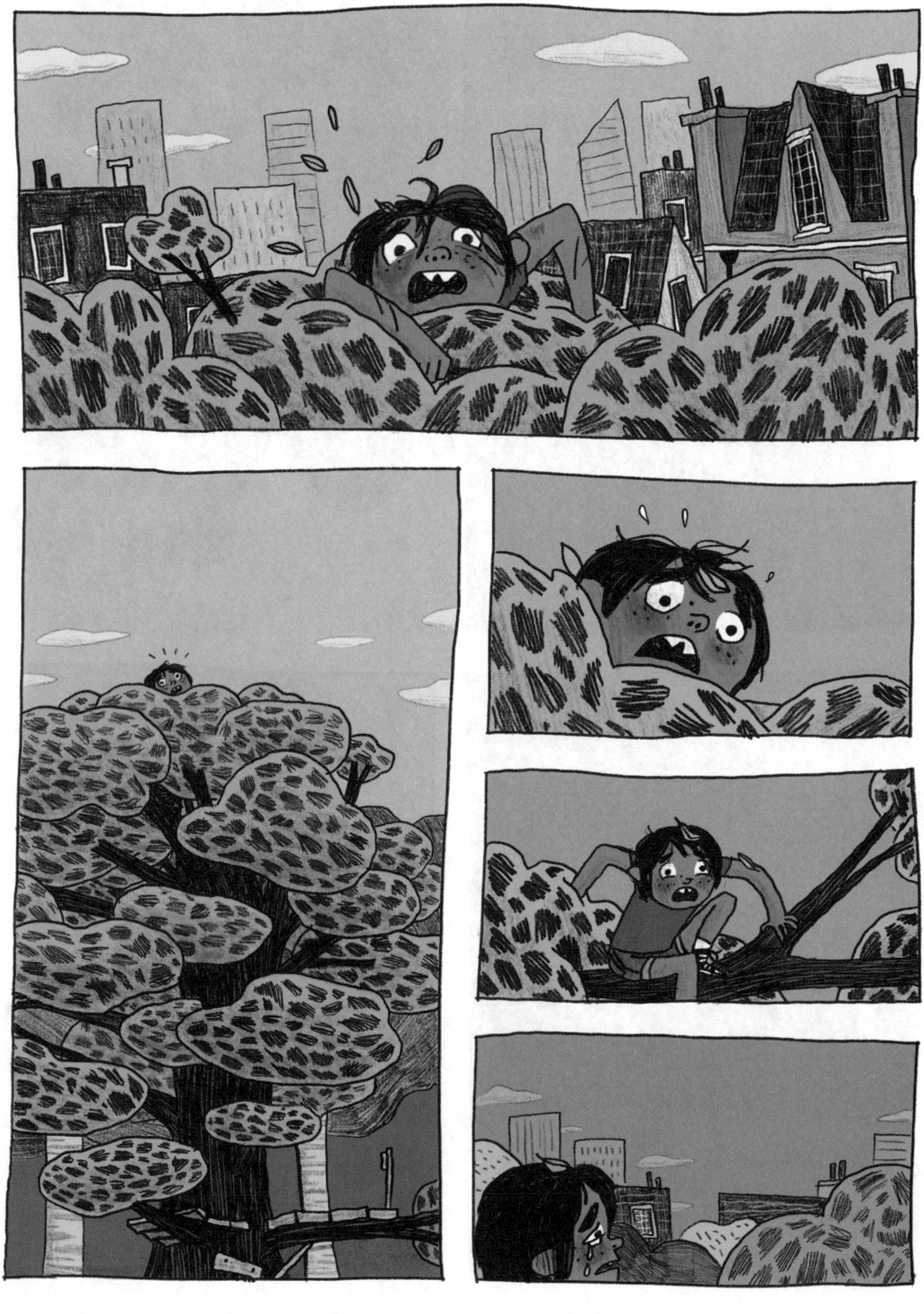

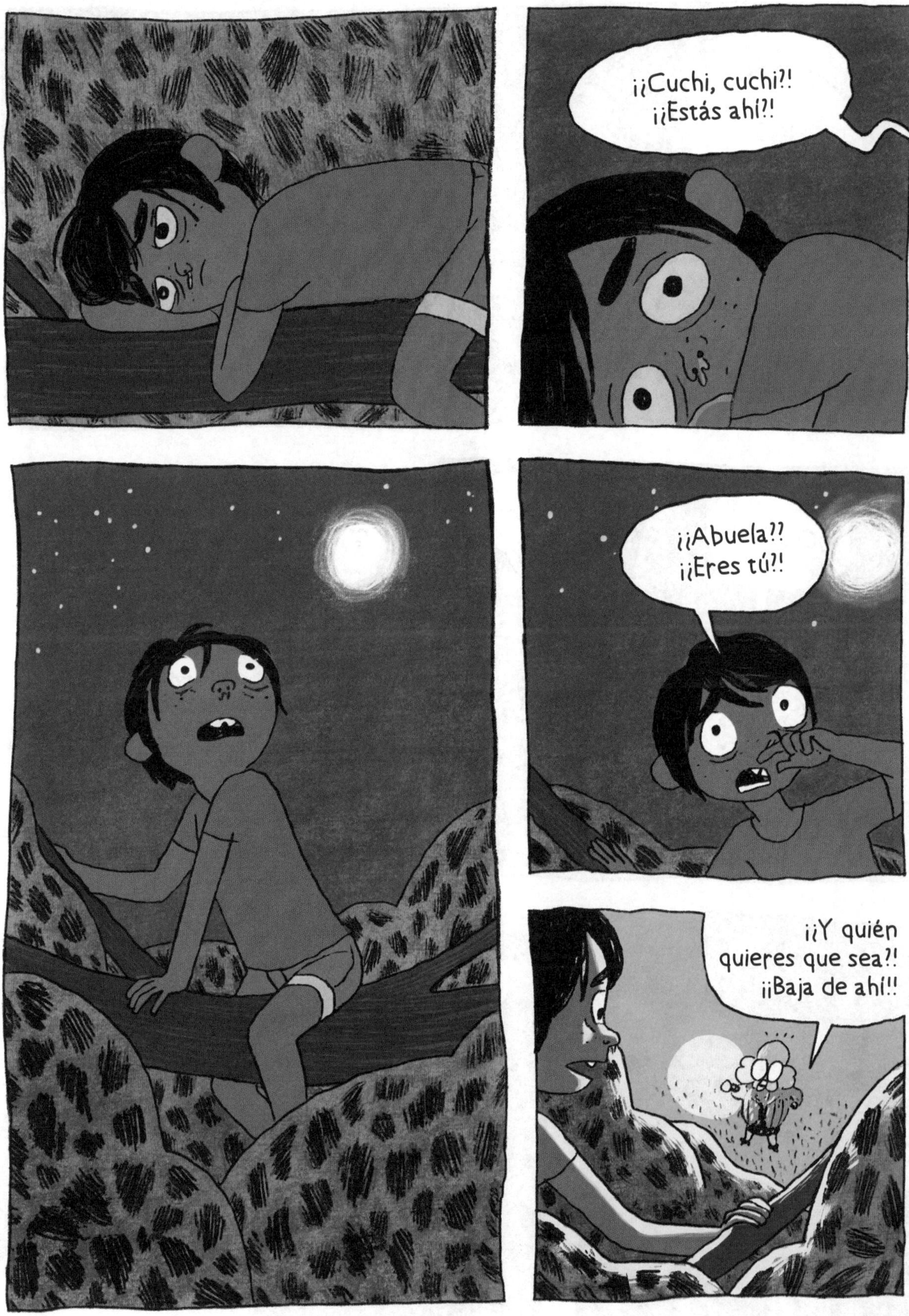
¡¿Cuchi, cuchi?!
¡¿Estás ahí?!
¡¿Abuela?!
¡¿Eres tú?!
¡¿Y quién quieres que sea?!
¡Baja de ahí!!

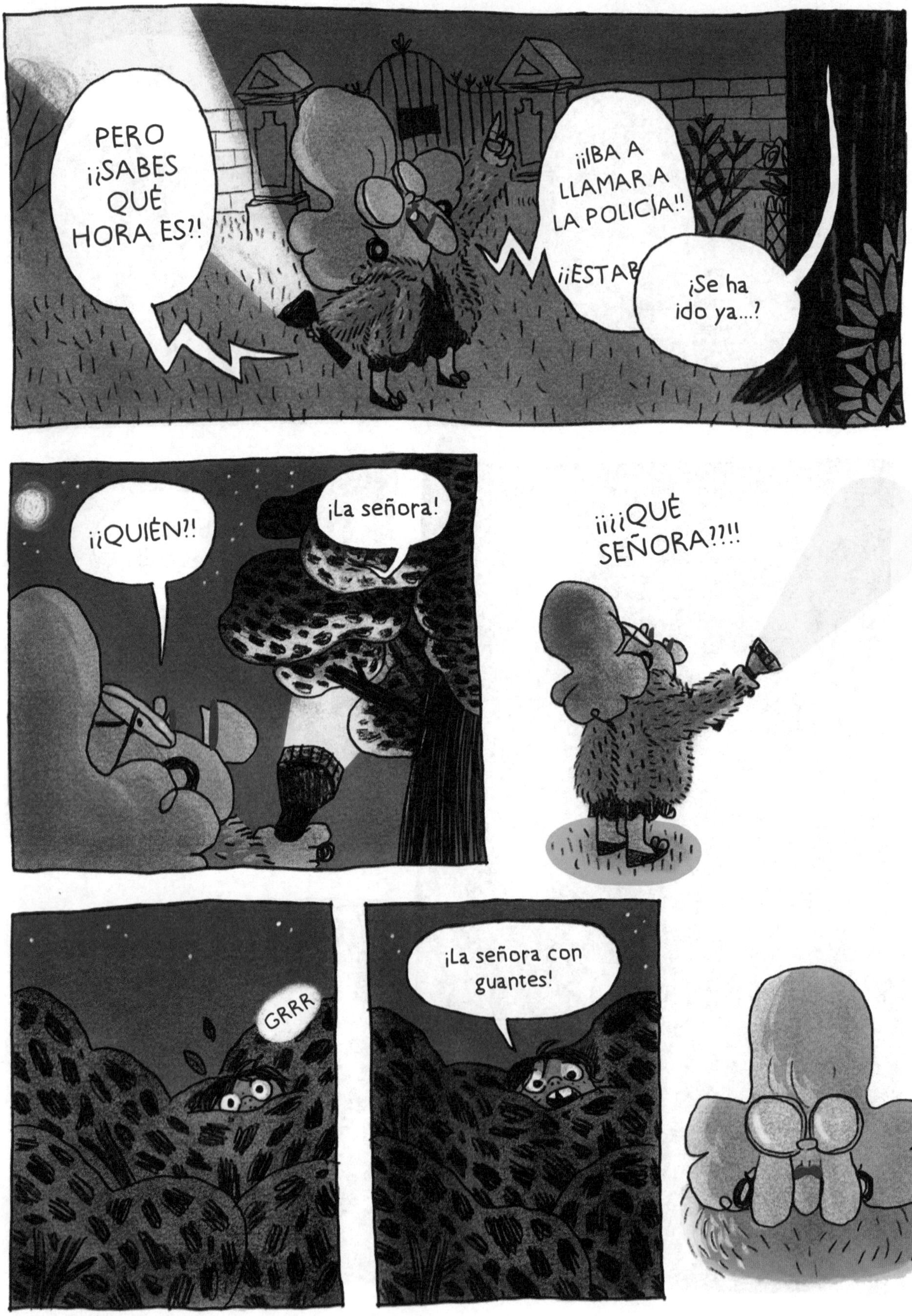
PERO ¡¡SABES QUÉ HORA ES?!
¡¡IBA A LLAMAR A LA POLICÍA!! ¡¡ESTAB
¿Se ha ido ya...?
¡¡QUIÉN?!
¡La señora!
¡¡¡QUÉ SEÑORA??!!
GRRR
¡La señora con guantes!

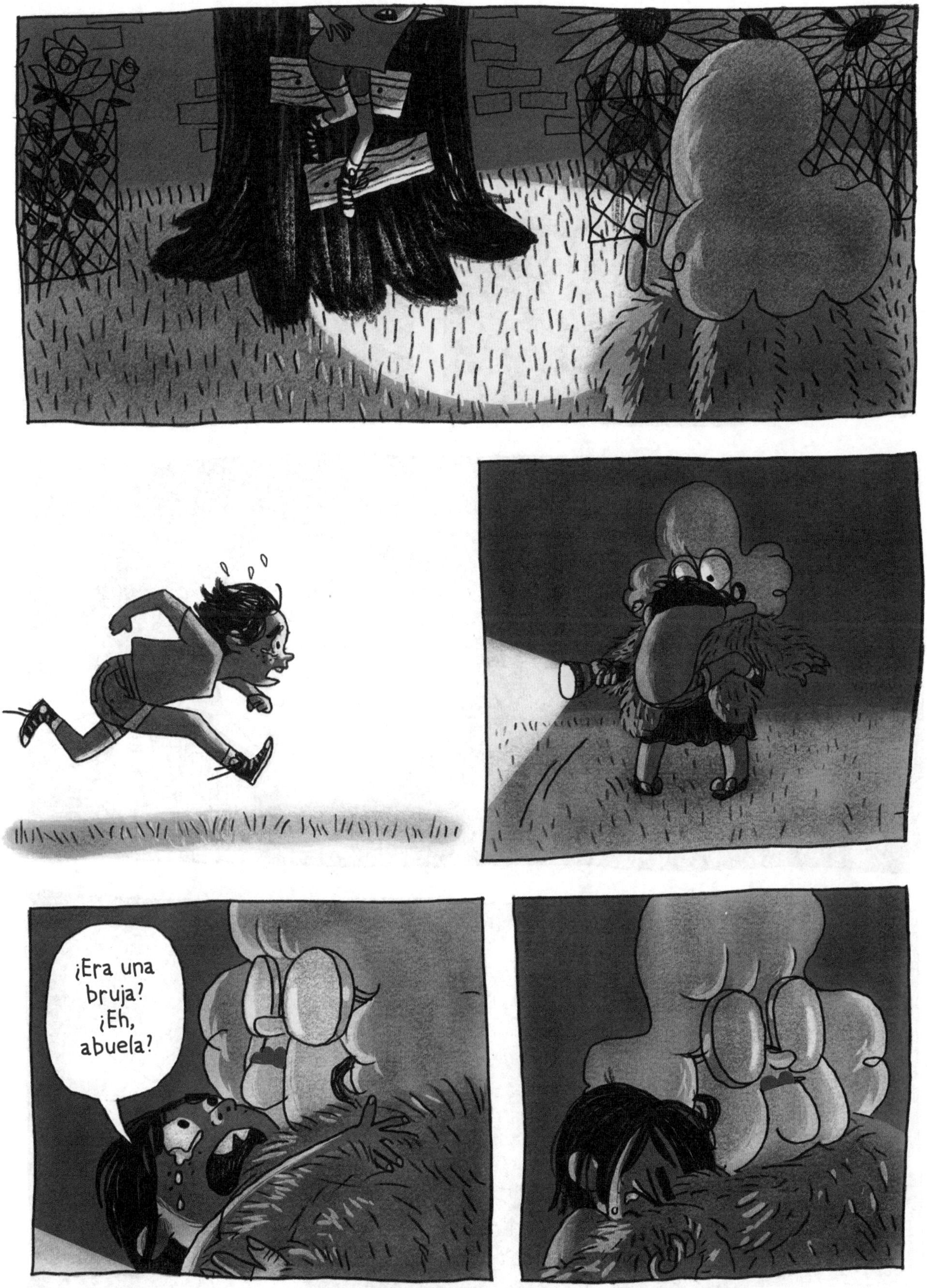
¡Era una bruja? ¡Eh, abuela?

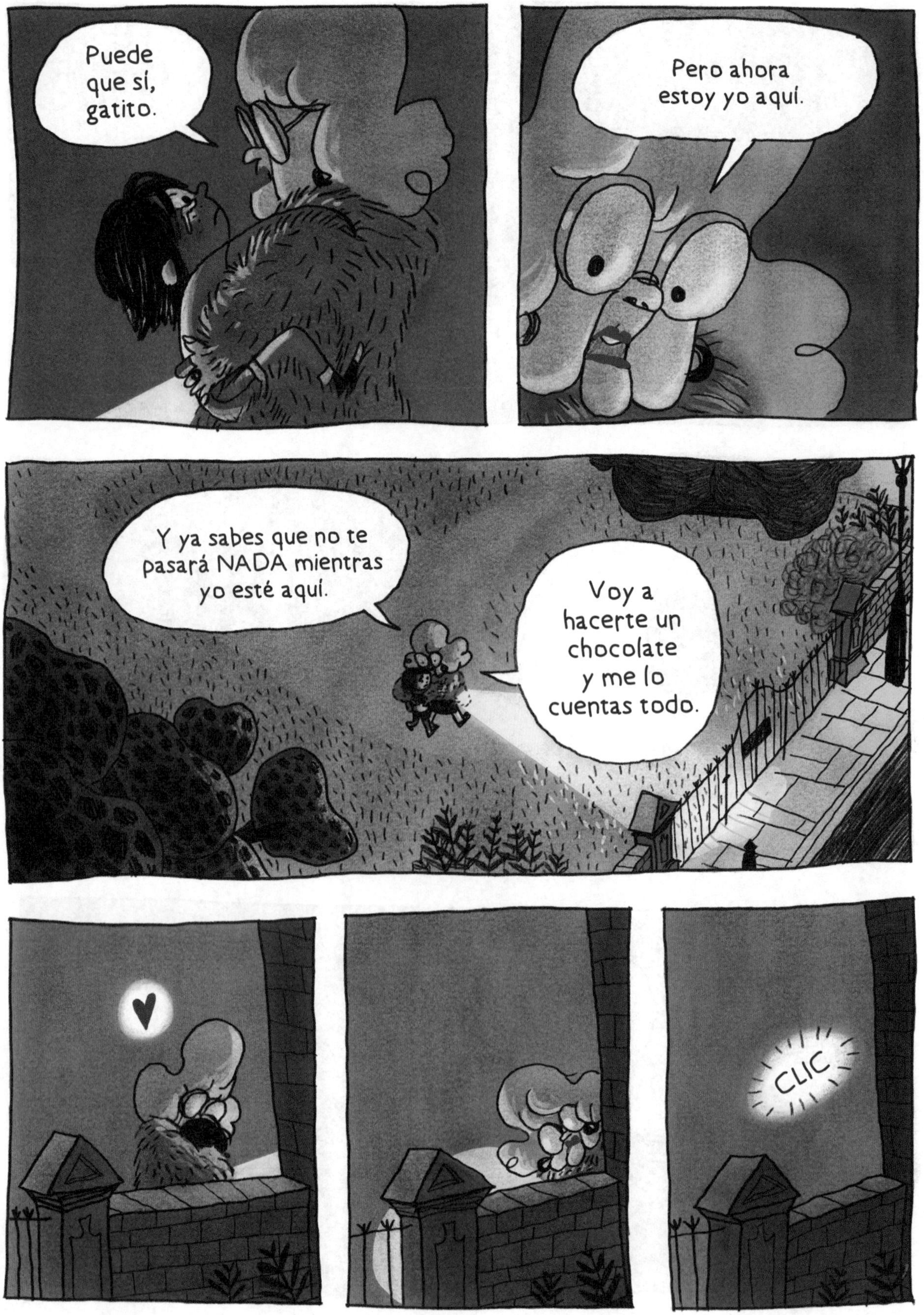
Puede que sí, gatito.
Pero ahora estoy yo aquí.
Y ya sabes que no te pasará NADA mientras yo esté aquí.
Voy a hacerte un chocolate y me lo cuentas todo.
CLIC

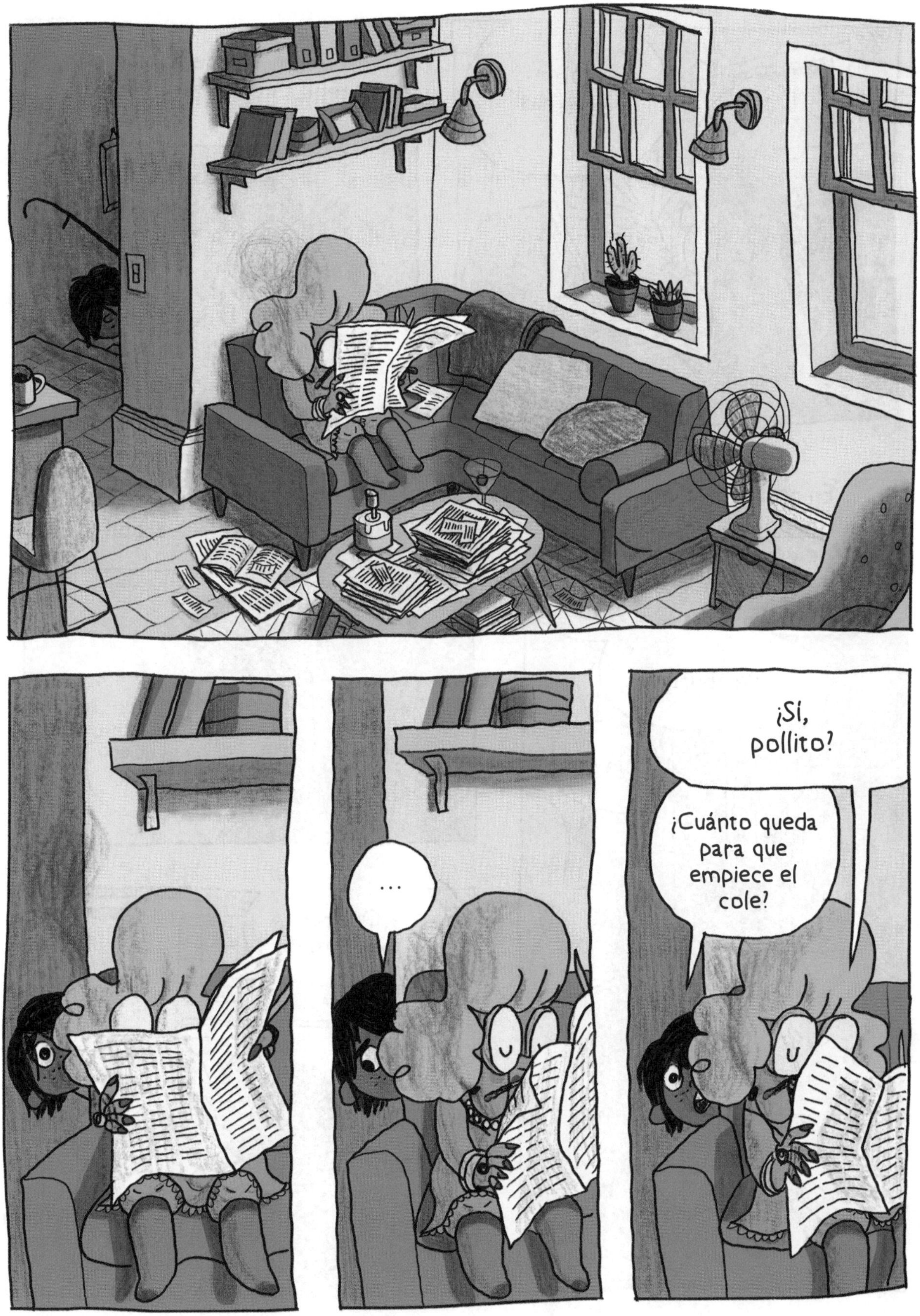
...
¡Sí,
pollito?
¿Cuánto queda para que empiece el cole?

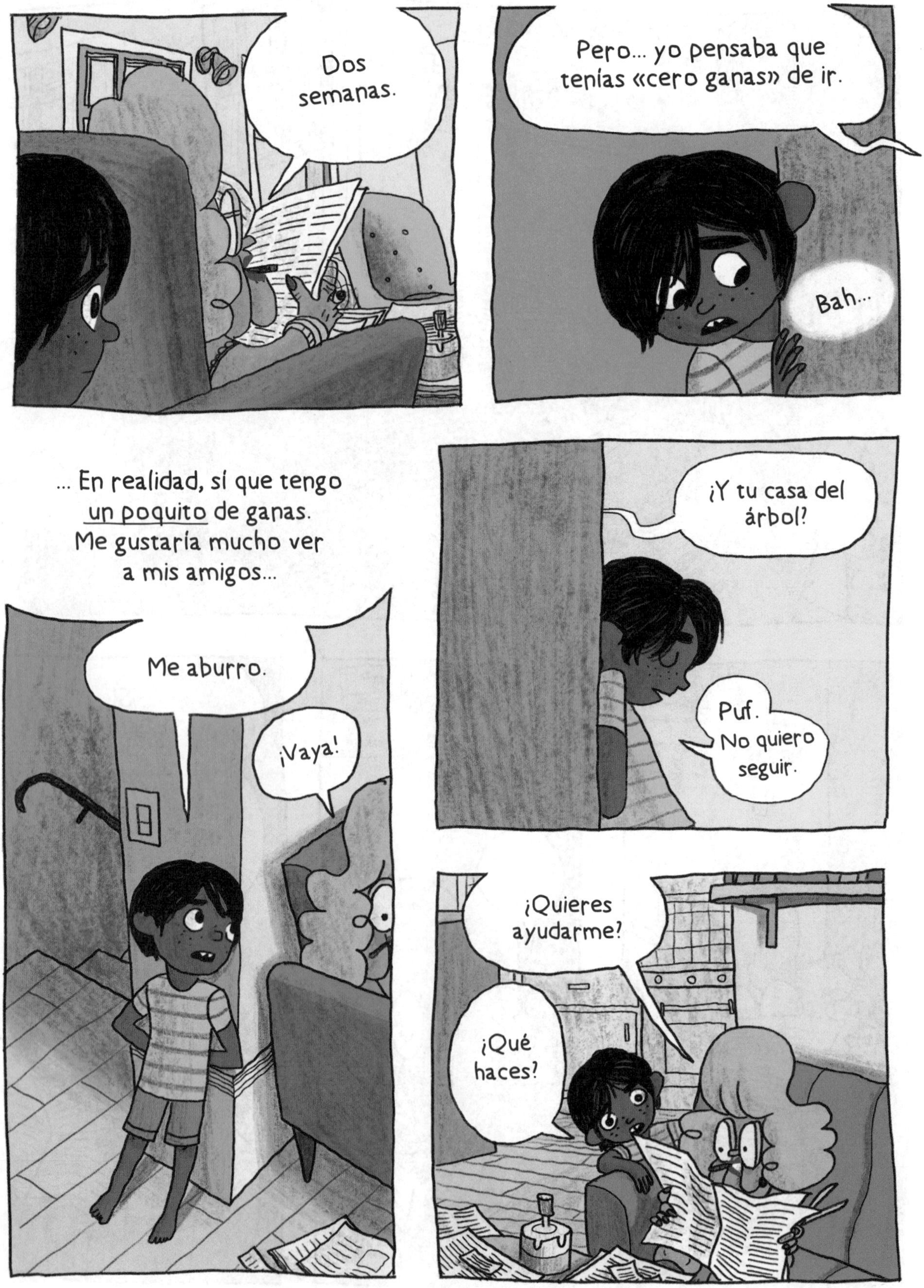
Dos semanas.
Pero... yo pensaba que tenías «cero ganas» de ir.
Bah...
... En realidad, sí que tengo un poquito de ganas. Me gustaría mucho ver a mis amigos...
Me aburro.
¡Vaya!
¿Y tu casa del árbol?
Puf. No quiero seguir.
¿Quieres ayudarme?
¿Qué haces?

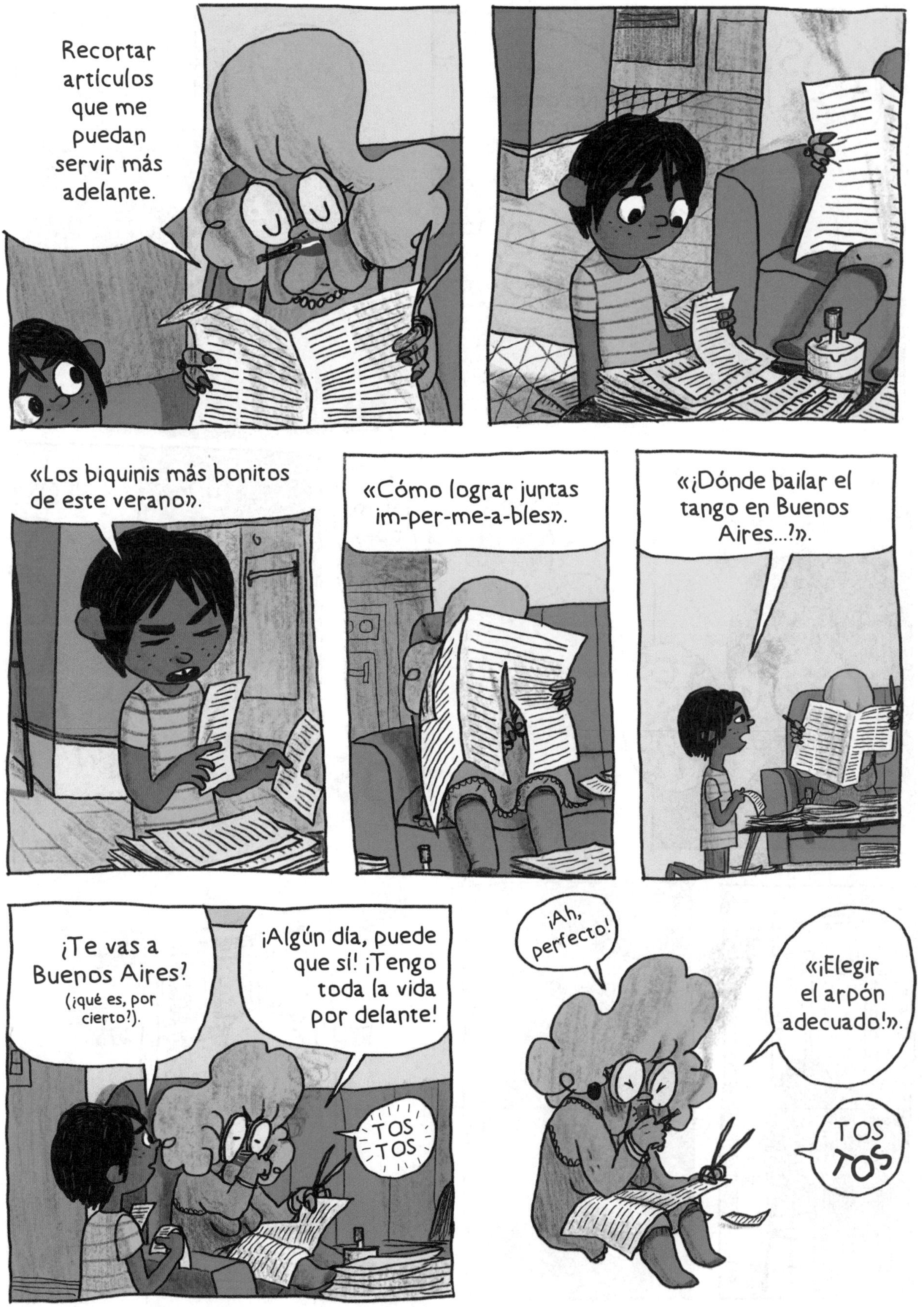
Recortar artículos que me puedan servir más adelante.
«Los biquinis más bonitos de este verano».
«Cómo lograr juntas im-per-me-a-bles».
«¿Dónde bailar el tango en Buenos Aires...?».
¿Te vas a Buenos Aires? (¿qué es, por cierto?).
¡Algún día, puede que sí! ¡Tengo toda la vida por delante!
TOS TOS
¡Ah, perfecto!
«¡Elegir el arpón adecuado!».
TOS TOS

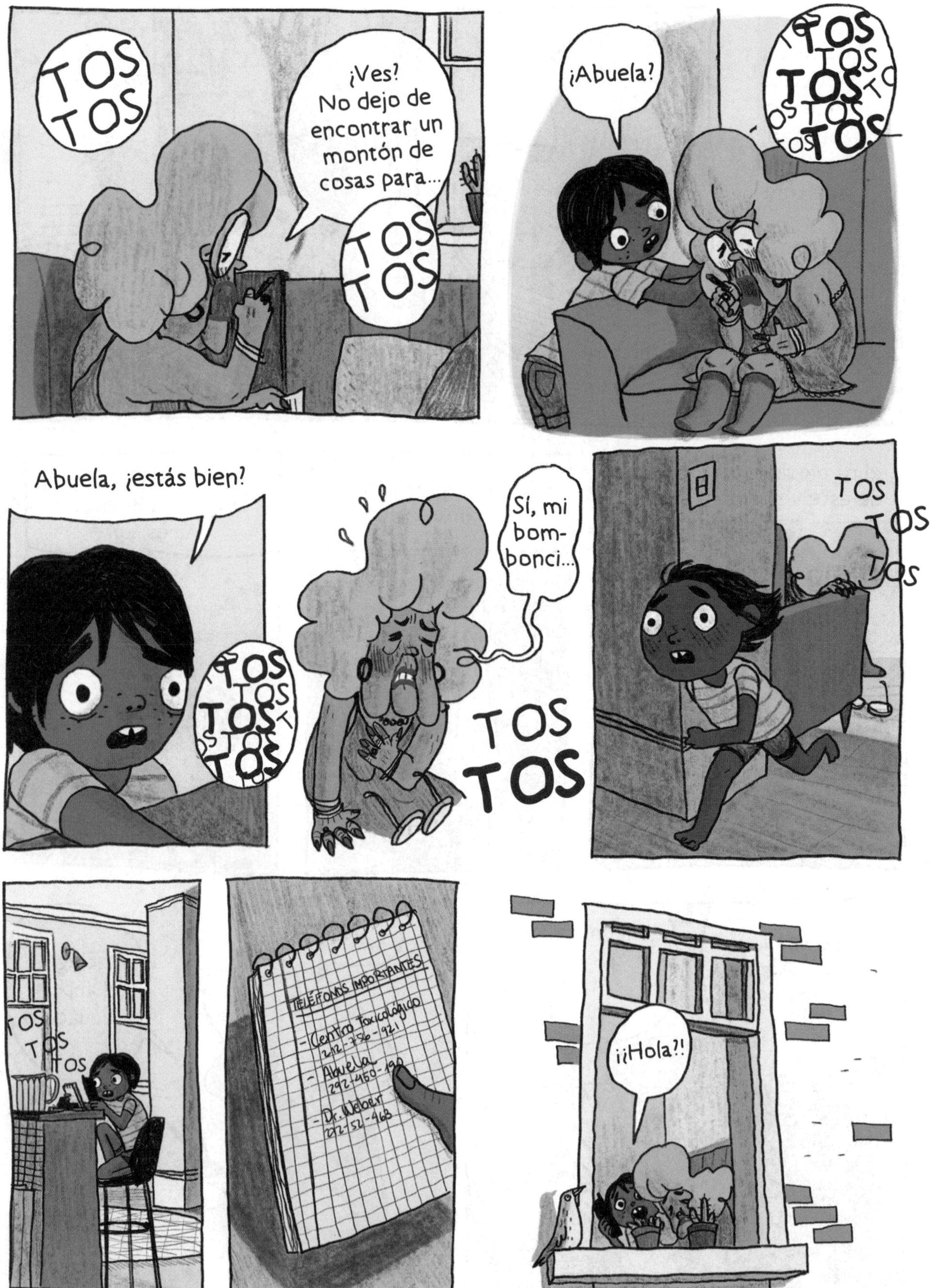
TOS TOS
¿Ves? No dejo de encontrar un montón de cosas para...
TOS TOS
¿Abuela?
TOS TOS TOS TOS TOS TOS
Abuela, ¿estás bien?
TOS TOS TOS TOS
Sí, mi bombonci...
TOS TOS
TOS TOS TOS
TOS TOS TOS
TELÉFONOS IMPORTANTES
- Centro Toxicológico 212-756-921
- Abuela 292-450-190
- Dr. Weber 292-52-463
¡¡Hola?!

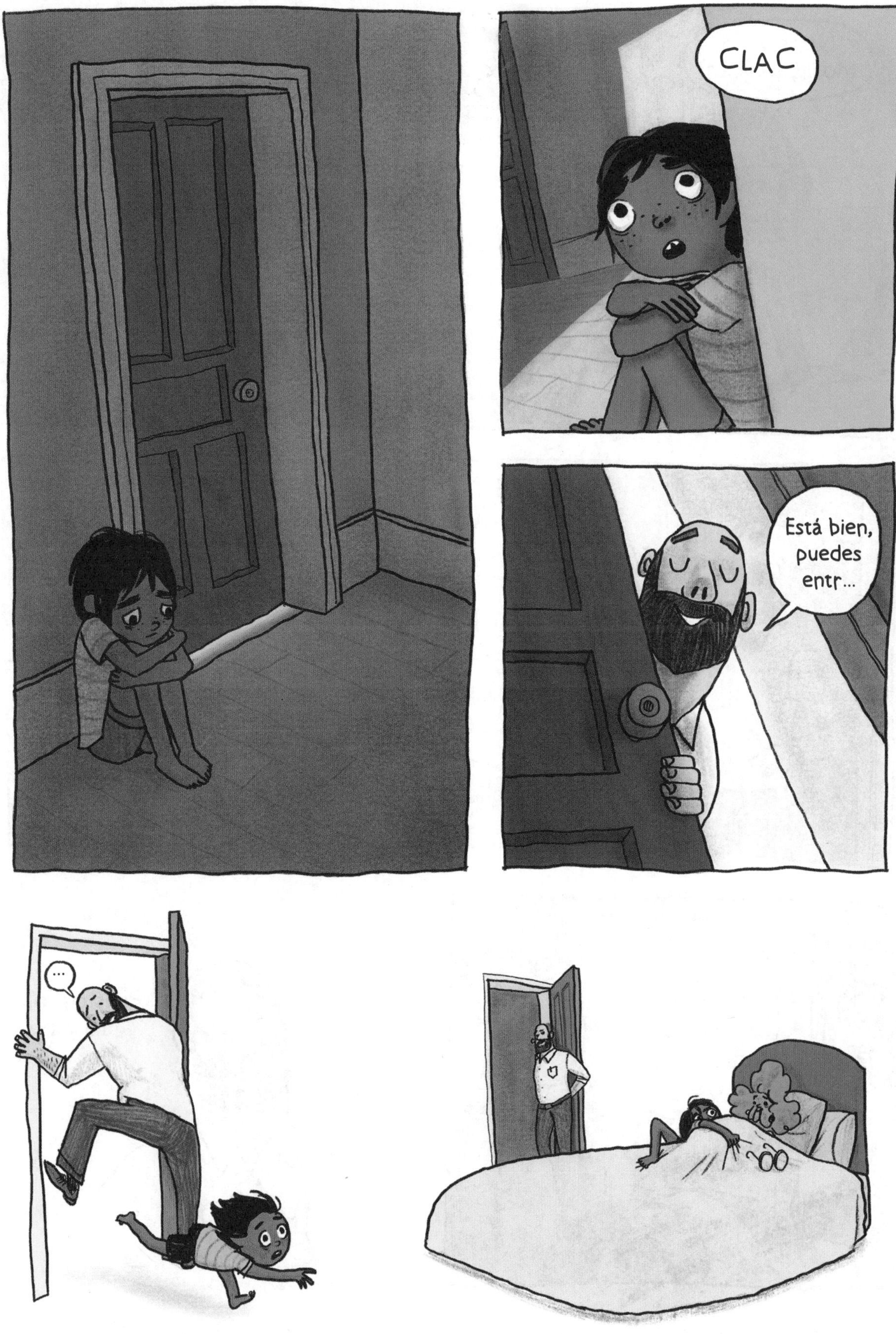
CLAC
Está bien, puedes entr...
...

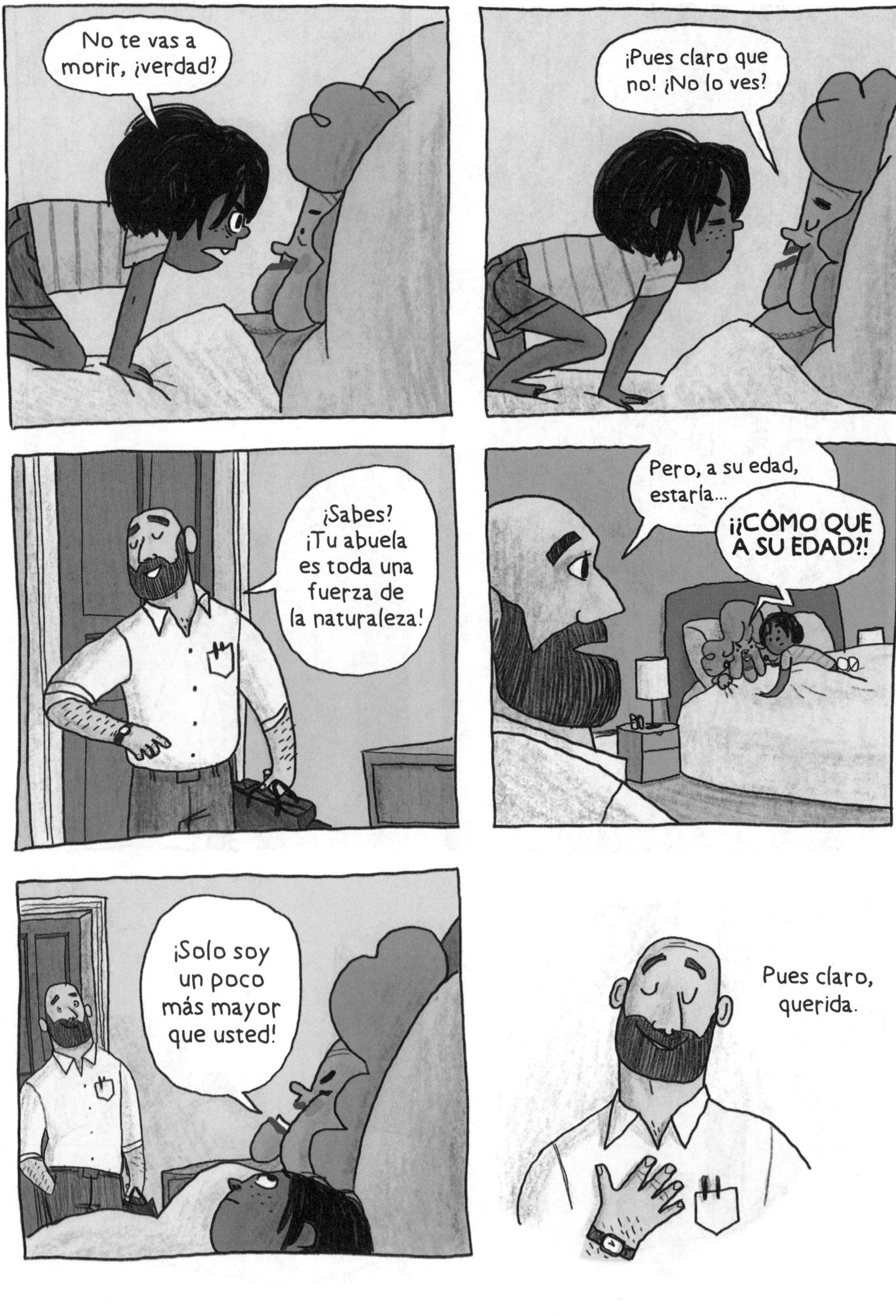
No te vas a morir, ¿verdad?
¡Pues claro que no! ¿No lo ves?
¿Sabes? ¡Tu abuela es toda una fuerza de la naturaleza!
Pero, a su edad, estaría...
¡¿CÓMO QUE A SU EDAD?!
¡Solo soy un poco más mayor que usted!
Pues claro, querida.

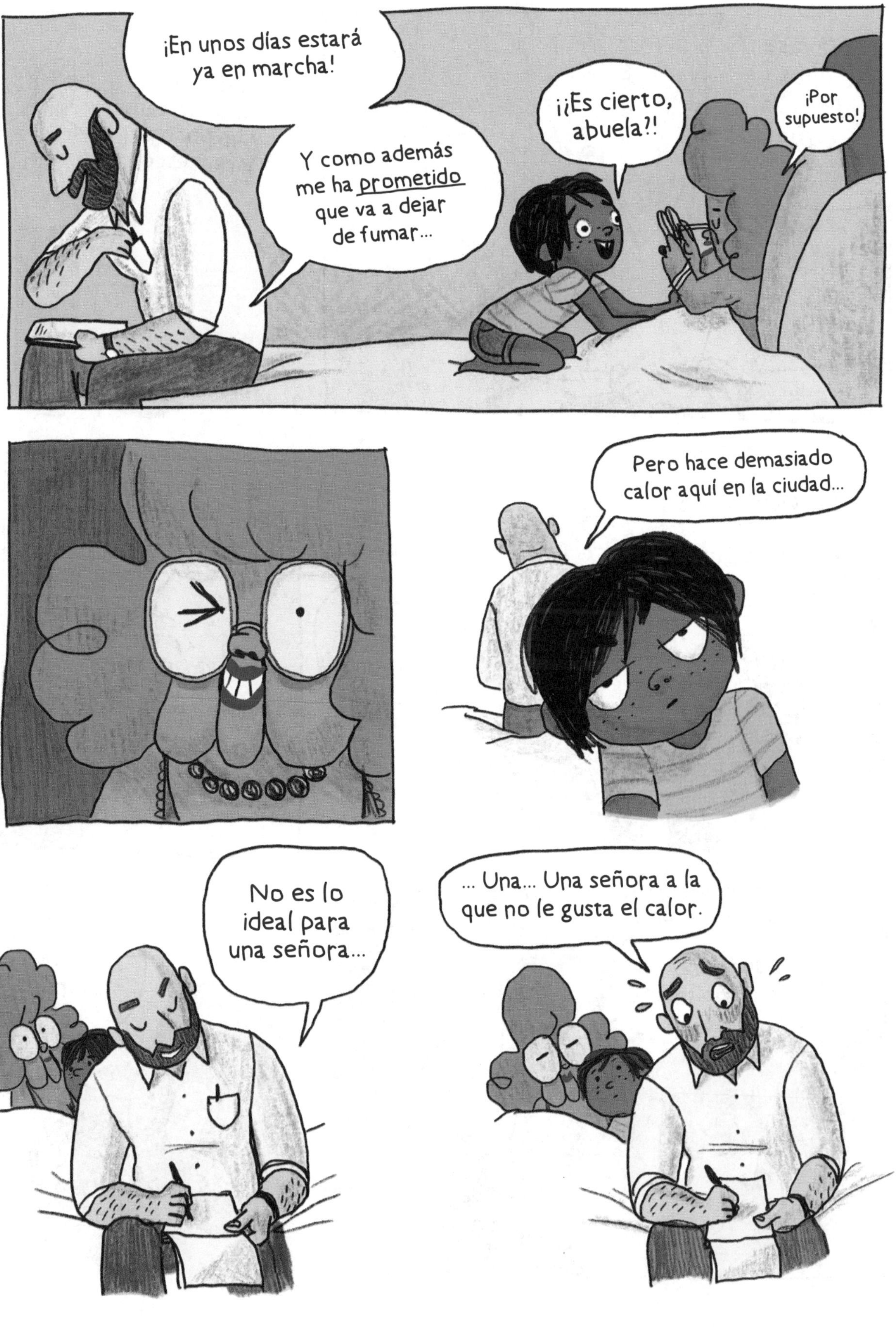

¡En unos días estará ya en marcha!
Y como además me ha prometido que va a dejar de fumar...
¡¿Es cierto, abuela?!
¡Por supuesto!
Pero hace demasiado calor aquí en la ciudad...
No es lo ideal para una señora...
... Una... Una señora a la que no le gusta el calor.

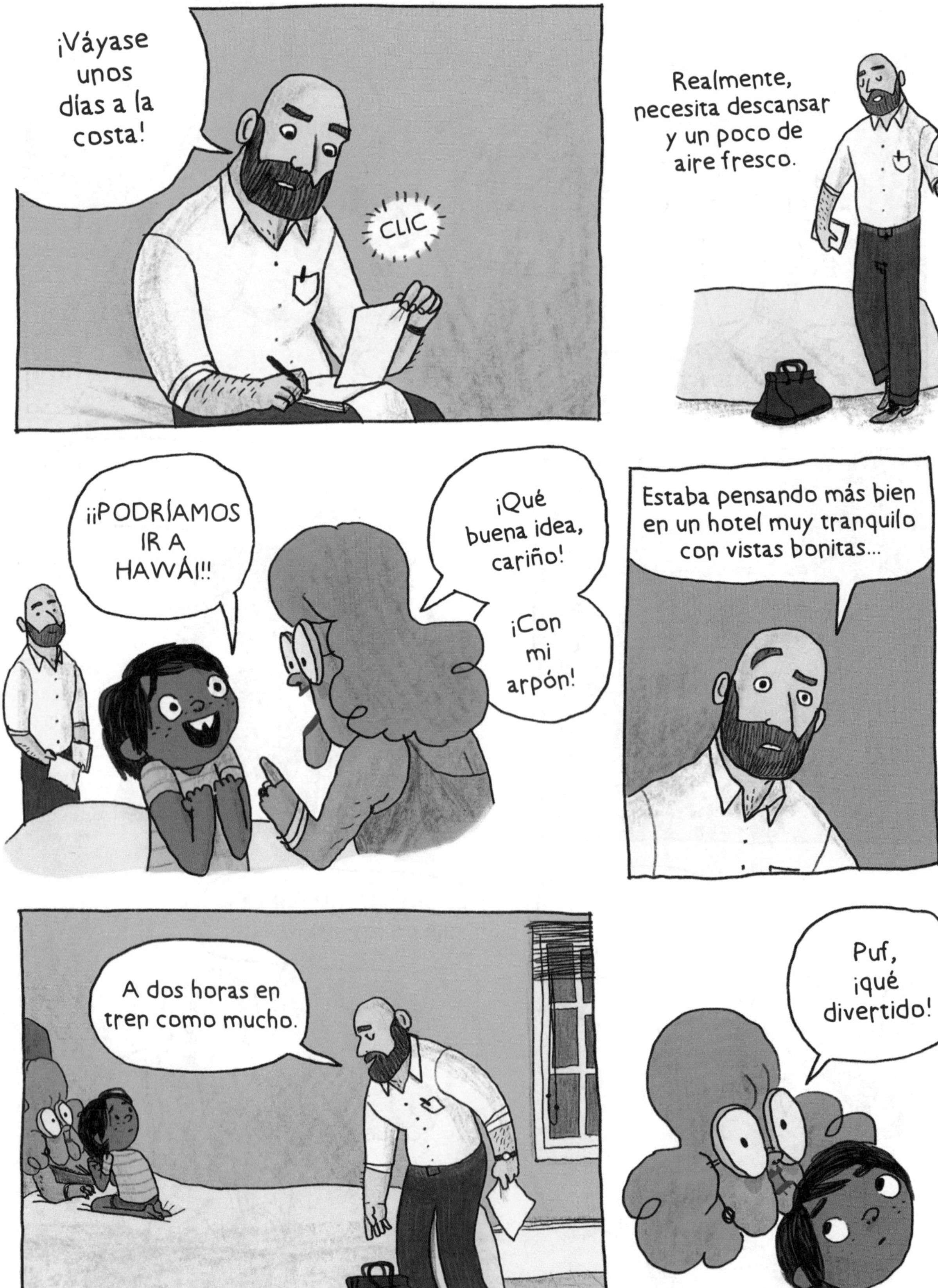
¡Váyase unos días a la costa!
CLIC
Realmente, necesita descansar y un poco de aire fresco.
¡¡PODRÍAMOS IR A HAWÁI!!
¡Qué buena idea, cariño!
¡Con mi arpón!
Estaba pensando más bien en un hotel muy tranquilo con vistas bonitas...
A dos horas en tren como mucho.
Puf, ¡qué divertido!

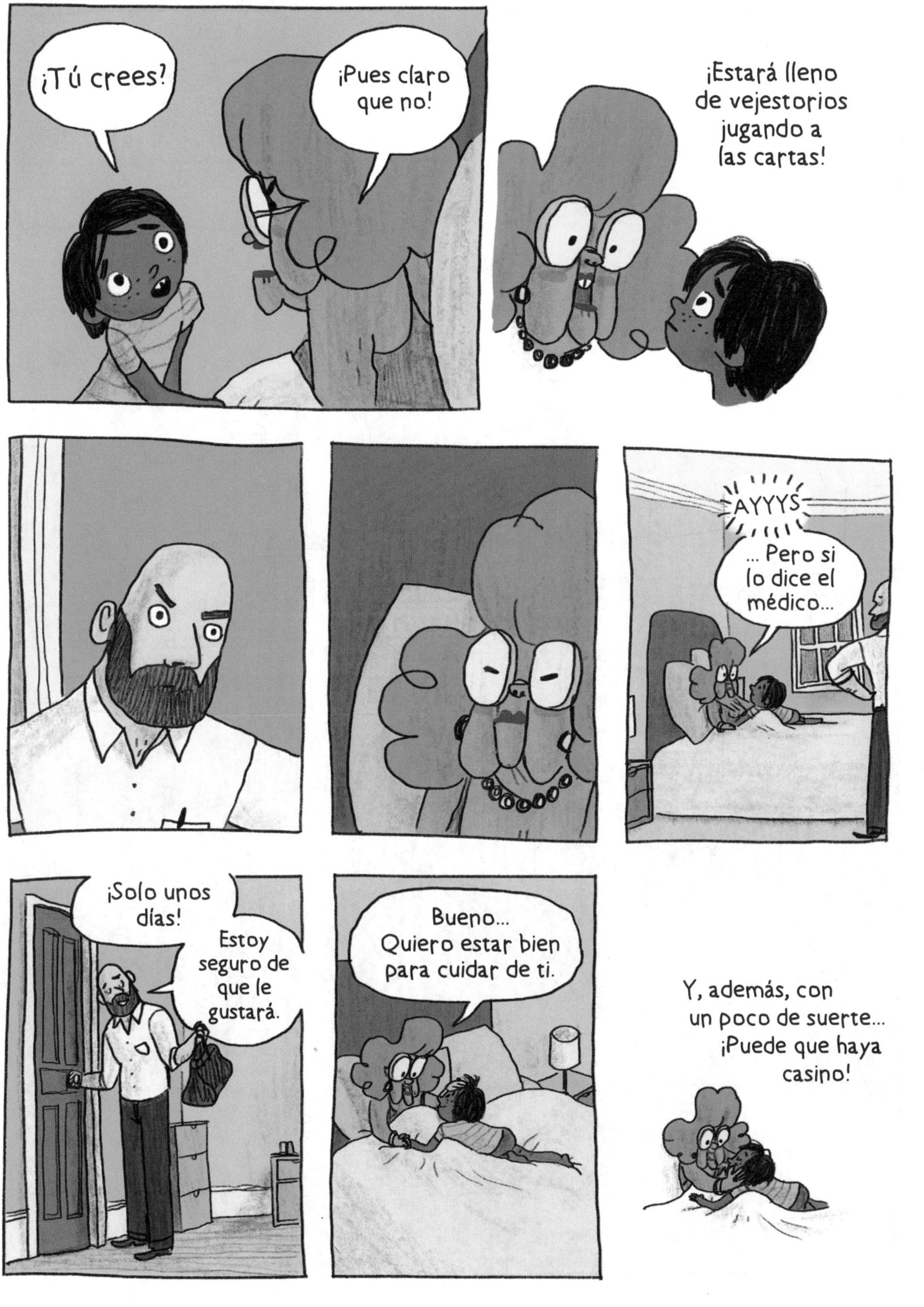
¡Tú crees?
¡Pues claro que no!
¡Estará lleno de vejestorios jugando a las cartas!
AYYYS
... Pero si lo dice el médico...
¡Solo unos días!
Estoy seguro de que le gustará.
Bueno... Quiero estar bien para cuidar de ti.
Y, además, con un poco de suerte... ¡Puede que haya casino!

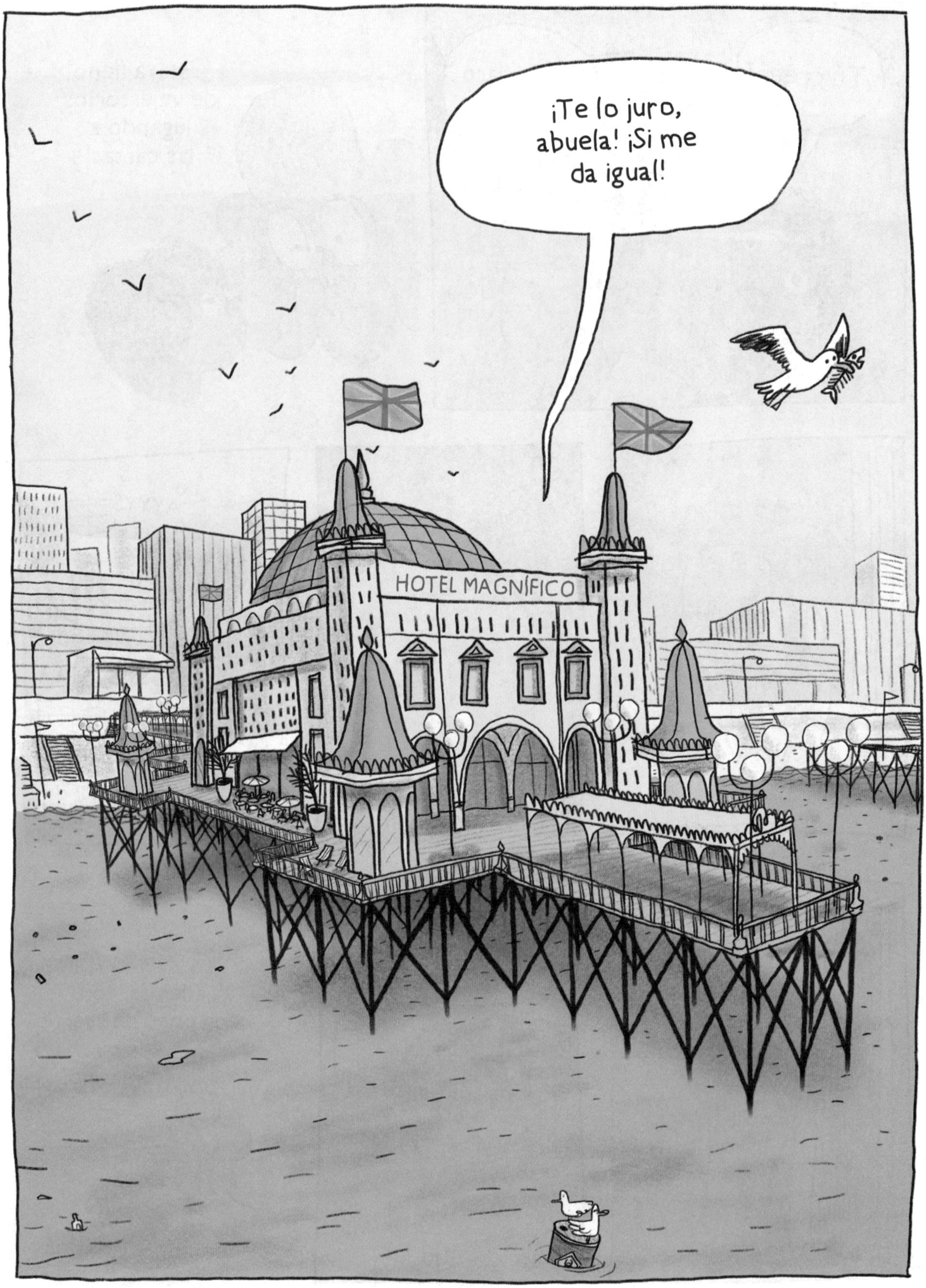
¡Te lo juro, abuela! ¡Si me da igual!
HOTEL MAGNÍFICO

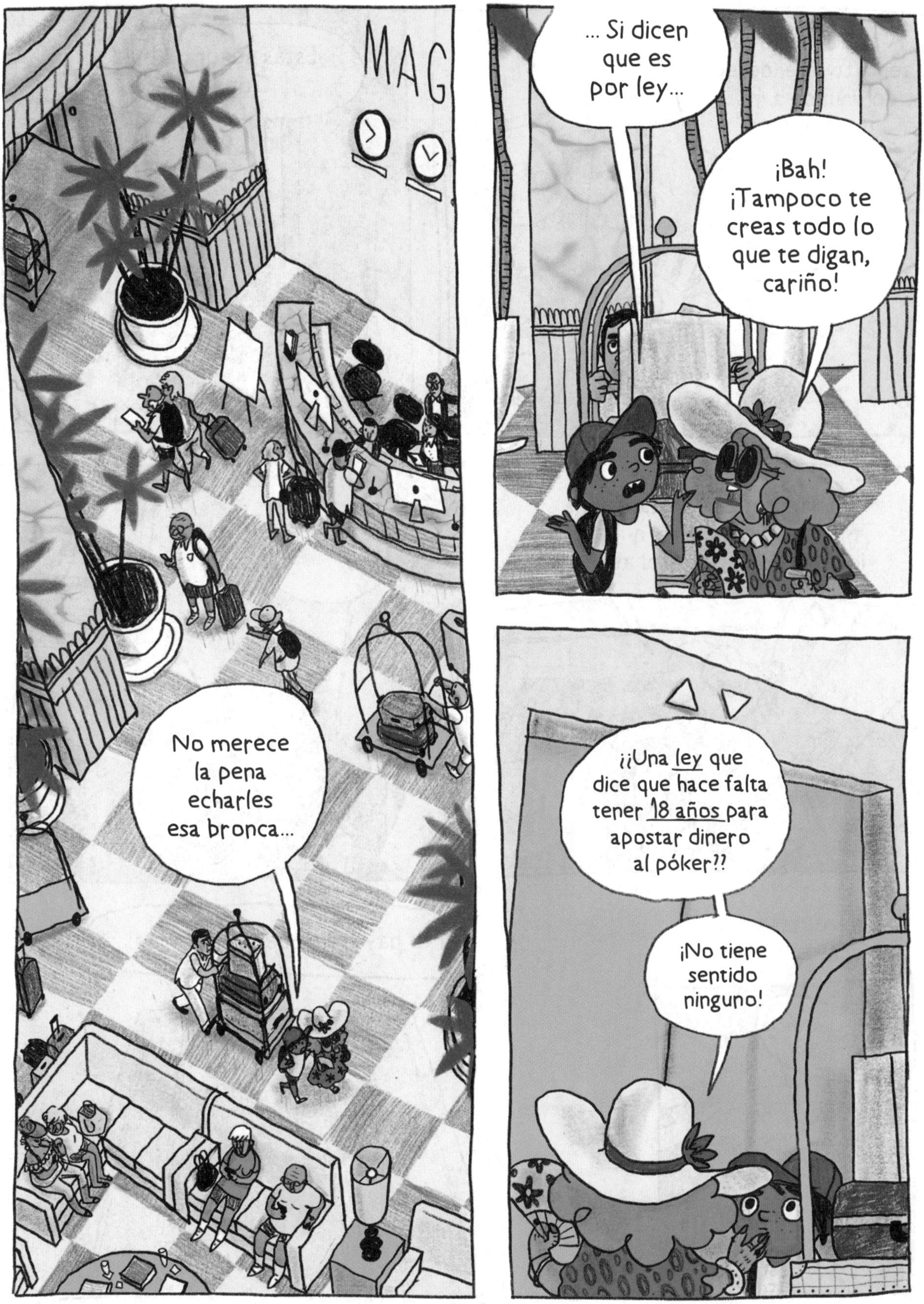
MAG
No merece la pena echarles esa bronca...
... Si dicen que es por ley...
¡Bah! ¡Tampoco te creas todo lo que te digan, cariño!
¡¡Una ley que dice que hace falta tener 18 años para apostar dinero al póker??
¡No tiene sentido ninguno!

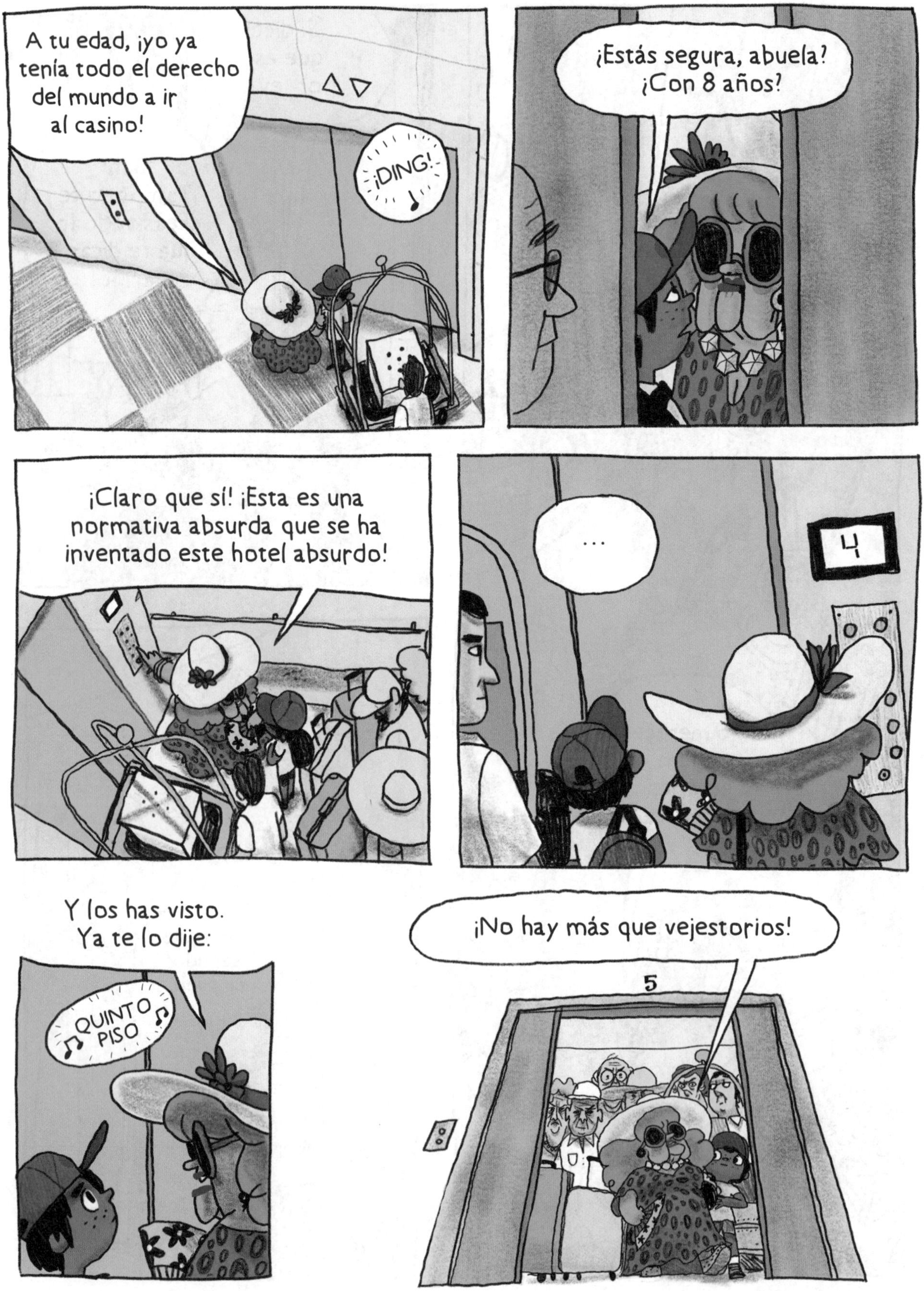
A tu edad, ¡yo ya tenía todo el derecho del mundo a ir al casino!
¡DING!
¿Estás segura, abuela? ¿Con 8 años?
¡Claro que sí! ¡Esta es una normativa absurda que se ha inventado este hotel absurdo!
...
4
Y los has visto. Ya te lo dije:
QUINTO PISO
¡No hay más que vejestorios!
5

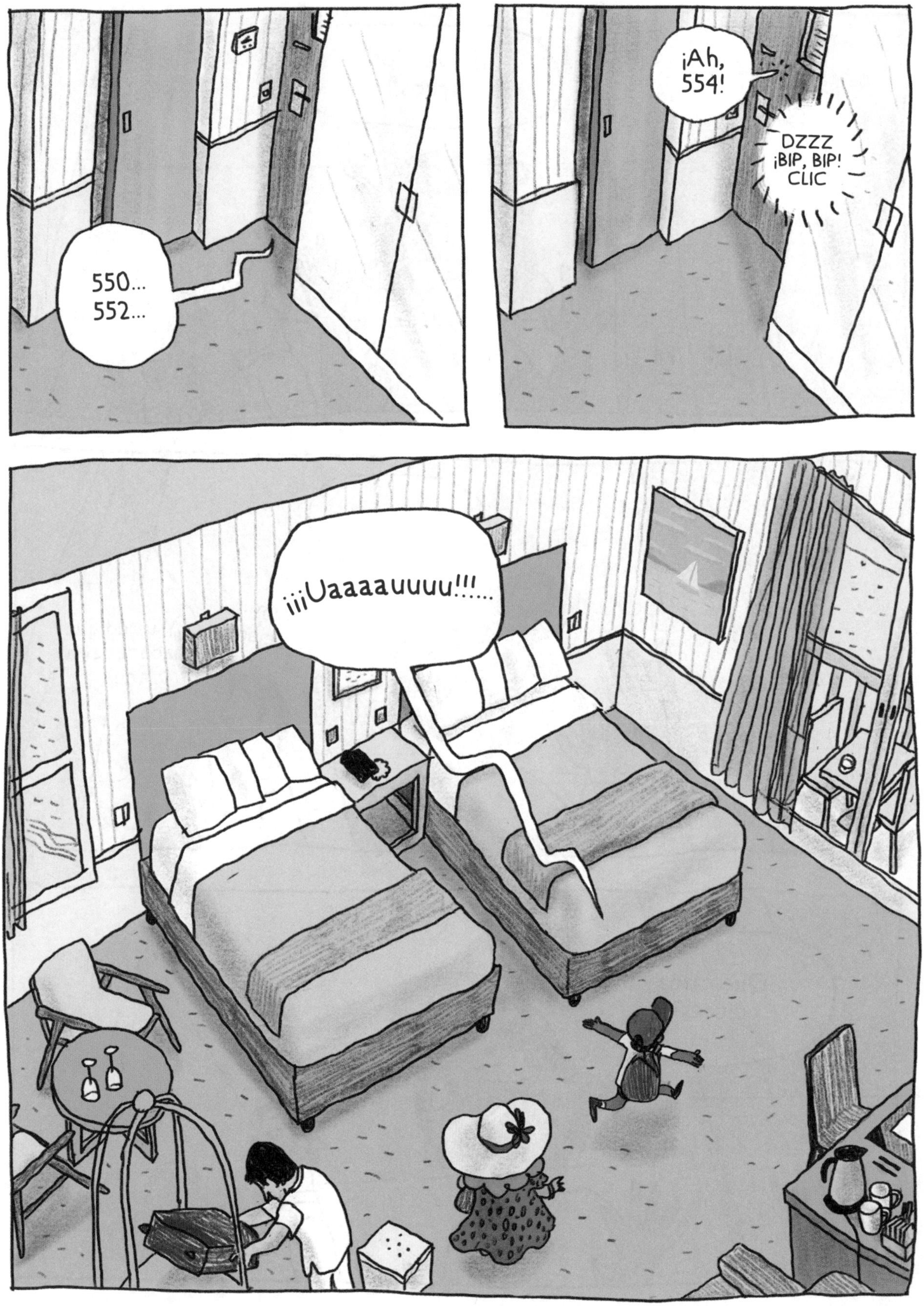
550...
552...
¡Ah,
554!
DZZZ
¡BIP, BIP!
CLIC
¡¡¡Uaaaauuuu!!!.....

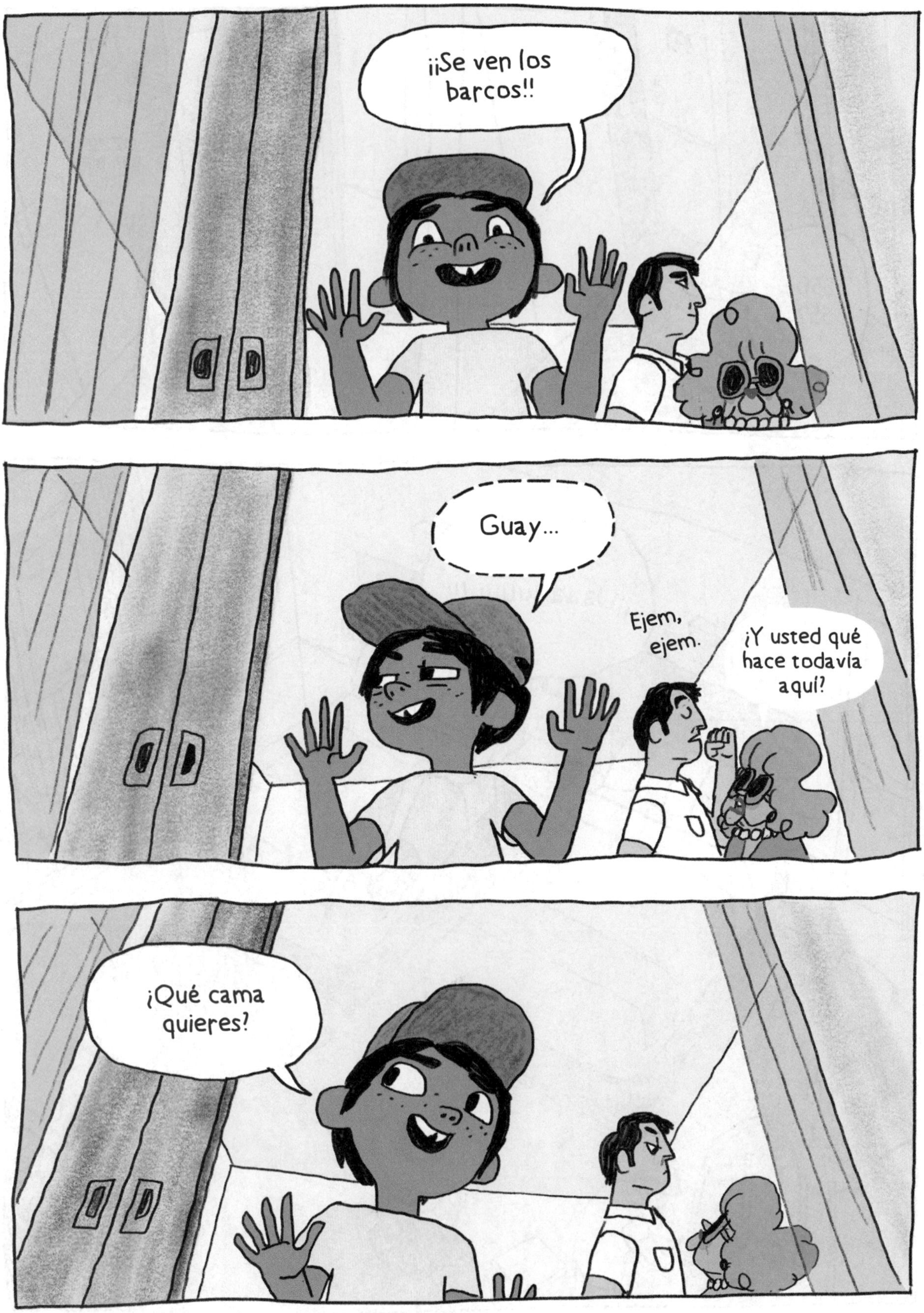
¡¡Se ven los barcos!!
Guay...
Ejem, ejem.
¿Y usted qué hace todavía aquí?
¿Qué cama quieres?

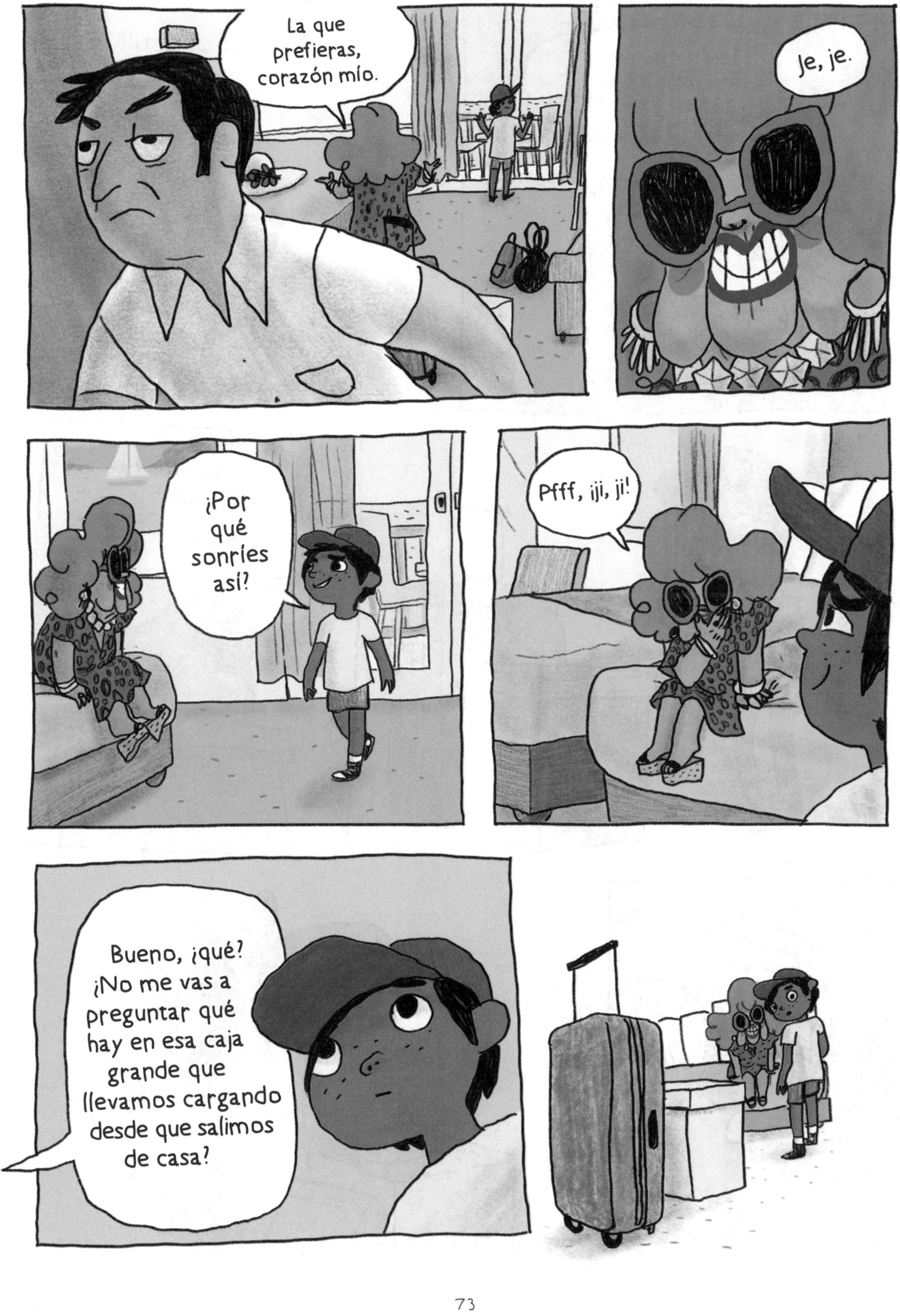
La que prefieras, corazón mío.
Je, je.
¿Por qué sonríes así?
Pfff, ¡ji, ji!
Bueno, ¿qué? ¿No me vas a preguntar qué hay en esa caja grande que llevamos cargando desde que salimos de casa?

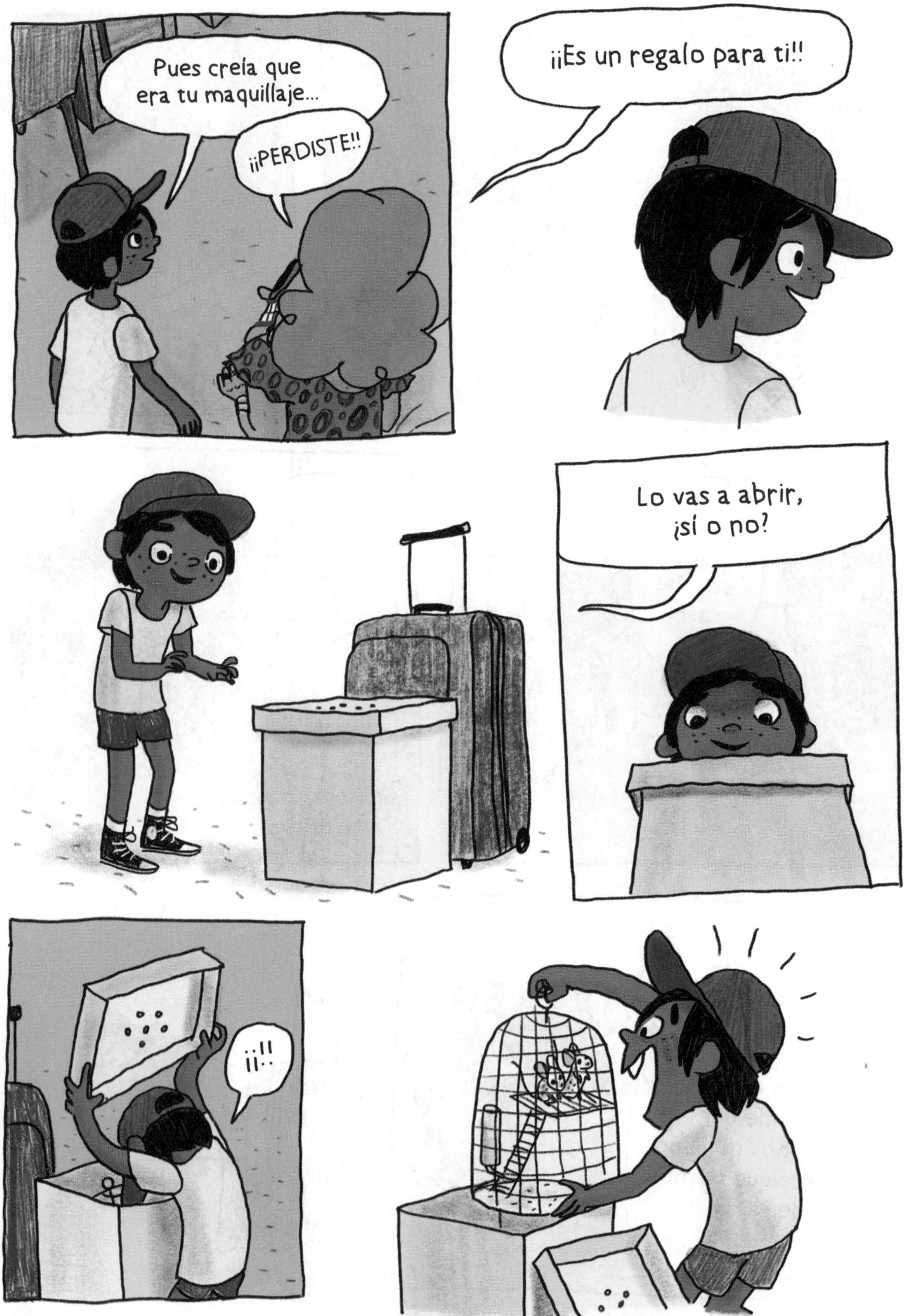

Pues creía que era tu maquillaje...
¡¡PERDISTE!!
¡¡Es un regalo para ti!!
Lo vas a abrir, ¿sí o no?
¡¡!!

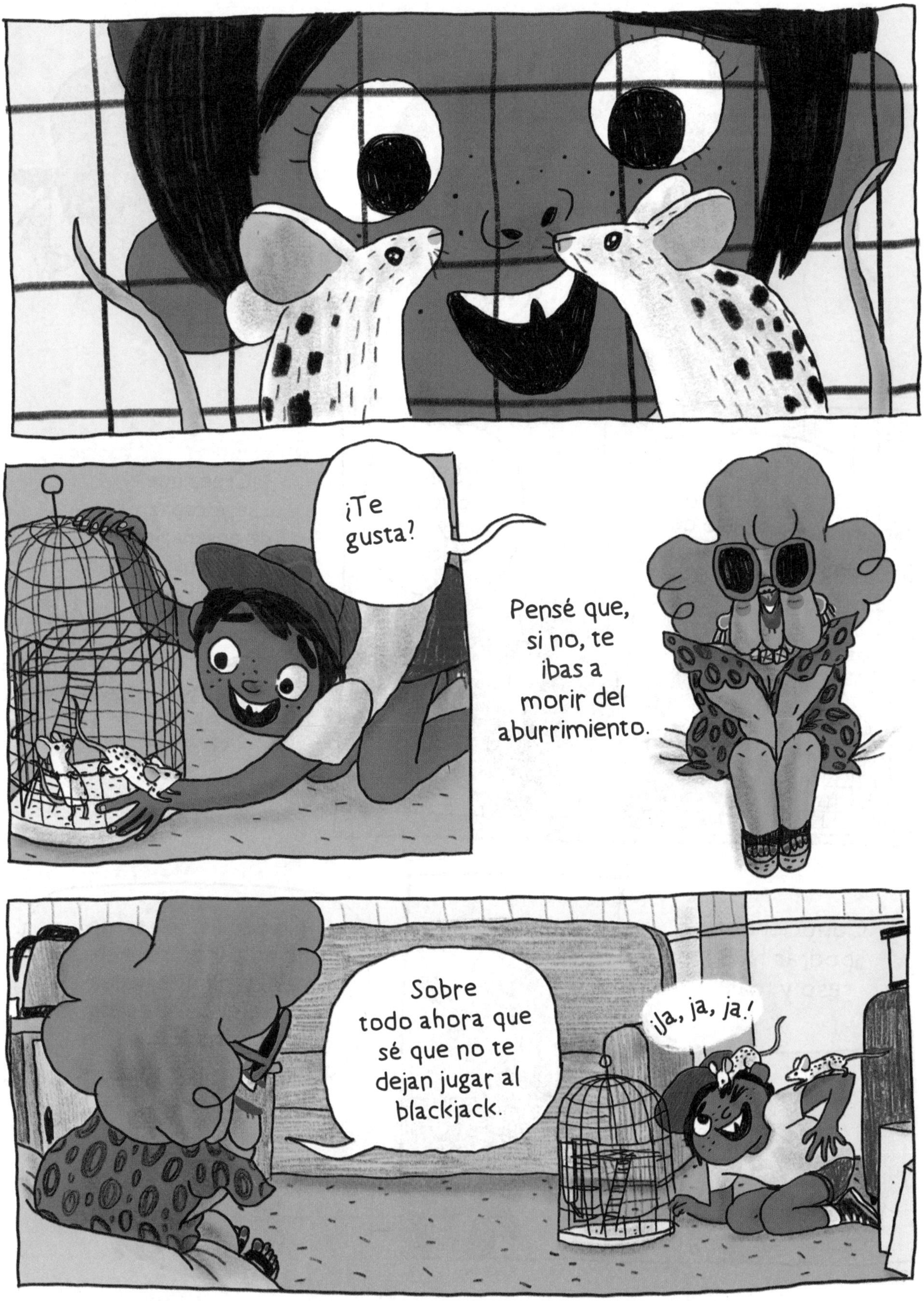
¿Te gusta?
Pensé que, si no, te ibas a morir del aburrimiento.
Sobre todo ahora que sé que no te dejan jugar al blackjack.
¡Ja, ja, ja!

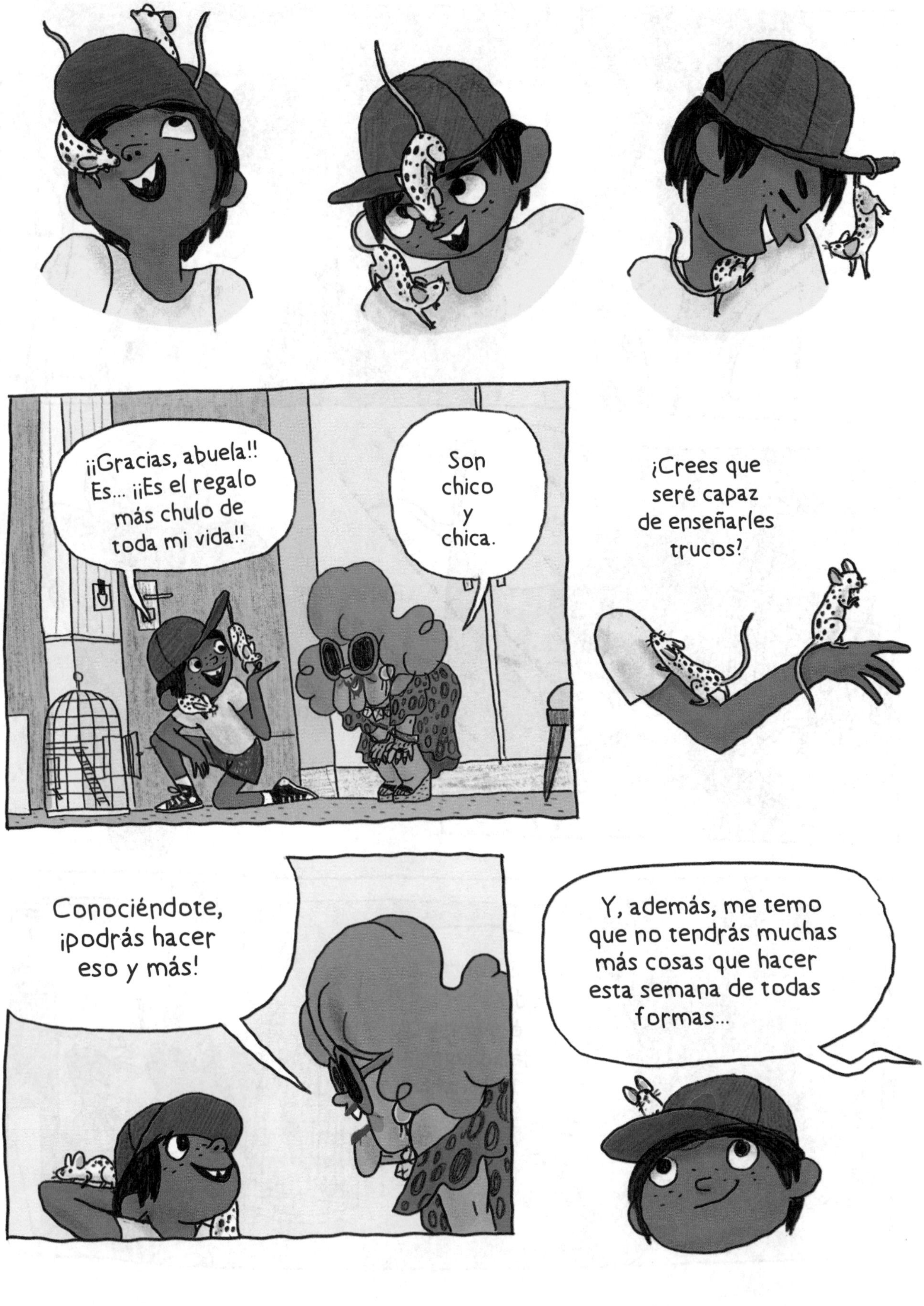

¡¡Gracias, abuela!! Es... ¡¡Es el regalo más chulo de toda mi vida!!
Son chico y chica.
¿Crees que seré capaz de enseñarles trucos?
Conociéndote, ¡podrás hacer eso y más!
Y, además, me temo que no tendrás muchas más cosas que hacer esta semana de todas formas...

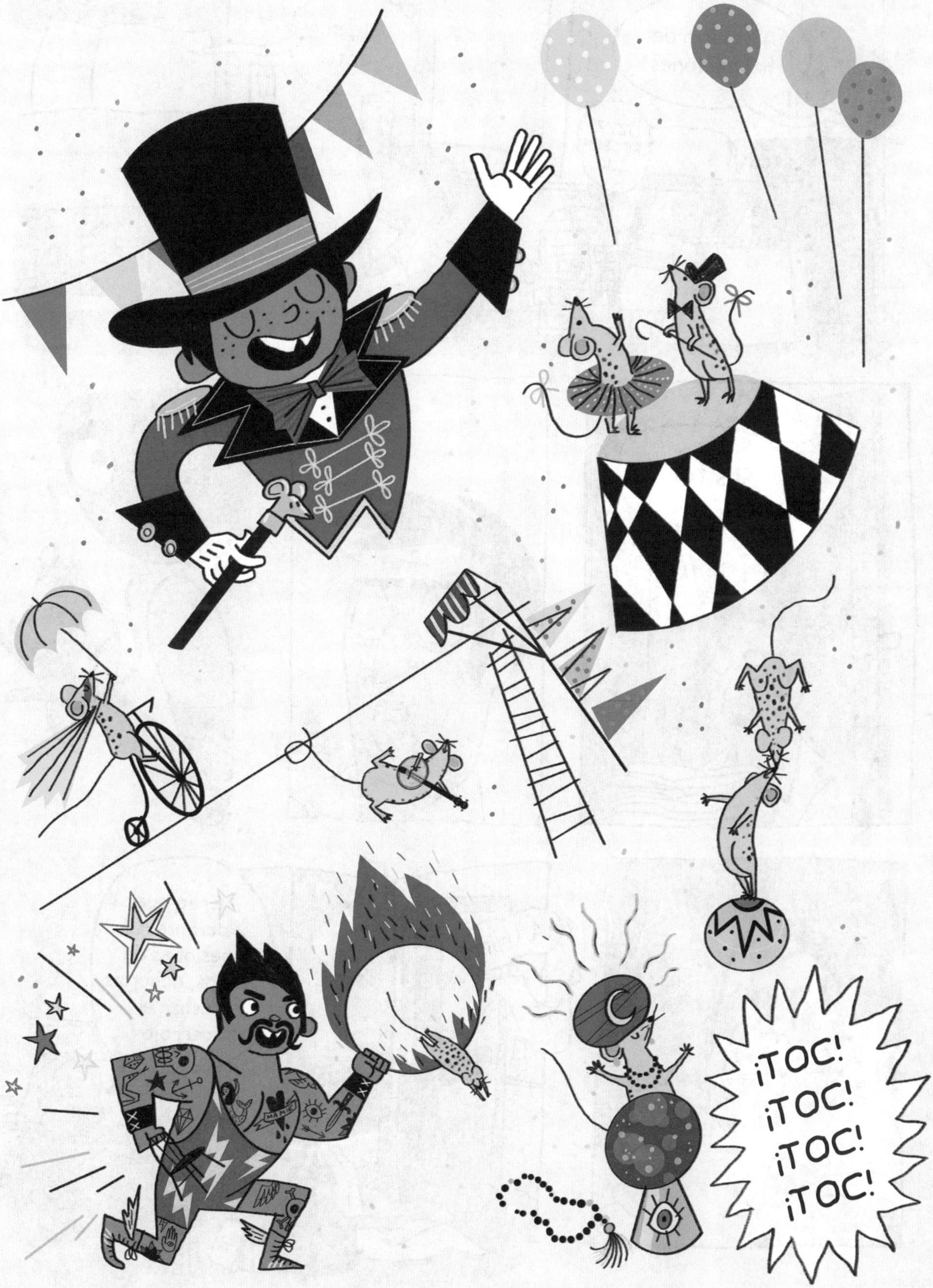
¡TOC!
¡TOC!
¡TOC!
¡TOC!

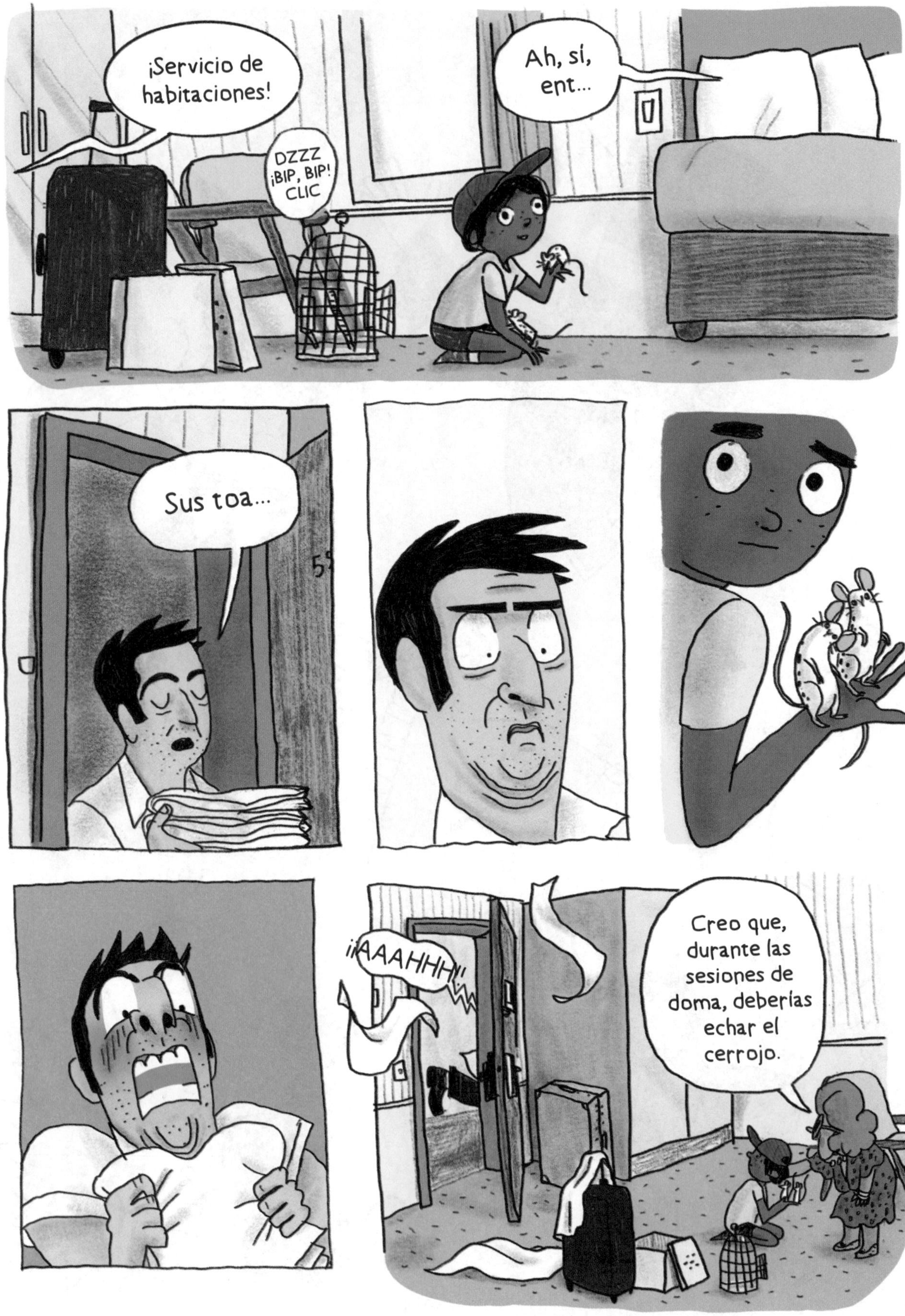
¡Servicio de habitaciones!
DZZZ ¡BIP, BIP! CLIC
Ah, sí, ent...
Sus toa...
¡¡AAAHHH!!
Creo que, durante las sesiones de doma, deberías echar el cerrojo.

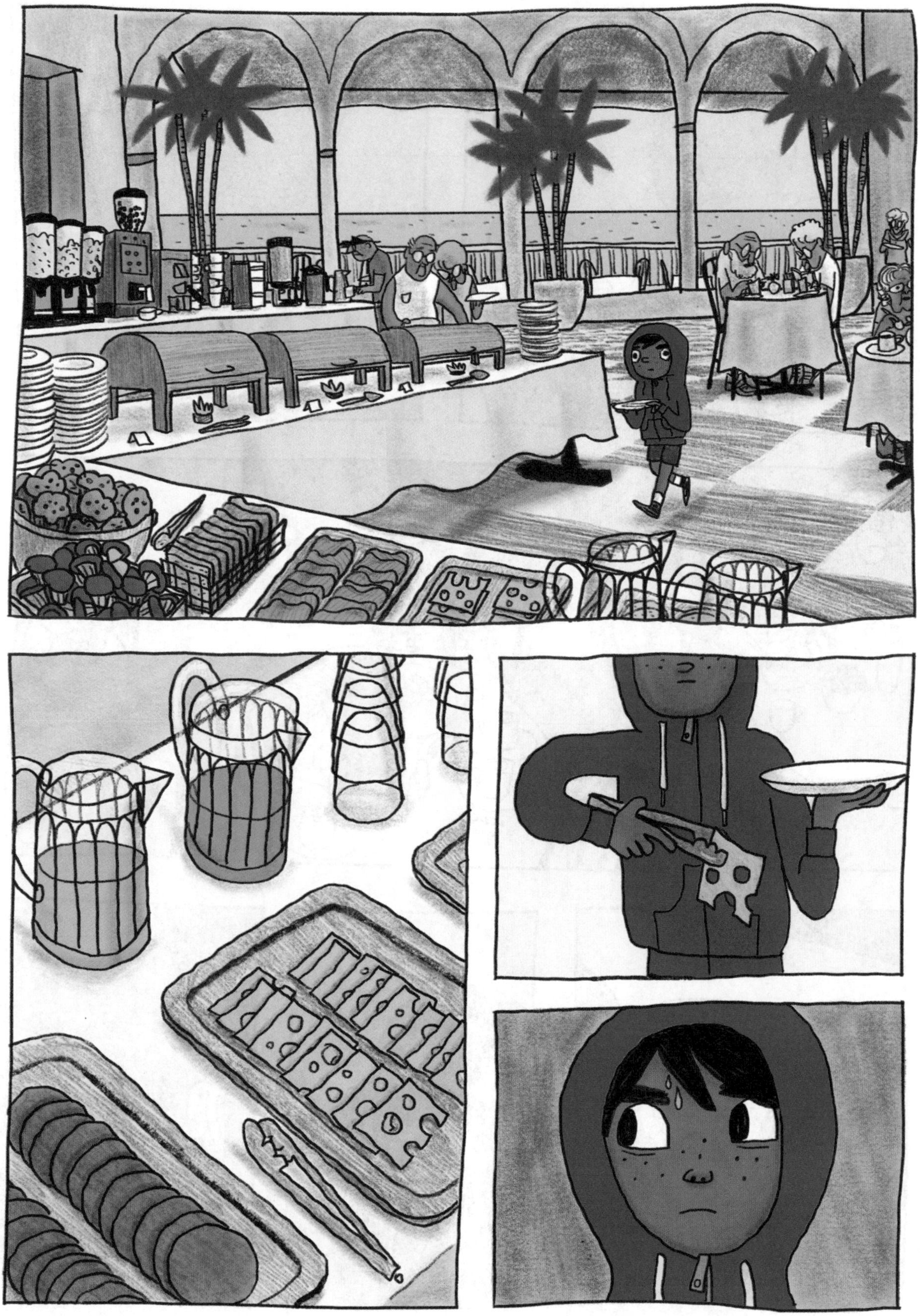

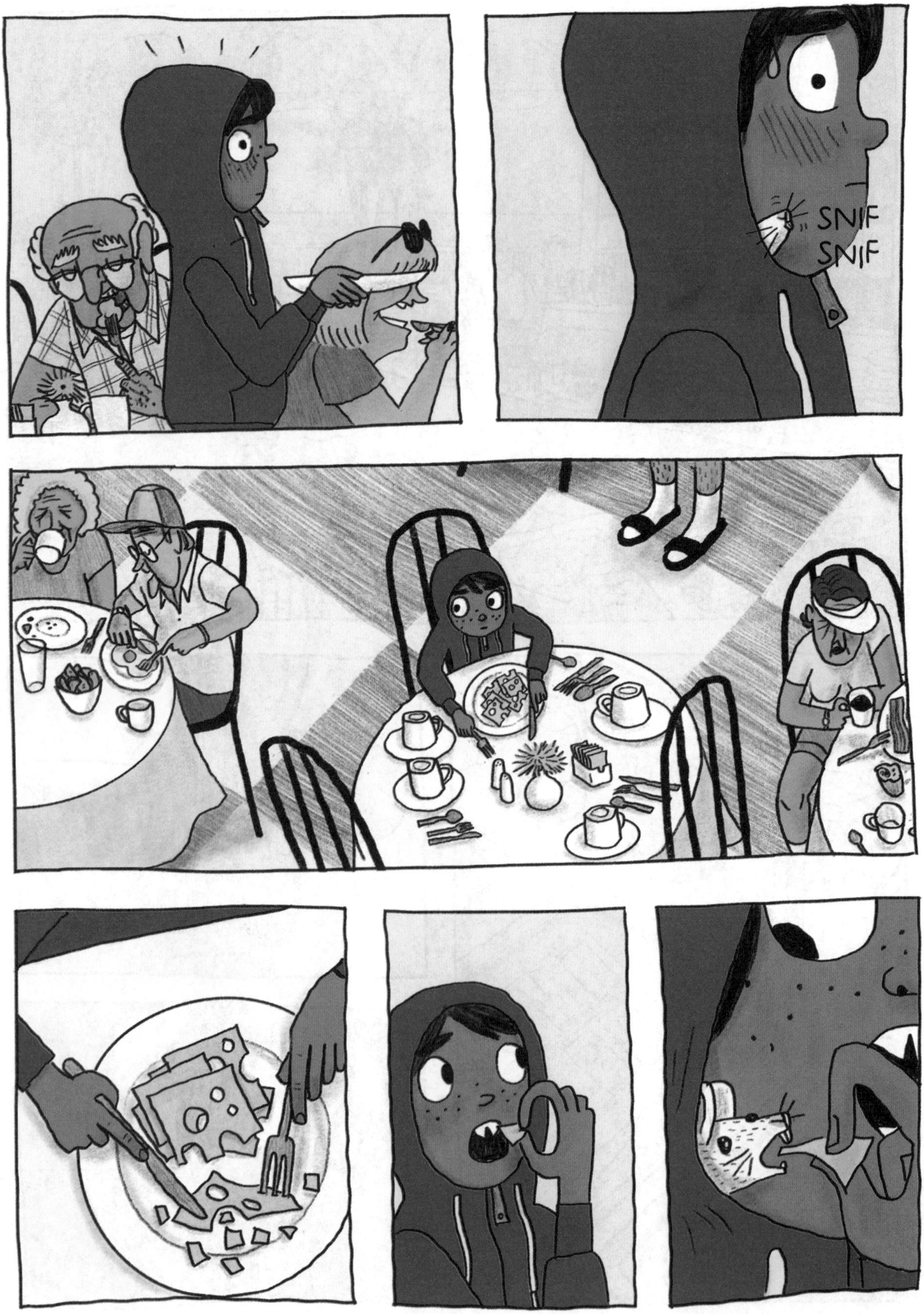
SNIF
SNIF

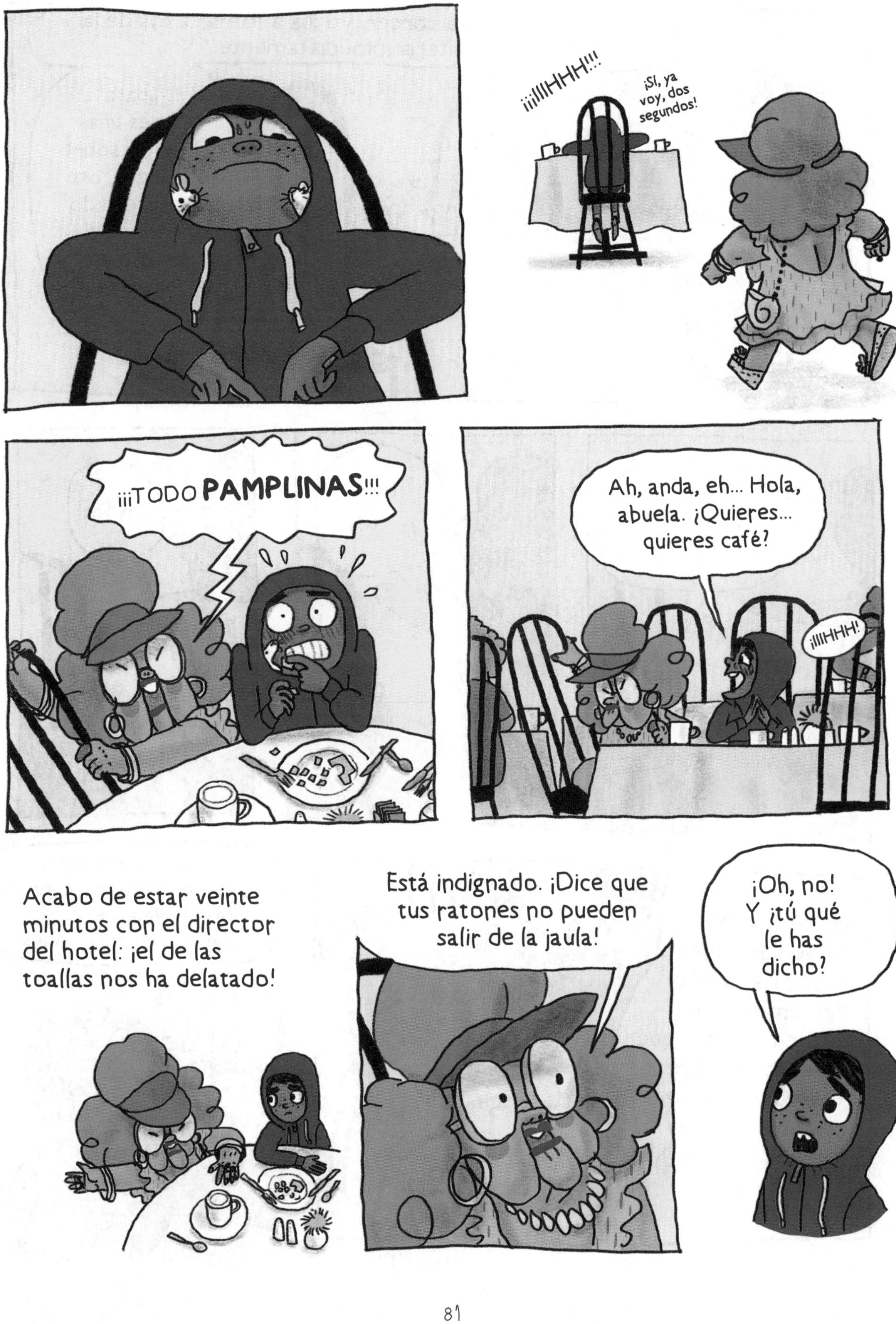
¡¡¡IIIIHHH!!!
¡SÍ, ya voy, dos segundos!
¡¡¡TODO PAMPLINAS!!!
Ah, anda, eh... Hola, abuela. ¿Quieres... quieres café?
¡IIIHHH!
Acabo de estar veinte minutos con el director del hotel: ¡el de las toallas nos ha delatado!
Está indignado. ¡Dice que tus ratones no pueden salir de la jaula!
¡Oh, no! Y ¿tú qué le has dicho?

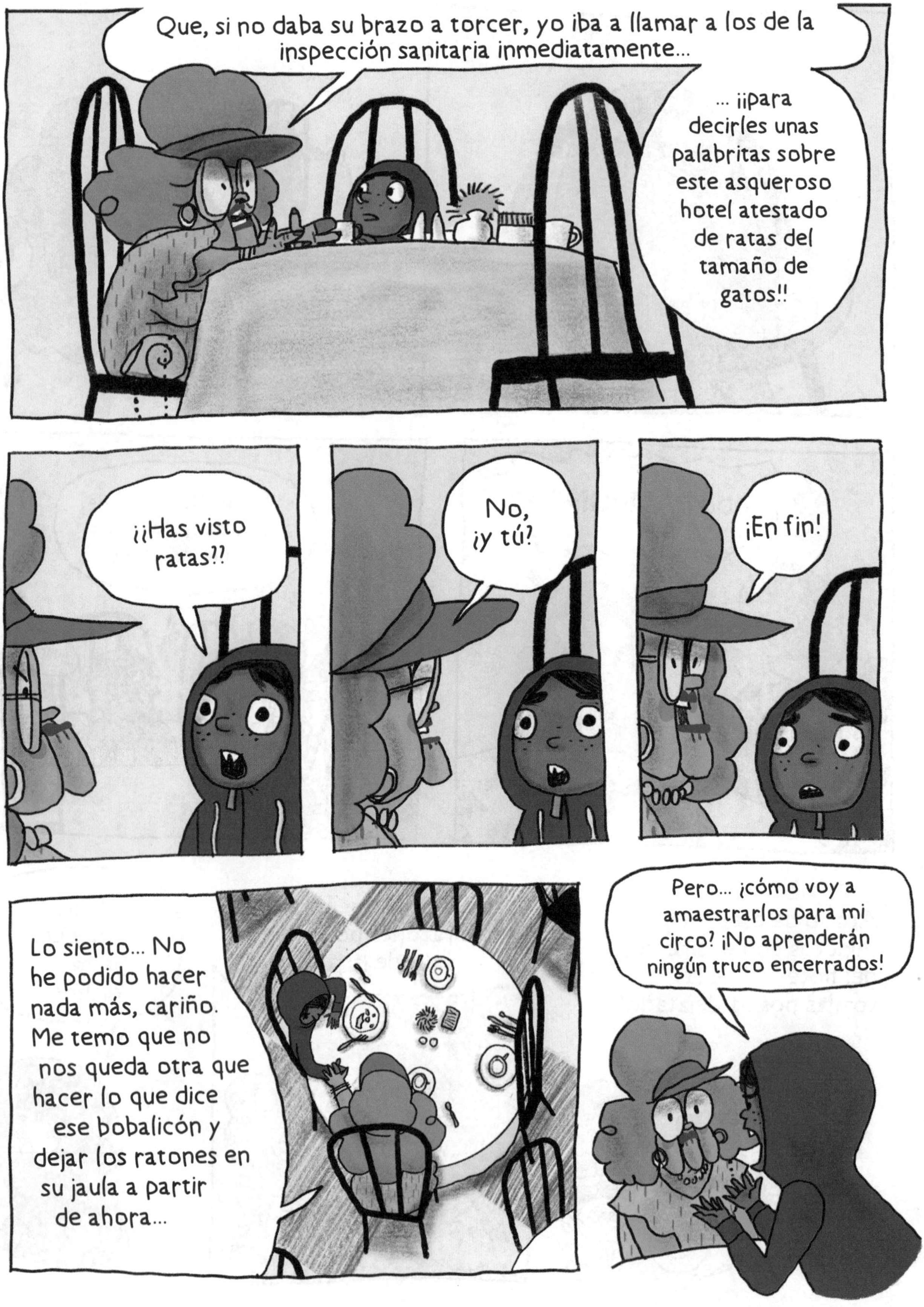
Que, si no daba su brazo a torcer, yo iba a llamar a los de la inspección sanitaria inmediatamente...
... ¡¡para decirles unas palabritas sobre este asqueroso hotel atestado de ratas del tamaño de gatos!!
¡¡Has visto ratas??
No, ¿y tú?
¡En fin!
Lo siento... No he podido hacer nada más, cariño. Me temo que no nos queda otra que hacer lo que dice ese bobalicón y dejar los ratones en su jaula a partir de ahora...
Pero... ¿cómo voy a amaestrarlos para mi circo? ¡No aprenderán ningún truco encerrados!

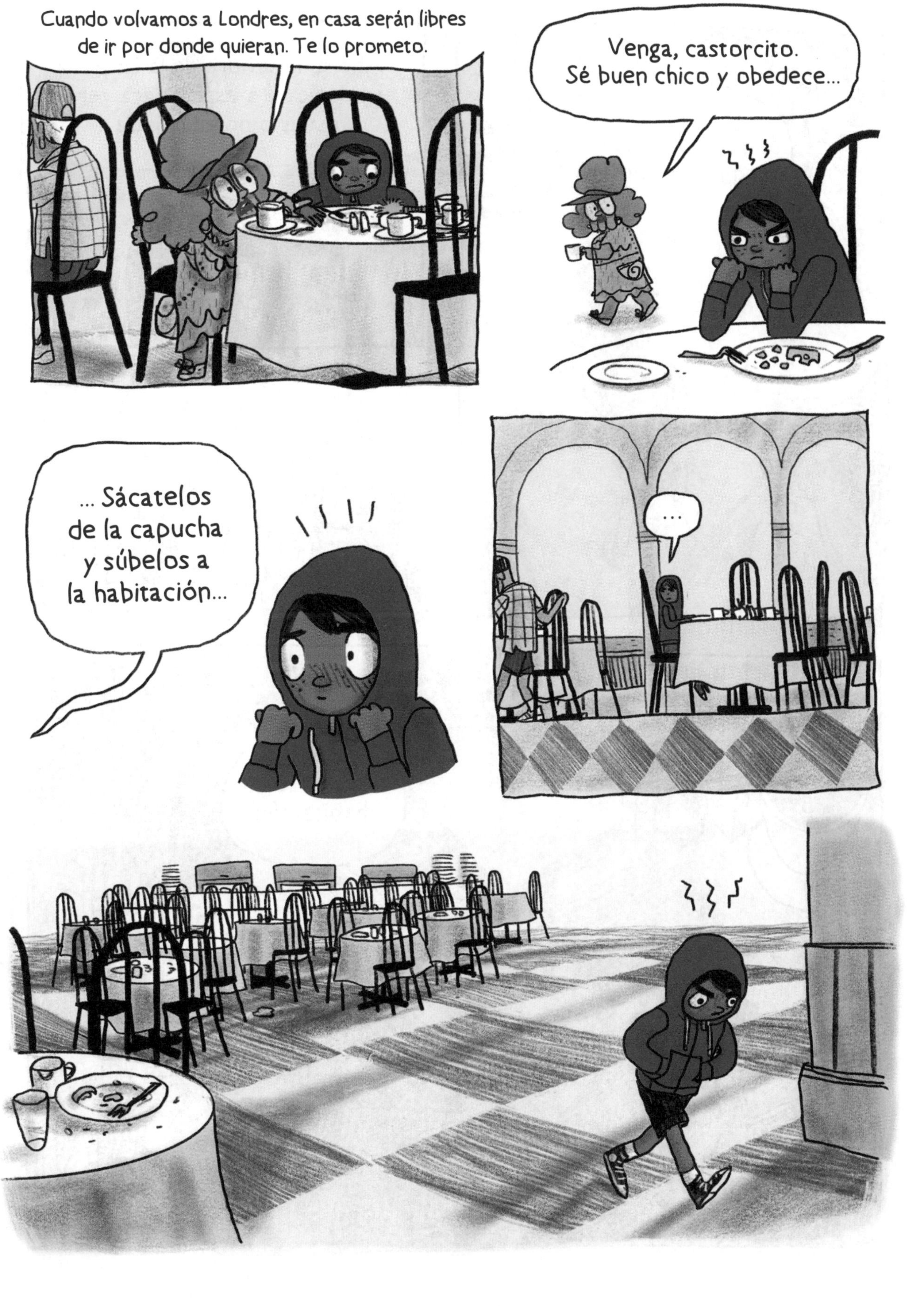
Cuando volvamos a Londres, en casa serán libres de ir por donde quieran. Te lo prometo.
Venga, castorcito. Sé buen chico y obedece...
... Sácatelos de la capucha y súbelos a la habitación...
...

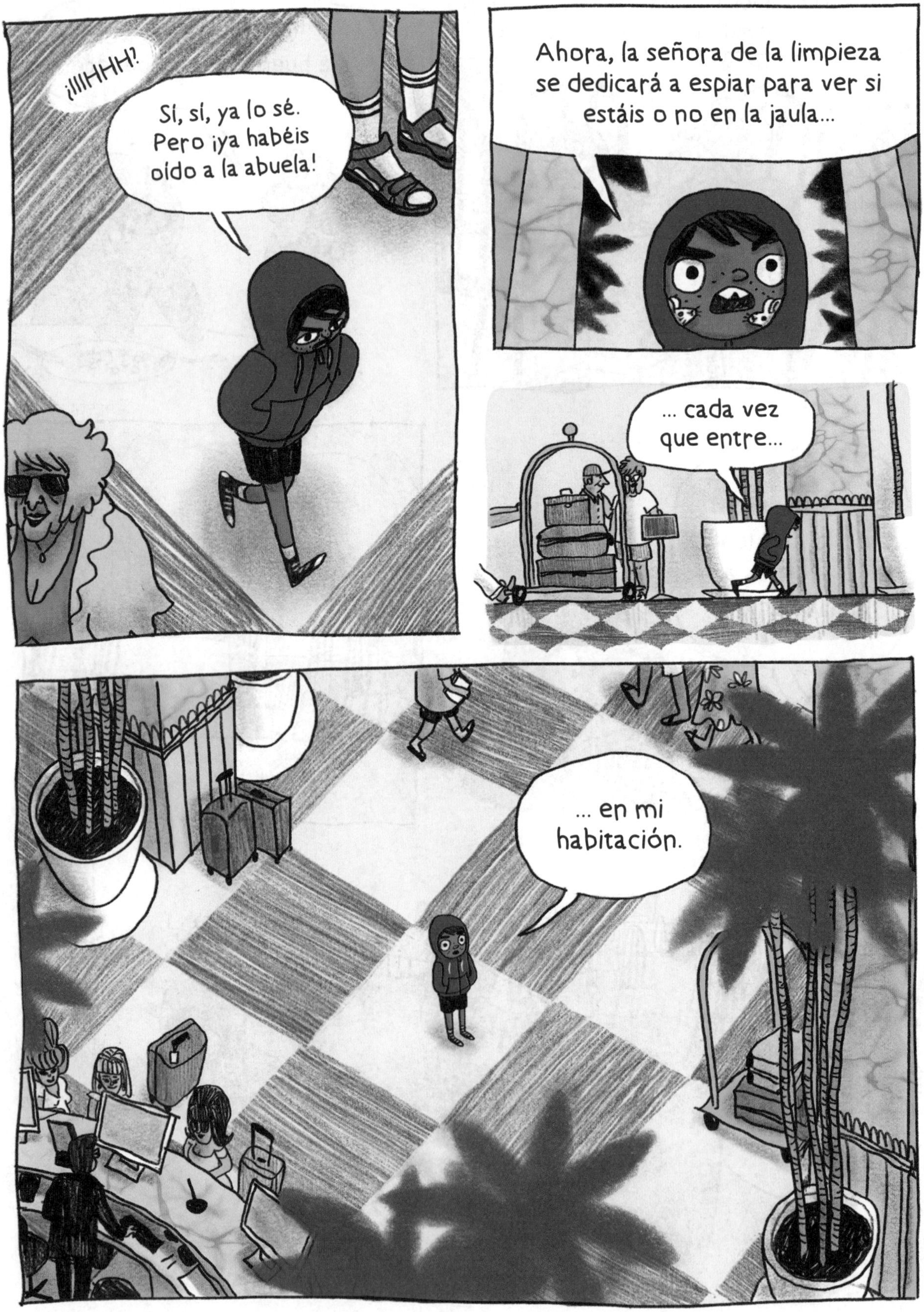
¡IIIHHH!
Sí, sí, ya lo sé. Pero ¡ya habéis oído a la abuela!
Ahora, la señora de la limpieza se dedicará a espiar para ver si estáis o no en la jaula...
... cada vez que entre...
... en mi habitación.

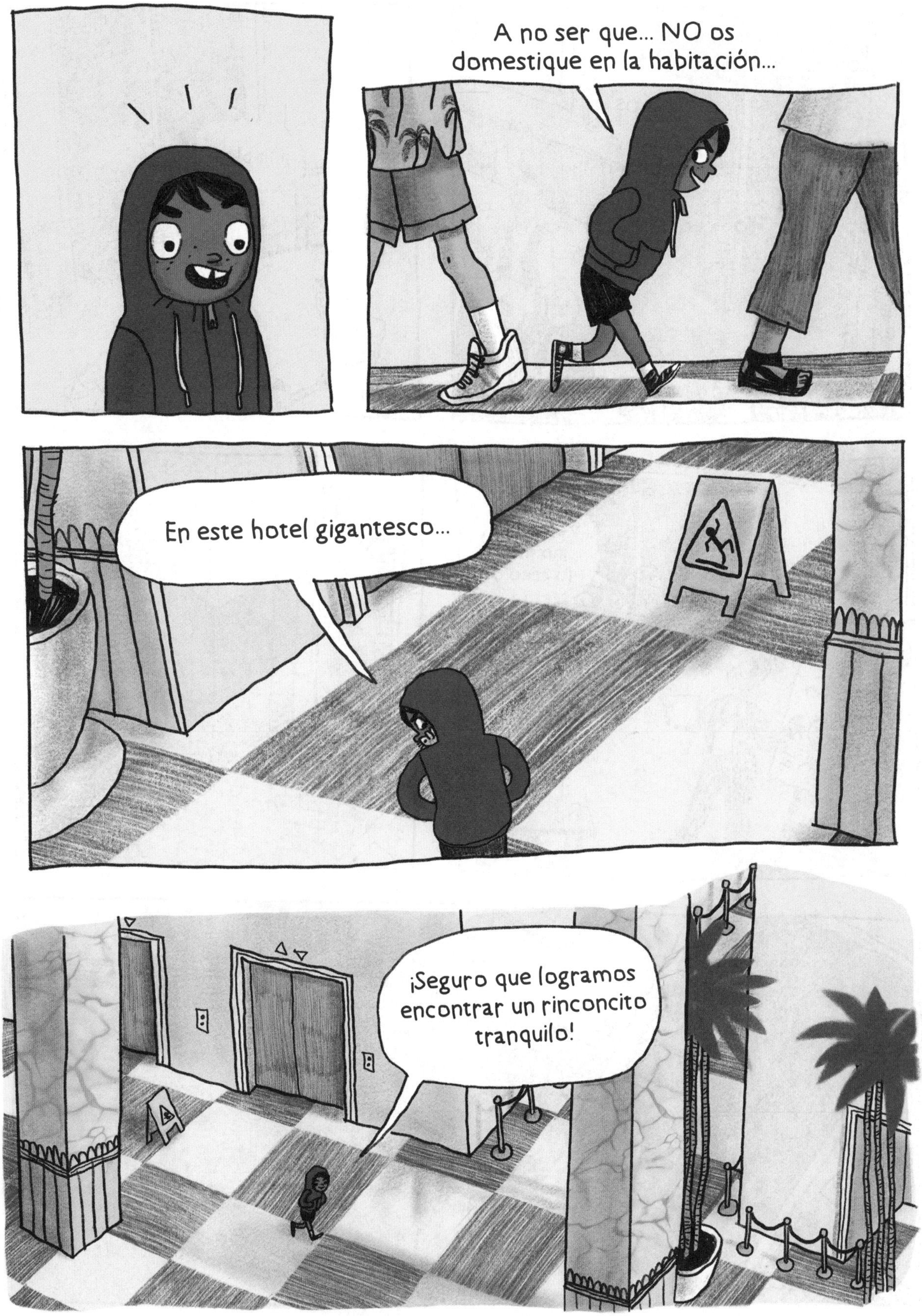
A no ser que... NO os domestique en la habitación...
En este hotel gigantesco...
¡Seguro que logramos encontrar un rinconcito tranquilo!

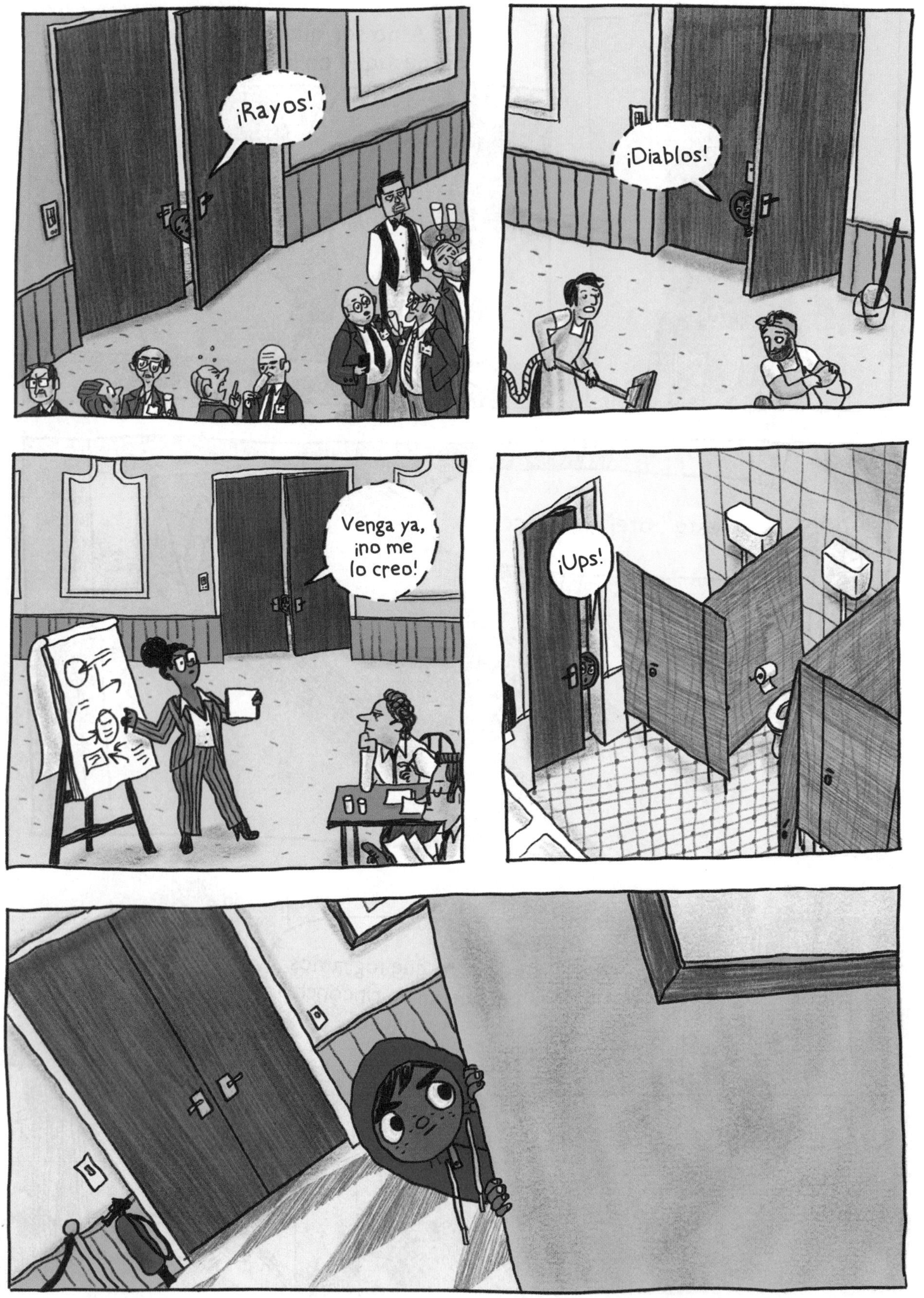
¡Rayos!
¡Diablos!
Venga ya, ¡no me lo creo!
¡Ups!

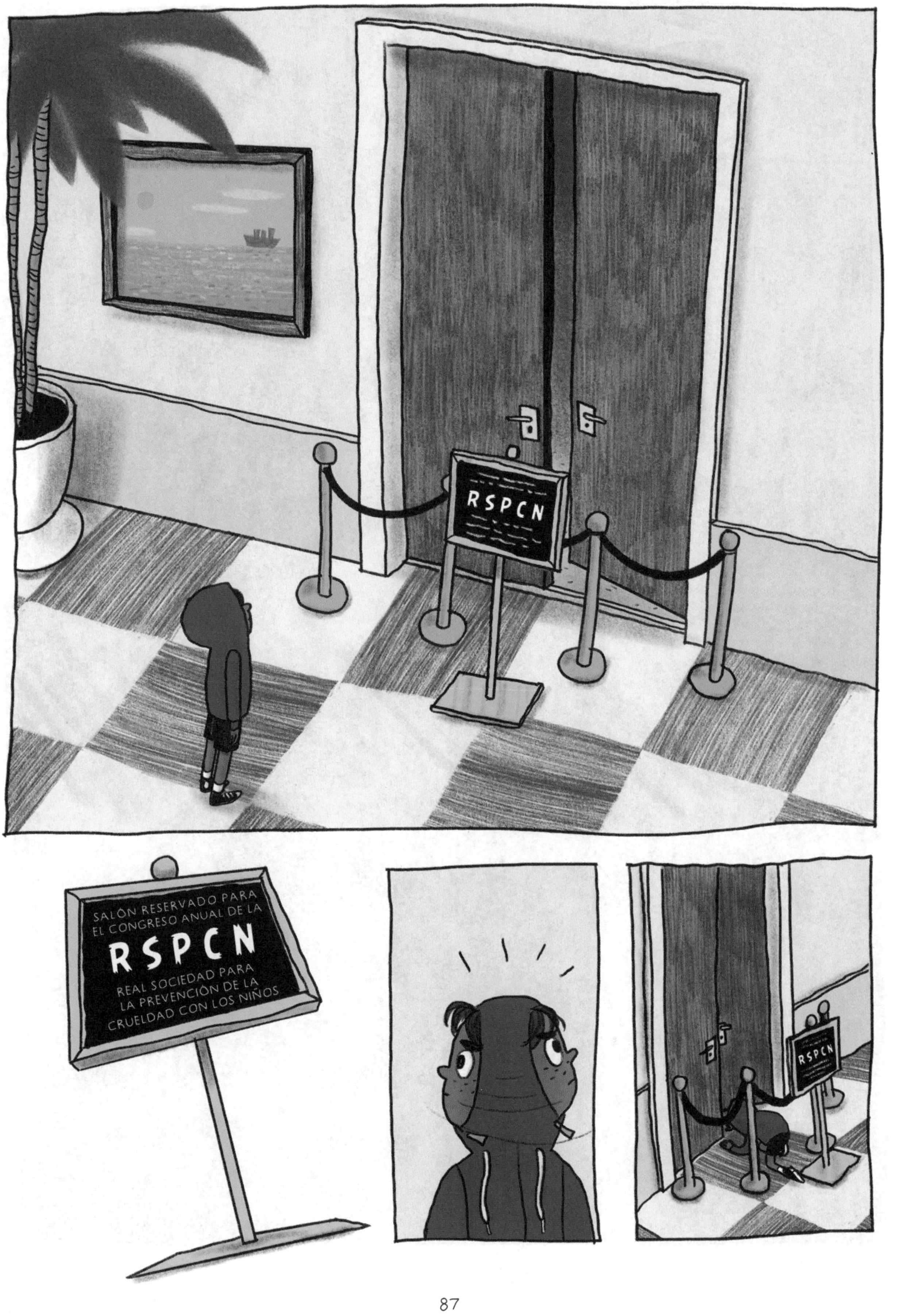
RSPCN
SALÓN RESERVADO PARA
EL CONGRESO ANUAL DE LA
RSPCN
REAL SOCIEDAD PARA
LA PREVENCIÓN DE LA
CRUELDAD CON LOS NIÑOS
RSPCN

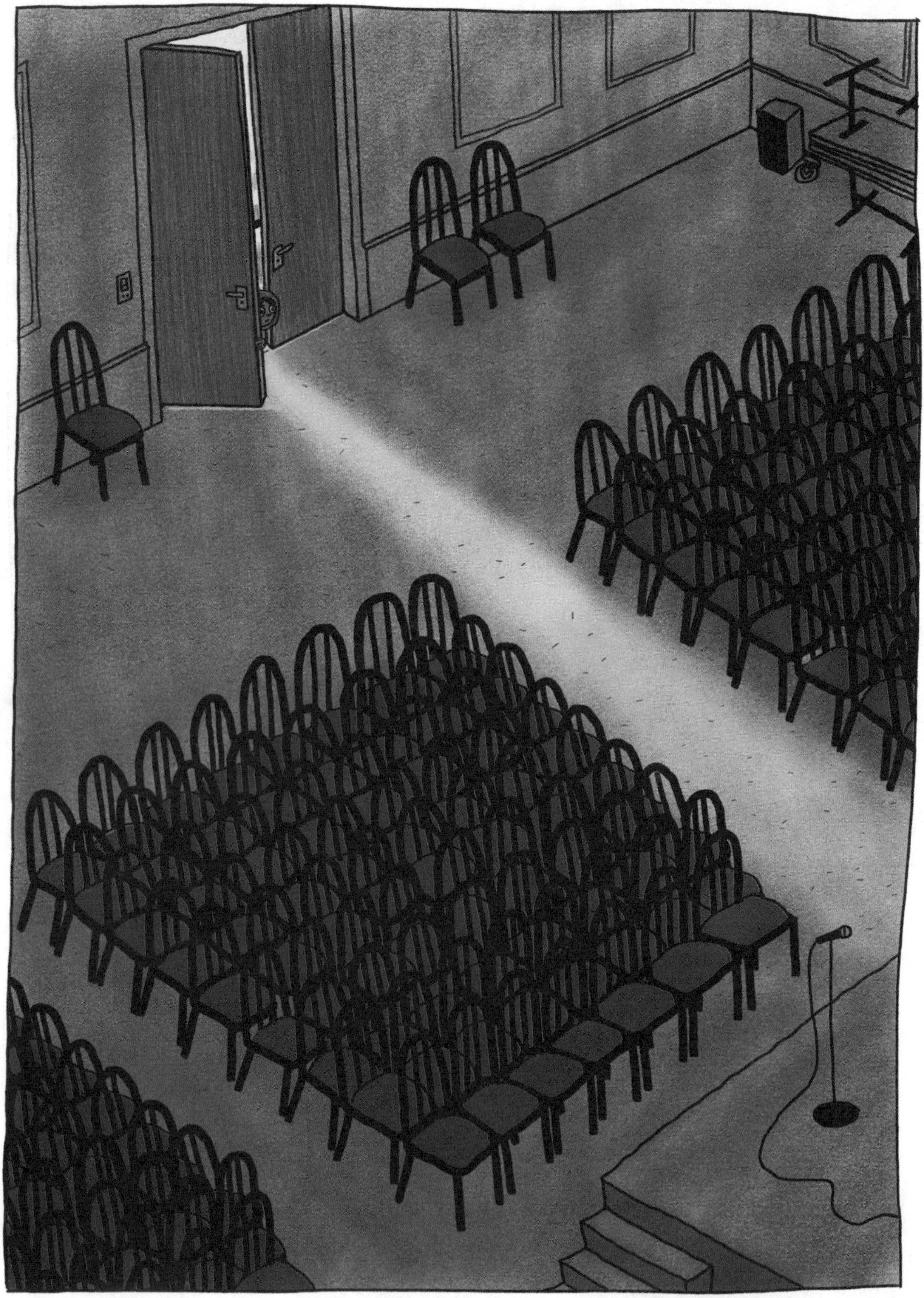

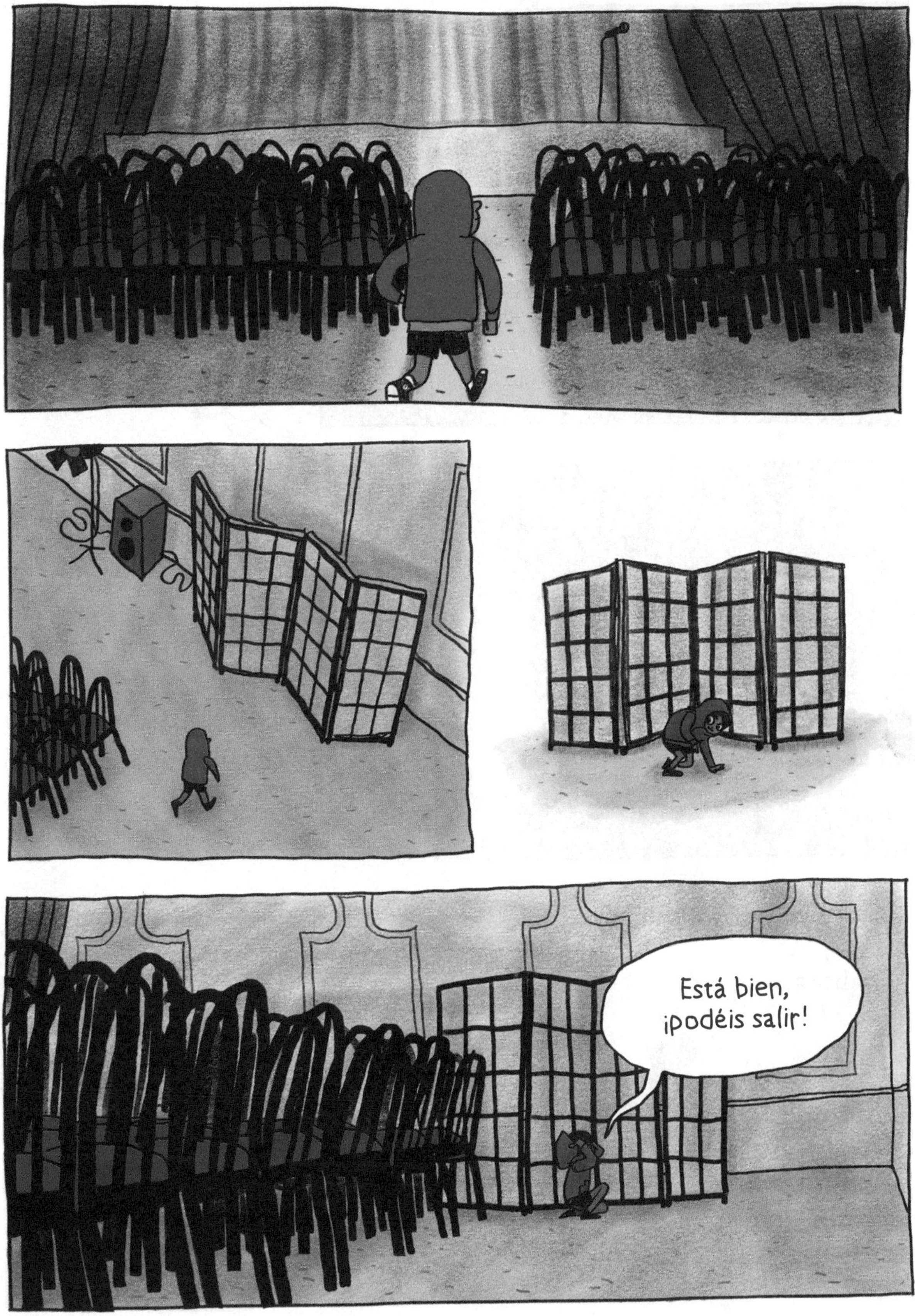
Está bien,
¡podéis salir!

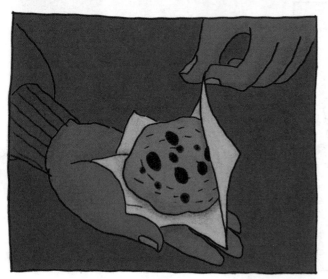

Vale,
y ahora...

¡Vamos a concentrarnos!

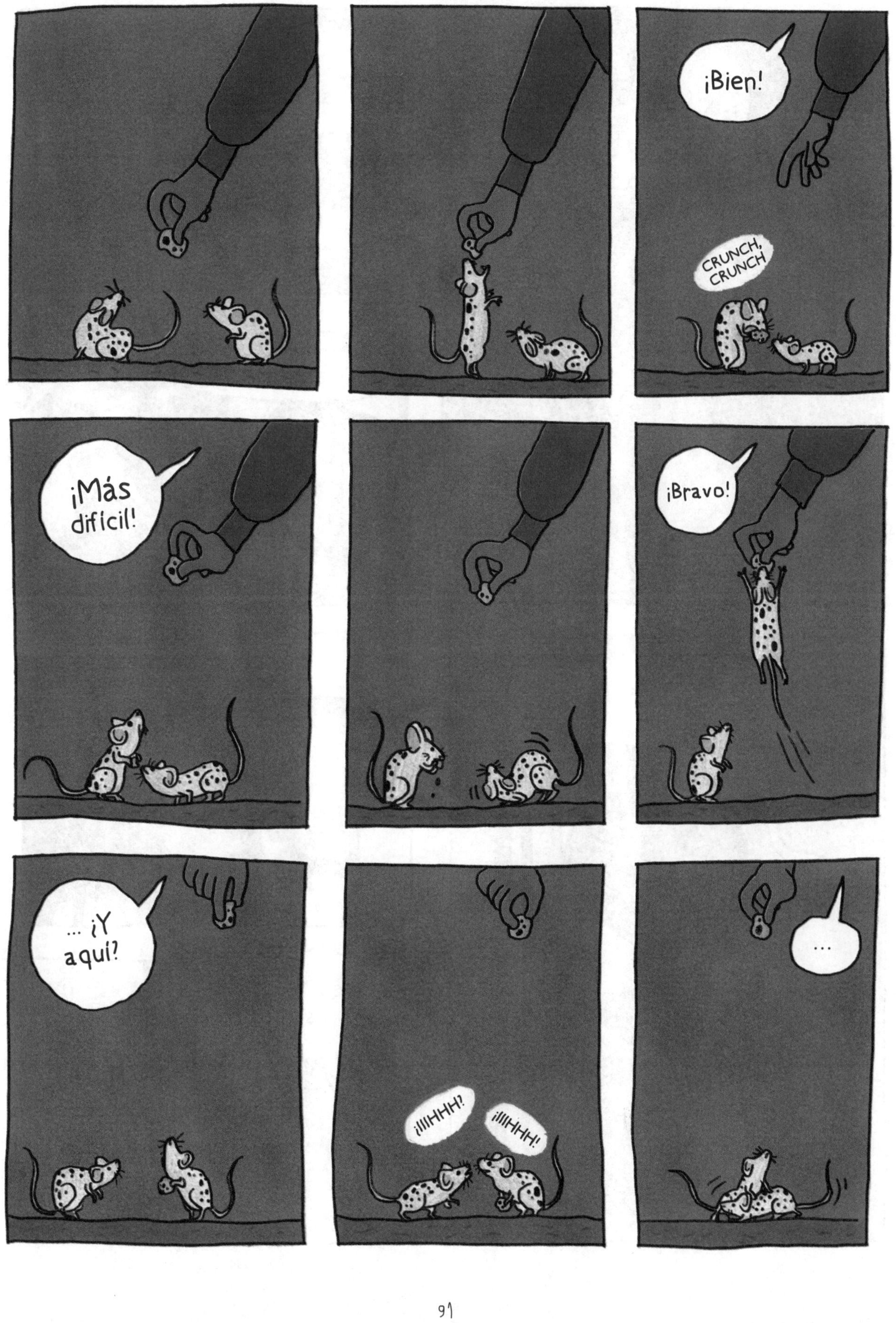
¡Bien!
CRUNCH, CRUNCH
¡Más difícil!
¡Bravo!
... ¡Y aquí?
¡IIIHHH!
¡IIIHHH!
...

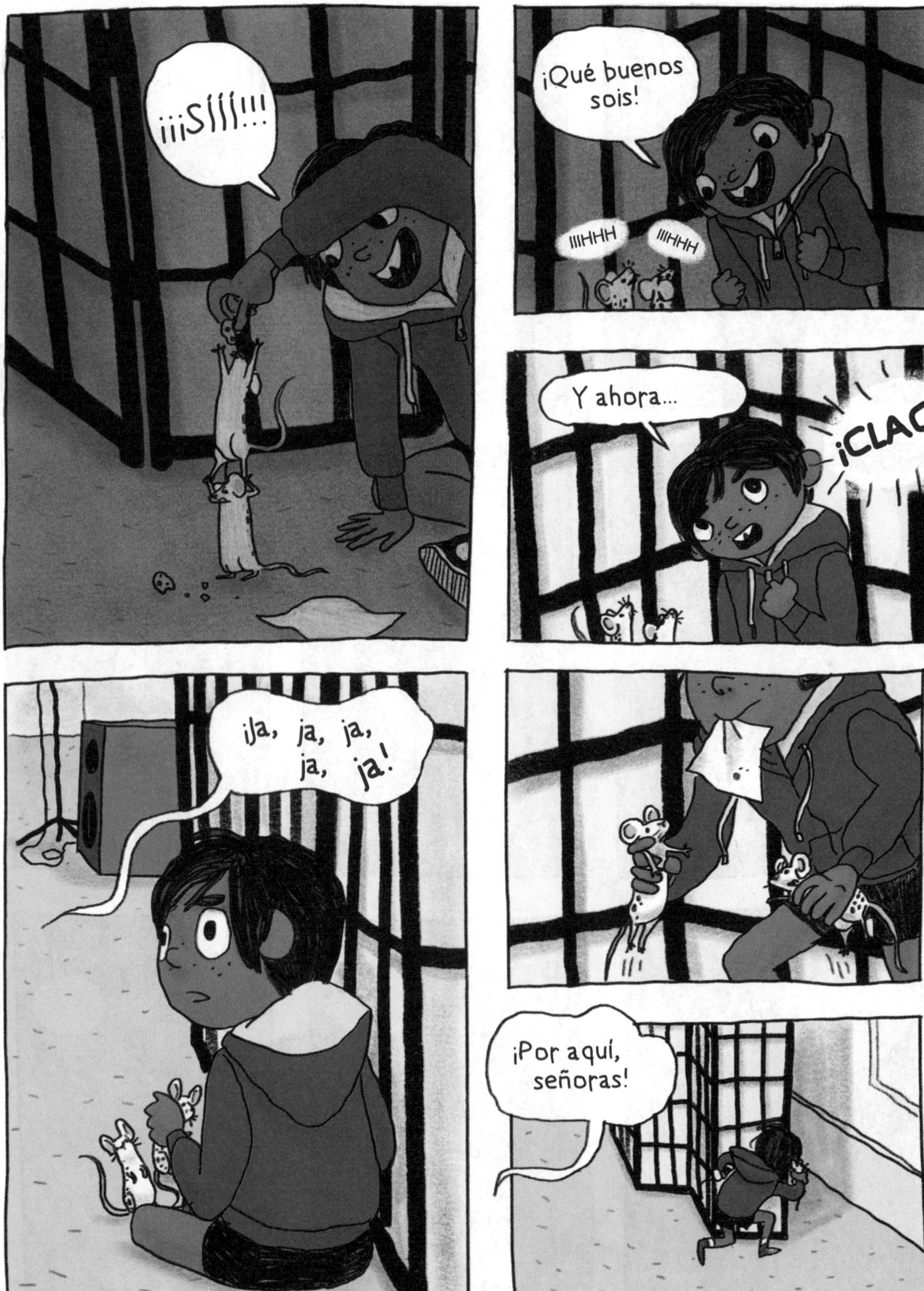
¡¡¡SÍÍÍ!!!
¡Qué buenos sois!
IIIHHH
IIIHHH
Y ahora...
¡CLAC!
¡Ja, ja, ja, ja, ja!
¡Por aquí, señoras!

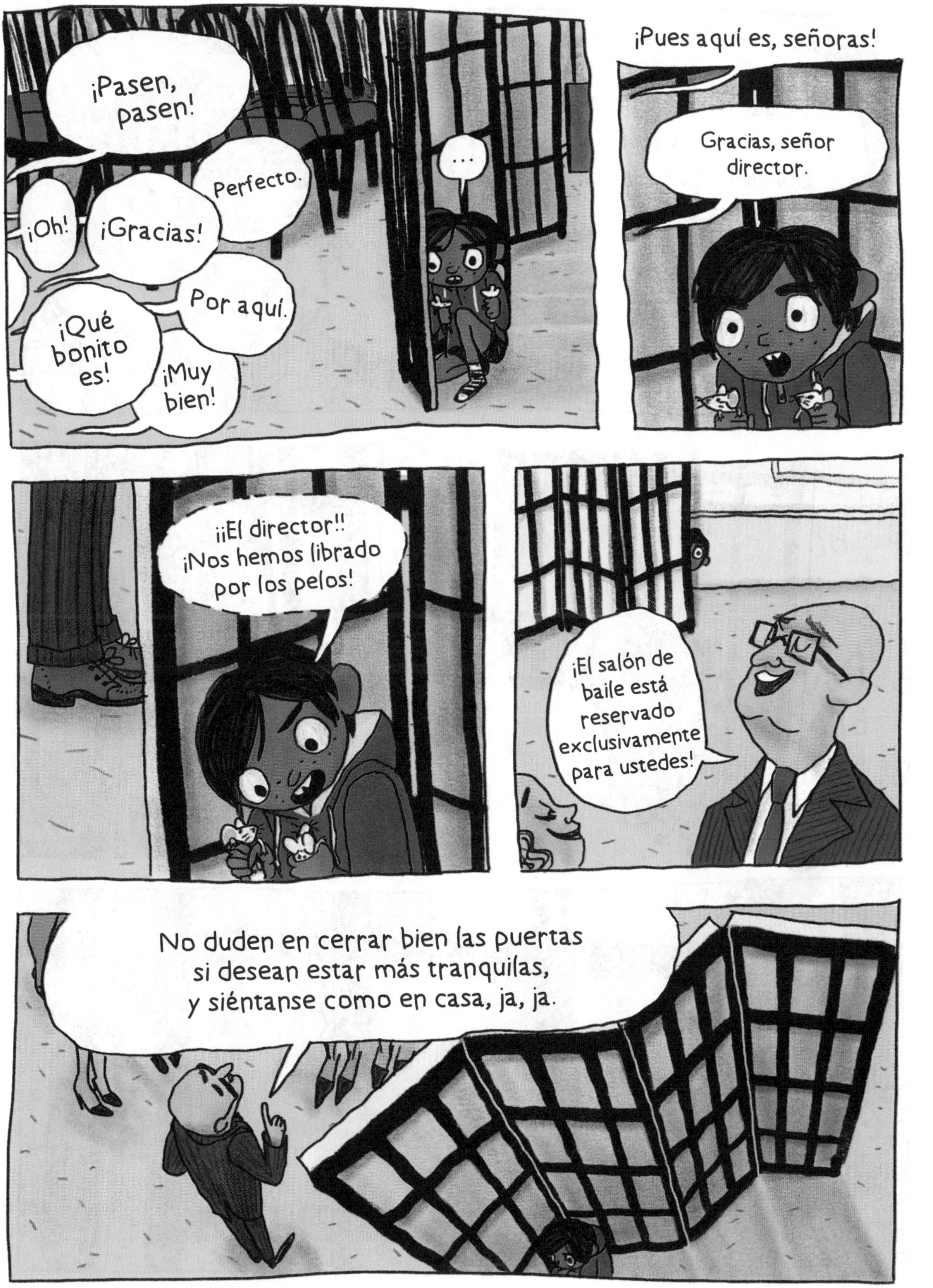
¡Pasen, pasen!
¡Oh!
¡Gracias!
Perfecto.
Por aquí.
¡Qué bonito es!
¡Muy bien!
...
¡Pues aquí es, señoras!
Gracias, señor director.
¡¡El director!! ¡Nos hemos librado por los pelos!
¡El salón de baile está reservado exclusivamente para ustedes!
No duden en cerrar bien las puertas si desean estar más tranquilas, y siéntanse como en casa, ja, ja.

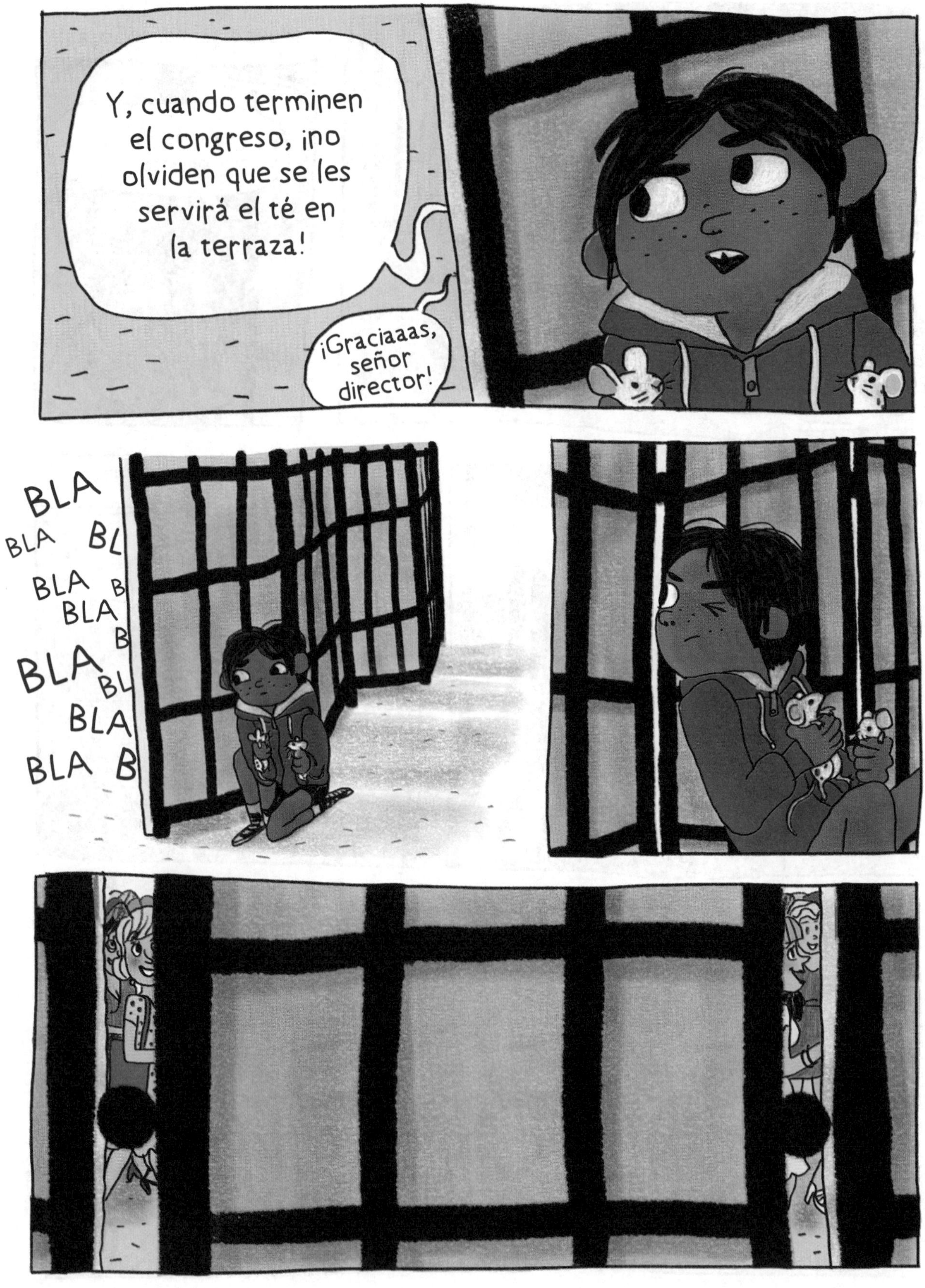
Y, cuando terminen el congreso, ¡no olviden que se les servirá el té en la terraza!
¡Graciaaas, señor director!
BLA BLA BL BLA B BLA B BLA BL BLA BLA B

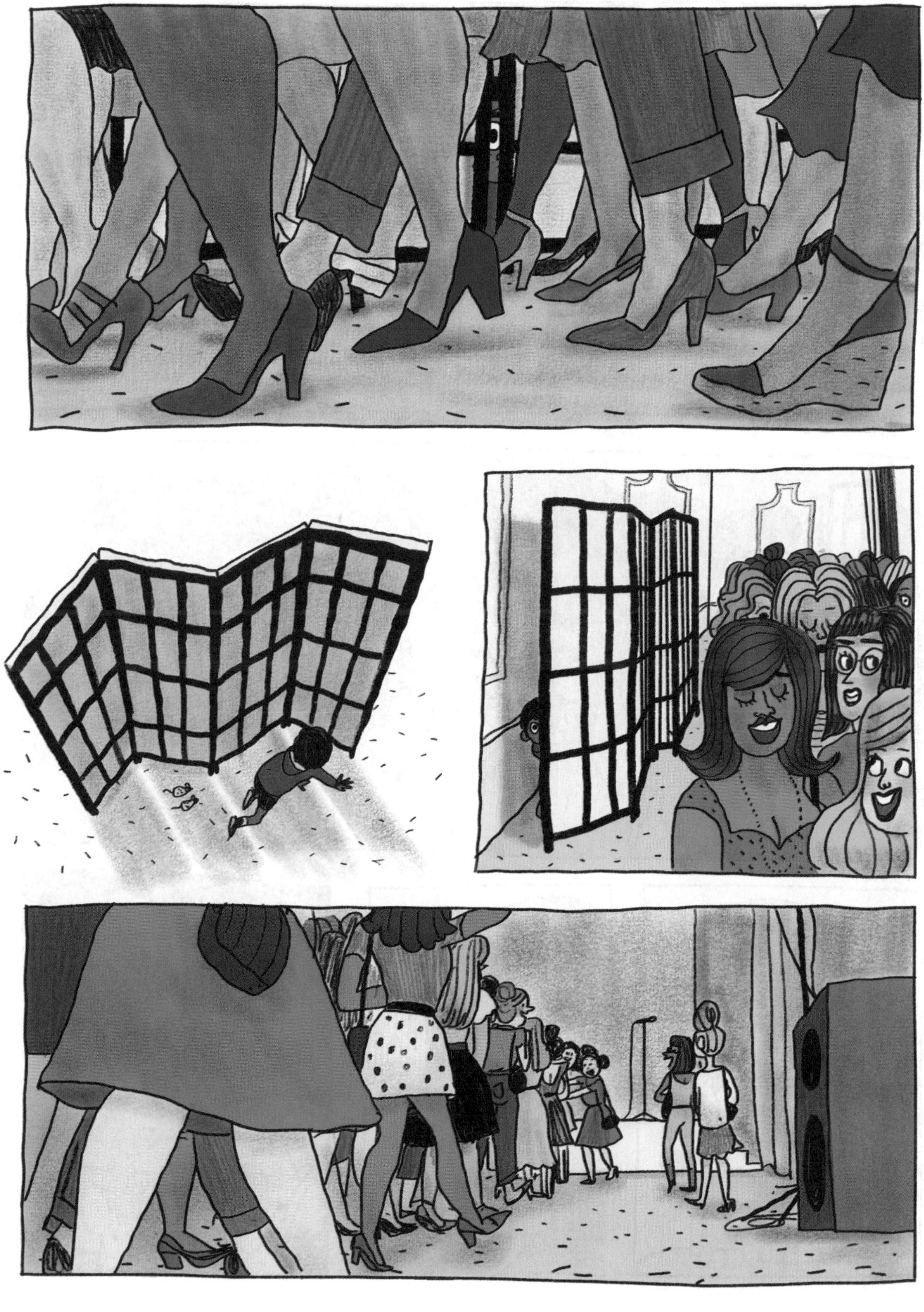

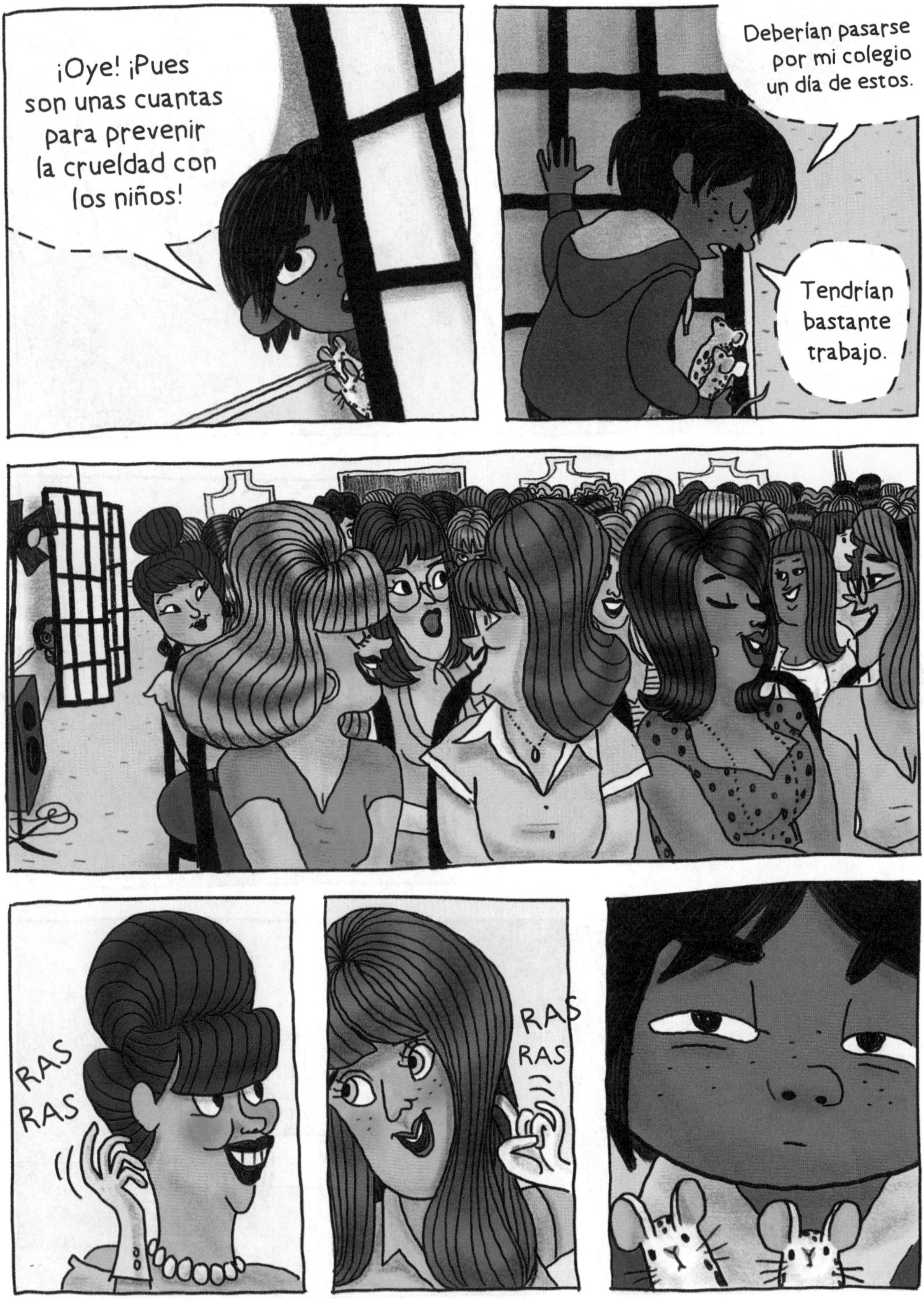

¡Oye! ¡Pues son unas cuantas para prevenir la crueldad con los niños!
Deberían pasarse por mi colegio un día de estos.
Tendrían bastante trabajo.
RAS RAS
RAS RAS

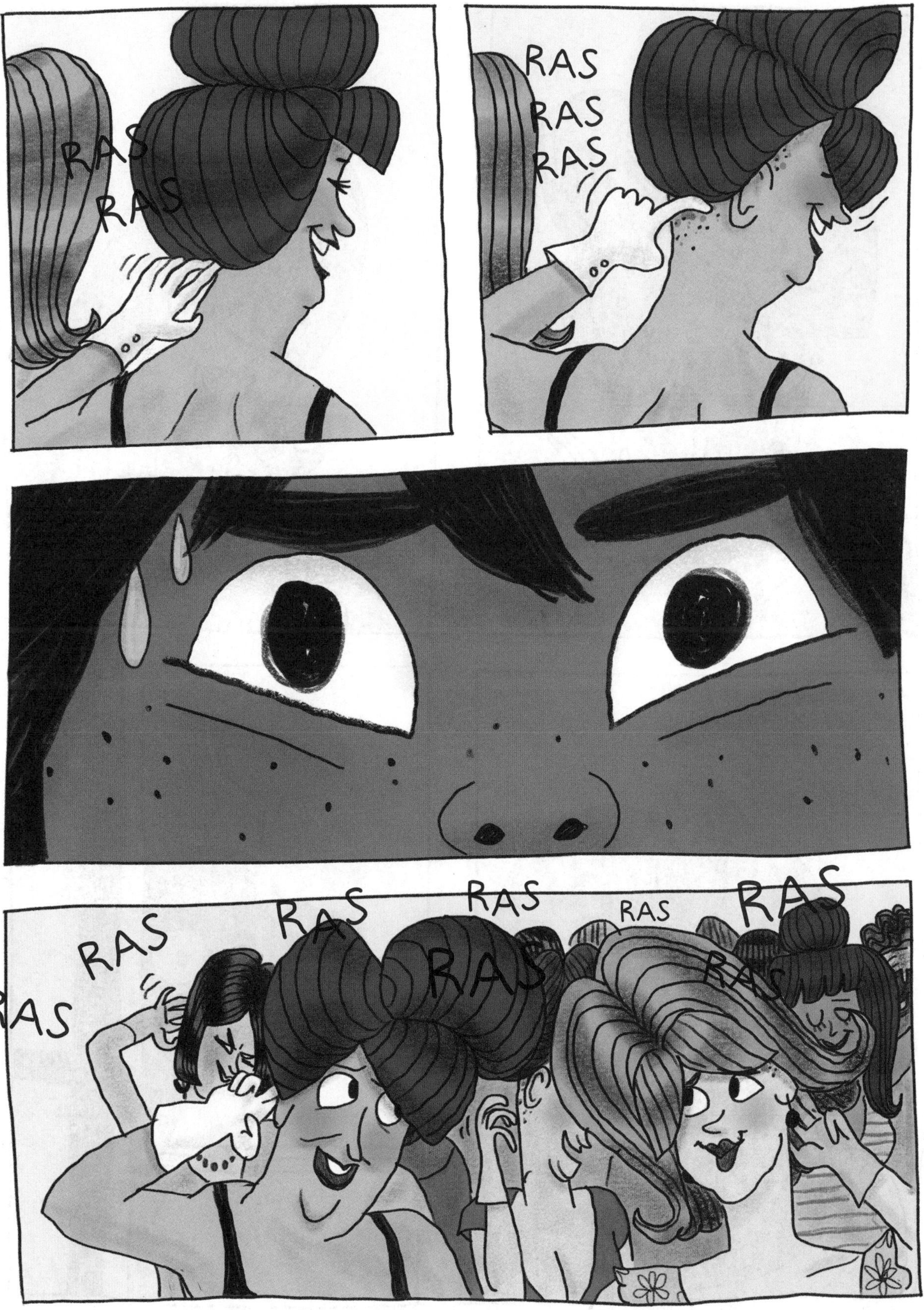
RAS
RAS
RAS
RAS
RAS
RAS
RAS
RAS
RAS
RAS
RAS
RAS
RAS
RAS
RAS

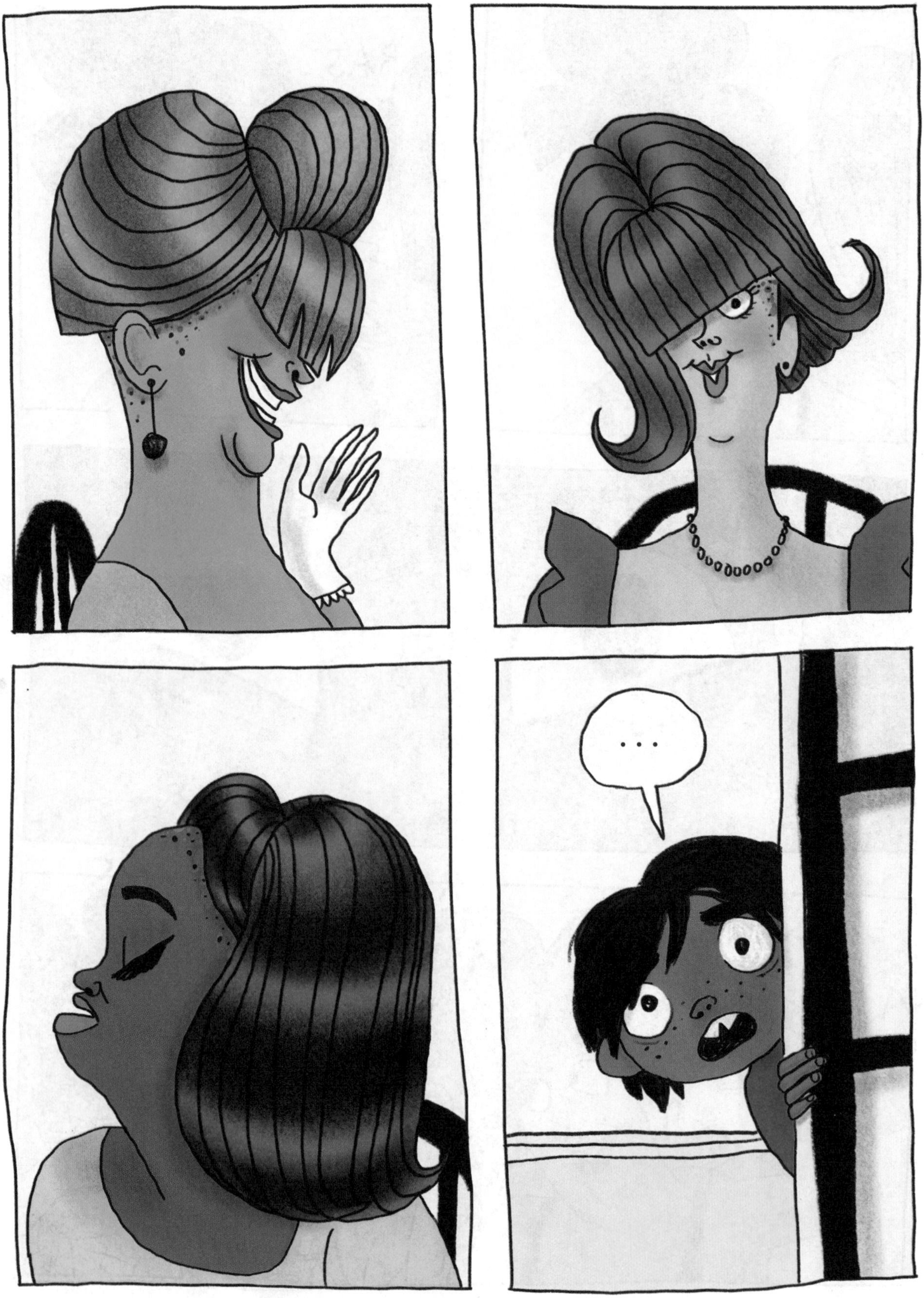
...

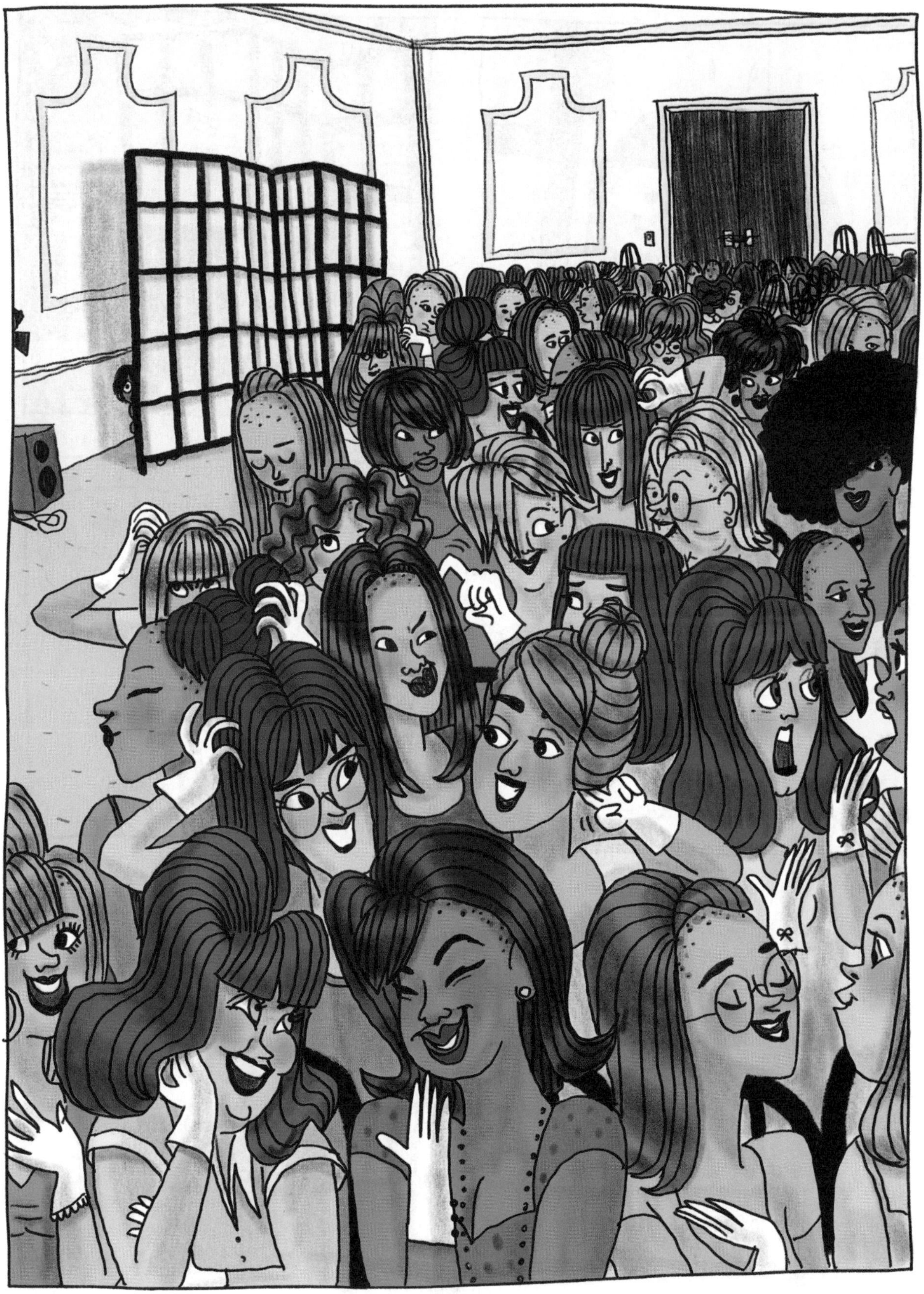

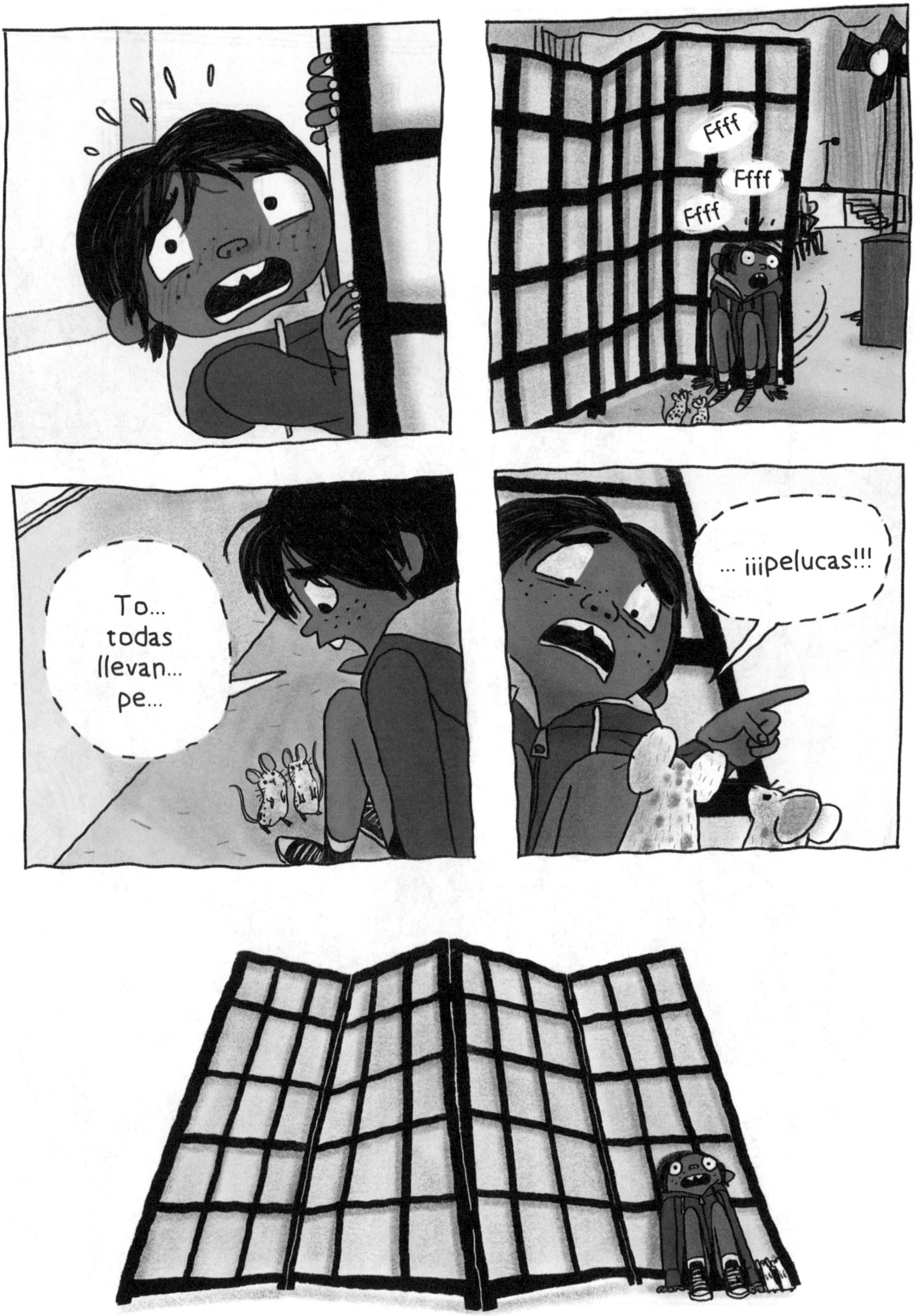

Ffff
Ffff
Ffff
To... todas llevan... pe...
... ¡¡¡pelucas!!!

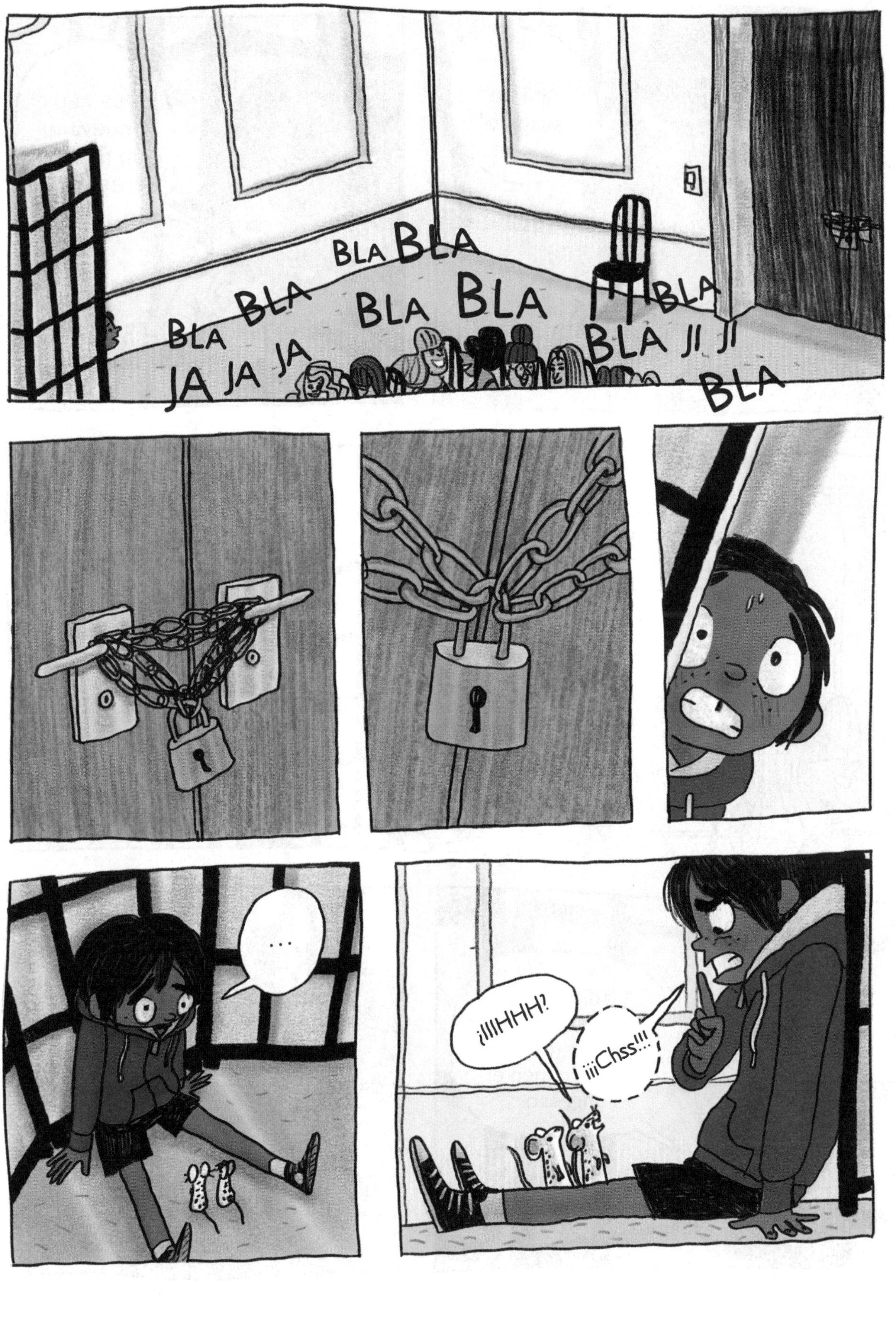
BLA BLA
BLA BLA
BLA BLA
BLA BLA
BLA
JA JA JA
BLA JI JI
BLA
...
¡¡¡IIIHHH!
¡¡¡Chss!!!

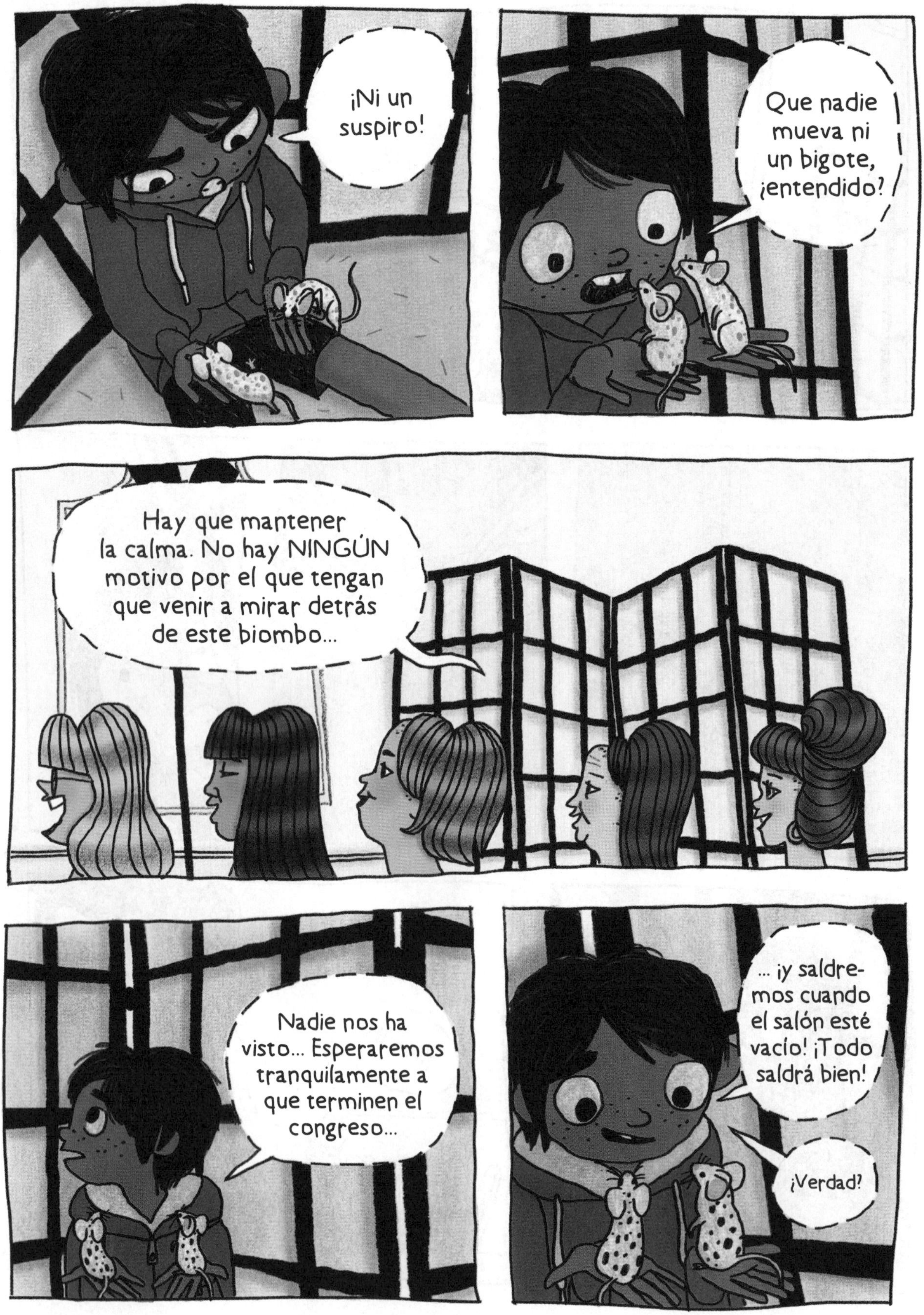
¡Ni un suspiro!
Que nadie mueva ni un bigote, ¡entendido?
Hay que mantener la calma. No hay NINGÚN motivo por el que tengan que venir a mirar detrás de este biombo...
Nadie nos ha visto... Esperaremos tranquilamente a que terminen el congreso...
... ¡y saldremos cuando el salón esté vacío! ¡Todo saldrá bien!
¿Verdad?

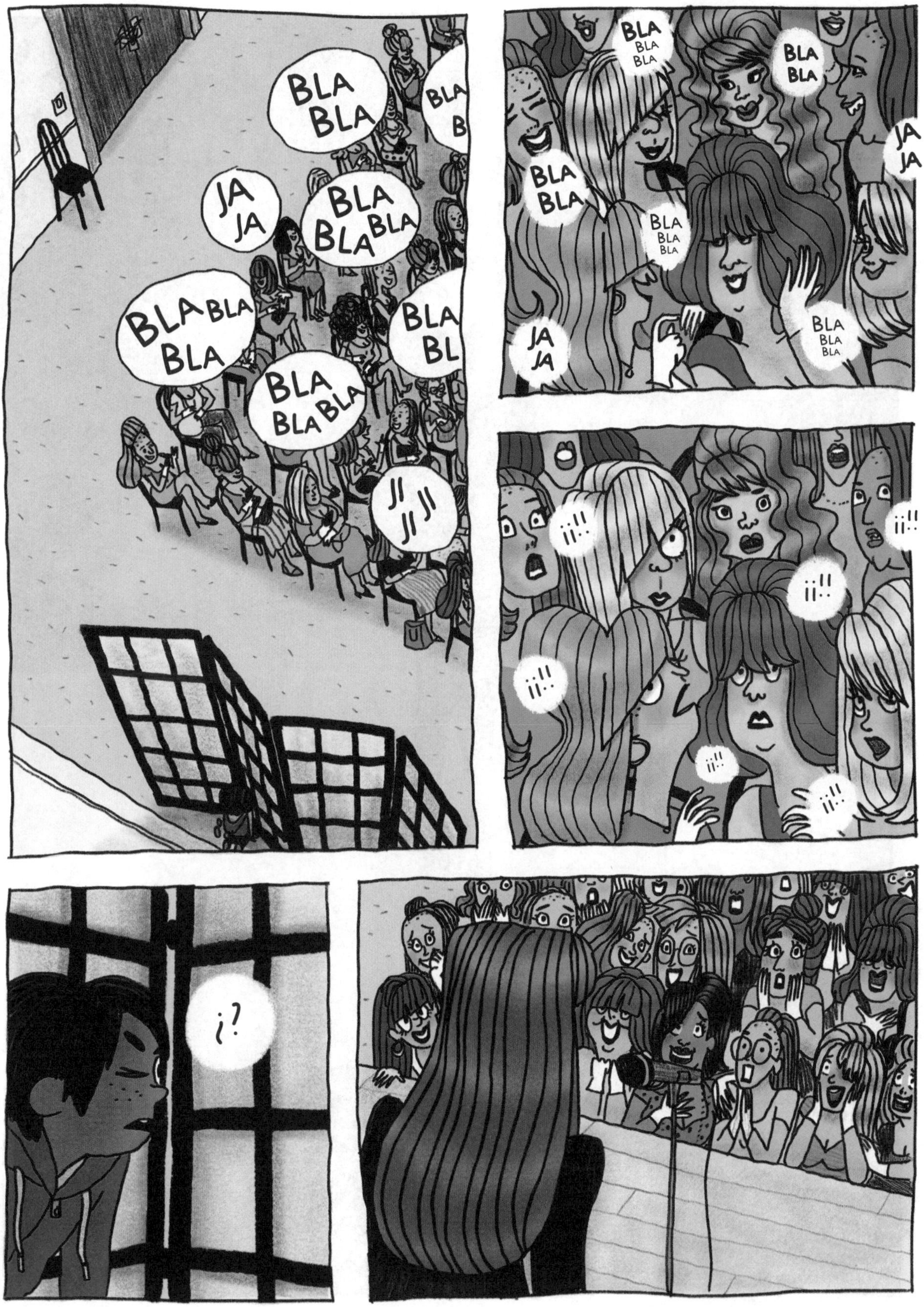
BLA BLA
JA JA
BLA BLA BLA
BLA BLA BLA
BLA BLA BLA
JI JI JI
BLA BLA BLA
BLA BLA
BLA BLA
BLA BLA BLA
JA JA
JA JA
BLA BLA BLA
¡¡!!
¡¡!!
¡¡!!
¡¡!!
¡¡!!
¡¡!!
¿?

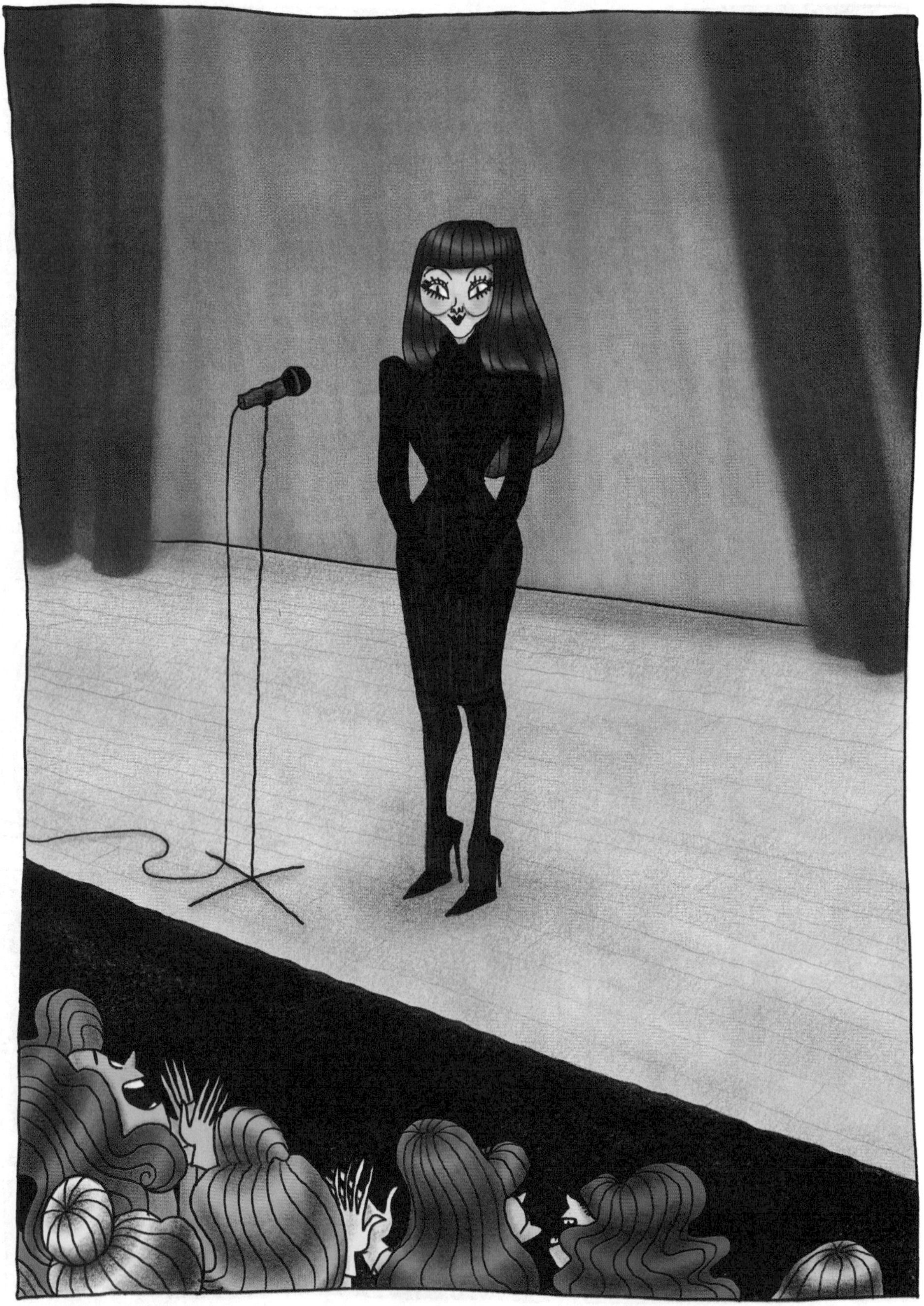

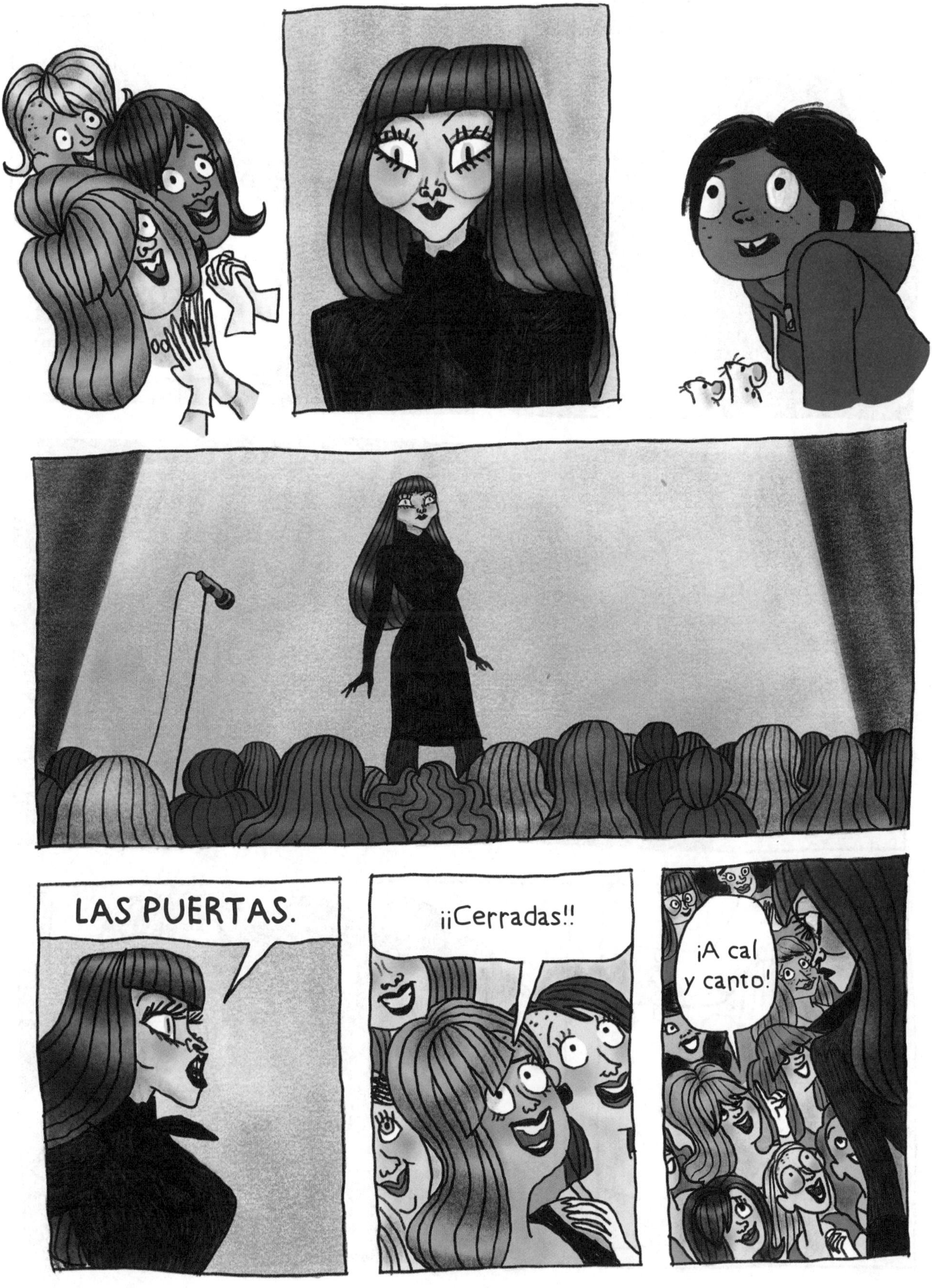
LAS PUERTAS.
¡¡Cerradas!!
¡A cal y canto!

QUITAOS...

... LOS GUANTES.

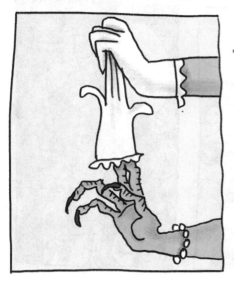

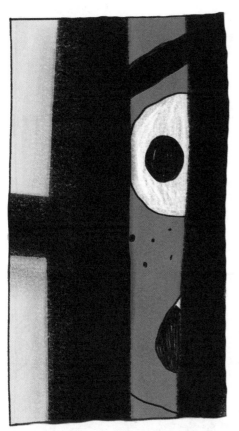

QUITAOS...

... ¡LOS ZAPATOS!

Ay, Dios, ¡gracias!

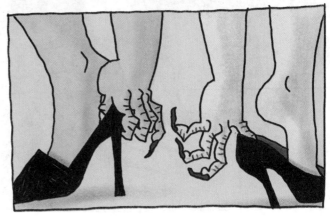

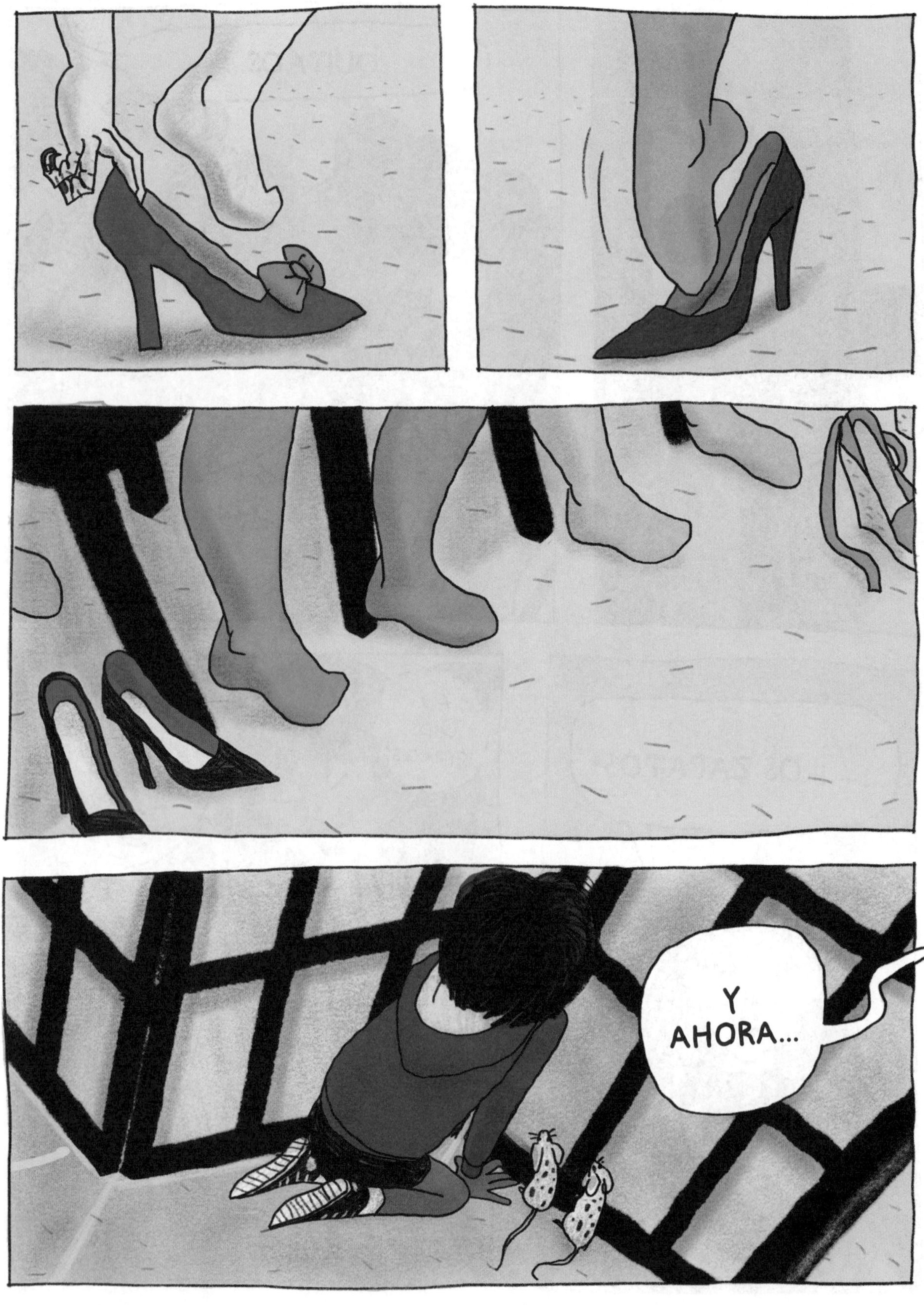
Y AHORA...

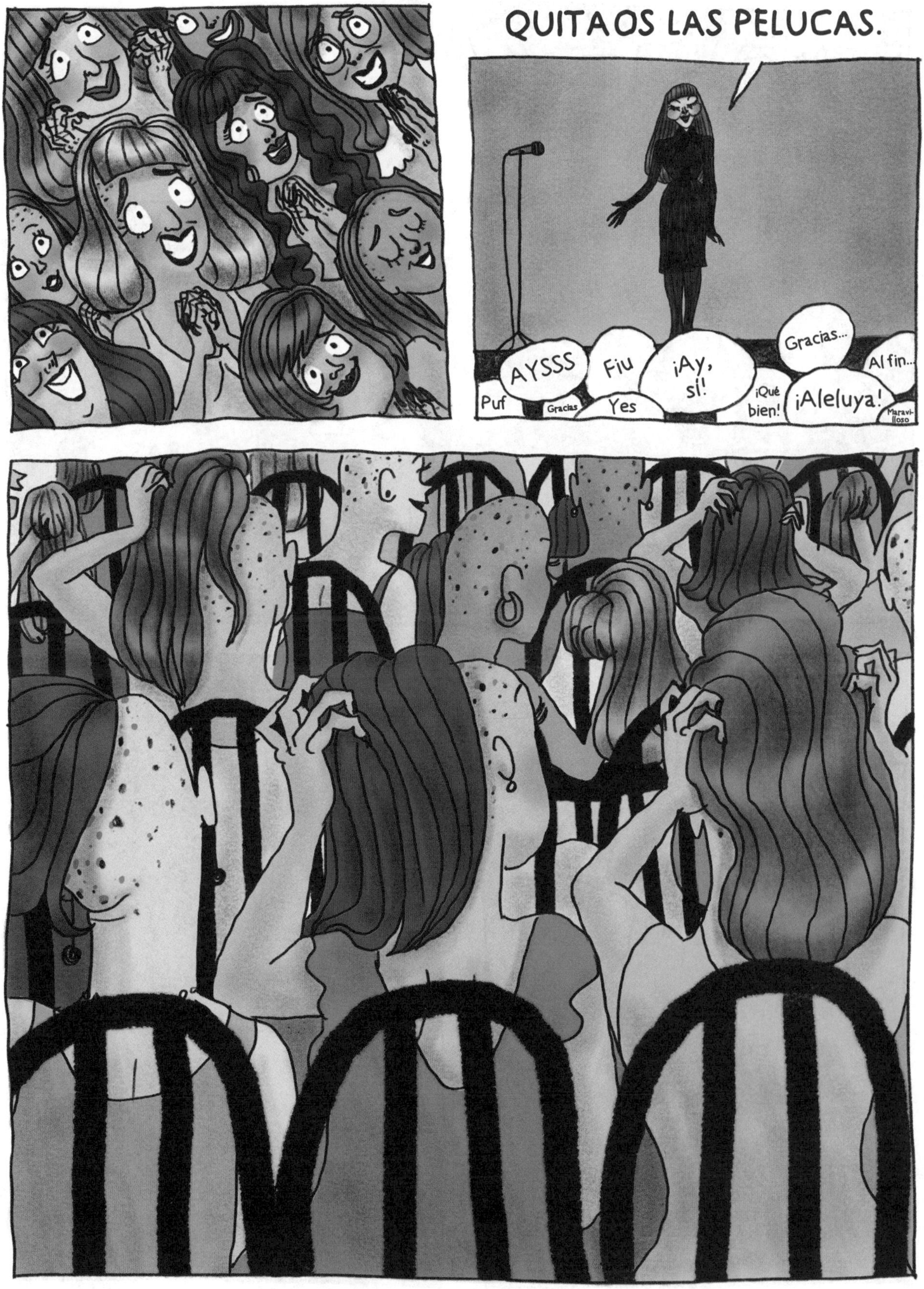
QUITAOS LAS PELUCAS.
AYSSS
Fiu
¡Ay, sí!
Gracias...
Al fin...
Puf
Gracias
Yes
¡Qué bien!
¡Aleluya!
Maravi-lloso

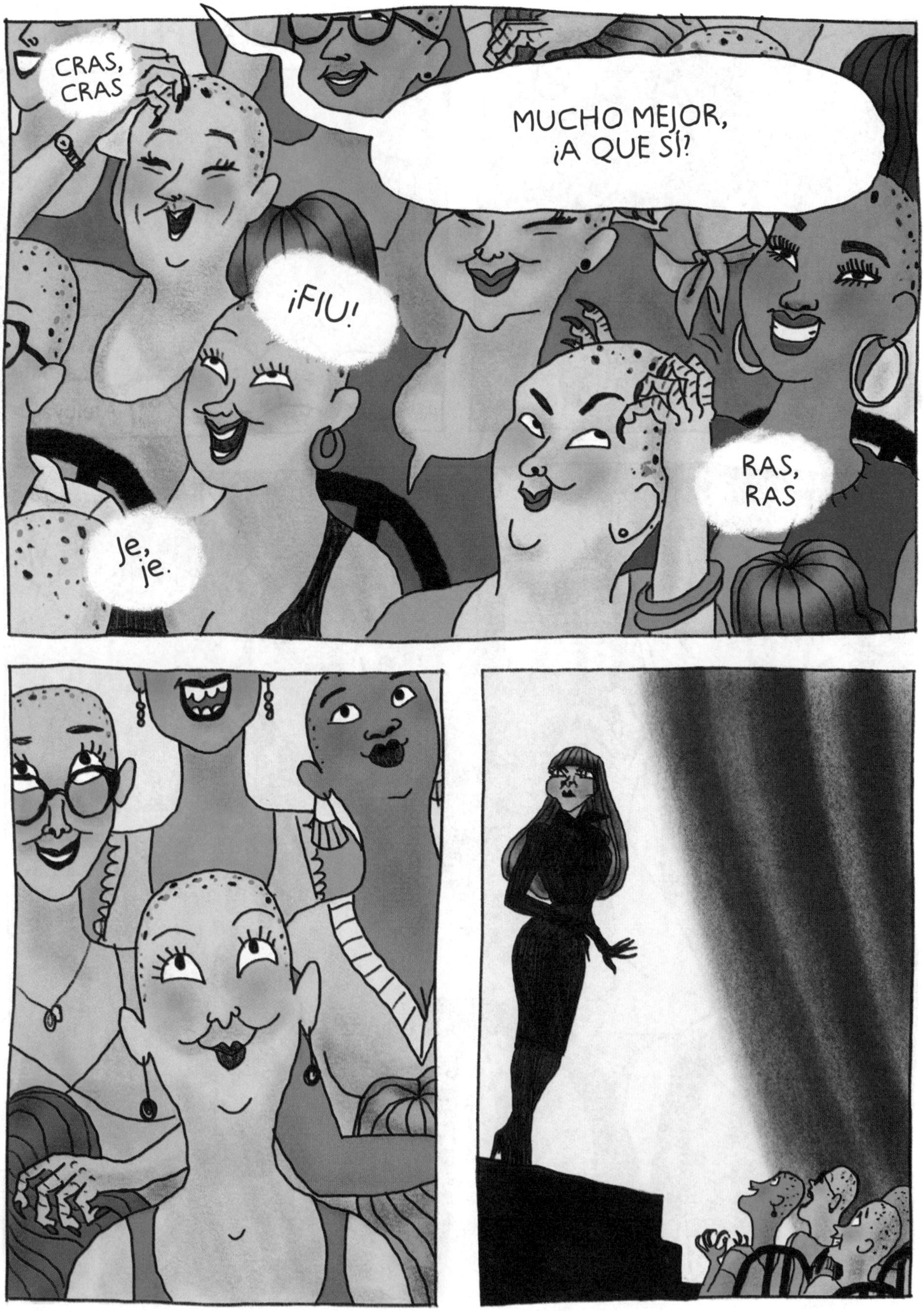
CRAS, CRAS
MUCHO MEJOR, ¡A QUE SÍ?
¡FIU!
RAS, RAS
Je, je.

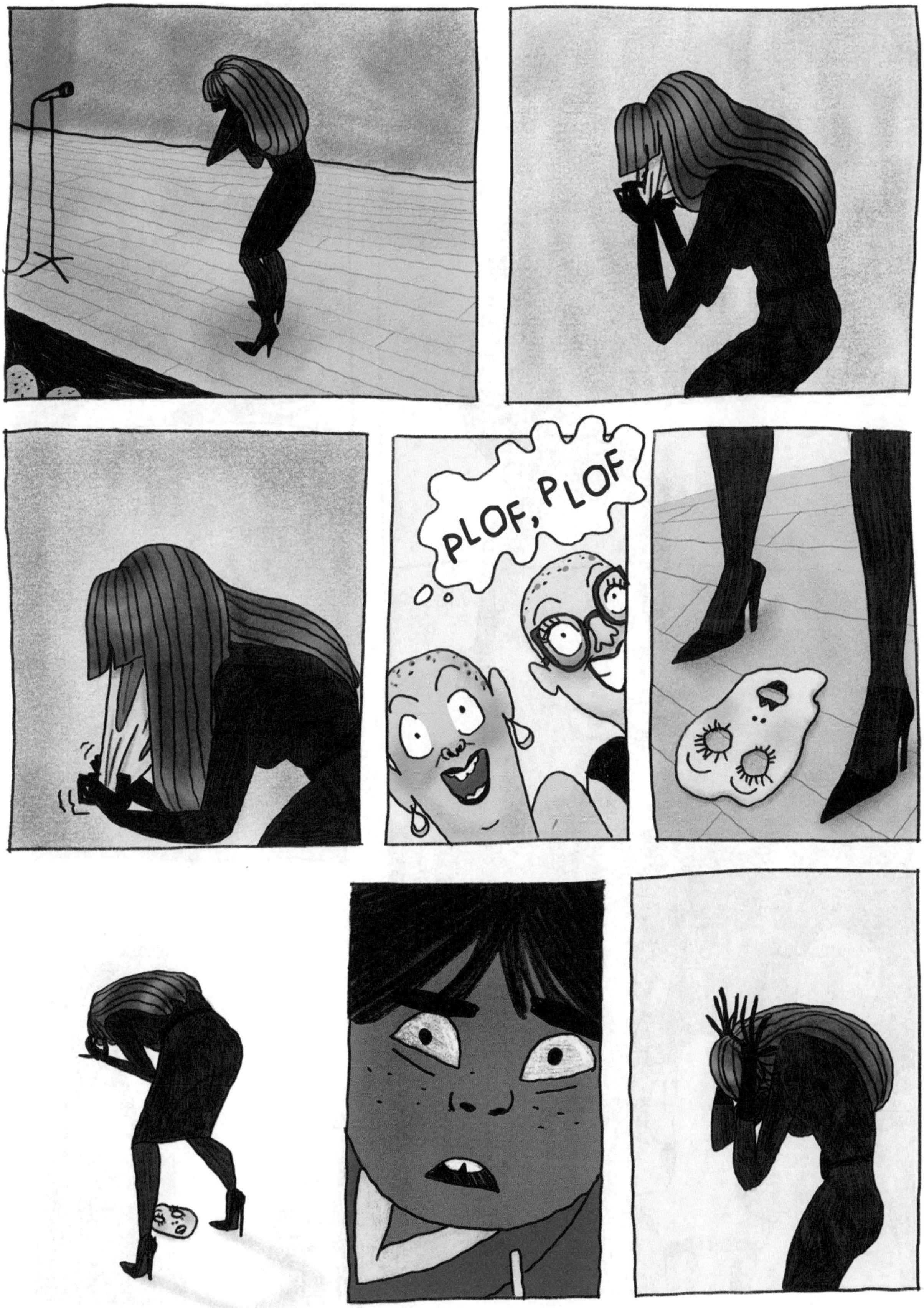
PLOF, PLOF

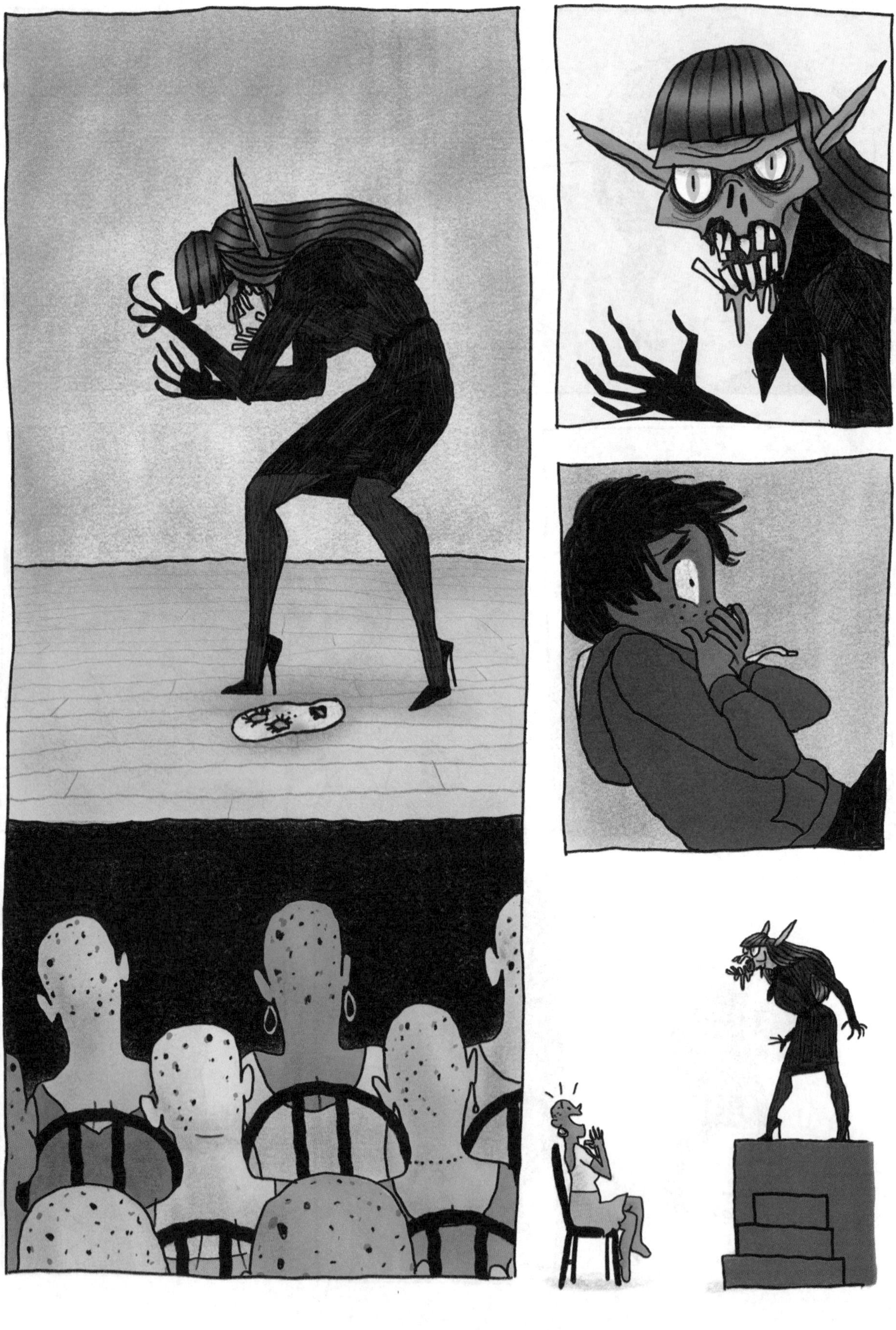

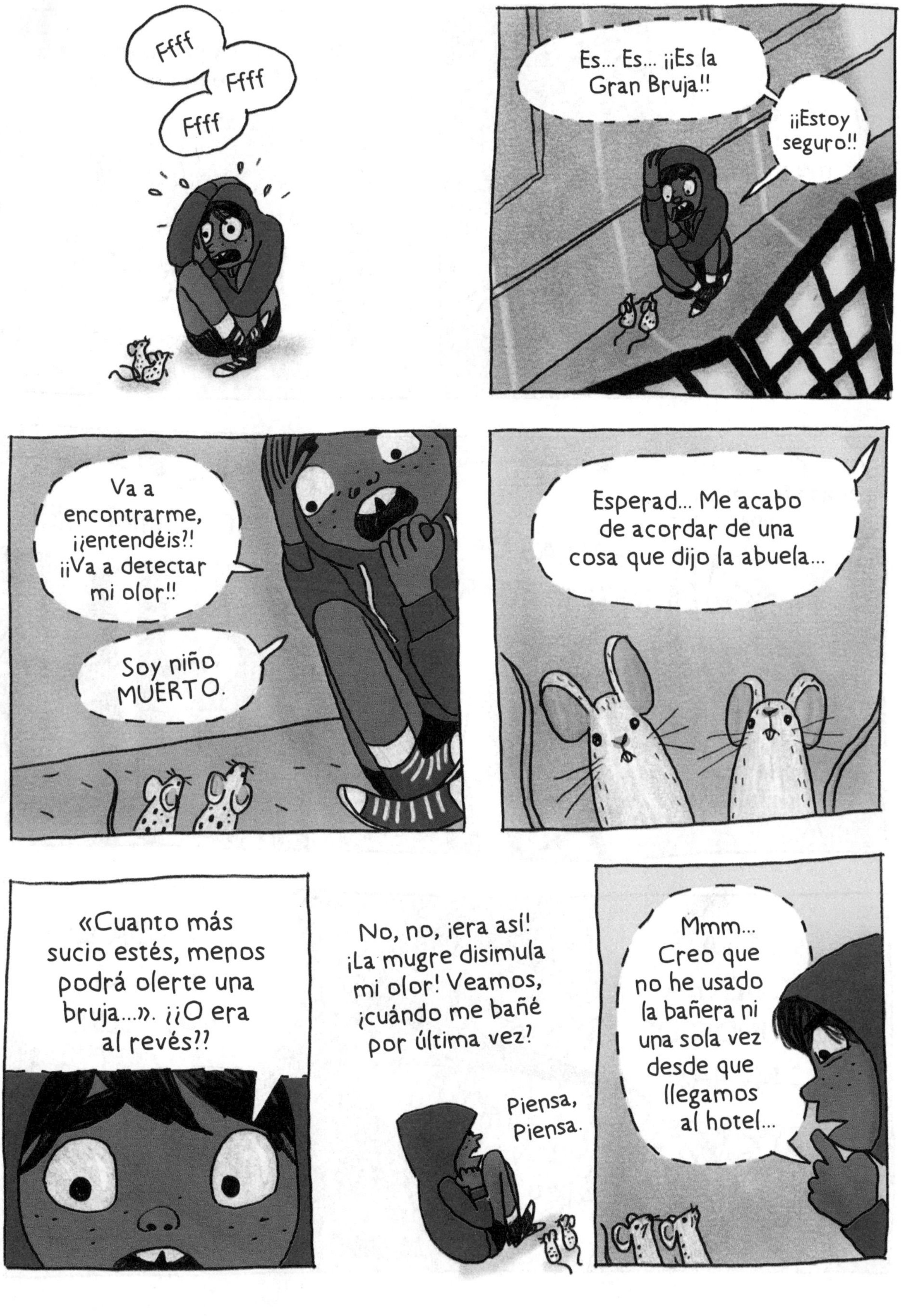
Ffff
Ffff
Ffff
Es... Es... ¡¡Es la Gran Bruja!!
¡¡Estoy seguro!!
Va a encontrarme, ¡¡entendéis?! ¡¡Va a detectar mi olor!!
Soy niño MUERTO.
Esperad... Me acabo de acordar de una cosa que dijo la abuela...
«Cuanto más sucio estés, menos podrá olerte una bruja...». ¡¡O era al revés??
No, no, ¡era así! ¡La mugre disimula mi olor! Veamos, ¿cuándo me bañé por última vez?
Piensa, Piensa.
Mmm... Creo que no he usado la bañera ni una sola vez desde que llegamos al hotel...

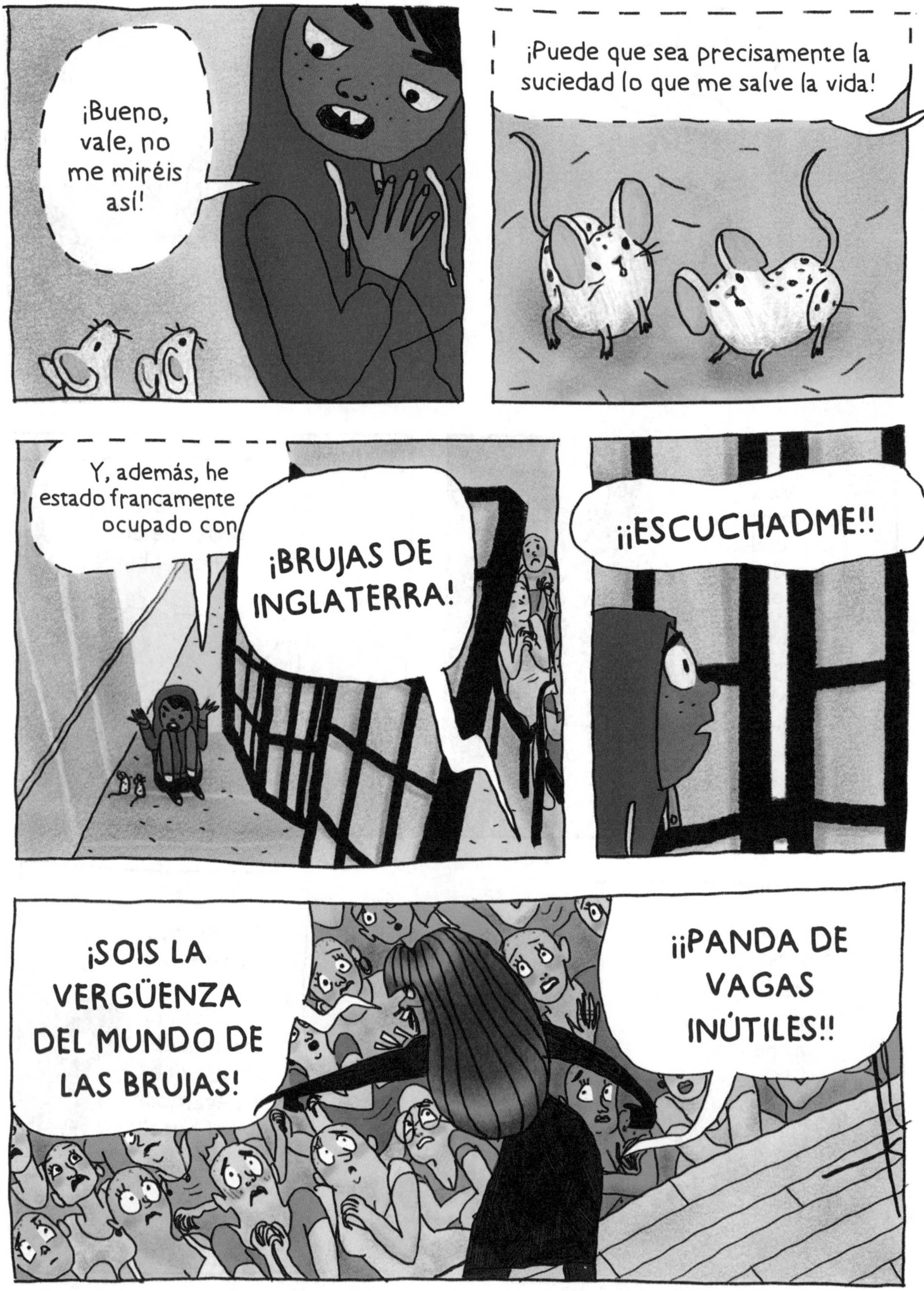
¡Bueno, vale, no me miréis así!
¡Puede que sea precisamente la suciedad lo que me salve la vida!
Y, además, he estado francamente ocupado con
¡BRUJAS DE INGLATERRA!
¡¡ESCUCHADME!!
¡SOIS LA VERGÜENZA DEL MUNDO DE LAS BRUJAS!
¡¡PANDA DE VAGAS INÚTILES!!

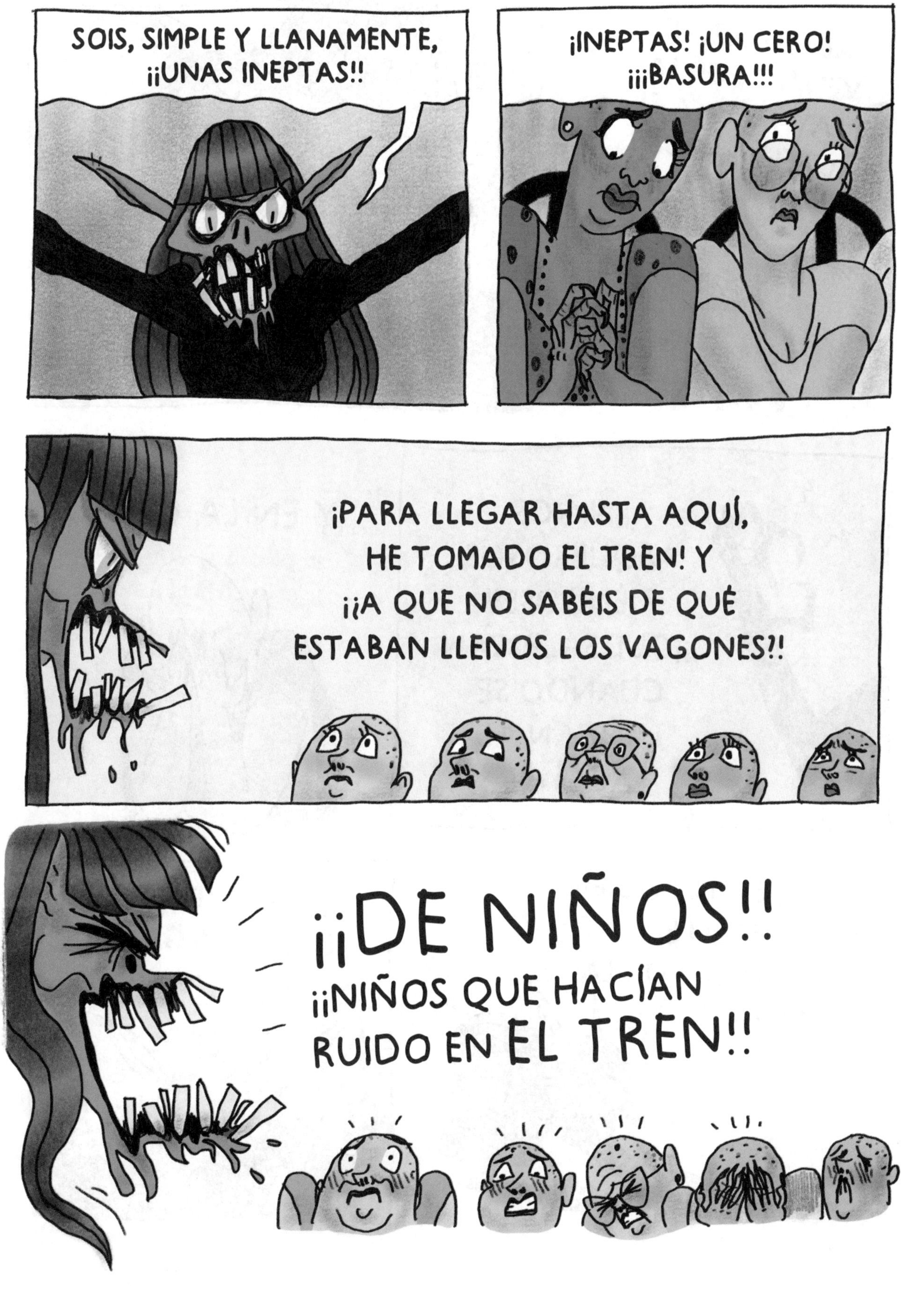
SOIS, SIMPLE Y LLANAMENTE, ¡¡UNAS INEPTAS!!
¡INEPTAS! ¡UN CERO! ¡¡¡BASURA!!!
¡PARA LLEGAR HASTA AQUÍ, HE TOMADO EL TREN! Y ¡¿A QUE NO SABÉIS DE QUÉ ESTABAN LLENOS LOS VAGONES?!
¡¡DE NIÑOS!! ¡¡NIÑOS QUE HACÍAN RUIDO EN EL TREN!!

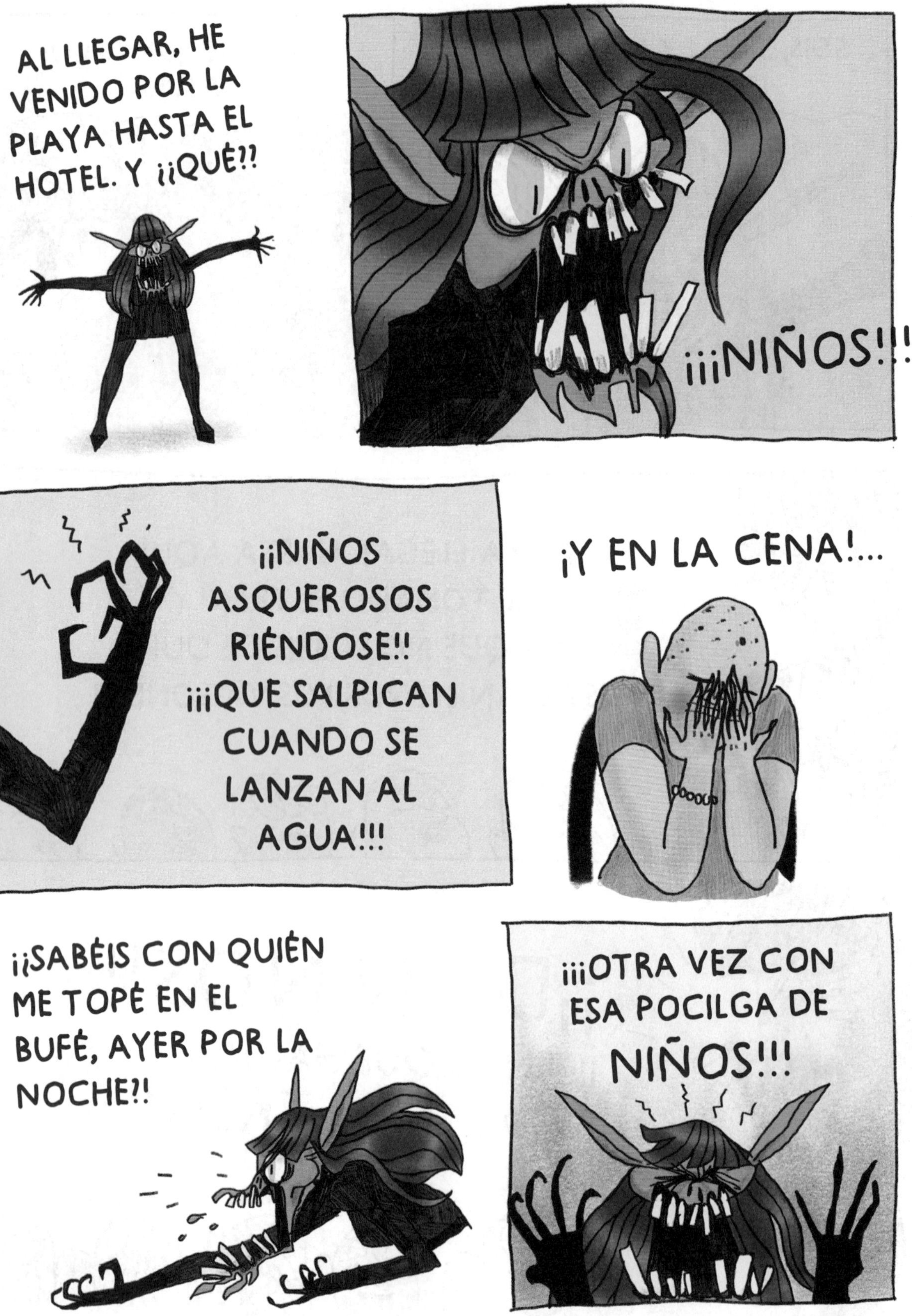
AL LLEGAR, HE VENIDO POR LA PLAYA HASTA EL HOTEL. Y ¡¡QUÉ?!
¡¡¡NIÑOS!!!
¡¡NIÑOS ASQUEROSOS RIÉNDOSE!! ¡¡¡QUE SALPICAN CUANDO SE LANZAN AL AGUA!!!
¡Y EN LA CENA!...
¡¡SABÉIS CON QUIÉN ME TOPÉ EN EL BUFÉ, AYER POR LA NOCHE?!
¡¡¡OTRA VEZ CON ESA POCILGA DE NIÑOS!!!

¡¡HABÍA UNO QUE INCLUSO ERUCTABA EN LA MESA!!

¡EN TODAS PARTES! ¡¡CIENTOS!! ¡¡MILES!!

Creo que ese era yo.

¡¡POR QUÉ TODAVÍA QUEDAN TANTOS NIÑOS?! ¡¡¡POR QUÉ SIGUEN VIVOS?!!

RAS RAS

¡¡¡¡POR QUÉ?!!!

¡¡¡A QUÉ OS ESTÁIS DEDICANDO?!!! ¡¡¡POR QUÉ NO LOS HABÉIS DESTRUIDO YA A TODOS?!!

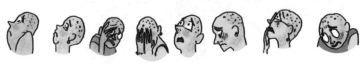

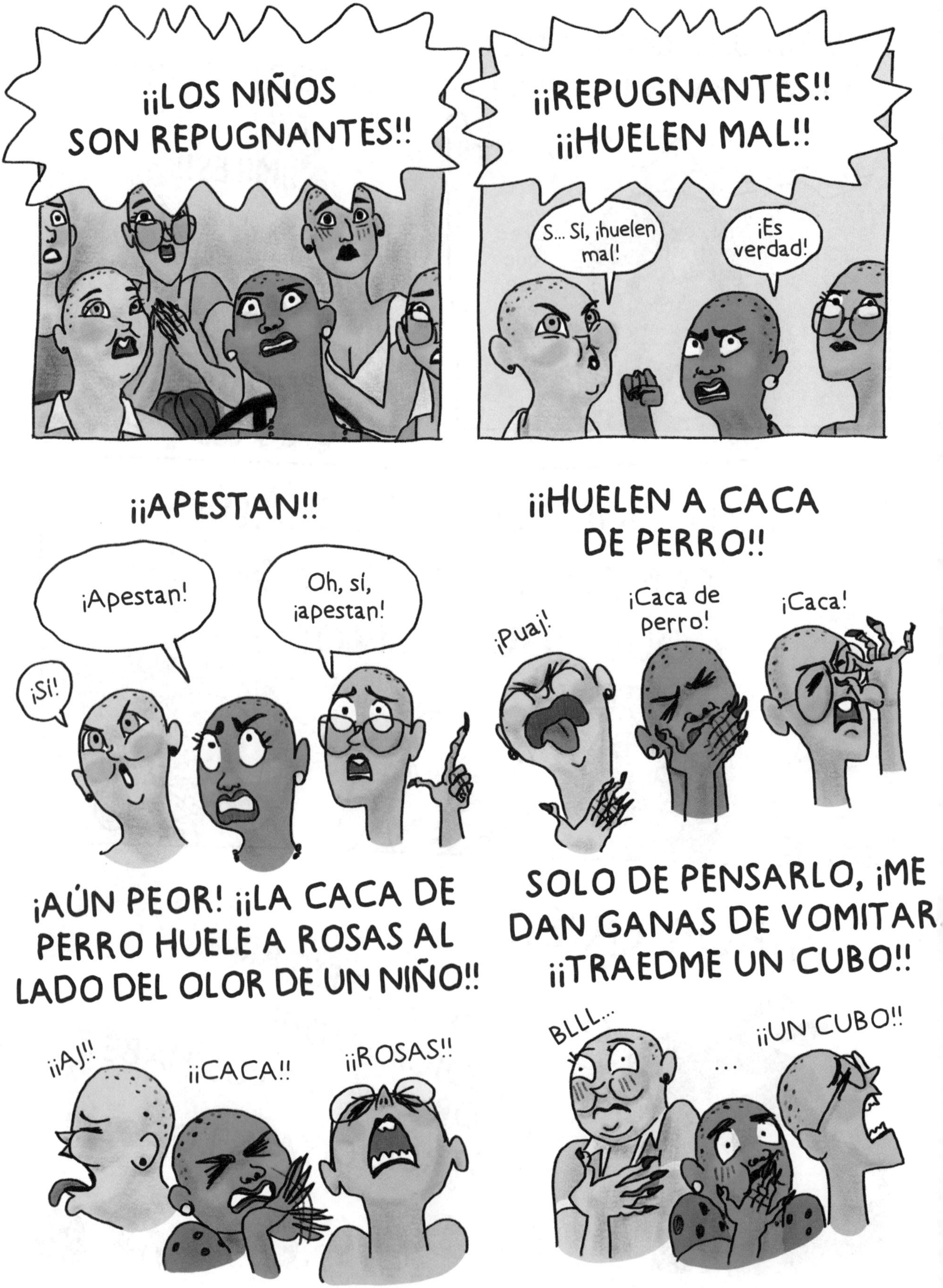
¡¡LOS NIÑOS SON REPUGNANTES!!
¡¡REPUGNANTES!! ¡¡HUELEN MAL!!
S... Sí, ¡huelen mal!
¡Es verdad!
¡¡APESTAN!!
¡Apestan!
Oh, sí, ¡apestan!
¡Sí!
¡¡HUELEN A CACA DE PERRO!!
¡Puaj!
¡Caca de perro!
¡Caca!
¡AÚN PEOR! ¡¡LA CACA DE PERRO HUELE A ROSAS AL LADO DEL OLOR DE UN NIÑO!!
¡¡AJ!!
¡¡CACA!!
¡¡ROSAS!!
SOLO DE PENSARLO, ¡ME DAN GANAS DE VOMITAR. ¡¡TRAEDME UN CUBO!!
BLLL...
...
¡¡UN CUBO!!

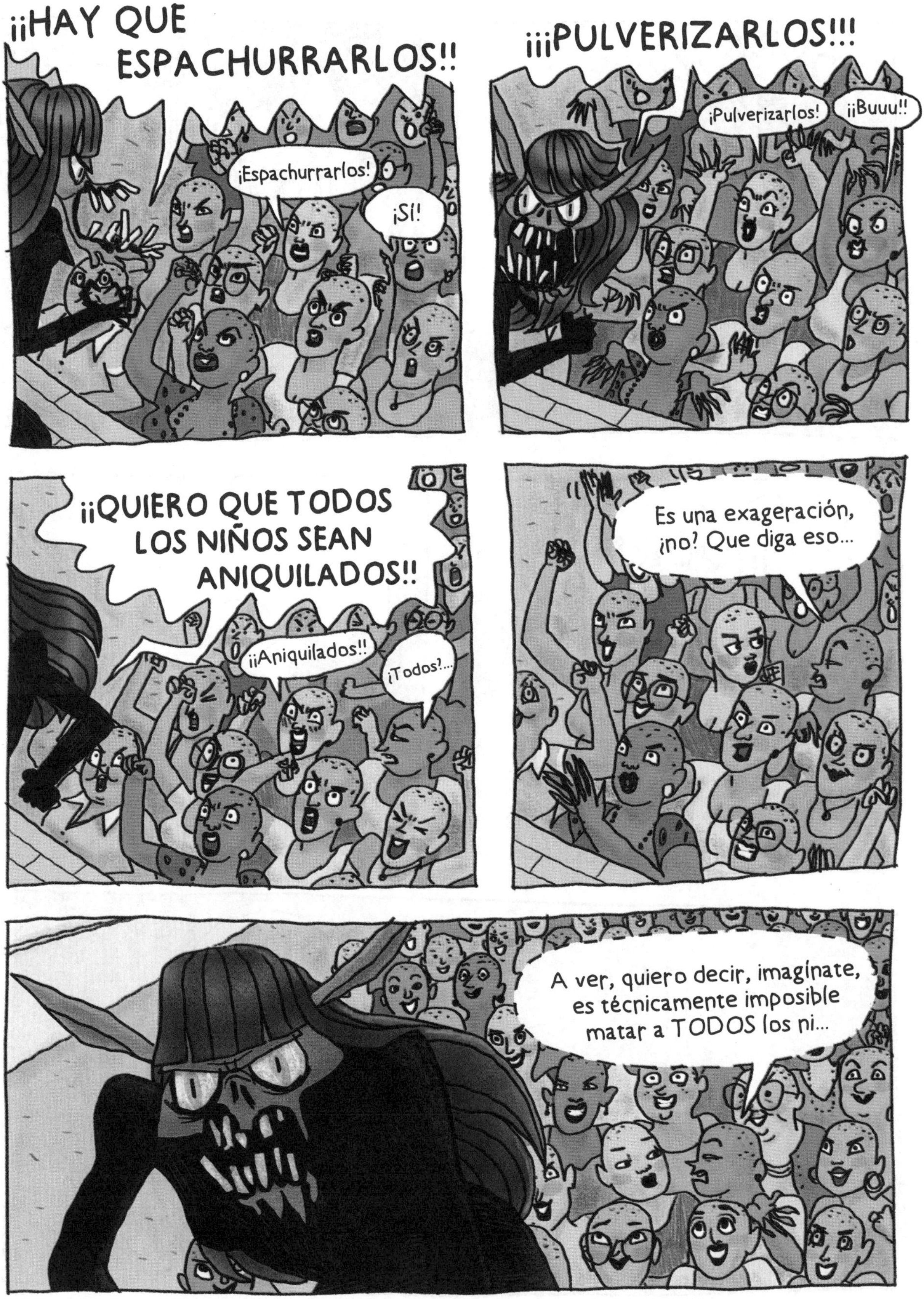
¡¡HAY QUE ESPACHURRARLOS!!
¡Espachurrarlos!
¡Sí!
¡¡¡PULVERIZARLOS!!!
¡Pulverizarlos!
¡¡Buuu!!
¡¡QUIERO QUE TODOS LOS NIÑOS SEAN ANIQUILADOS!!
¡¡Aniquilados!!
¿Todos?...
Es una exageración, ¿no? Que diga eso...
A ver, quiero decir, imagínate, es técnicamente imposible matar a TODOS los ni...

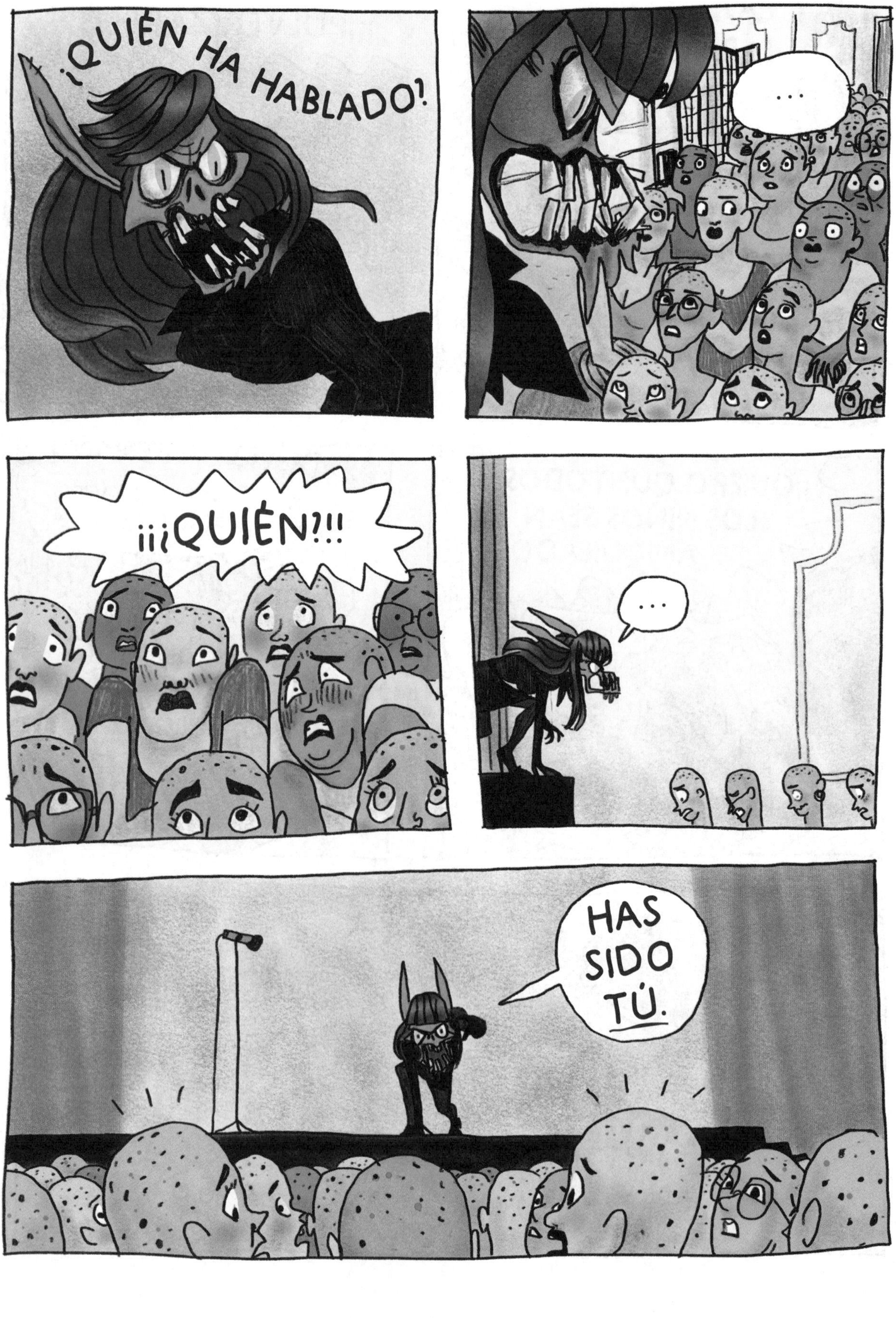
¡QUIÉN HA HABLADO?
...
¡¡¡QUIÉN?!!
...
HAS SIDO TÚ.

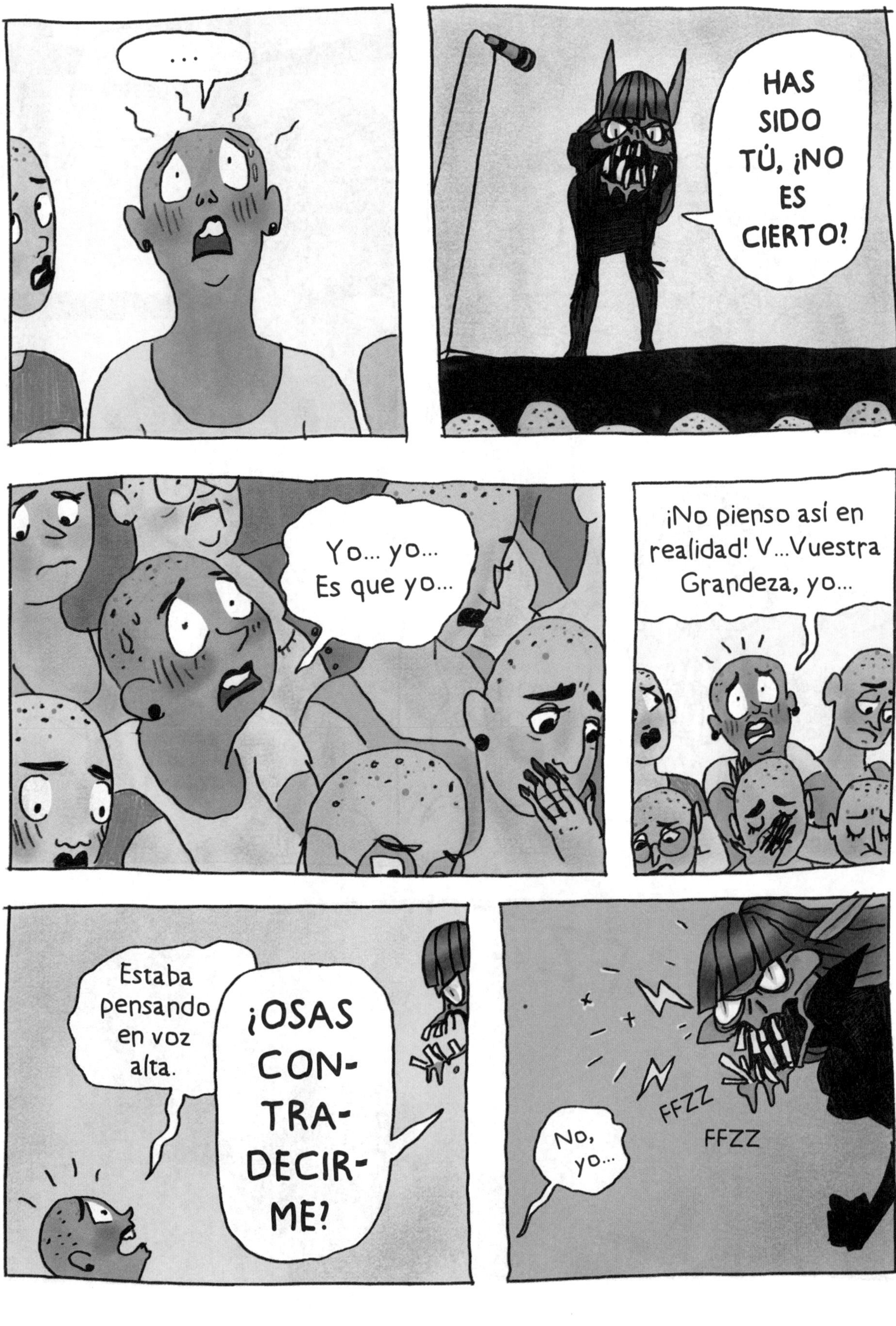
...
HAS SIDO TÚ, ¡NO ES CIERTO?
Yo... yo... Es que yo...
¡No pienso así en realidad! V...Vuestra Grandeza, yo...
Estaba pensando en voz alta.
¡OSAS CONTRA-DECIRME?
FFZZ
FFZZ
No, yo...

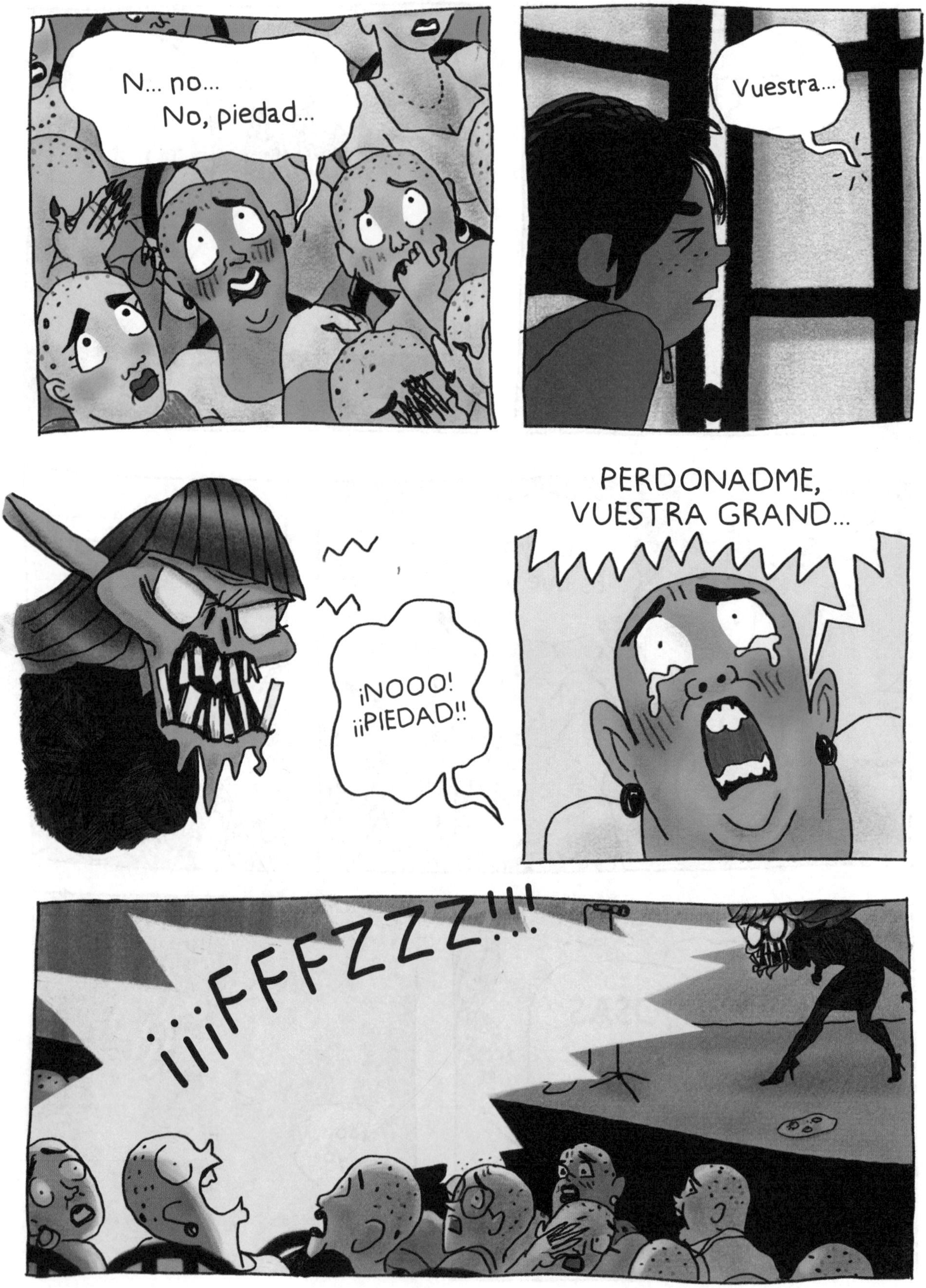
N... no...
No, piedad...
Vuestra...
PERDONADME, VUESTRA GRAND...
¡NOOO! ¡¡PIEDAD!!
¡¡¡FFFZZZ!!!

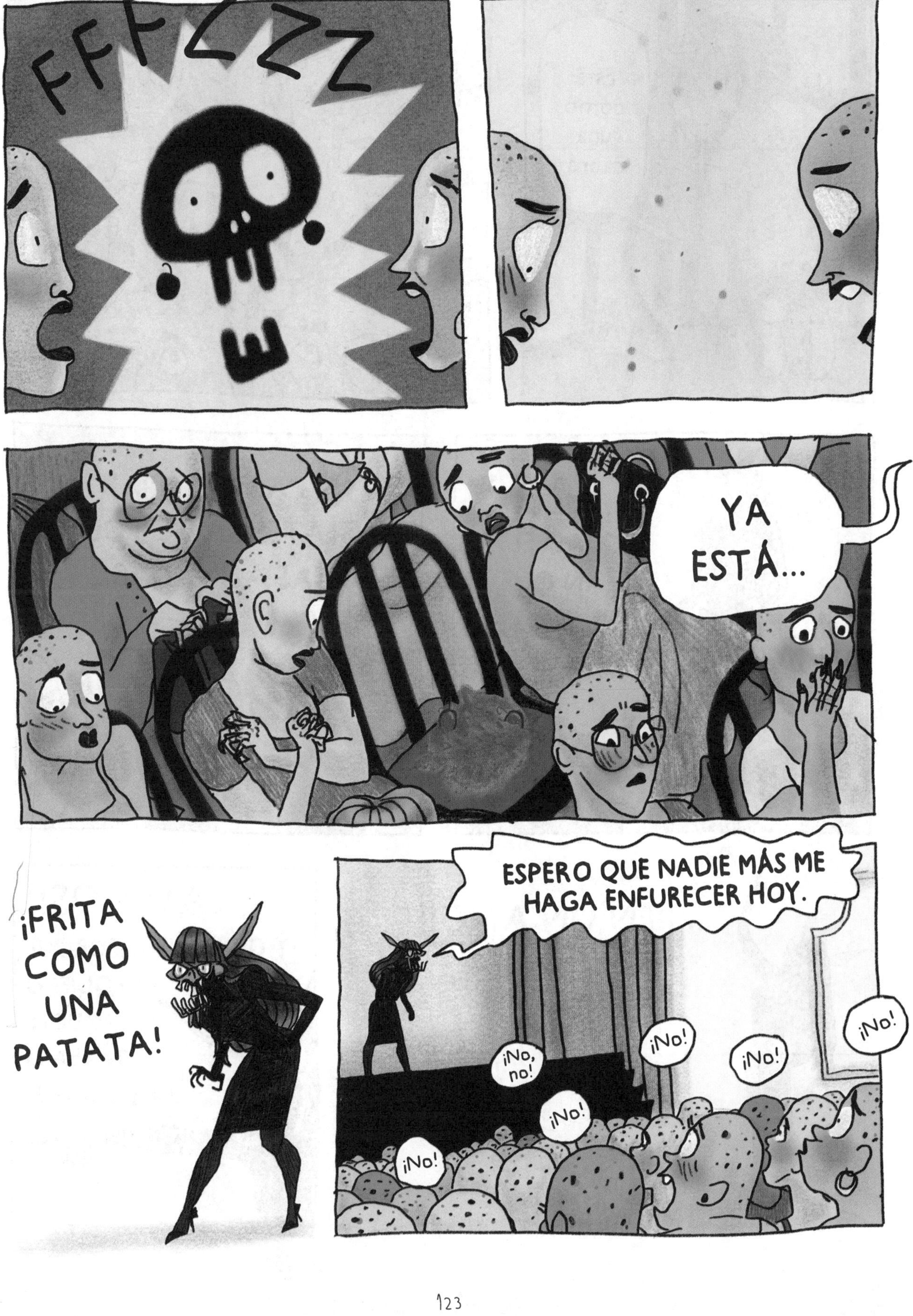
FFFZZZZ
YA ESTÁ...
¡FRITA COMO UNA PATATA!
ESPERO QUE NADIE MÁS ME HAGA ENFURECER HOY.
¡No, no!
¡No!
¡No!
¡No!
¡No!
¡No!

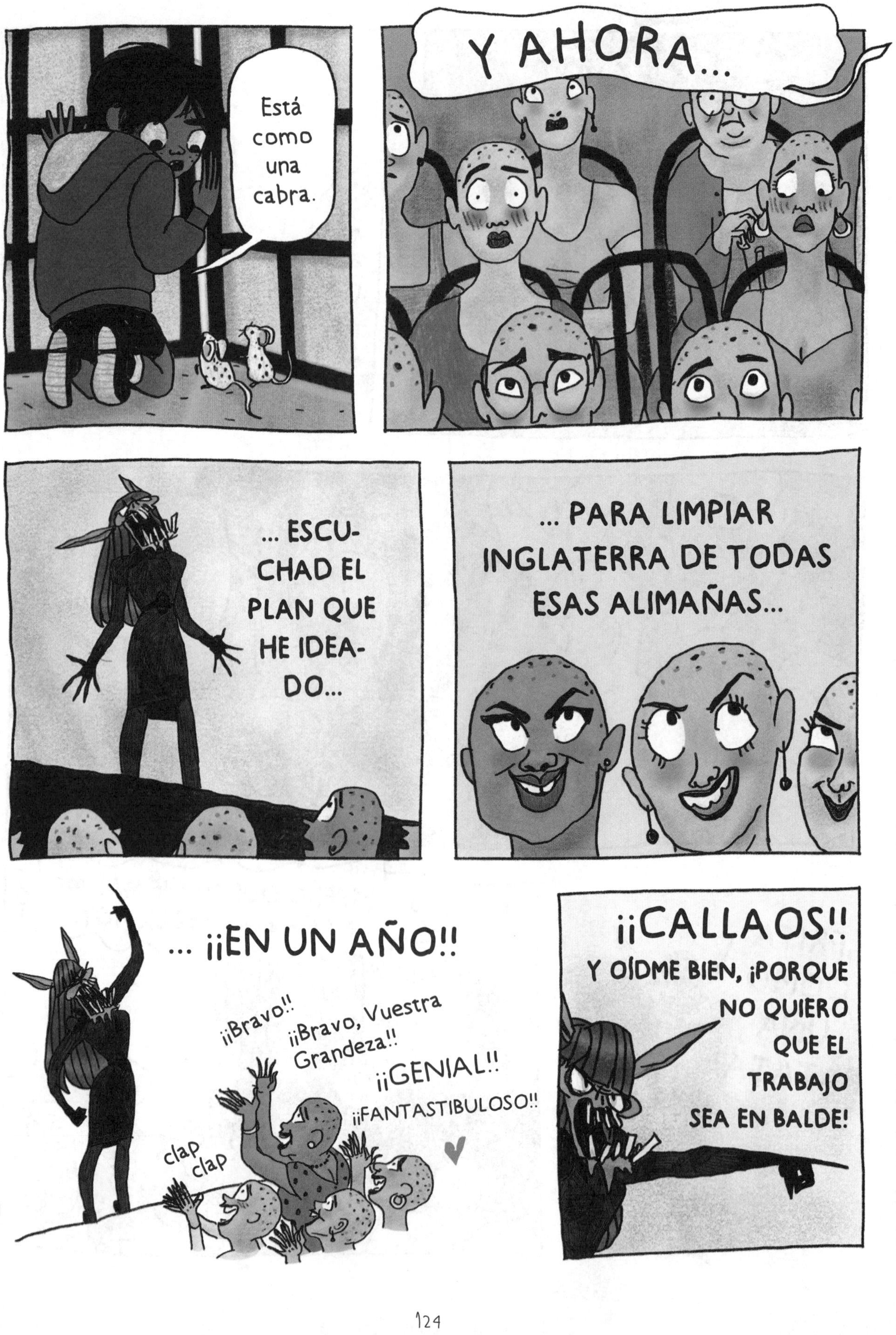
Está como una cabra.
Y AHORA...
... ESCUCHAD EL PLAN QUE HE IDEADO...
... PARA LIMPIAR INGLATERRA DE TODAS ESAS ALIMAÑAS...
... ¡¡EN UN AÑO!!
¡¡Bravo!!
¡¡Bravo, Vuestra Grandeza!!
¡¡GENIAL!!
¡¡FANTASTIBULOSO!!
clap clap
¡¡CALLAOS!!
Y OÍDME BIEN, ¡PORQUE NO QUIERO QUE EL TRABAJO SEA EN BALDE!

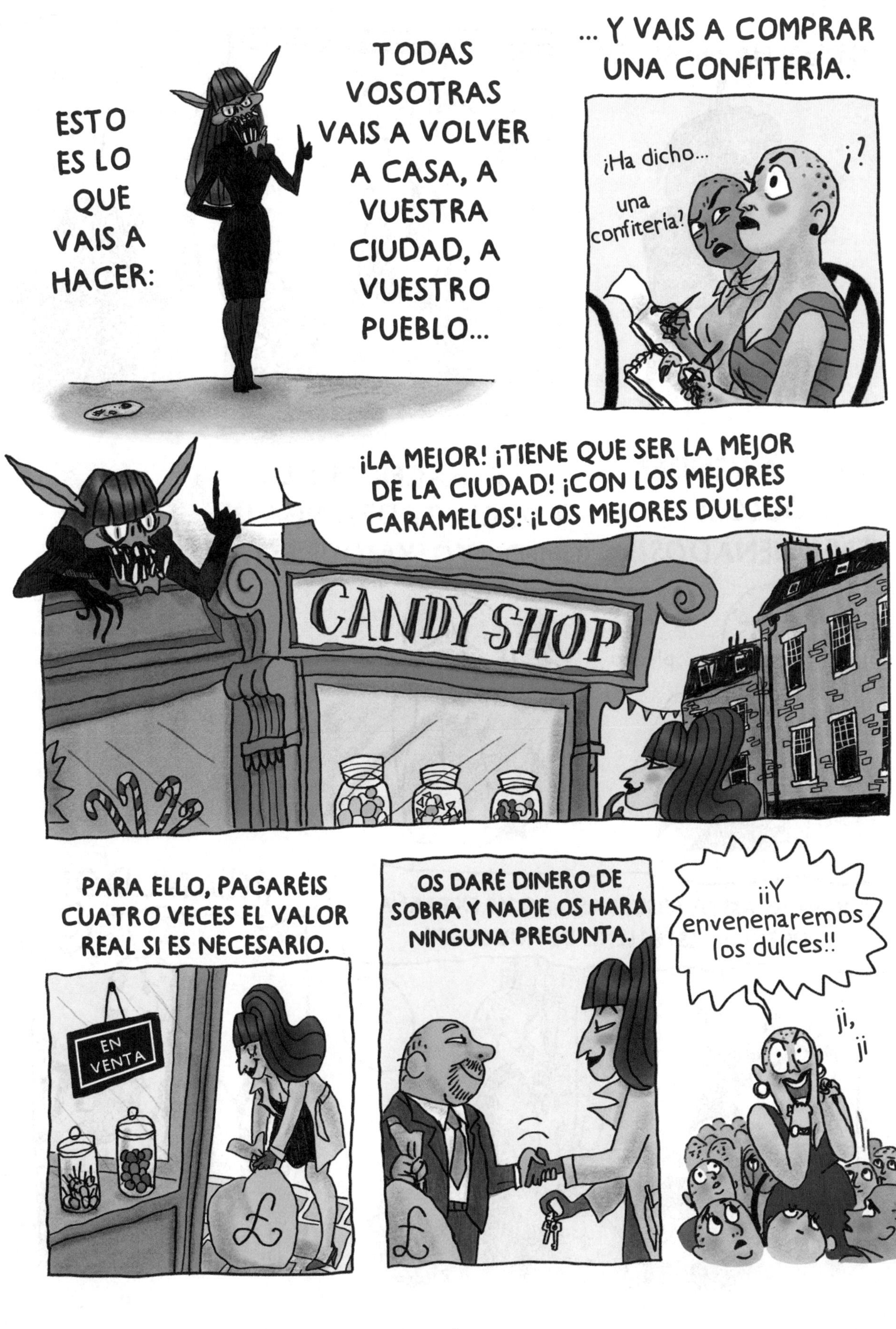
ESTO ES LO QUE VAIS A HACER:
TODAS VOSOTRAS VAIS A VOLVER A CASA, A VUESTRA CIUDAD, A VUESTRO PUEBLO...
... Y VAIS A COMPRAR UNA CONFITERÍA.
¿Ha dicho... una confitería?
¿?
¡LA MEJOR! ¡TIENE QUE SER LA MEJOR DE LA CIUDAD! ¡CON LOS MEJORES CARAMELOS! ¡LOS MEJORES DULCES!
CANDY SHOP
PARA ELLO, PAGARÉIS CUATRO VECES EL VALOR REAL SI ES NECESARIO.
EN VENTA
OS DARÉ DINERO DE SOBRA Y NADIE OS HARÁ NINGUNA PREGUNTA.
¡¡Y envenenaremos los dulces!!
ji, ji

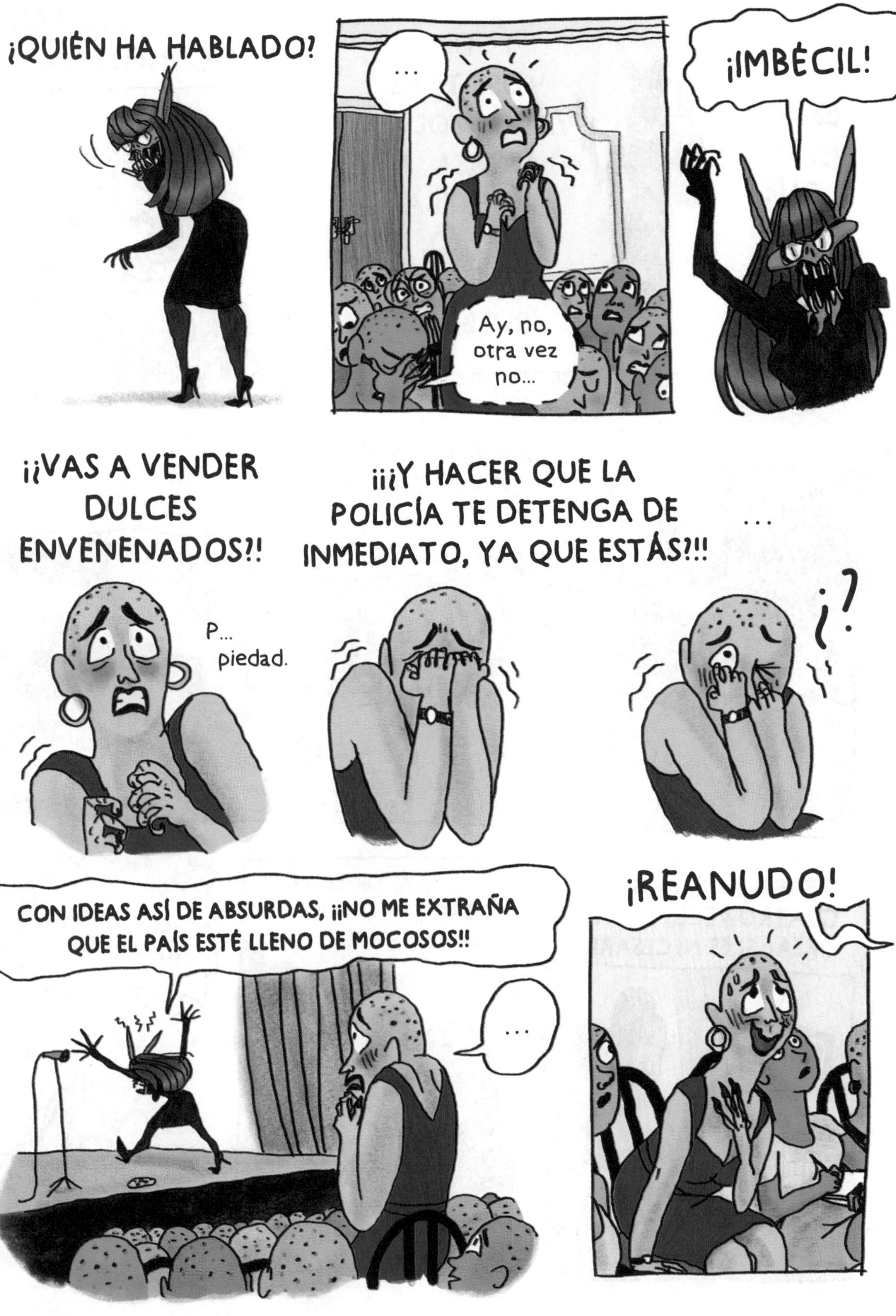

¿QUIÉN HA HABLADO?
...
Ay, no, otra vez no...
¡IMBÉCIL!
¡¿VAS A VENDER DULCES ENVENENADOS?!
P... piedad.
¡¡¡Y HACER QUE LA POLICÍA TE DETENGA DE INMEDIATO, YA QUE ESTÁS?!!
...
¿?
CON IDEAS ASÍ DE ABSURDAS, ¡¡NO ME EXTRAÑA QUE EL PAÍS ESTÉ LLENO DE MOCOSOS!!
...
¡REANUDO!

PERO ¡LA PRÓXIMA QUE ME INTERRUMPA VA A SABER LO QUE ES UNA BUENA BARBACOA!

¡COMO IBA DICIENDO!

TODAS TENDRÉIS UNA CONFITERÍA PRECIOSA.

LA ABRIRÉIS AL PÚBLICO EN UNA FECHA CONCRETA Y CELEBRARÉIS UNA GRAN FIESTA PARA LA OCASIÓN.

¡INAUGURACIÓN

GRAN VELADA ¡ESPECIAL!

Un bombón o dulce GRATIS para cada niño.

¡DULCES GRATIS! OBVIAMENTE, ¡ESOS ASQUEROSOS NIÑITOS IRÁN EN MASA!

QUÉ ASCO ME DAN.

Y VOSOTRAS PREPARARÉIS ESTE MARAVILLOSO EVENTO ECHÁNDOLES A LOS DULCES...

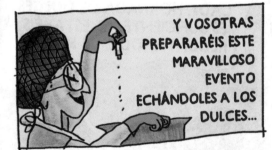

... UN PEQUEÑO SECRETO CASERO... UN INGREDIENTE ESPECIAL QUE HE INVENTADO YO...

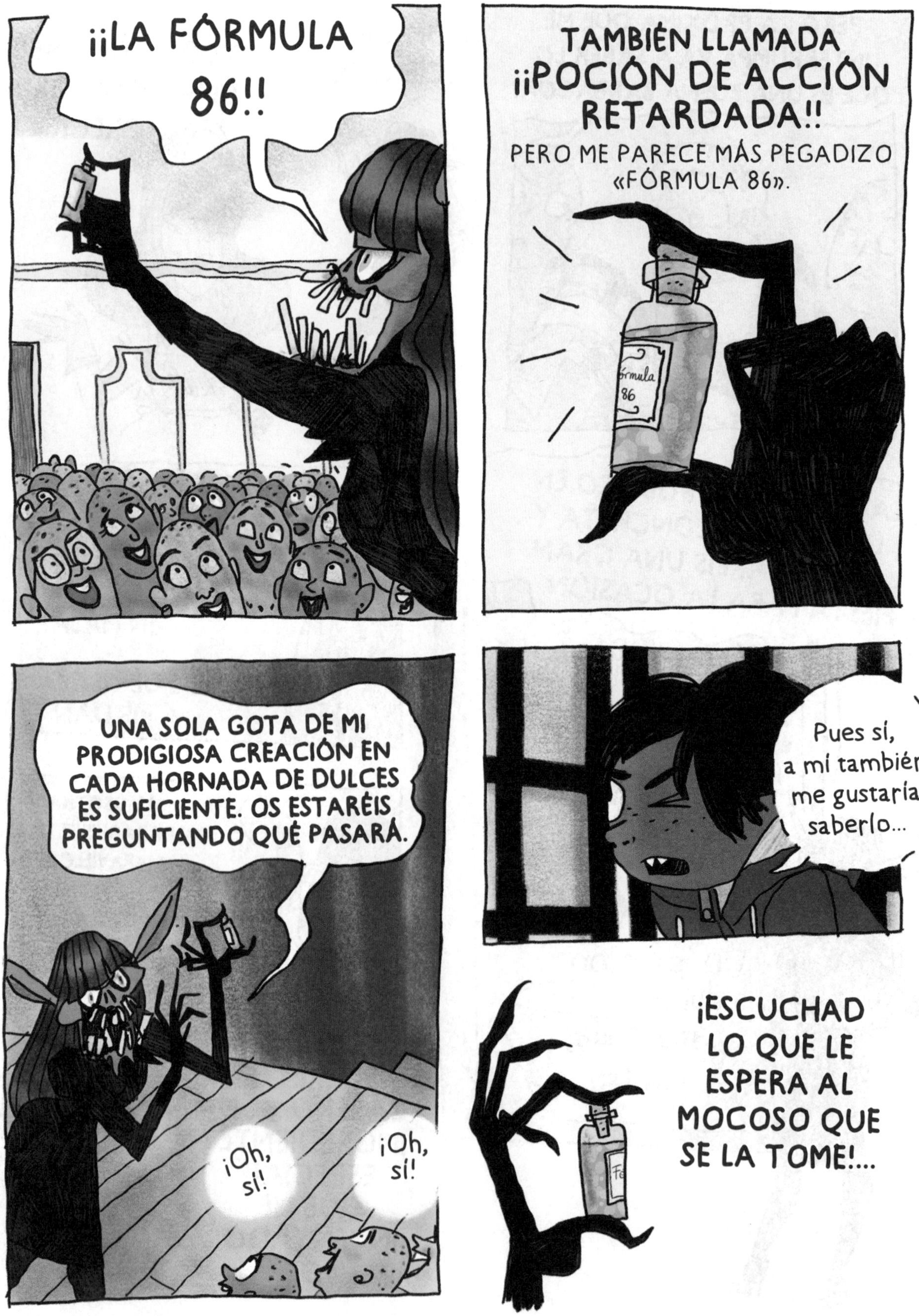
¡¡LA FÓRMULA 86!!
TAMBIÉN LLAMADA ¡¡POCIÓN DE ACCIÓN RETARDADA!! PERO ME PARECE MÁS PEGADIZO «FÓRMULA 86».
Fórmula 86
UNA SOLA GOTA DE MI PRODIGIOSA CREACIÓN EN CADA HORNADA DE DULCES ES SUFICIENTE. OS ESTARÉIS PREGUNTANDO QUÉ PASARÁ.
¡Oh, sí!
¡Oh, sí!
Pues sí, a mí también me gustaría saberlo...
¡ESCUCHAD LO QUE LE ESPERA AL MOCOSO QUE SE LA TOME!...

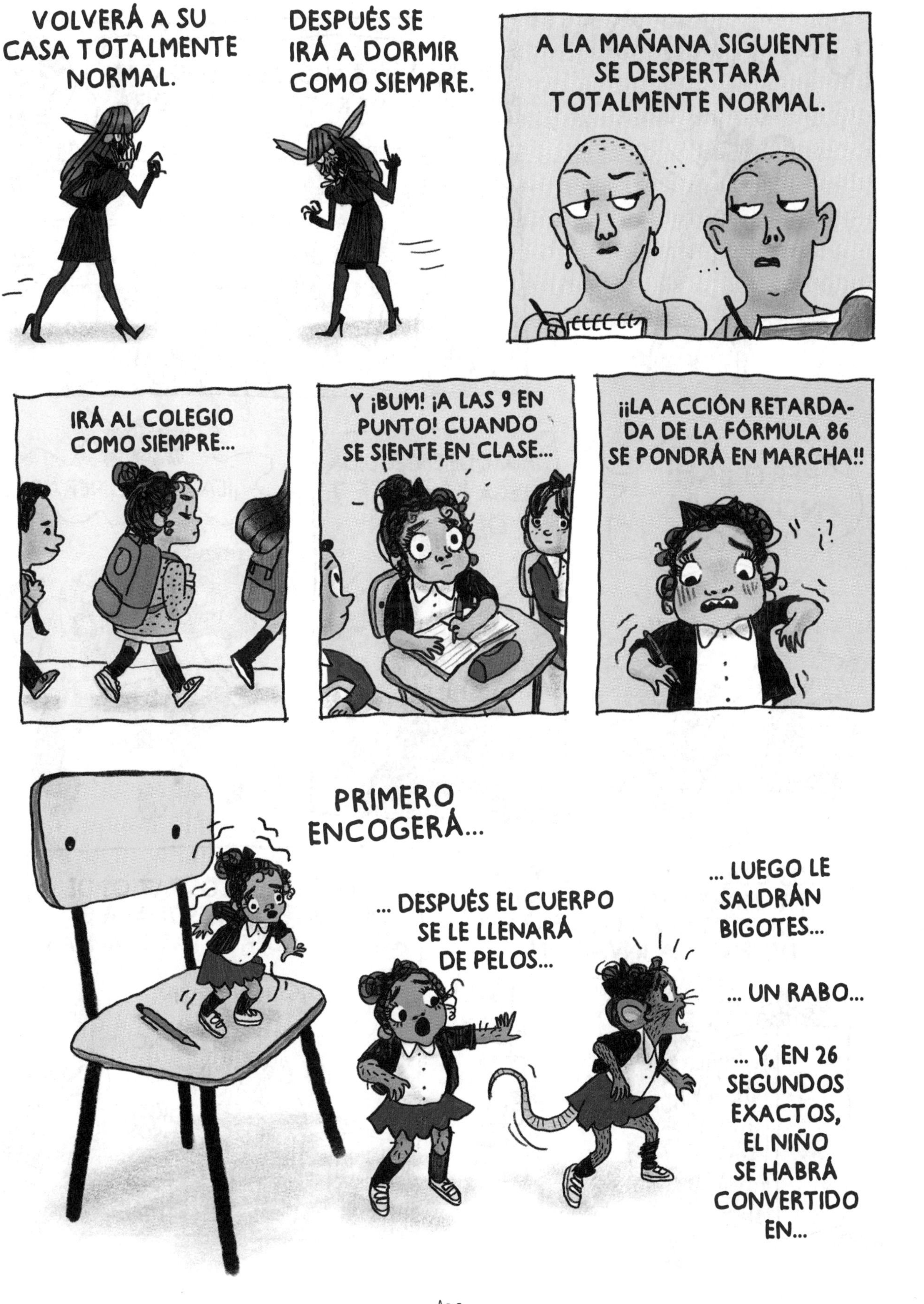
VOLVERÁ A SU CASA TOTALMENTE NORMAL.
DESPUÉS SE IRÁ A DORMIR COMO SIEMPRE.
A LA MAÑANA SIGUIENTE SE DESPERTARÁ TOTALMENTE NORMAL.
IRÁ AL COLEGIO COMO SIEMPRE...
Y ¡BUM! ¡A LAS 9 EN PUNTO! CUANDO SE SIENTE EN CLASE...
¡¡LA ACCIÓN RETARDADA DE LA FÓRMULA 86 SE PONDRÁ EN MARCHA!!
¿?
PRIMERO ENCOGERÁ...
... DESPUÉS EL CUERPO SE LE LLENARÁ DE PELOS...
... LUEGO LE SALDRÁN BIGOTES...
... UN RABO...
... Y, EN 26 SEGUNDOS EXACTOS, EL NIÑO SE HABRÁ CONVERTIDO EN...

¡¡UN RATÓN!!

¡LAS AULAS SE INUNDARÁN DE RATONES! ¡¡CUNDIRÁ EL PÁNICO!!

PERO ¡¡AHÍ NO ACABA TODO!!

¡Bravo!

CLAP CLAP
CLAP CLAP
CLAP CLAP
CLAP CLAP

¡Bravo!

¡PORQUE ENSEGUIDA LLEGA **LA FASE 2** DE MI PLAN!

¡¡LAS RATONERAS!!

LOS COLEGIOS INSTALARÁN TRAMPAS PARA RATONES POR TODAS PARTES PARA DETENER LA INVASIÓN...

Aa Bb Cc Dd Ee
Ff Gg Hh Ii Jj
Kk Ll Mm Nn Ññ
Oo Pp Qq Rr
Ss Tt Uu Vv
Ww Xx Yy Zz

¡Y EN TODOS LOS PATIOS DE INGLATERRA RESONARÁ EL ALEGRE CRUJIR DE LAS TRAMPAS!

¡CLAC! ¡CLAC! ¡CLAC!
¡CLAC! ¡CLAC!
¡CLAC!

Y ¡ADIÓS, MOCOSOS!

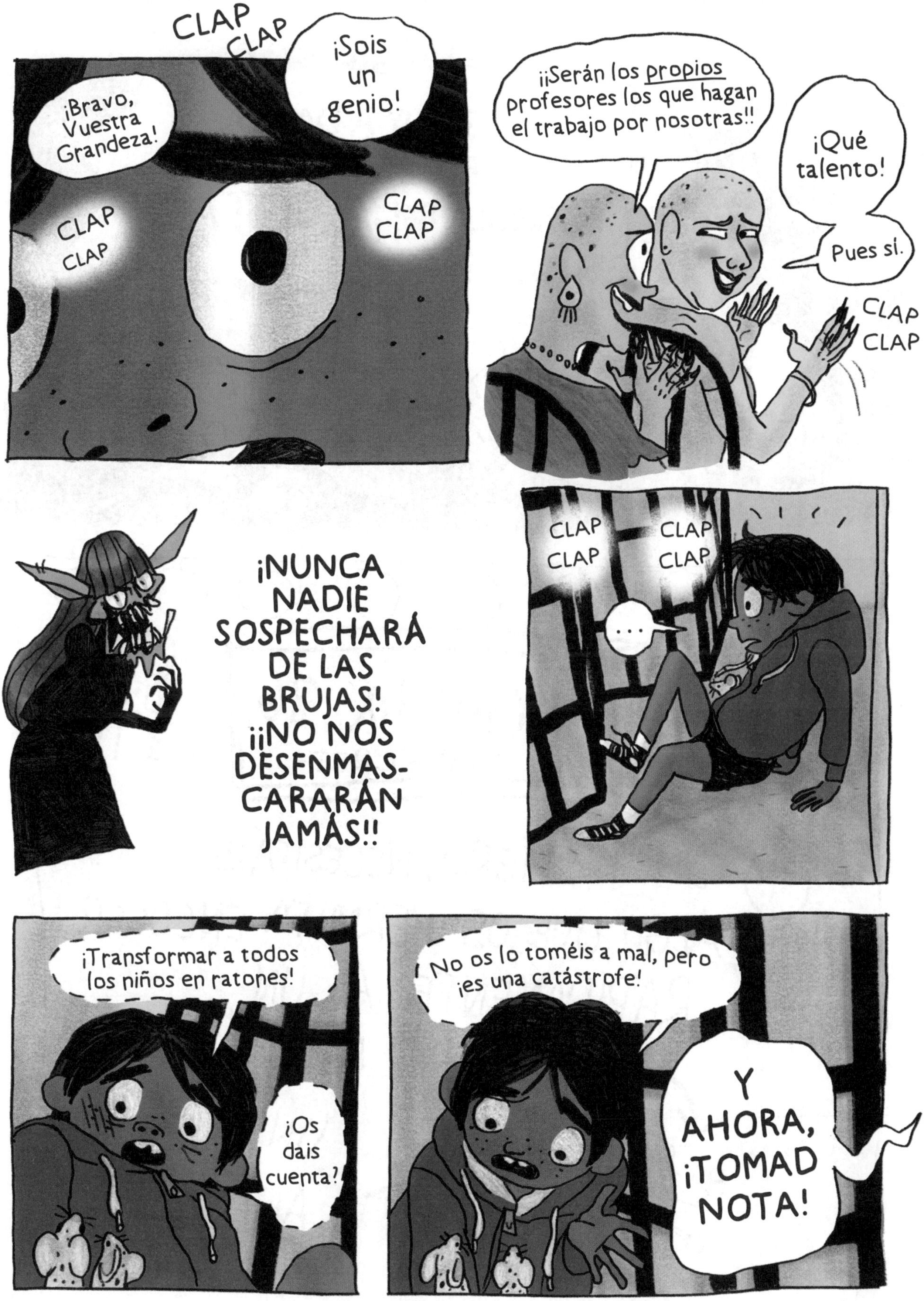
CLAP CLAP
¡Sois un genio!
¡Bravo, Vuestra Grandeza!
CLAP CLAP
CLAP CLAP
¡¡Serán los propios profesores los que hagan el trabajo por nosotras!!
¡Qué talento!
Pues sí.
CLAP CLAP
¡NUNCA NADIE SOSPECHARÁ DE LAS BRUJAS! ¡¡NO NOS DESENMASCARARÁN JAMÁS!!
CLAP CLAP
CLAP CLAP
...
¡Transformar a todos los niños en ratones!
¡Os dais cuenta?
No os lo toméis a mal, pero ¡es una catástrofe!
Y AHORA, ¡TOMAD NOTA!

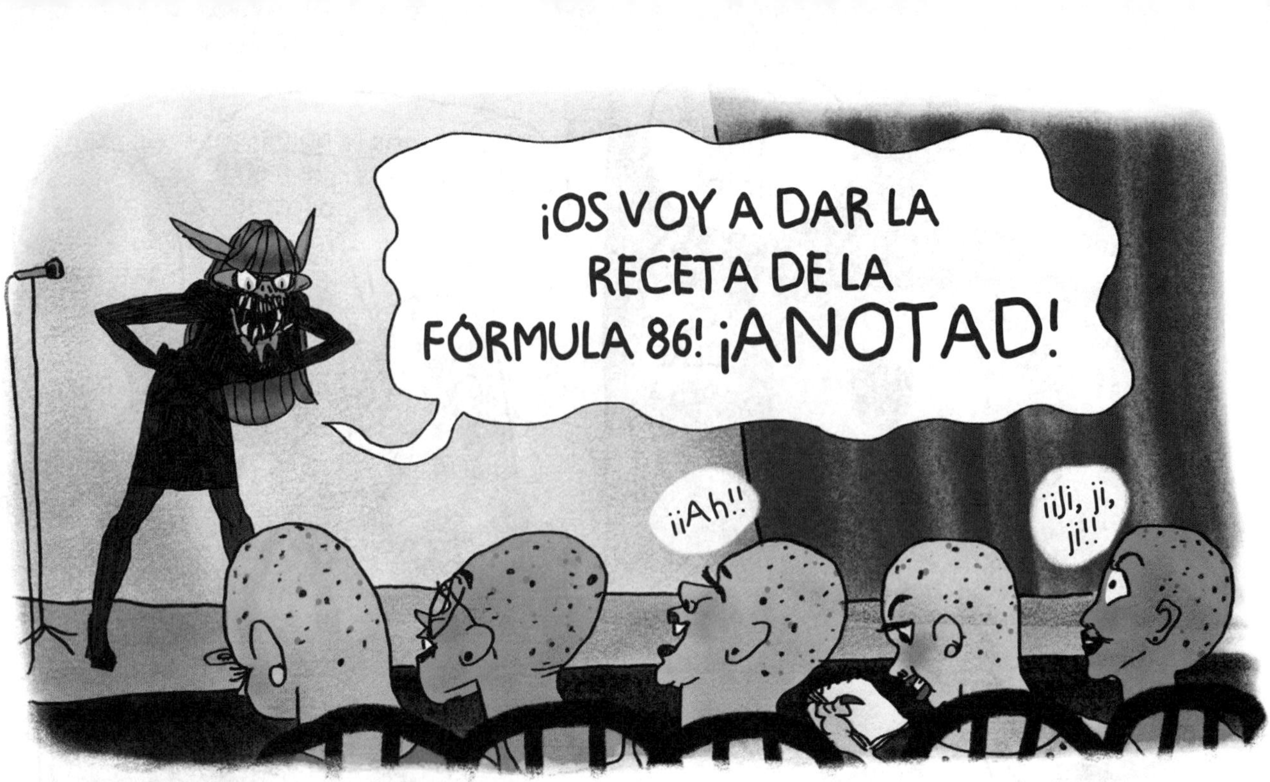
¡OS VOY A DAR LA RECETA DE LA FÓRMULA 86! ¡ANOTAD!
¡¡Ah!!
¡¡Ji, ji, ji!!

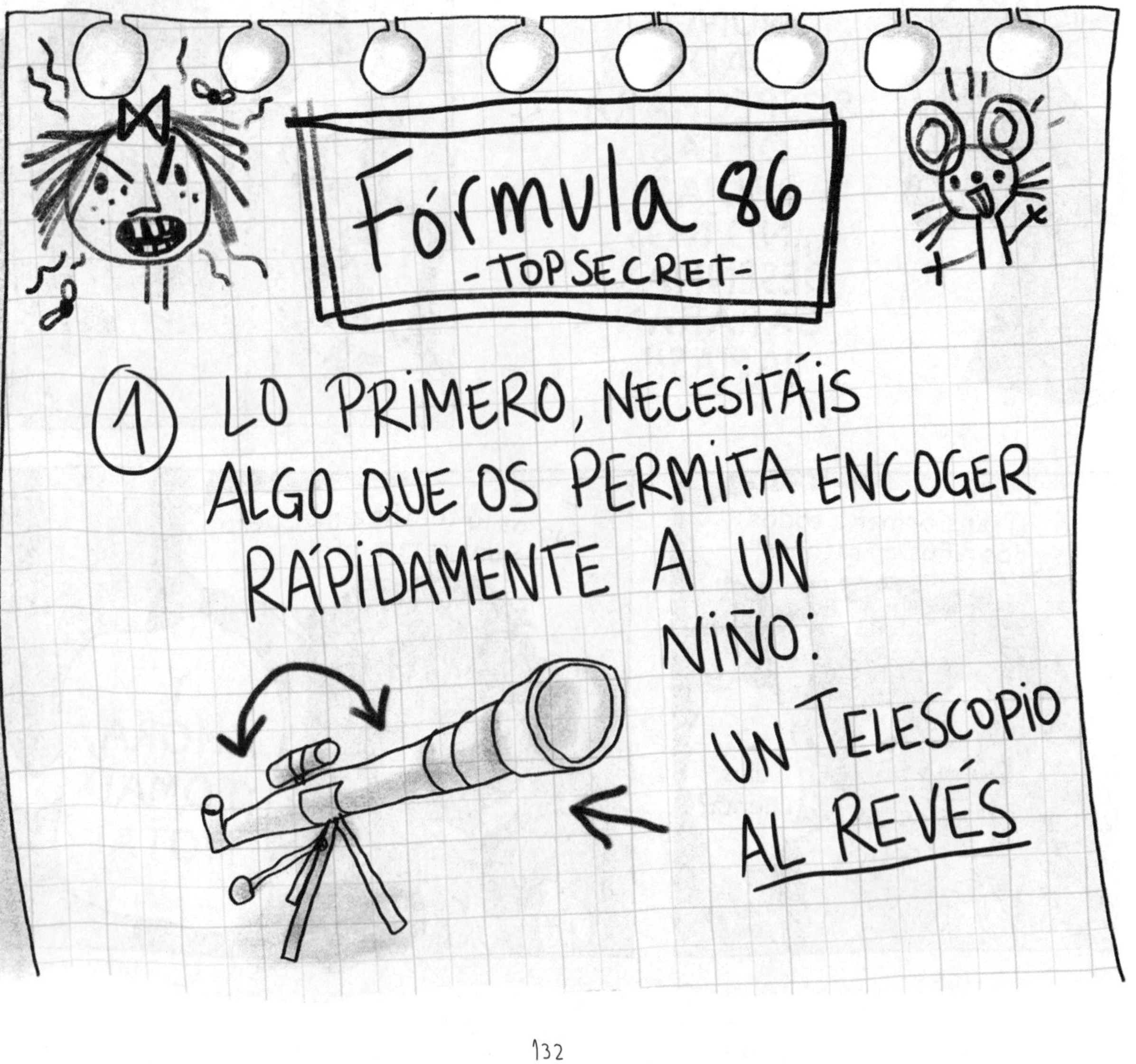
Fórmula 86
-TOP SECRET-
1 LO PRIMERO, NECESITÁIS ALGO QUE OS PERMITA ENCOGER RÁPIDAMENTE A UN NIÑO:
UN TELESCOPIO AL REVÉS

SUJETÁIS UN TELESCOPIO POR EL LADO MÁS ESTRECHO Y LO HERVÍS HASTA QUE SE ABLANDE.

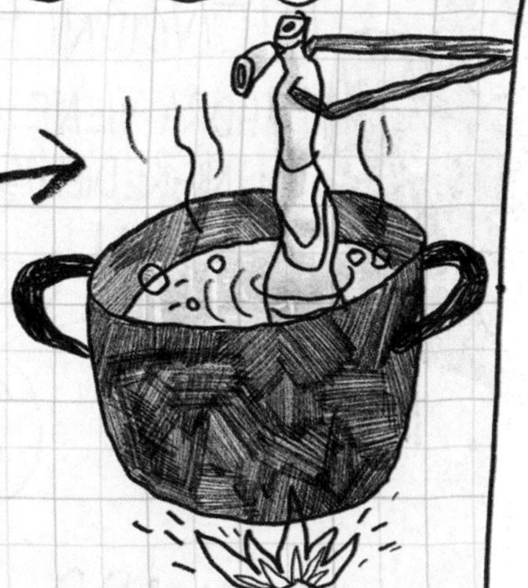

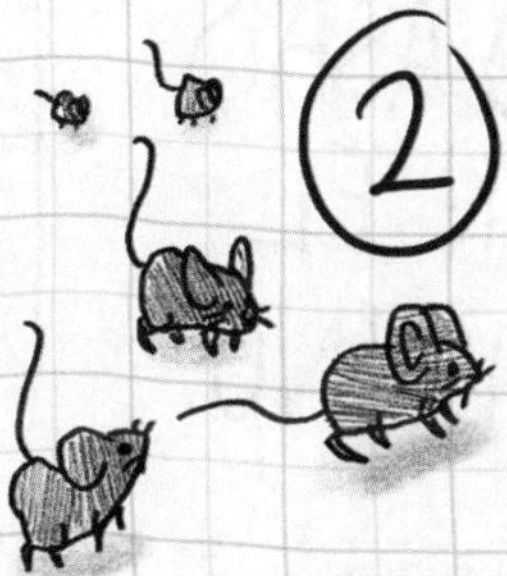

② DESPUÉS AÑADÍS 45 RATONES PARDOS.

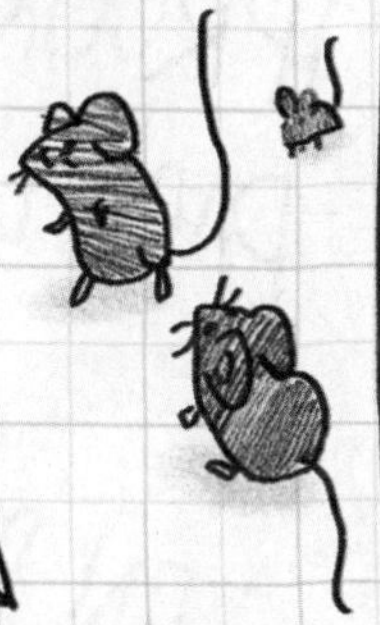

LOS RABOS

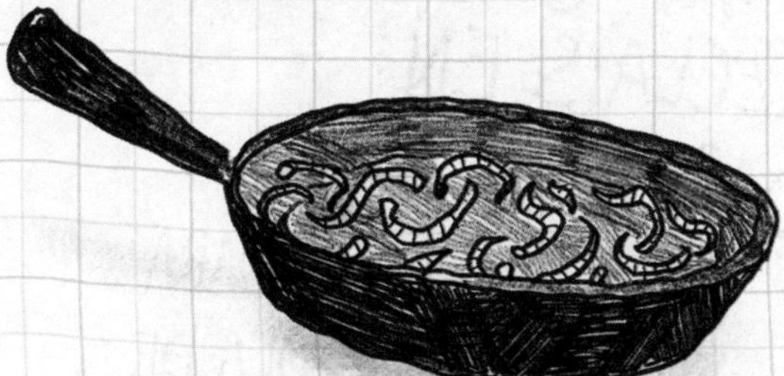

FREÍDLOS EN UNA SARTÉN HASTA QUE ESTÉN CRUJIENTES.

LOS CUERPOS

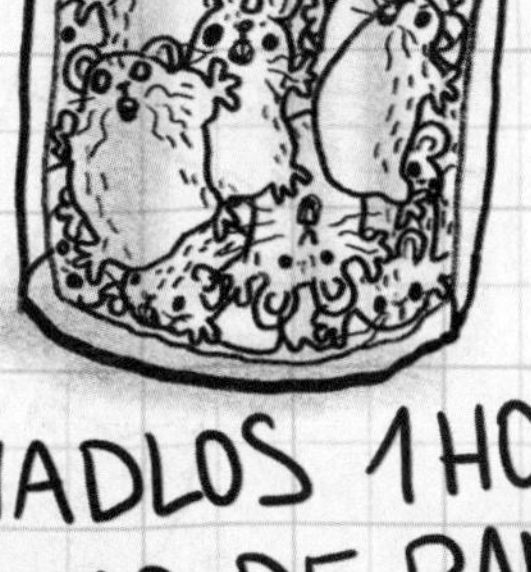

MARINADLOS 1 HORA EN ZUMO DE RANA.

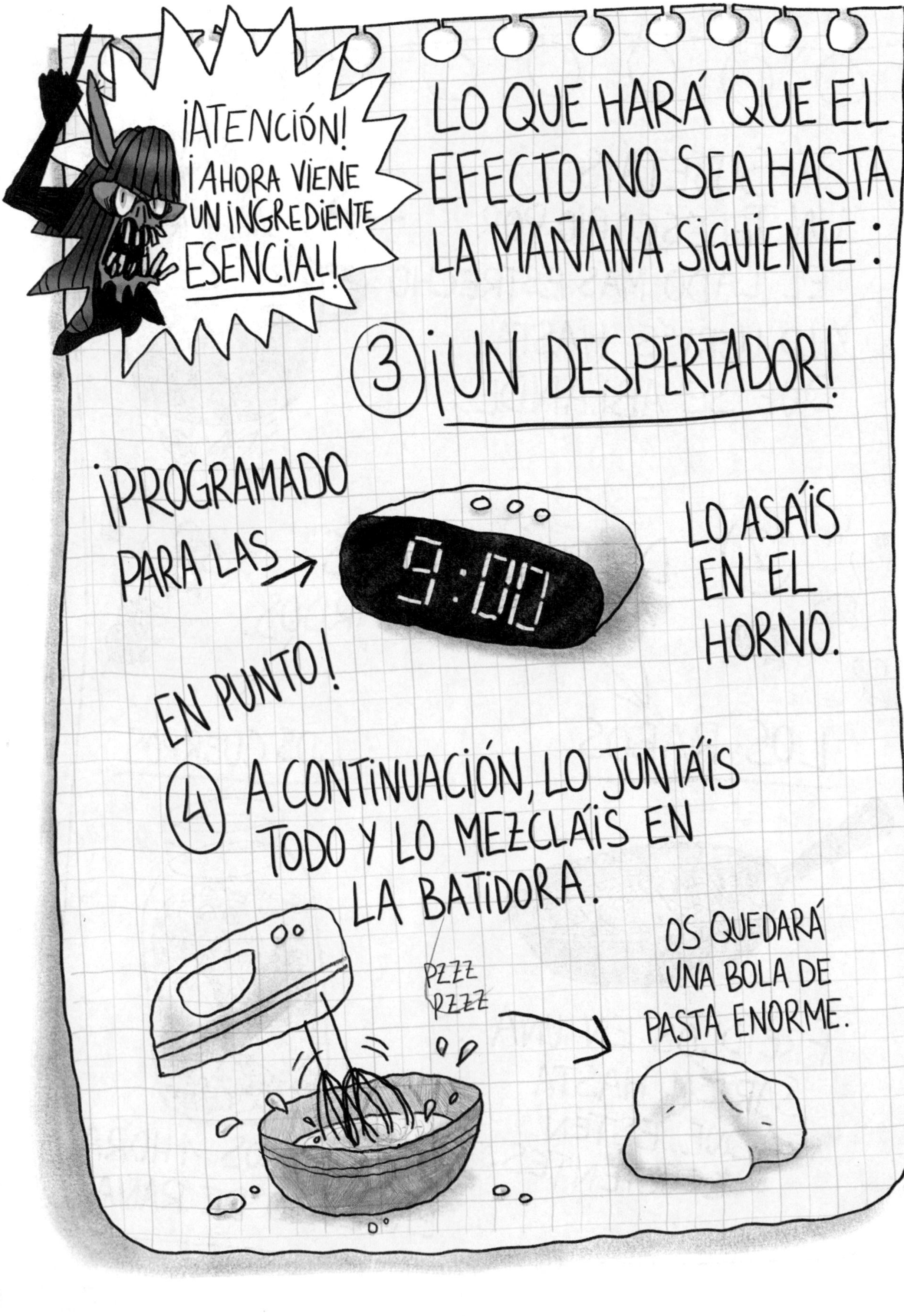
¡ATENCIÓN! ¡AHORA VIENE UN INGREDIENTE ESENCIAL!
LO QUE HARÁ QUE EL EFECTO NO SEA HASTA LA MAÑANA SIGUIENTE:
3 ¡UN DESPERTADOR!
¡PROGRAMADO PARA LAS
9:00
EN PUNTO!
LO ASÁIS EN EL HORNO.
4 A CONTINUACIÓN, LO JUNTÁIS TODO Y LO MEZCLÁIS EN LA BATIDORA.
PZZZ PZZZ
OS QUEDARÁ UNA BOLA DE PASTA ENORME.

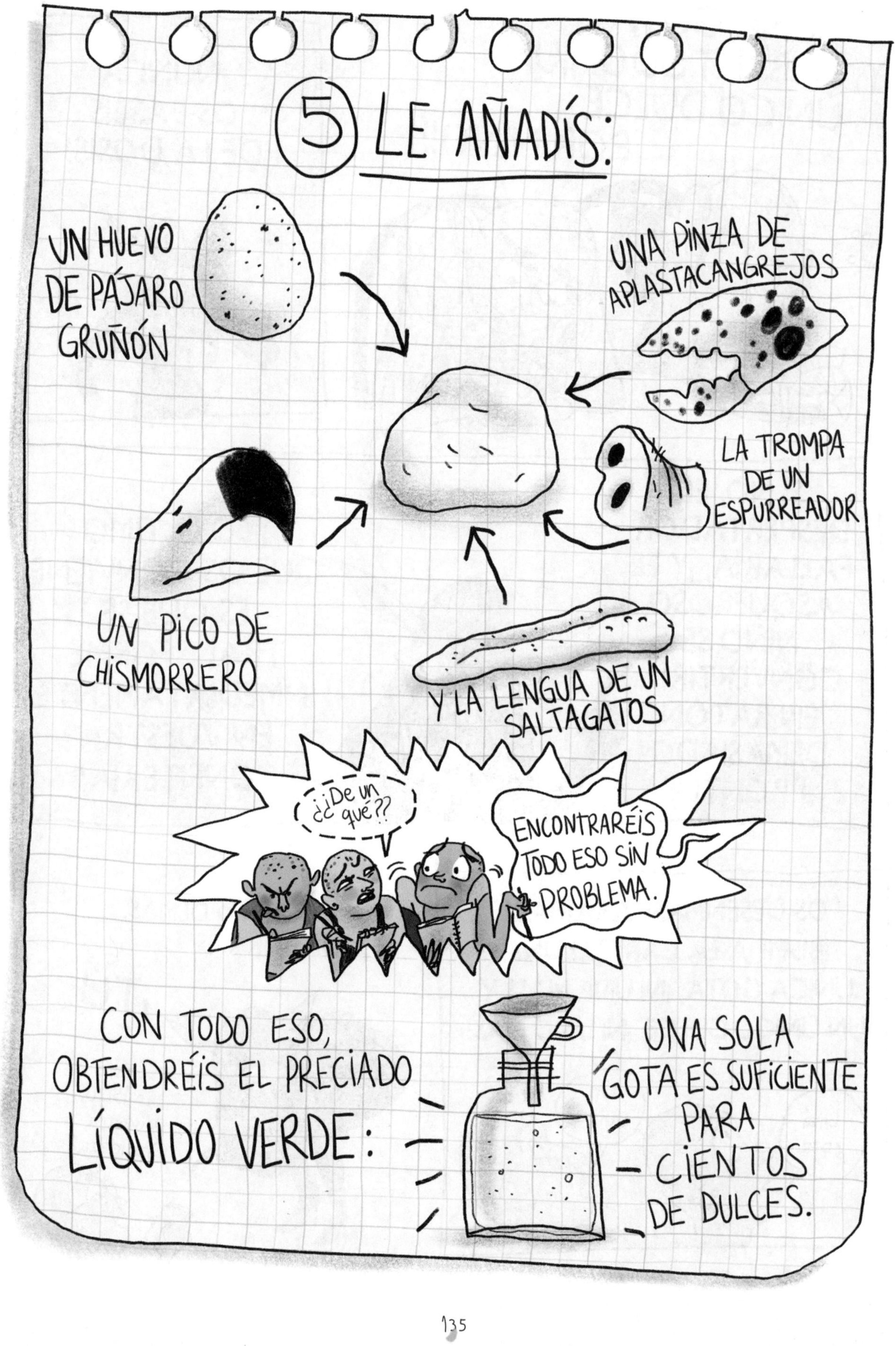
5 LE AÑADÍS:
UN HUEVO DE PÁJARO GRUÑÓN
UNA PINZA DE APLASTACANGREJOS
LA TROMPA DE UN ESPURREADOR
UN PICO DE CHISMORRERO
Y LA LENGUA DE UN SALTAGATOS
¿¿De un qué??
ENCONTRARÉIS TODO ESO SIN PROBLEMA.
CON TODO ESO, OBTENDRÉIS EL PRECIADO
LÍQUIDO VERDE:
UNA SOLA GOTA ES SUFICIENTE PARA CIENTOS DE DULCES.

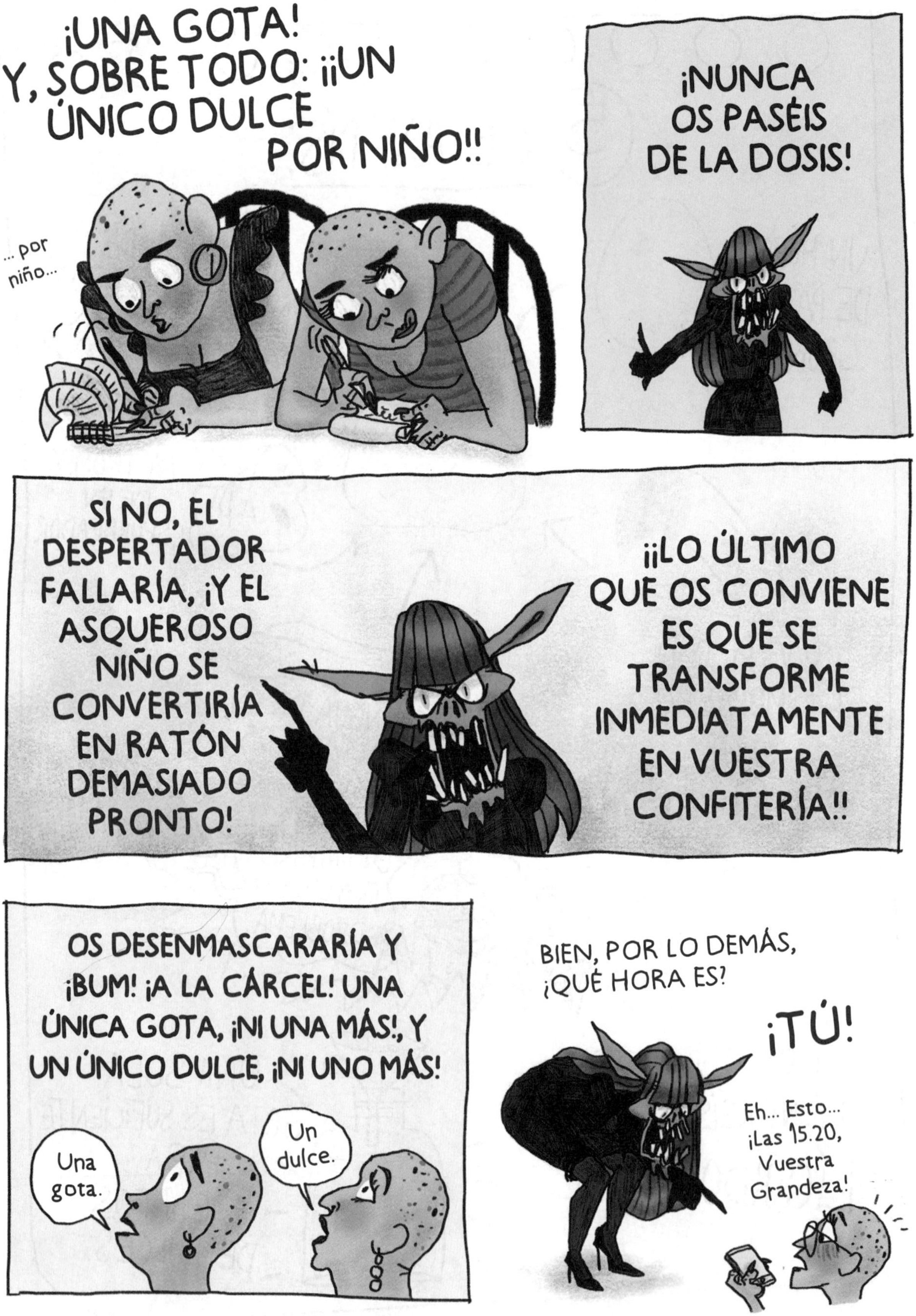
¡UNA GOTA!
Y, SOBRE TODO: ¡¡UN ÚNICO DULCE POR NIÑO!!
... por niño...
¡NUNCA OS PASÉIS DE LA DOSIS!
SI NO, EL DESPERTADOR FALLARÍA, ¡Y EL ASQUEROSO NIÑO SE CONVERTIRÍA EN RATÓN DEMASIADO PRONTO!
¡¡LO ÚLTIMO QUE OS CONVIENE ES QUE SE TRANSFORME INMEDIATAMENTE EN VUESTRA CONFITERÍA!!
OS DESENMASCARARÍA Y ¡BUM! ¡A LA CÁRCEL! UNA ÚNICA GOTA, ¡NI UNA MÁS!, Y UN ÚNICO DULCE, ¡NI UNO MÁS!
Una gota.
Un dulce.
BIEN, POR LO DEMÁS, ¿QUÉ HORA ES?
¡TÚ!
Eh... Esto... ¡Las 15.20, Vuestra Grandeza!

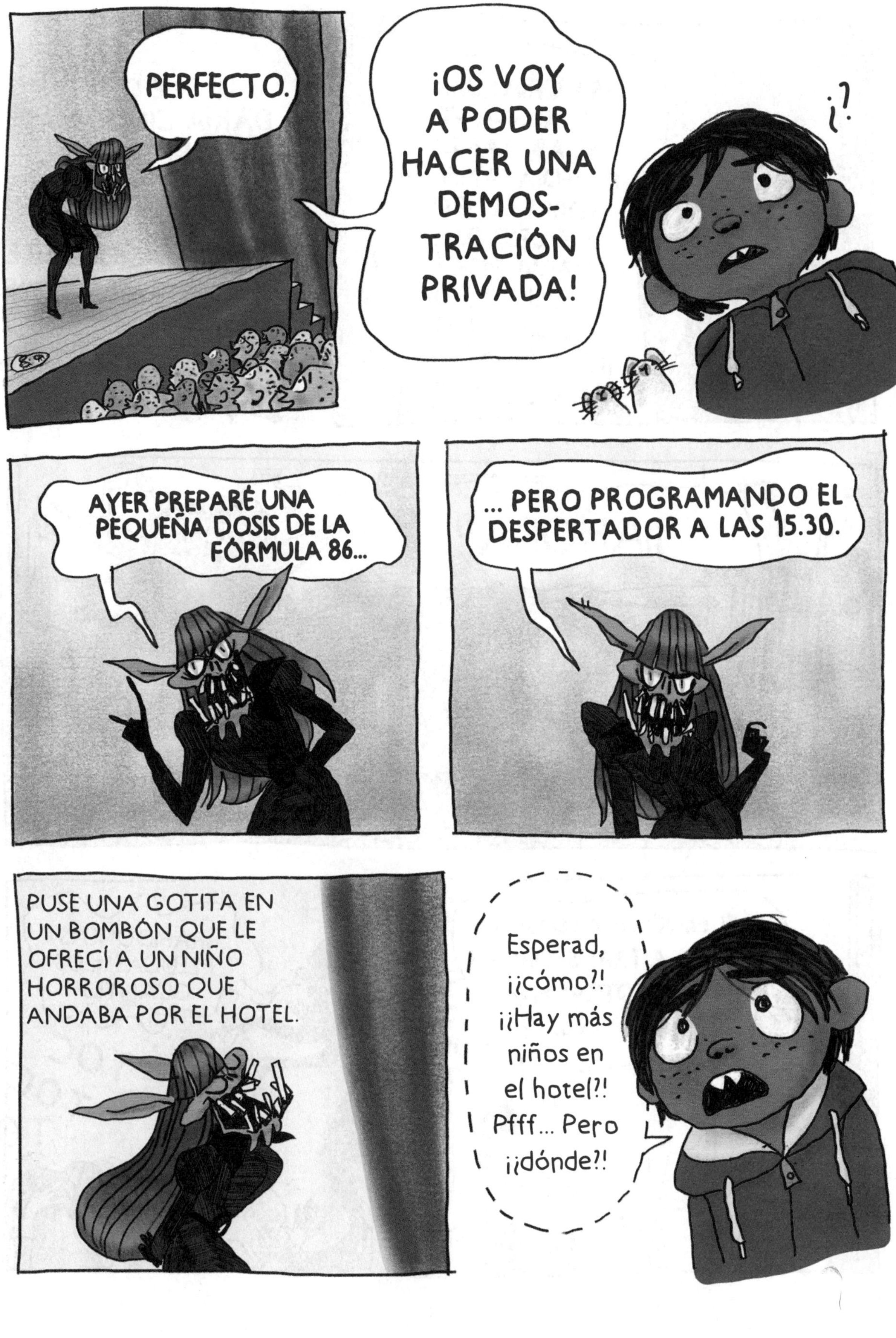
PERFECTO.
¡OS VOY A PODER HACER UNA DEMOS-TRACIÓN PRIVADA!
¿?
AYER PREPARÉ UNA PEQUEÑA DOSIS DE LA FÓRMULA 86...
... PERO PROGRAMANDO EL DESPERTADOR A LAS 15.30.
PUSE UNA GOTITA EN UN BOMBÓN QUE LE OFRECÍ A UN NIÑO HORROROSO QUE ANDABA POR EL HOTEL.
Esperad, ¡¿cómo?! ¡¿Hay más niños en el hotel?! Pfff... Pero ¡¿dónde?!

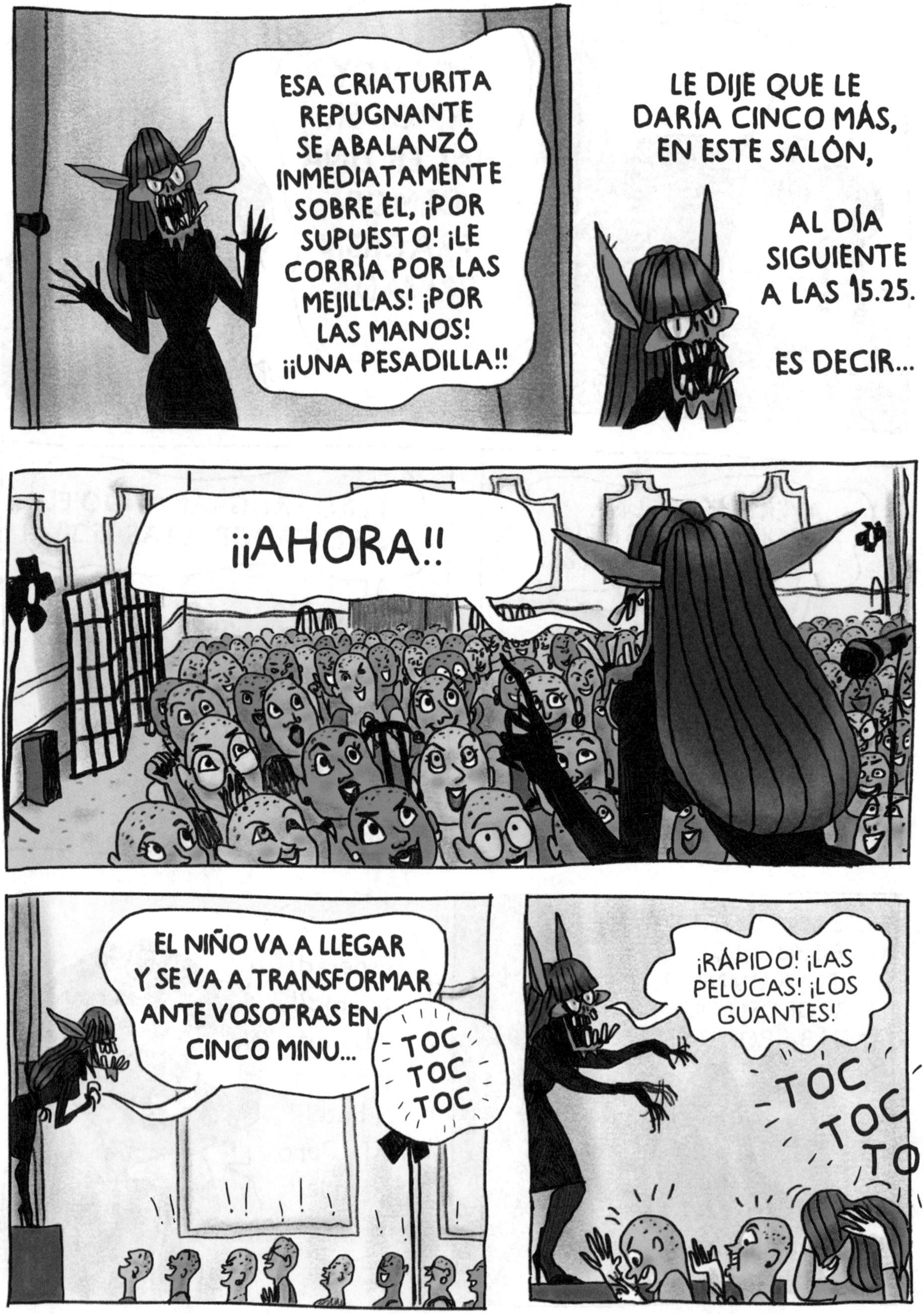
ESA CRIATURITA REPUGNANTE SE ABALANZÓ INMEDIATAMENTE SOBRE ÉL, ¡POR SUPUESTO! ¡LE CORRÍA POR LAS MEJILLAS! ¡POR LAS MANOS! ¡¡UNA PESADILLA!!
LE DIJE QUE LE DARÍA CINCO MÁS, EN ESTE SALÓN,
AL DÍA SIGUIENTE A LAS 15.25.
ES DECIR...
¡¡AHORA!!
EL NIÑO VA A LLEGAR Y SE VA A TRANSFORMAR ANTE VOSOTRAS EN CINCO MINU...
TOC TOC TOC
¡RÁPIDO! ¡LAS PELUCAS! ¡LOS GUANTES!
TOC TOC TOC

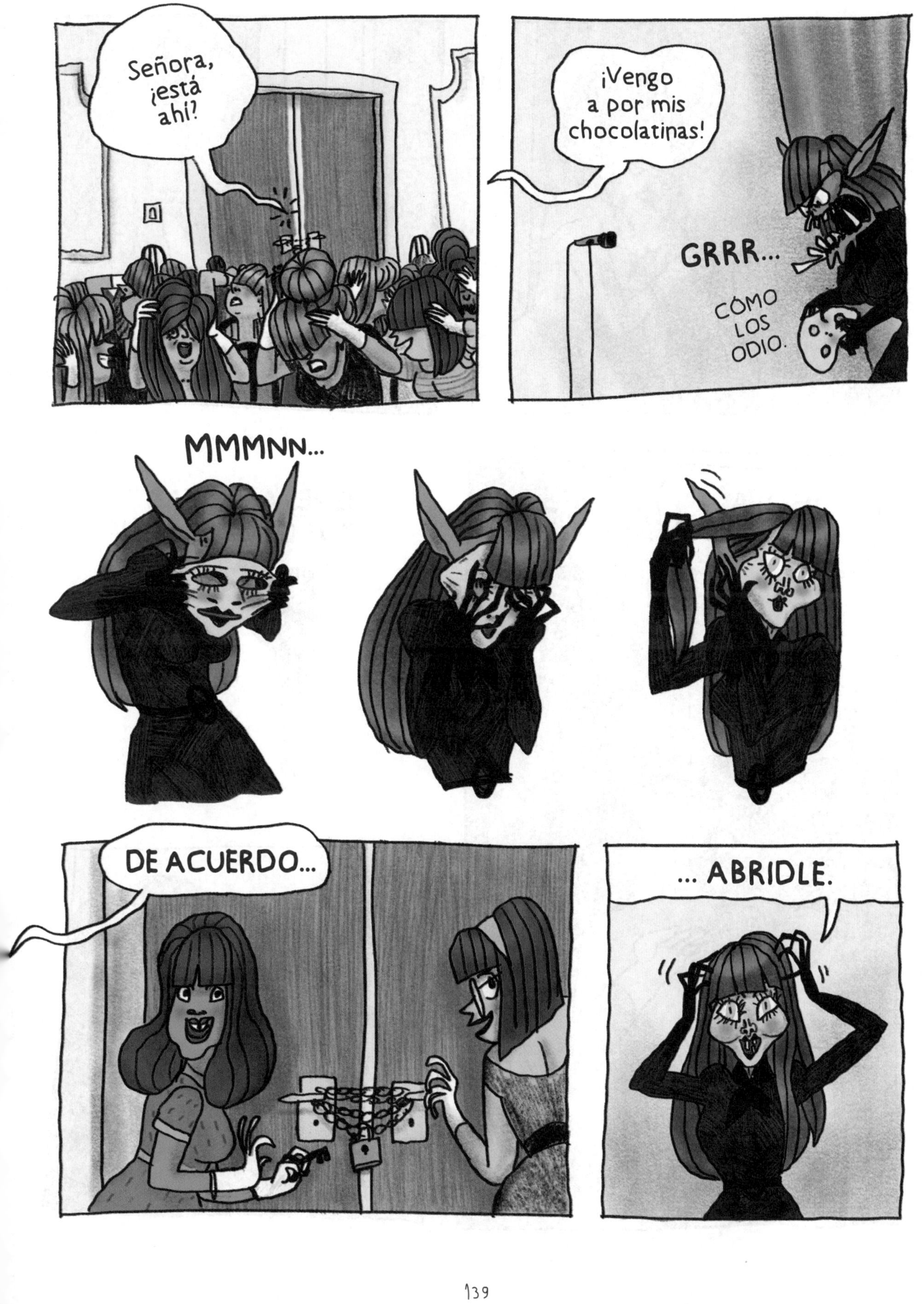
Señora, ¿está ahí?
¡Vengo a por mis chocolatinas!
GRRR...
CÓMO LOS ODIO.
MMMNN...
DE ACUERDO...
... ABRIDLE.

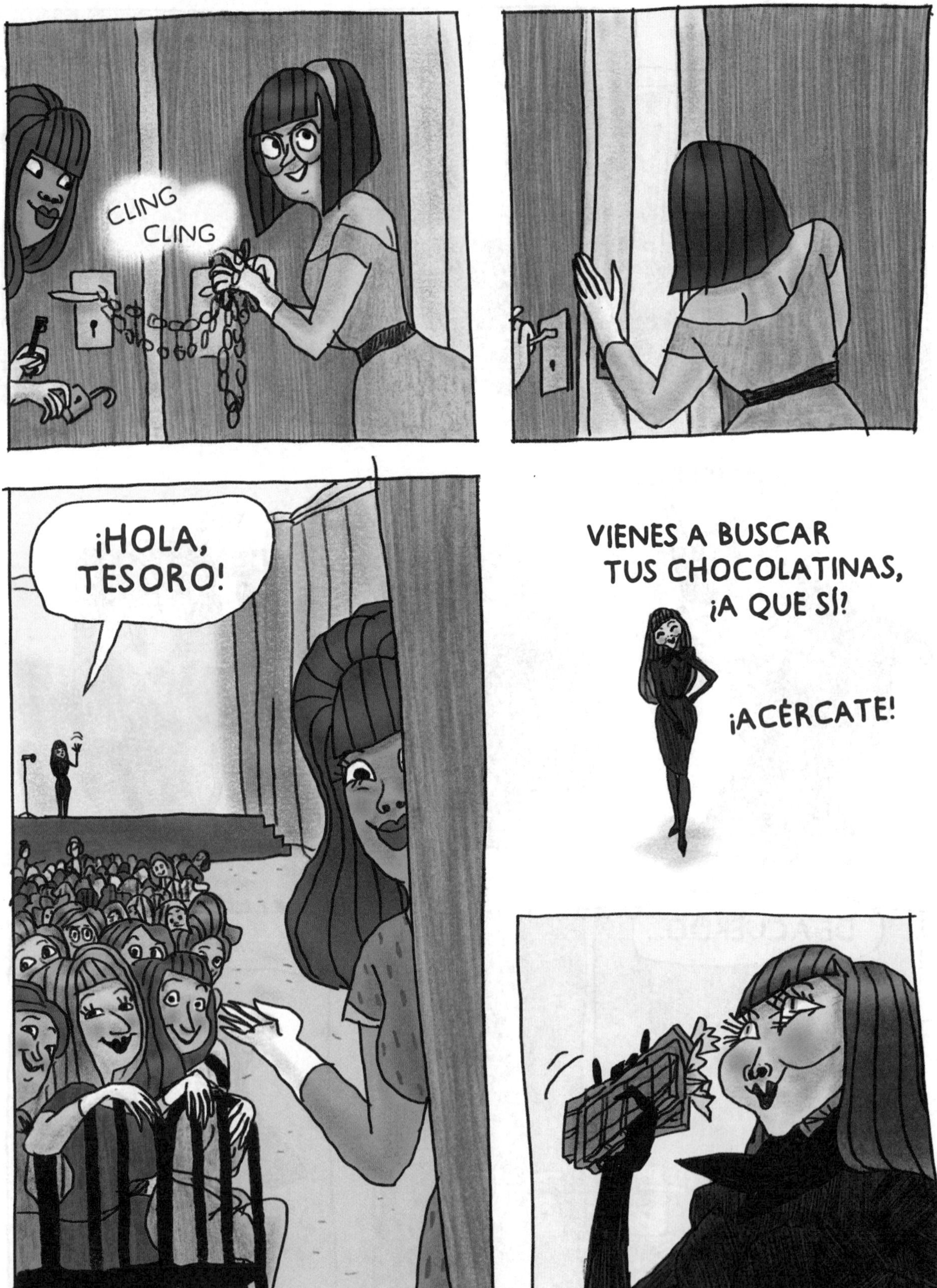
CLING
CLING
¡HOLA, TESORO!
VIENES A BUSCAR TUS CHOCOLATINAS, ¡A QUE SÍ?
¡ACÉRCATE!

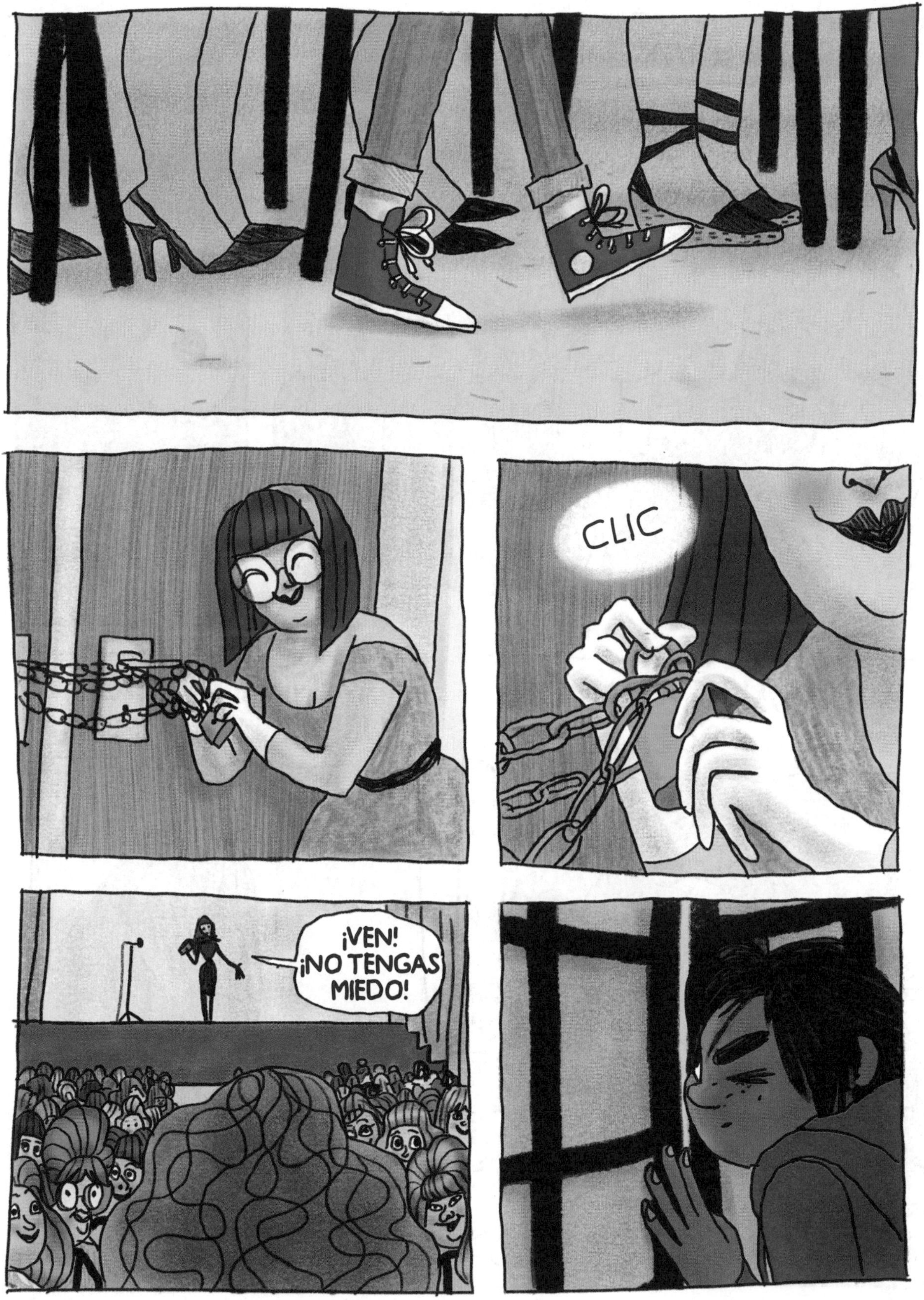
CLIC
¡VEN! ¡NO TENGAS MIEDO!

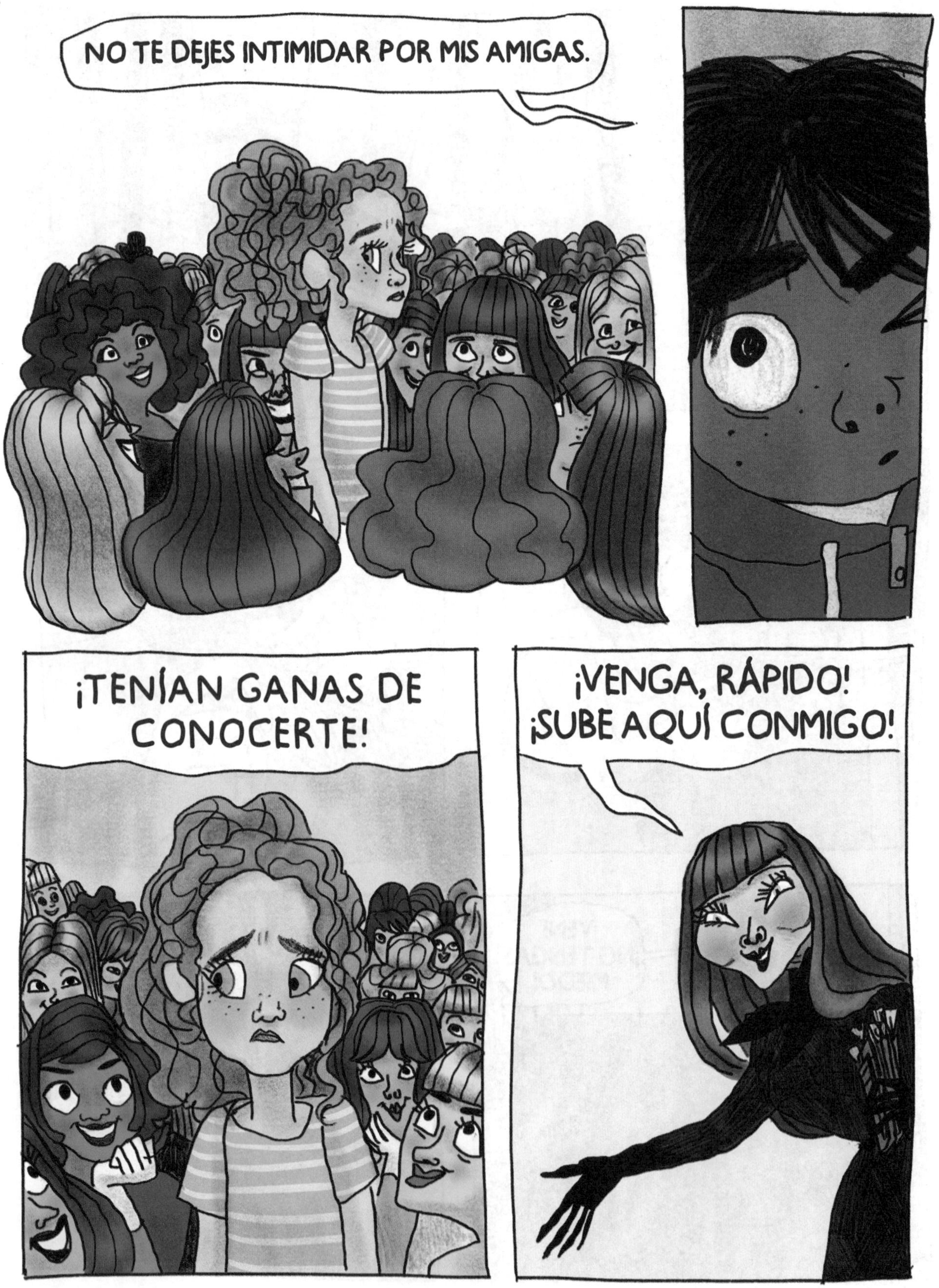
NO TE DEJES INTIMIDAR POR MIS AMIGAS.
¡TENÍAN GANAS DE CONOCERTE!
¡VENGA, RÁPIDO! ¡SUBE AQUÍ CONMIGO!

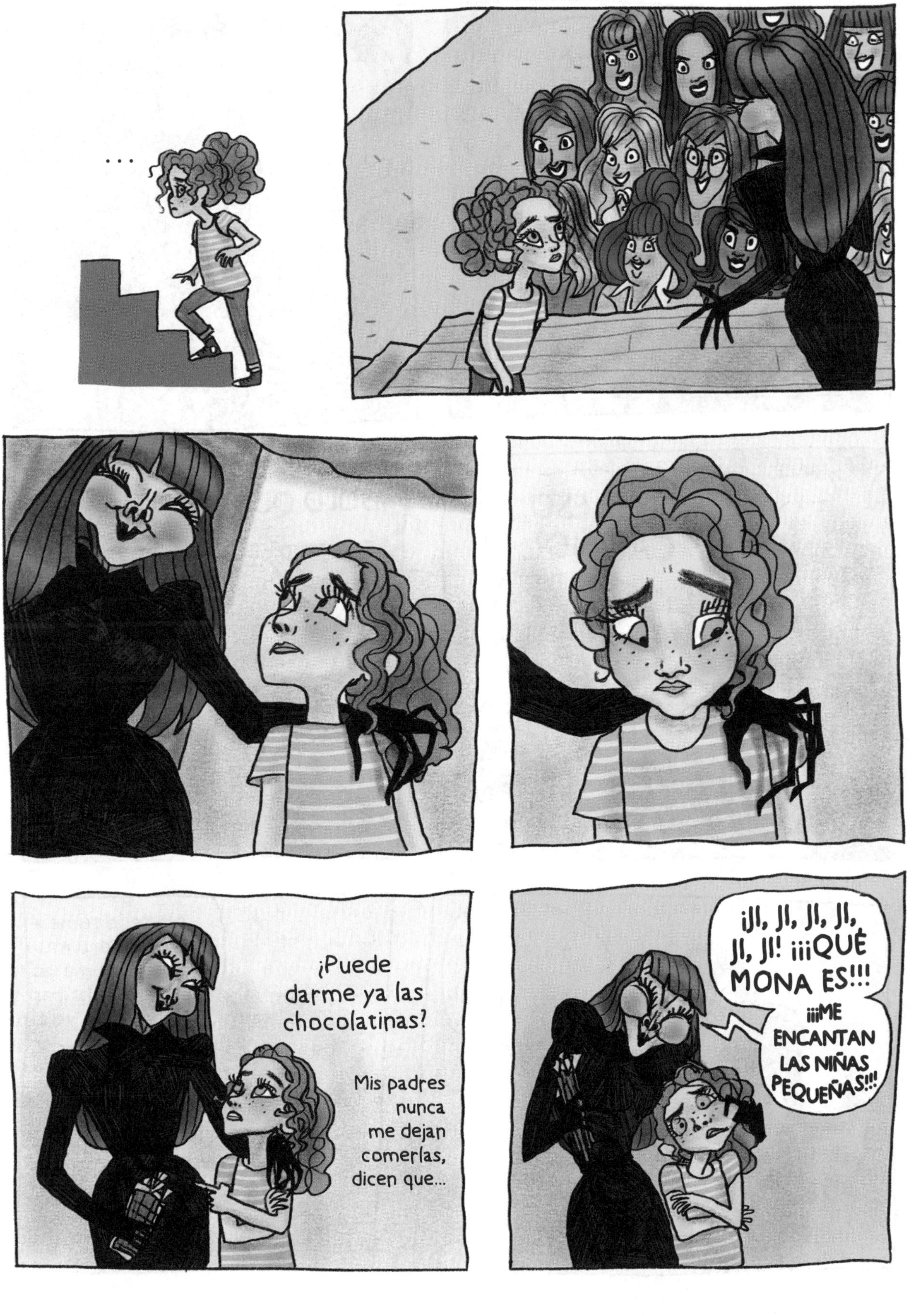
...
¿Puede darme ya las chocolatinas?
Mis padres nunca me dejan comerlas, dicen que...
¡JI, JI, JI, JI, JI, JI! ¡¡¡QUÉ MONA ES!!!
¡¡¡ME ENCANTAN LAS NIÑAS PEQUEÑAS!!!

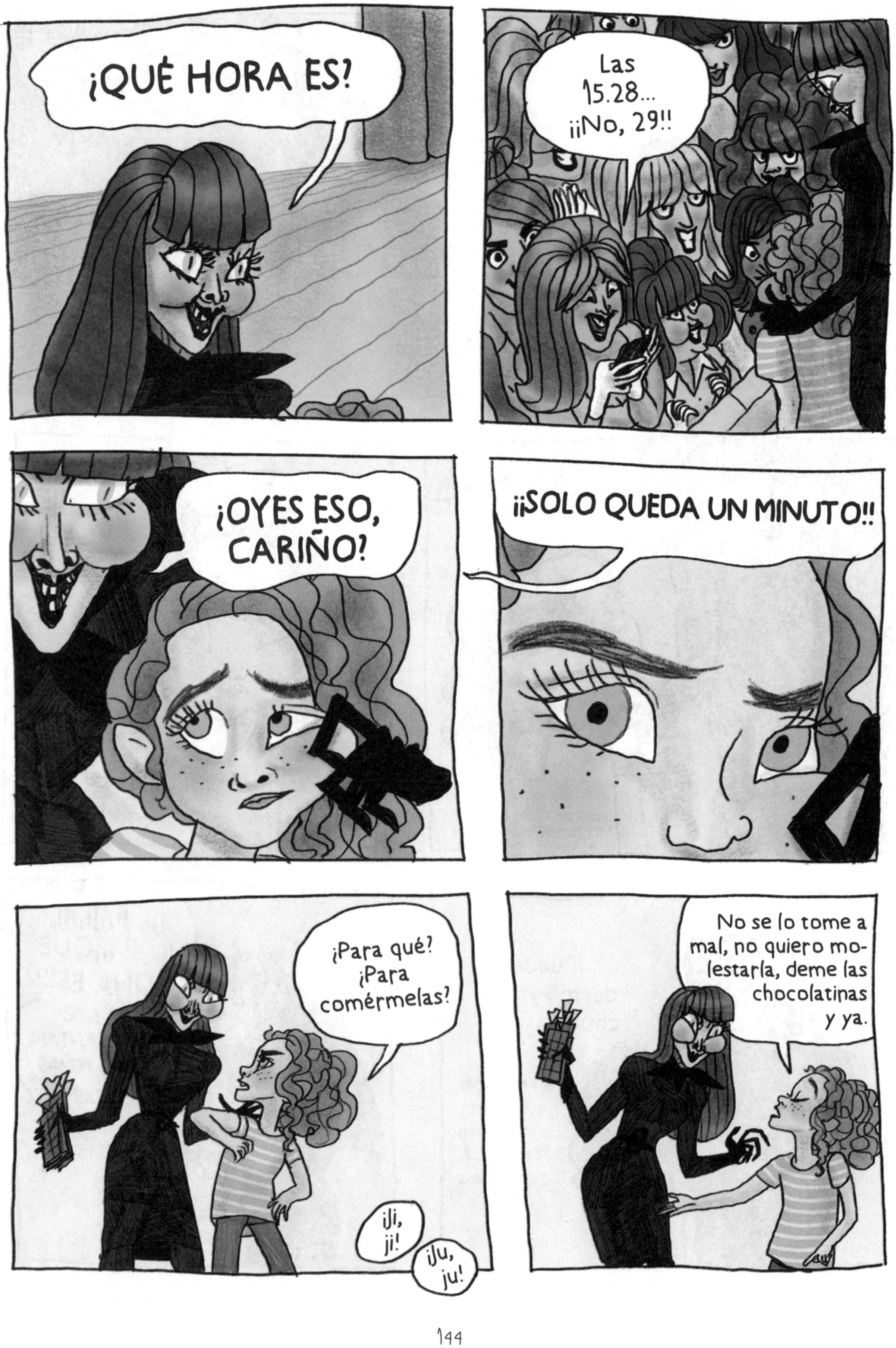
¿QUÉ HORA ES?
Las 15.28... ¡¡No, 29!!
¿OYES ESO, CARIÑO?
¡¡SOLO QUEDA UN MINUTO!!
¿Para qué? ¿Para comérmelas?
¡Ji, ji!
¡Ju, ju!
No se lo tome a mal, no quiero molestarla, deme las chocolatinas y ya.

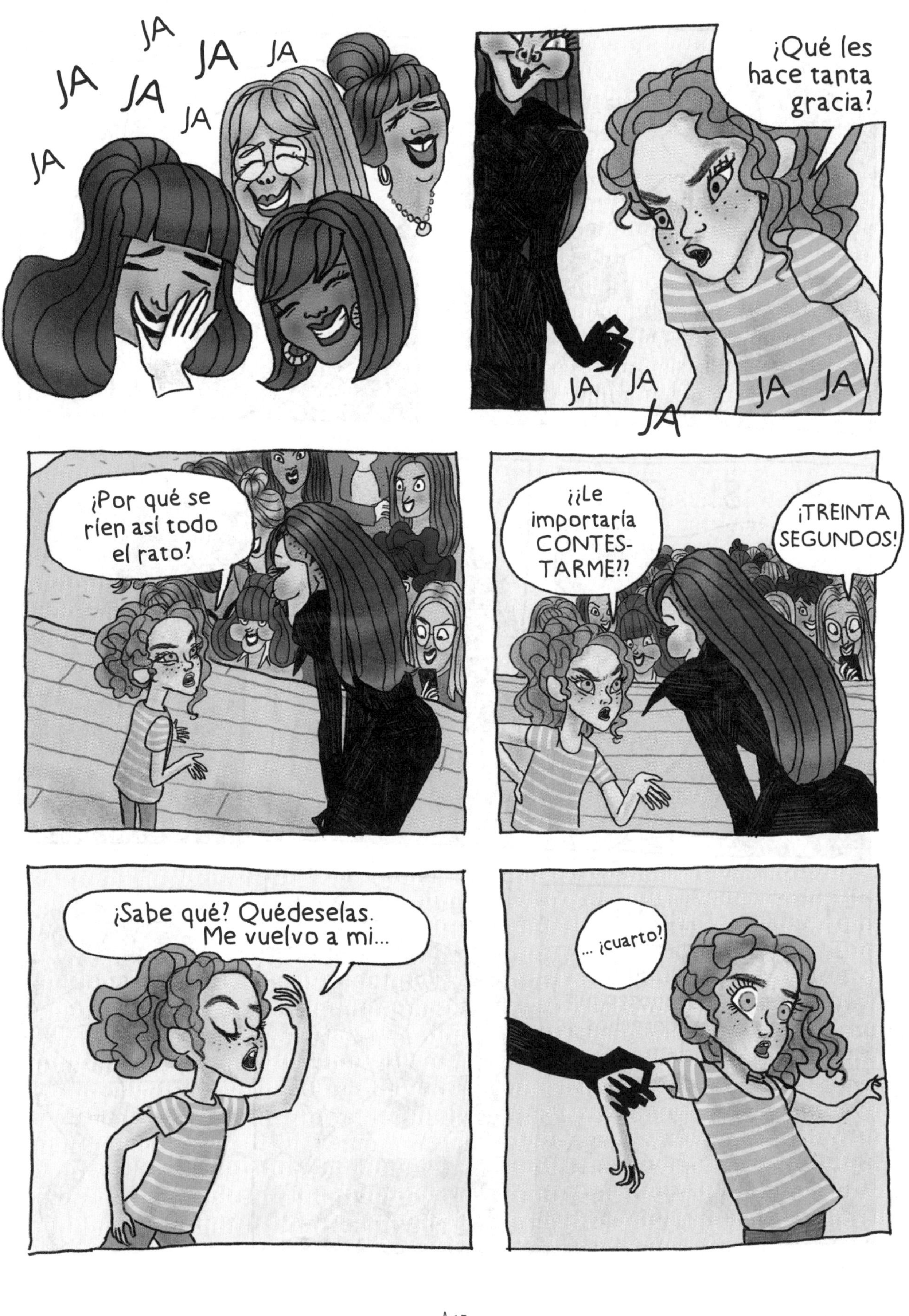
JA JA JA JA JA JA JA
¿Qué les hace tanta gracia?
JA JA JA JA JA
¿Por qué se ríen así todo el rato?
¡¡Le importaría CONTESTARME??
¡TREINTA SEGUNDOS!
¿Sabe qué? Quédeselas. Me vuelvo a mi...
... ¿cuarto?

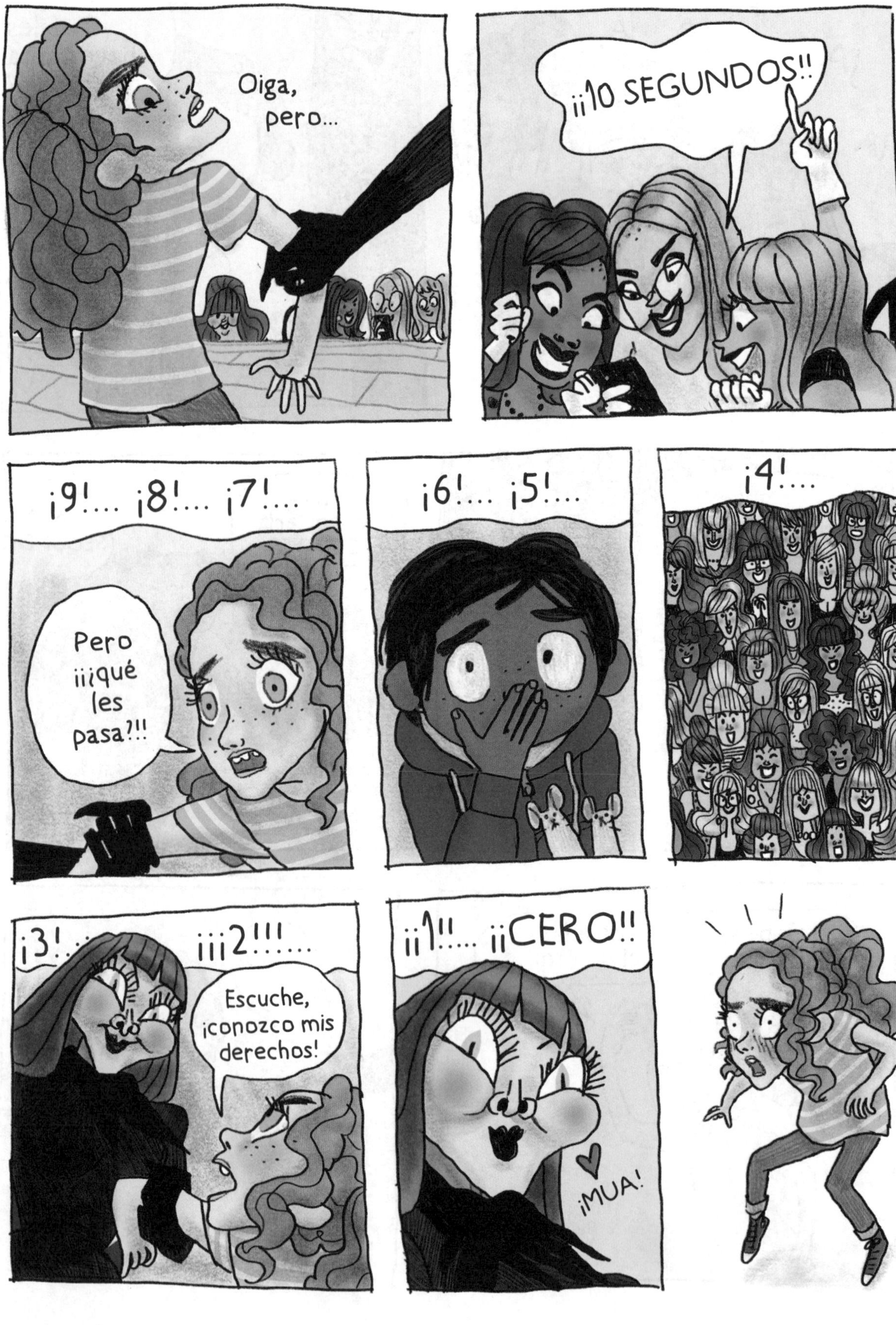
Oiga, pero...
¡¡10 SEGUNDOS!!
¡9!... ¡8!... ¡7!...
Pero ¡¡¿qué les pasa?!!
¡6!... ¡5!...
¡4!...
¡3!...
¡¡¡2!!!...
Escuche, ¡conozco mis derechos!
¡¡1!!... ¡¡CERO!!
¡MUA!

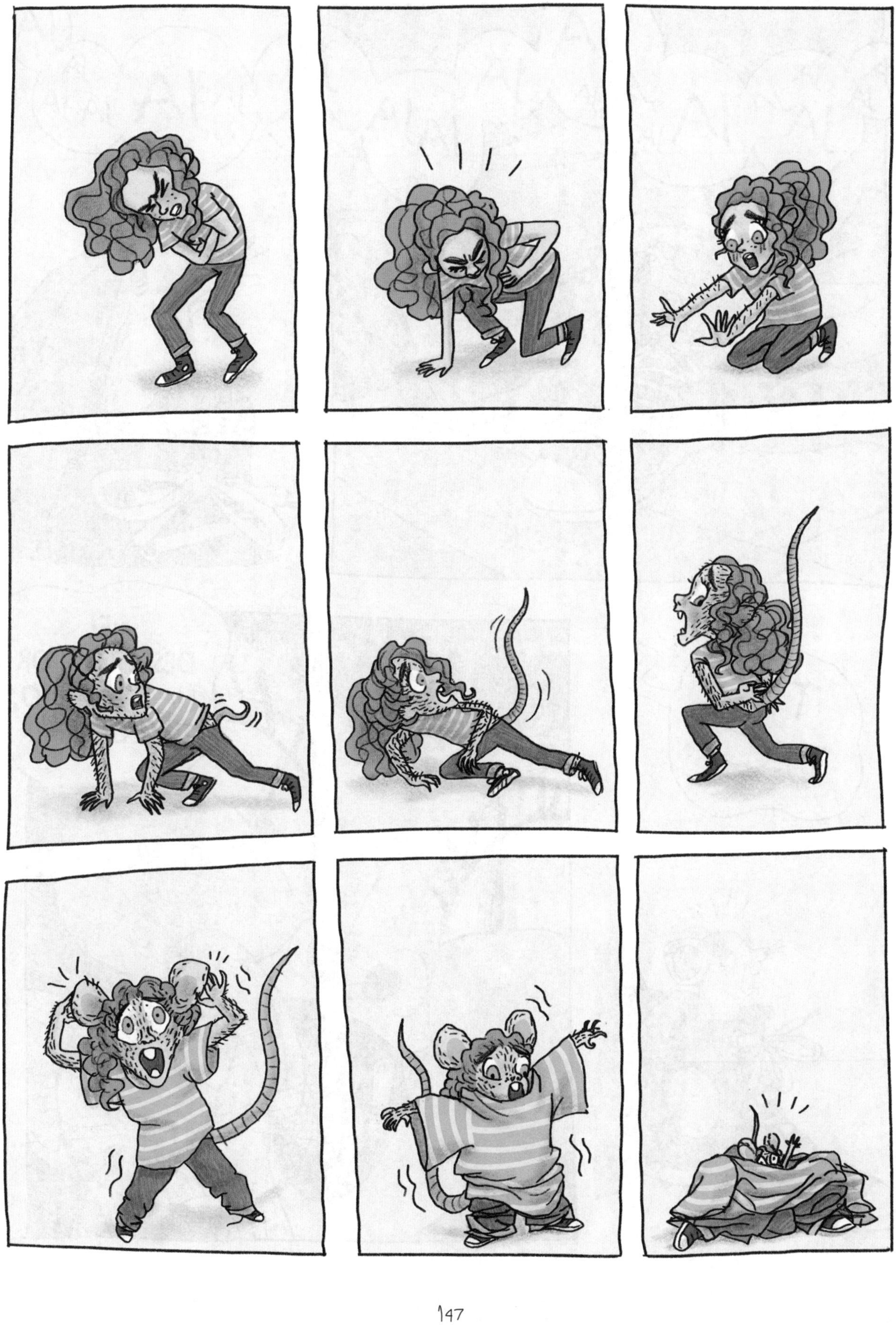

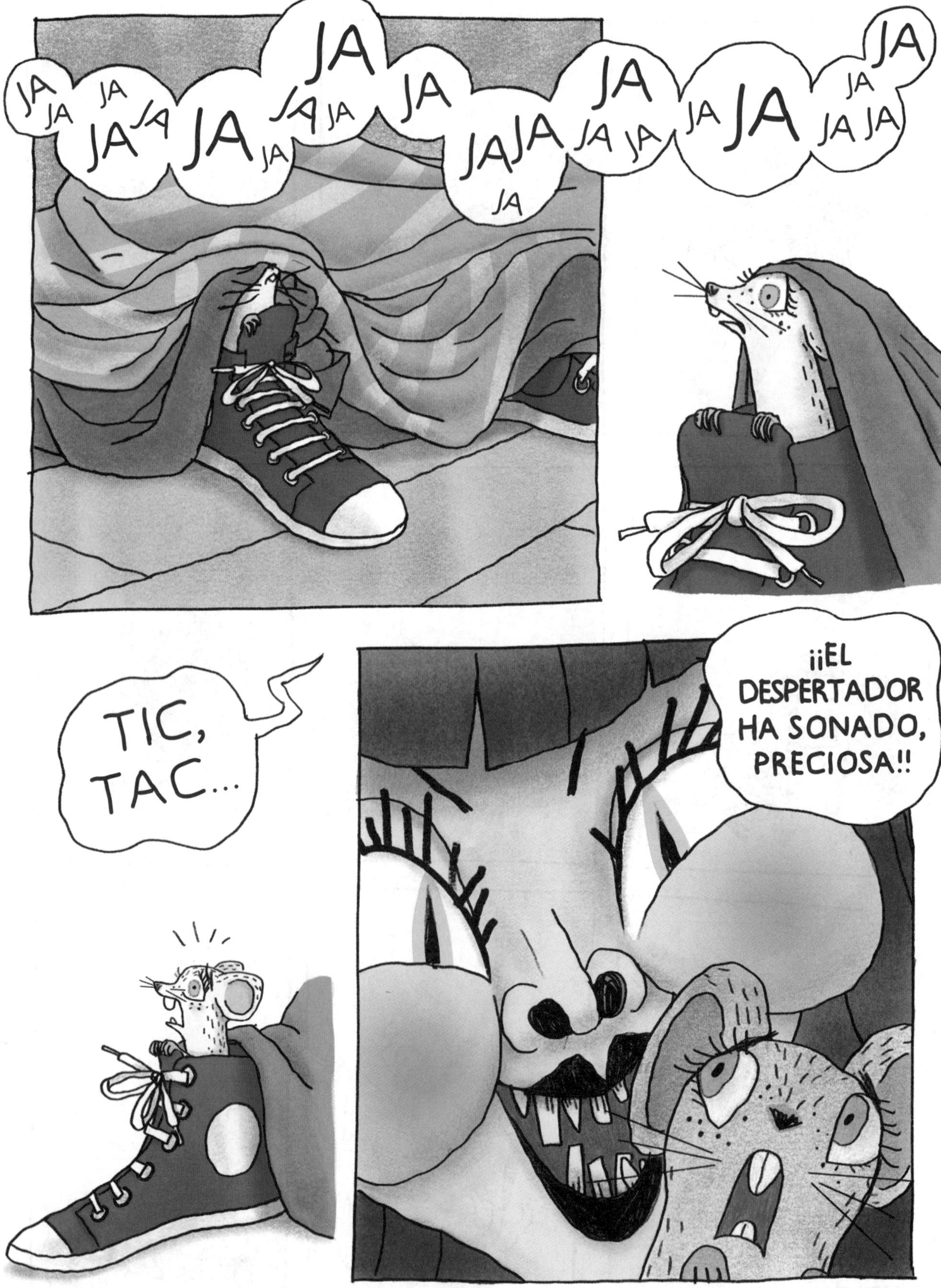

JA JA
JA JA JA
JA JA JA
JA JA JA
JA
JA JA JA
JA JA JA JA
JA JA
JA JA JA JA
TIC, TAC...
¡¡EL DESPERTADOR HA SONADO, PRECIOSA!!

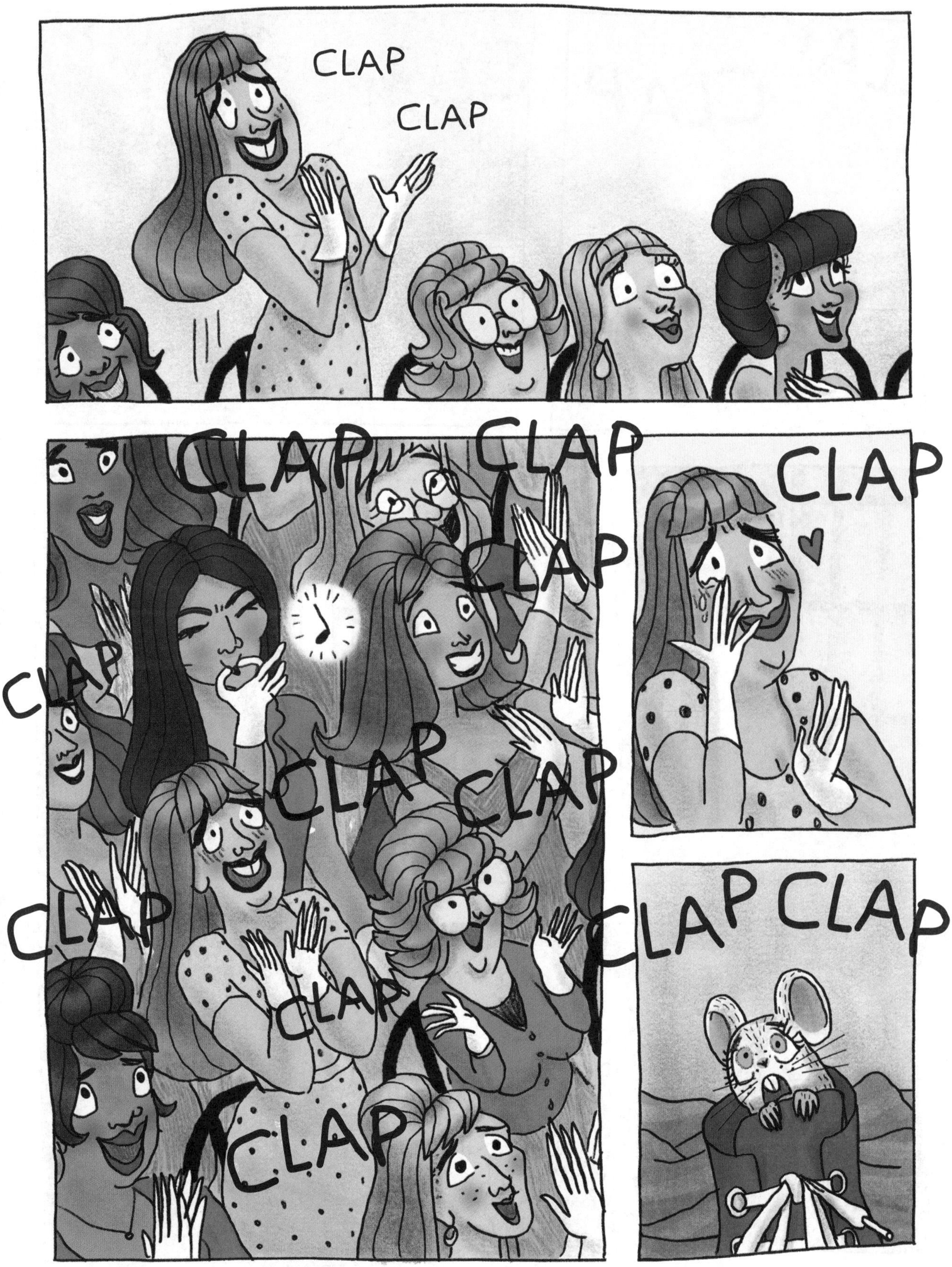
CLAP
CLAP
CLAP
CLAP
CLAP
CLAP
CLAP
CLAP
CLAP
CLAP
CLAP
CLAP
CLAP
CLAP

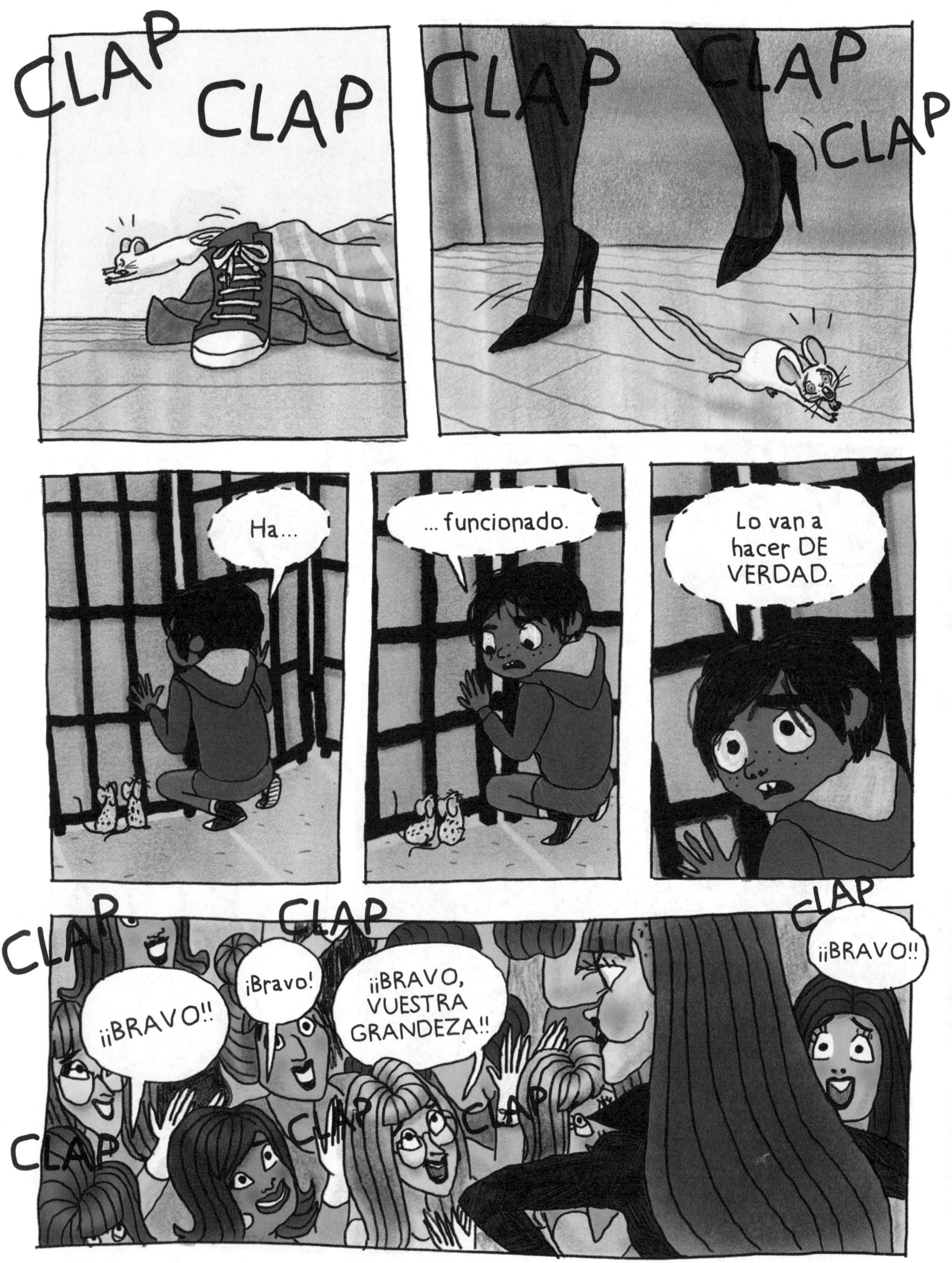
CLAP
CLAP
CLAP
CLAP
CLAP
Ha…
… funcionado.
Lo van a hacer DE VERDAD.
CLAP
CLAP
CLAP
¡¡BRAVO!!
¡Bravo!
¡¡BRAVO, VUESTRA GRANDEZA!!
¡¡BRAVO!!
CLAP
CLAP
CLAP

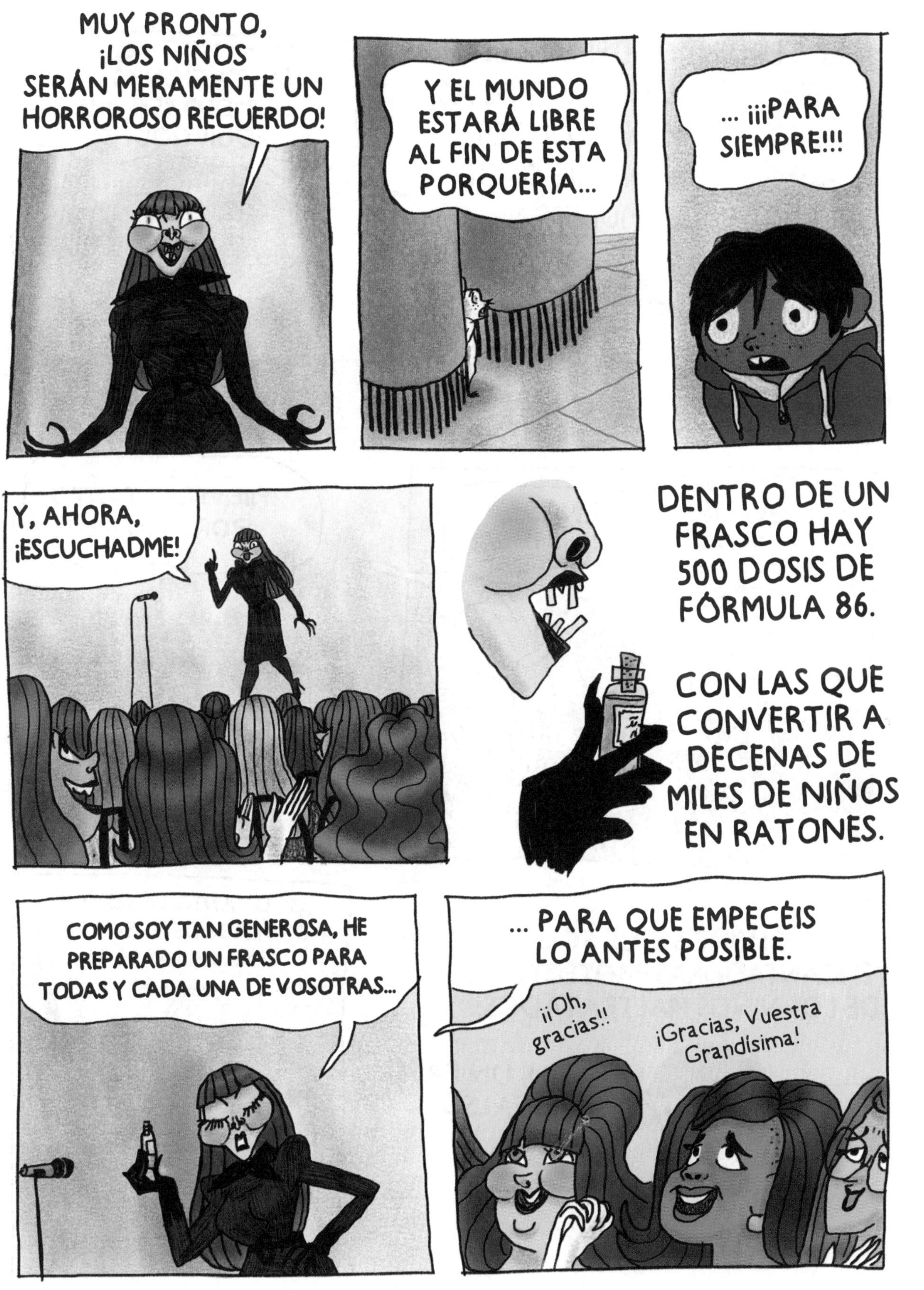
MUY PRONTO, ¡LOS NIÑOS SERÁN MERAMENTE UN HORROROSO RECUERDO!
Y EL MUNDO ESTARÁ LIBRE AL FIN DE ESTA PORQUERÍA...
... ¡¡¡PARA SIEMPRE!!!
Y, AHORA, ¡ESCUCHADME!
DENTRO DE UN FRASCO HAY 500 DOSIS DE FÓRMULA 86.
CON LAS QUE CONVERTIR A DECENAS DE MILES DE NIÑOS EN RATONES.
COMO SOY TAN GENEROSA, HE PREPARADO UN FRASCO PARA TODAS Y CADA UNA DE VOSOTRAS...
... PARA QUE EMPECÉIS LO ANTES POSIBLE.
¡¡Oh, gracias!!
¡Gracias, Vuestra Grandísima!

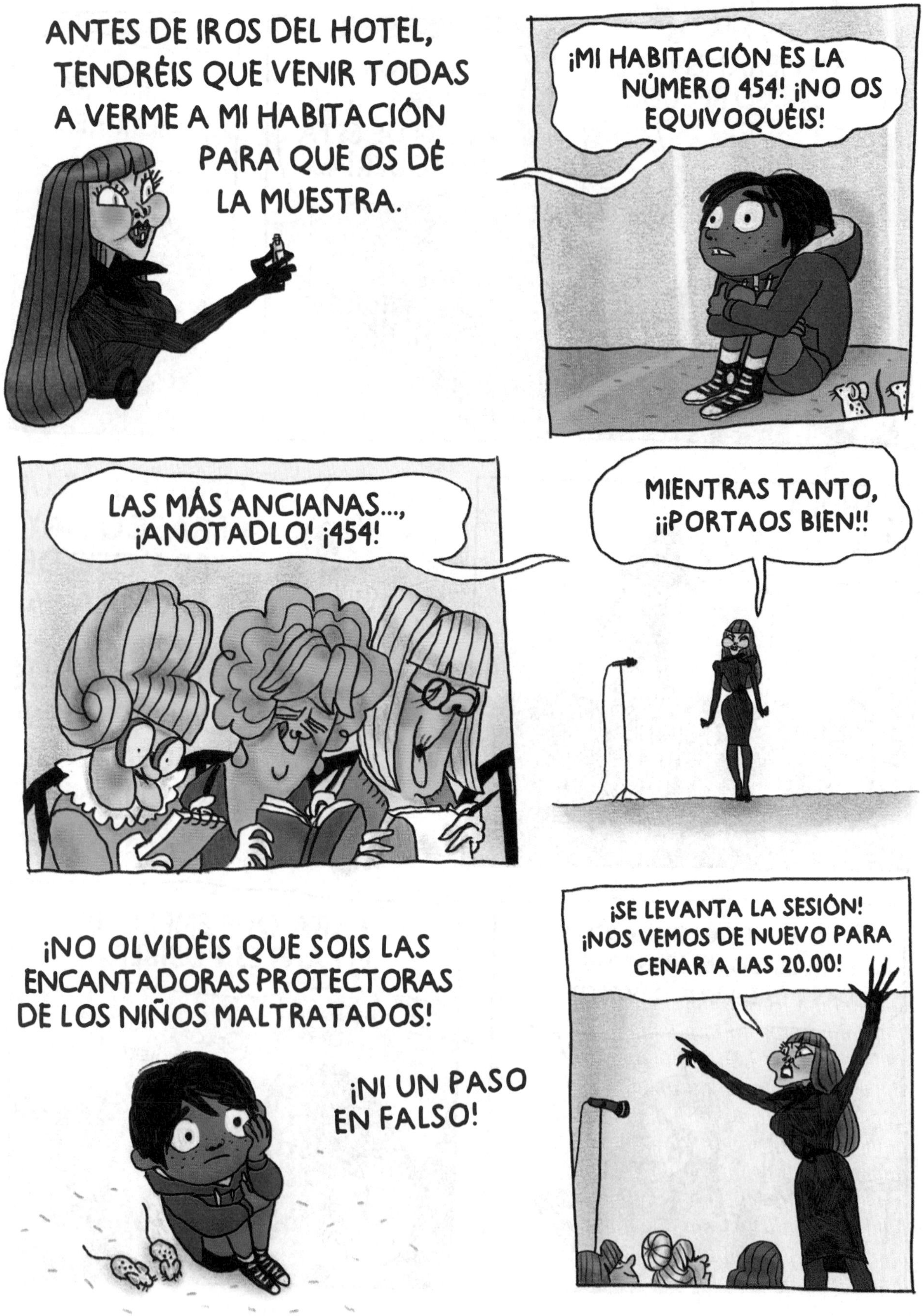
ANTES DE IROS DEL HOTEL, TENDRÉIS QUE VENIR TODAS A VERME A MI HABITACIÓN PARA QUE OS DÉ LA MUESTRA.
¡MI HABITACIÓN ES LA NÚMERO 454! ¡NO OS EQUIVOQUÉIS!
LAS MÁS ANCIANAS..., ¡ANOTADLO! ¡454!
MIENTRAS TANTO, ¡¡PORTAOS BIEN!!
¡NO OLVIDÉIS QUE SOIS LAS ENCANTADORAS PROTECTORAS DE LOS NIÑOS MALTRATADOS!
¡NI UN PASO EN FALSO!
¡SE LEVANTA LA SESIÓN! ¡NOS VEMOS DE NUEVO PARA CENAR A LAS 20.00!

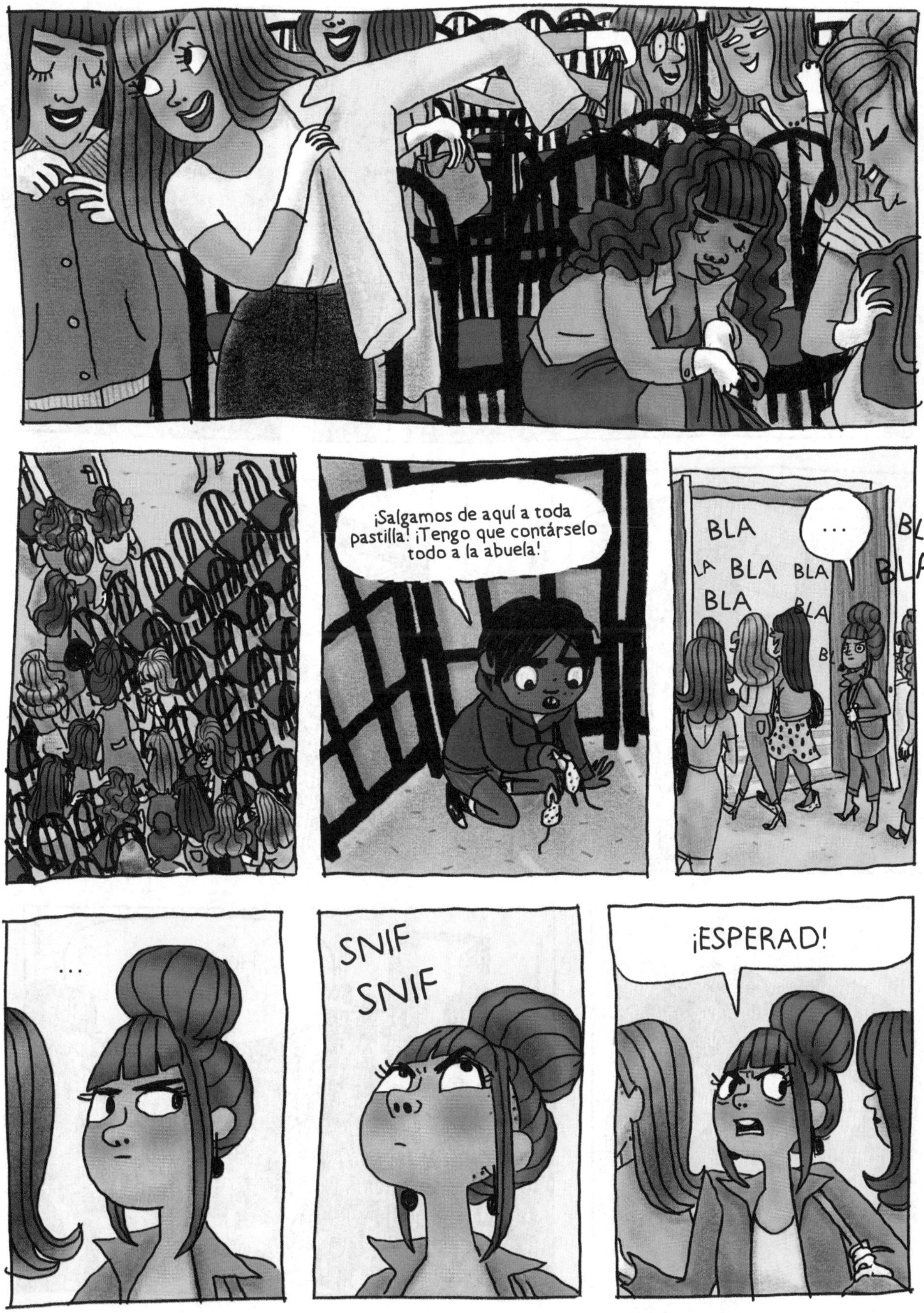
¡Salgamos de aquí a toda pastilla! ¡Tengo que contárselo todo a la abuela!
BLA
...
BLA
LA BLA BLA
BLA
BLA
...
SNIF SNIF
¡ESPERAD!

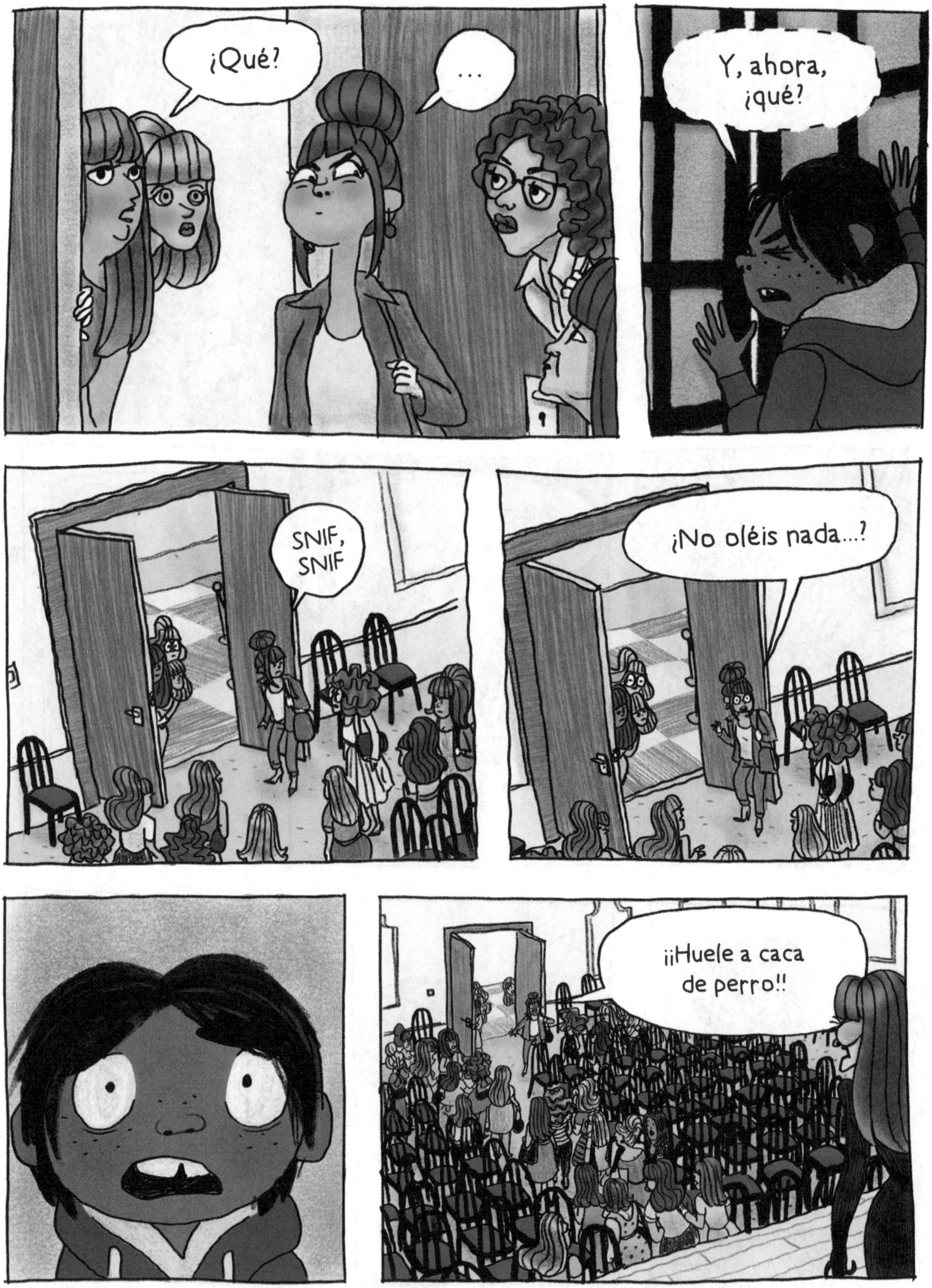
¿Qué?
...
Y, ahora, ¿qué?
SNIF, SNIF
¿No oléis nada...?
¡¡Huele a caca de perro!!

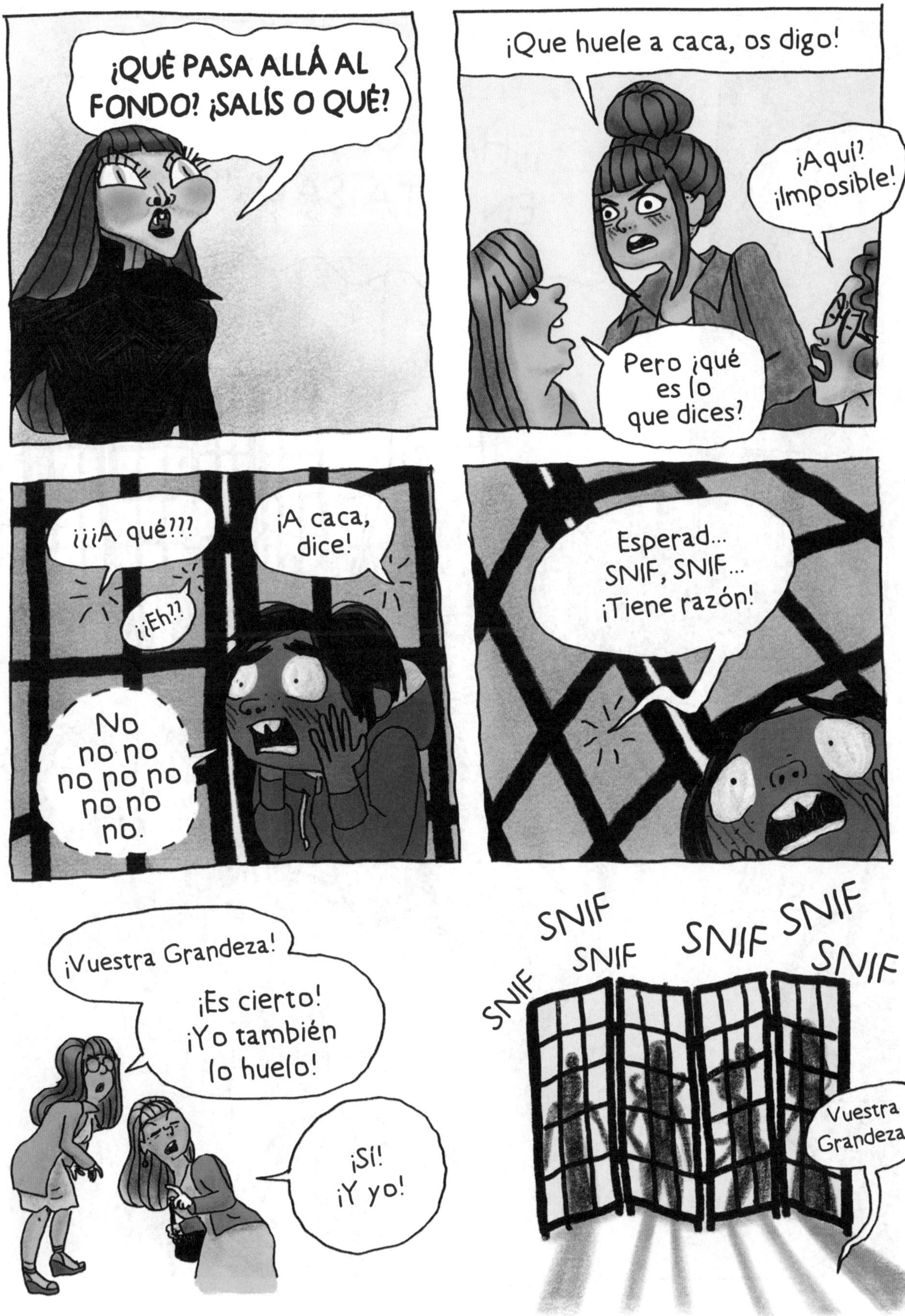
¡QUÉ PASA ALLÁ AL FONDO? ¡SALÍS O QUÉ?
¡Que huele a caca, os digo!
¡Aquí? ¡Imposible!
Pero ¿qué es lo que dices?
¡¡¡A qué???
¡A caca, dice!
¡¡Eh??
No no no no no no no no no.
Esperad... SNIF, SNIF... ¡Tiene razón!
¡Vuestra Grandeza!
¡Es cierto! ¡Yo también lo huelo!
¡Sí! ¡Y yo!
SNIF
SNIF
SNIF
SNIF
SNIF
SNIF
Vuestra Grandeza...

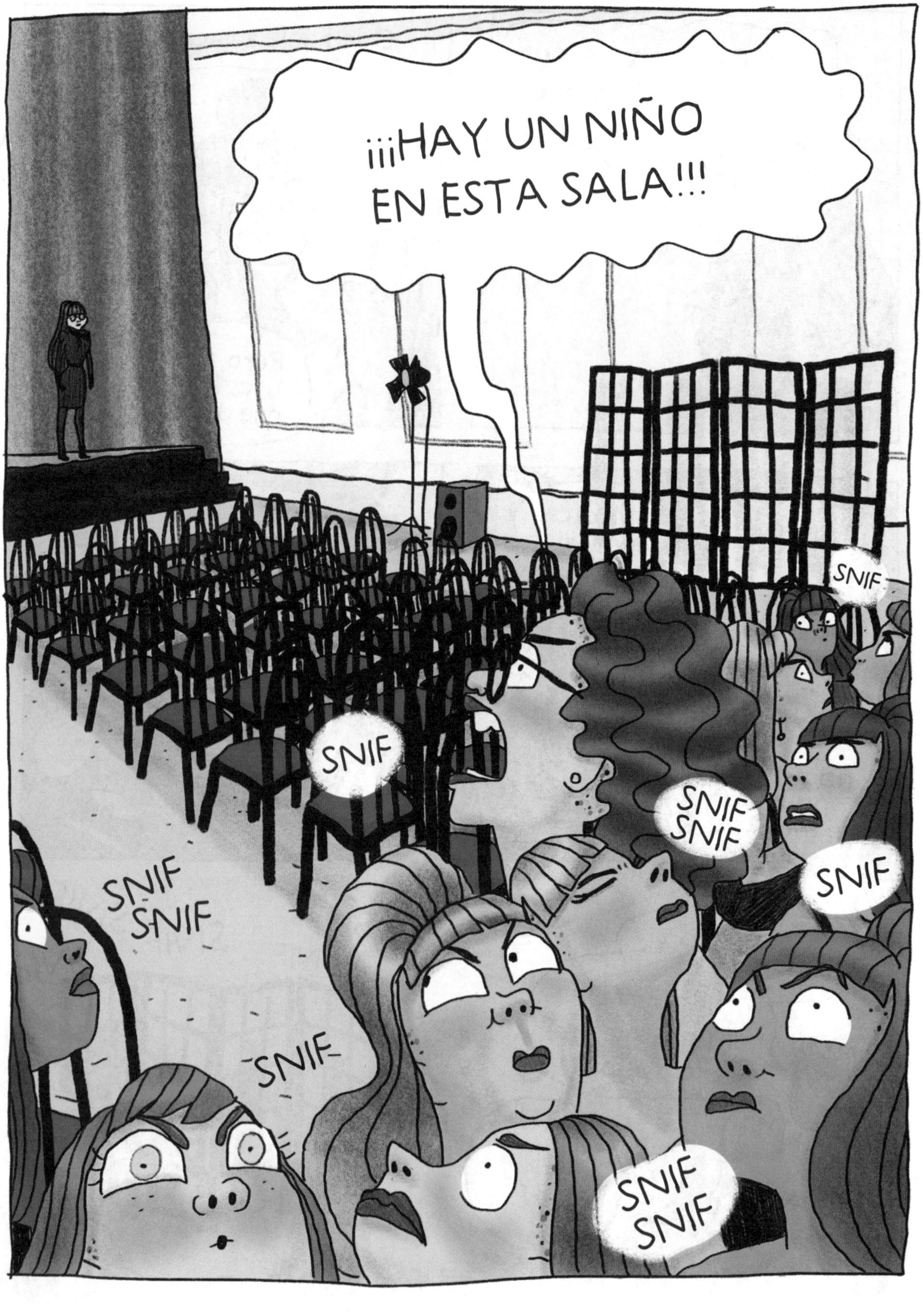
¡¡¡HAY UN NIÑO
EN ESTA SALA!!!
SNIF
SNIF
SNIF
SNIF
SNIF
SNIF
SNIF
SNIF
SNIF
SNIF
SNIF
SNIF

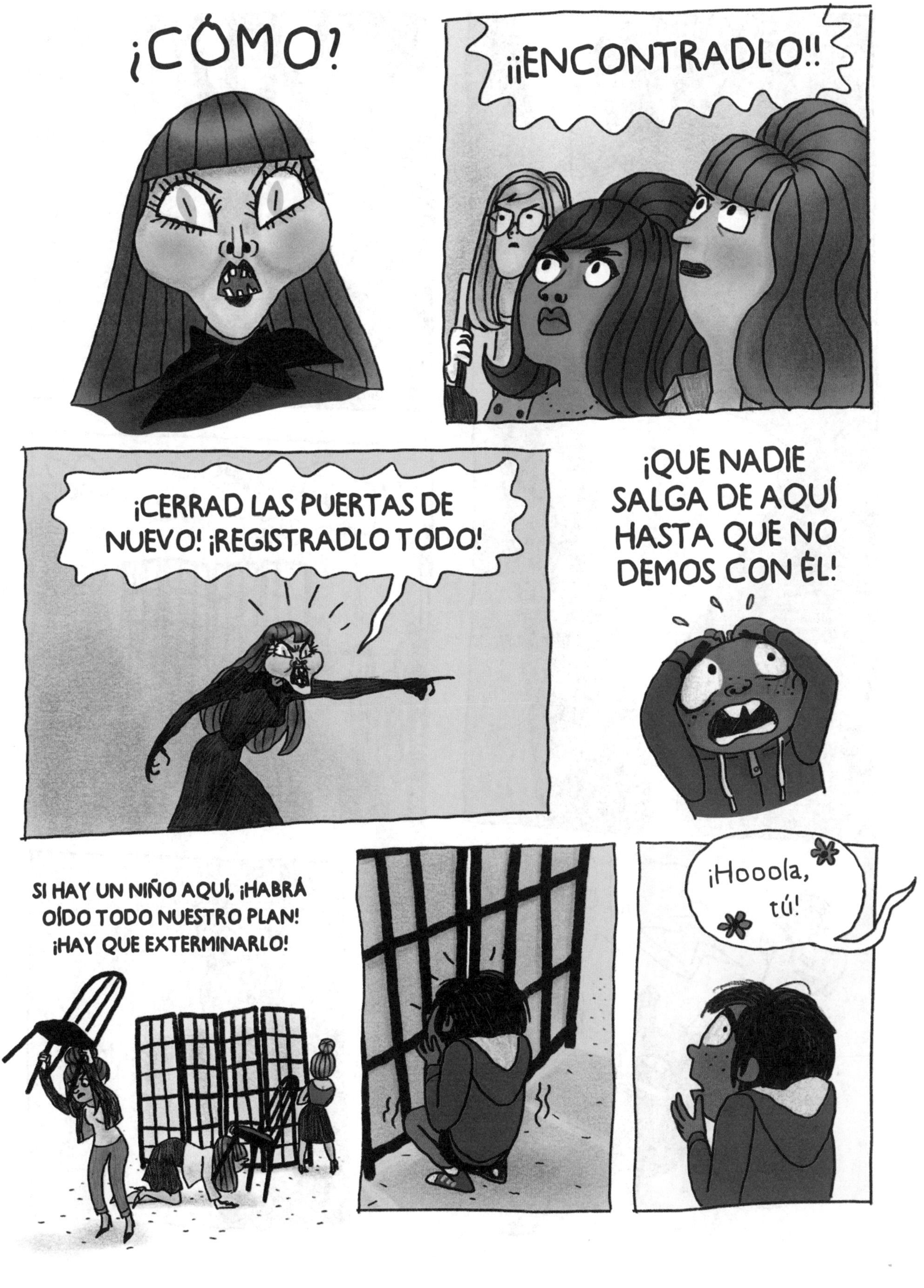
¡CÓMO?
¡¡ENCONTRADLO!!
¡CERRAD LAS PUERTAS DE NUEVO! ¡REGISTRADLO TODO!
¡QUE NADIE SALGA DE AQUÍ HASTA QUE NO DEMOS CON ÉL!
SI HAY UN NIÑO AQUÍ, ¡HABRÁ OÍDO TODO NUESTRO PLAN! ¡HAY QUE EXTERMINARLO!
¡Hooola, tú!

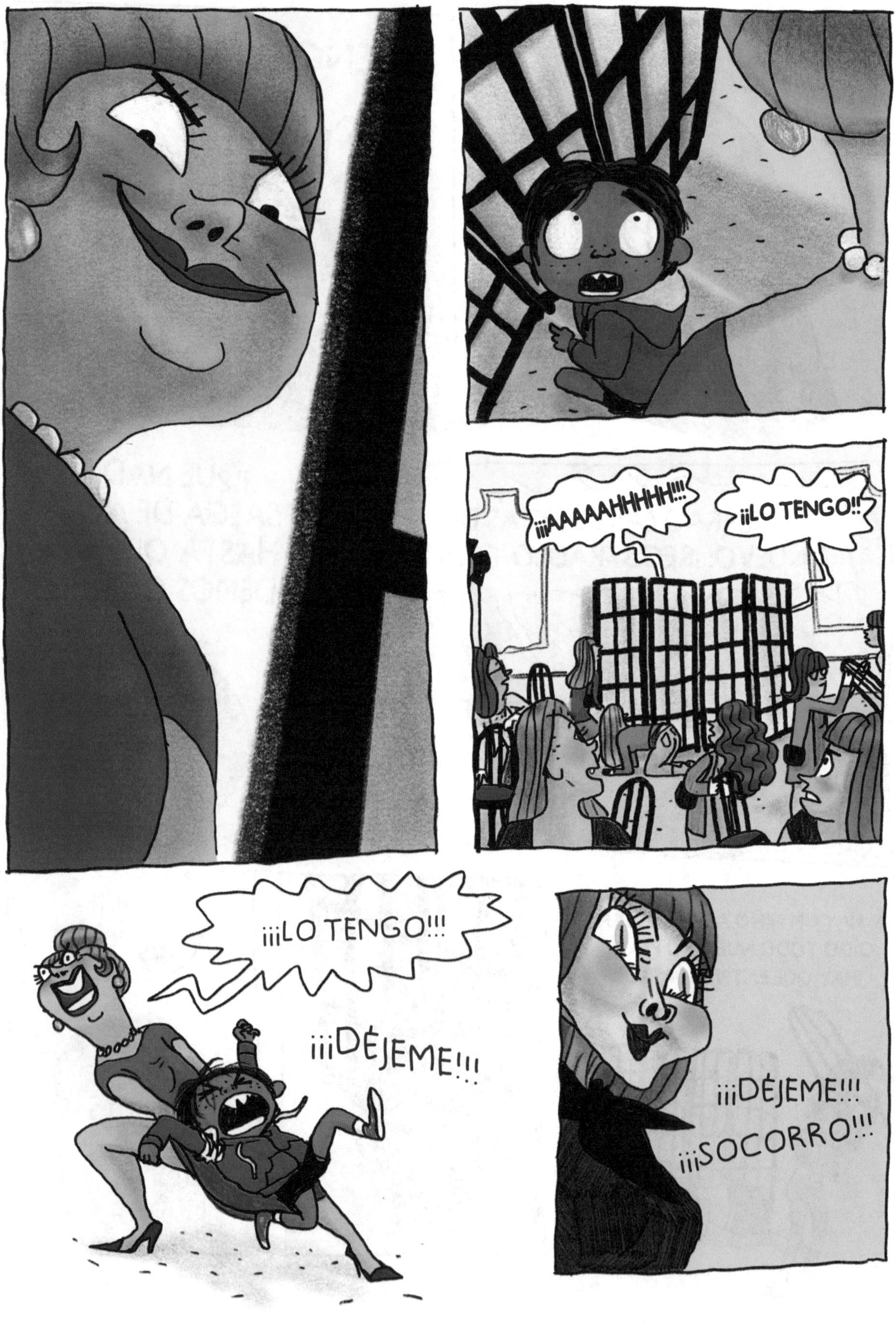

¡¡¡AAAAAHHHHH!!!
¡¡LO TENGO!!
¡¡¡LO TENGO!!!
¡¡¡DÉJEME!!!
¡¡¡DÉJEME!!!
¡¡¡SOCORRO!!!

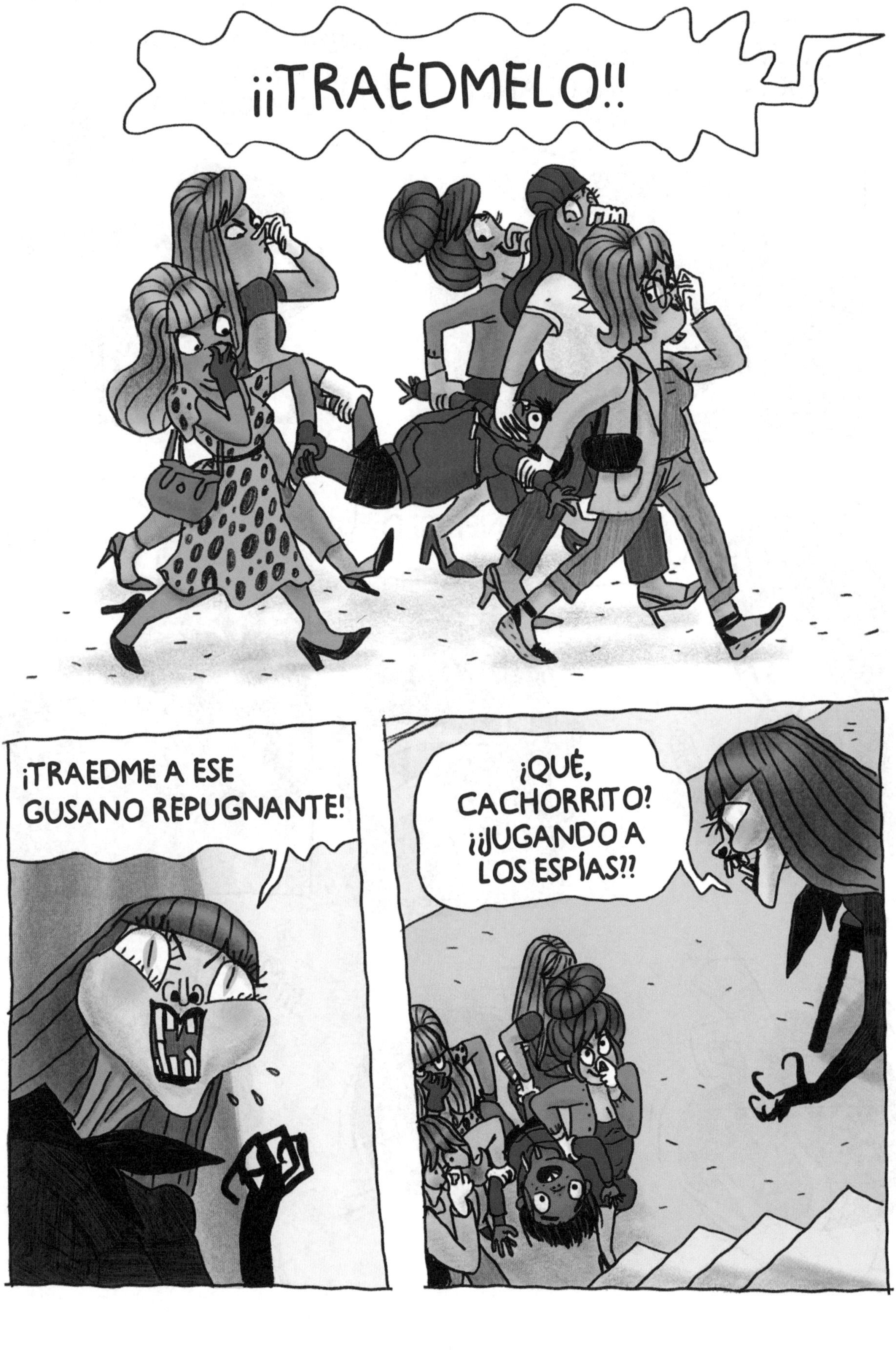
¡¡TRAÉDMELO!!
¡TRAEDME A ESE GUSANO REPUGNANTE!
¿QUÉ, CACHORRITO? ¡¿JUGANDO A LOS ESPÍAS?!

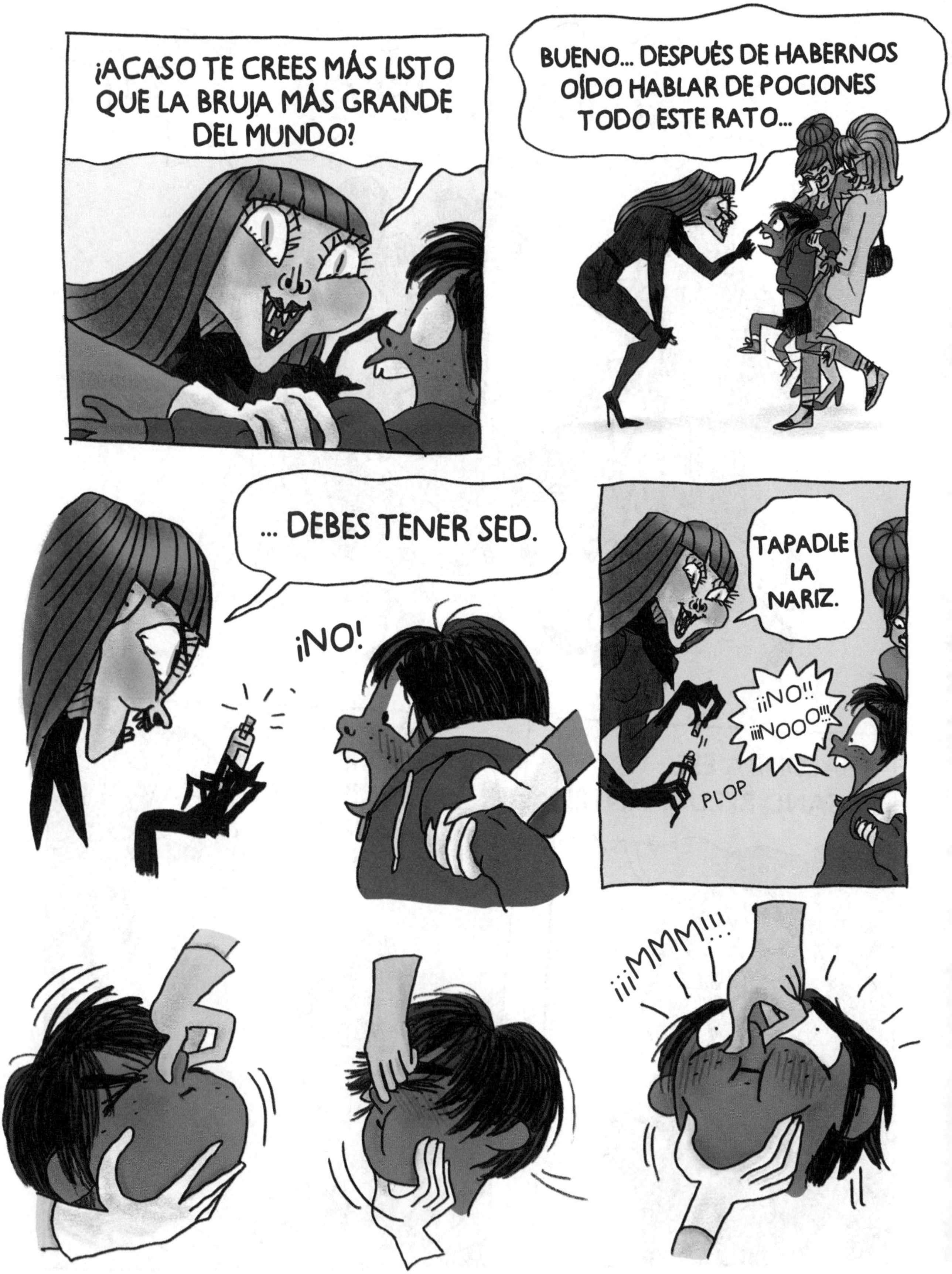
¡ACASO TE CREES MÁS LISTO QUE LA BRUJA MÁS GRANDE DEL MUNDO?
BUENO... DESPUÉS DE HABERNOS OÍDO HABLAR DE POCIONES TODO ESTE RATO...
... DEBES TENER SED.
¡NO!
TAPADLE LA NARIZ.
¡¡NO!! ¡¡¡NOOO!!!
PLOP
¡¡¡MMM!!!

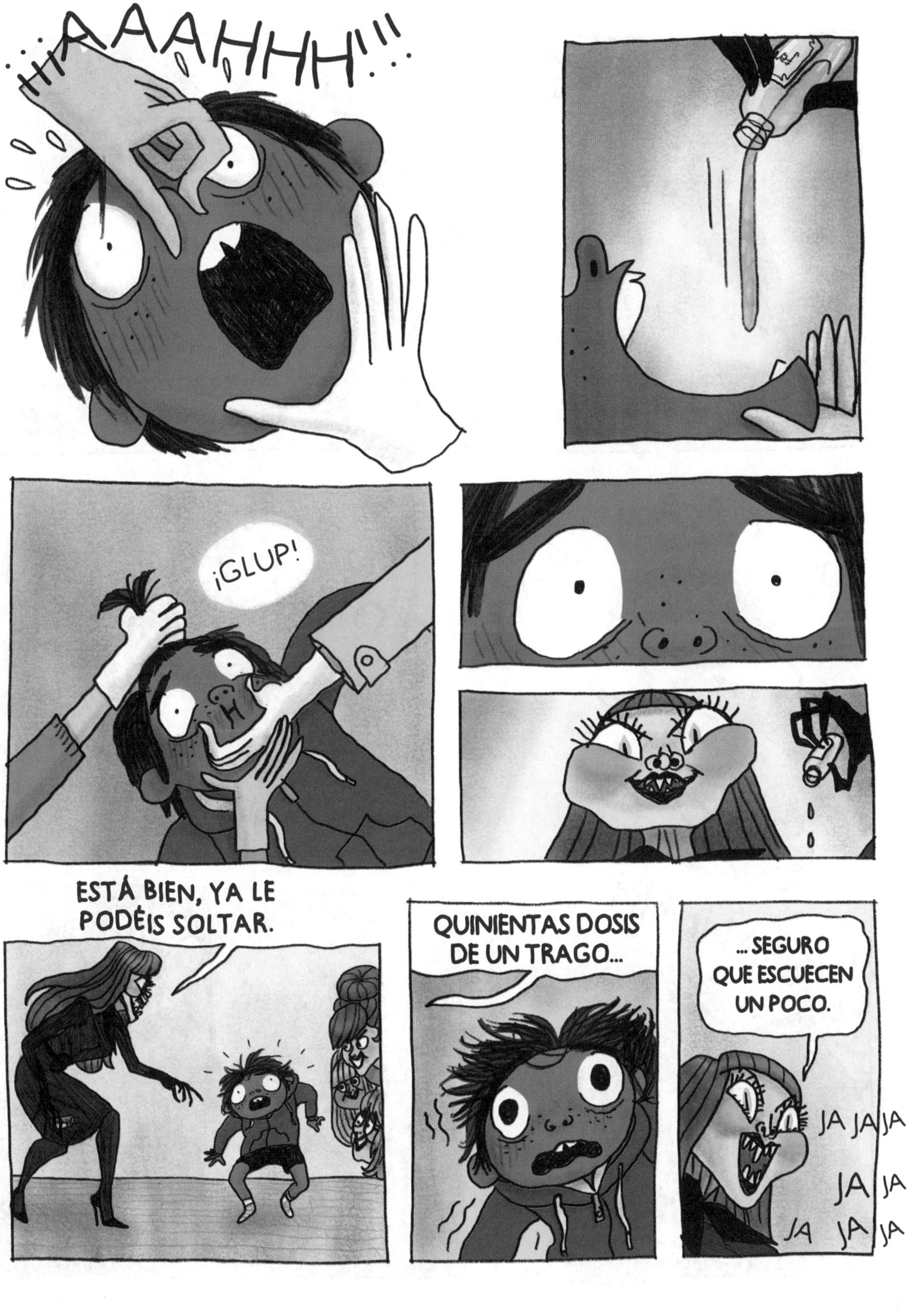
¡AAAHHH!
¡GLUP!
ESTÁ BIEN, YA LE PODÉIS SOLTAR.
QUINIENTAS DOSIS DE UN TRAGO...
... SEGURO QUE ESCUECEN UN POCO.
JA JA JA
JA JA
JA JA JA

AAAAAAAAAHHHHHHH

AAAAAAHHHHH

...

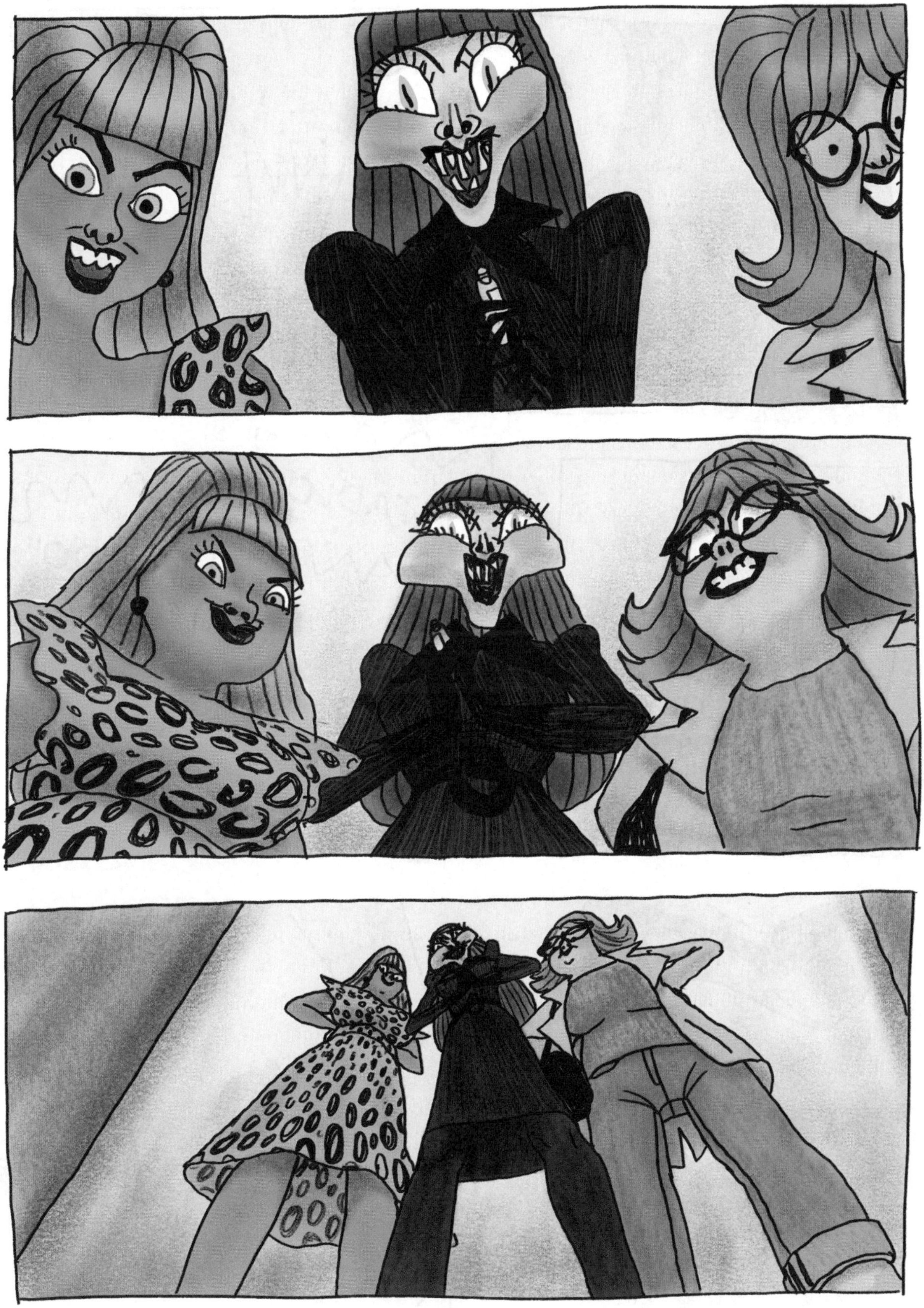

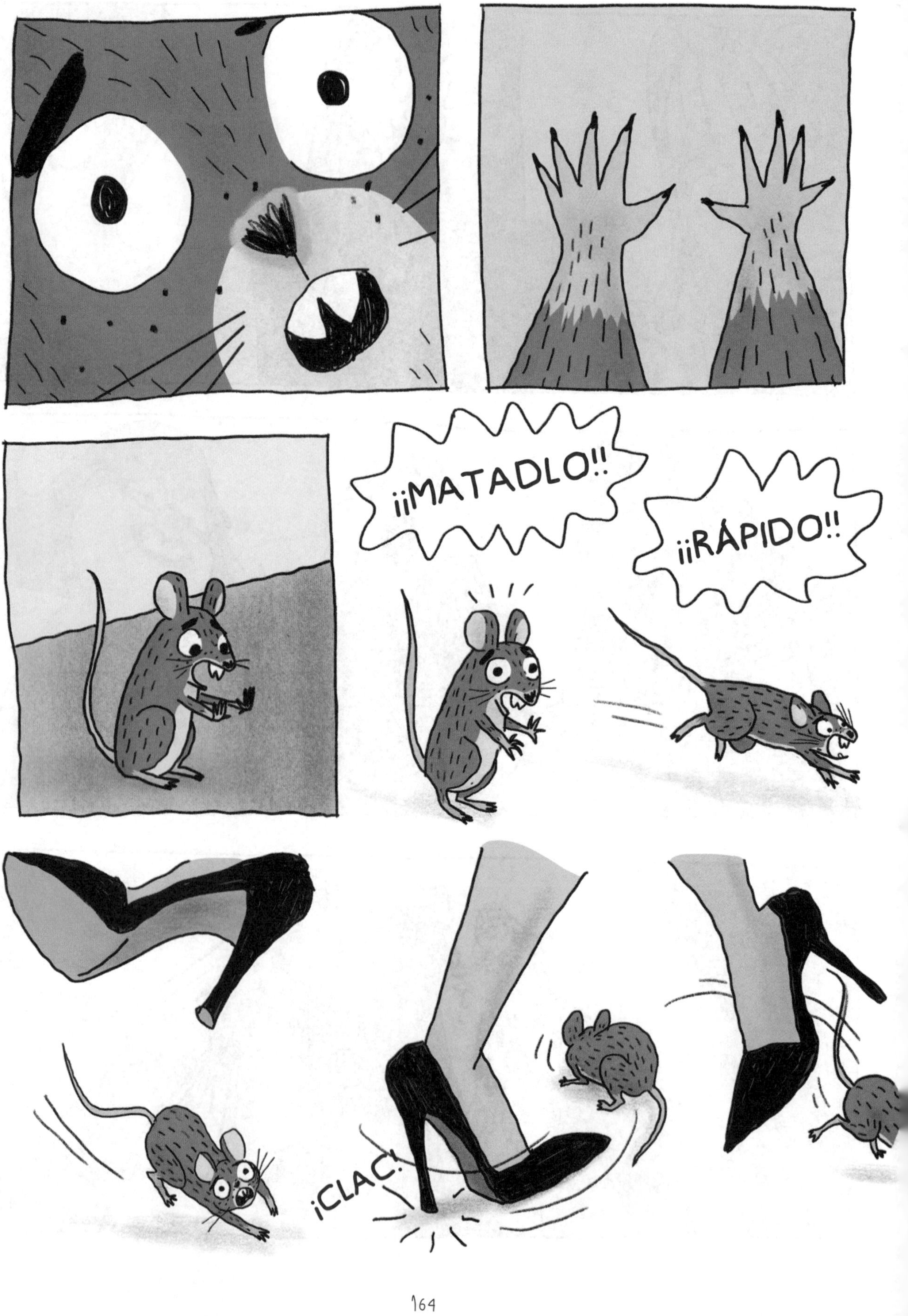
¡¡MATADLO!!
¡¡RÁPIDO!!
¡CLAC!

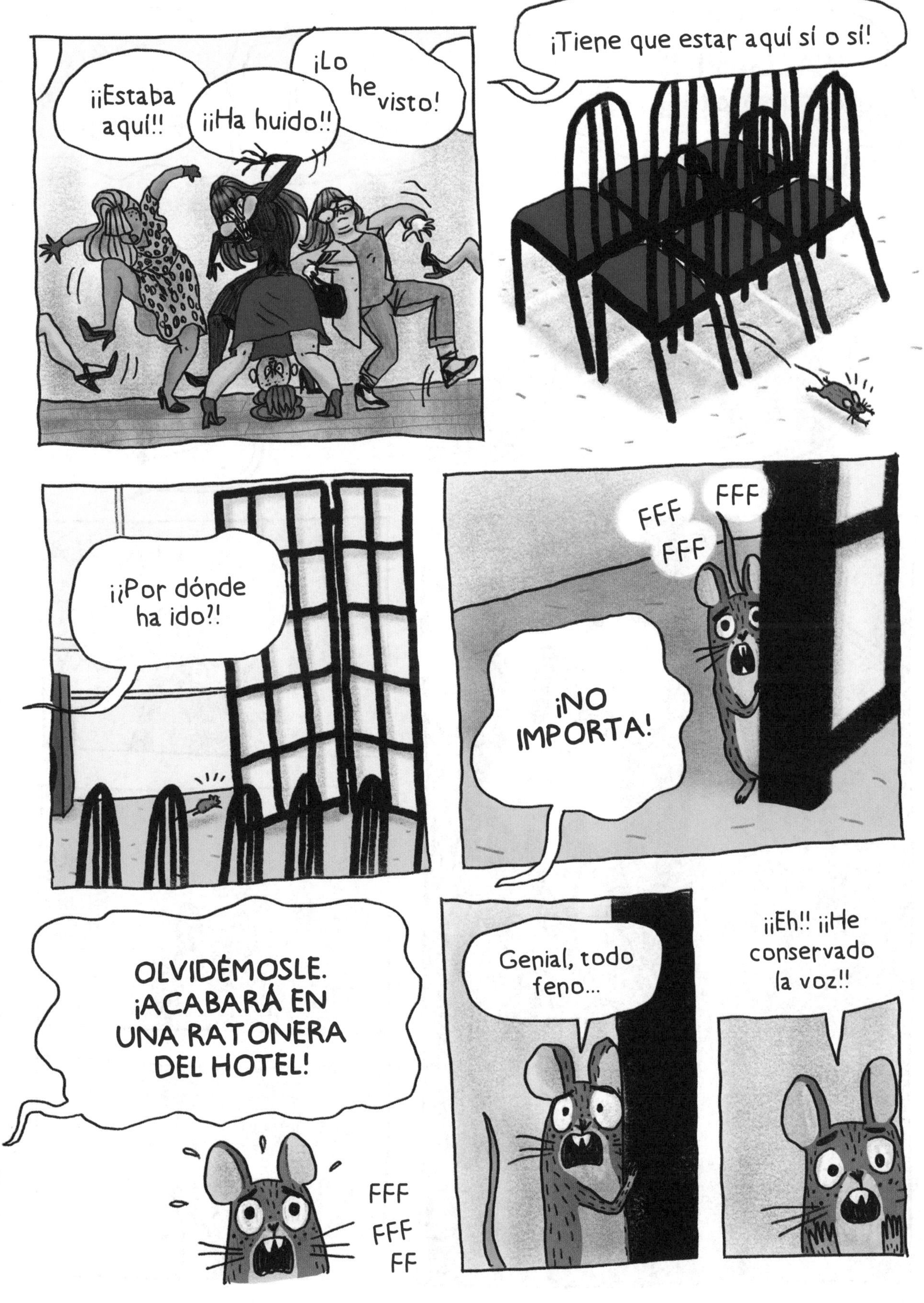
¡¡Estaba aquí!!
¡¡Ha huido!!
¡Lo he visto!
¡Tiene que estar aquí sí o sí!
¡¿Por dónde ha ido?!
FFF
FFF
FFF
¡NO IMPORTA!
OLVIDÉMOSLE. ¡ACABARÁ EN UNA RATONERA DEL HOTEL!
FFF
FFF
FF
Genial, todo feno...
¡¡Eh!! ¡¡He conservado la voz!!

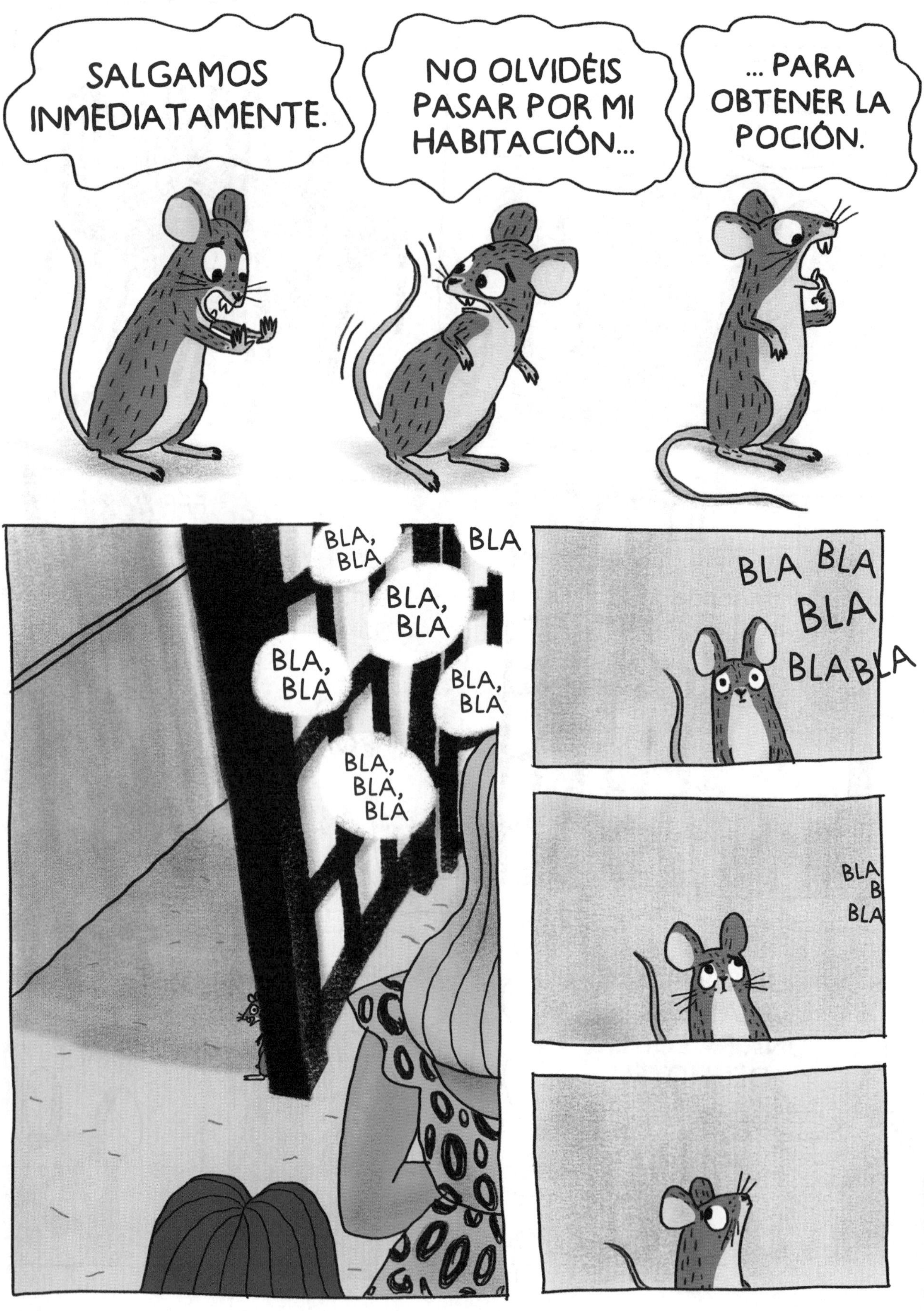
SALGAMOS INMEDIATAMENTE.
NO OLVIDÉIS PASAR POR MI HABITACIÓN...
... PARA OBTENER LA POCIÓN.
BLA, BLA
BLA
BLA, BLA
BLA, BLA
BLA, BLA
BLA, BLA, BLA
BLA BLA
BLA
BLABLA
BLA
B
BLA

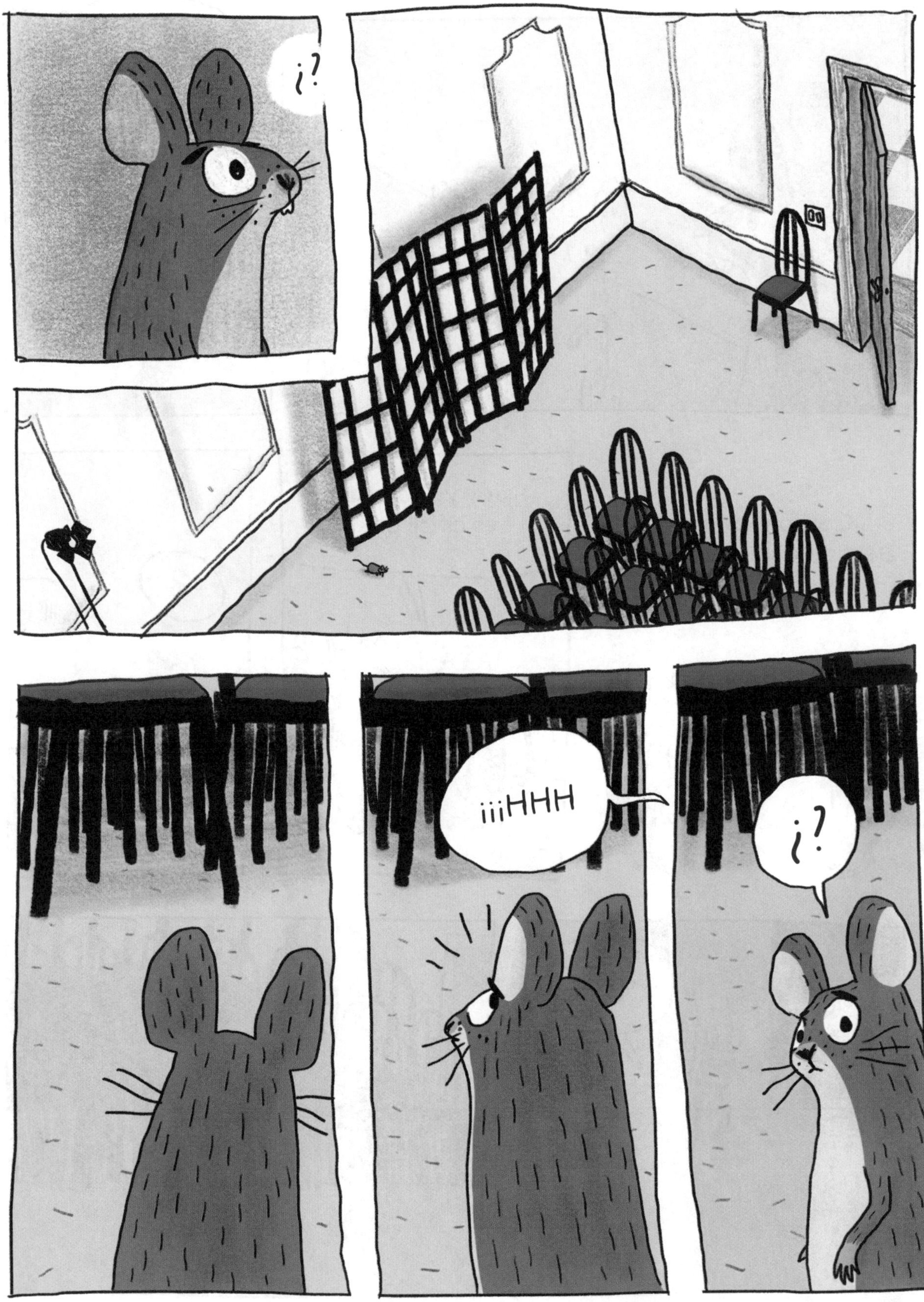
¿?
¡¡¡HHH
¿?

¡¡Cómo me alegro de veros, chicos!!

¡¡Soy yo!! Sé que es difícil de...

...

¡¡¡llIIHHH!!!

... creer.

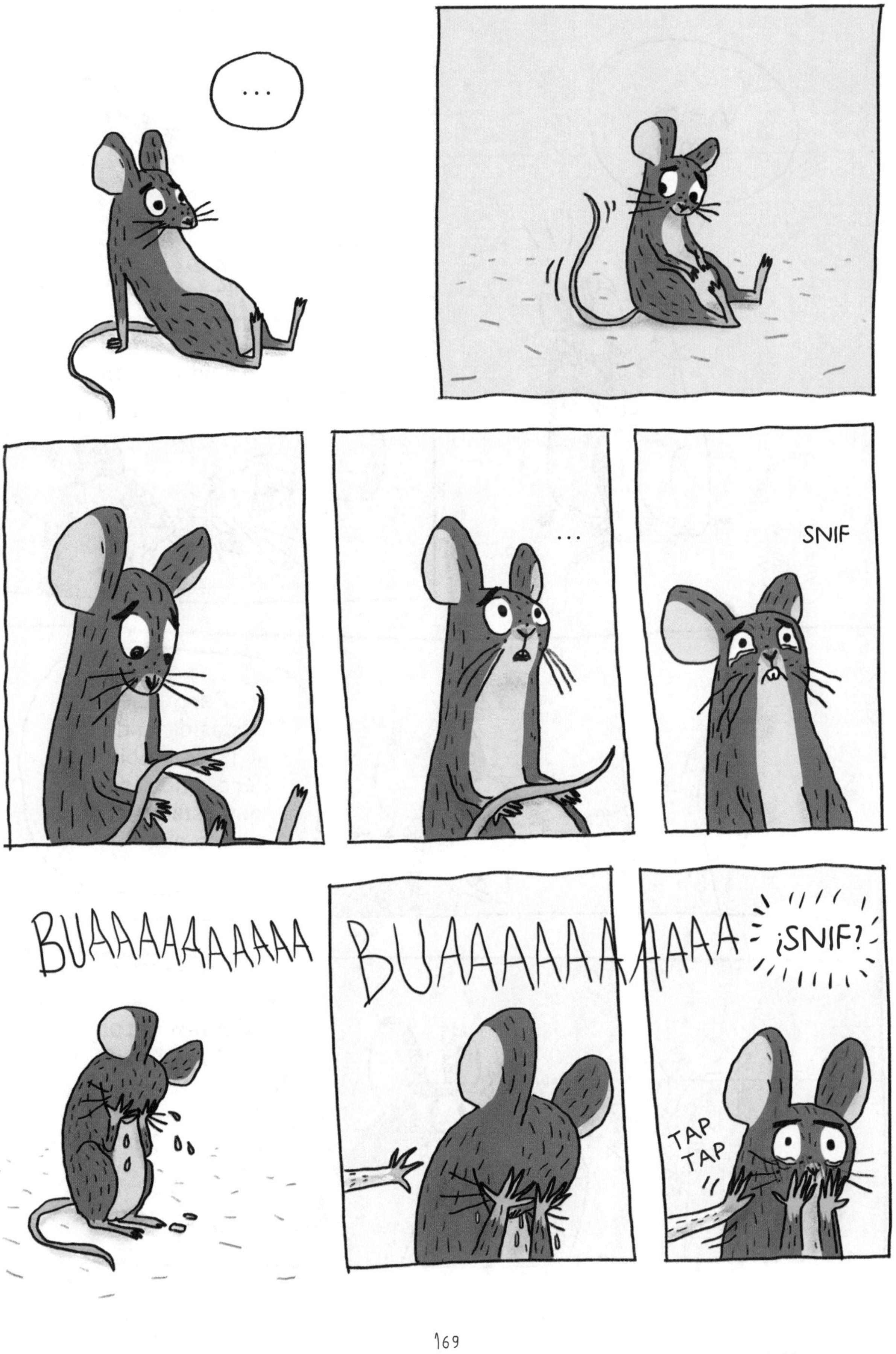
...
...
SNIF
BUAAAAAAAAAA
BUAAAAAAAAAAA
¡SNIF?
TAP TAP

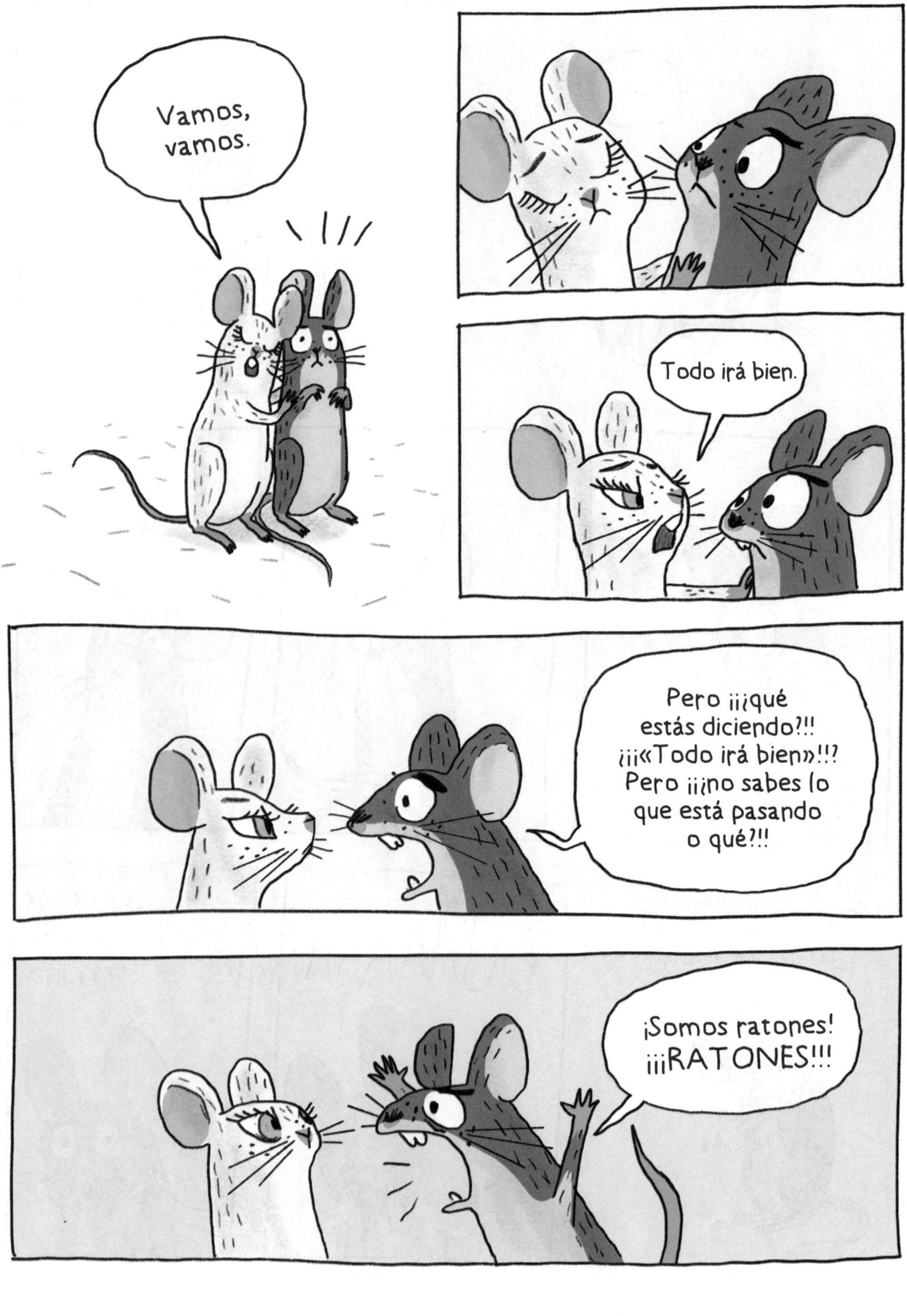
Vamos, vamos.
Todo irá bien.
Pero ¡¡¿qué estás diciendo?!! ¡¡¡«Todo irá bien»!!? Pero ¡¡¿no sabes lo que está pasando o qué?!!
¡Somos ratones! ¡¡¡RATONES!!!

Ya me había dado cuenta, ¡gracias!

Solo intentaba animarte, ¡vale?

¡Pues, mira! ¡No funciona muy bien!

Te da corte que yo te haya visto llorar.

¡Para nada!

Sí. Pero es una reacción normal. Un mecanismo de defensa.

¿Por qué hablas así?

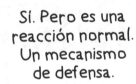

No reprimas tus emociones. ¿Tienes miedo? ¡Estás enfadado?

Intenta expresar con palabras lo que sient...

¡¡Oye, déjame!!

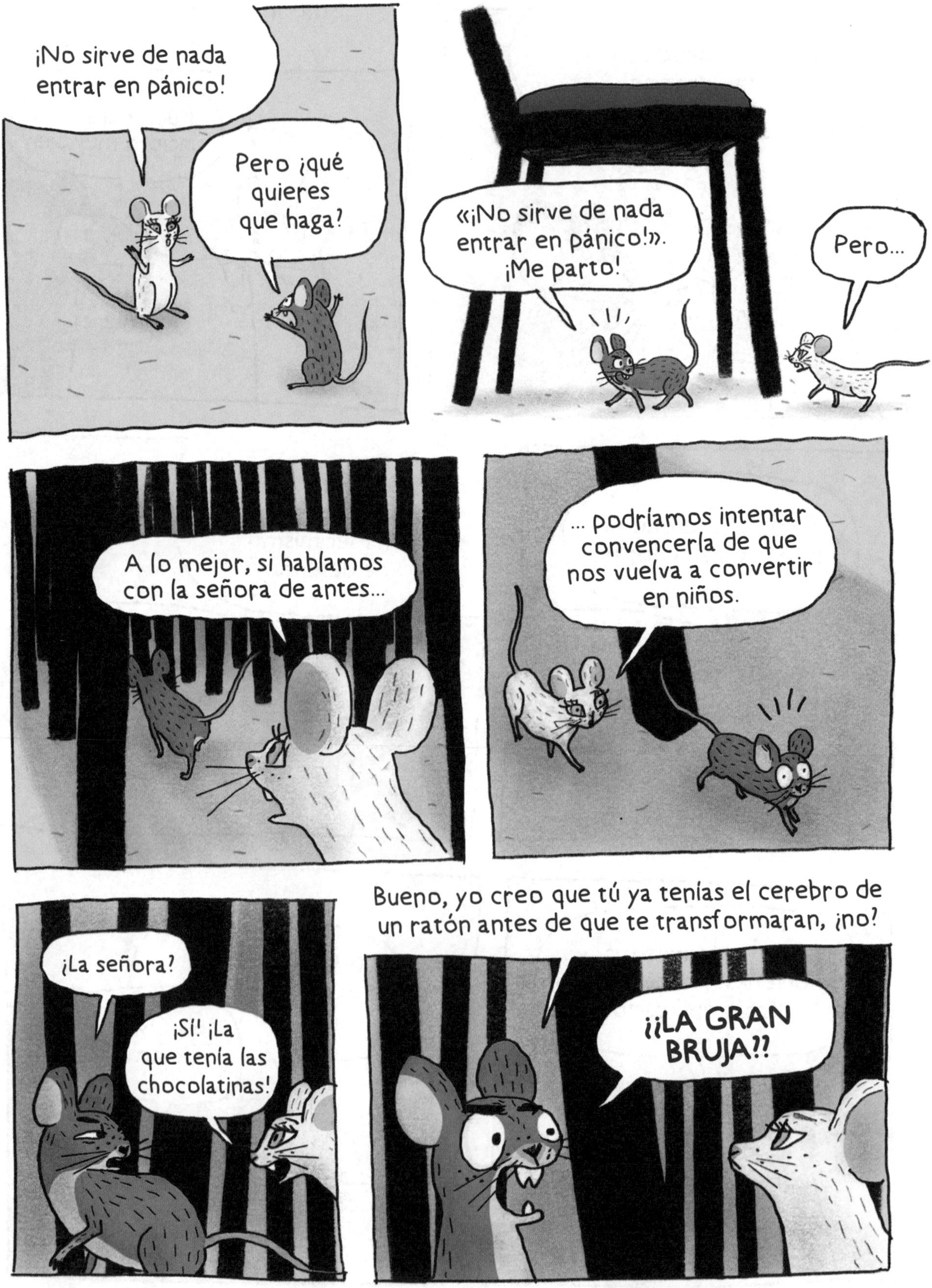
¡No sirve de nada entrar en pánico!
Pero ¿qué quieres que haga?
«¡No sirve de nada entrar en pánico!». ¡Me parto!
Pero...
A lo mejor, si hablamos con la señora de antes...
... podríamos intentar convencerla de que nos vuelva a convertir en niños.
¿La señora?
¡Sí! ¡La que tenía las chocolatinas!
Bueno, yo creo que tú ya tenías el cerebro de un ratón antes de que te transformaran, ¿no?
¡¿LA GRAN BRUJA?!

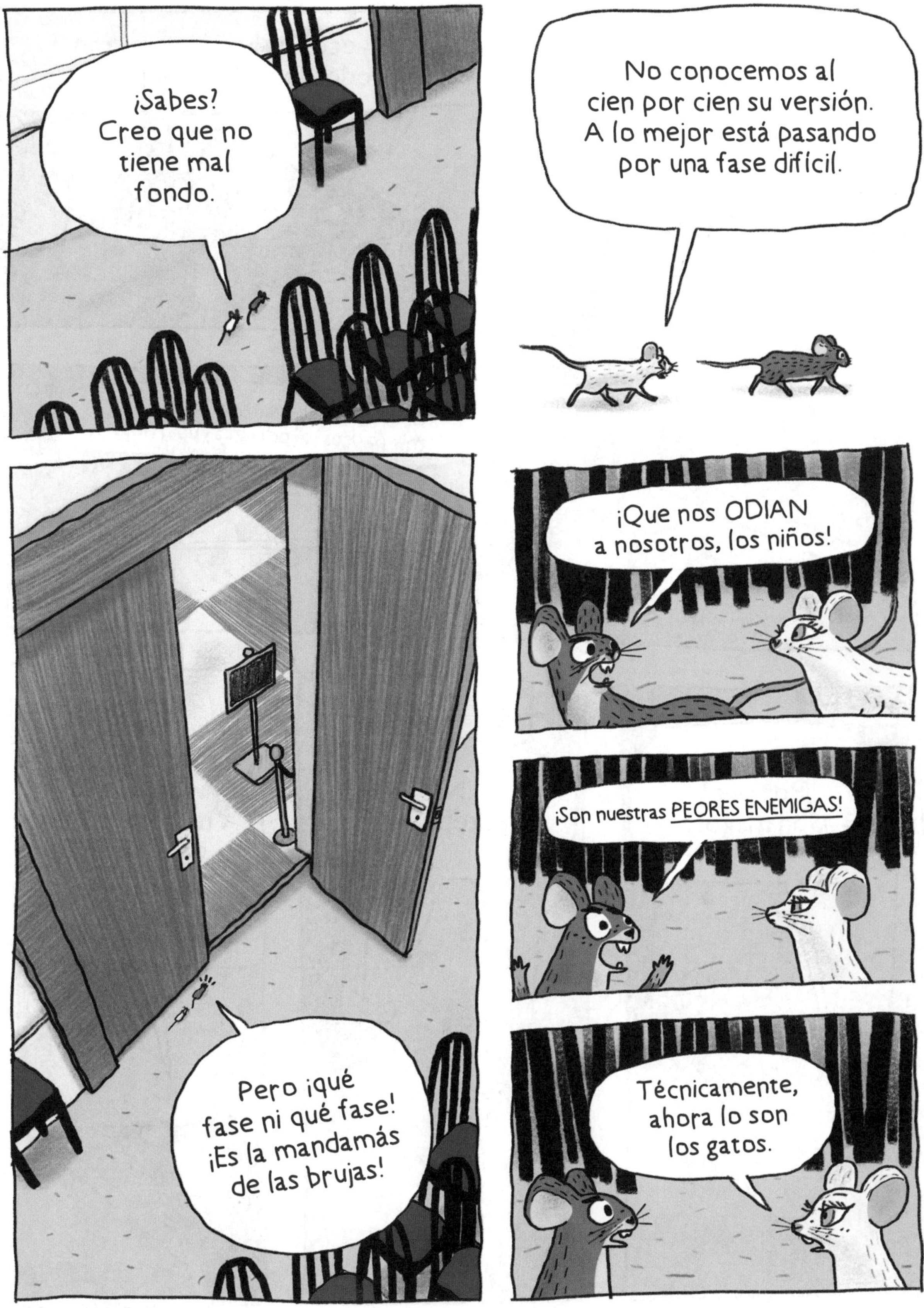
¿Sabes? Creo que no tiene mal fondo.
No conocemos al cien por cien su versión. A lo mejor está pasando por una fase difícil.
Pero ¡qué fase ni qué fase! ¡Es la mandamás de las brujas!
¡Que nos ODIAN a nosotros, los niños!
¡Son nuestras PEORES ENEMIGAS!
Técnicamente, ahora lo son los gatos.

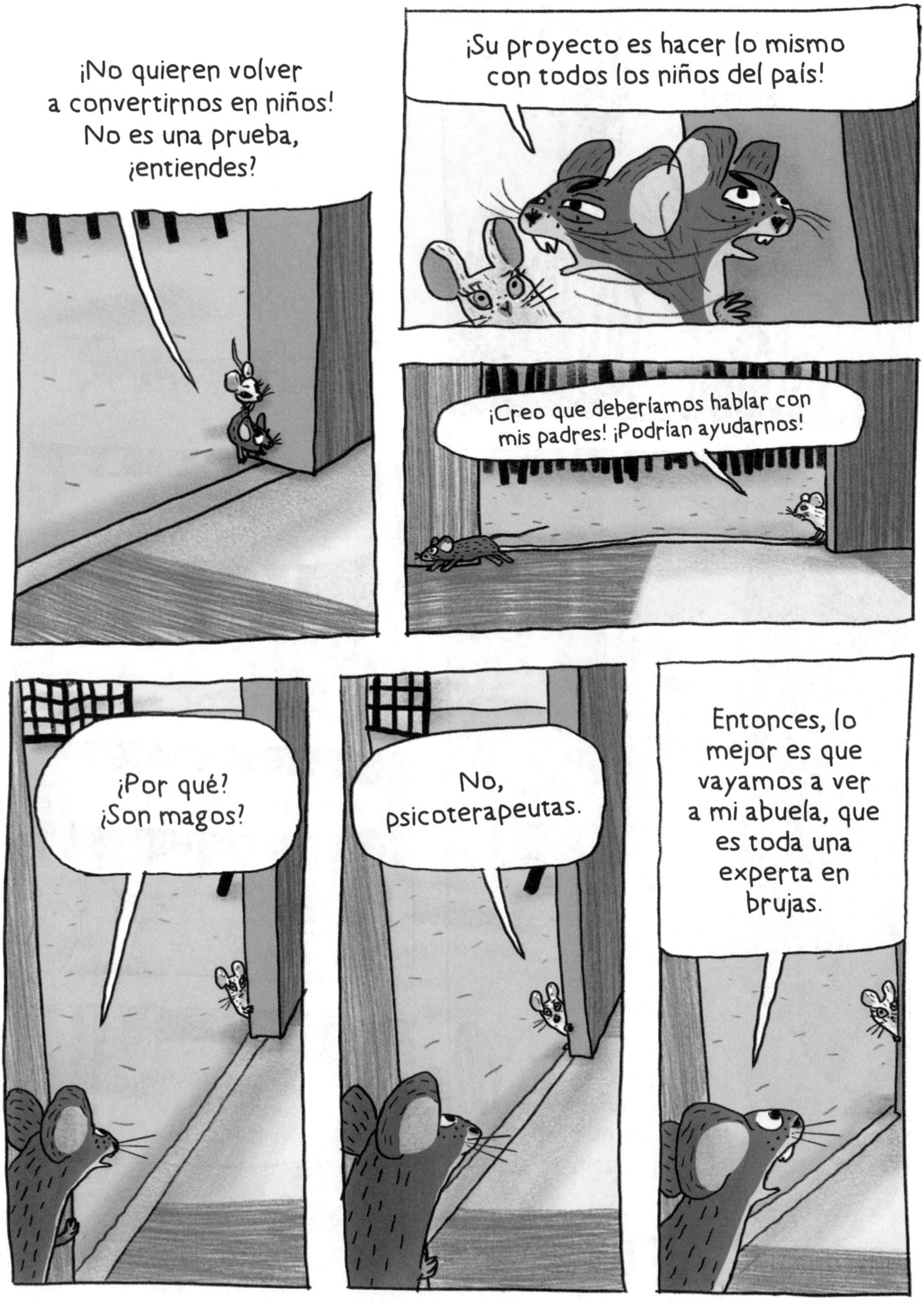
¡No quieren volver a convertirnos en niños! No es una prueba, ¿entiendes?
¡Su proyecto es hacer lo mismo con todos los niños del país!
¡Creo que deberíamos hablar con mis padres! ¡Podrían ayudarnos!
¿Por qué? ¿Son magos?
No, psicoterapeutas.
Entonces, lo mejor es que vayamos a ver a mi abuela, que es toda una experta en brujas.

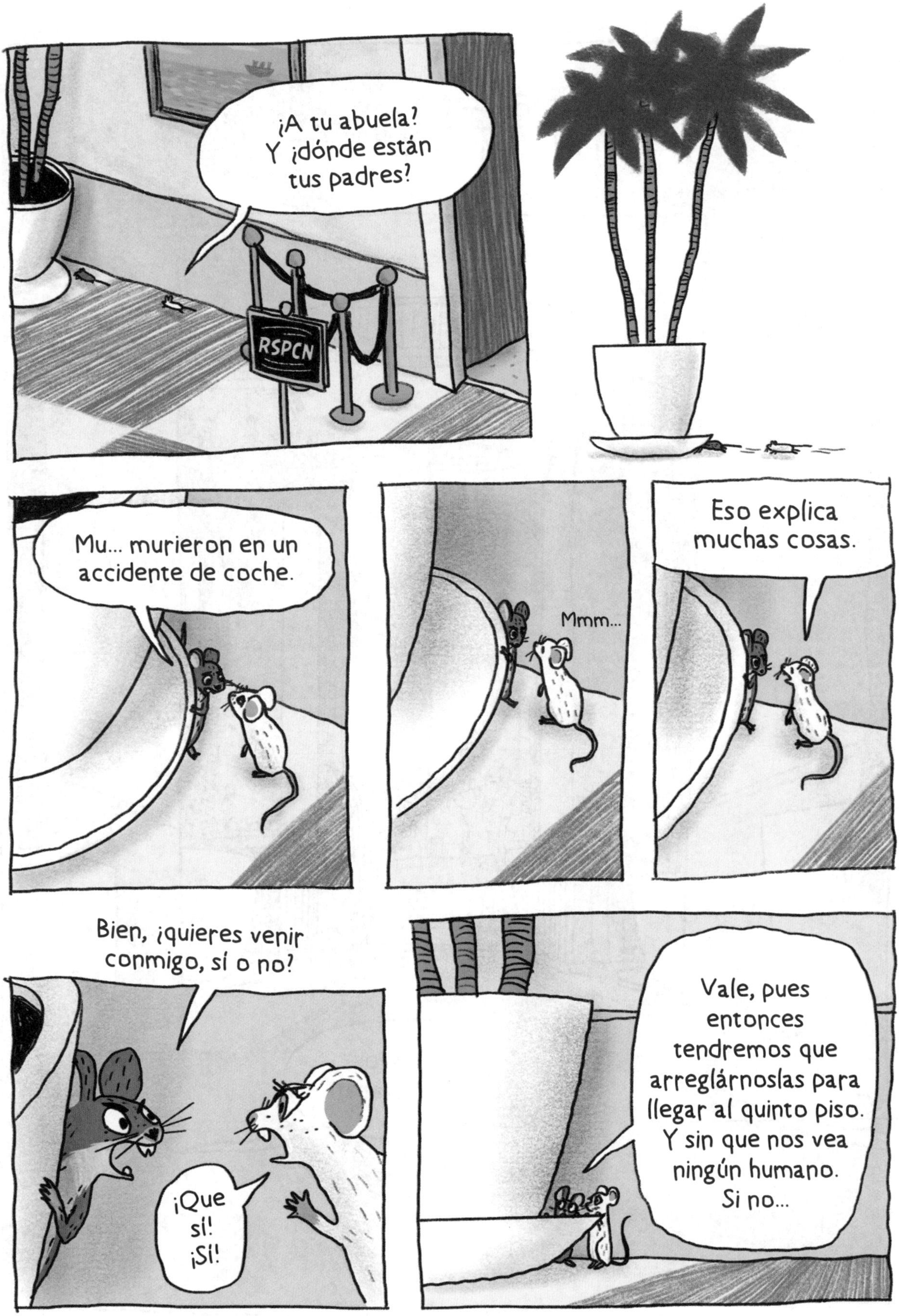
¡A tu abuela?
Y ¿dónde están tus padres?
RSPCN
Mu... murieron en un accidente de coche.
Mmm...
Eso explica muchas cosas.
Bien, ¿quieres venir conmigo, sí o no?
¡Que sí! ¡Sí!
Vale, pues entonces tendremos que arreglárnoslas para llegar al quinto piso. Y sin que nos vea ningún humano. Si no...

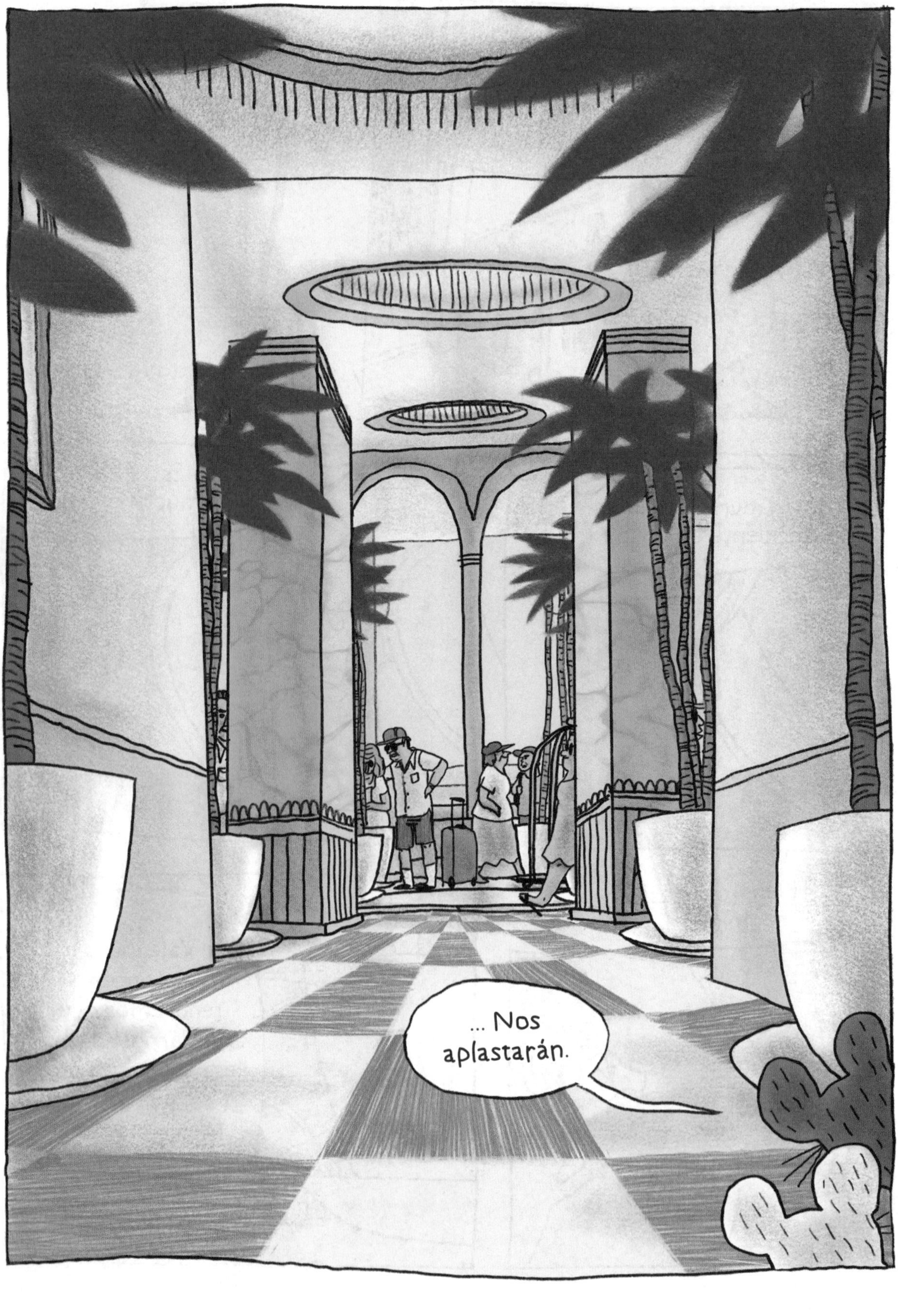
... Nos aplastarán.

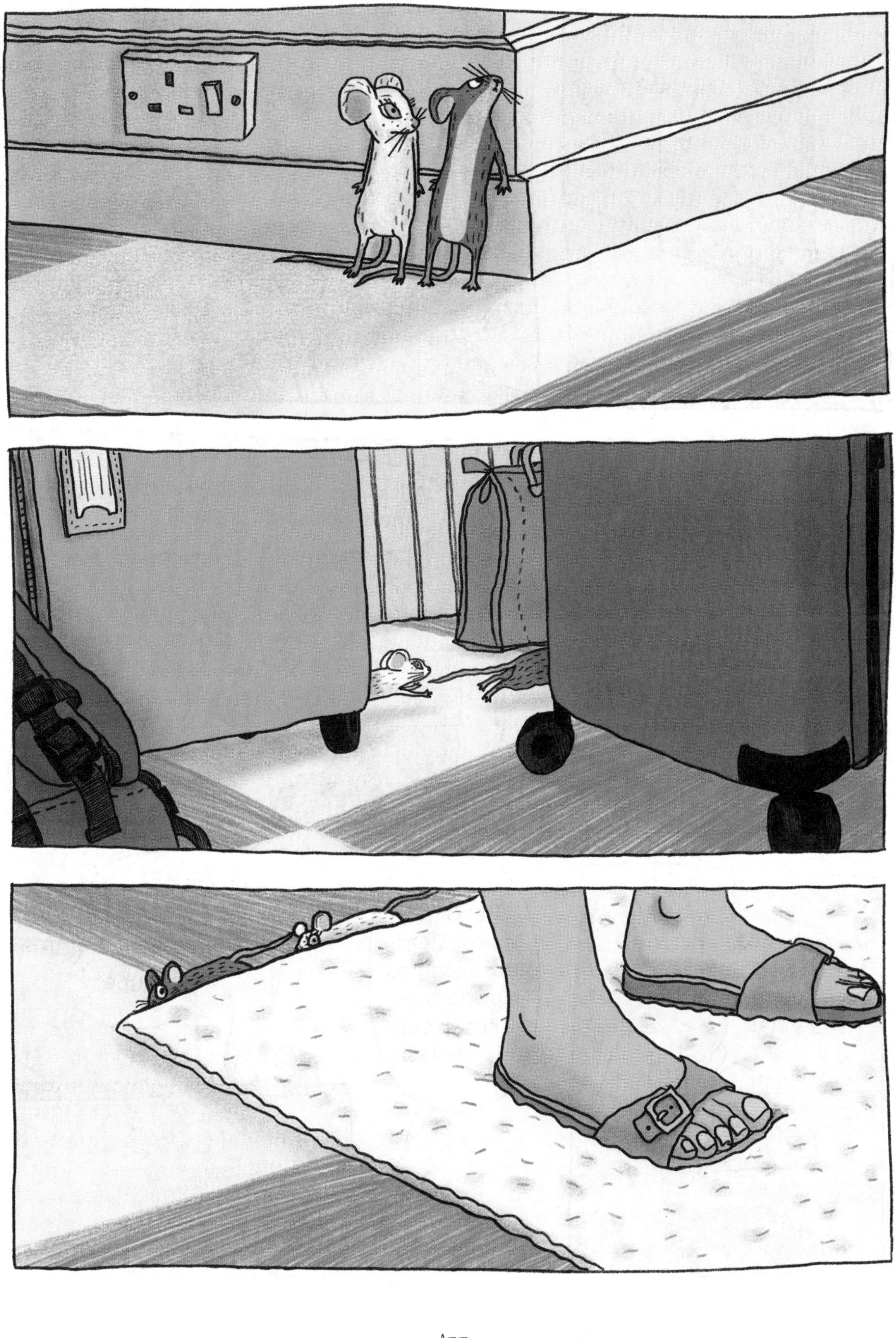

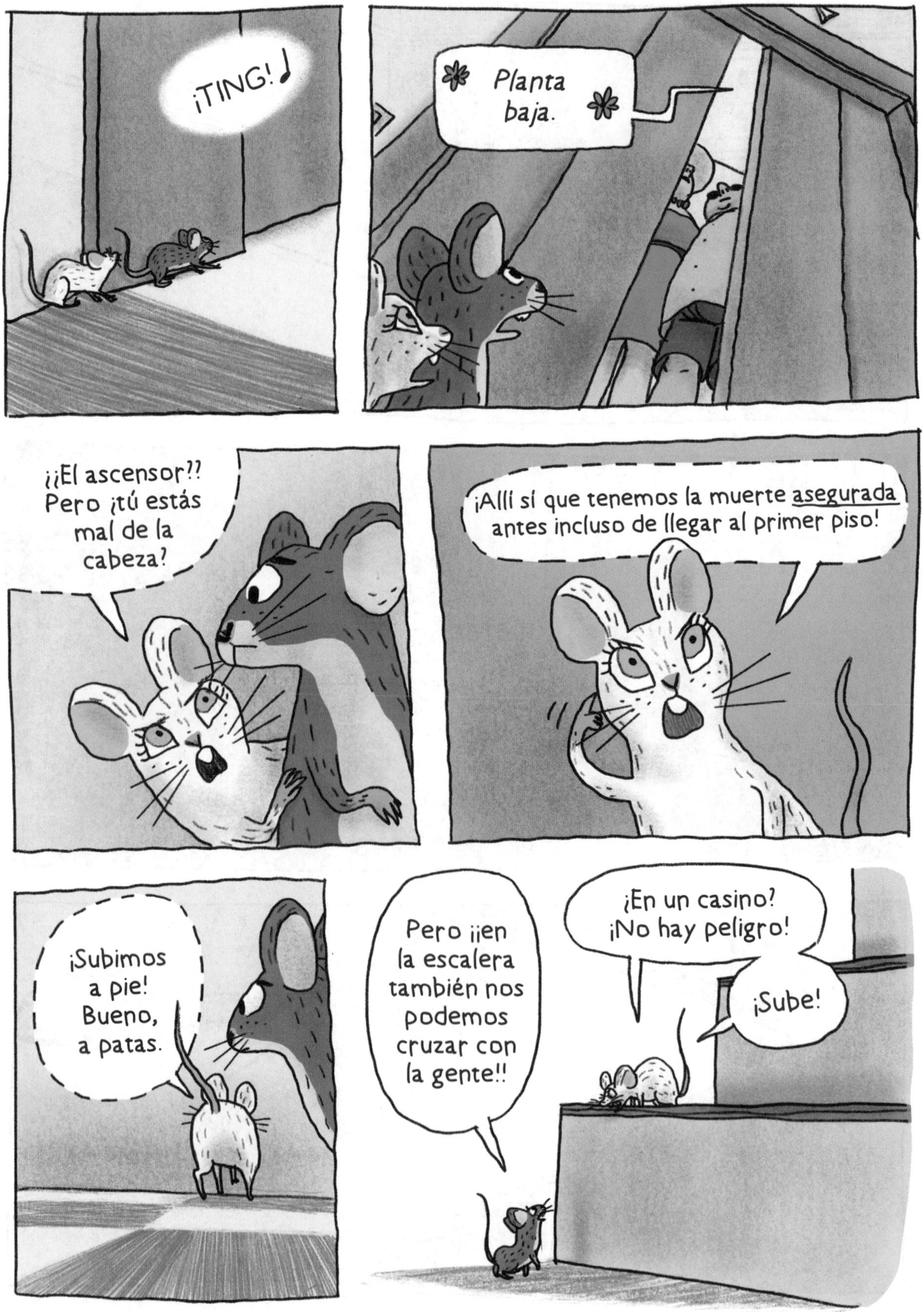
¡TING!
Planta baja.
¡¿El ascensor?? Pero ¡tú estás mal de la cabeza?
¡Allí sí que tenemos la muerte asegurada antes incluso de llegar al primer piso!
¡Subimos a pie! Bueno, a patas.
Pero ¡¡en la escalera también nos podemos cruzar con la gente!!
¡En un casino? ¡No hay peligro!
¡Sube!

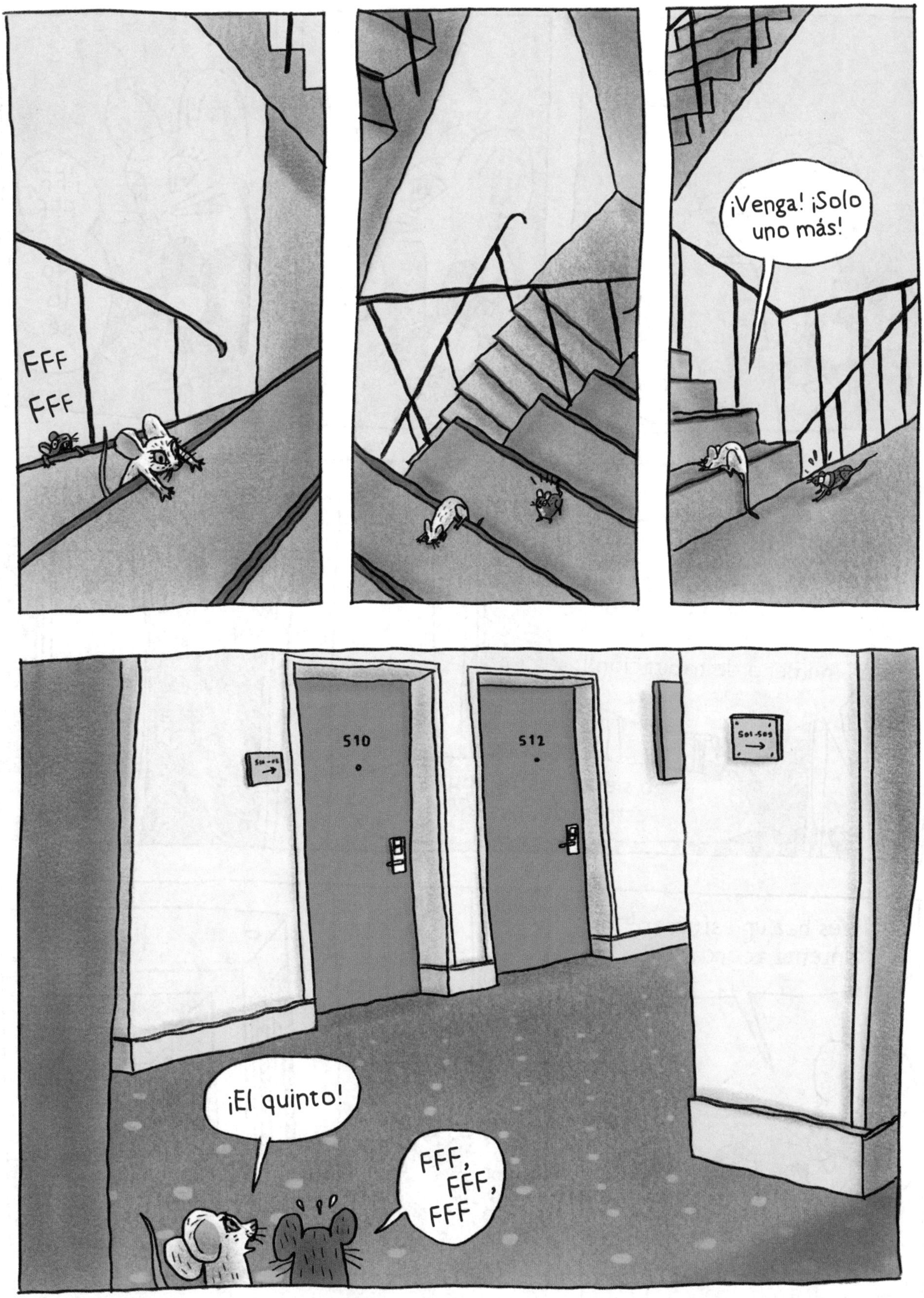
FFF
FFF
¡Venga! ¡Solo uno más!
510
512
¡El quinto!
FFF, FFF, FFF

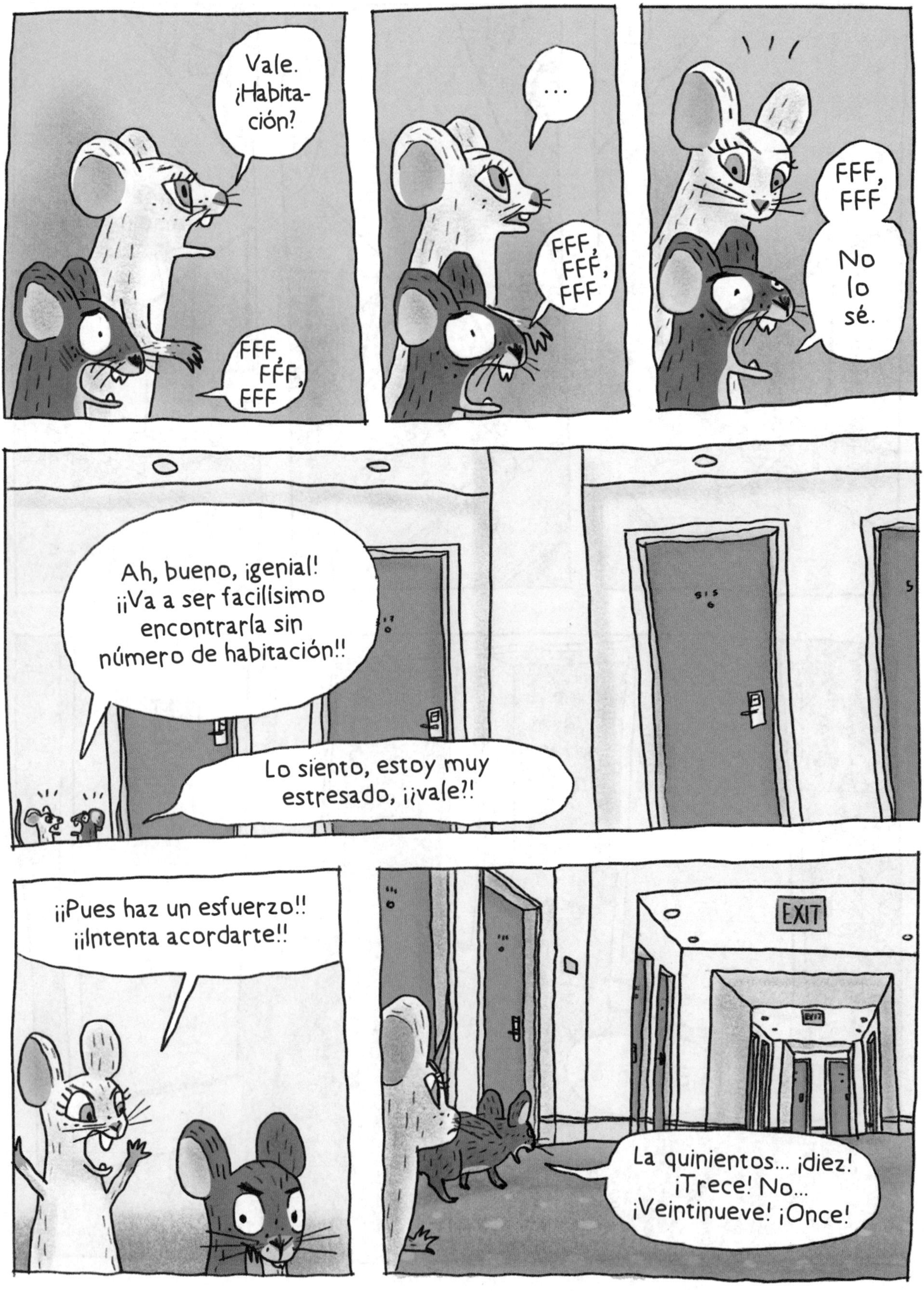
Vale. ¡Habitación?
FFF, FFF, FFF
...
FFF, FFF, FFF
FFF, FFF
No lo sé.
Ah, bueno, ¡genial! ¡¡Va a ser facilísimo encontrarla sin número de habitación!!
Lo siento, estoy muy estresado, ¡¿vale?!
¡¡Pues haz un esfuerzo!! ¡¡Intenta acordarte!!
EXIT
La quinientos... ¡diez! ¡Trece! No... ¡Veintinueve! ¡Once!

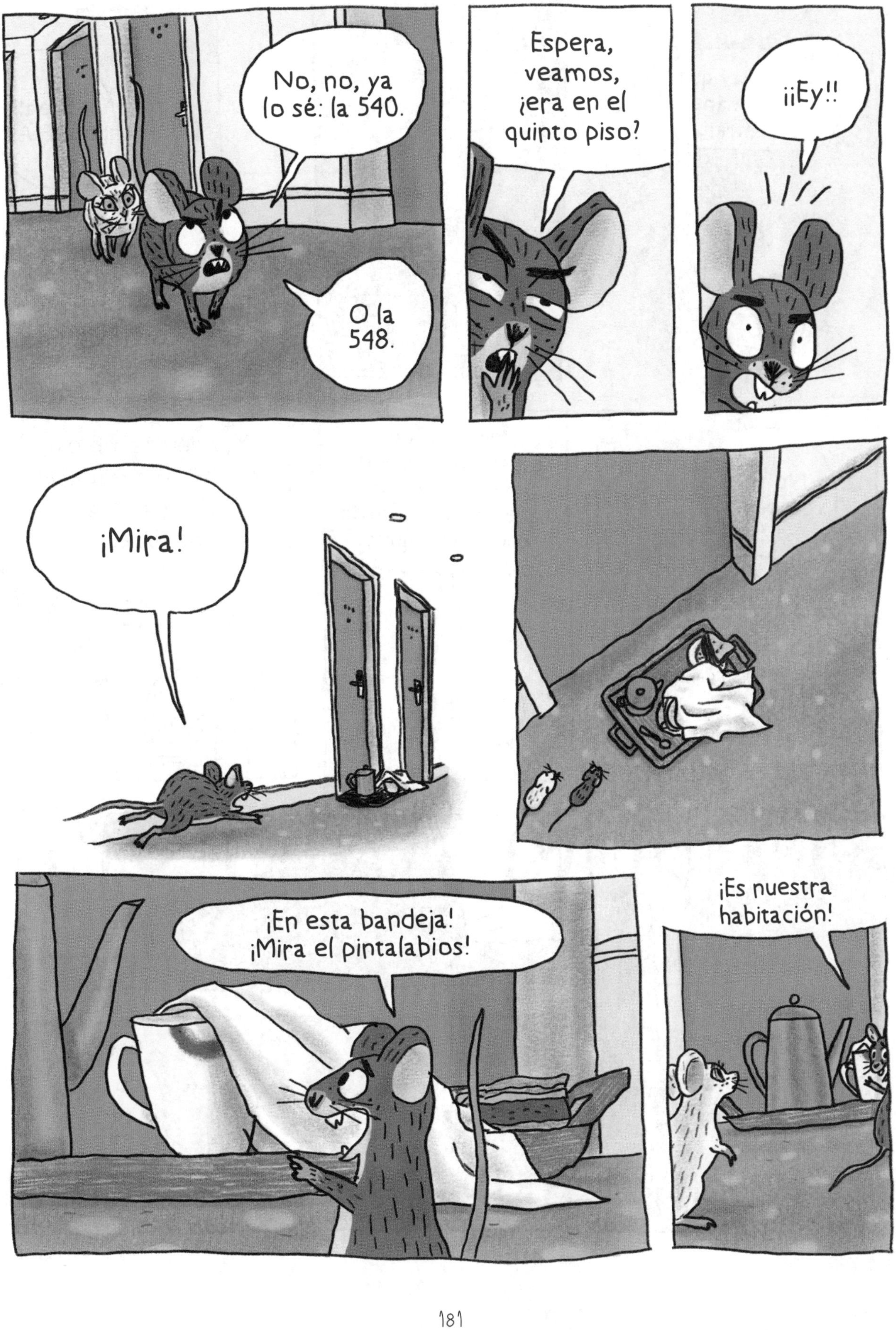
No, no, ya lo sé: la 540.
O la 548.
Espera, veamos, ¿era en el quinto piso?
¡¡Ey!!
¡Mira!
¡En esta bandeja! ¡Mira el pintalabios!
¡Es nuestra habitación!

Ahora hay que hallar la manera de entrar.

5 5 4

¡TIP!
¡TIP!
¡TIP!

¡¡Abuela!! ¡¡¡ABUELA!!!

No te canses.

¡TIP! ¡TIP!
¡TIP! ¡TIP!
¡TIP!

Mira, para el espectro audible de un oído humano, haces el mismo ruido que un mosquito.

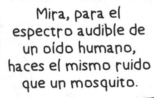

TIP TIP
TIP
TIP

Y, además, no es por ser desagradable, pero a su edad tu abue...

PUM
PUM

PUM PUM

PUM

Ay, no...

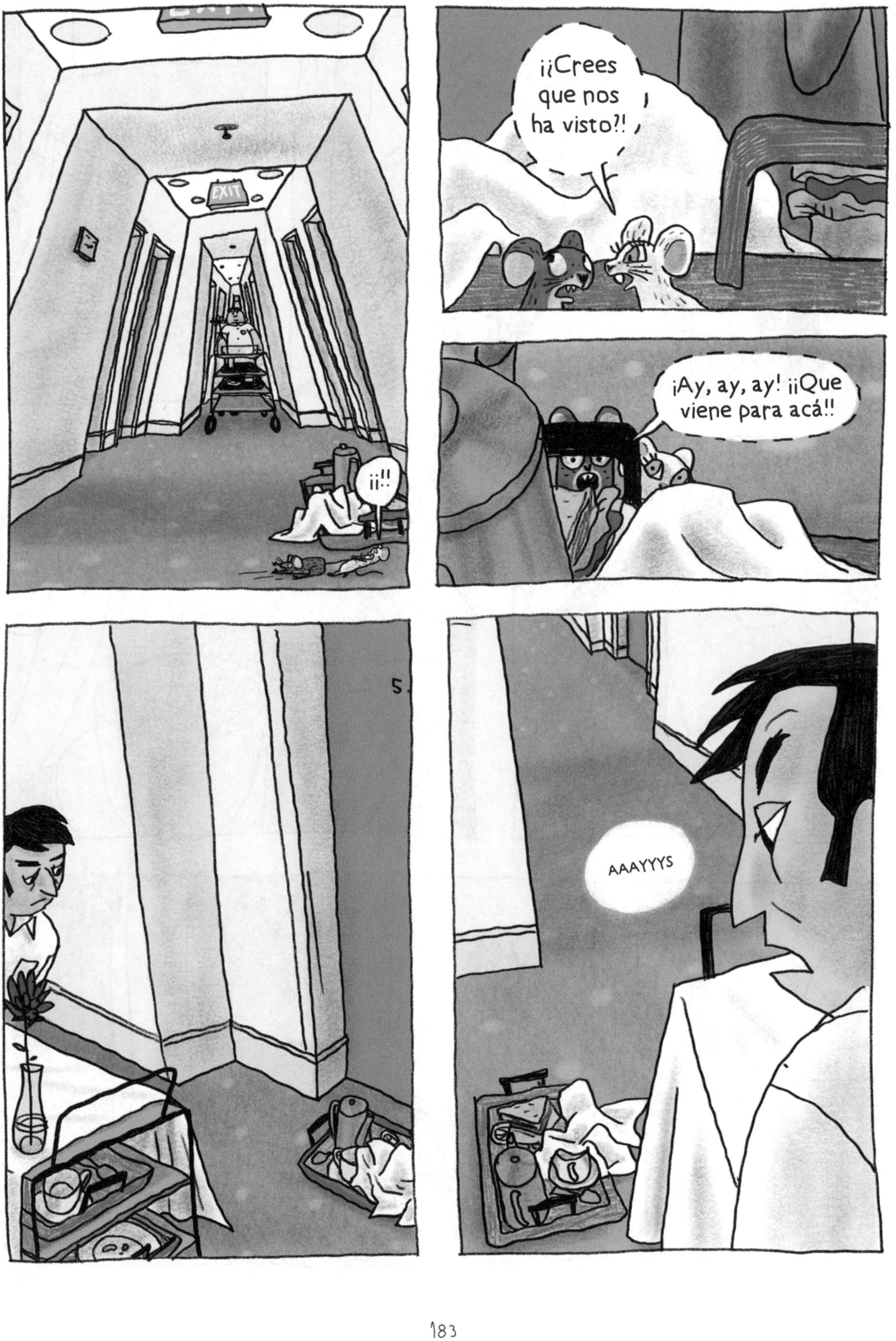
EXIT
¡¡!!
¡¡Crees que nos ha visto?!
¡Ay, ay, ay! ¡¡Que viene para acá!!
AAAYYYS

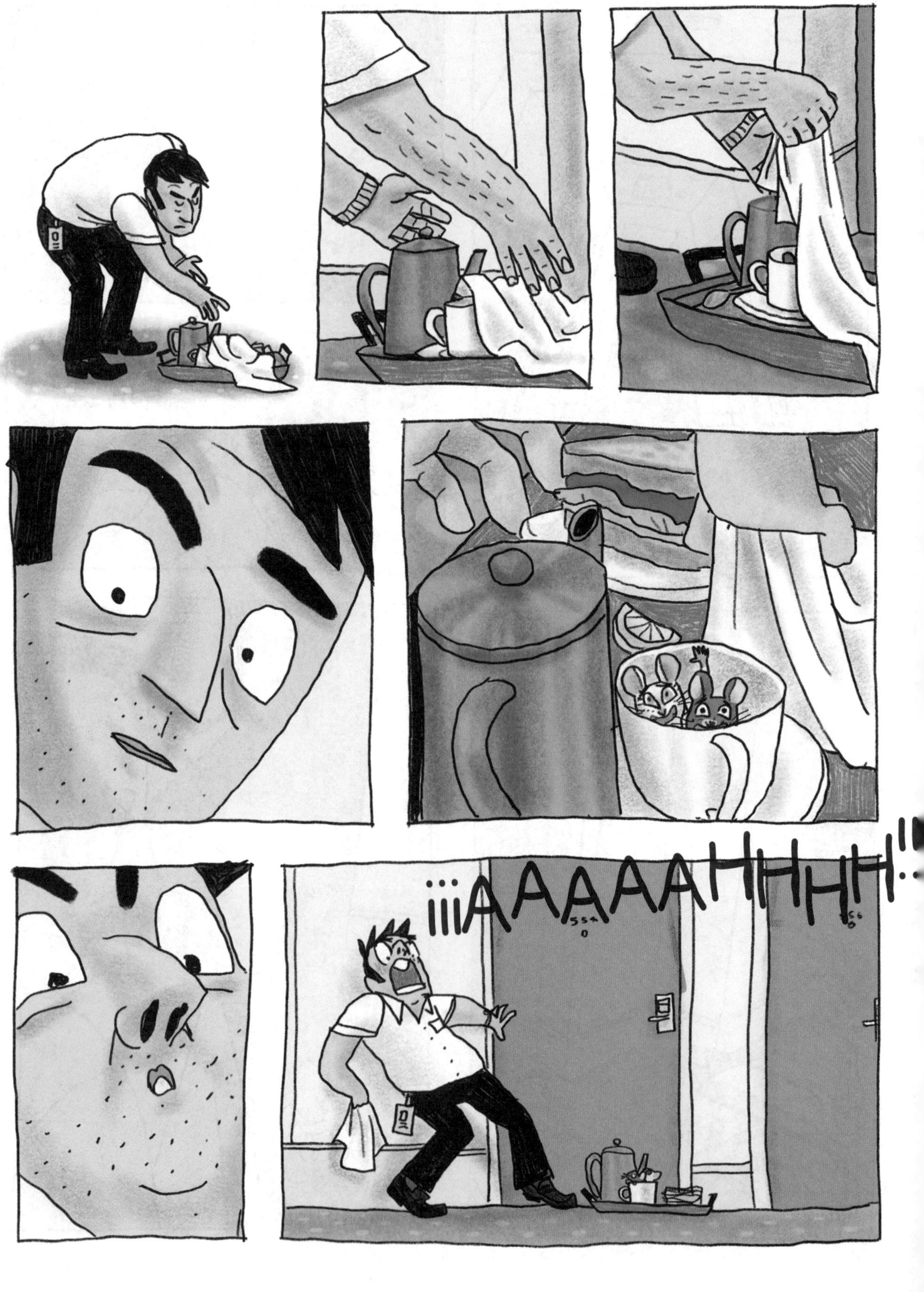
¡¡¡AAAAAHHHH!!!

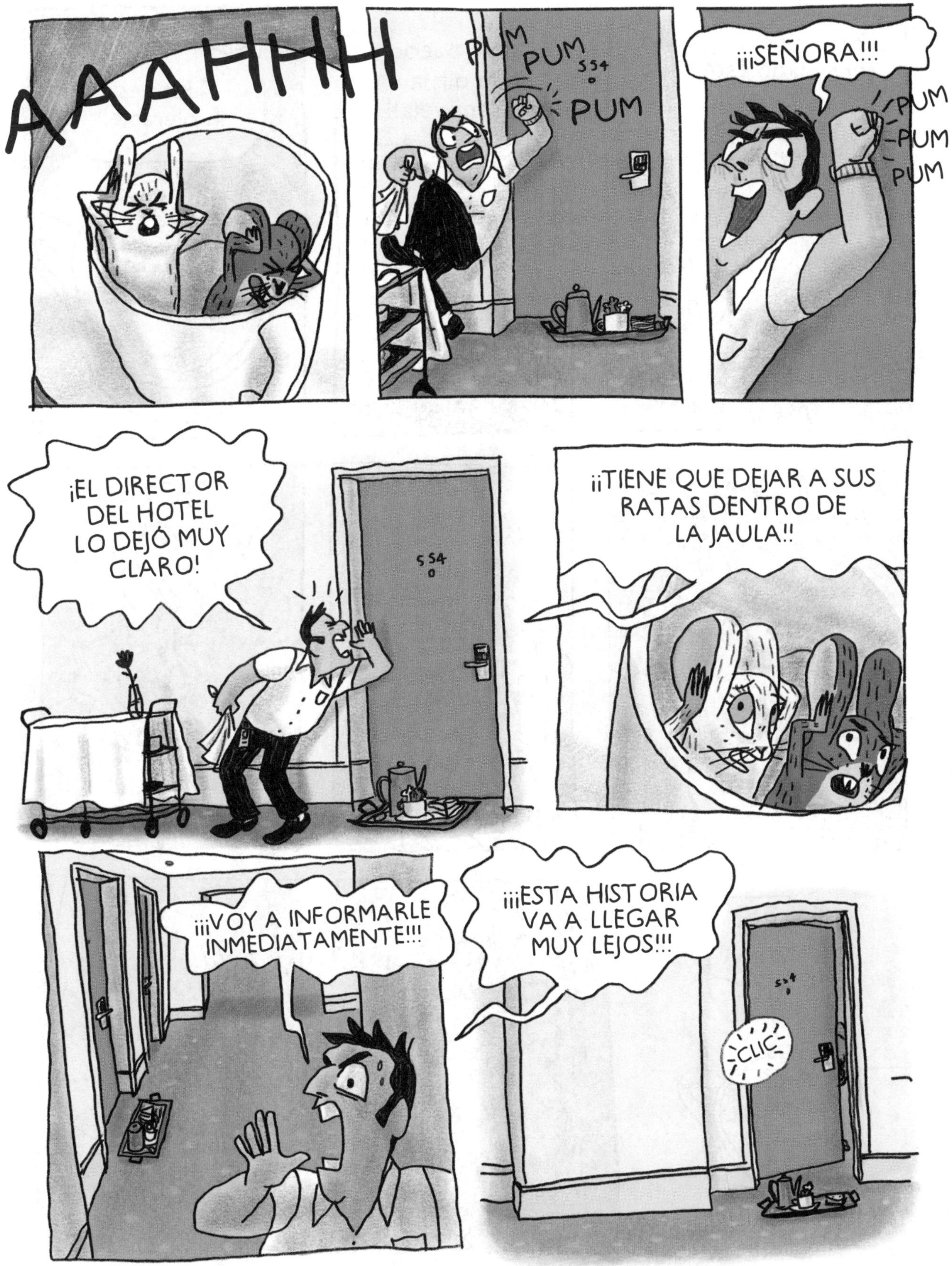
AAAHHHH
PUM PUM PUM
554
¡¡¡SEÑORA!!!
PUM PUM PUM
¡EL DIRECTOR DEL HOTEL LO DEJÓ MUY CLARO!
554
¡¡TIENE QUE DEJAR A SUS RATAS DENTRO DE LA JAULA!!
¡¡¡VOY A INFORMARLE INMEDIATAMENTE!!!
¡¡¡ESTA HISTORIA VA A LLEGAR MUY LEJOS!!!
554
CLIC

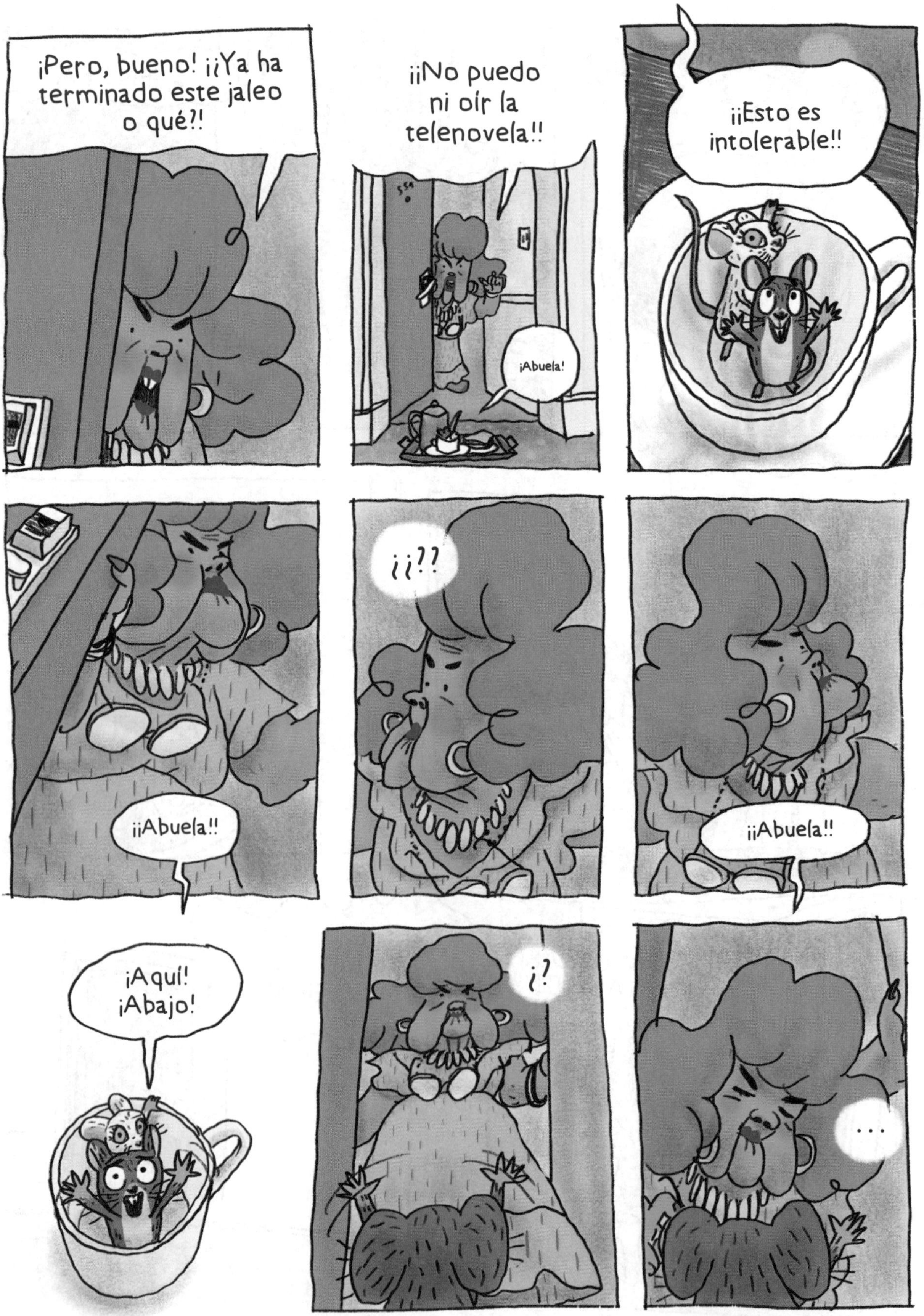
¡Pero, bueno! ¡¿Ya ha terminado este jaleo o qué?!
¡¡No puedo ni oír la telenovela!!
¡Abuela!
¡¡Esto es intolerable!!
¡¡Abuela!!
¿¿??
¡¡Abuela!!
¡Aquí! ¡Abajo!
¿?
...

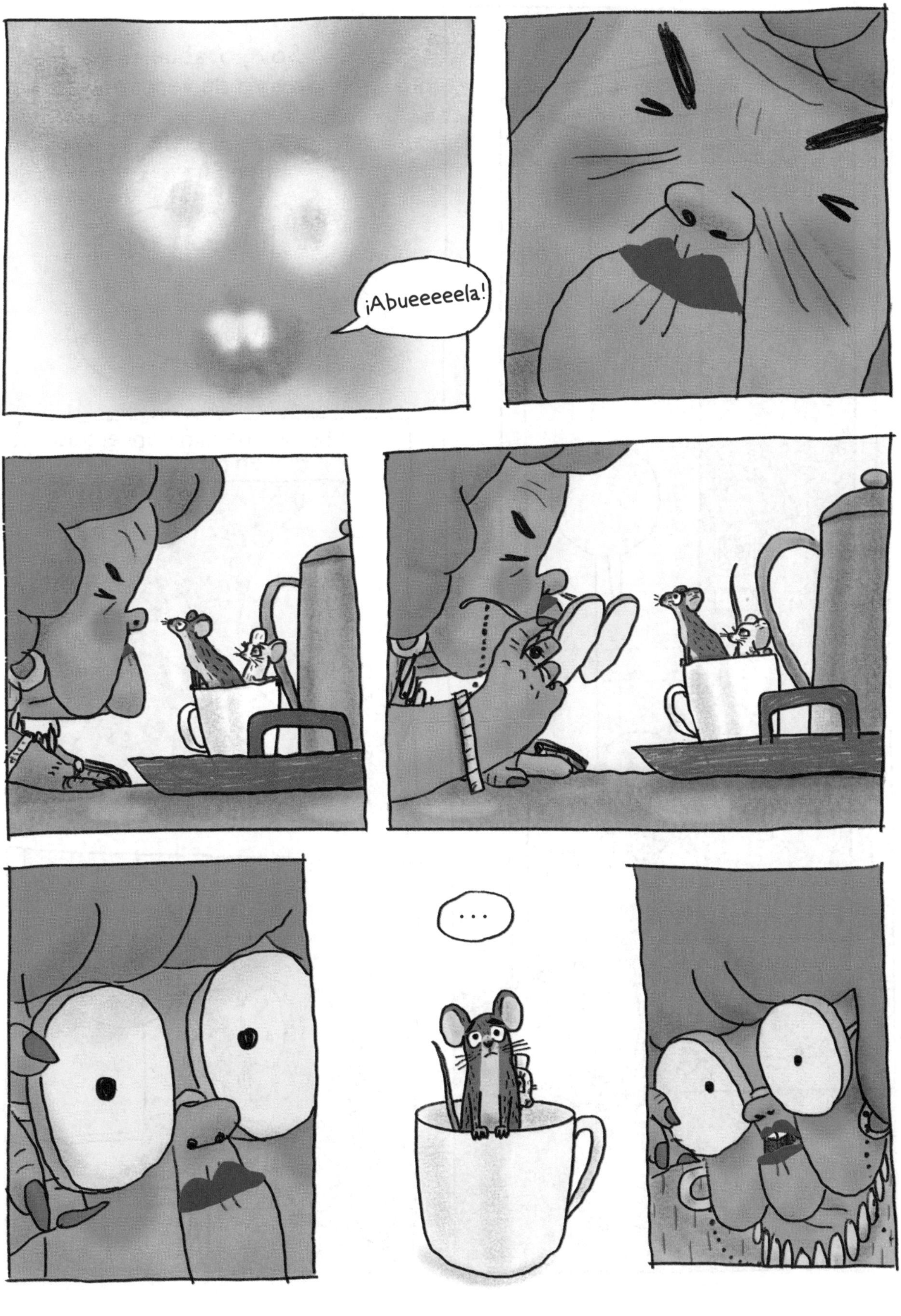
¡Abueeeeela!
...

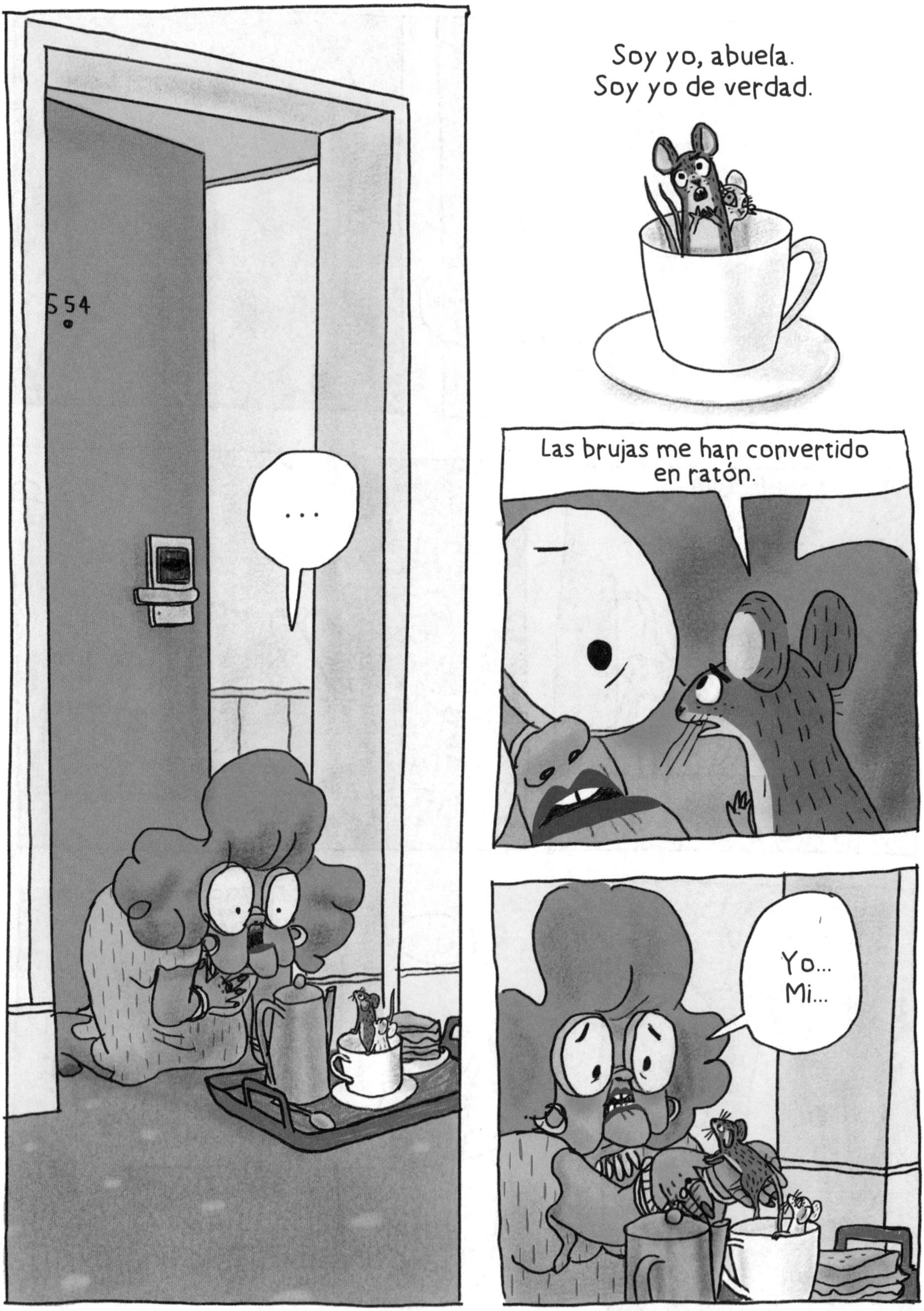
...
Soy yo, abuela. Soy yo de verdad.
Las brujas me han convertido en ratón.
Yo... Mi...

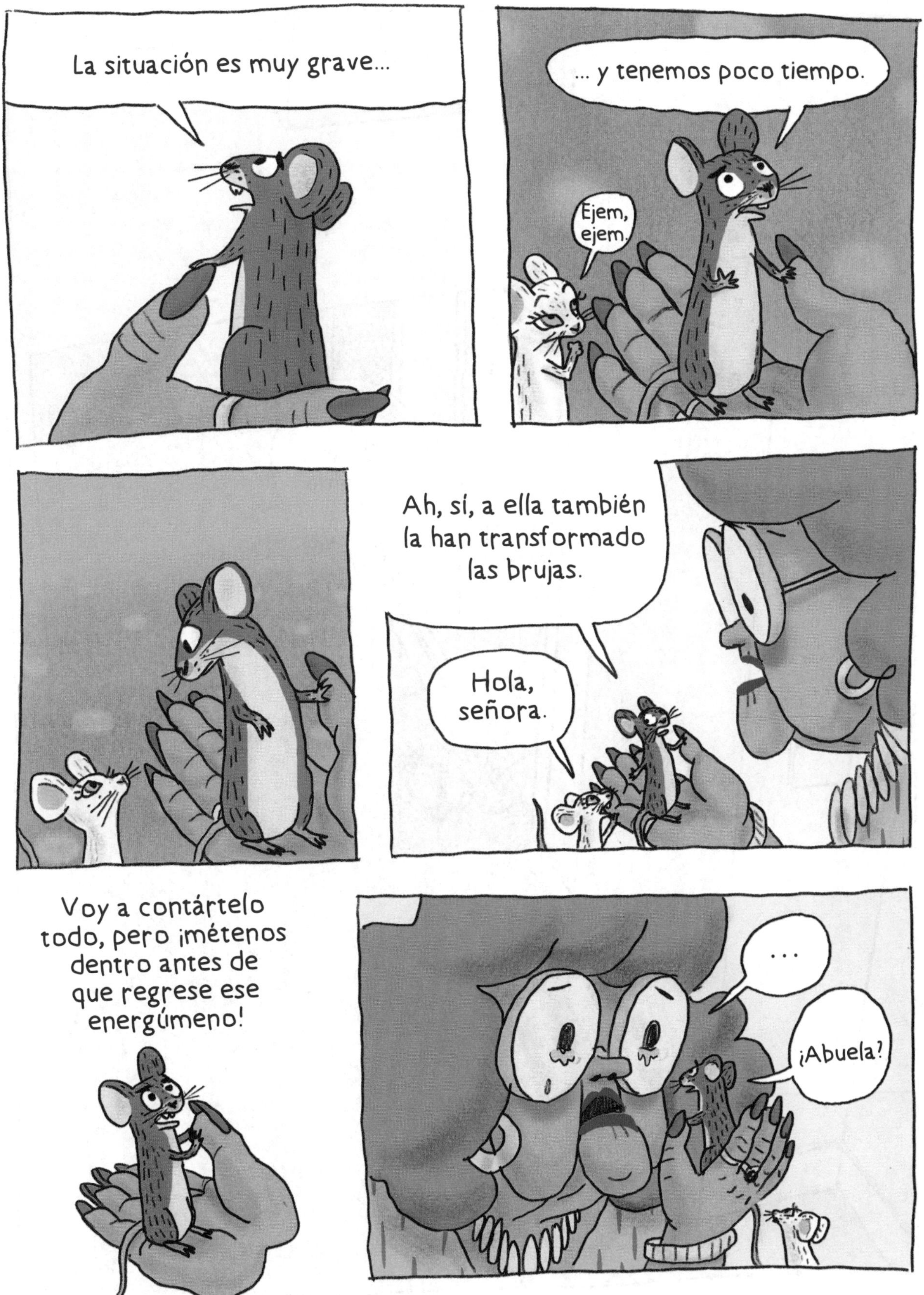
La situación es muy grave...
... y tenemos poco tiempo.
Ejem, ejem.
Ah, sí, a ella también la han transformado las brujas.
Hola, señora.
Voy a contártelo todo, pero ¡métenos dentro antes de que regrese ese energúmeno!
...
¿Abuela?

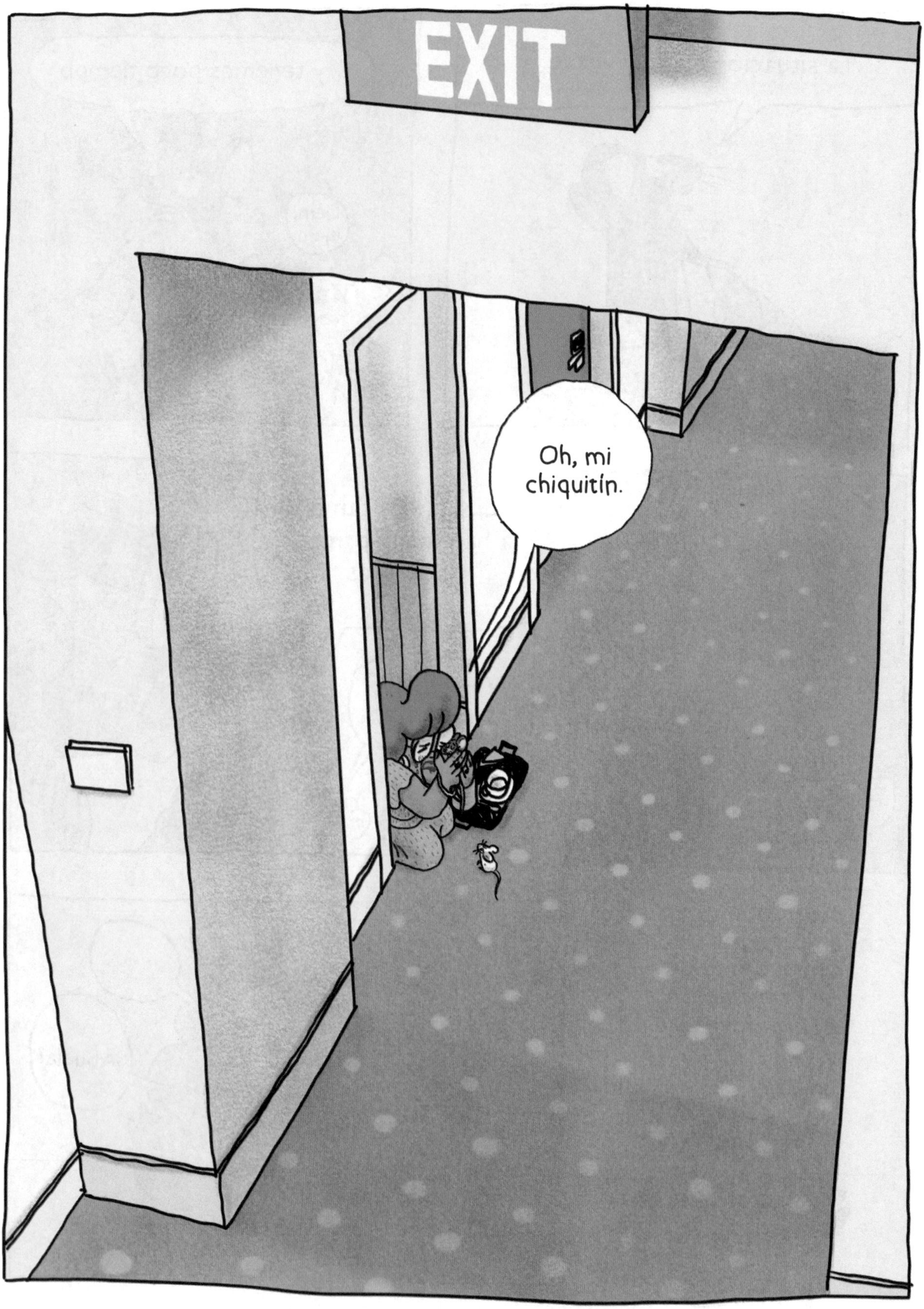
EXIT
Oh, mi chiquitín.

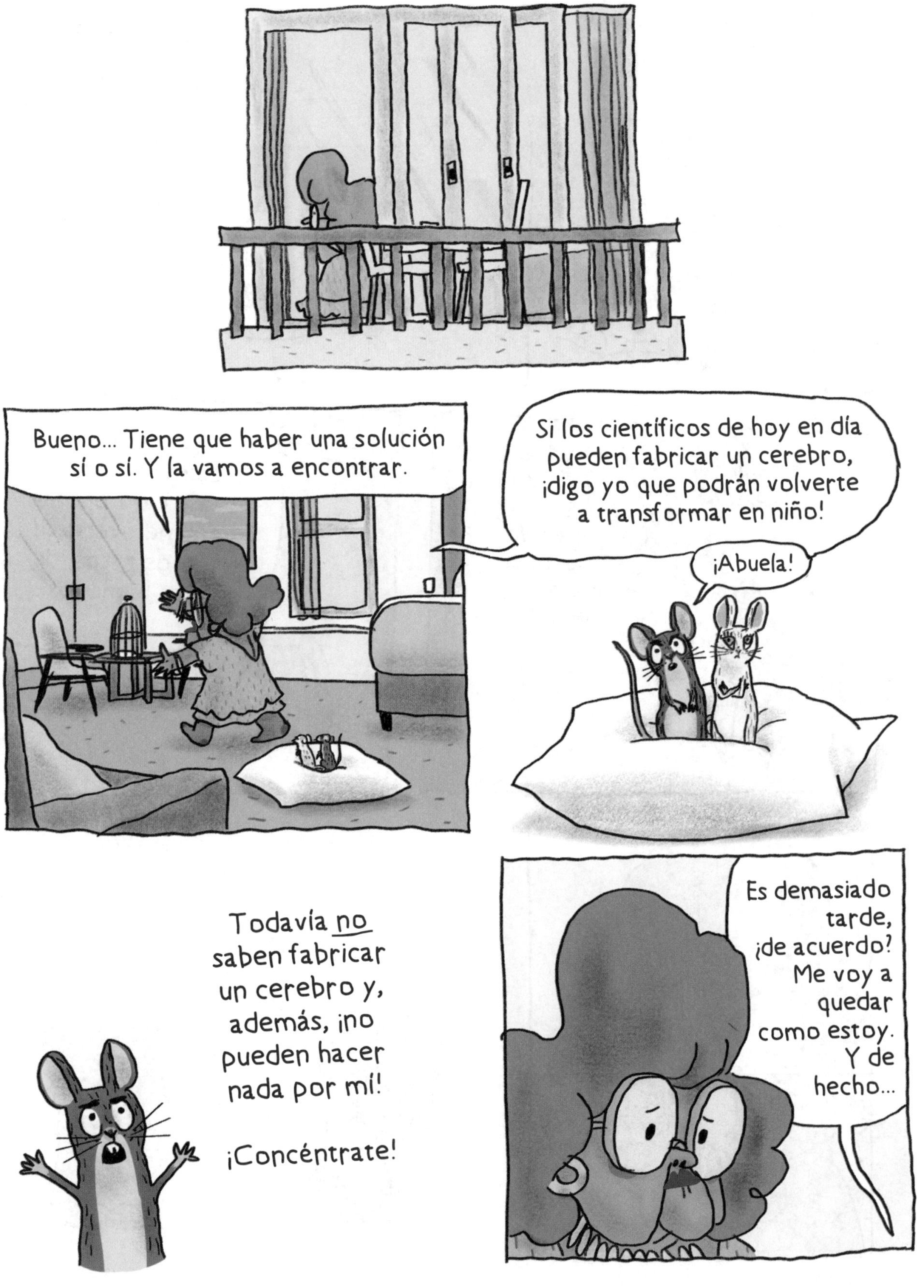
Bueno... Tiene que haber una solución sí o sí. Y la vamos a encontrar.
Si los científicos de hoy en día pueden fabricar un cerebro, ¡digo yo que podrán volverte a transformar en niño!
¡Abuela!
Todavía no saben fabricar un cerebro y, además, ¡no pueden hacer nada por mí!
¡Concéntrate!
Es demasiado tarde, ¿de acuerdo? Me voy a quedar como estoy. Y de hecho...

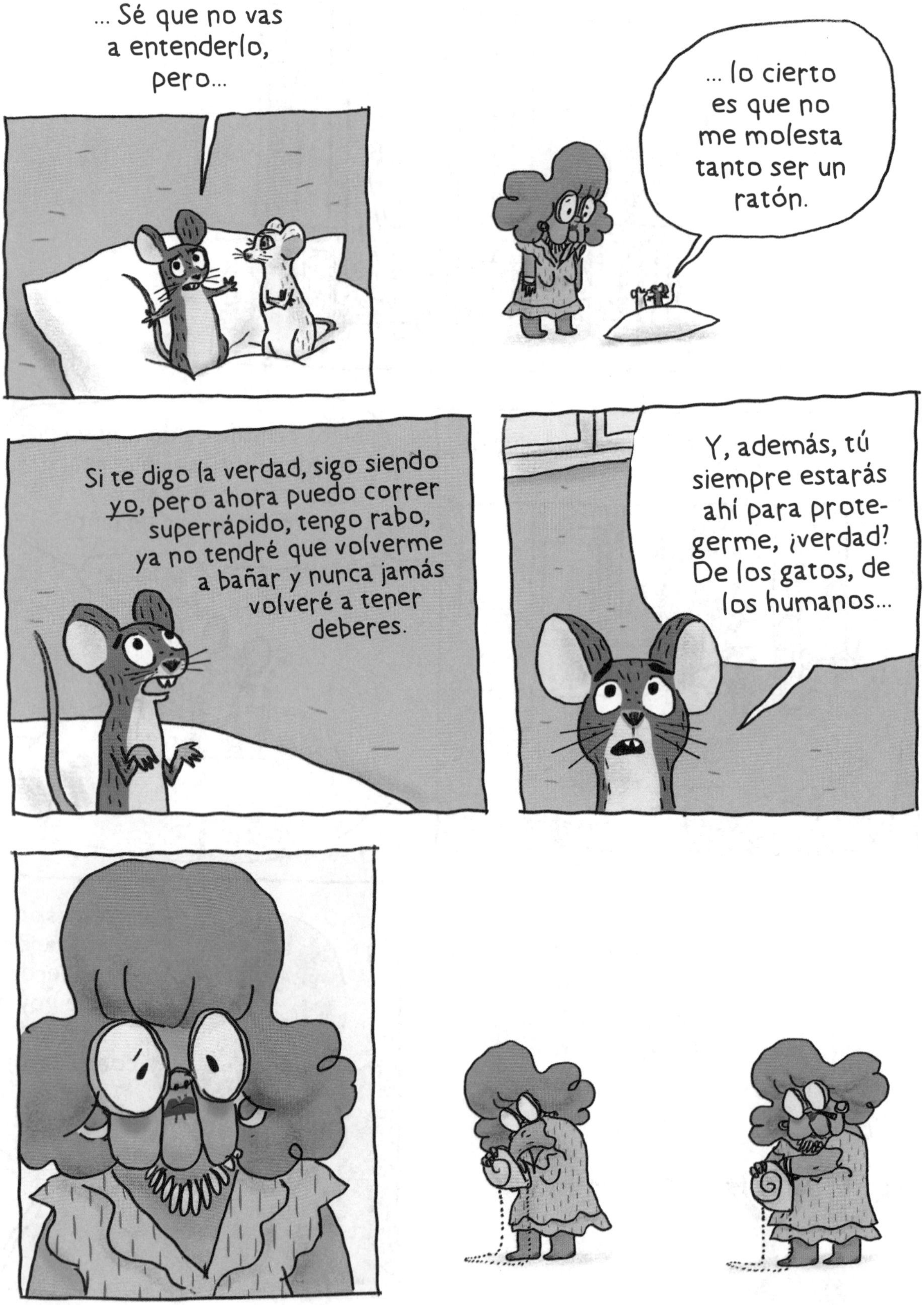
... Sé que no vas a entenderlo, pero...
... lo cierto es que no me molesta tanto ser un ratón.
Si te digo la verdad, sigo siendo yo, pero ahora puedo correr superrápido, tengo rabo, ya no tendré que volverme a bañar y nunca jamás volveré a tener deberes.
Y, además, tú siempre estarás ahí para protegerme, ¿verdad? De los gatos, de los humanos...

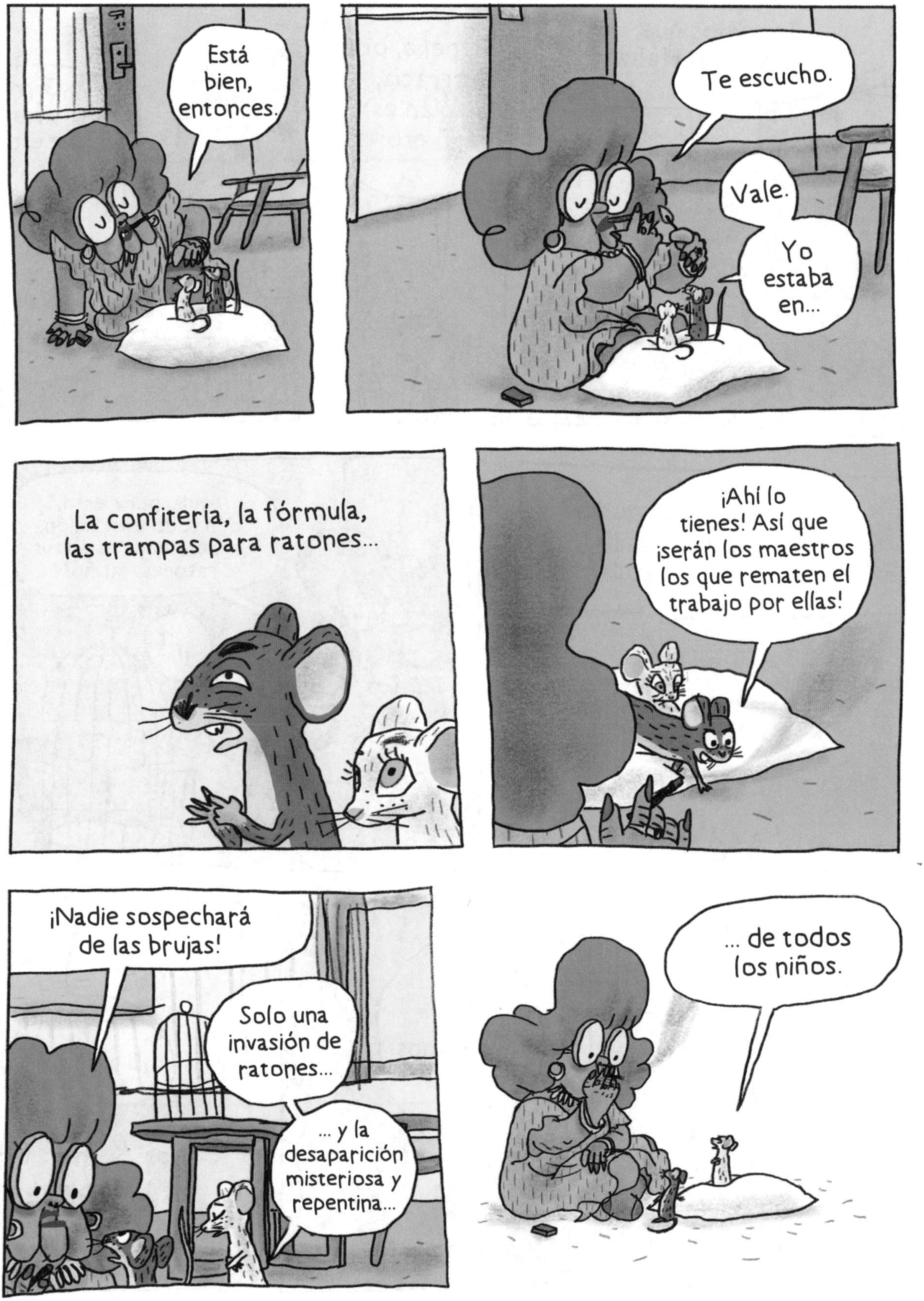
Está bien, entonces.
Te escucho.
Vale.
Yo estaba en...
La confitería, la fórmula, las trampas para ratones...
¡Ahí lo tienes! Así que ¡serán los maestros los que rematen el trabajo por ellas!
¡Nadie sospechará de las brujas!
Solo una invasión de ratones...
... y la desaparición misteriosa y repentina...
... de todos los niños.

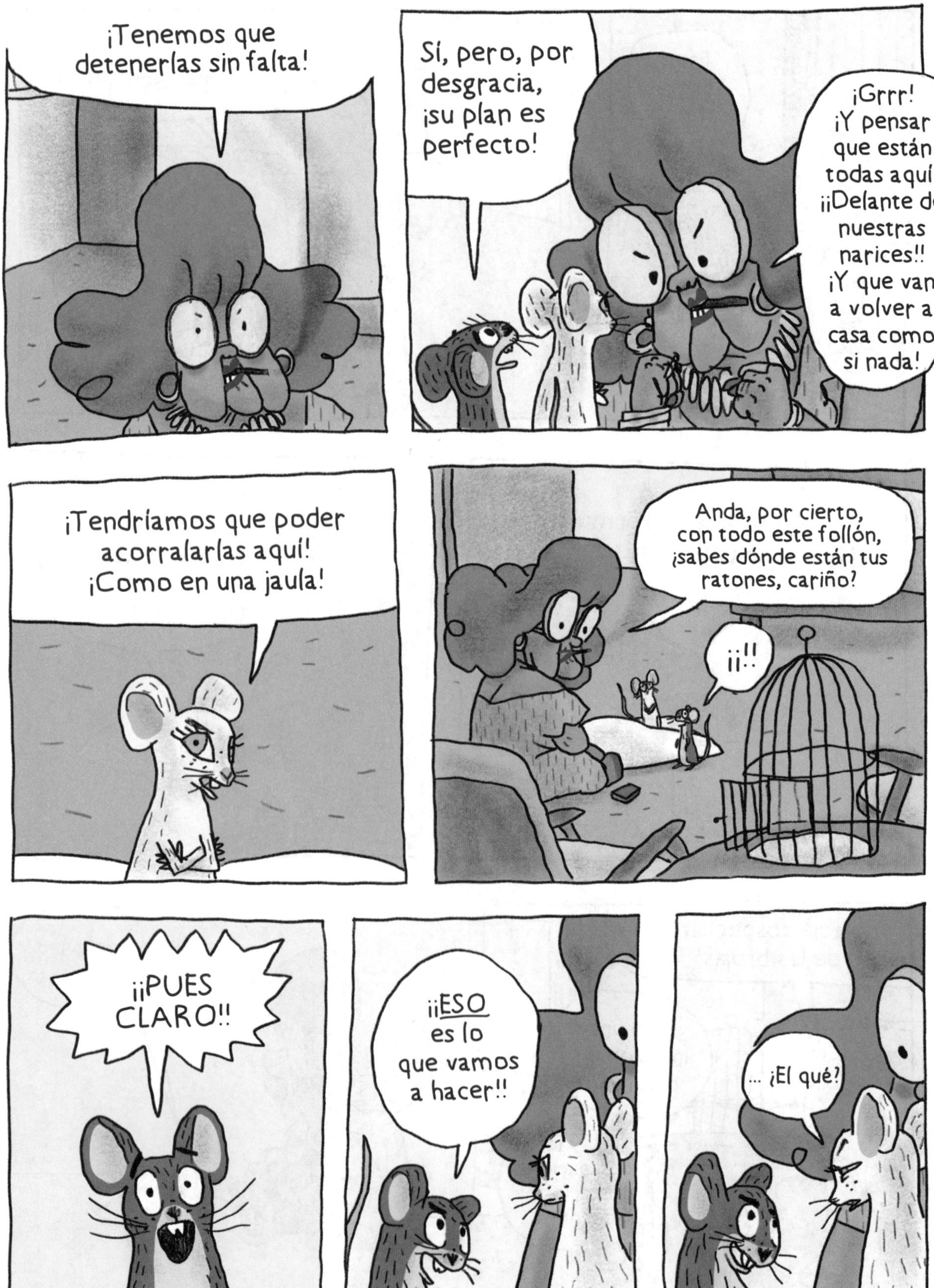
¡Tenemos que detenerlas sin falta!
Sí, pero, por desgracia, ¡su plan es perfecto!
¡Grrr! ¡Y pensar que están todas aquí! ¡¡Delante de nuestras narices!! ¡Y que van a volver a casa como si nada!
¡Tendríamos que poder acorralarlas aquí! ¡Como en una jaula!
Anda, por cierto, con todo este follón, ¿sabes dónde están tus ratones, cariño?
¡¡..!!
¡¡PUES CLARO!!
¡¡ESO es lo que vamos a hacer!!
... ¿El qué?

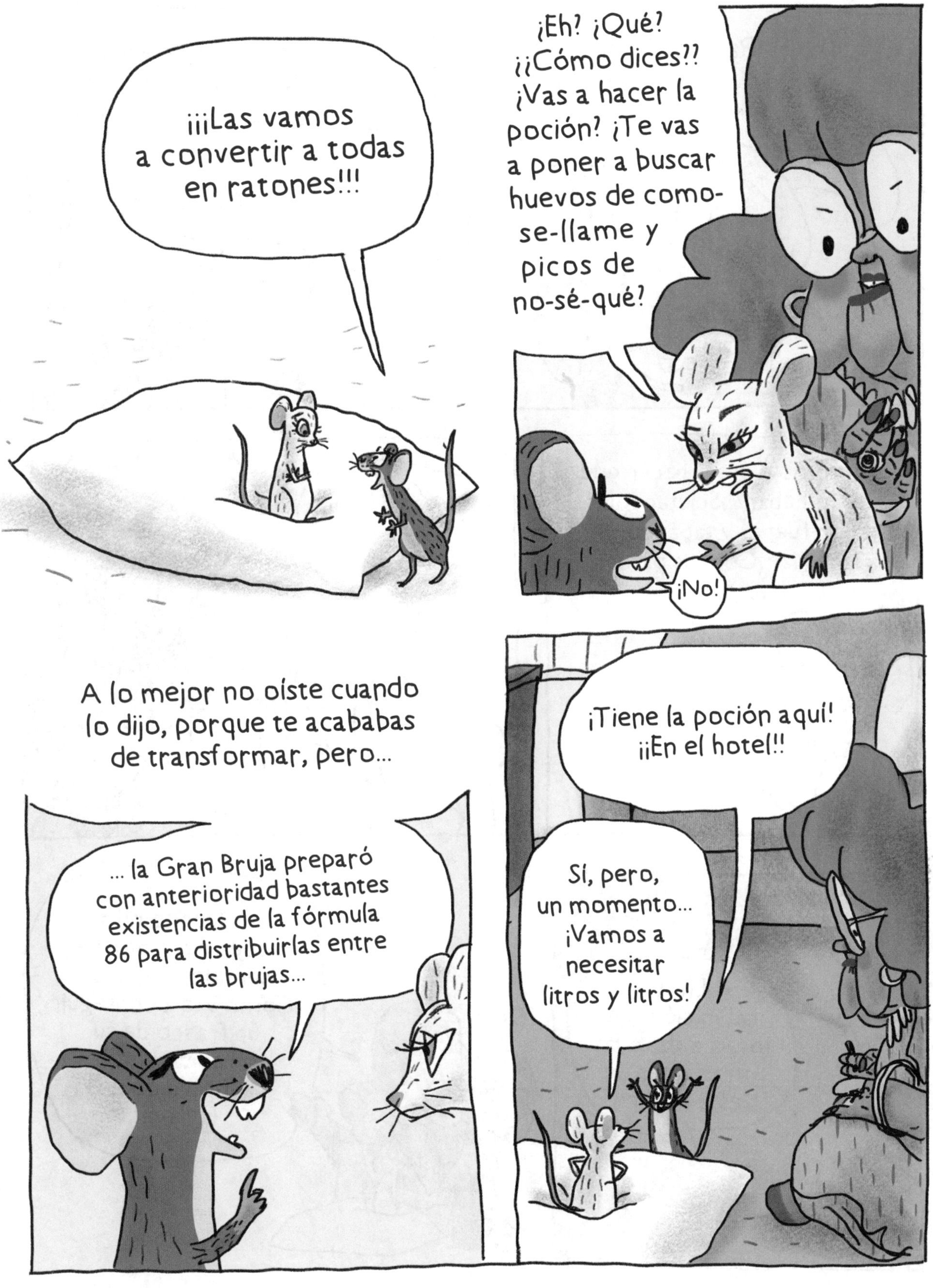

¡¡¡Las vamos a convertir a todas en ratones!!!
¿Eh? ¿Qué? ¿¿Cómo dices?? ¿Vas a hacer la poción? ¿Te vas a poner a buscar huevos de como-se-llame y picos de no-sé-qué?
¡No!
A lo mejor no oíste cuando lo dijo, porque te acababas de transformar, pero...
... la Gran Bruja preparó con anterioridad bastantes existencias de la fórmula 86 para distribuirlas entre las brujas...
¡Tiene la poción aquí! ¡¡En el hotel!!
Sí, pero, un momento... ¡Vamos a necesitar litros y litros!

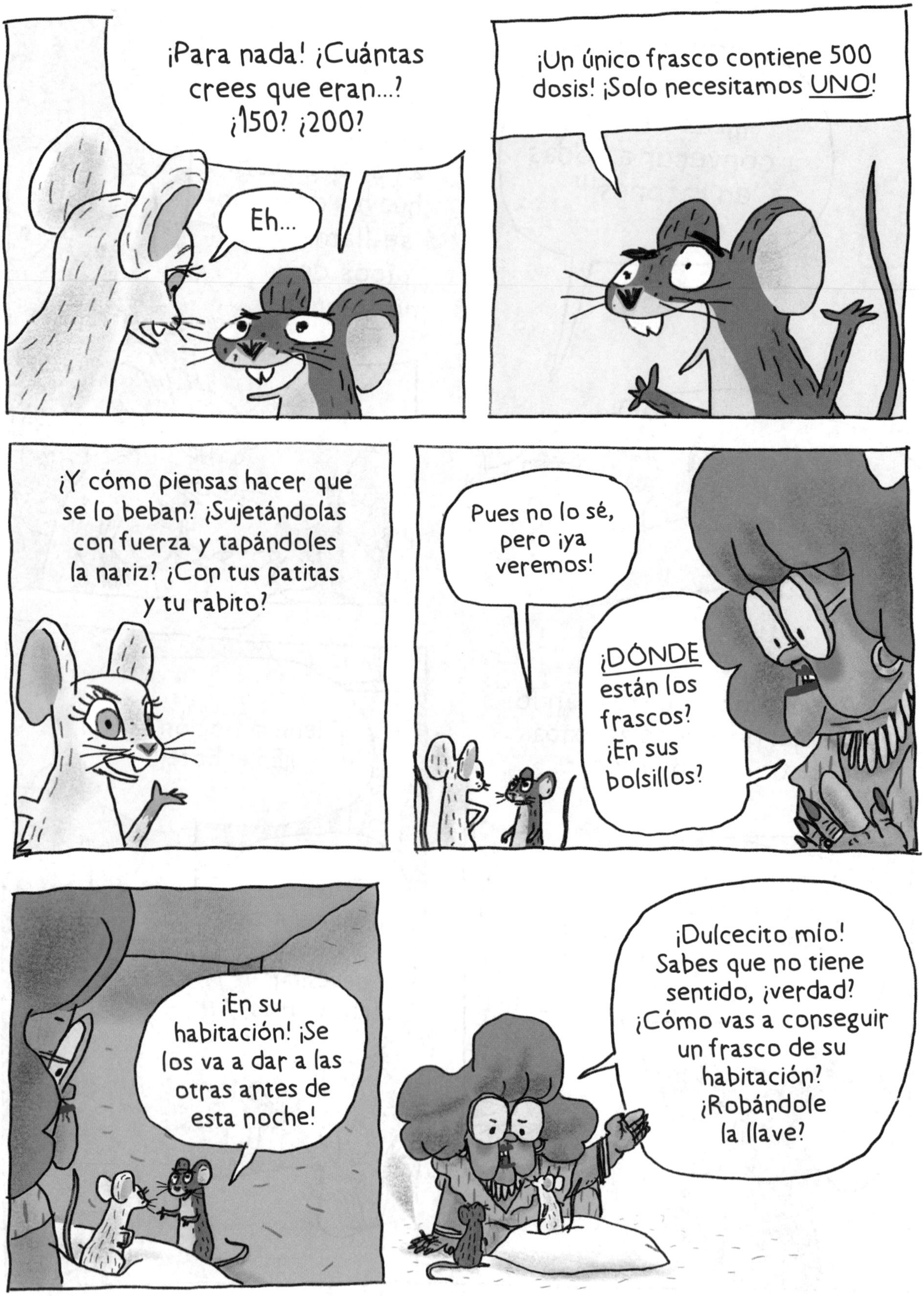
¡Para nada! ¿Cuántas crees que eran...? ¿150? ¿200?
Eh...
¡Un único frasco contiene 500 dosis! ¡Solo necesitamos UNO!
¿Y cómo piensas hacer que se lo beban? ¿Sujetándolas con fuerza y tapándoles la nariz? ¿Con tus patitas y tu rabito?
Pues no lo sé, pero ¡ya veremos!
¿DÓNDE están los frascos? ¿En sus bolsillos?
¡En su habitación! ¡Se los va a dar a las otras antes de esta noche!
¡Dulcecito mío! Sabes que no tiene sentido, ¿verdad? ¿Cómo vas a conseguir un frasco de su habitación? ¿Robándole la llave?

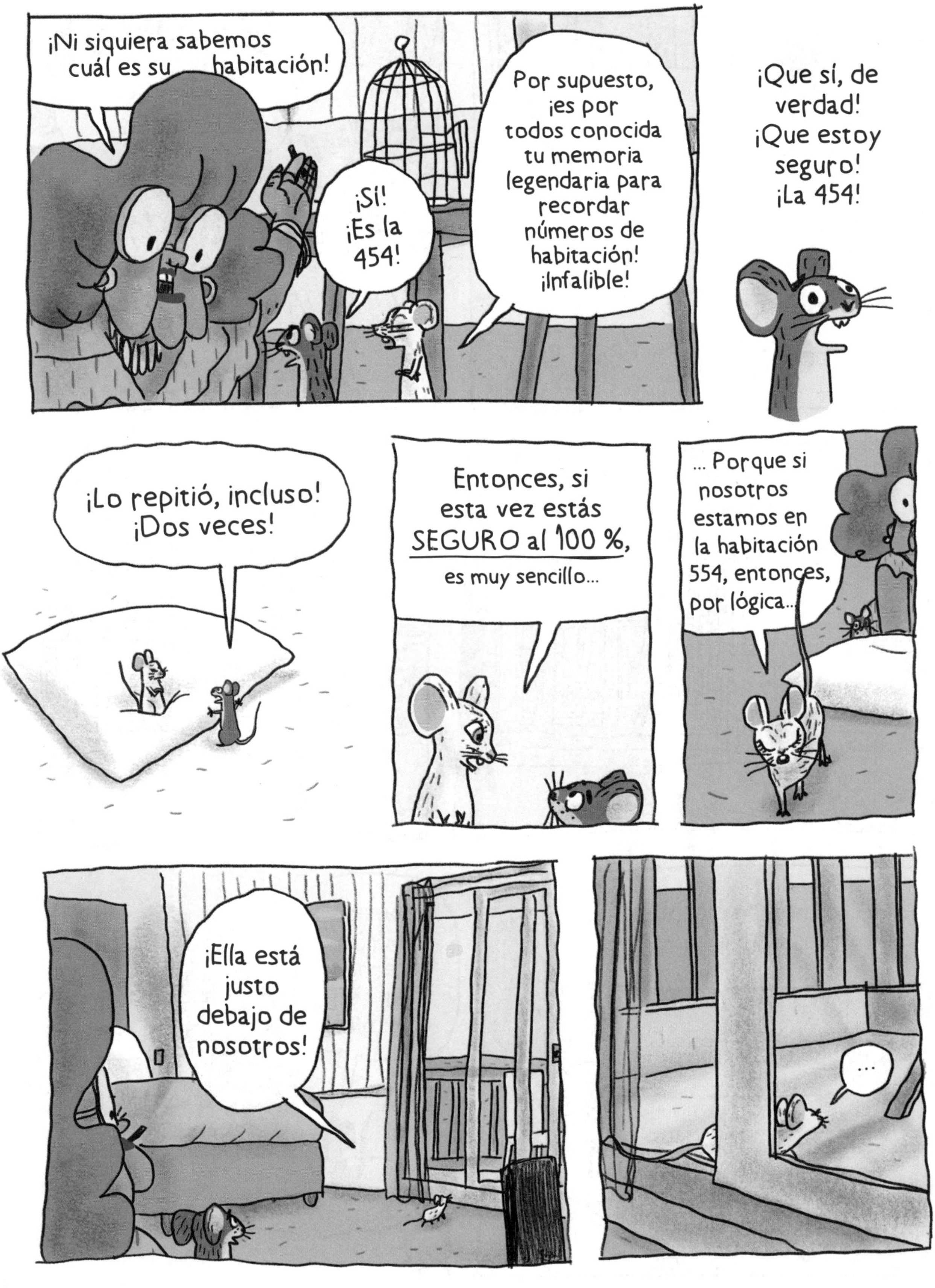
¡Ni siquiera sabemos cuál es su habitación!
¡Sí! ¡Es la 454!
Por supuesto, ¡es por todos conocida tu memoria legendaria para recordar números de habitación! ¡Infalible!
¡Que sí, de verdad! ¡Que estoy seguro! ¡La 454!
¡Lo repitió, incluso! ¡Dos veces!
Entonces, si esta vez estás SEGURO al 100 %, es muy sencillo...
... Porque si nosotros estamos en la habitación 554, entonces, por lógica...
¡Ella está justo debajo de nosotros!
...

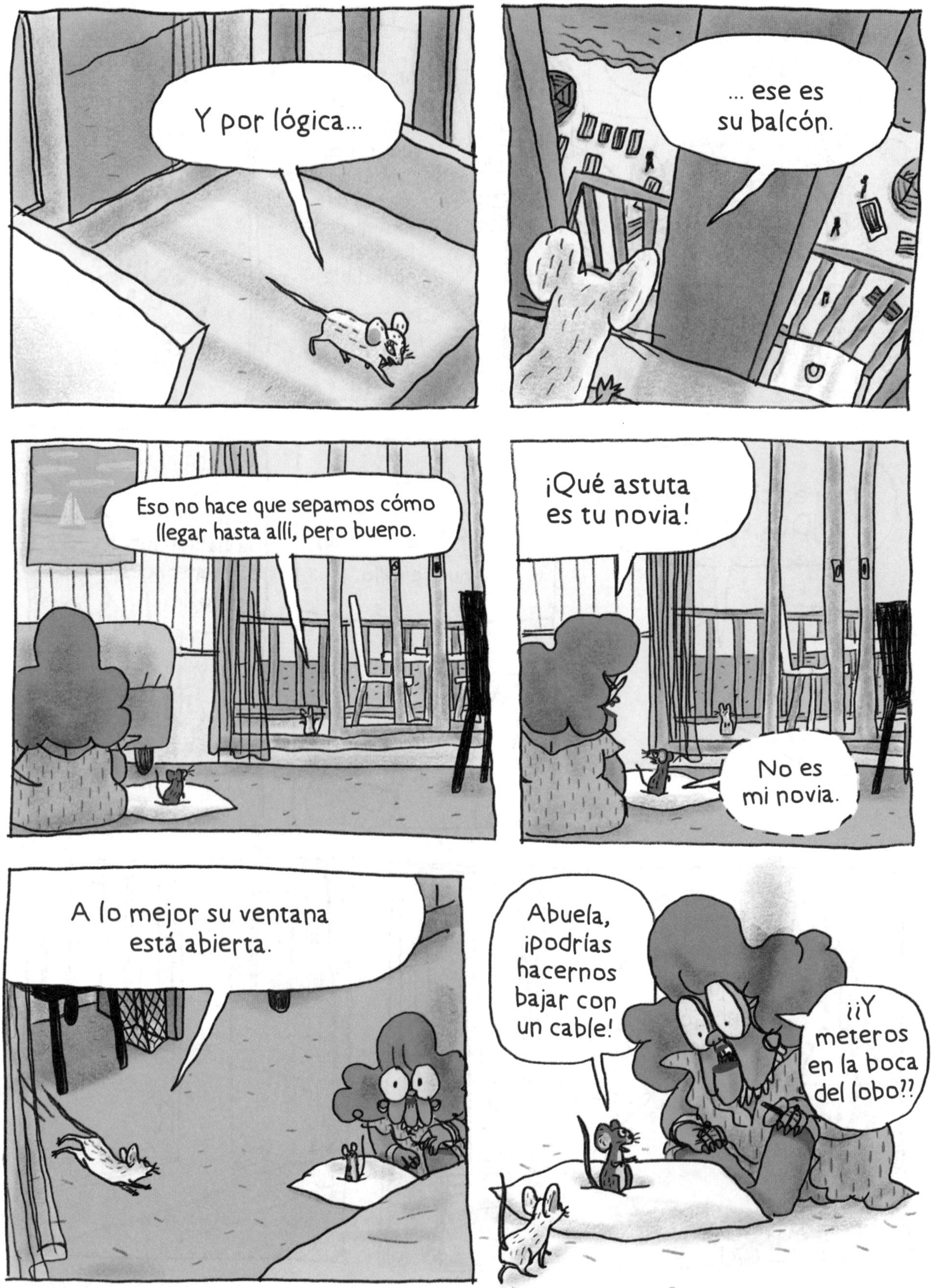
Y por lógica...
... ese es su balcón.
Eso no hace que sepamos cómo llegar hasta allí, pero bueno.
¡Qué astuta es tu novia!
No es mi novia.
A lo mejor su ventana está abierta.
Abuela, ¿podrías hacernos bajar con un cable!
¡¿Y meteros en la boca del lobo?!

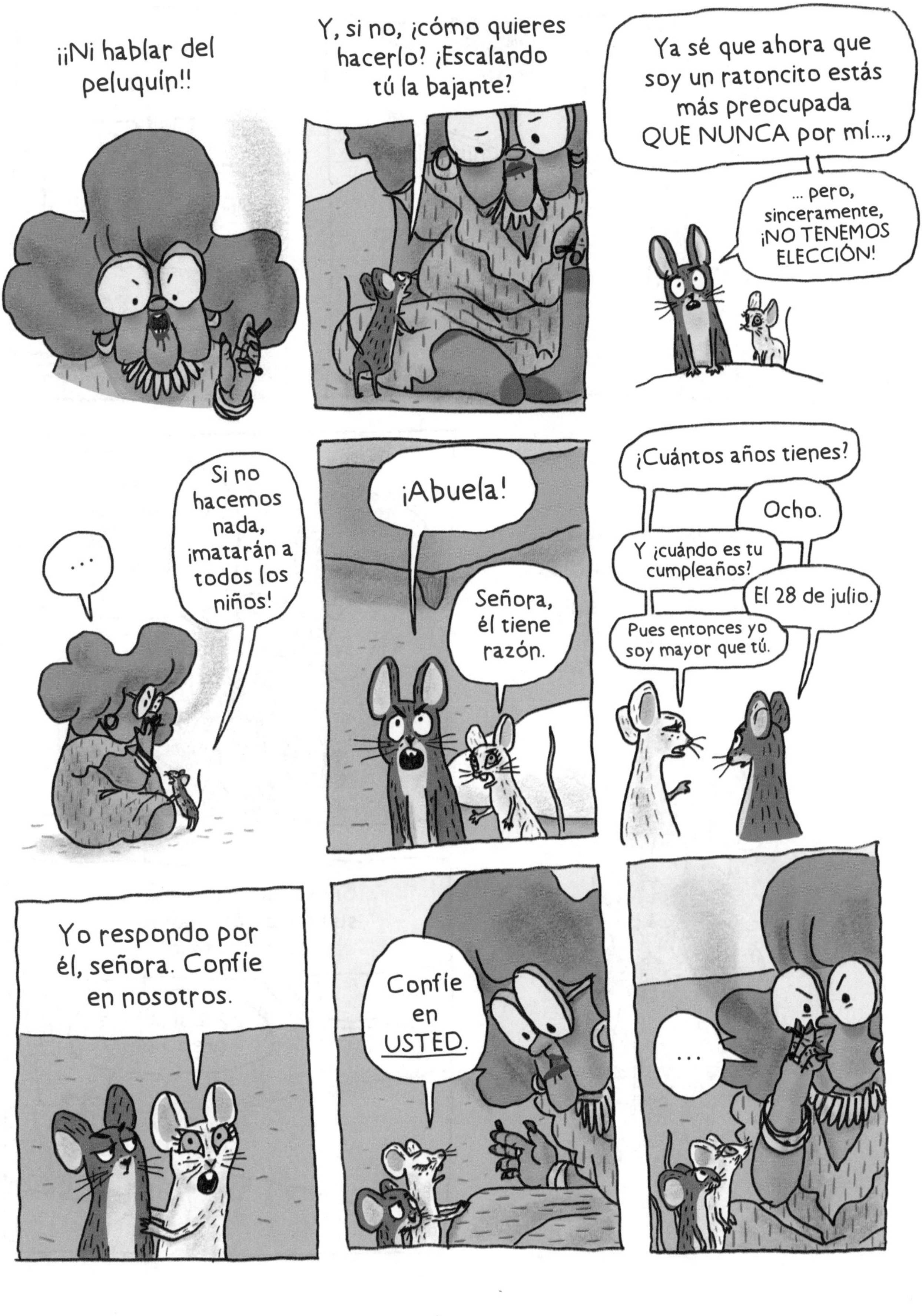
¡¡Ni hablar del peluquín!!
Y, si no, ¿cómo quieres hacerlo? ¿Escalando tú la bajante?
Ya sé que ahora que soy un ratoncito estás más preocupada QUE NUNCA por mí...,
... pero, sinceramente, ¡NO TENEMOS ELECCIÓN!
...
Si no hacemos nada, ¡matarán a todos los niños!
¡Abuela!
Señora, él tiene razón.
¿Cuántos años tienes?
Ocho.
Y ¿cuándo es tu cumpleaños?
El 28 de julio.
Pues entonces yo soy mayor que tú.
Yo respondo por él, señora. Confíe en nosotros.
Confíe en USTED.
...

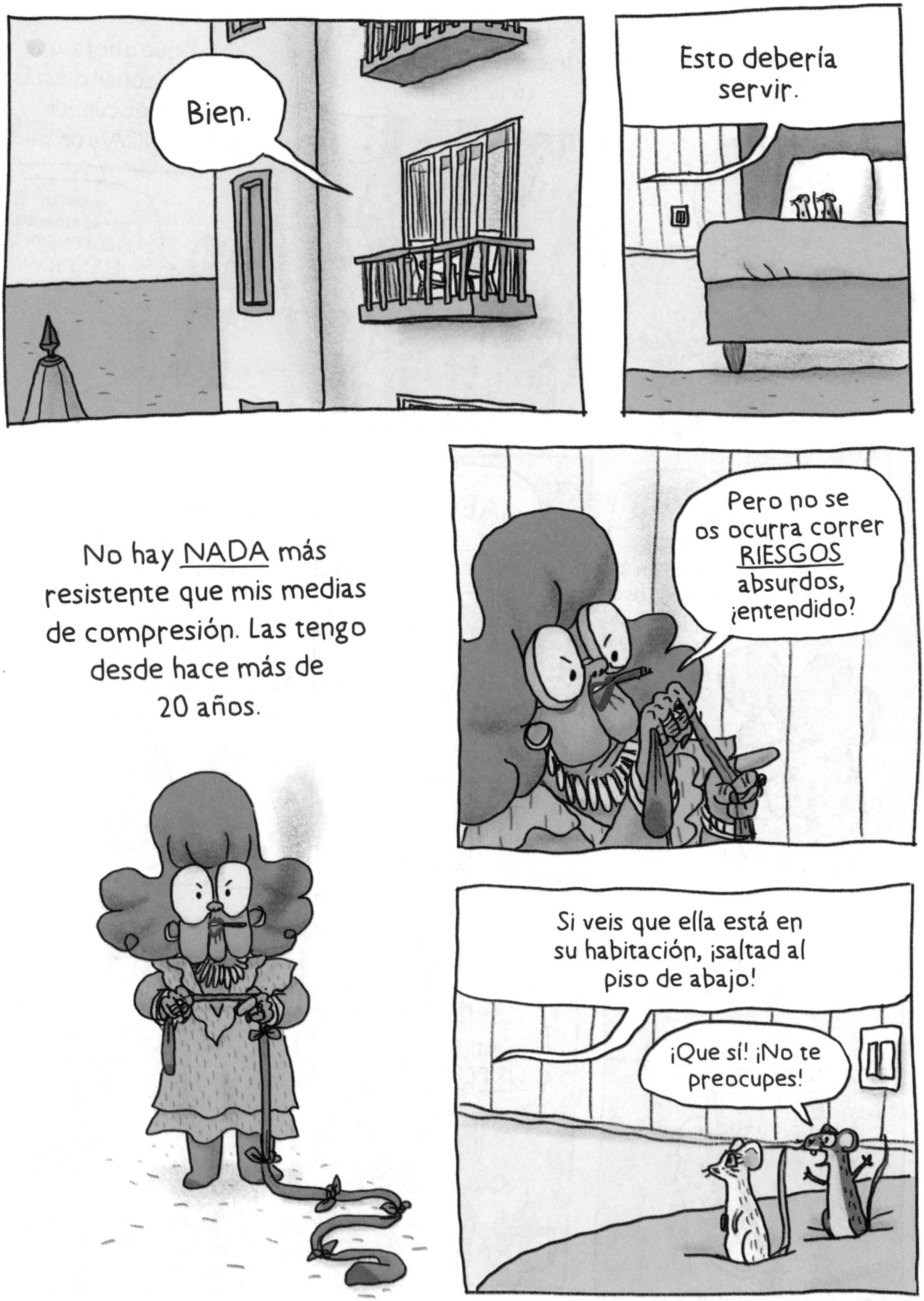
Bien.
Esto debería servir.
No hay NADA más resistente que mis medias de compresión. Las tengo desde hace más de 20 años.
Pero no se os ocurra correr RIESGOS absurdos, ¡entendido?
Si veis que ella está en su habitación, ¡saltad al piso de abajo!
¡Que sí! ¡No te preocupes!

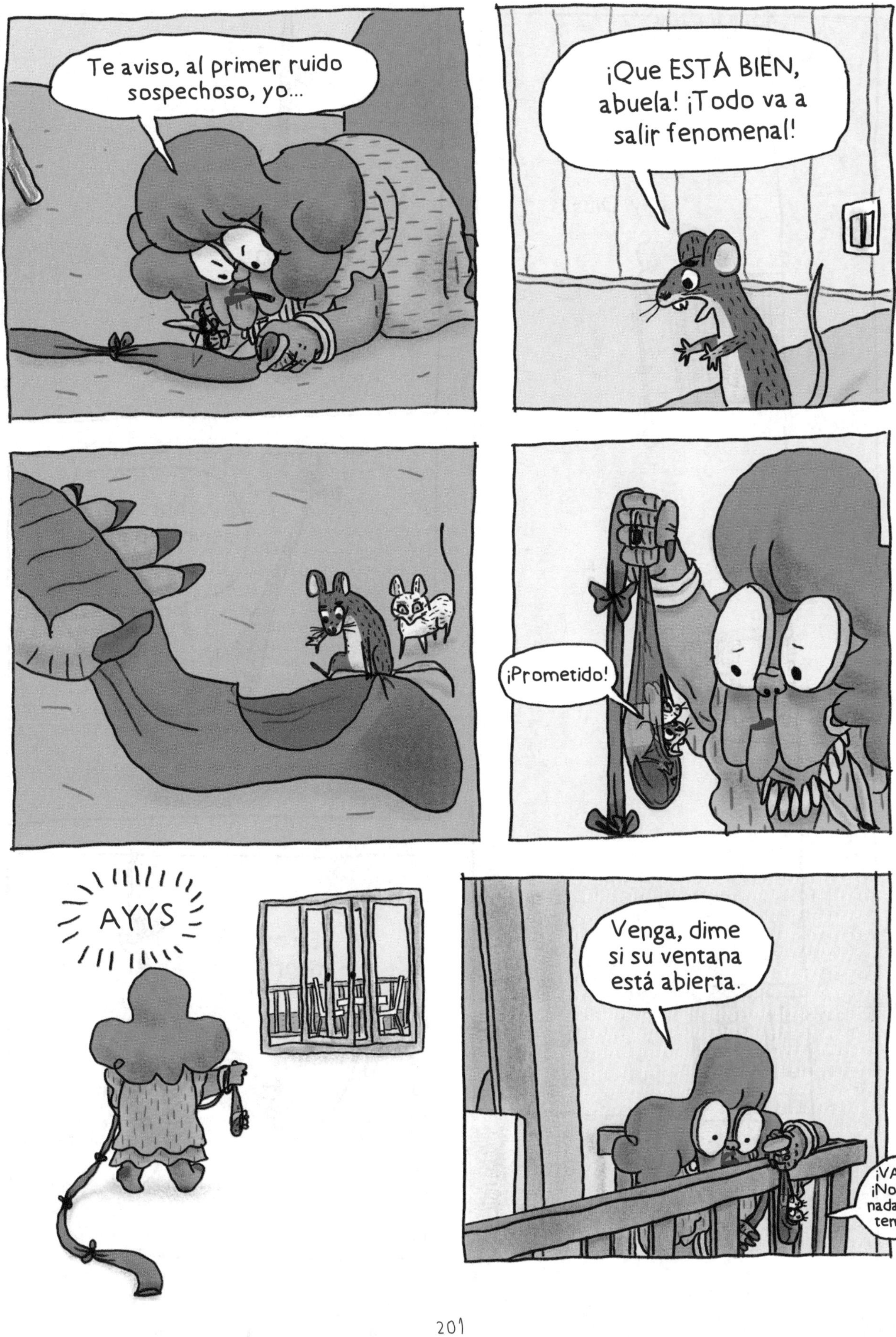
Te aviso, al primer ruido sospechoso, yo...
¡Que ESTÁ BIEN, abuela! ¡Todo va a salir fenomenal!
¡Prometido!
AYYS
Venga, dime si su ventana está abierta.
¡VALE! ¡No hay nada que temer!

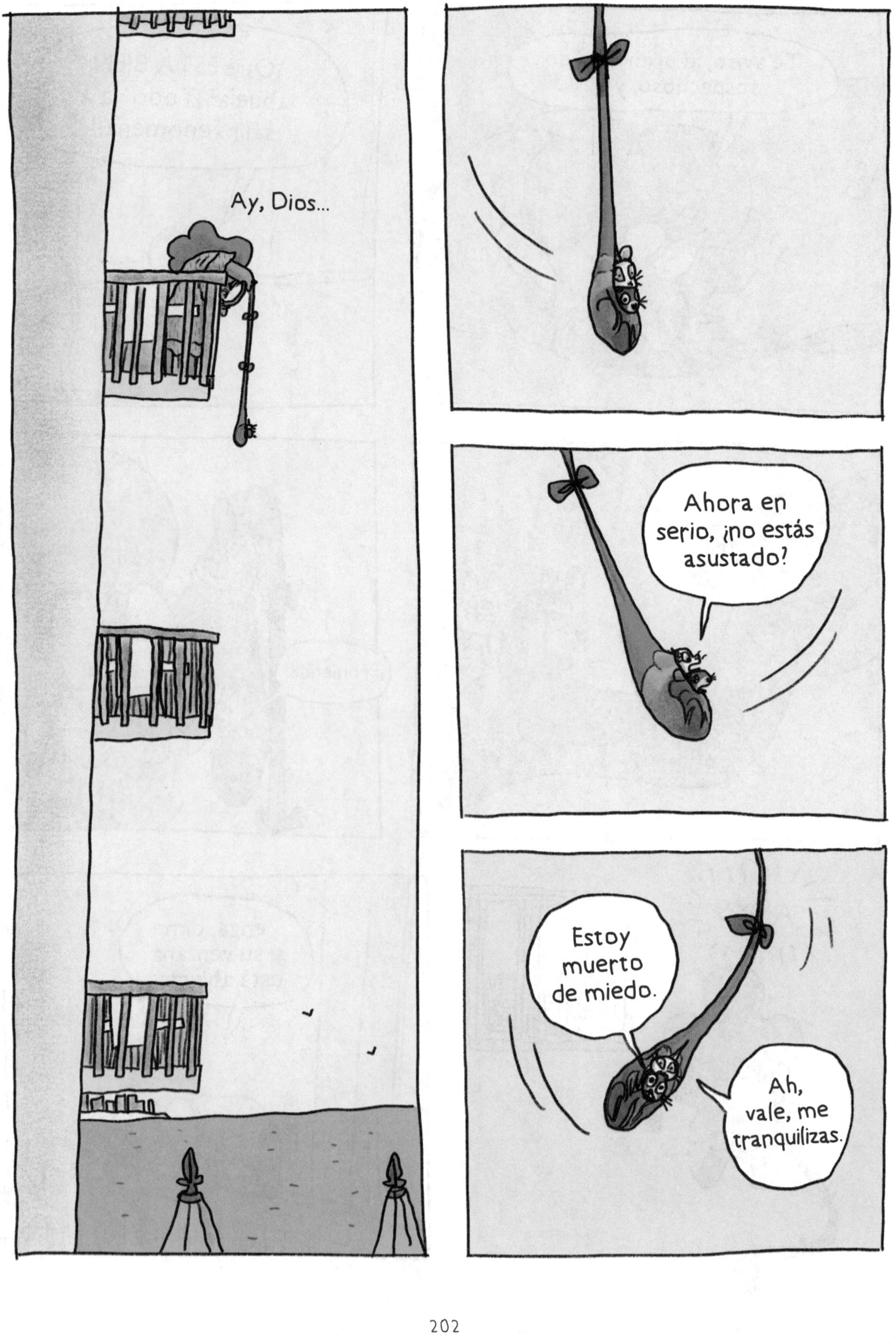
Ay, Dios...
Ahora en serio, ¡no estás asustado?
Estoy muerto de miedo.
Ah, vale, me tranquilizas.

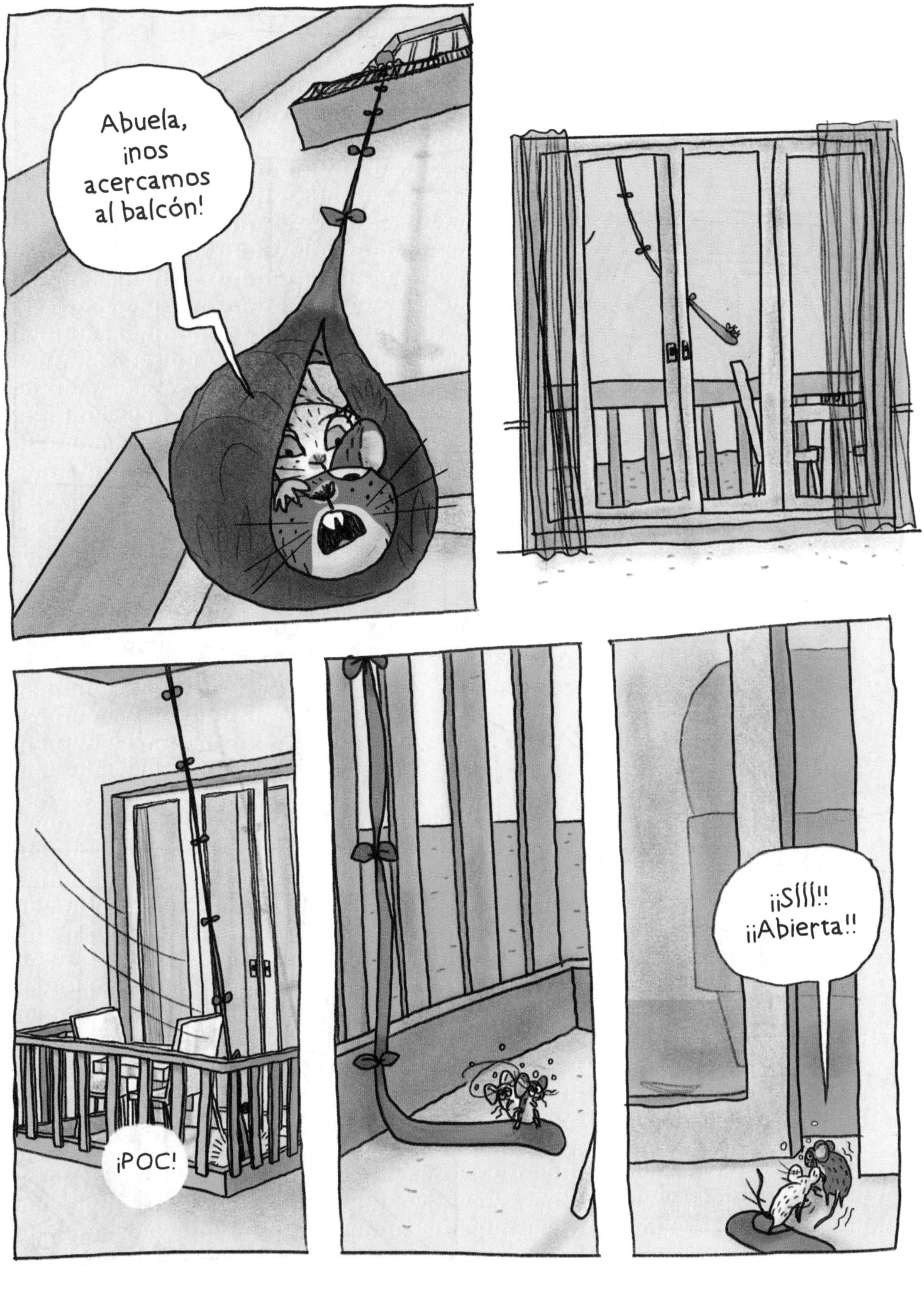
Abuela, ¡nos acercamos al balcón!
¡POC!
¡¡SÍÍÍ!! ¡¡Abierta!!

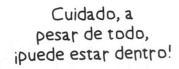

Cuidado, a pesar de todo, ¡puede estar dentro!

¡A mí me da la sensación de que aquí no hay nadie!

¡Quizá está en el baño?

No sé si las brujas hacen pis...

Bueno, en teoría, beben, así que...

¡Eh! ¡Vamos!

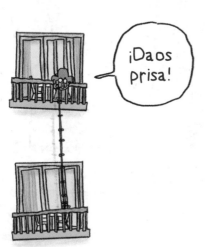

¡Daos prisa!

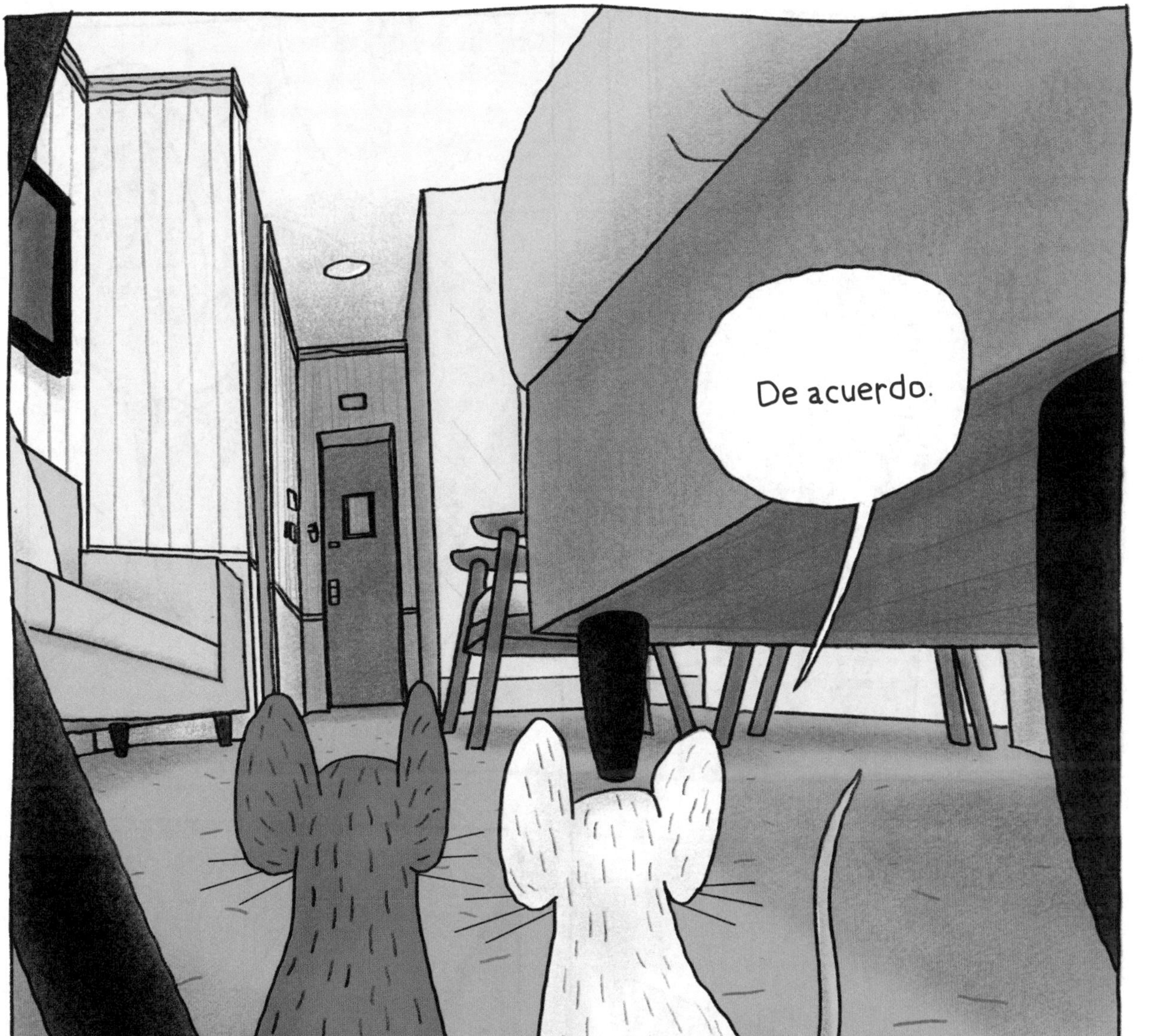
De acuerdo.

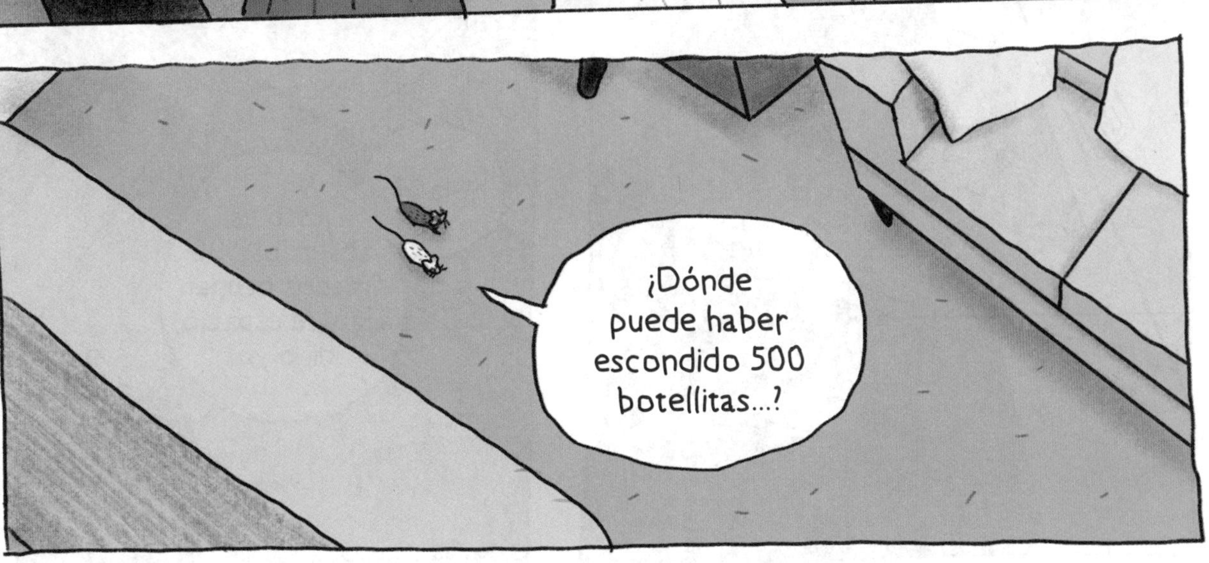
¿Dónde puede haber escondido 500 botellitas...?

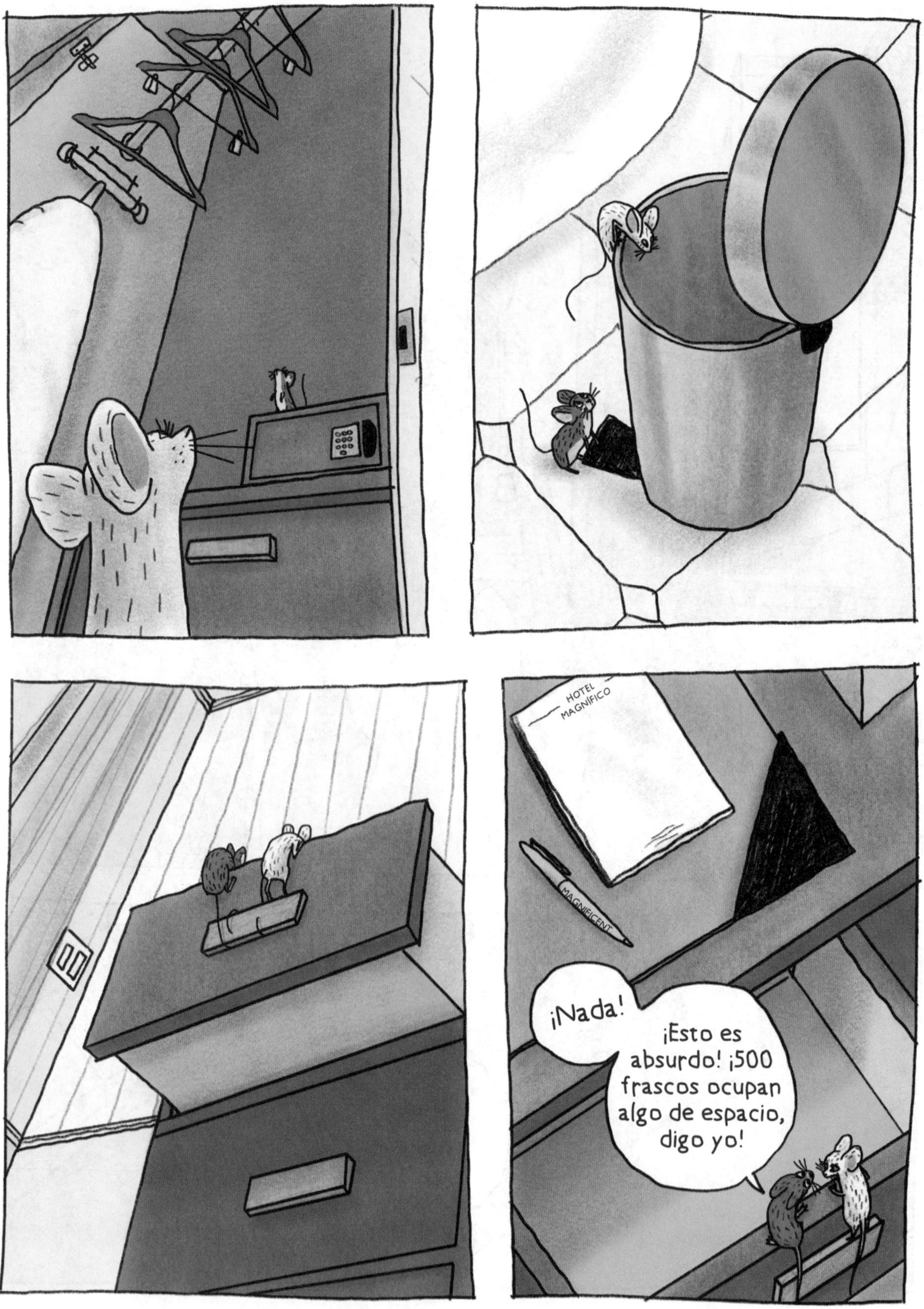
HOTEL MAGNÍFICO
MAGNIFICENT
¡Nada!
¡Esto es absurdo! ¡500 frascos ocupan algo de espacio, digo yo!

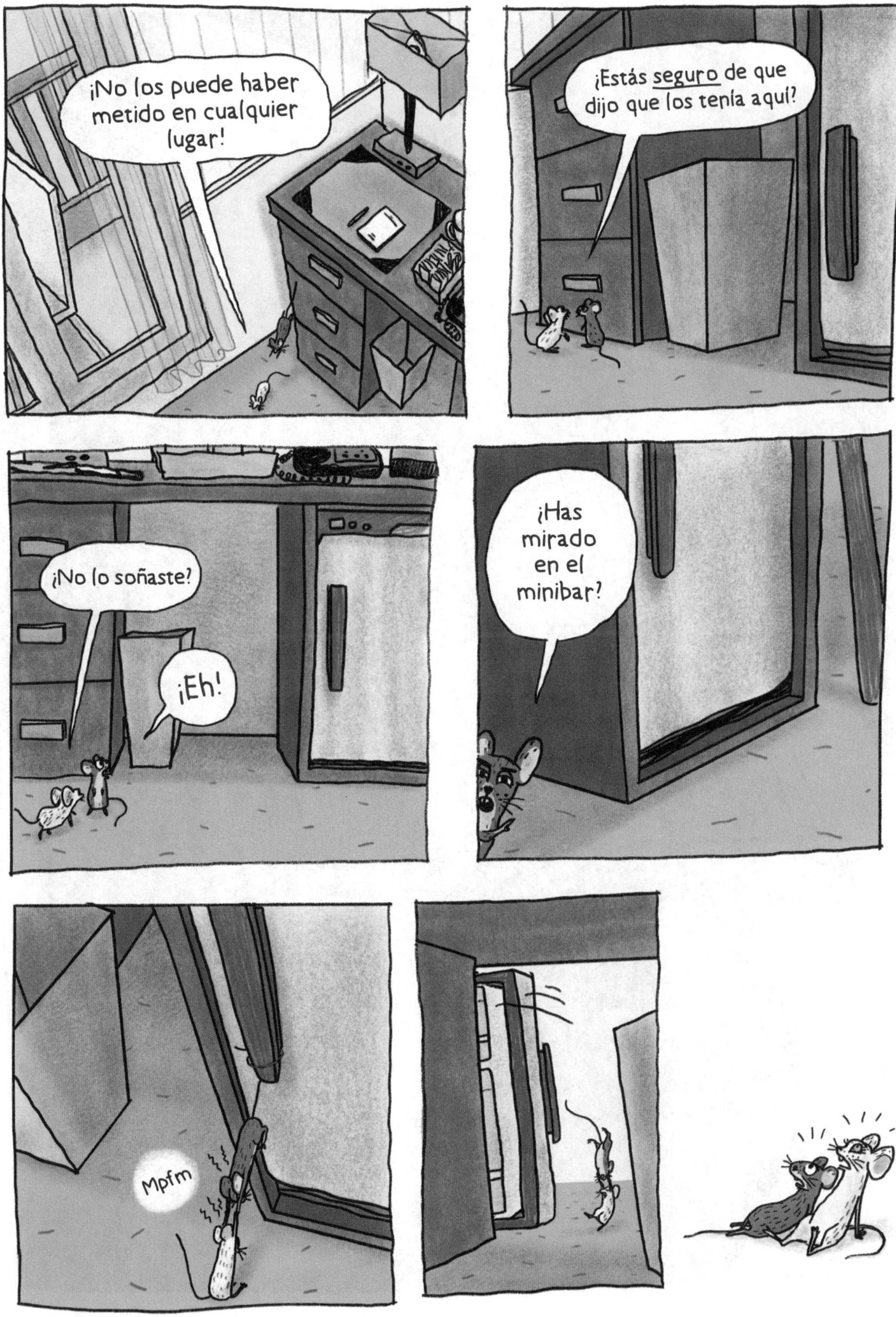
¡No los puede haber metido en cualquier lugar!
¿Estás seguro de que dijo que los tenía aquí?
¿No lo soñaste?
¡Eh!
¿Has mirado en el minibar?
Mpfm

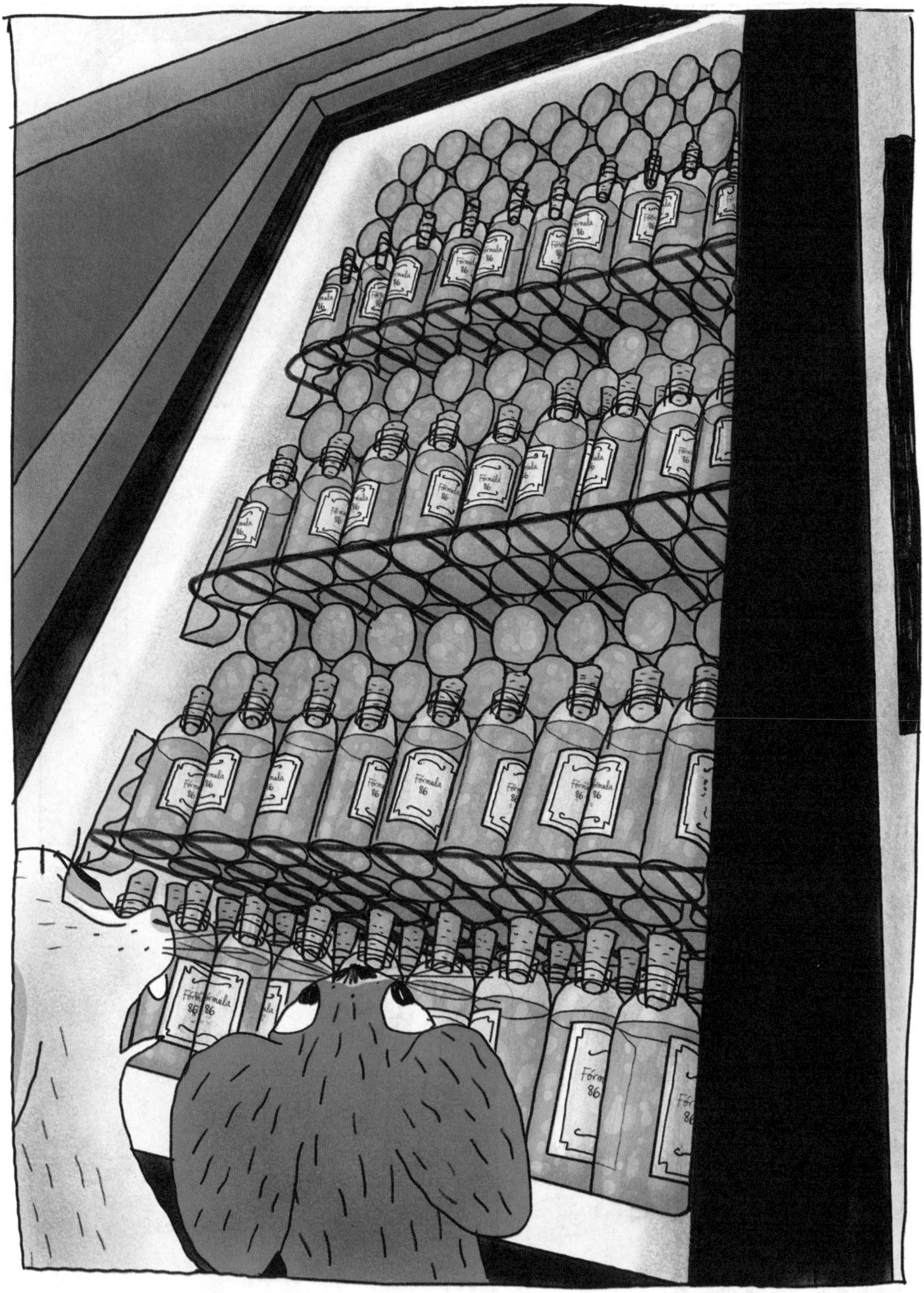
Fórmula 86

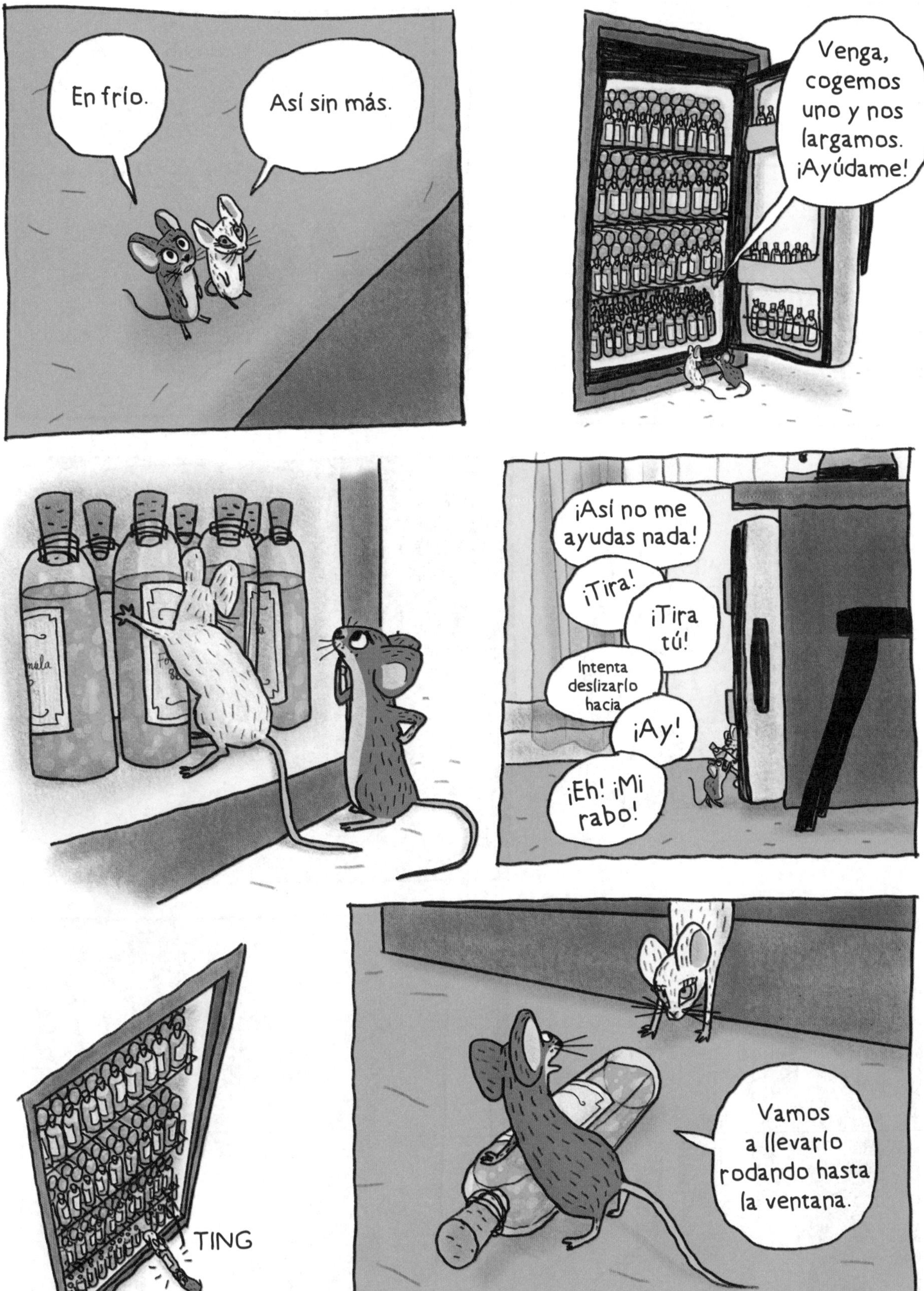
En frío.
Así sin más.
Venga, cogemos uno y nos largamos. ¡Ayúdame!
¡Así no me ayudas nada!
¡Tira!
¡Tira tú!
Intenta deslizarlo hacia
¡Ay!
¡Eh! ¡Mi rabo!
TING
Vamos a llevarlo rodando hasta la ventana.

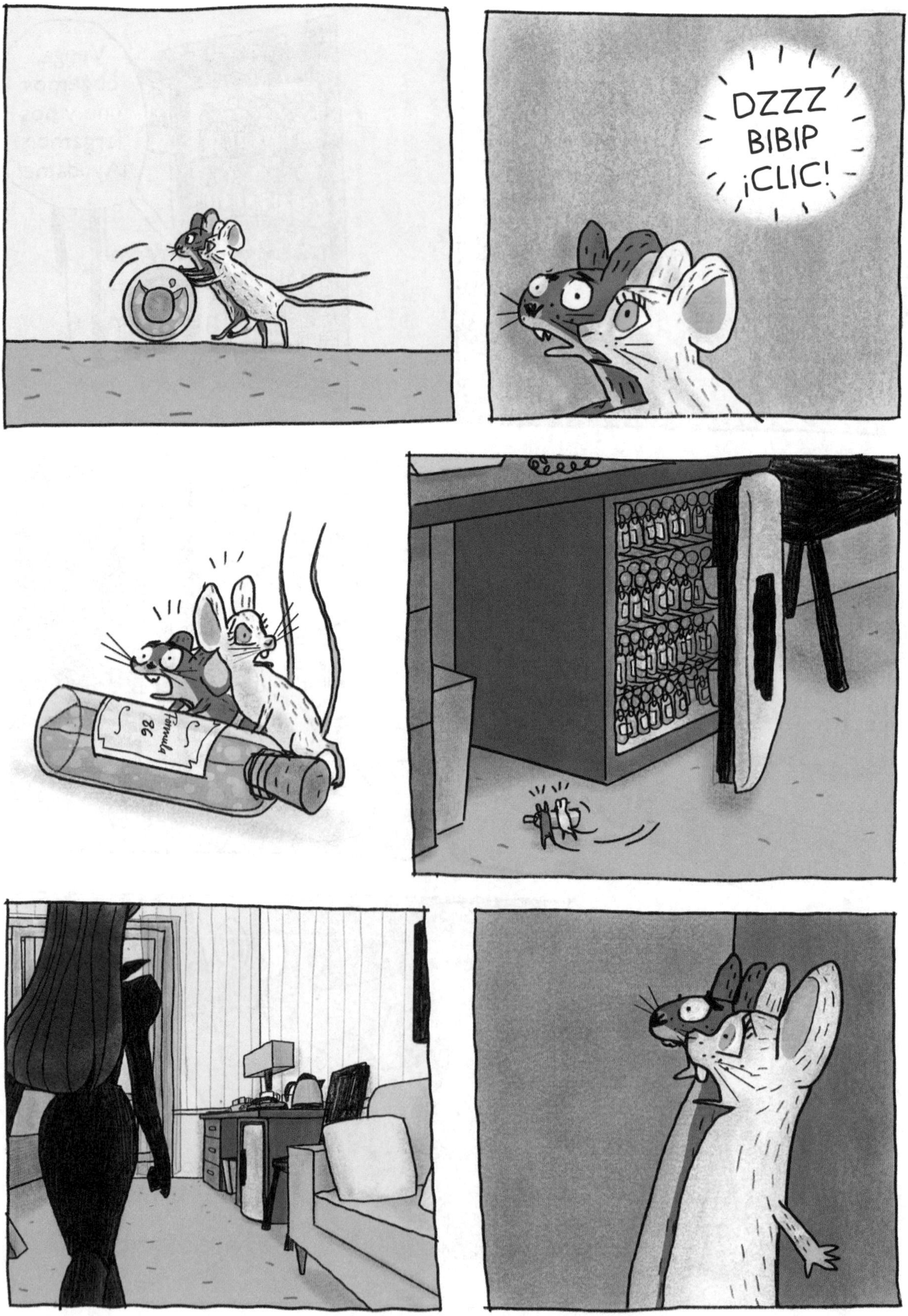
DZZZ
BIBIP
¡CLIC!
Fórmula 86

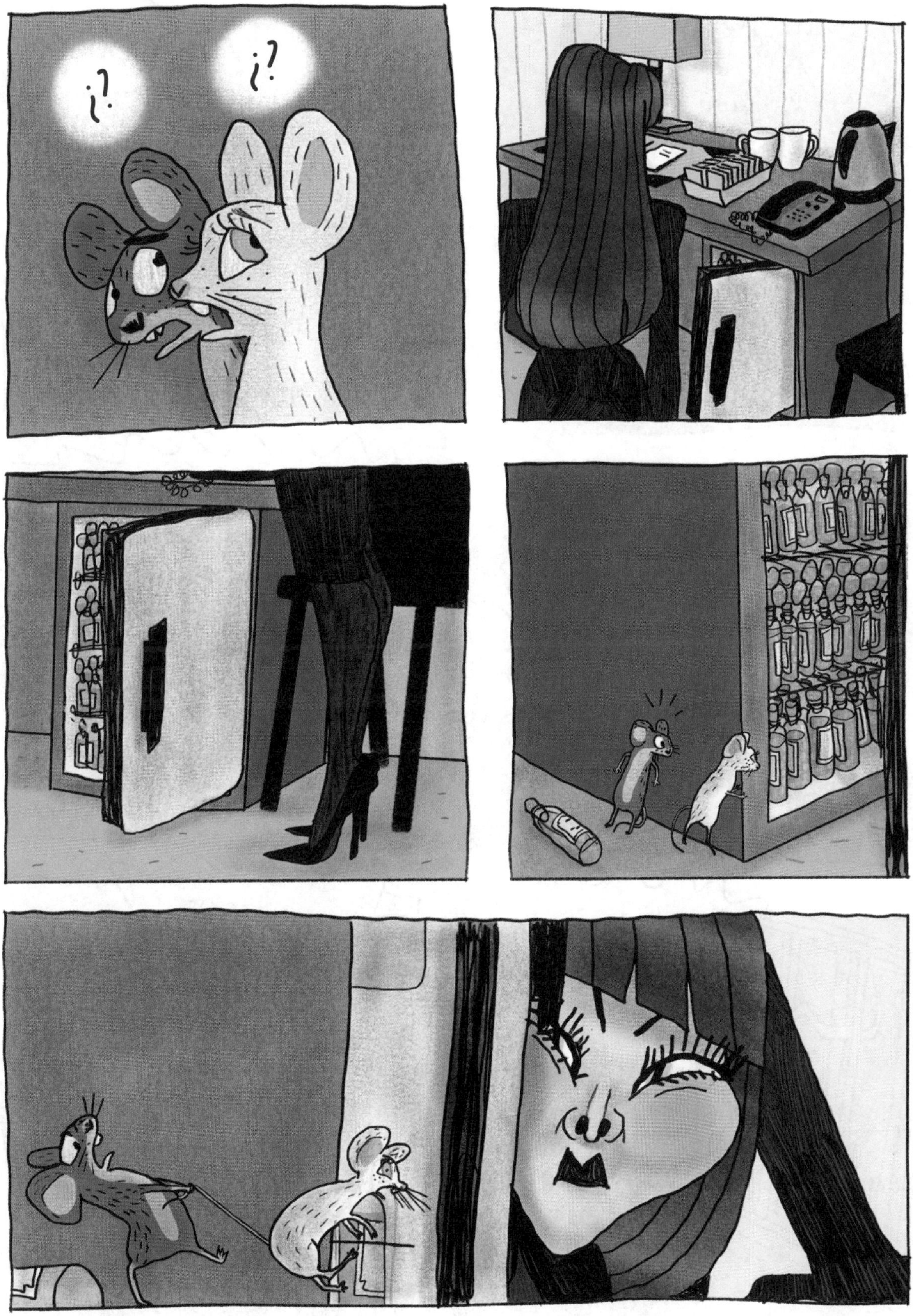
¿?
¿?

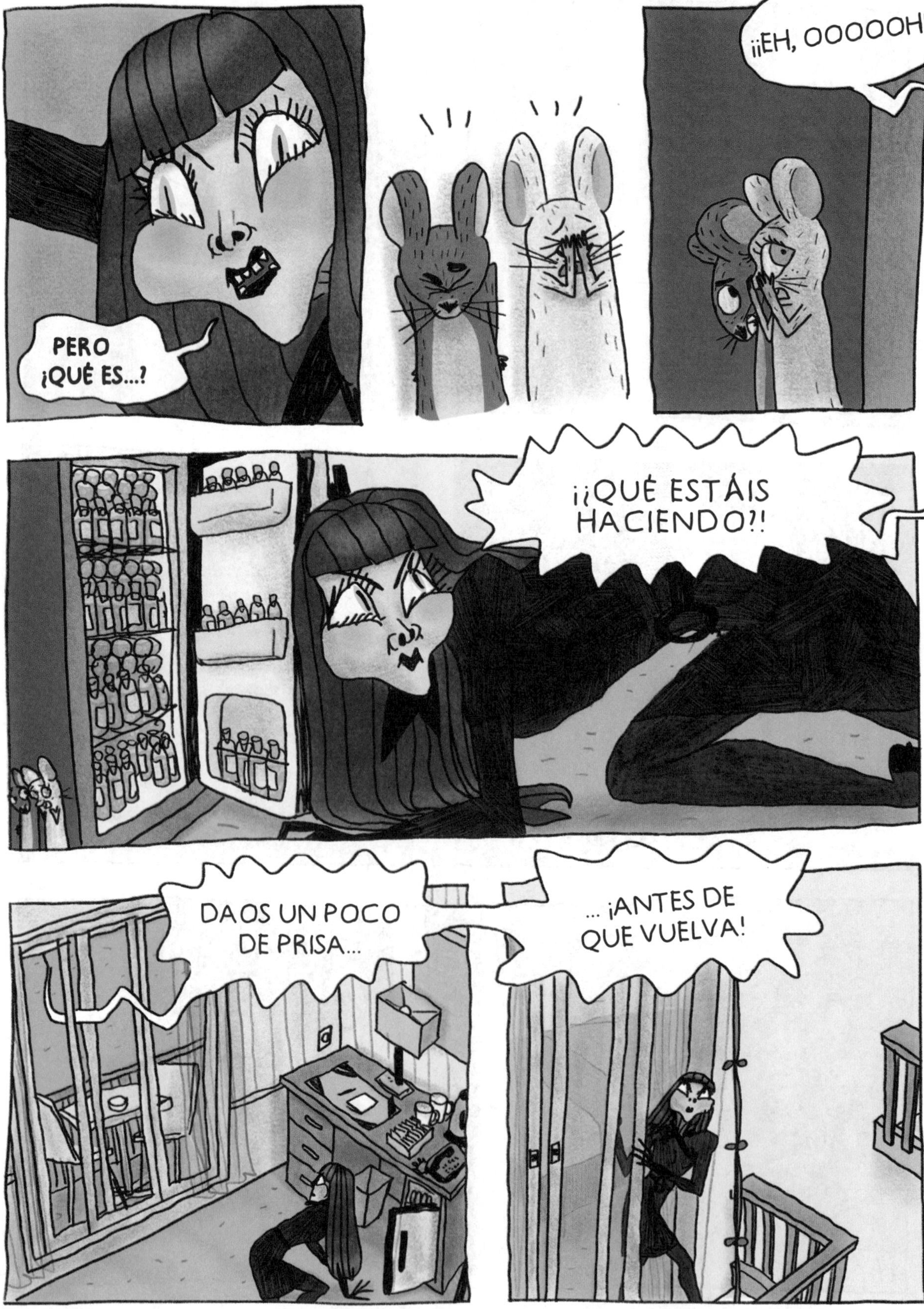
PERO ¿QUÉ ES...?
¡¡EH, OOOOOH!!
¡¡QUÉ ESTÁIS HACIENDO?!
DAOS UN POCO DE PRISA...
... ¡ANTES DE QUE VUELVA!

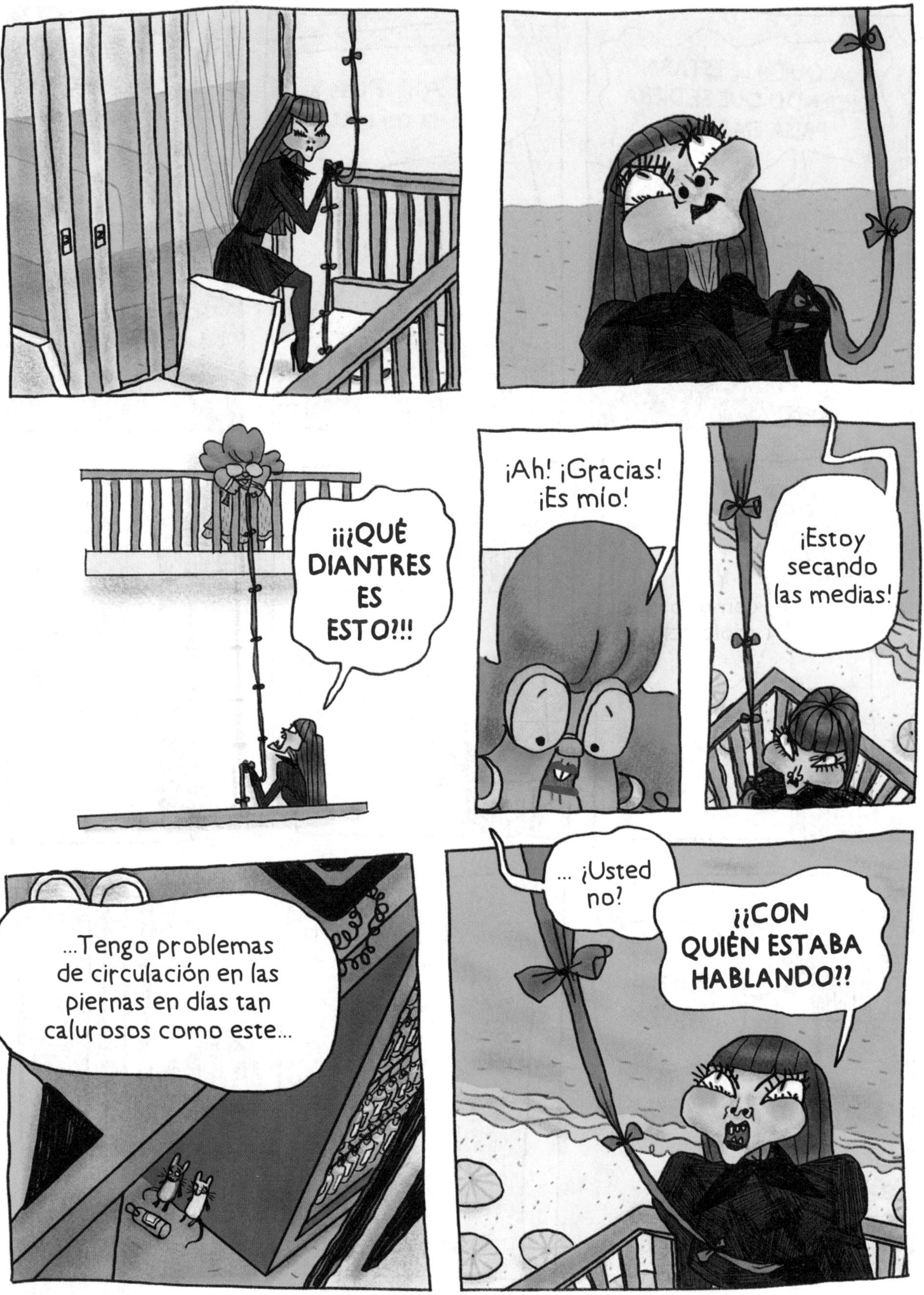
¡¡¡QUÉ DIANTRES ES ESTO?!!
¡Ah! ¡Gracias! ¡Es mío!
¡Estoy secando las medias!
...Tengo problemas de circulación en las piernas en días tan calurosos como este...
... ¿Usted no?
¡¡CON QUIÉN ESTABA HABLANDO?!

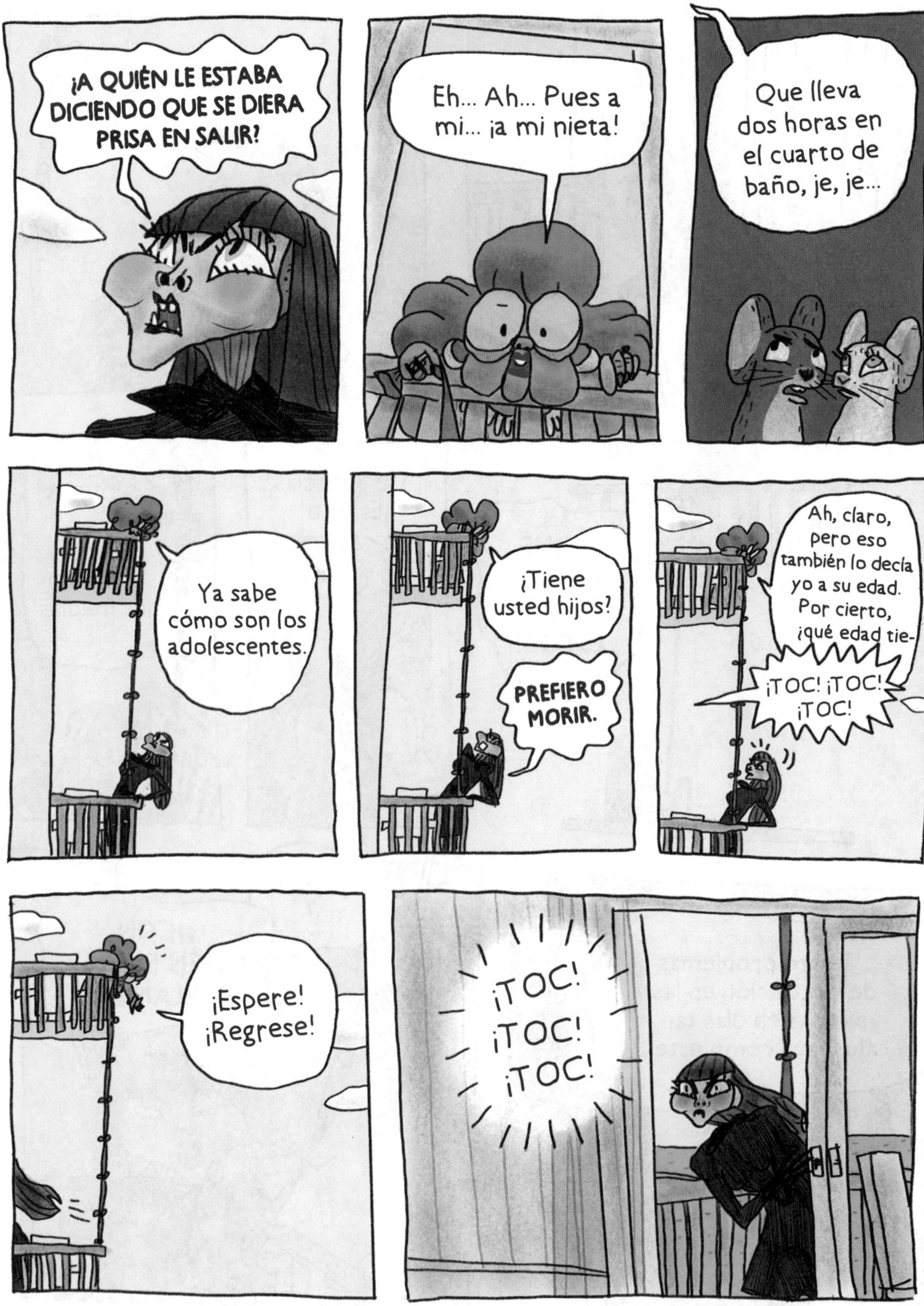

¡A QUIÉN LE ESTABA DICIENDO QUE SE DIERA PRISA EN SALIR?
Eh... Ah... Pues a mí... ¡a mi nieta!
Que lleva dos horas en el cuarto de baño, je, je...
Ya sabe cómo son los adolescentes.
¿Tiene usted hijos?
PREFIERO MORIR.
Ah, claro, pero eso también lo decía yo a su edad. Por cierto, ¿qué edad tie-
¡TOC! ¡TOC! ¡TOC!
¡Espere! ¡Regrese!
¡TOC! ¡TOC! ¡TOC!

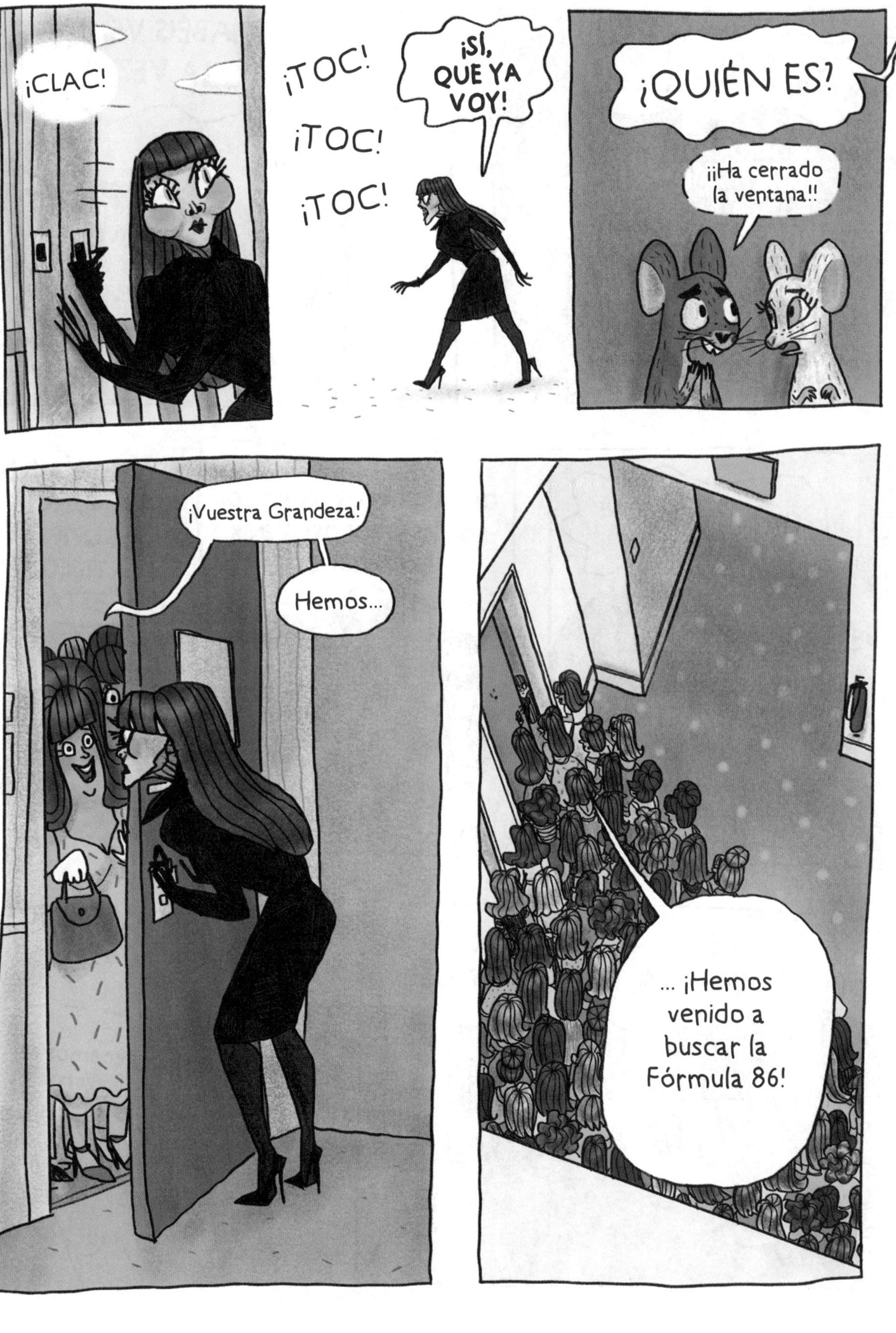
¡CLAC!
¡TOC!
¡TOC!
¡TOC!
¡SÍ, QUE YA VOY!
¿QUIÉN ES?
¡¡Ha cerrado la ventana!!
¡Vuestra Grandeza!
Hemos...
... ¡Hemos venido a buscar la Fórmula 86!

PERO... ¡¡QUÉ CLASE DE PANDA DE ESTÚPIDAS SOIS?!

HABÉIS... ¡¡¡HABÉIS VENIDO TODAS A LA VEZ?!!

¡QUÉ DISCRECIÓN! ¡BRAVO!

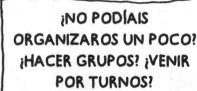

¡NO PODÍAIS ORGANIZAROS UN POCO? ¡HACER GRUPOS? ¡VENIR POR TURNOS?

¡¡LO PODÍAIS HABER ANUNCIADO A BOMBO Y PLATILLO, YA QUE ESTAMOS!!

AYSS ¡BIEN! ¡INTENTAREMOS HACER UNA FILA, POR LO MENOS!

NO, ESPERAD, HAGAMOS TRES EQUIPOS...

NO...

¡Tenemos que largarnos!

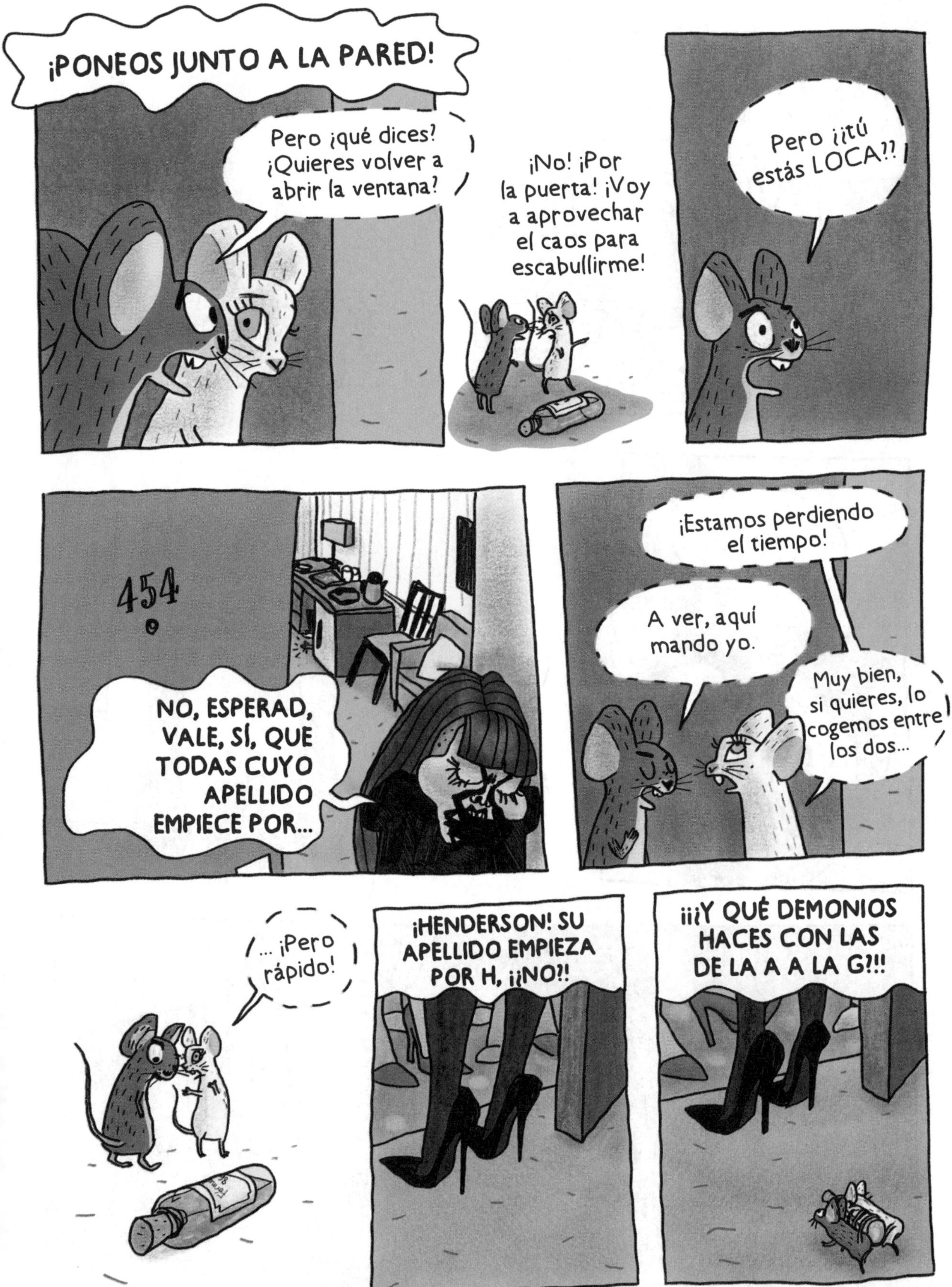
¡PONEOS JUNTO A LA PARED!
Pero ¿qué dices? ¿Quieres volver a abrir la ventana?
¡No! ¡Por la puerta! ¡Voy a aprovechar el caos para escabullirme!
Pero ¡¡tú estás LOCA!?
454
NO, ESPERAD, VALE, SÍ, QUE TODAS CUYO APELLIDO EMPIECE POR...
¡Estamos perdiendo el tiempo!
A ver, aquí mando yo.
Muy bien, si quieres, lo cogemos entre los dos...
... ¡Pero rápido!
¡HENDERSON! SU APELLIDO EMPIEZA POR H, ¡¡NO?!
¡¡¡Y QUÉ DEMONIOS HACES CON LAS DE LA A A LA G?!!

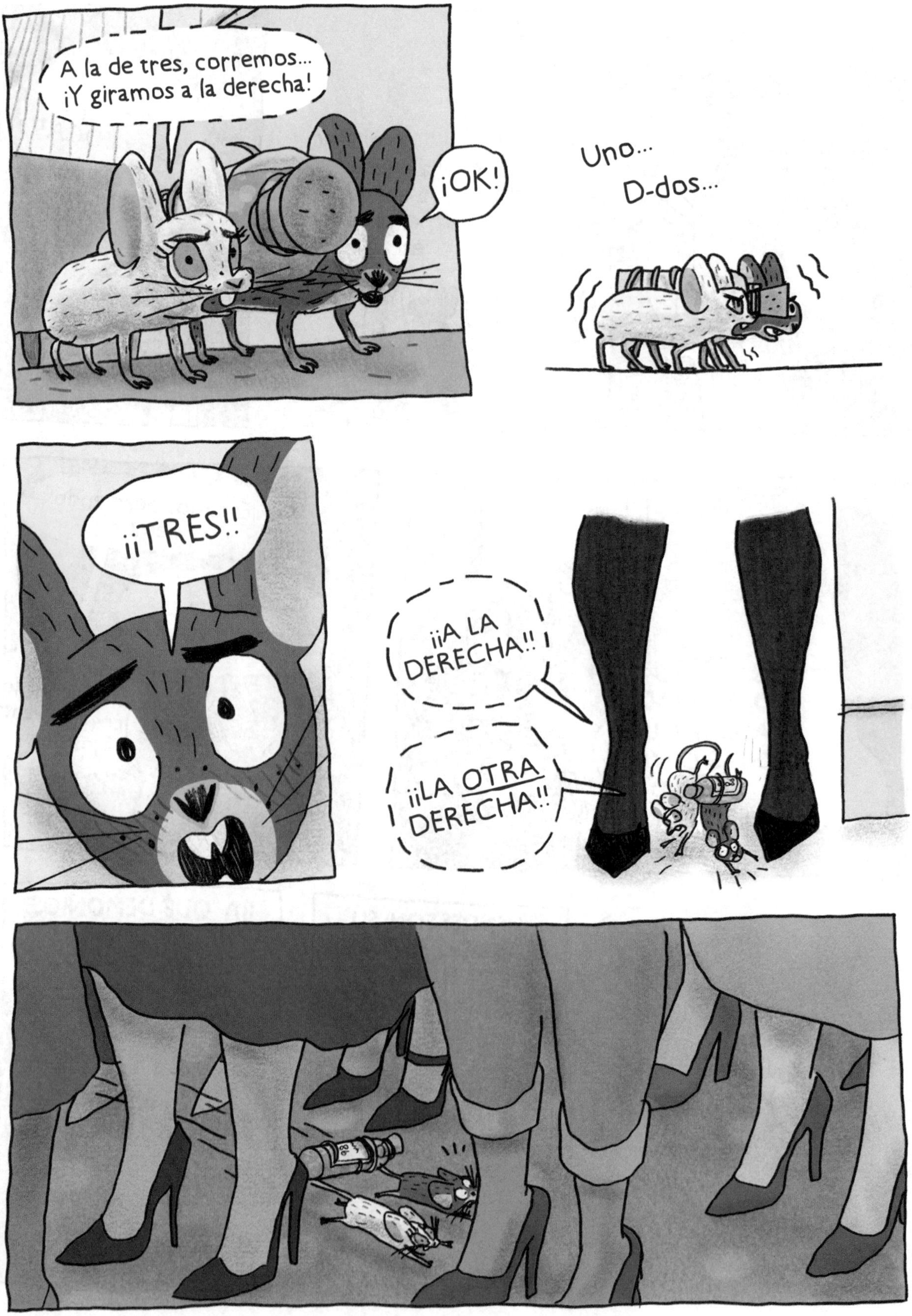
A la de tres, corremos...
¡Y giramos a la derecha!
¡OK!
Uno...
D-dos...
¡¡TRES!!
¡¡A LA DERECHA!!
¡¡LA OTRA DERECHA!!

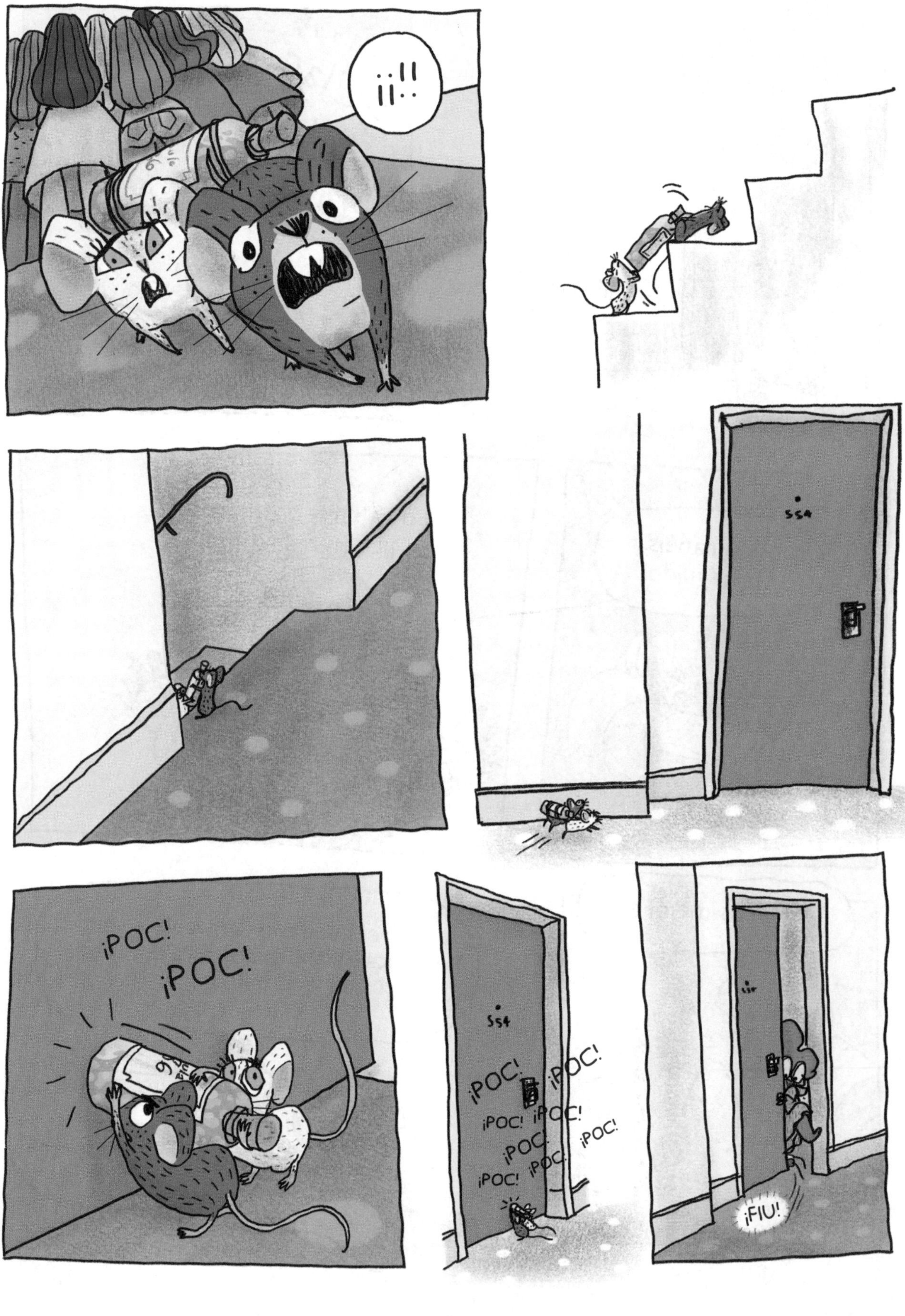
¡¡!!
554
¡POC!
¡POC!
¡POC!
¡POC!
¡POC!
¡POC!
¡POC!
¡POC!
¡POC!
¡POC!
¡FIU!

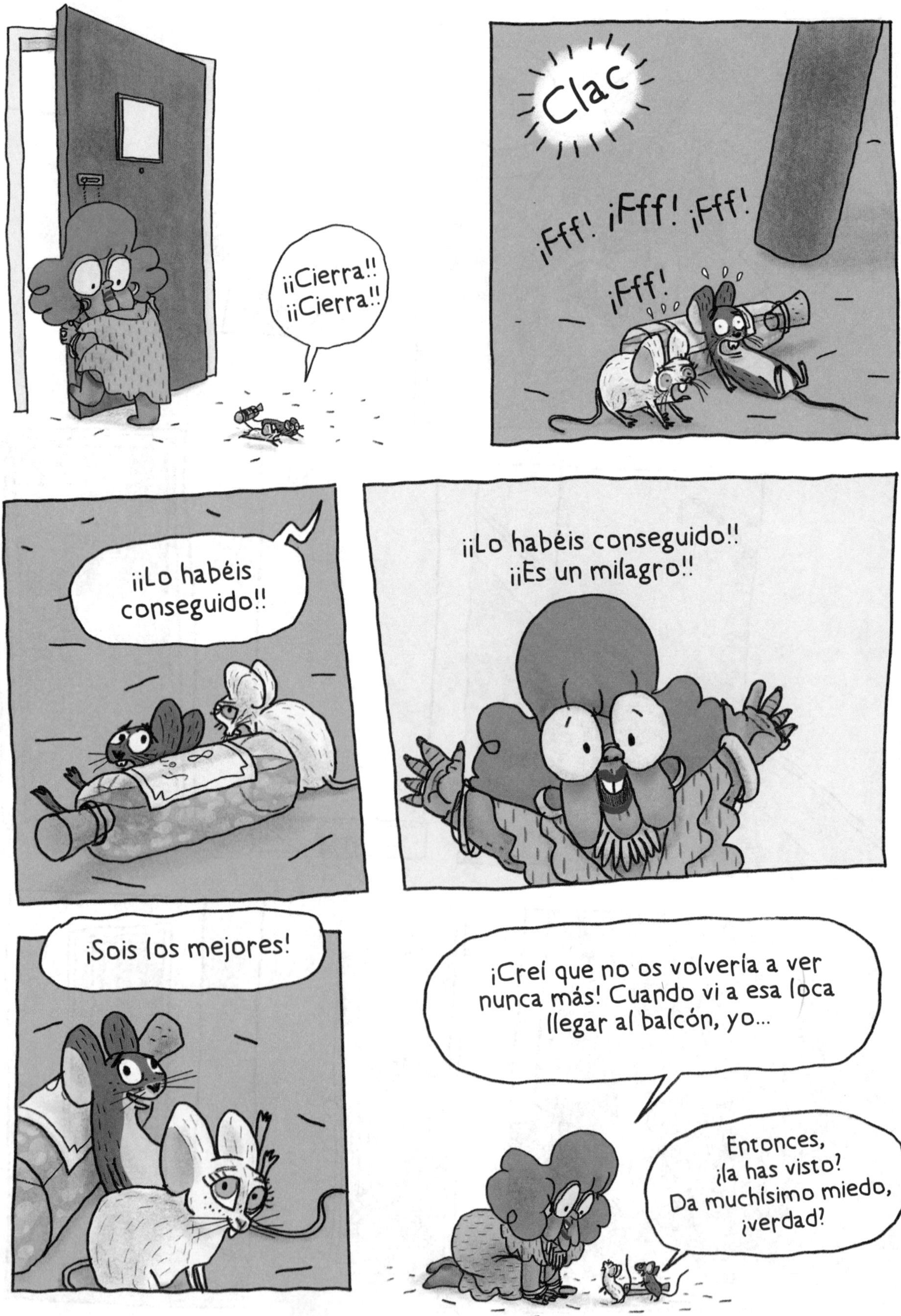
¡¡Cierra!! ¡¡Cierra!!
Clac
¡Fff! ¡Fff! ¡Fff!
¡Fff!
¡¡Lo habéis conseguido!!
¡¡Lo habéis conseguido!! ¡¡Es un milagro!!
¡Sois los mejores!
¡Creí que no os volvería a ver nunca más! Cuando vi a esa loca llegar al balcón, yo...
Entonces, ¿la has visto? Da muchísimo miedo, ¿verdad?

¡Su rostro falso es increíble! ¡¡De veras es una máscara?! ¡¡TIENE que comercializarla!! Porque yo estaría dispuesta a pagar una...

¡Abuela!

Ay, sí, ¡qué alivio! ¡Creí que os iba a matar!

Sí, nosotros también.

Y, ahora, ¿qué hacemos con esto?

Seguimos sin saber...

... ¡cómo obligarlas a bebérselo!

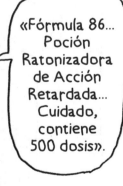

«Fórmula 86... Poción Ratonizadora de Acción Retardada... Cuidado, contiene 500 dosis».

Podría hacer un cóctel verde estupendo con esto, ¡y servirles una ronda!

Mmm... Con ginebra y una pizca de vermú...

Y ¡cómo vas a convencer al barman de que te deje hacerlo?

Además, ¿quién dice que beban alcohol?

¡Pero, bueno, por favor! ¡Qué pregunta más tonta!

Creo que lo mejor será verter la poción en la comida.

¡Sí!

Pronto será la hora de cenar, ¿no?

¡Y han quedado todas en el restaurante del hotel a las 20.00!

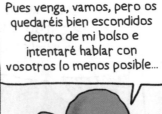

Pues venga, vamos, pero os quedaréis bien escondidos dentro de mi bolso e intentaré hablar con vosotros lo menos posible...

No me apetece nada que me tomen por una abuela loca que habla sola.

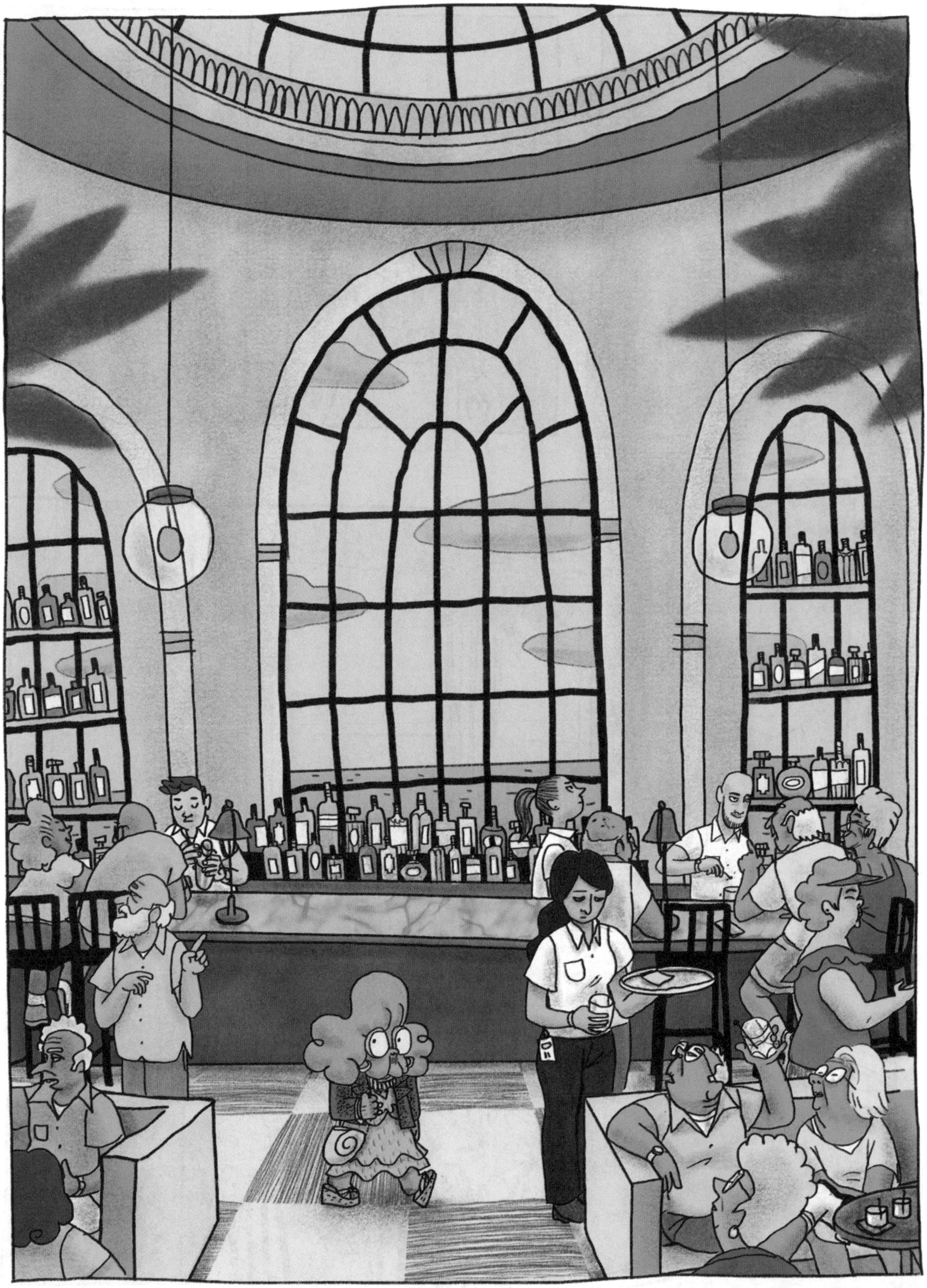

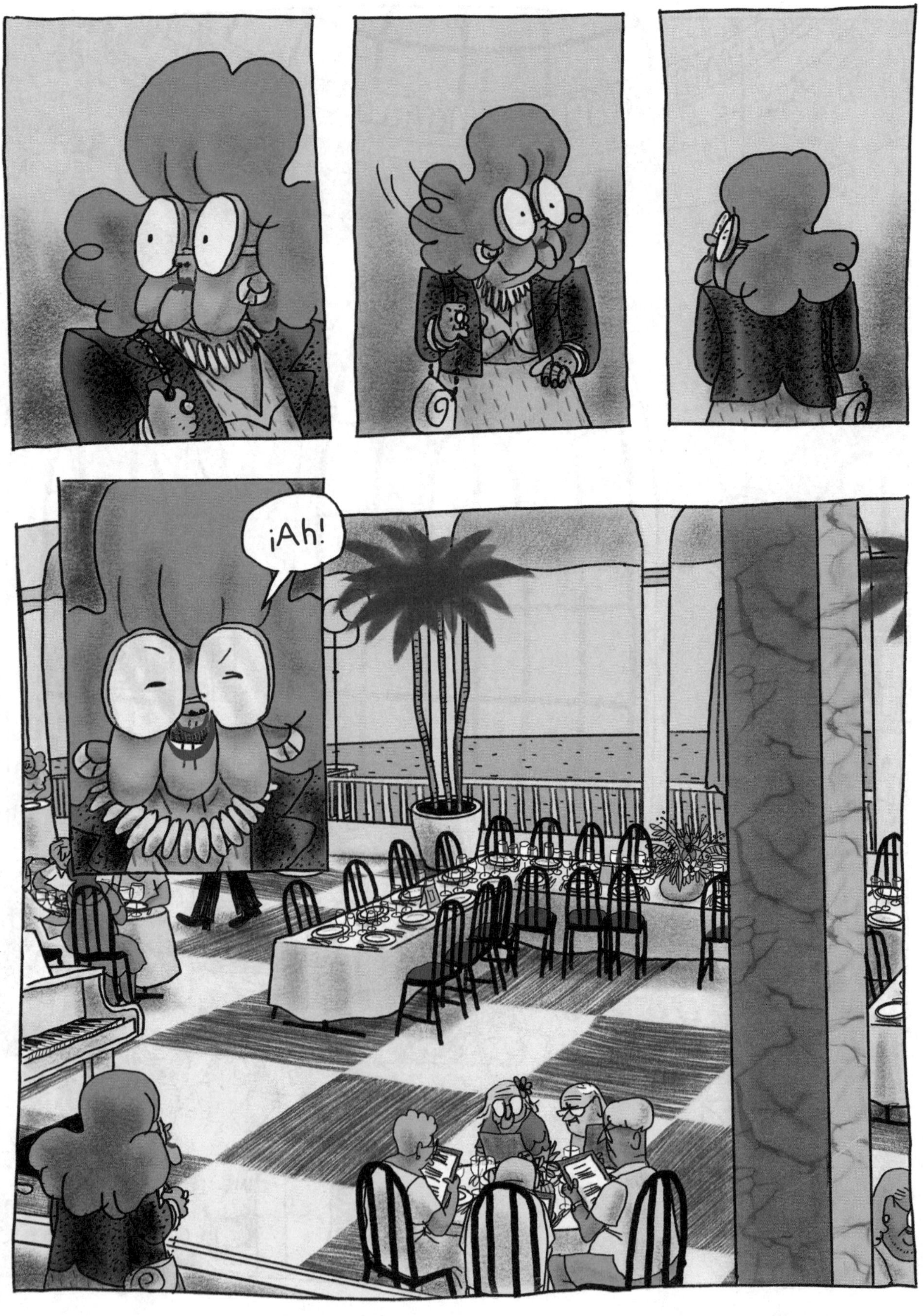
¡Ah!

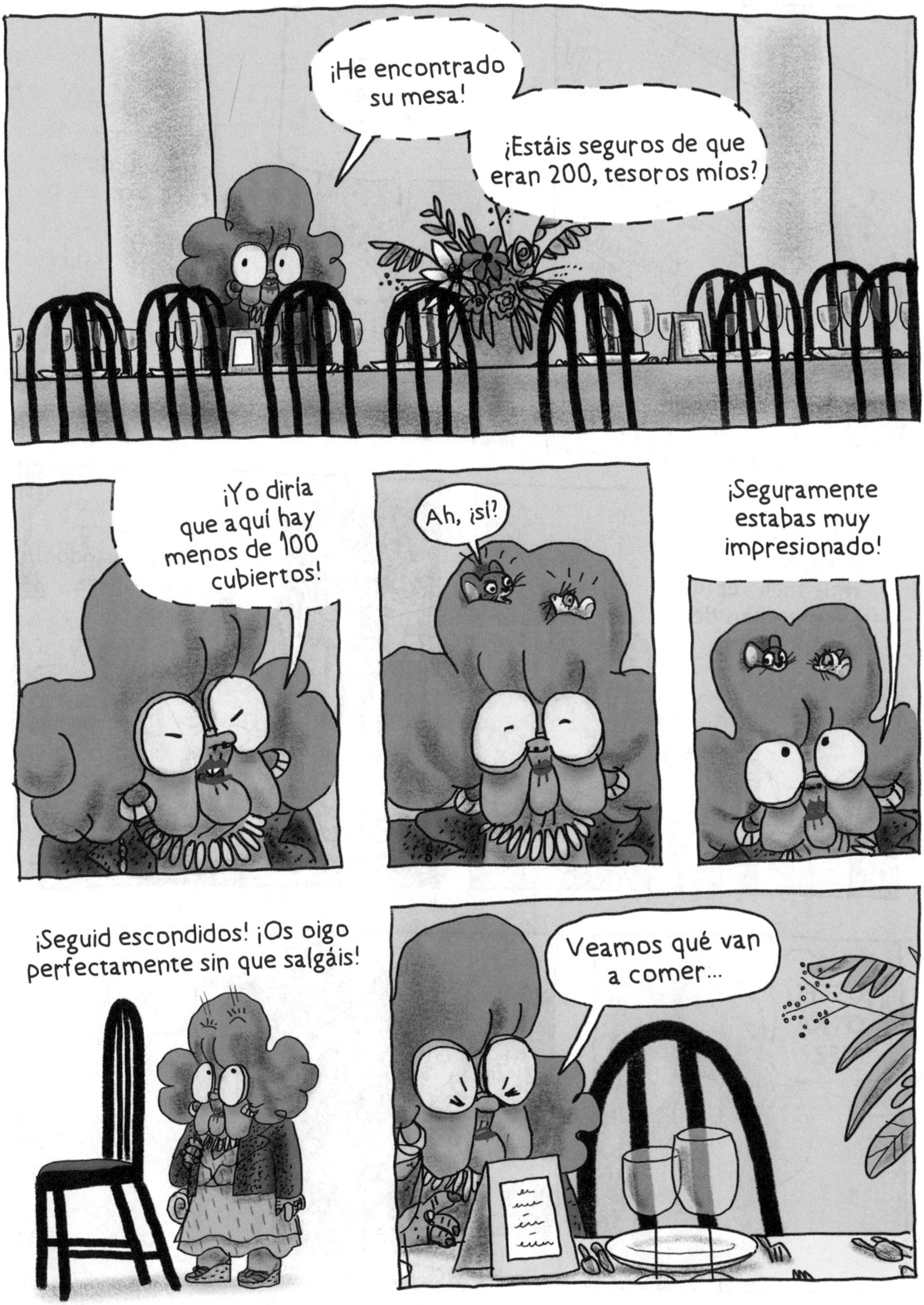
¡He encontrado su mesa!
¡Estáis seguros de que eran 200, tesoros míos?
¡Yo diría que aquí hay menos de 100 cubiertos!
Ah, ¿sí?
¡Seguramente estabas muy impresionado!
¡Seguid escondidos! ¡Os oigo perfectamente sin que salgáis!
Veamos qué van a comer...

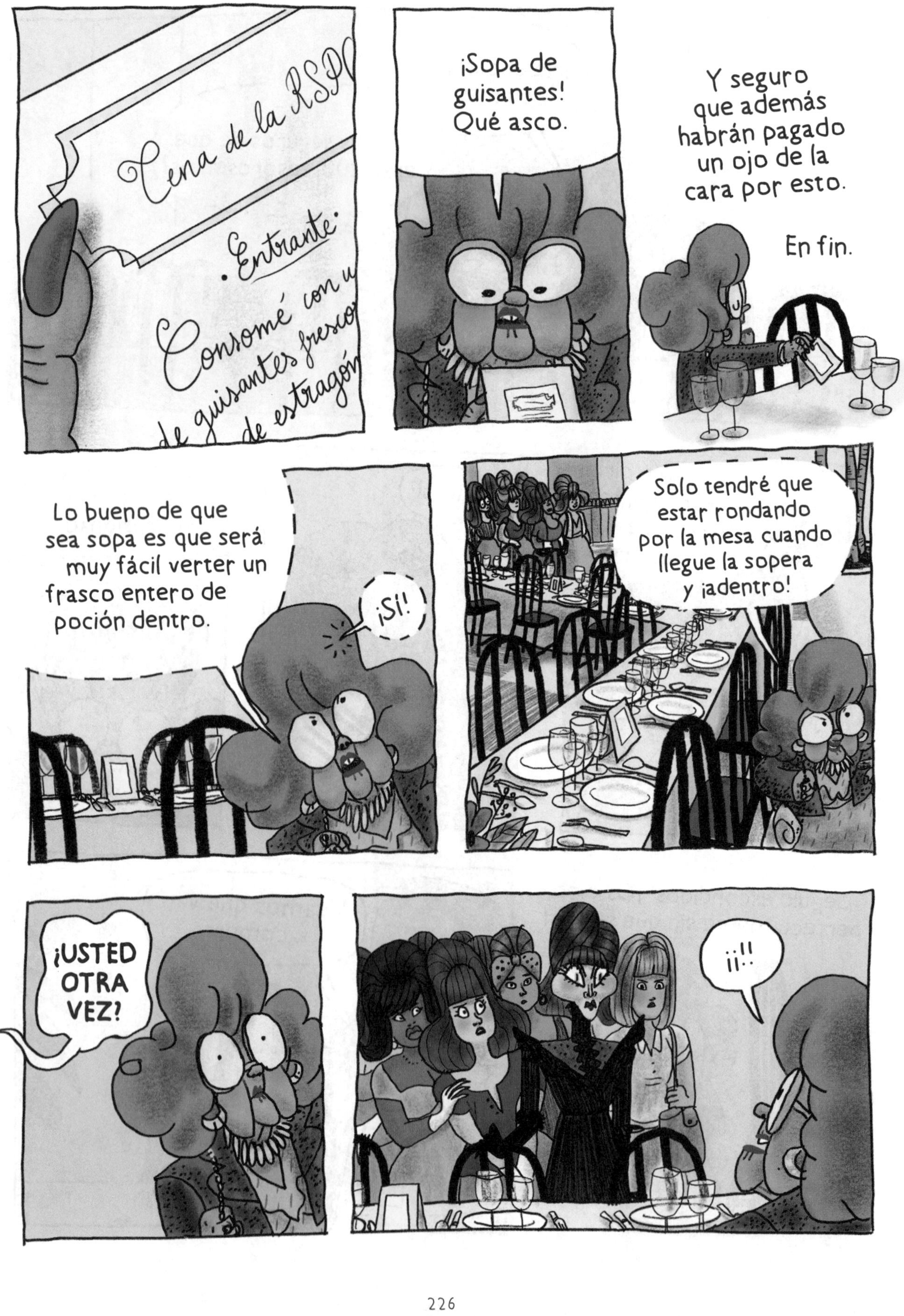

Cena de la RSP
Entrante:
Consomé con u
de guisantes fresco
de estragón
¡Sopa de guisantes! Qué asco.
Y seguro que además habrán pagado un ojo de la cara por esto.
En fin.
Lo bueno de que sea sopa es que será muy fácil verter un frasco entero de poción dentro.
¡Sí!
Solo tendré que estar rondando por la mesa cuando llegue la sopera y ¡adentro!
¡USTED OTRA VEZ?
¡¡..!!

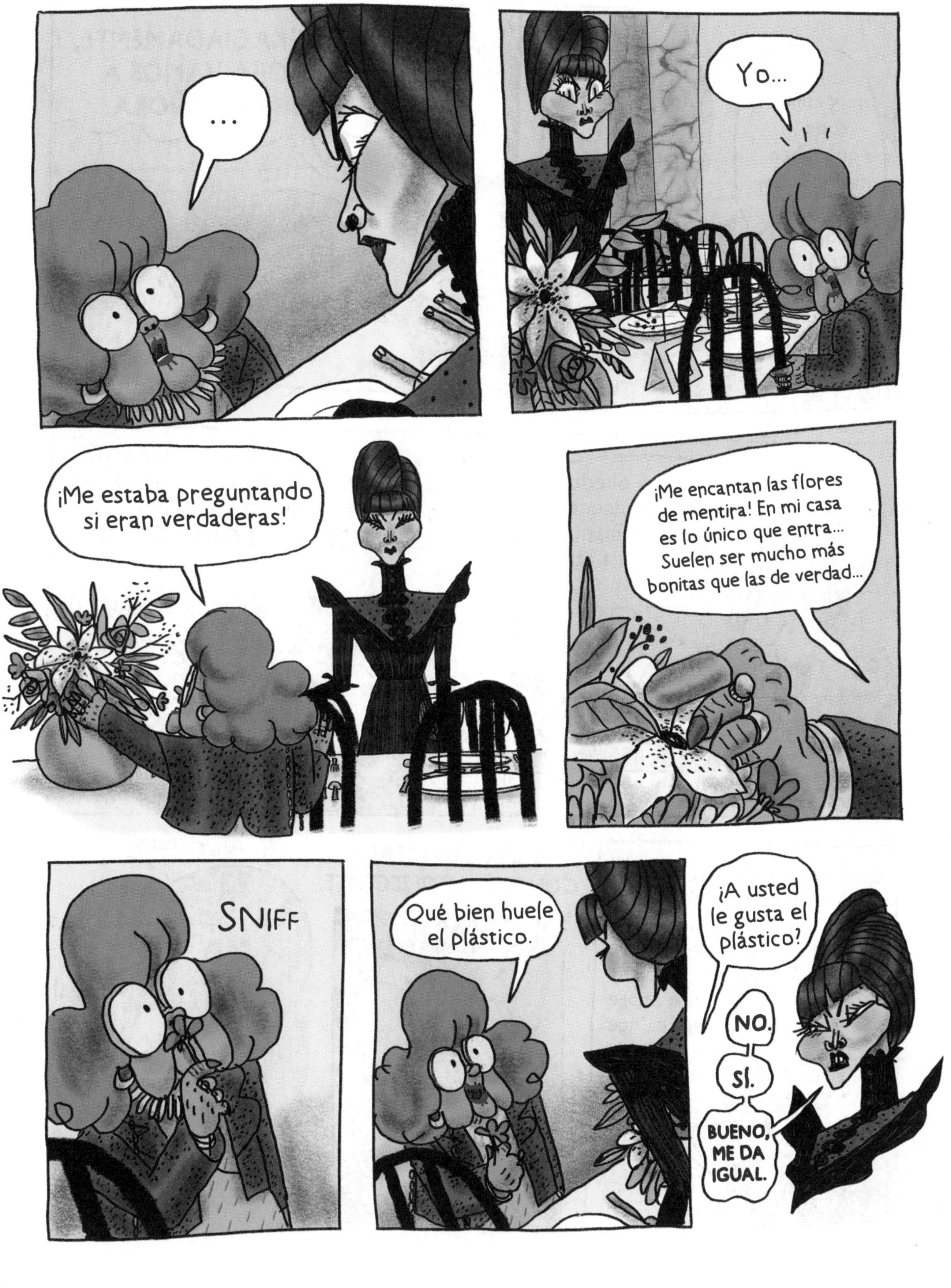
...
Yo...
¡Me estaba preguntando si eran verdaderas!
¡Me encantan las flores de mentira! En mi casa es lo único que entra... Suelen ser mucho más bonitas que las de verdad...
SNIFF
Qué bien huele el plástico.
¡A usted le gusta el plástico?
NO.
SÍ.
BUENO, ME DA IGUAL.

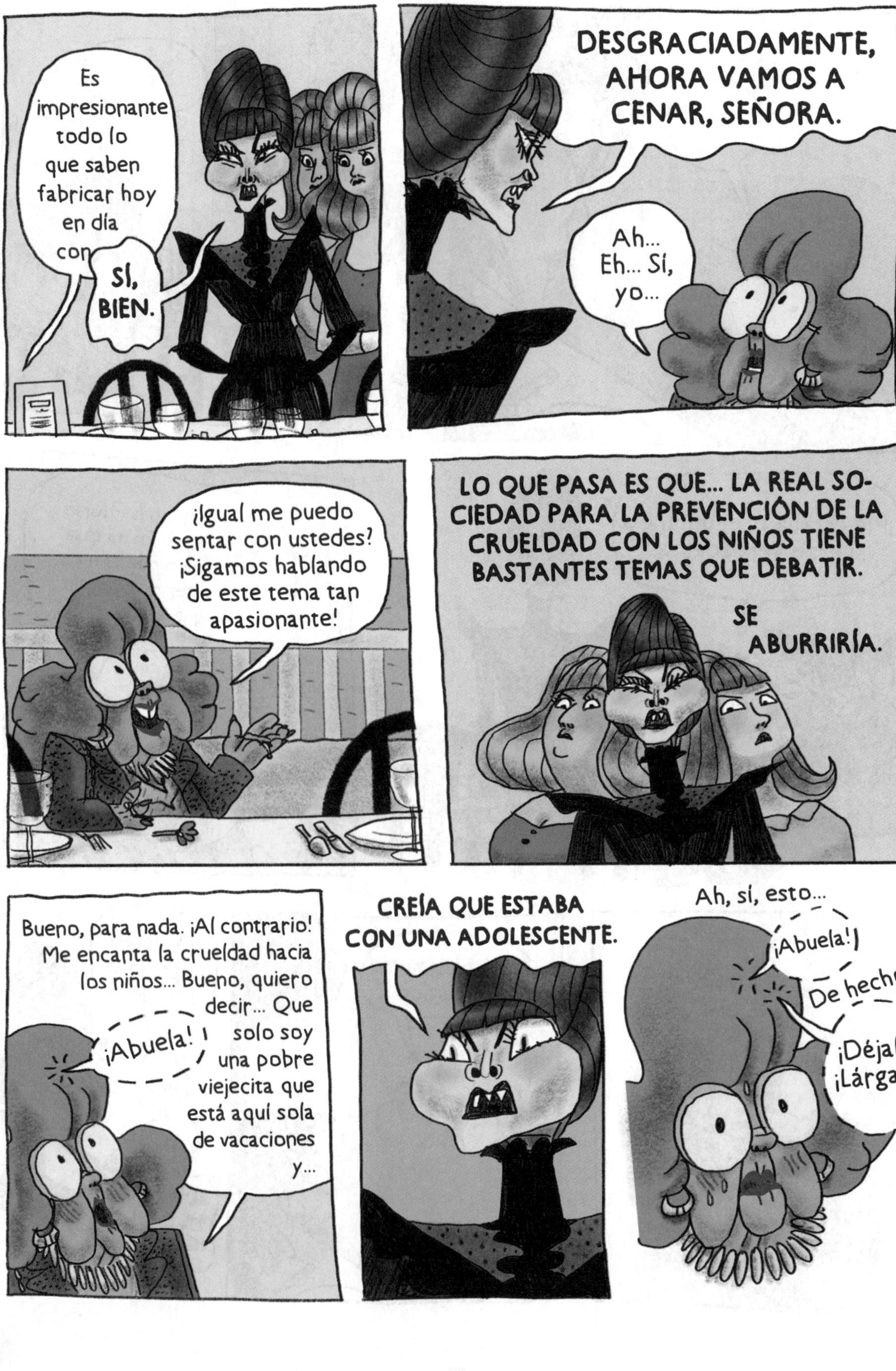

Es impresionante todo lo que saben fabricar hoy en día con
SÍ, BIEN.
DESGRACIADAMENTE, AHORA VAMOS A CENAR, SEÑORA.
Ah... Eh... Sí, yo...
¿Igual me puedo sentar con ustedes? ¡Sigamos hablando de este tema tan apasionante!
LO QUE PASA ES QUE... LA REAL SOCIEDAD PARA LA PREVENCIÓN DE LA CRUELDAD CON LOS NIÑOS TIENE BASTANTES TEMAS QUE DEBATIR.
SE ABURRIRÍA.
Bueno, para nada. ¡Al contrario! Me encanta la crueldad hacia los niños... Bueno, quiero decir... Que solo soy una pobre viejecita que está aquí sola de vacaciones y...
¡Abuela!
CREÍA QUE ESTABA CON UNA ADOLESCENTE.
Ah, sí, esto...
¡Abuela!
De hecho...
¡Déjalo! ¡Lárgate!

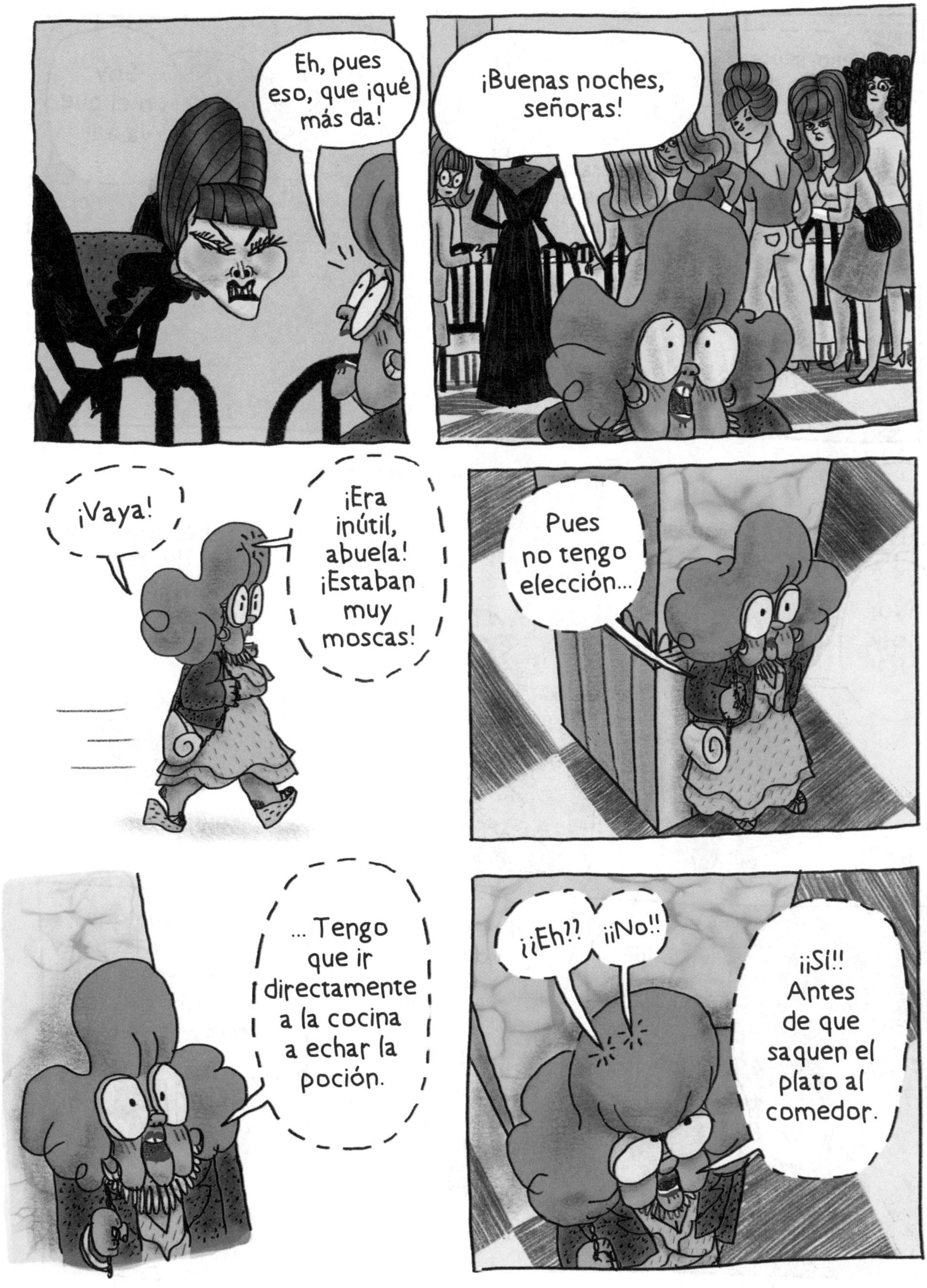
Eh, pues eso, que ¡qué más da!
¡Buenas noches, señoras!
¡Vaya!
¡Era inútil, abuela! ¡Estaban muy moscas!
Pues no tengo elección...
... Tengo que ir directamente a la cocina a echar la poción.
¡¿Eh?!
¡¡No!!
¡¡Sí!! Antes de que saquen el plato al comedor.

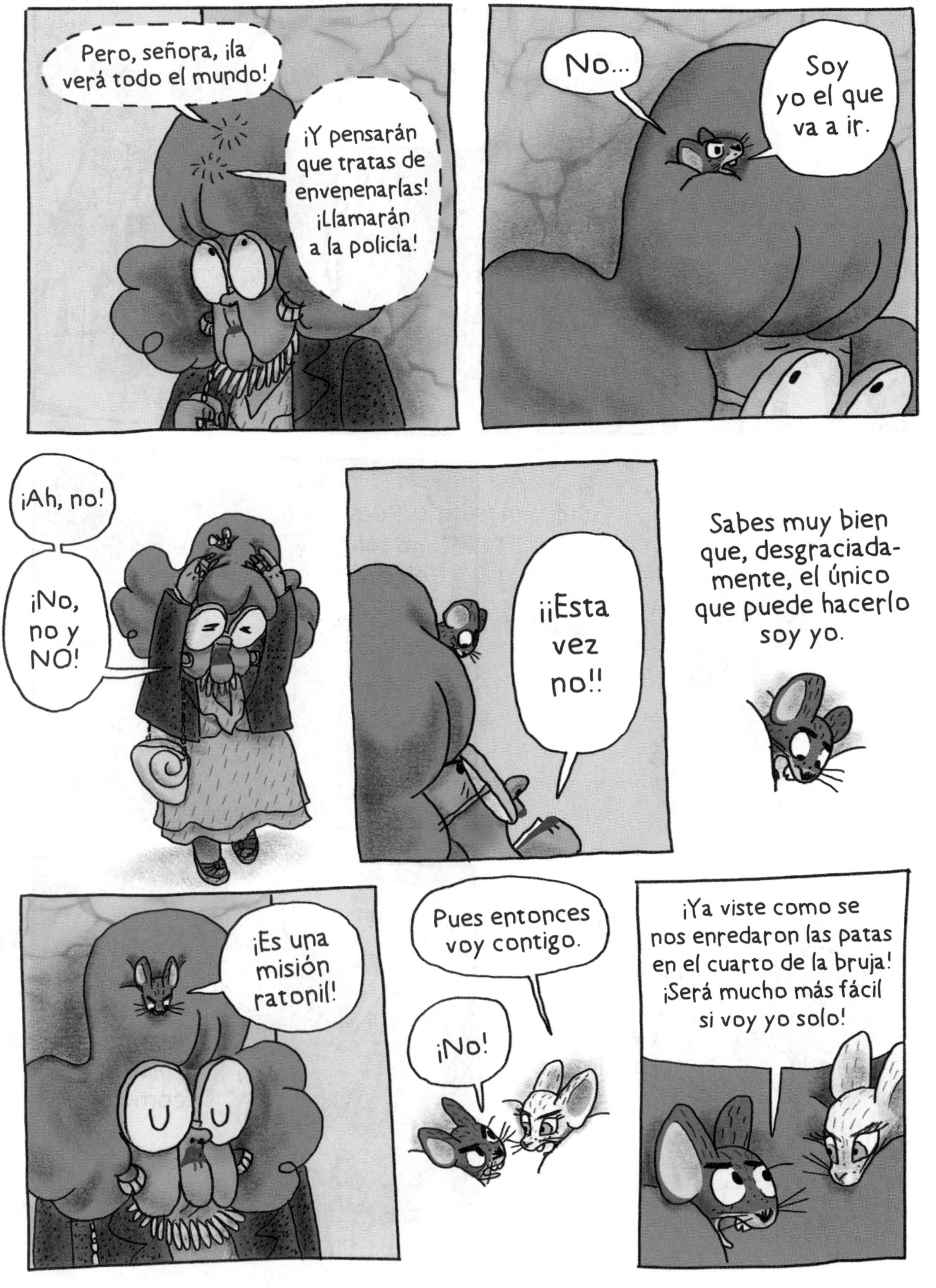
Pero, señora, ¡la verá todo el mundo!
¡Y pensarán que tratas de envenenarlas! ¡Llamarán a la policía!
No...
Soy yo el que va a ir.
¡Ah, no!
¡No, no y NO!
¡¡Esta vez no!!
Sabes muy bien que, desgraciada-mente, el único que puede hacerlo soy yo.
¡Es una misión ratonil!
Pues entonces voy contigo.
¡No!
¡Ya viste como se nos enredaron las patas en el cuarto de la bruja! ¡Será mucho más fácil si voy yo solo!

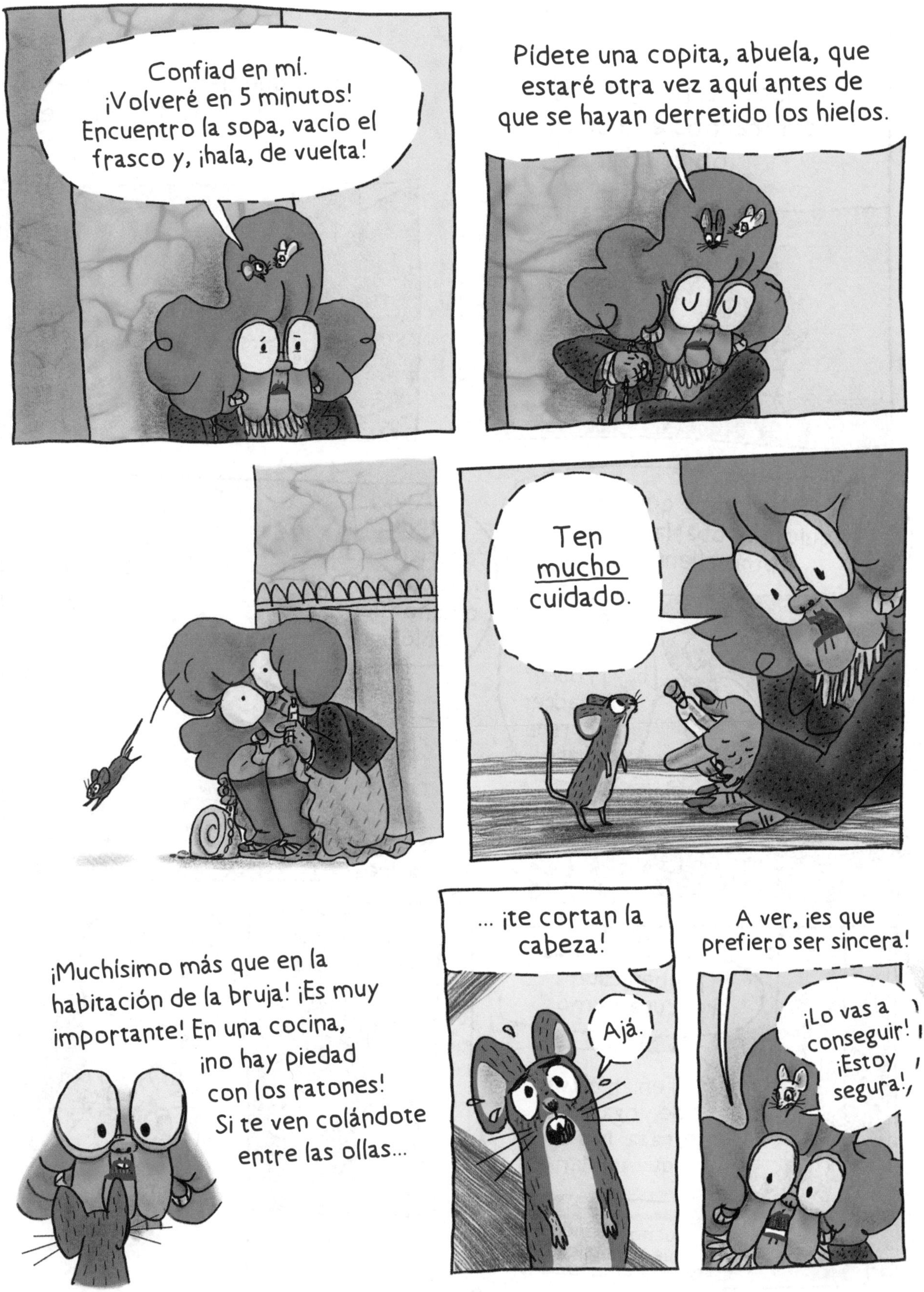

Confiad en mí. ¡Volveré en 5 minutos! Encuentro la sopa, vacío el frasco y, ¡hala, de vuelta!
Pídete una copita, abuela, que estaré otra vez aquí antes de que se hayan derretido los hielos.
Ten mucho cuidado.
¡Muchísimo más que en la habitación de la bruja! ¡Es muy importante! En una cocina, ¡no hay piedad con los ratones! Si te ven colándote entre las ollas...
... ¡te cortan la cabeza!
Ajá.
A ver, ¡es que prefiero ser sincera!
¡Lo vas a conseguir! ¡Estoy segura!

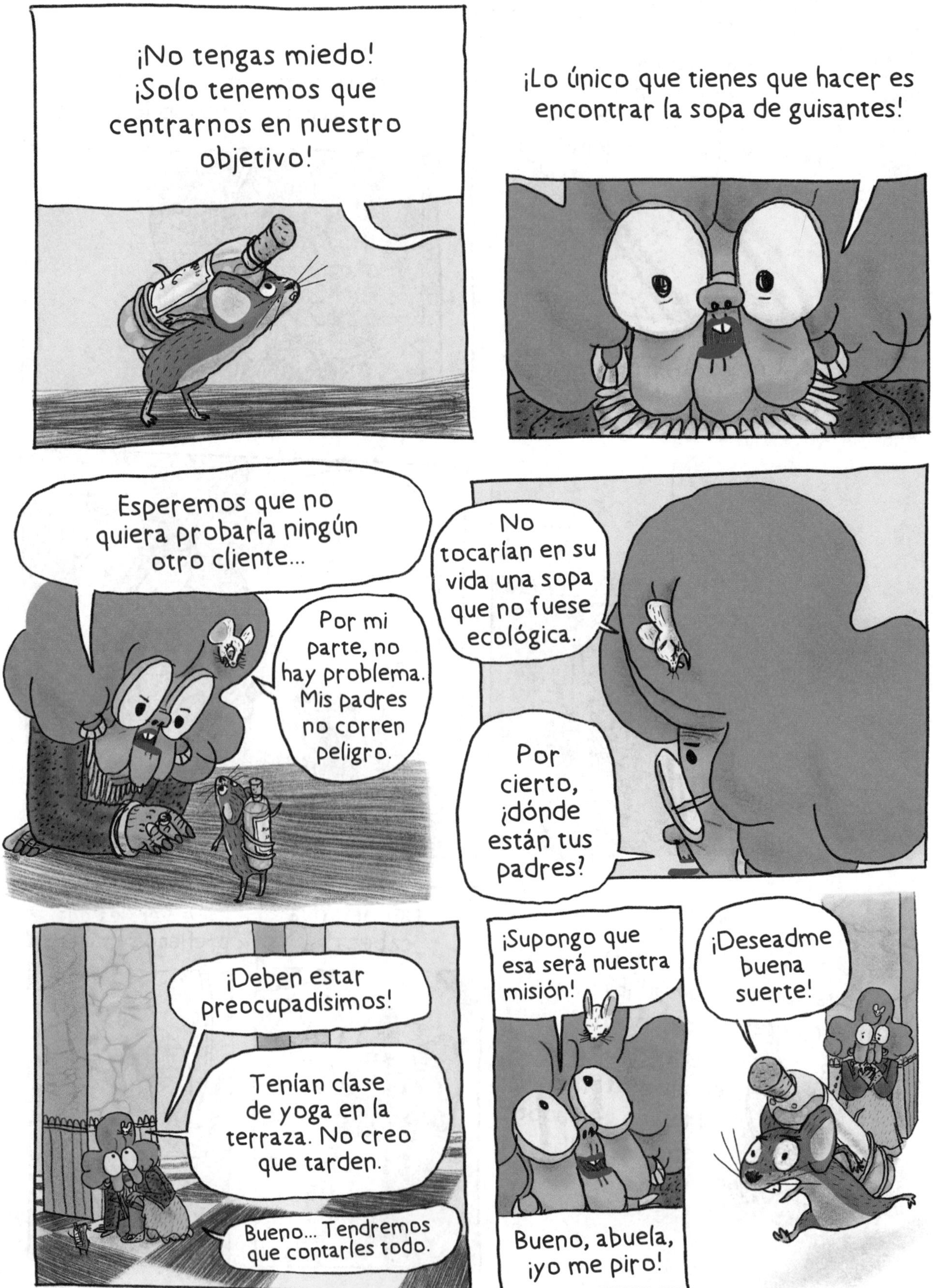
¡No tengas miedo! ¡Solo tenemos que centrarnos en nuestro objetivo!
¡Lo único que tienes que hacer es encontrar la sopa de guisantes!
Esperemos que no quiera probarla ningún otro cliente...
Por mi parte, no hay problema. Mis padres no corren peligro.
No tocarían en su vida una sopa que no fuese ecológica.
Por cierto, ¿dónde están tus padres?
¡Deben estar preocupadísimos!
Tenían clase de yoga en la terraza. No creo que tarden.
Bueno... Tendremos que contarles todo.
¡Supongo que esa será nuestra misión!
Bueno, abuela, ¡yo me piro!
¡Deseadme buena suerte!

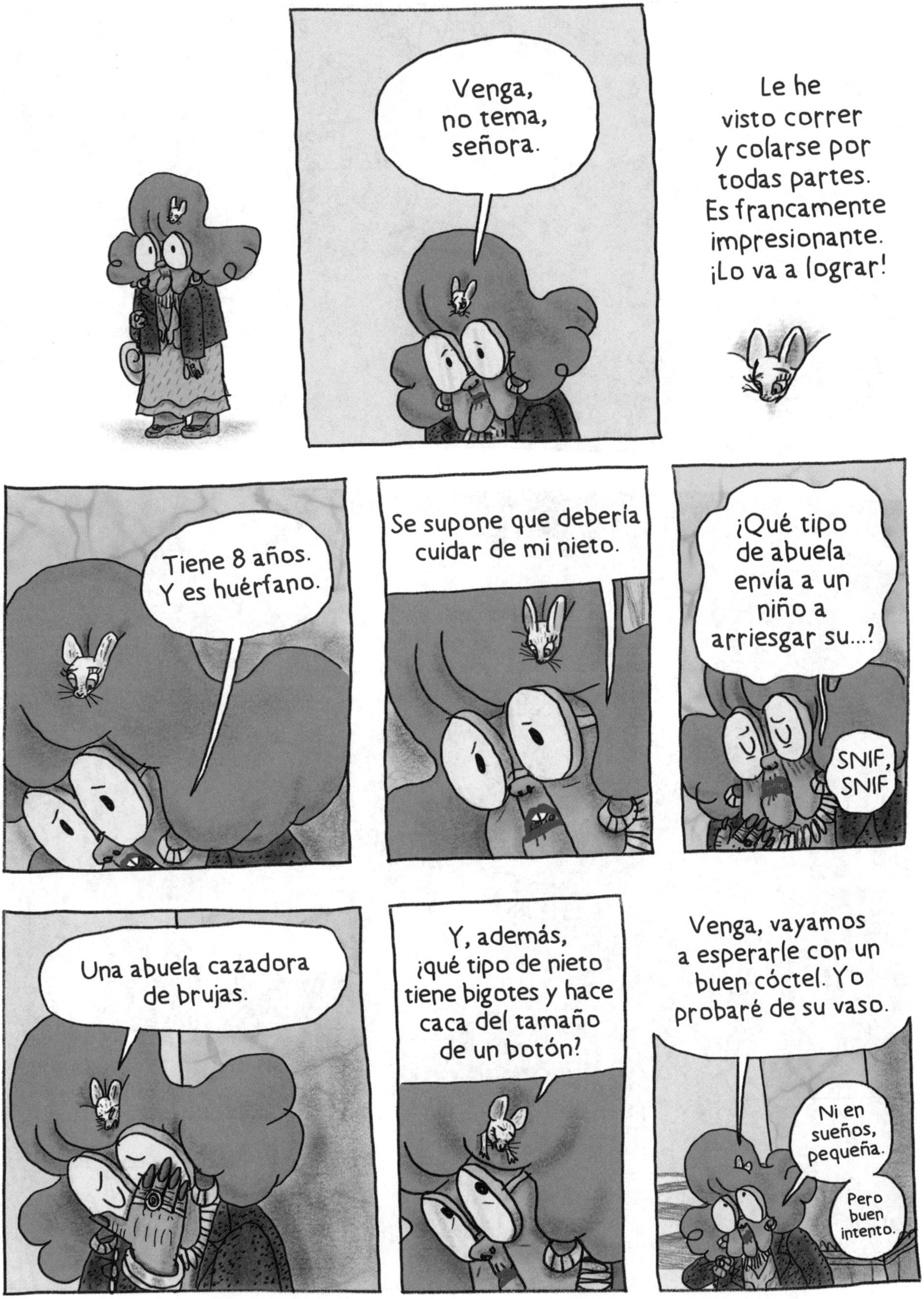
Venga, no tema, señora.
Le he visto correr y colarse por todas partes. Es francamente impresionante. ¡Lo va a lograr!
Tiene 8 años. Y es huérfano.
Se supone que debería cuidar de mi nieto.
¿Qué tipo de abuela envía a un niño a arriesgar su...?
SNIF, SNIF
Una abuela cazadora de brujas.
Y, además, ¿qué tipo de nieto tiene bigotes y hace caca del tamaño de un botón?
Venga, vayamos a esperarle con un buen cóctel. Yo probaré de su vaso.
Ni en sueños, pequeña.
Pero buen intento.

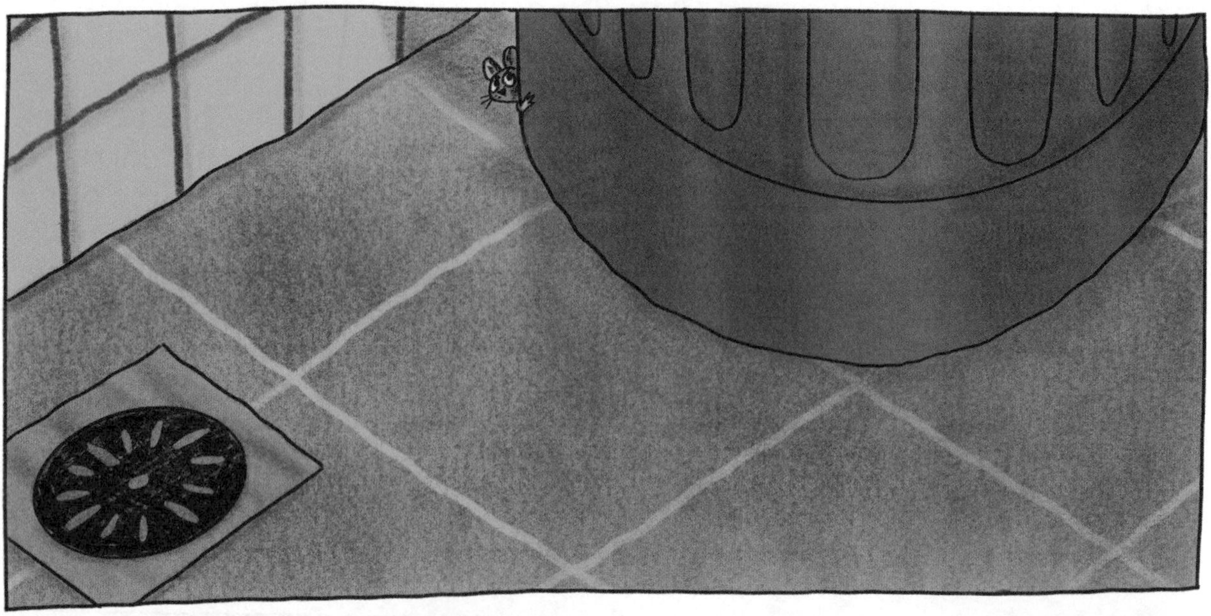

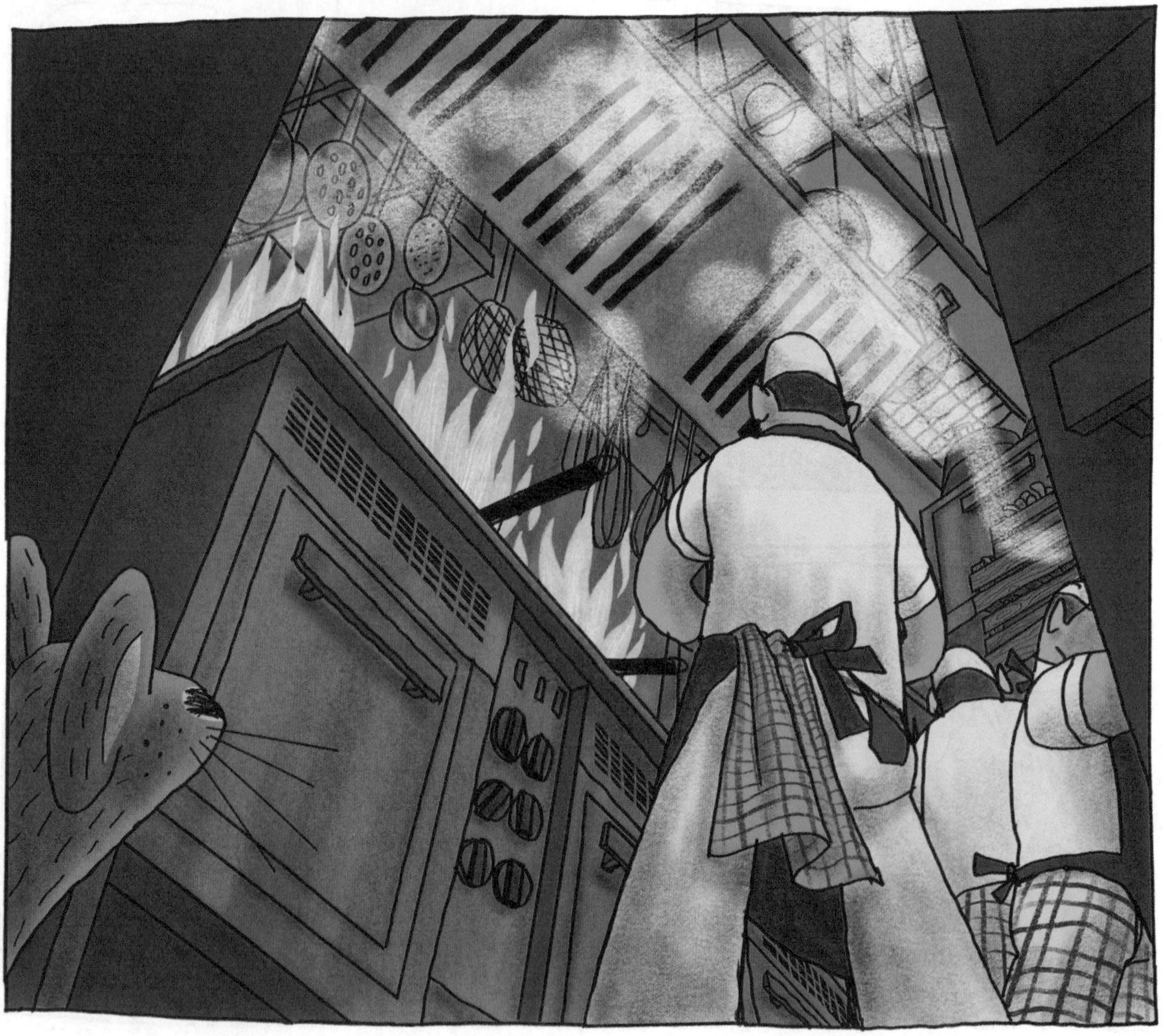

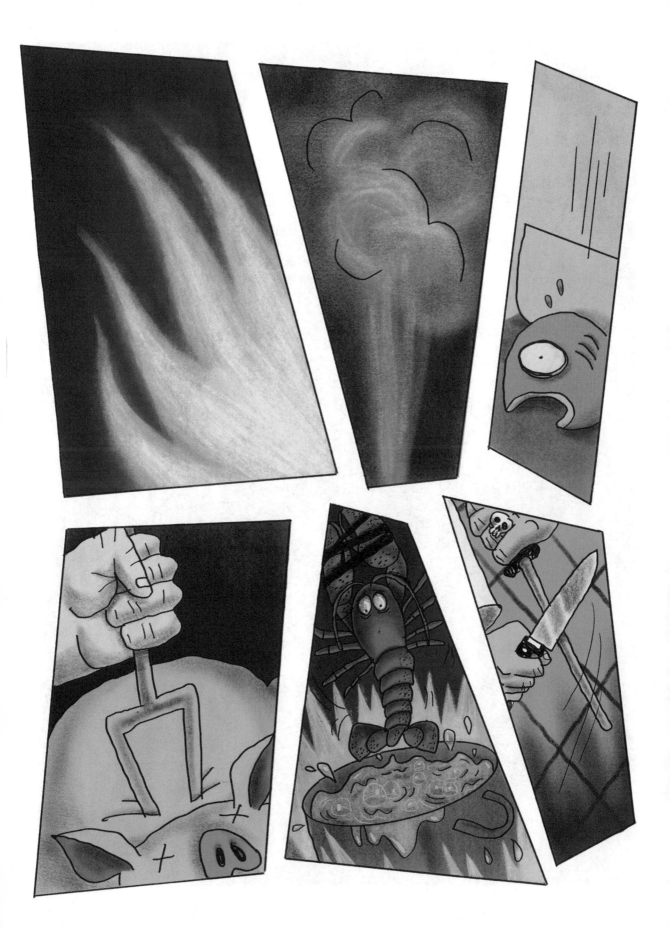

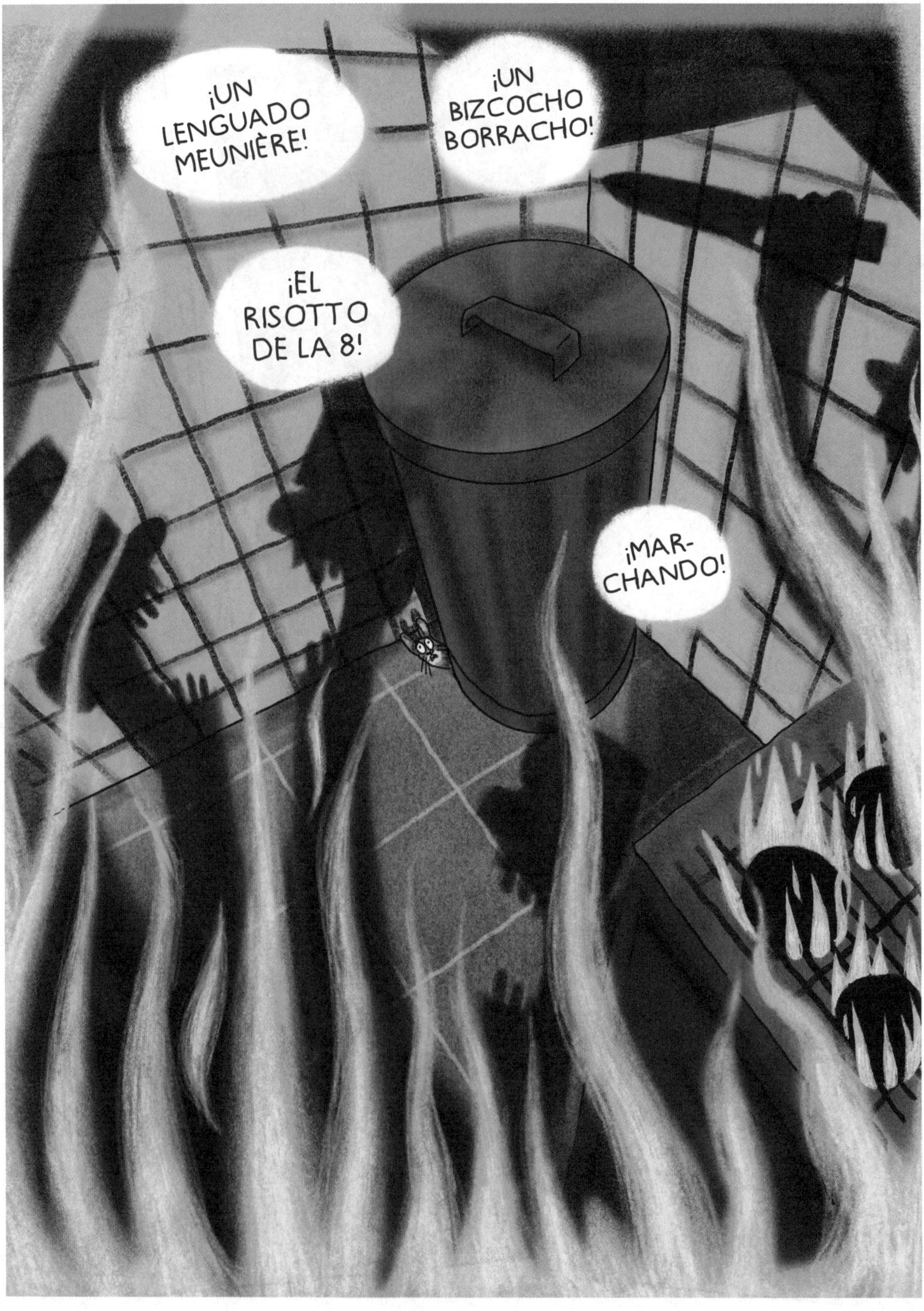
¡UN LENGUADO MEUNIÈRE!
¡UN BIZCOCHO BORRACHO!
¡EL RISOTTO DE LA 8!
¡MAR-CHANDO!

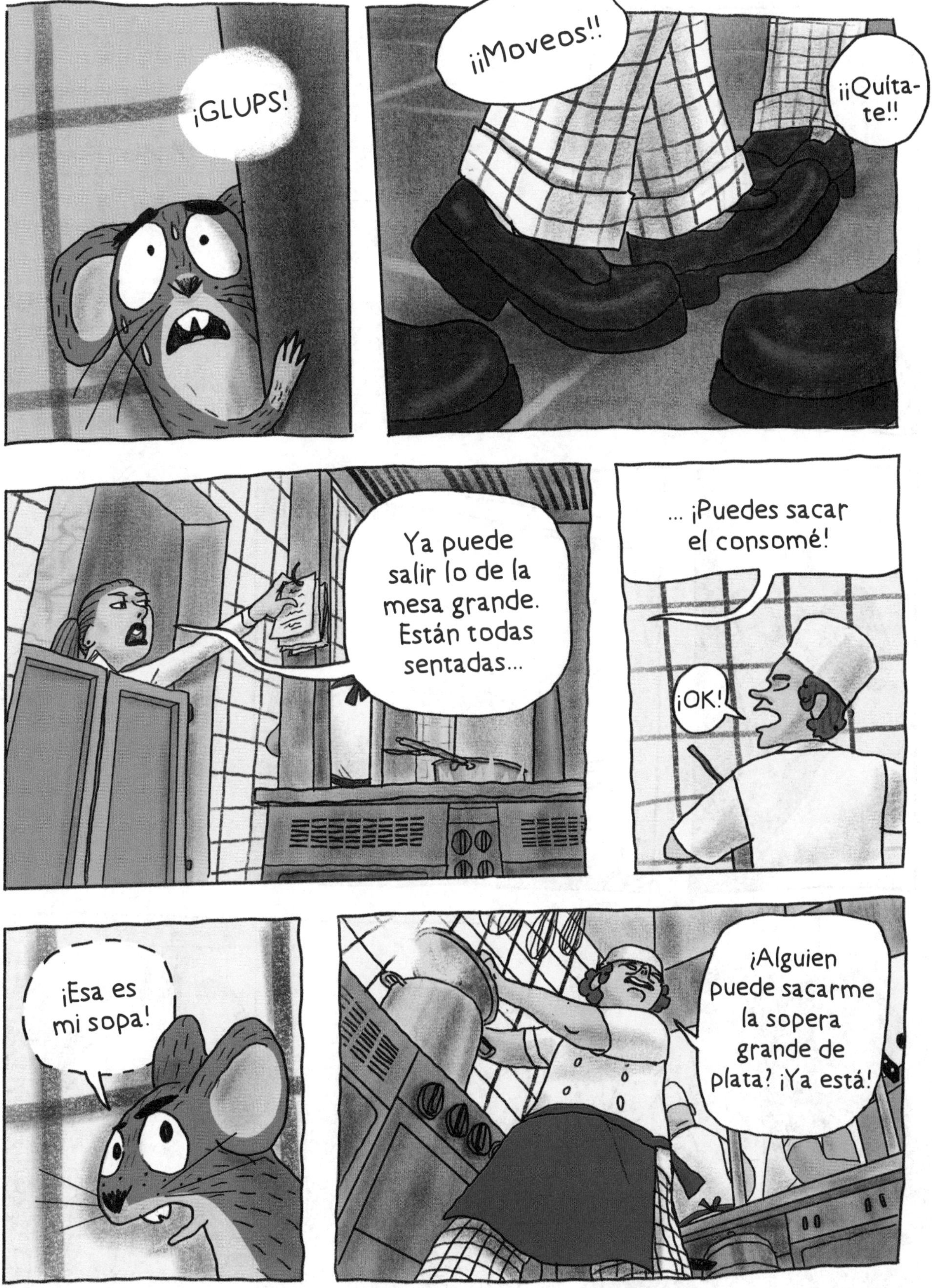

¡GLUPS!
¡¡Moveos!!
¡¡Quíta-te!!
Ya puede salir lo de la mesa grande. Están todas sentadas...
... ¡Puedes sacar el consomé!
¡OK!
¡Esa es mi sopa!
¡Alguien puede sacarme la sopera grande de plata? ¡Ya está!

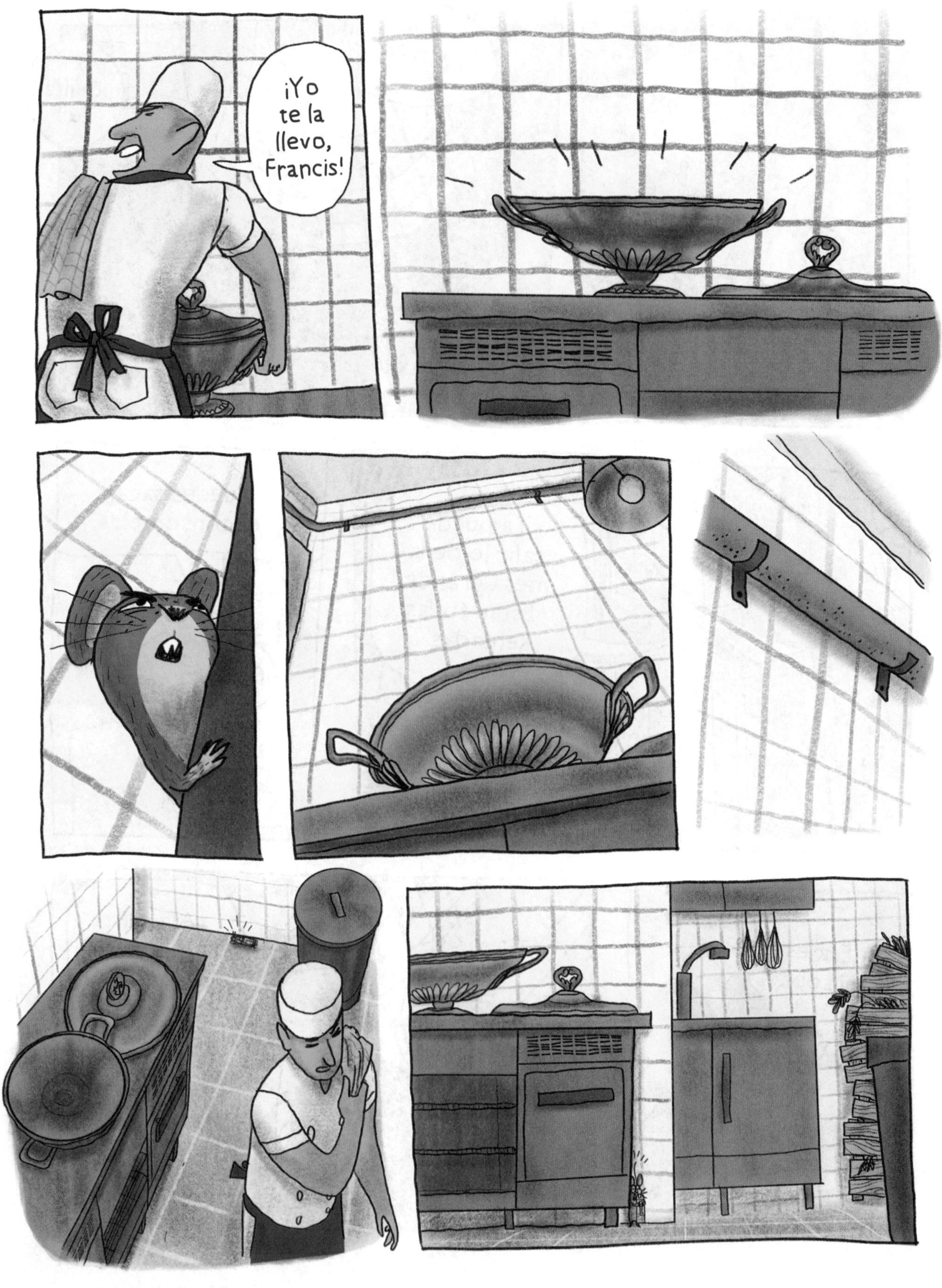
¡Yo te la llevo, Francis!

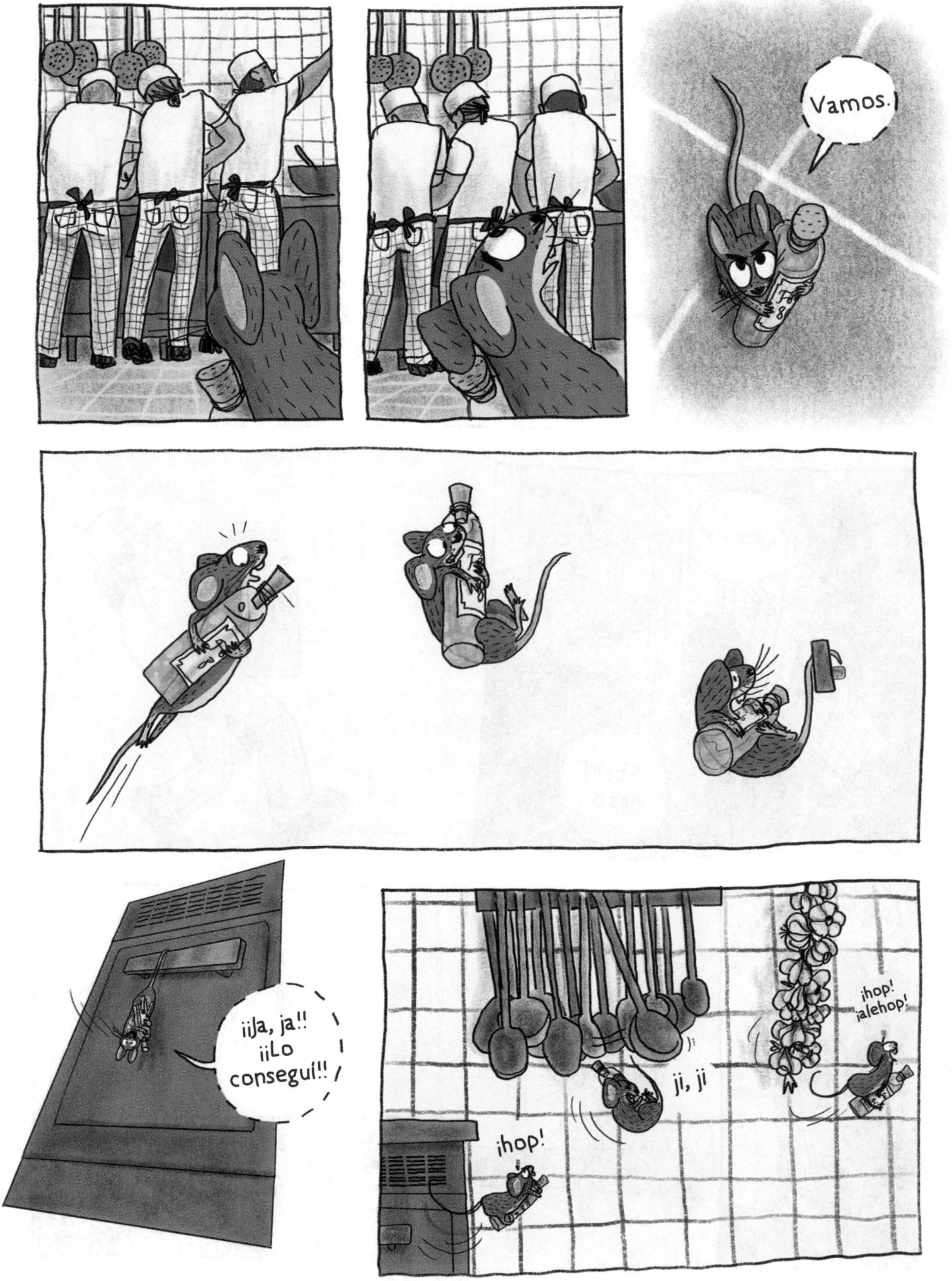
Vamos.
¡¡Ja, ja!! ¡¡Lo conseguí!!
¡hop! ¡alehop!
ji, ji
¡hop!

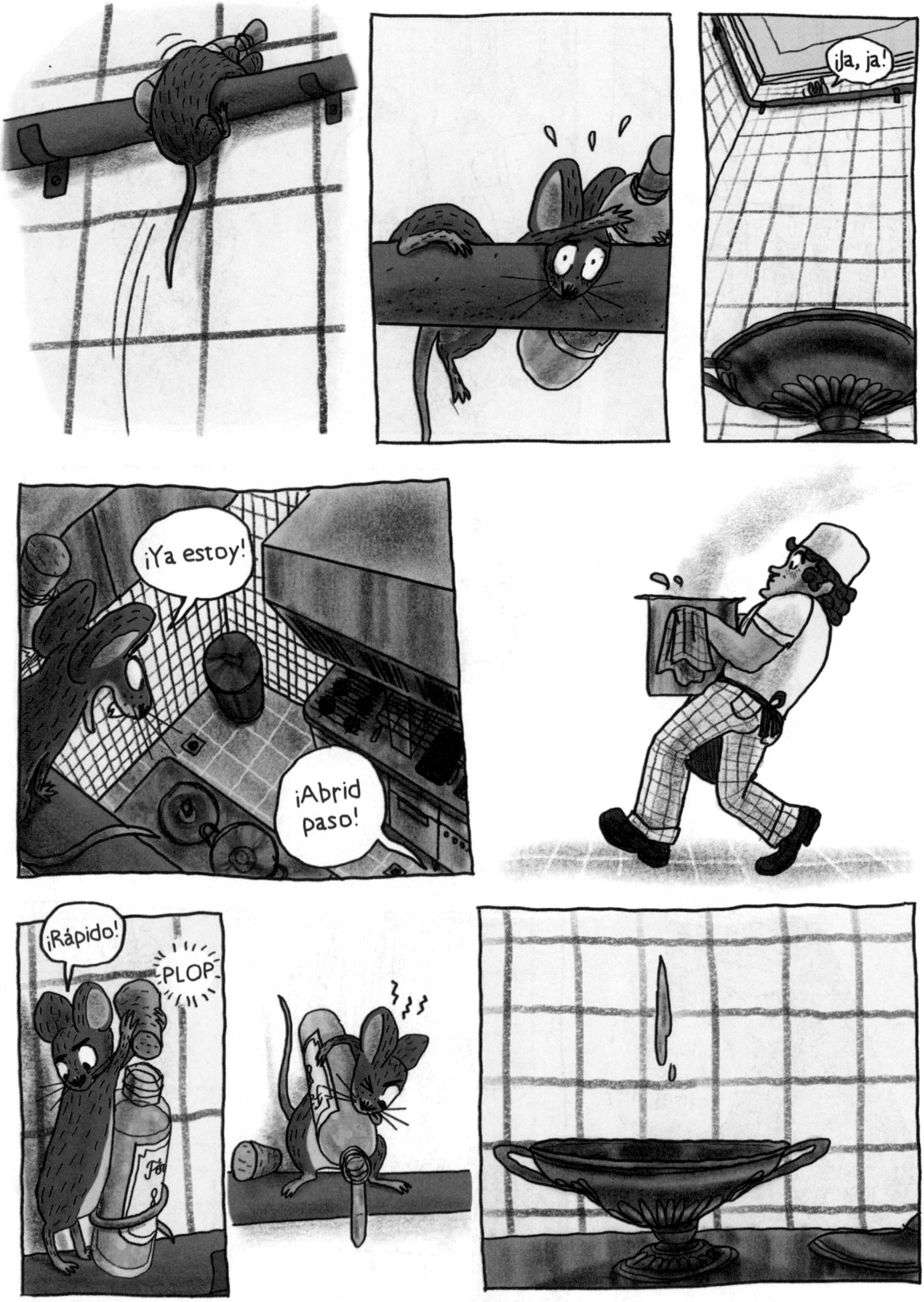

¡Ja, ja!
¡Ya estoy!
¡Abrid paso!
¡Rápido!
PLOP

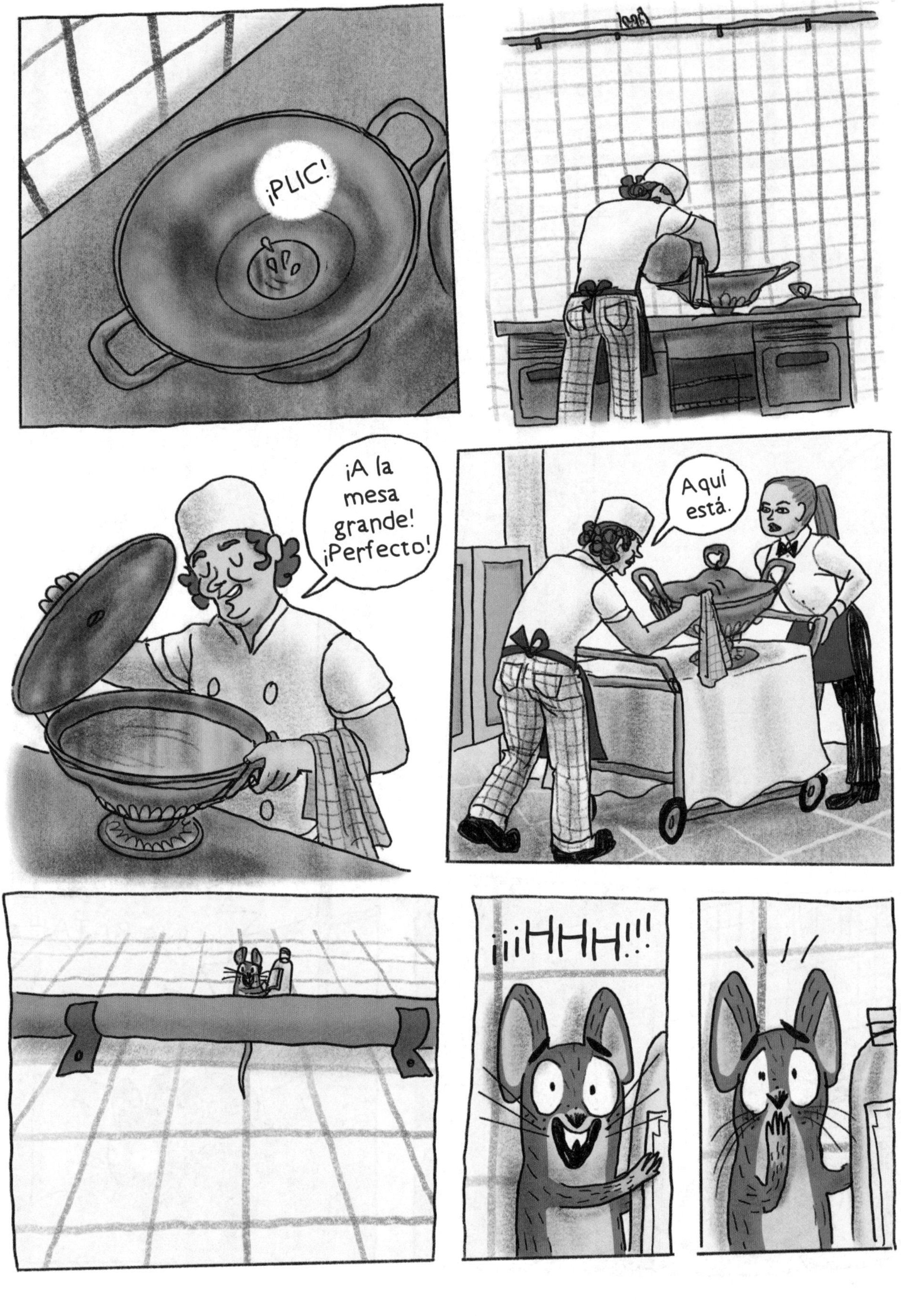
¡PLIC!
¡A la mesa grande! ¡Perfecto!
Aquí está.
¡¡¡HHH!!!

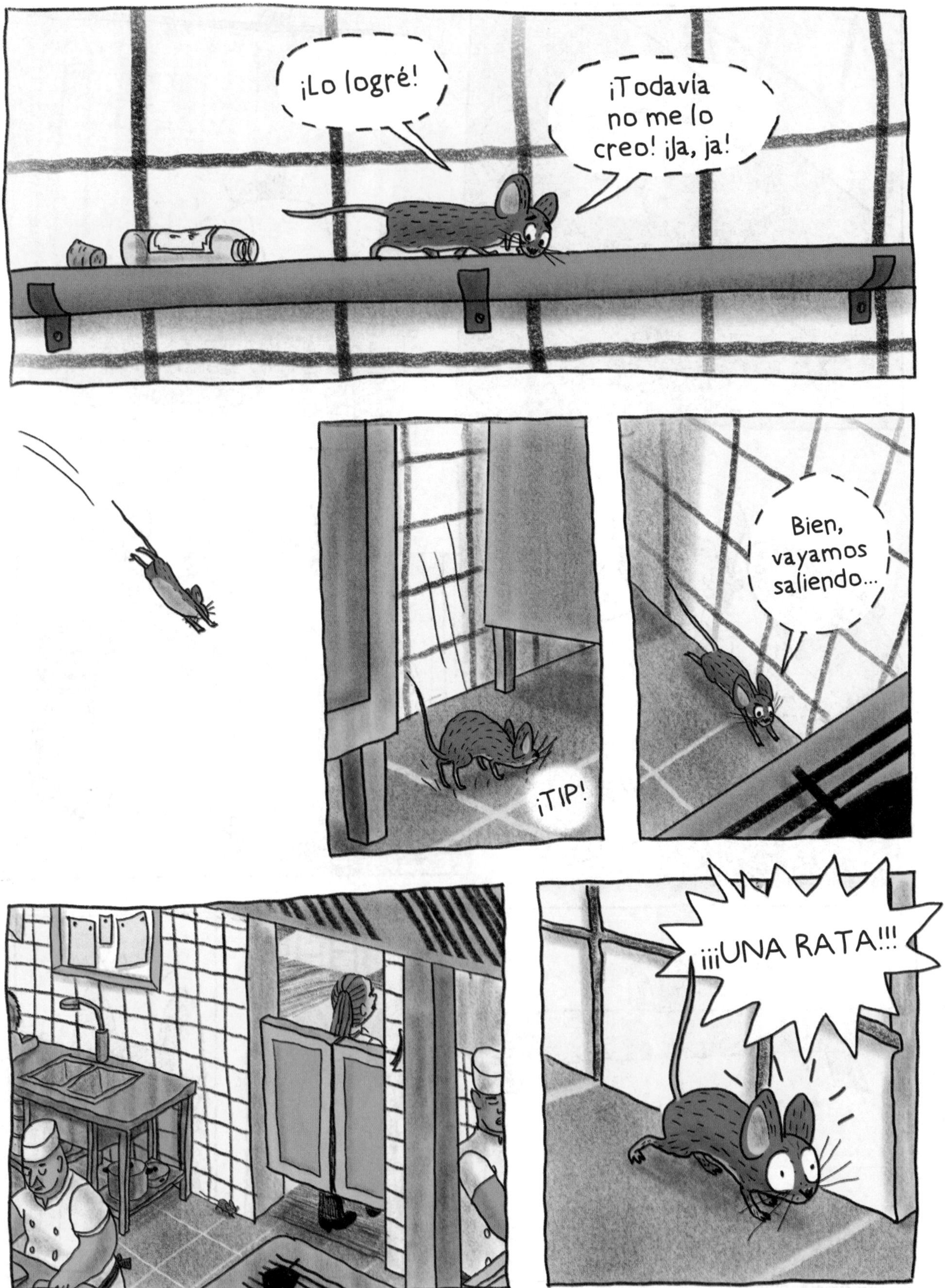
¡Lo logré!
¡Todavía no me lo creo! ¡Ja, ja!
¡TIP!
Bien, vayamos saliendo...
¡¡¡UNA RATA!!!

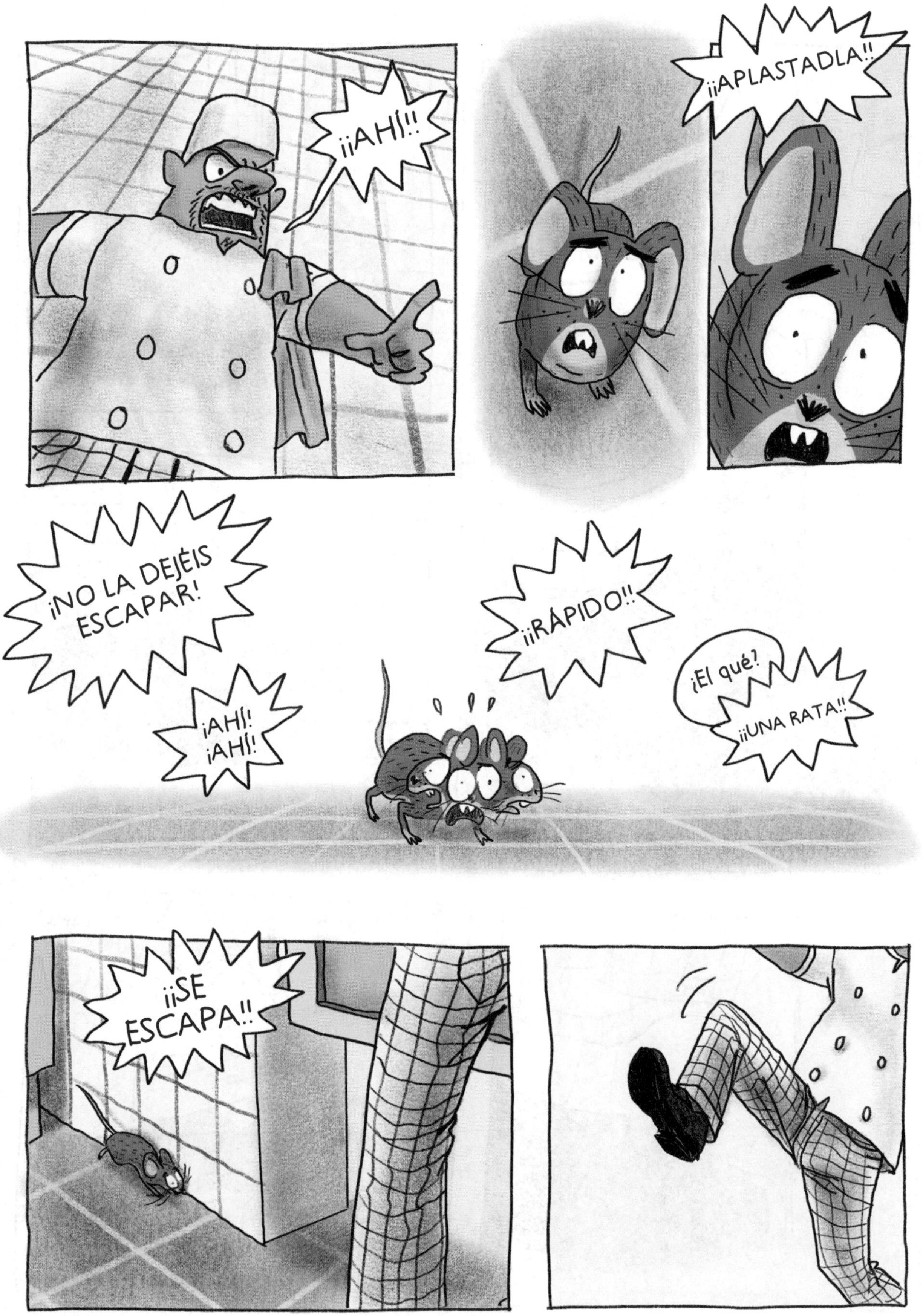
¡¡AHÍ!!
¡¡APLASTADLA!!
¡NO LA DEJÉIS ESCAPAR!
¡¡RÁPIDO!!
¡AHÍ! ¡AHÍ!
¿El qué?
¡¡UNA RATA!!
¡¡SE ESCAPA!!

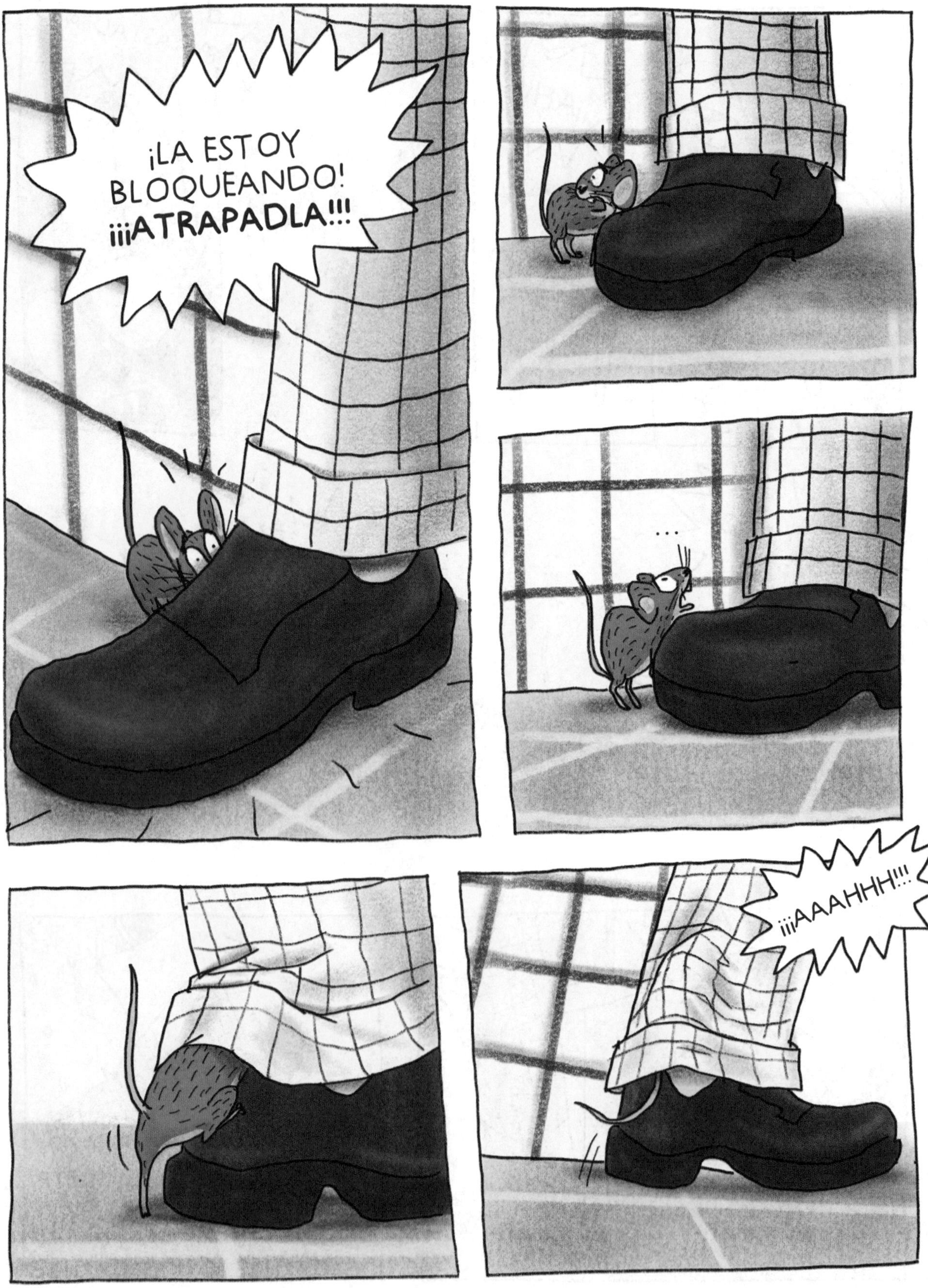
¡LA ESTOY BLOQUEANDO! ¡¡¡ATRAPADLA!!!
...
¡¡¡AAAHHH!!!

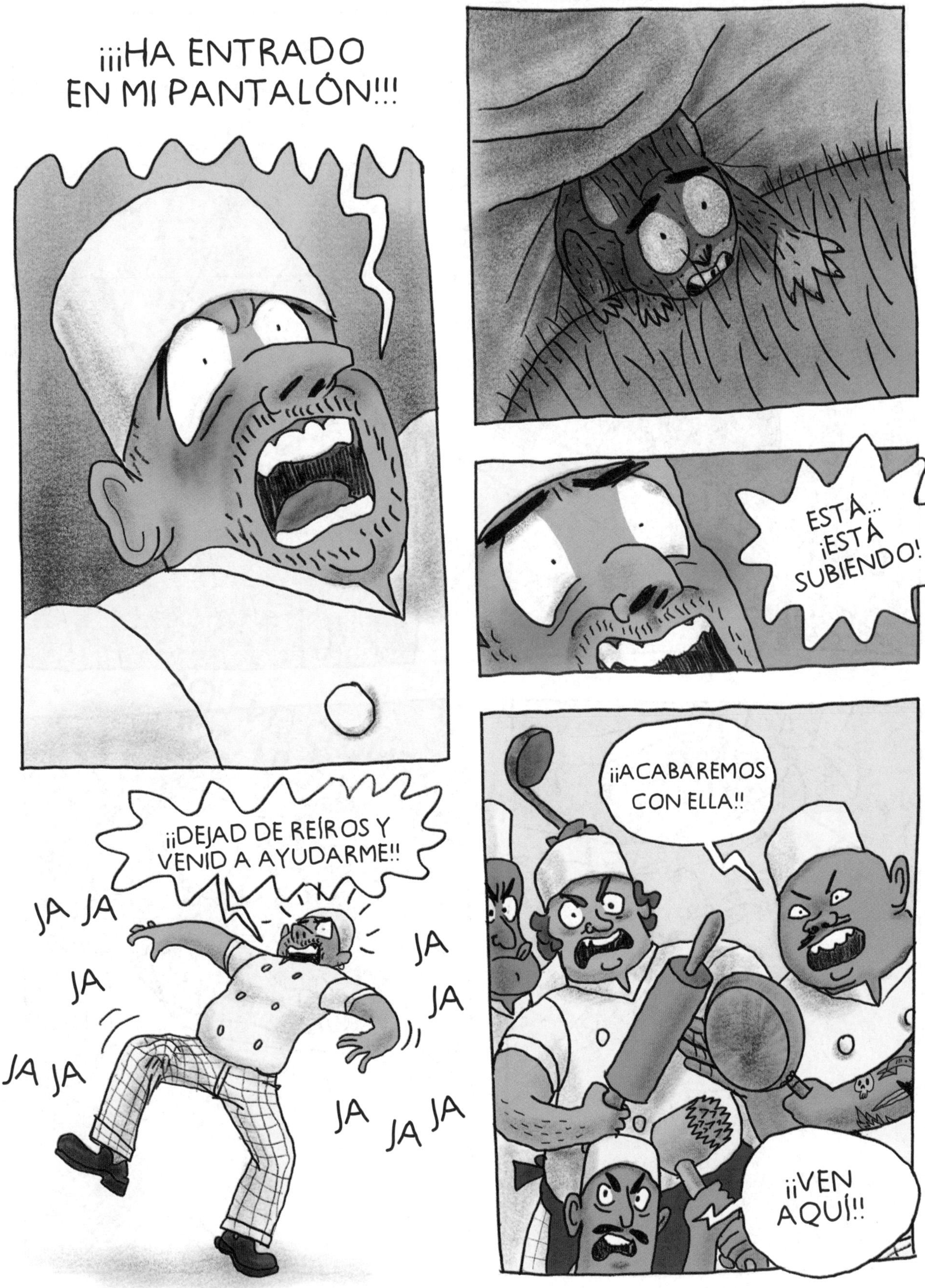
¡¡¡HA ENTRADO EN MI PANTALÓN!!!
ESTÁ... ¡ESTÁ SUBIENDO!
¡¡DEJAD DE REÍROS Y VENID A AYUDARME!!
JA JA
JA
JA JA
JA
JA
JA
JA JA
¡¡ACABAREMOS CON ELLA!!
¡¡VEN AQUÍ!!

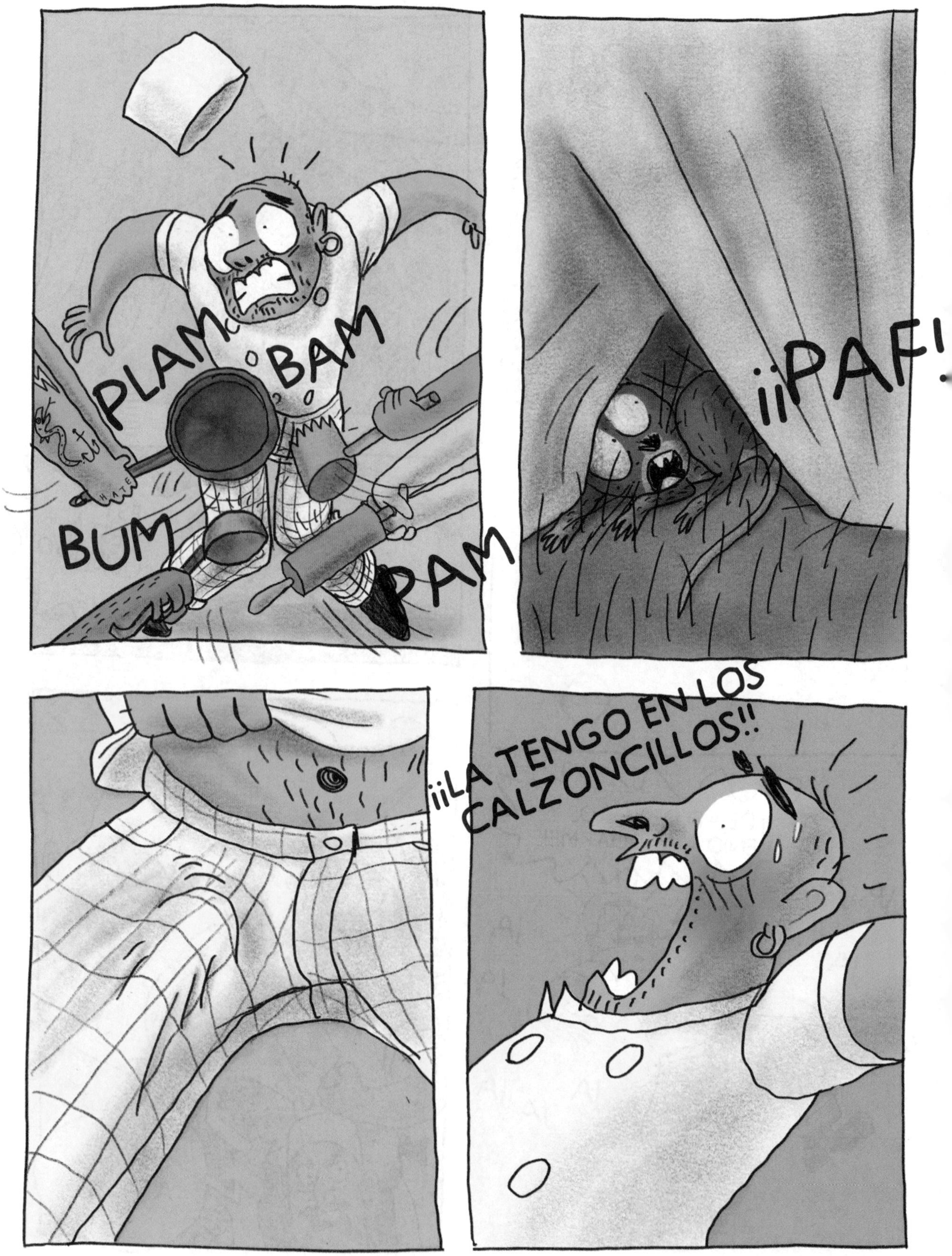
PLAM
BAM
BUM
PAM
¡¡PAF!!
¡¡LA TENGO EN LOS CALZONCILLOS!!

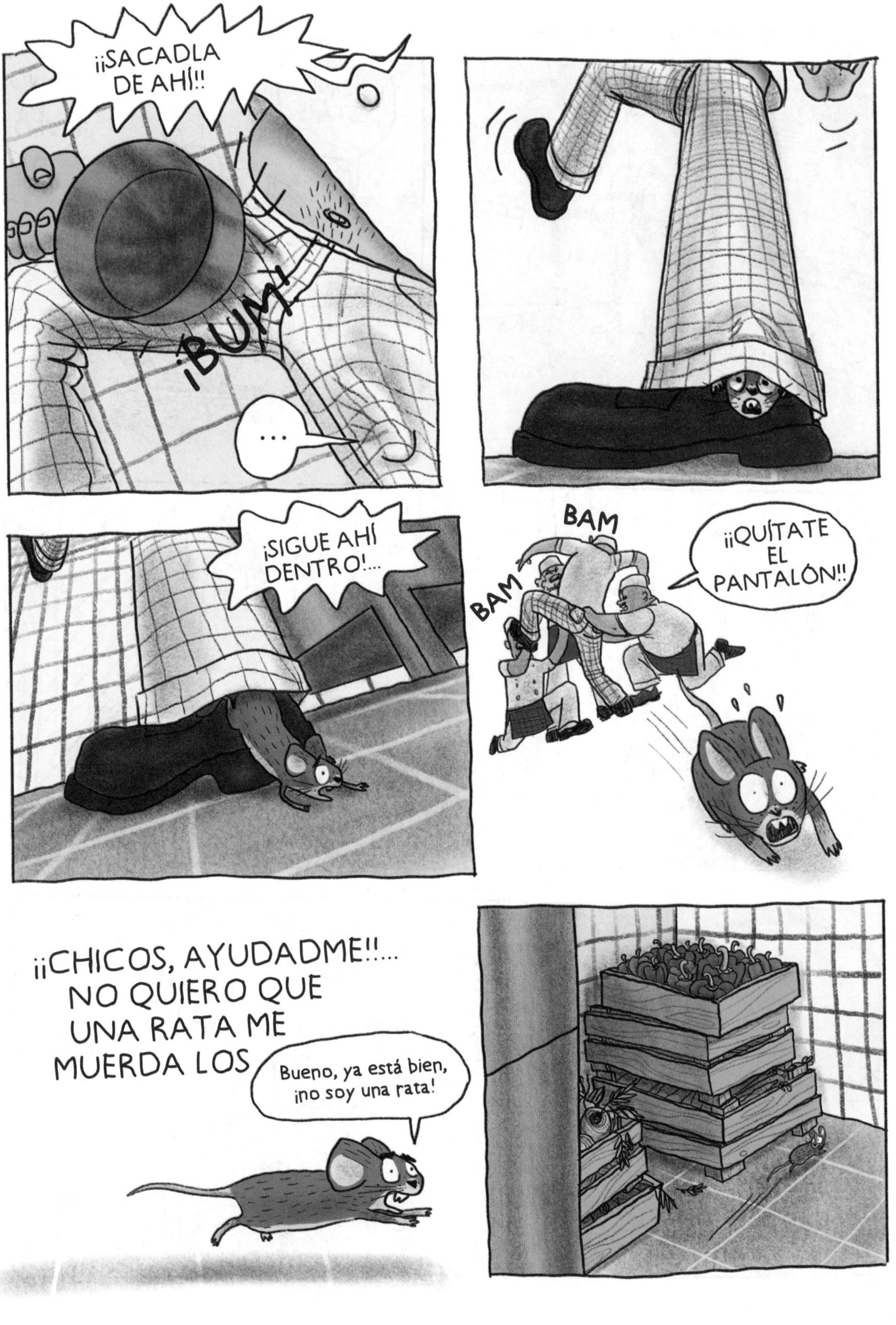
¡¡SACADLA DE AHÍ!!
¡BUM!
...
¡SIGUE AHÍ DENTRO!...
BAM
BAM
¡¡QUÍTATE EL PANTALÓN!!
¡¡CHICOS, AYUDADME!!... NO QUIERO QUE UNA RATA ME MUERDA LOS
Bueno, ya está bien, ¡no soy una rata!

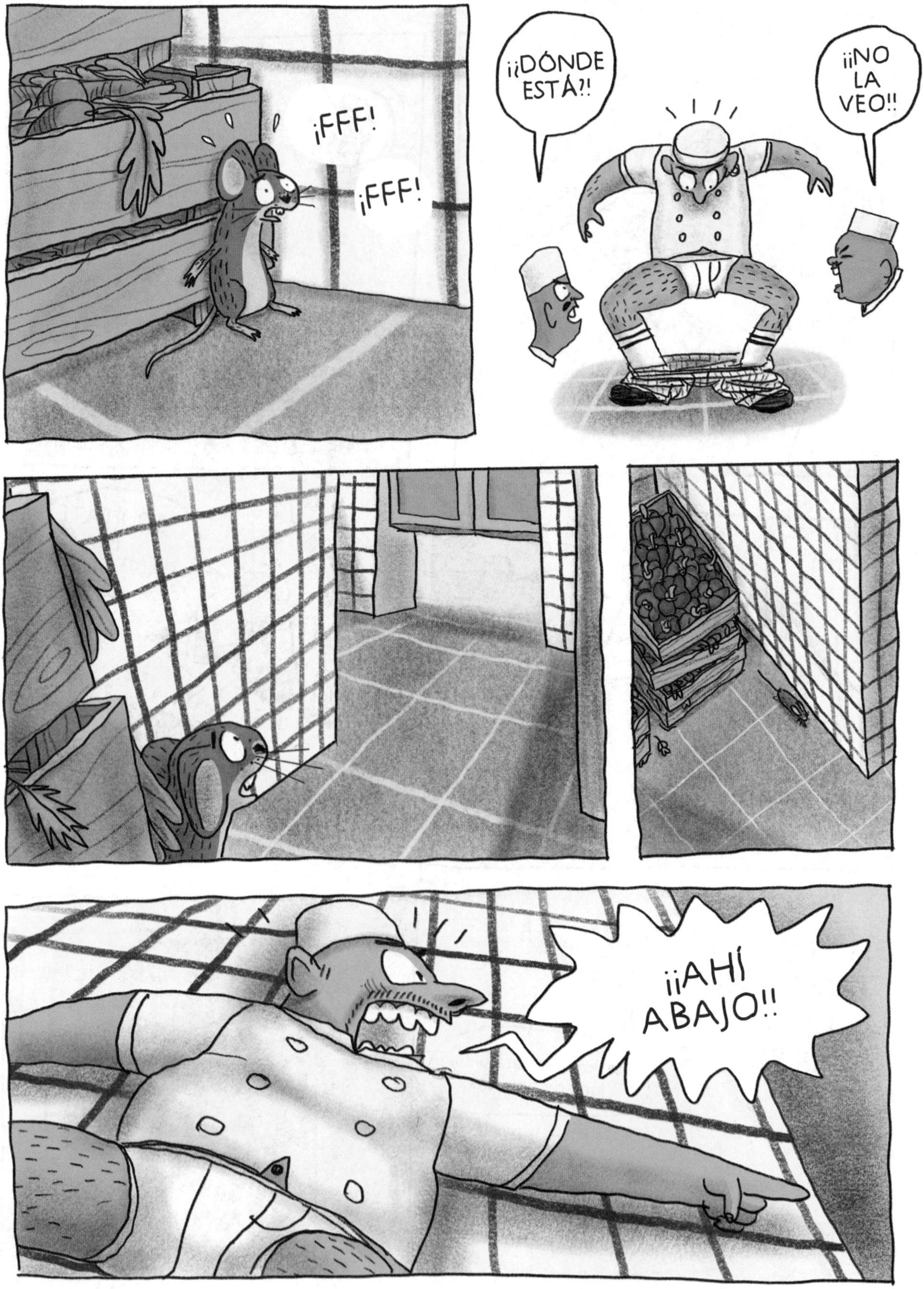

¡FFF!
¡FFF!
¡¿DÓNDE ESTÁ?!
¡¡NO LA VEO!!
¡¡AHÍ ABAJO!!

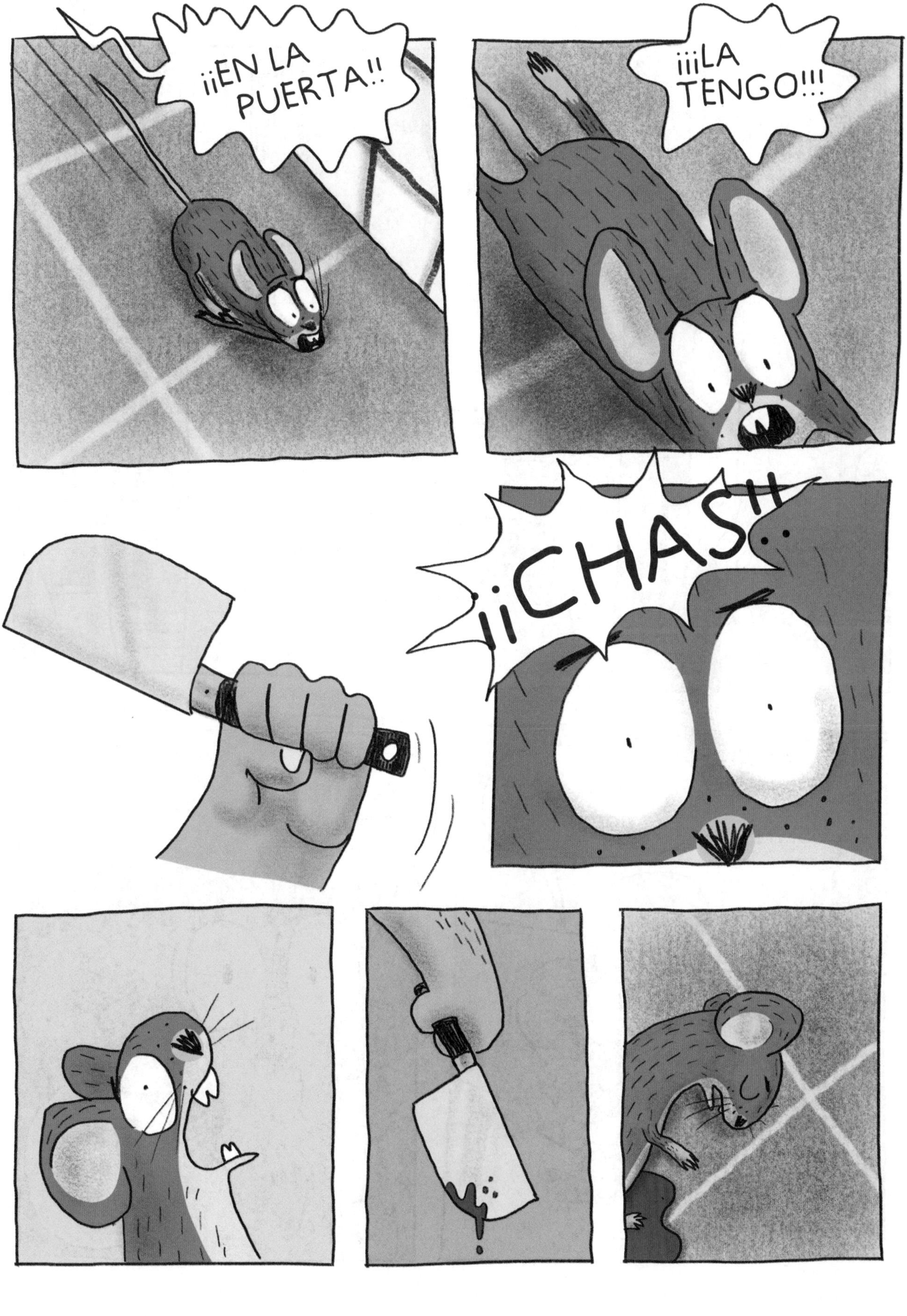
¡¡EN LA PUERTA!!
¡¡¡LA TENGO!!!
¡¡CHAS!!

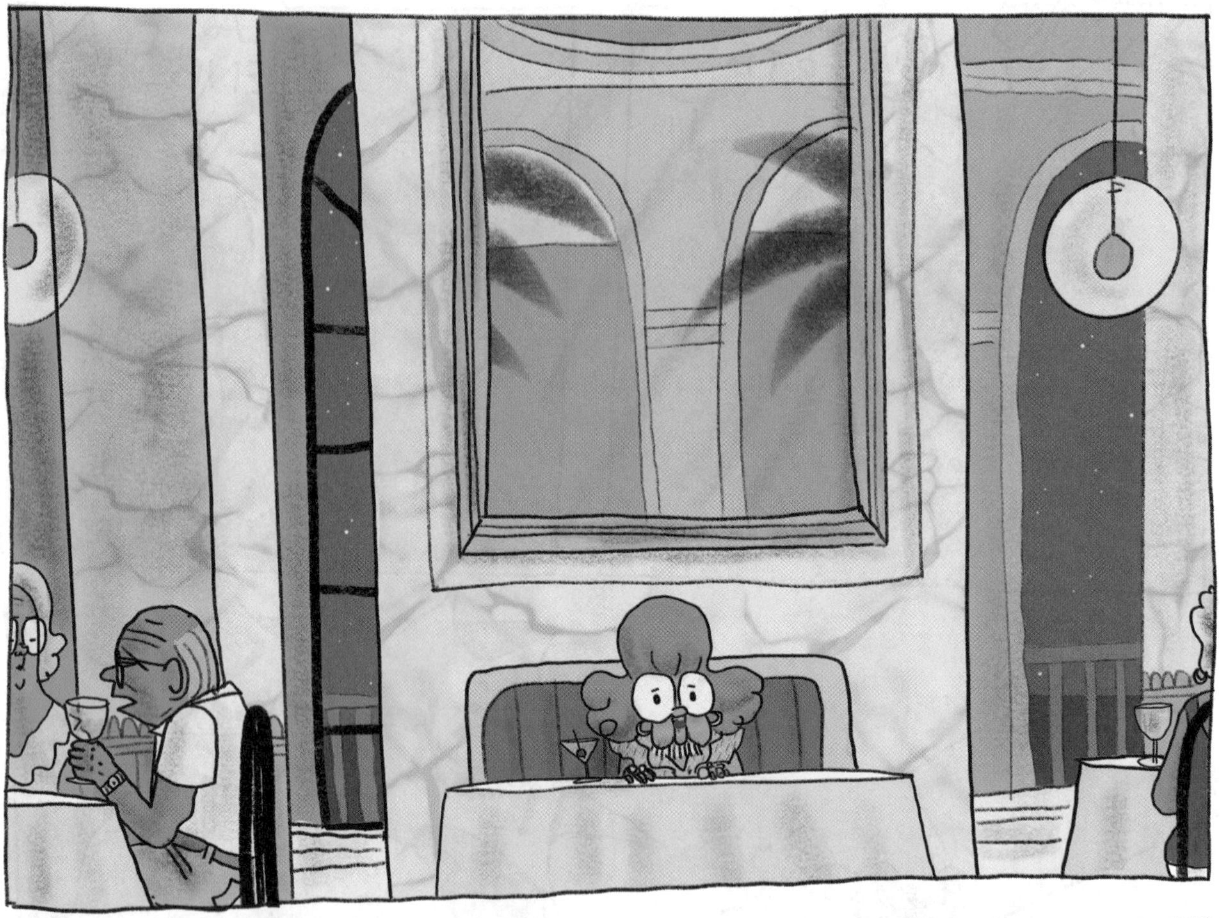

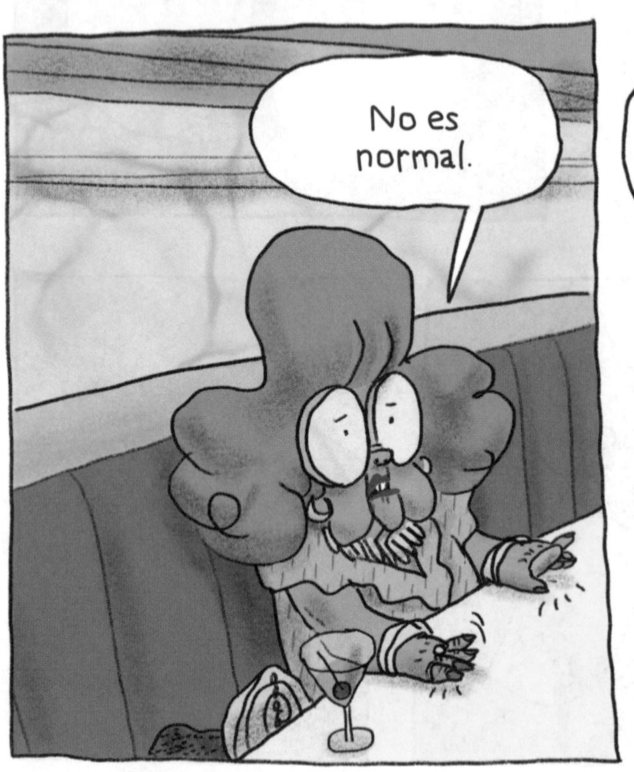
No es normal.

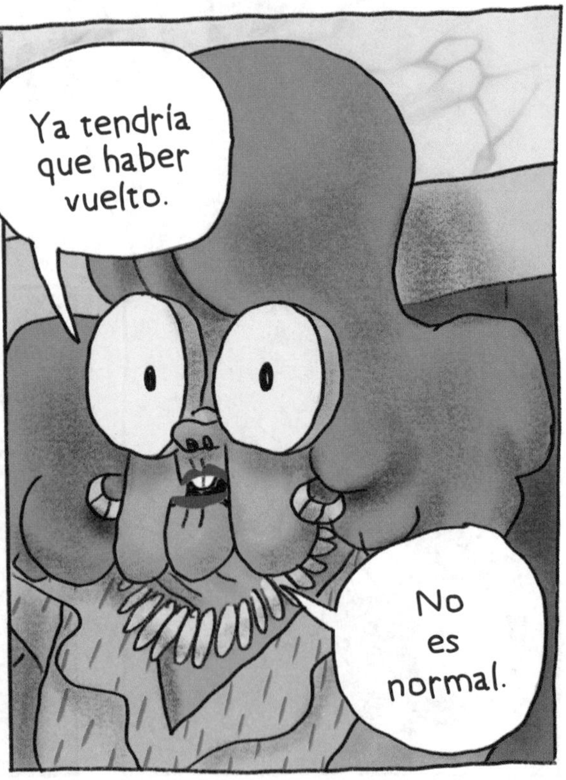
Ya tendría que haber vuelto.
No es normal.

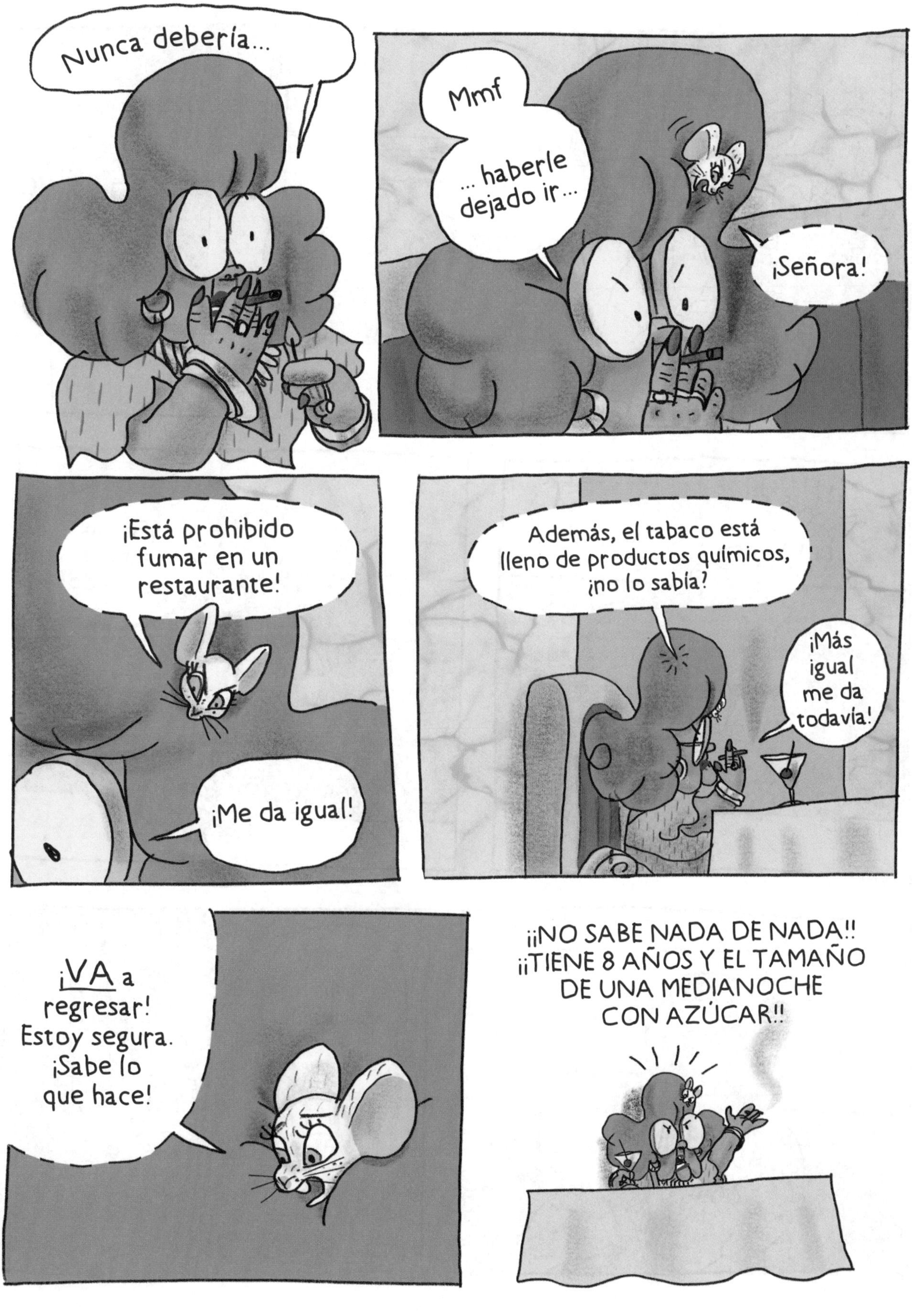
Nunca debería...
Mmf
... haberle dejado ir...
¡Señora!
¡Está prohibido fumar en un restaurante!
¡Me da igual!
Además, el tabaco está lleno de productos químicos, ¿no lo sabía?
¡Más igual me da todavía!
¡VA a regresar! Estoy segura. ¡Sabe lo que hace!
¡¡NO SABE NADA DE NADA!! ¡¡TIENE 8 AÑOS Y EL TAMAÑO DE UNA MEDIANOCHE CON AZÚCAR!!

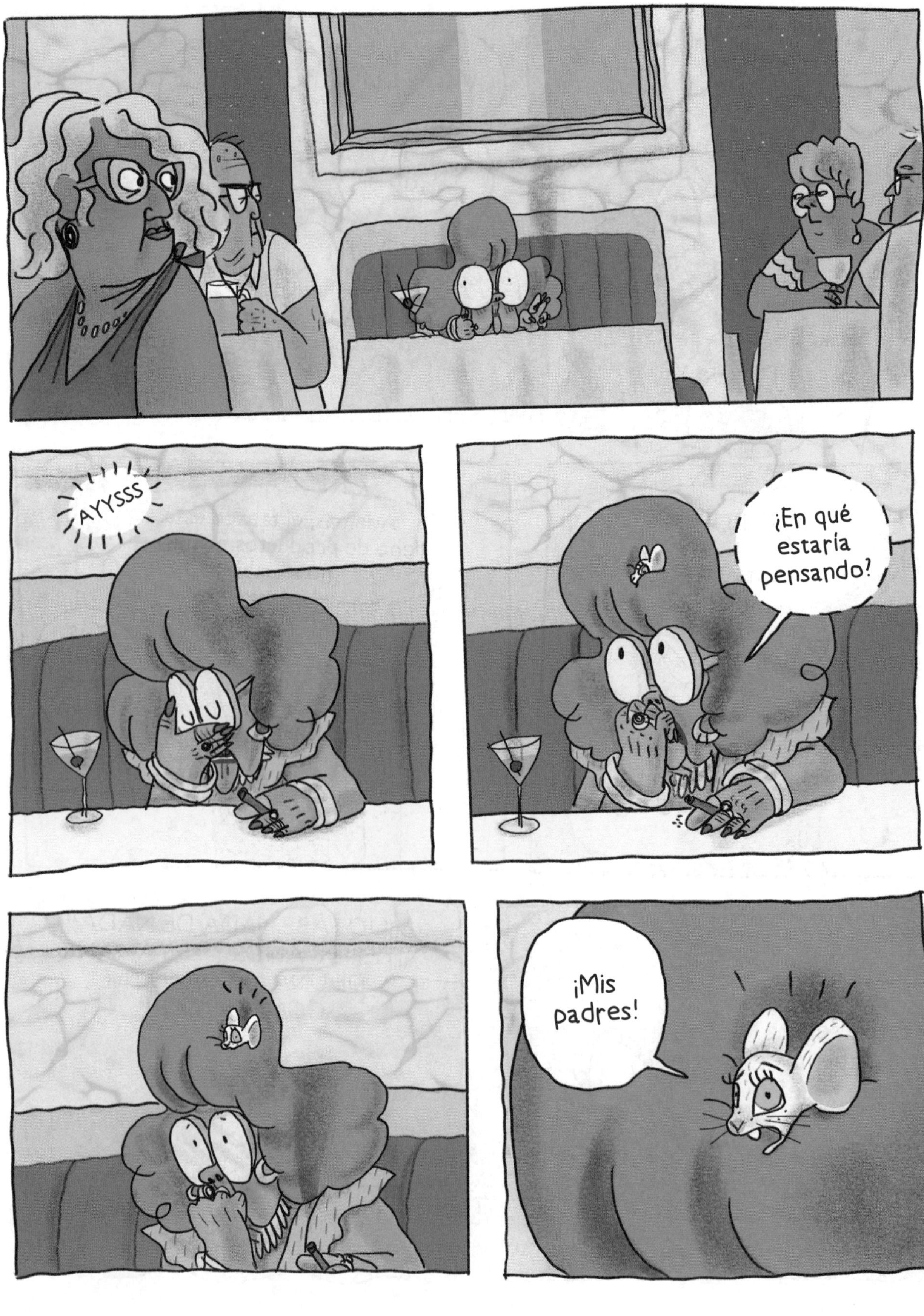
AYYSSS
¿En qué estaría pensando?
¡Mis padres!

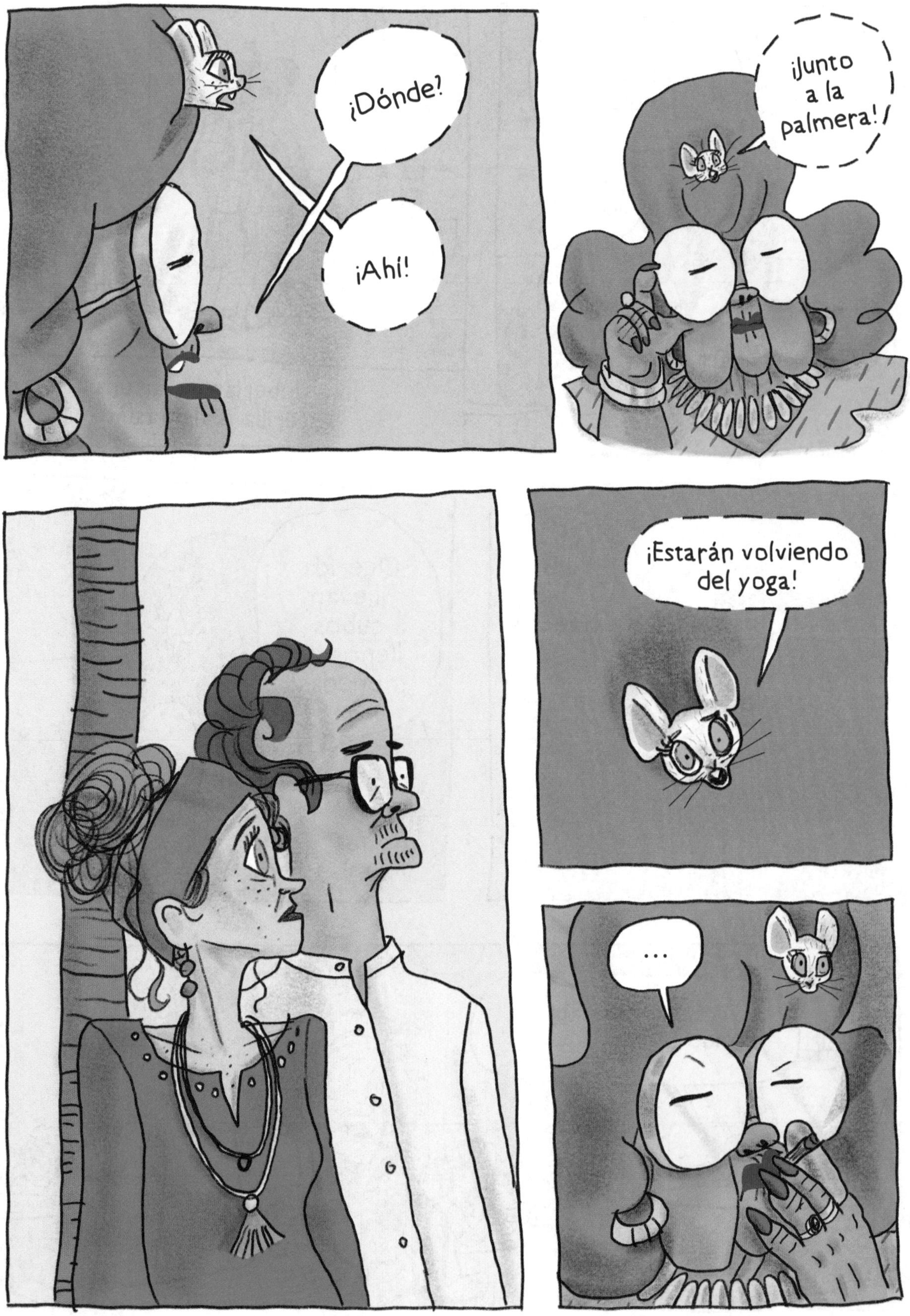
¿Dónde?
¡Ahí!
¡Junto a la palmera!
¡Estarán volviendo del yoga!
...

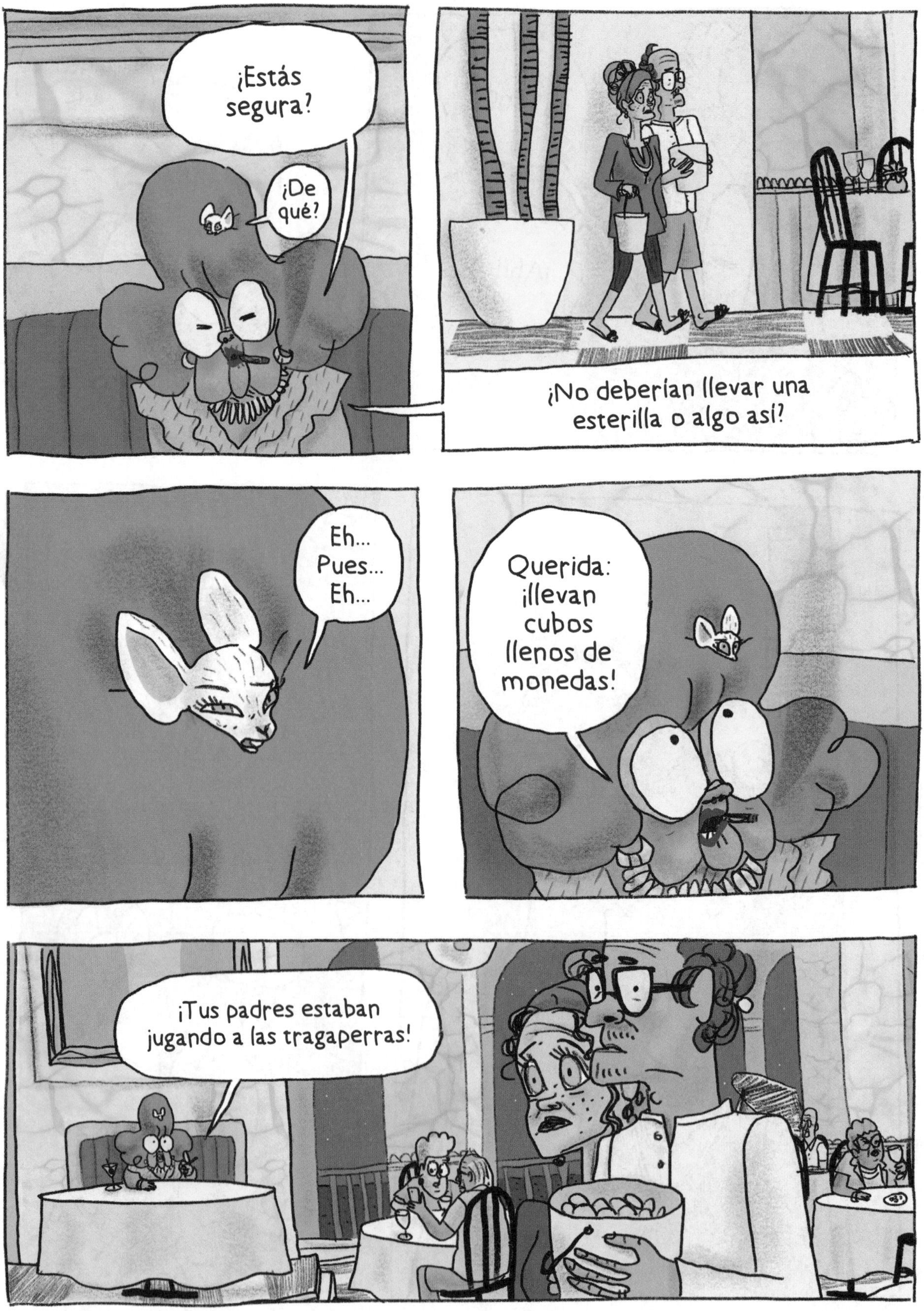
¡Estás segura?
¡De qué?
¡No deberían llevar una esterilla o algo así?
Eh... Pues... Eh...
Querida: ¡llevan cubos llenos de monedas!
¡Tus padres estaban jugando a las tragaperras!

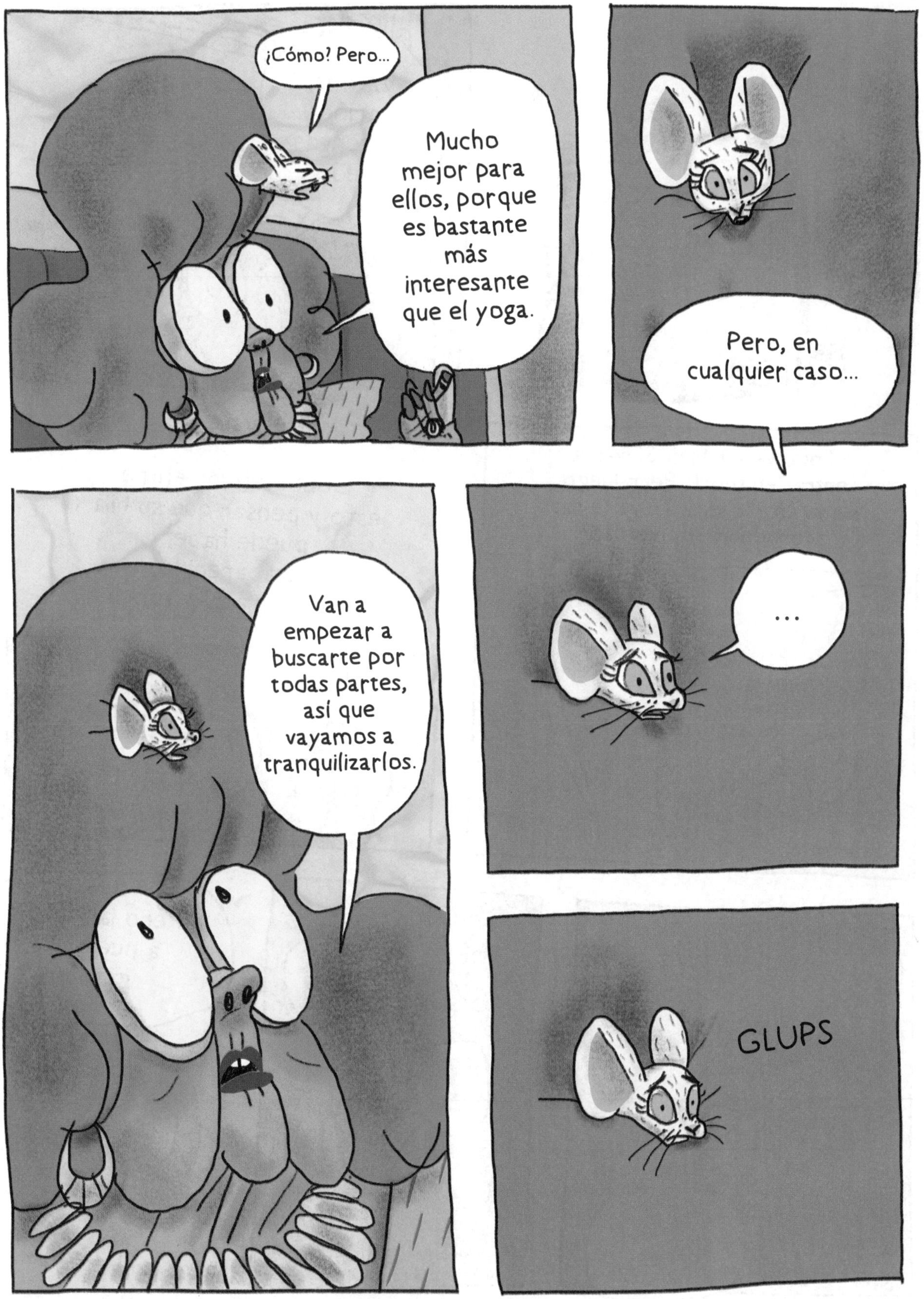
¡Cómo? Pero...
Mucho mejor para ellos, porque es bastante más interesante que el yoga.
Pero, en cualquier caso...
Van a empezar a buscarte por todas partes, así que vayamos a tranquilizarlos.
...
GLUPS

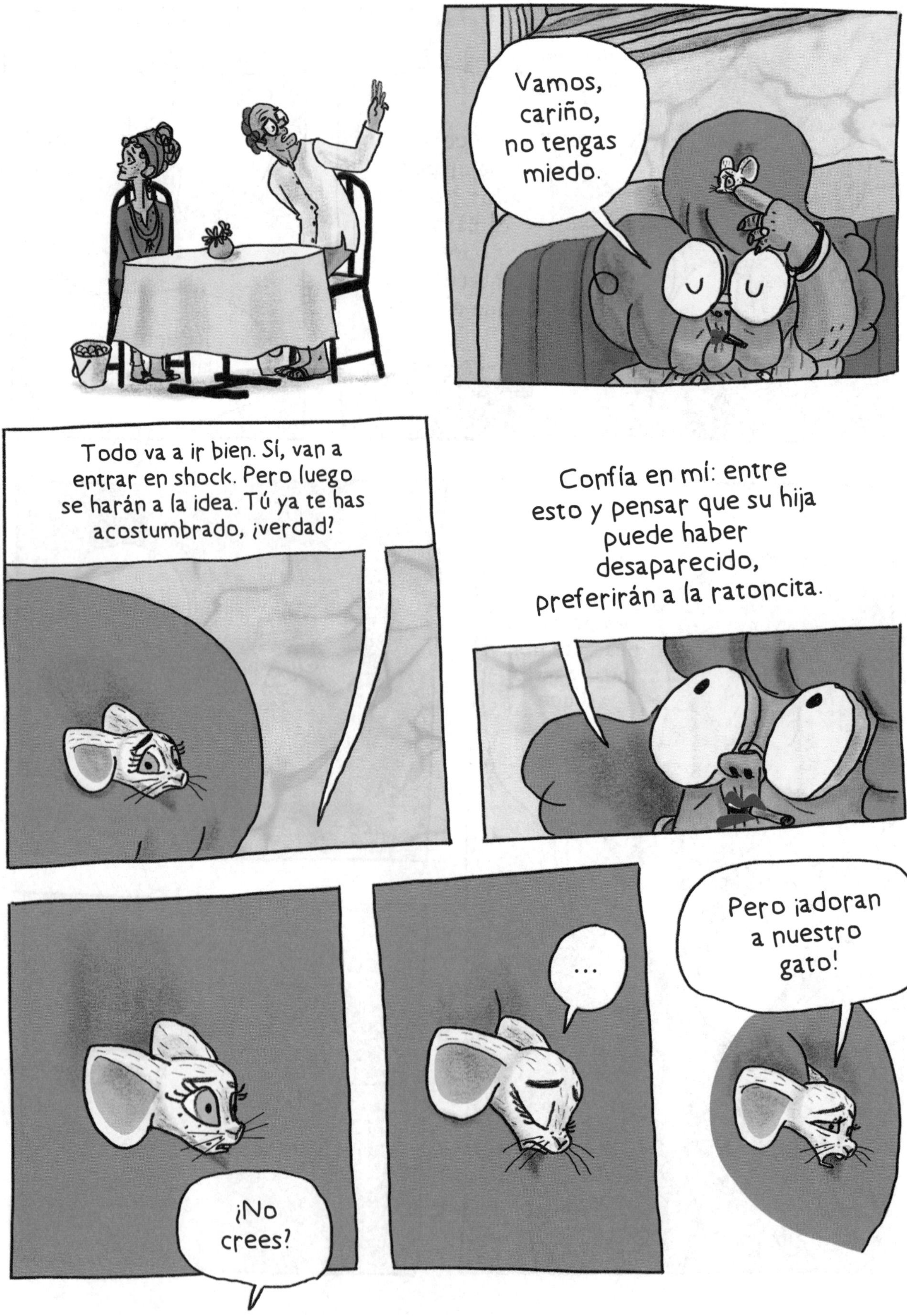
Vamos, cariño, no tengas miedo.
Todo va a ir bien. Sí, van a entrar en shock. Pero luego se harán a la idea. Tú ya te has acostumbrado, ¿verdad?
Confía en mí: entre esto y pensar que su hija puede haber desaparecido, preferirán a la ratoncita.
¿No crees?
...
Pero ¡adoran a nuestro gato!

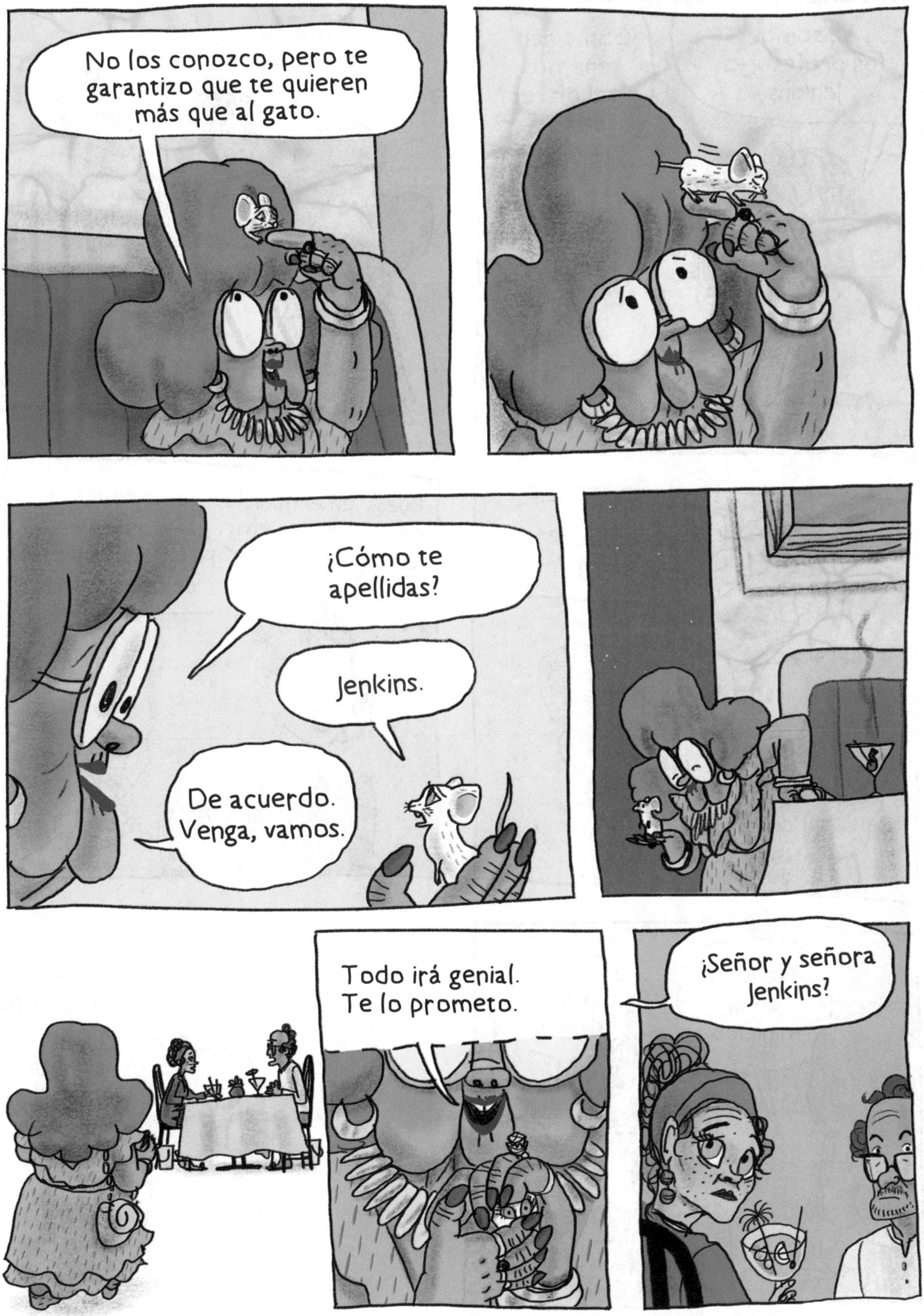
No los conozco, pero te garantizo que te quieren más que al gato.
¿Cómo te apellidas?
Jenkins.
De acuerdo. Venga, vamos.
Todo irá genial. Te lo prometo.
¿Señor y señora Jenkins?

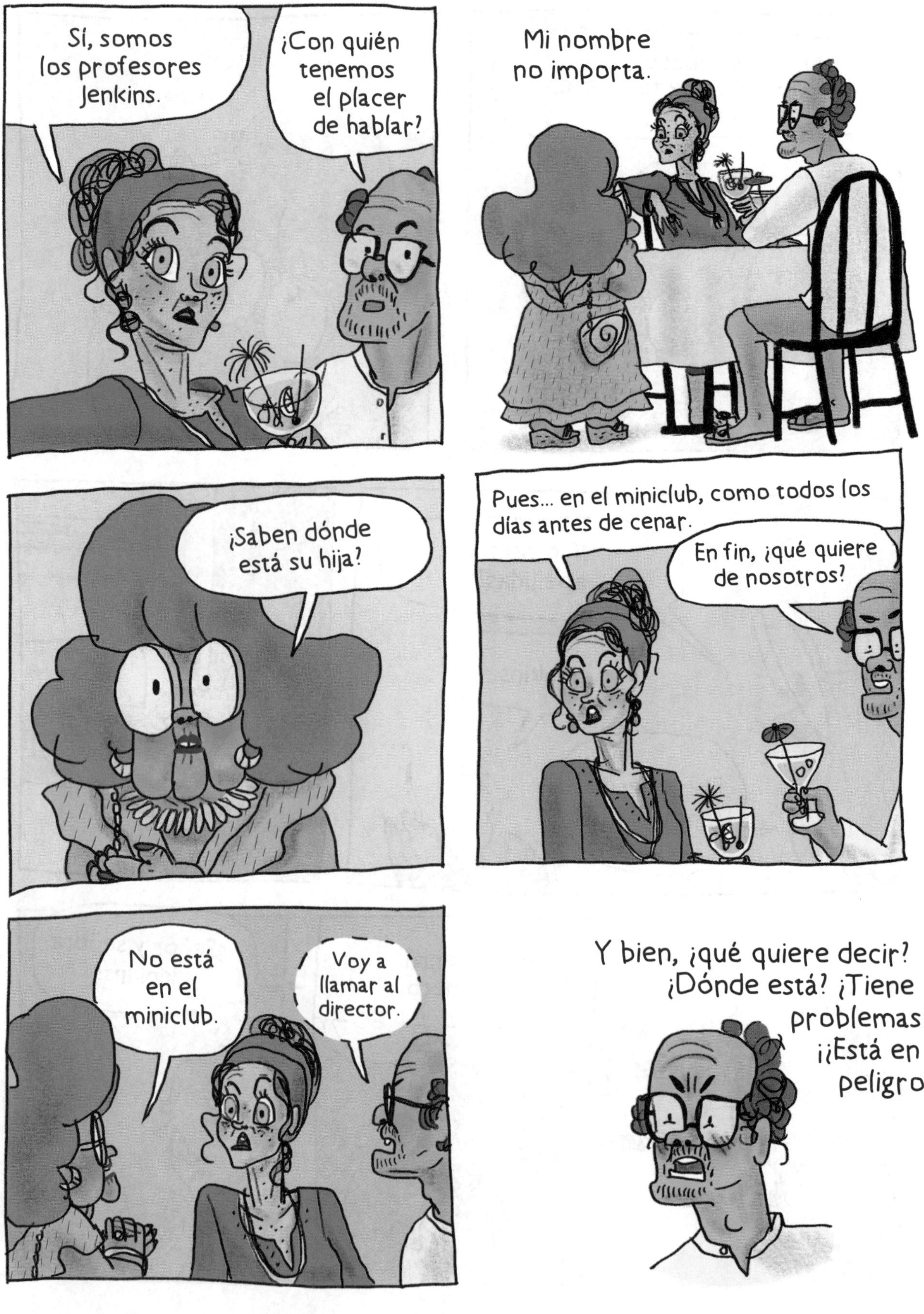
Sí, somos los profesores Jenkins.
¿Con quién tenemos el placer de hablar?
Mi nombre no importa.
¿Saben dónde está su hija?
Pues... en el miniclub, como todos los días antes de cenar.
En fin, ¿qué quiere de nosotros?
No está en el miniclub.
Voy a llamar al director.
Y bien, ¿qué quiere decir? ¿Dónde está? ¿Tiene problemas? ¡¿Está en peligro?!

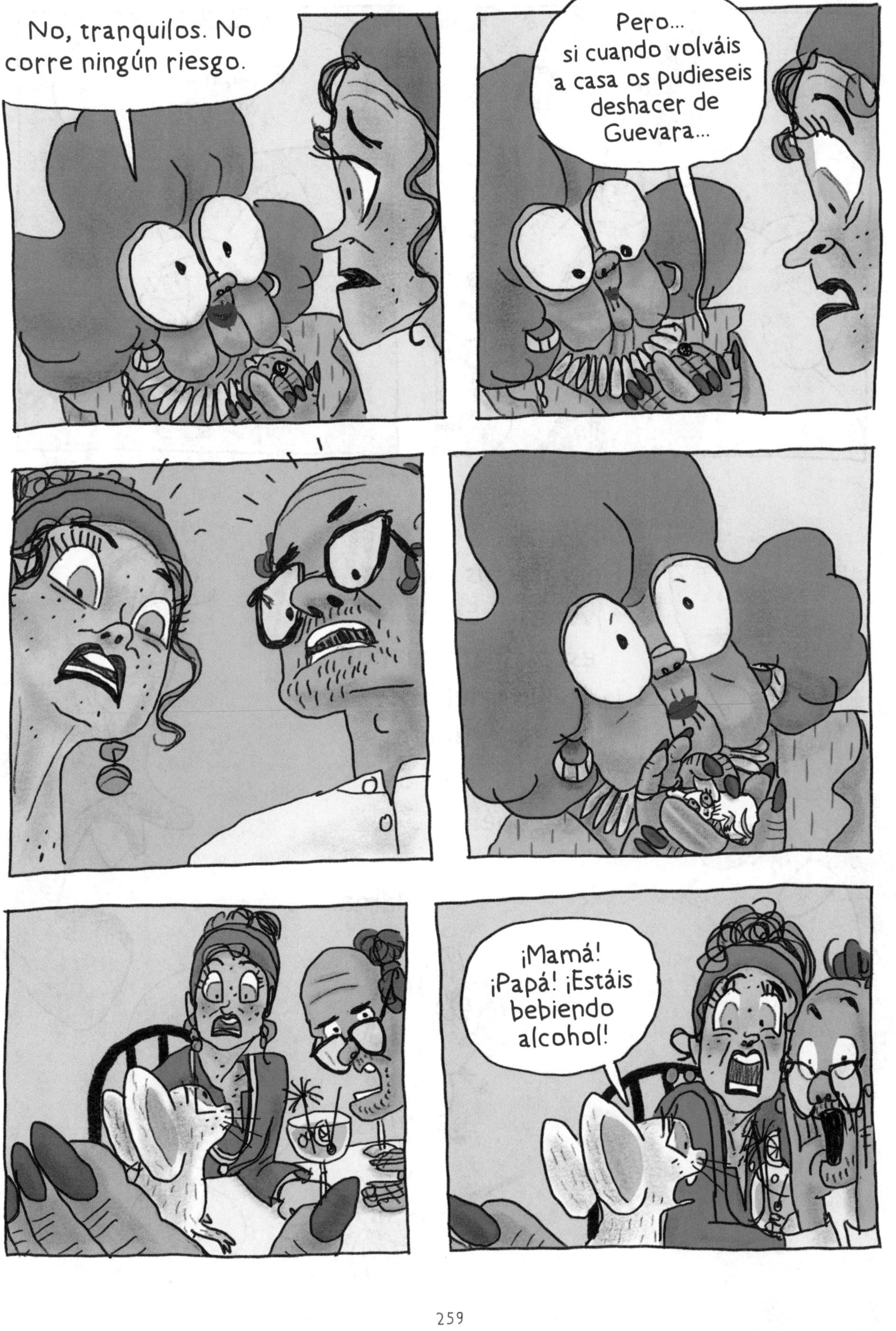
No, tranquilos. No corre ningún riesgo.
Pero... si cuando volváis a casa os pudieseis deshacer de Guevara...
¡Mamá! ¡Papá! ¡Estáis bebiendo alcohol!

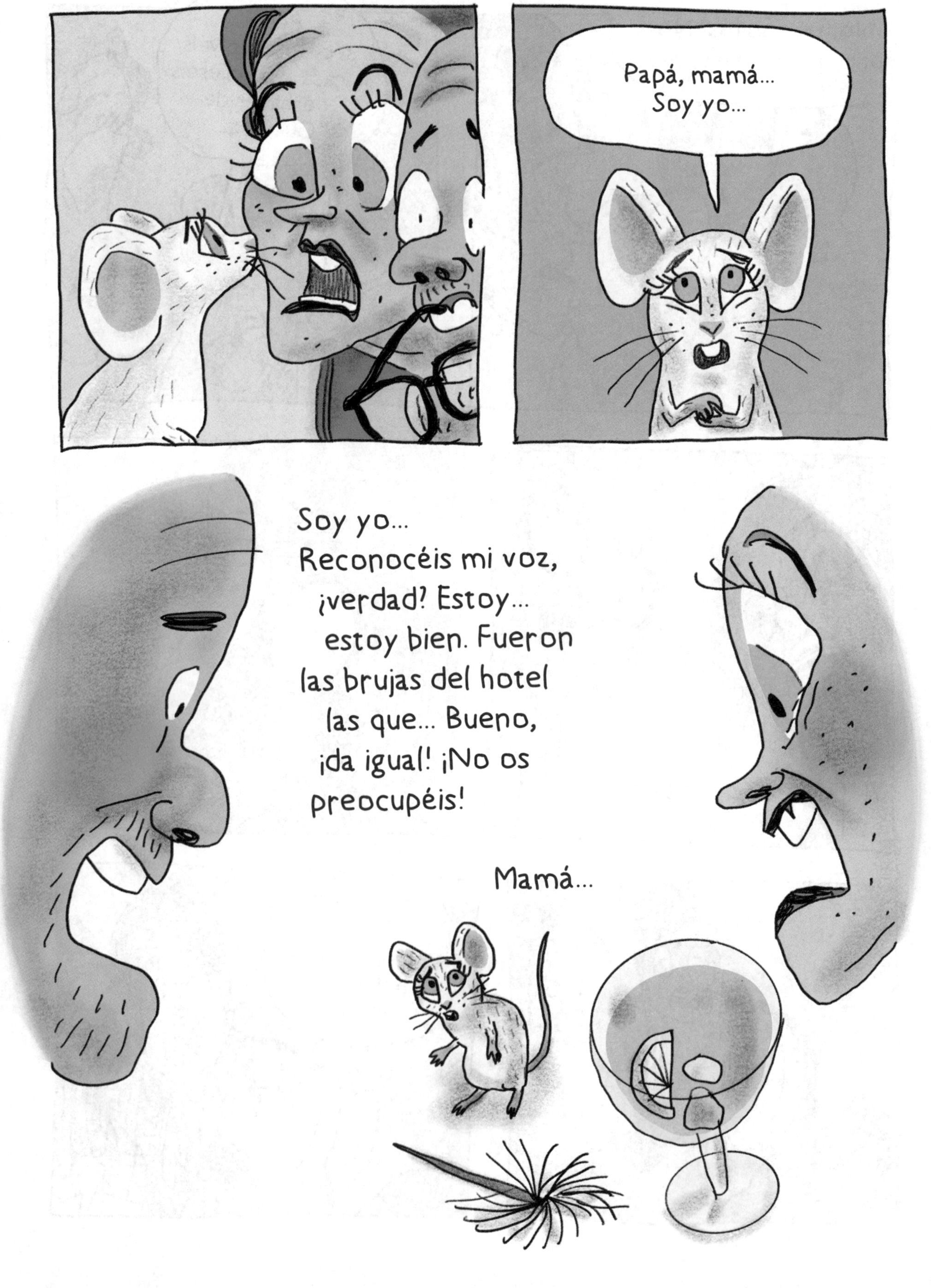
Papá, mamá...
Soy yo...
Soy yo...
Reconocéis mi voz, ¿verdad? Estoy... estoy bien. Fueron las brujas del hotel las que... Bueno, ¡da igual! ¡No os preocupéis!
Mamá...

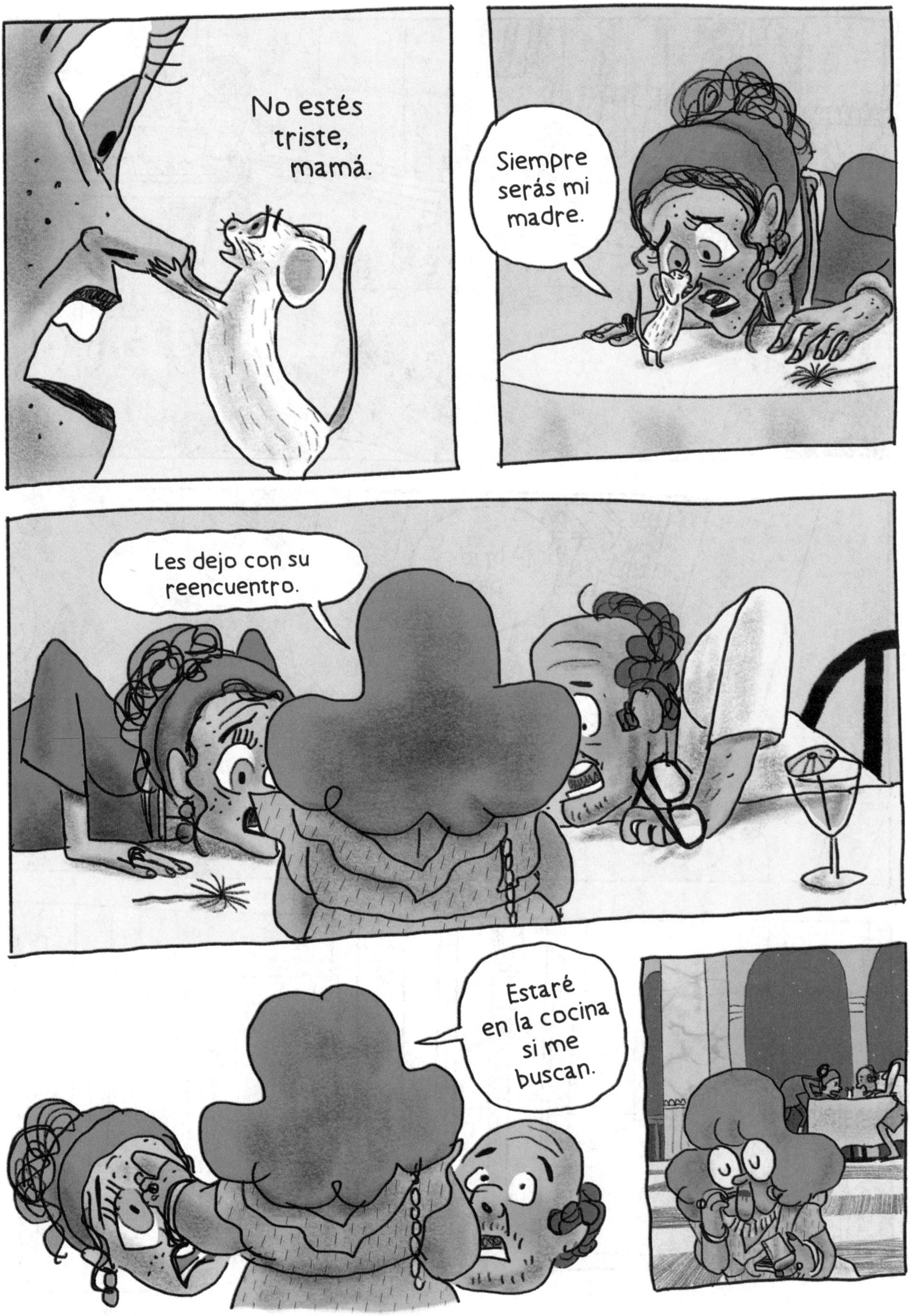
No estés triste, mamá.
Siempre serás mi madre.
Les dejo con su reencuentro.
Estaré en la cocina si me buscan.

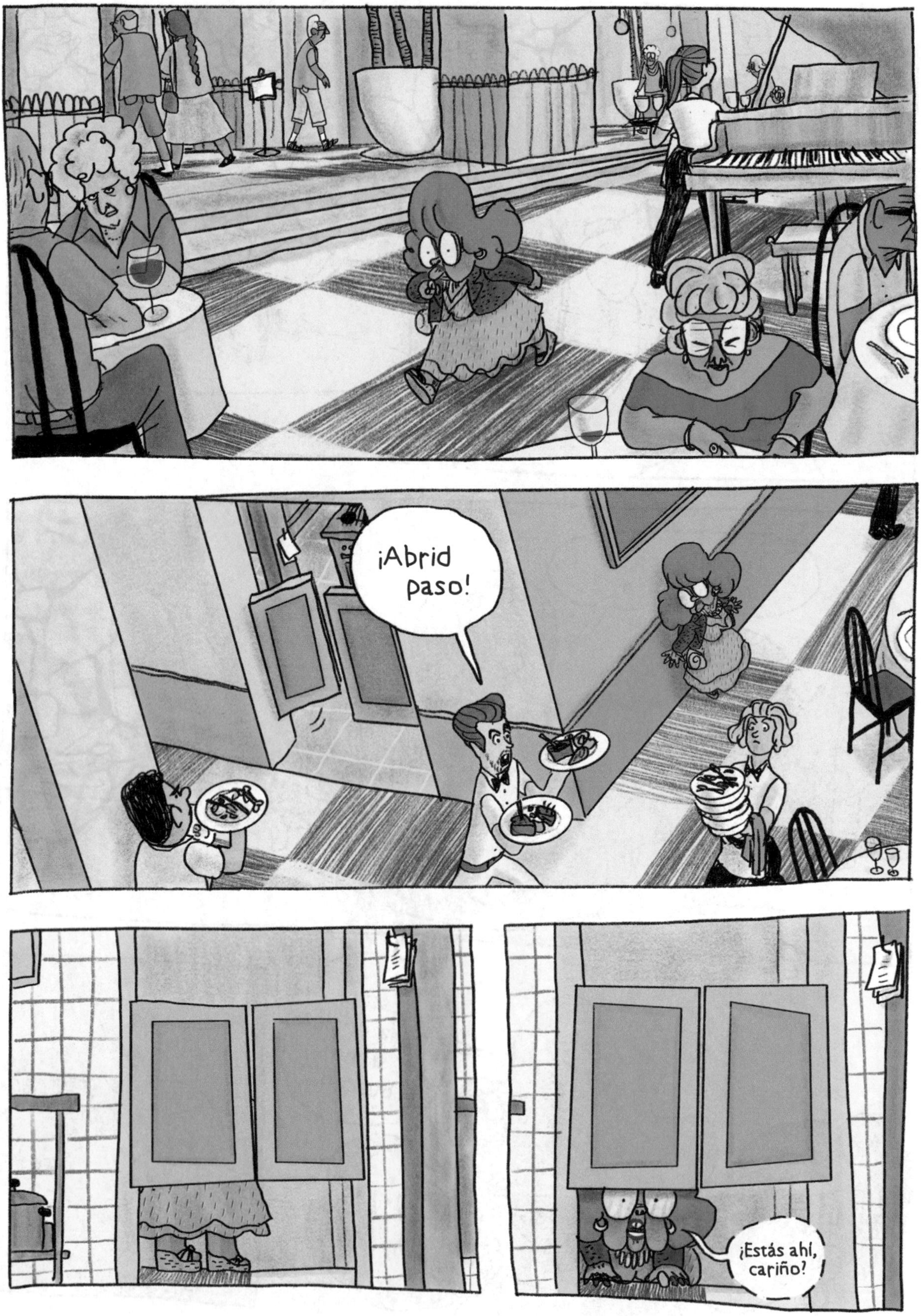
¡Abrid paso!
¡Estás ahí, cariño?

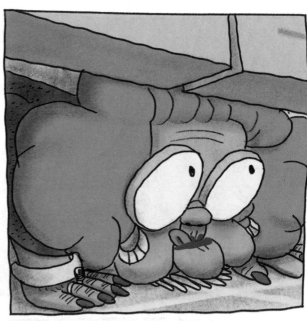

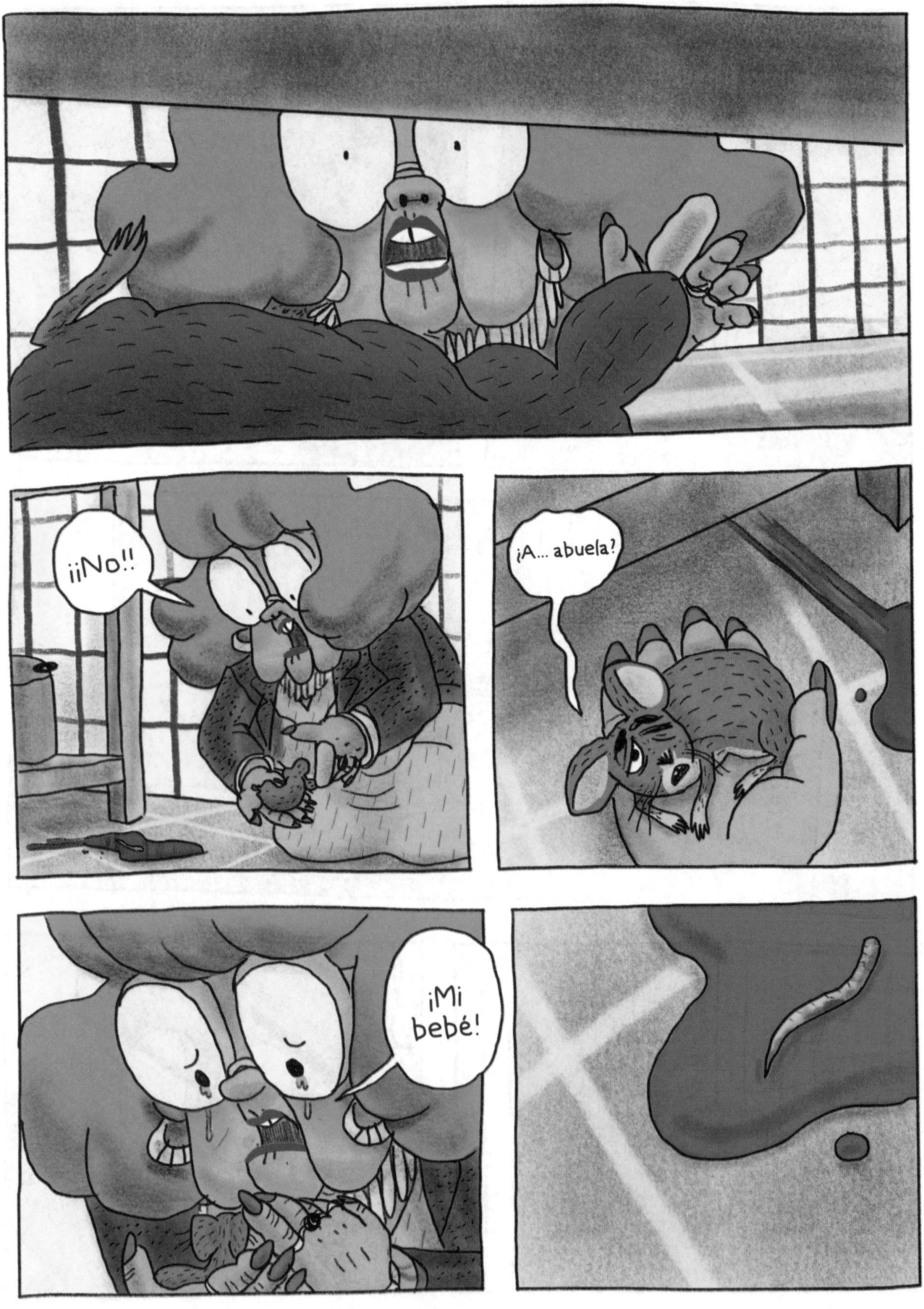
¡¡No!!
¡A... abuela?
¡Mi bebé!

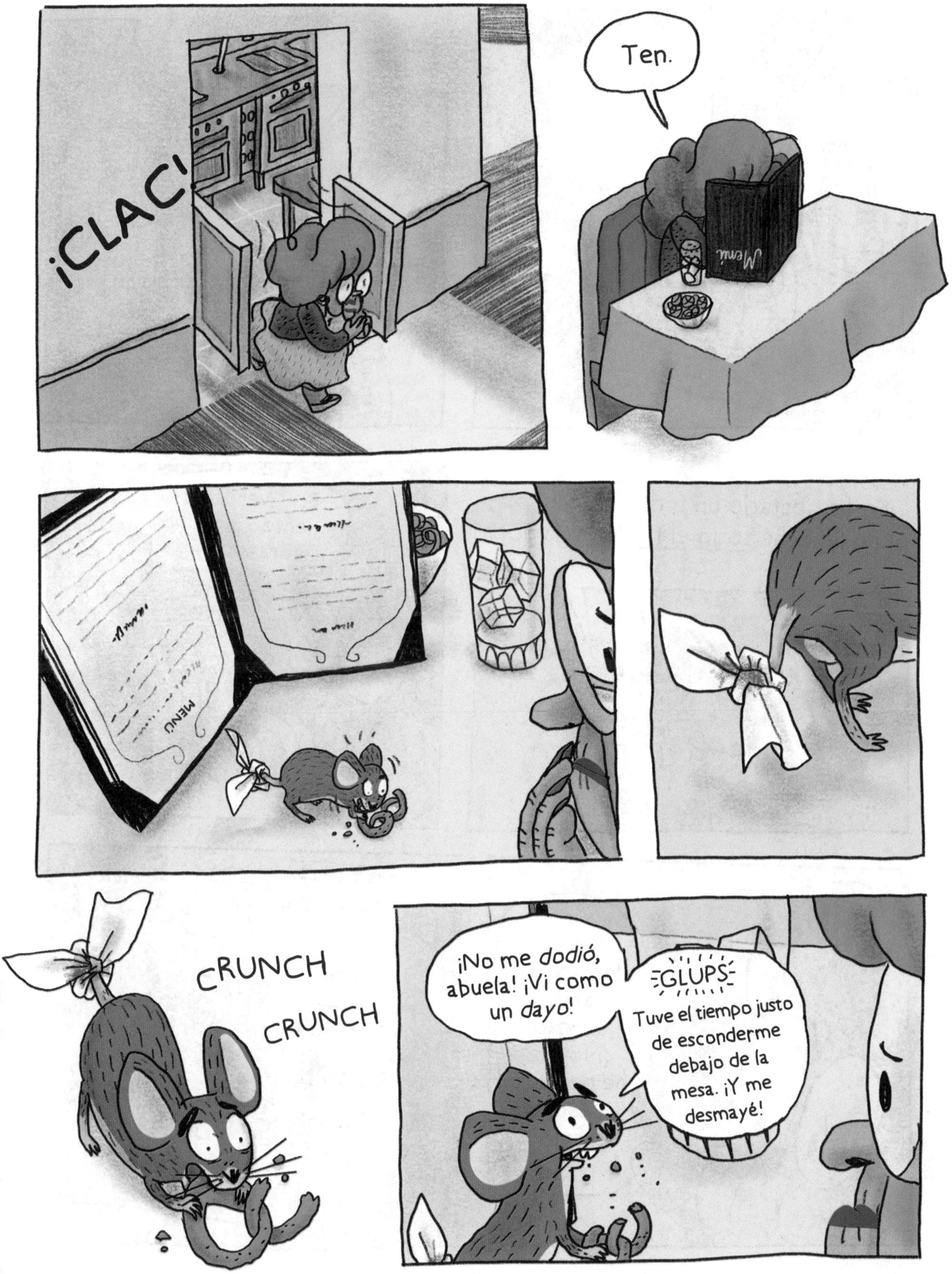
¡CLAC!
Ten.
CRUNCH
CRUNCH
¡No me *dodió*, abuela! ¡Vi como un *dayo*!
GLUPS
Tuve el tiempo justo de esconderme debajo de la mesa. ¡Y me desmayé!

Ay, cariño mío.

Pero... ¡lo CONSEGUÍ!

Me ha costado un trozo de mi cola, pero ¡le eché todo el frasco a la sopa!

Eres verdaderamente... increíble, corazón mío.

No es demasiado tarde, ¿verdad? ¡No me he perdido el espectáculo?

No, mira...

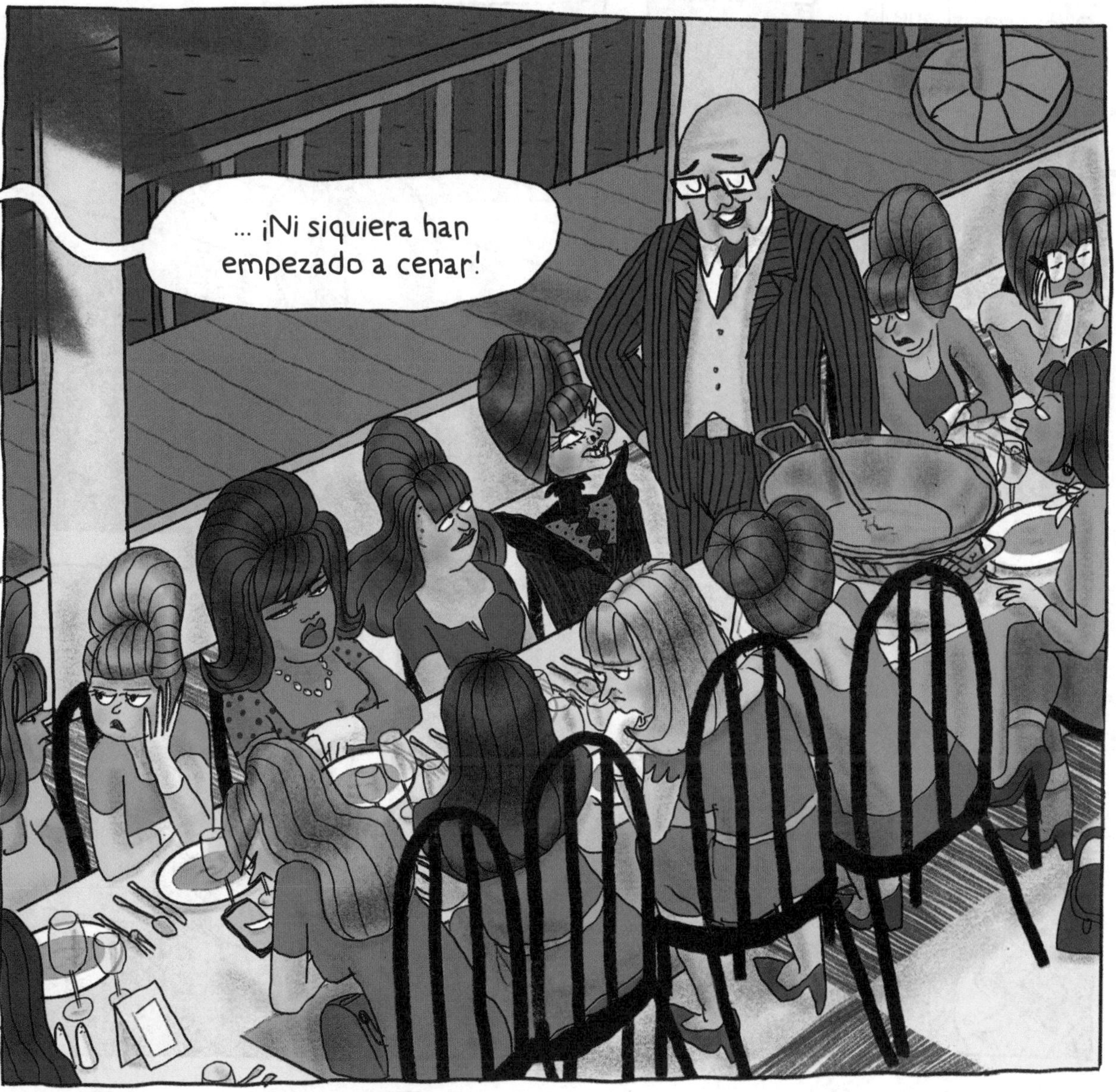
... ¡Ni siquiera han empezado a cenar!

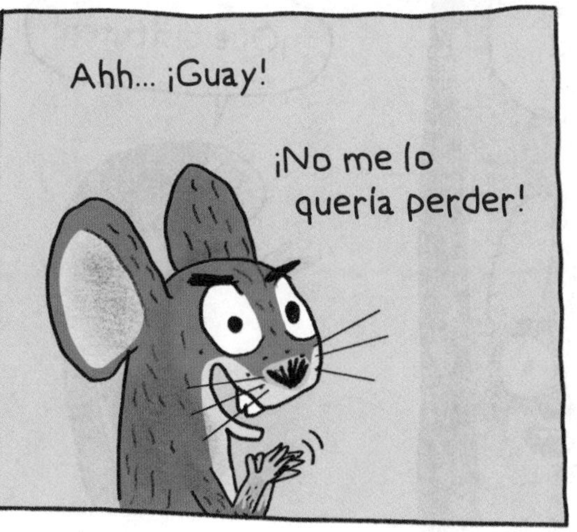
Ahh... ¡Guay!
¡No me lo quería perder!

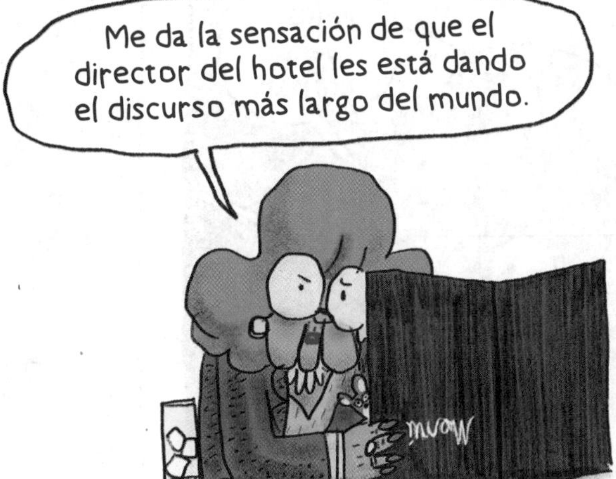
Me da la sensación de que el director del hotel les está dando el discurso más largo del mundo.
mvaw

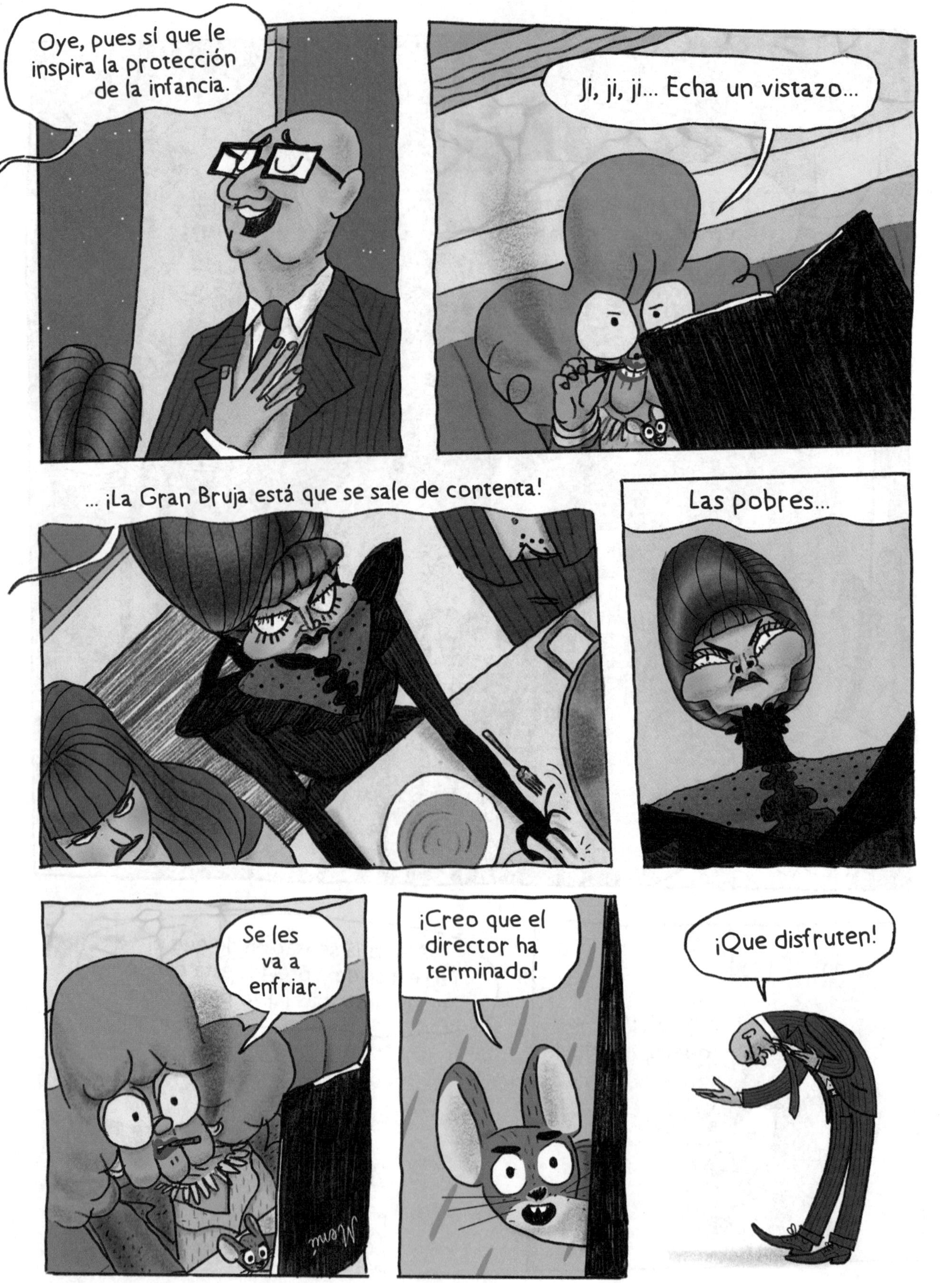

Oye, pues sí que le inspira la protección de la infancia.
Ji, ji, ji... Echa un vistazo...
... ¡La Gran Bruja está que se sale de contenta!
Las pobres...
Se les va a enfriar.
¡Creo que el director ha terminado!
¡Que disfruten!

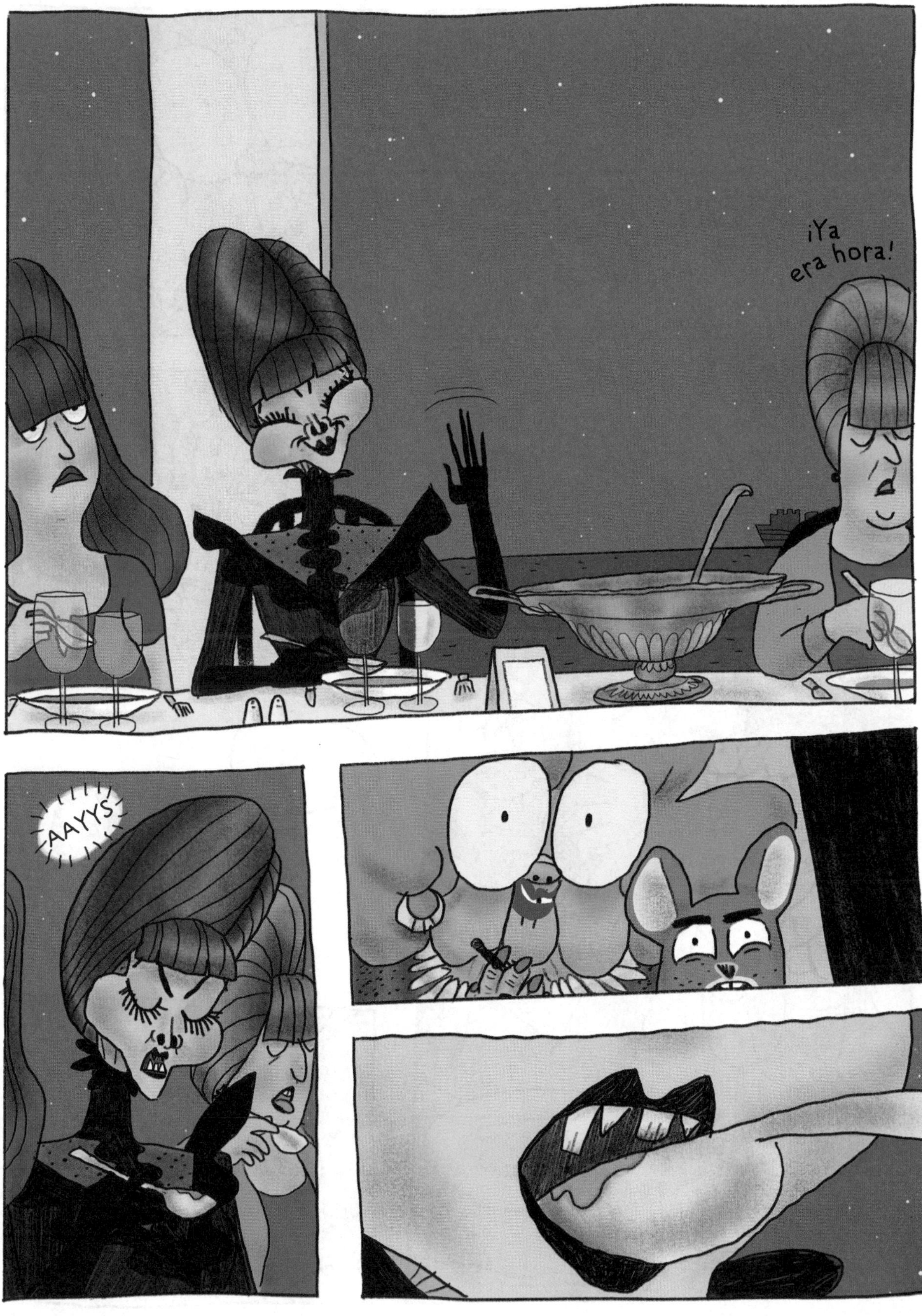
¡Ya era hora!
AAYYS

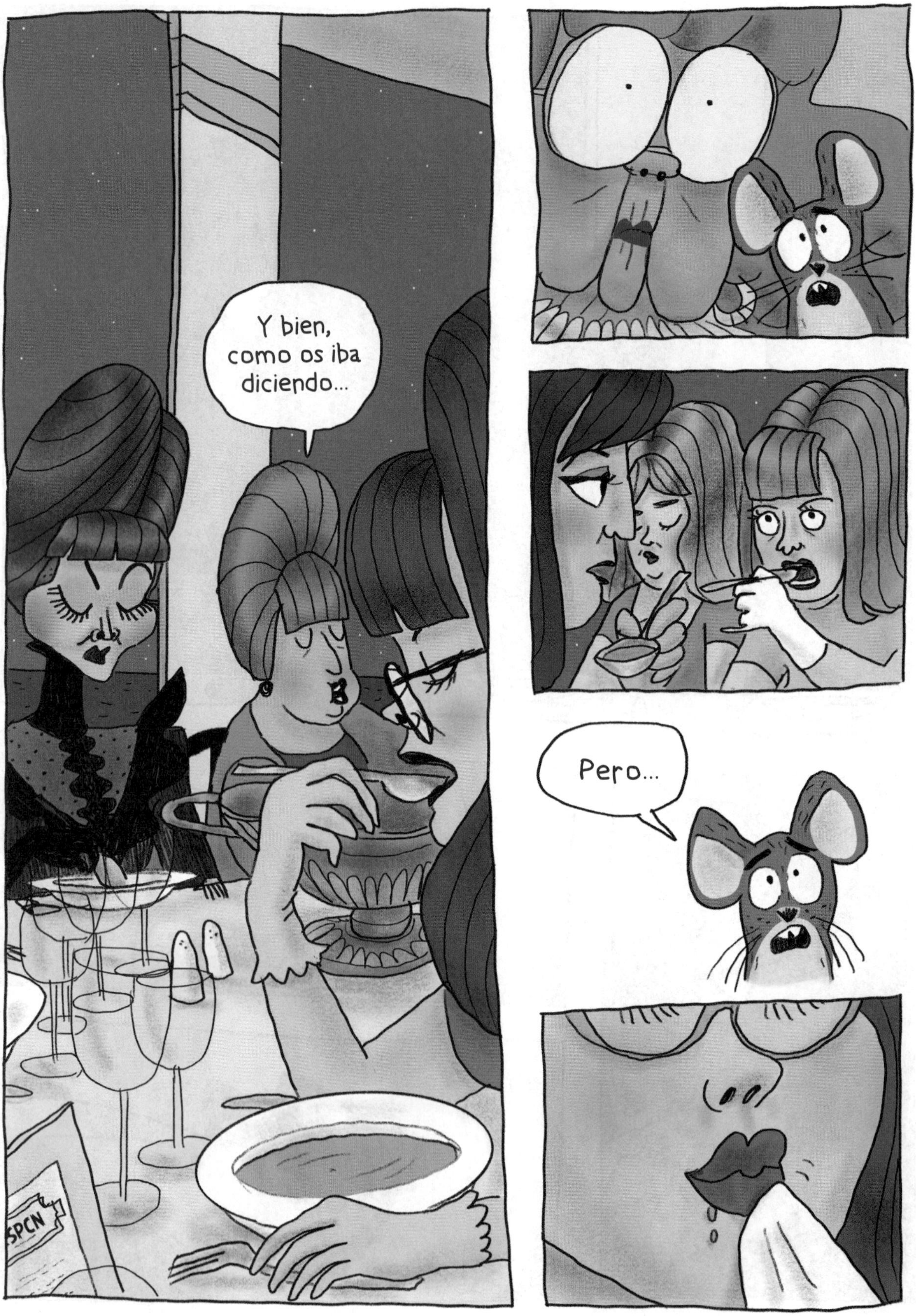
Y bien, como os iba diciendo...
SPCN
Pero...

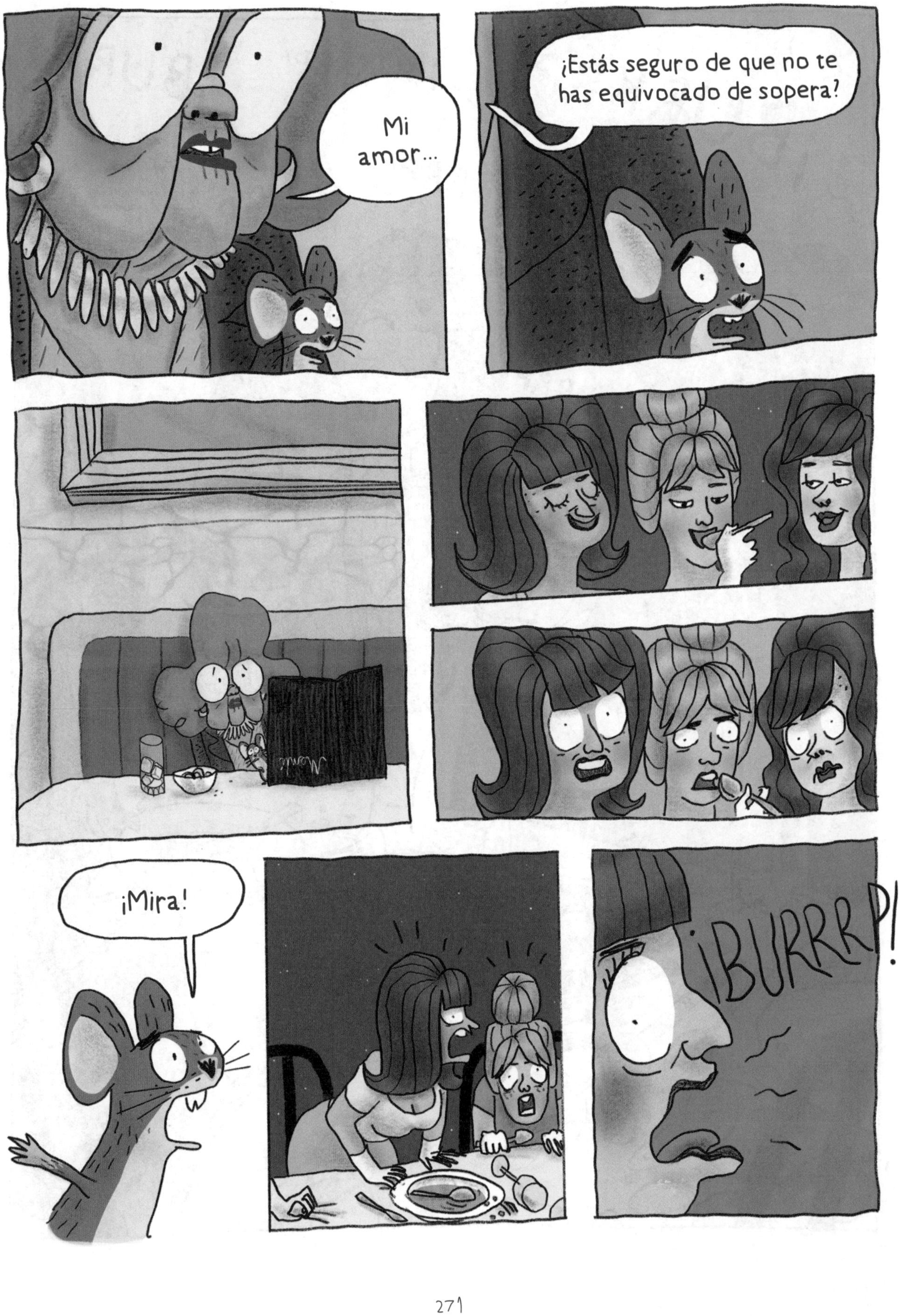
Mi amor...
¿Estás seguro de que no te has equivocado de sopera?
¡Mira!
¡BURRRP!

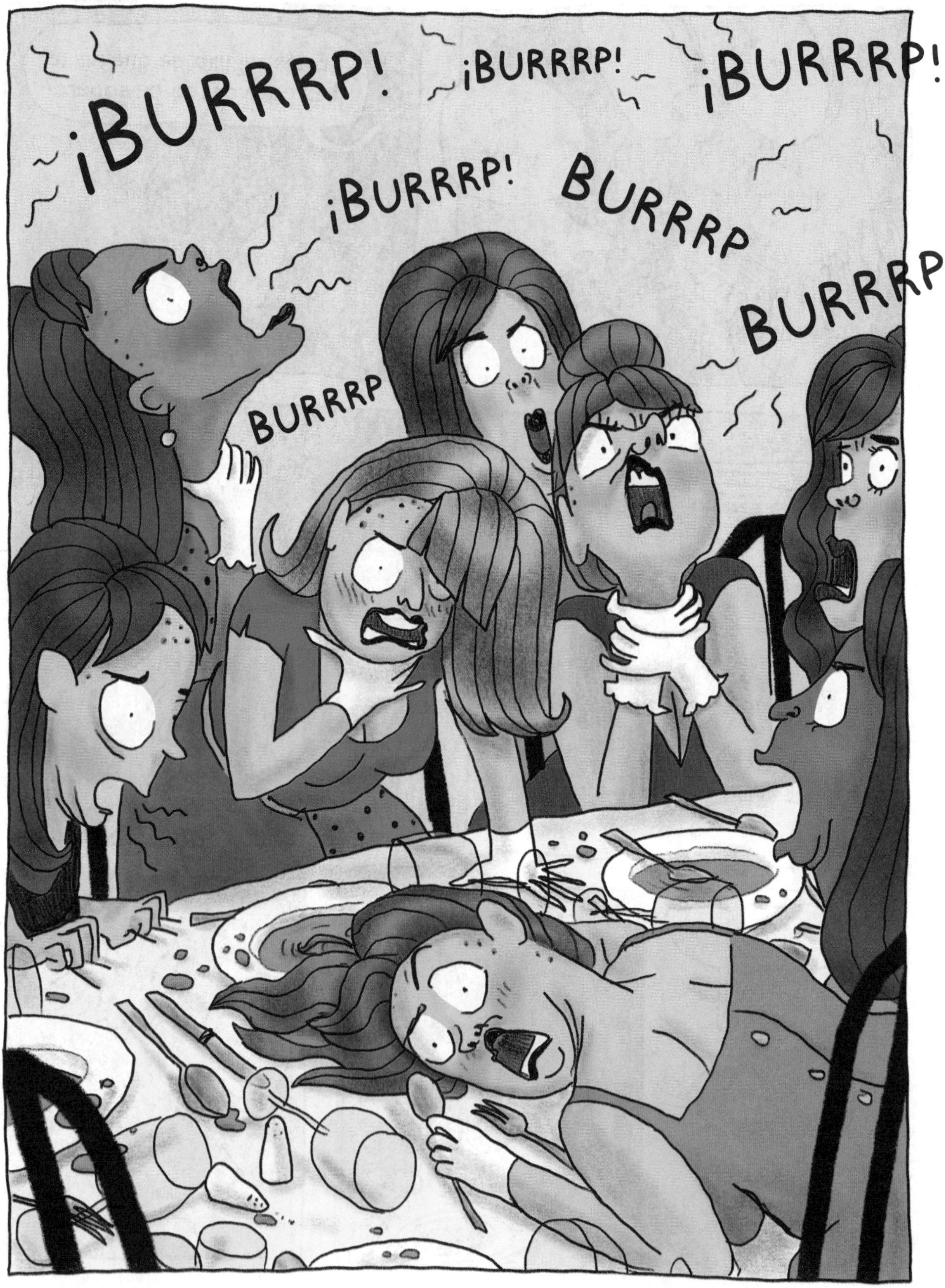
¡BURRRP!
¡BURRRP!
¡BURRRRP!
¡BURRRP!
BURRRRP
BURRRRP
BURRRP

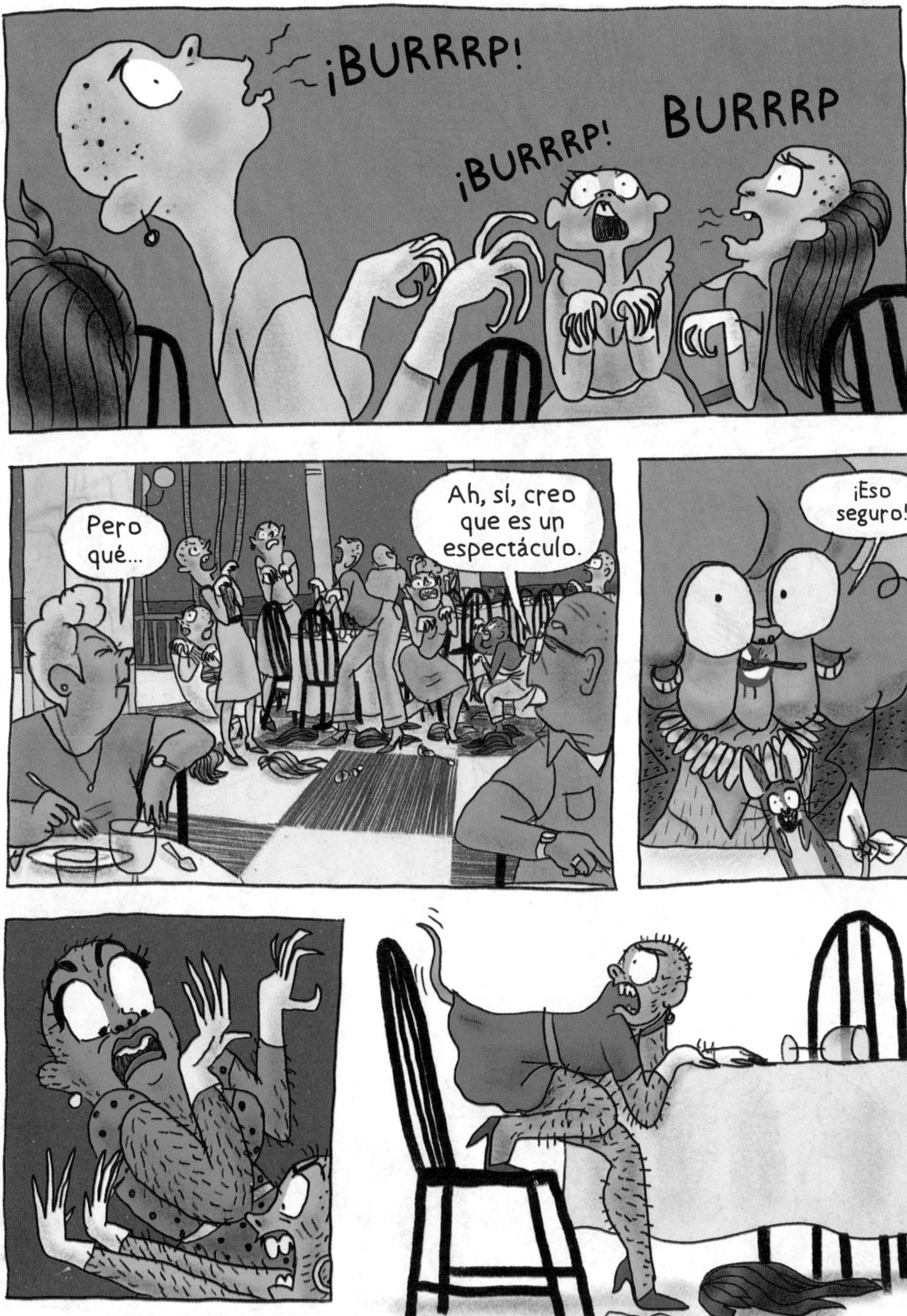
¡BURRRP!
¡BURRRP!
BURRRP
Pero qué...
Ah, sí, creo que es un espectáculo.
¡Eso seguro!

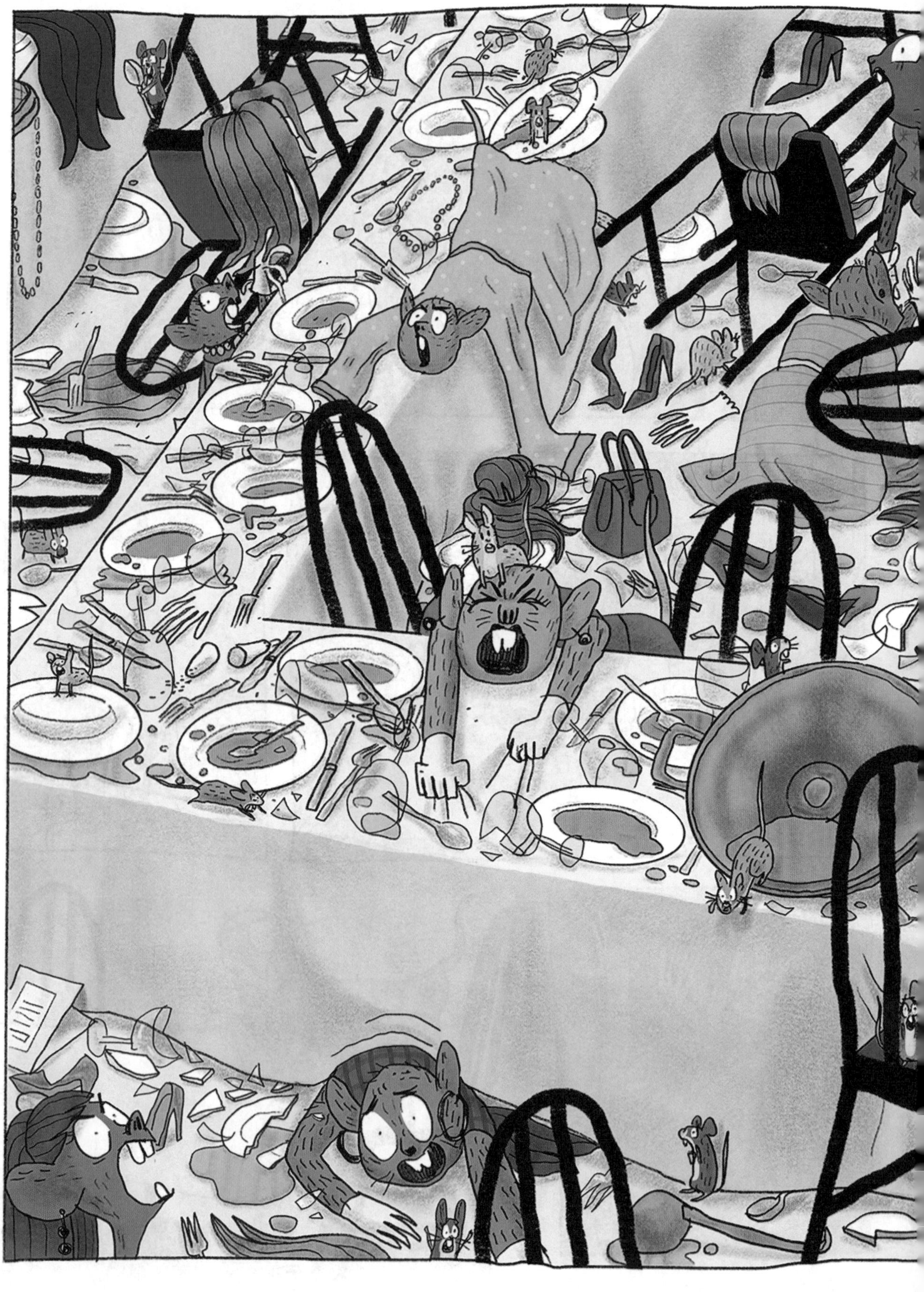

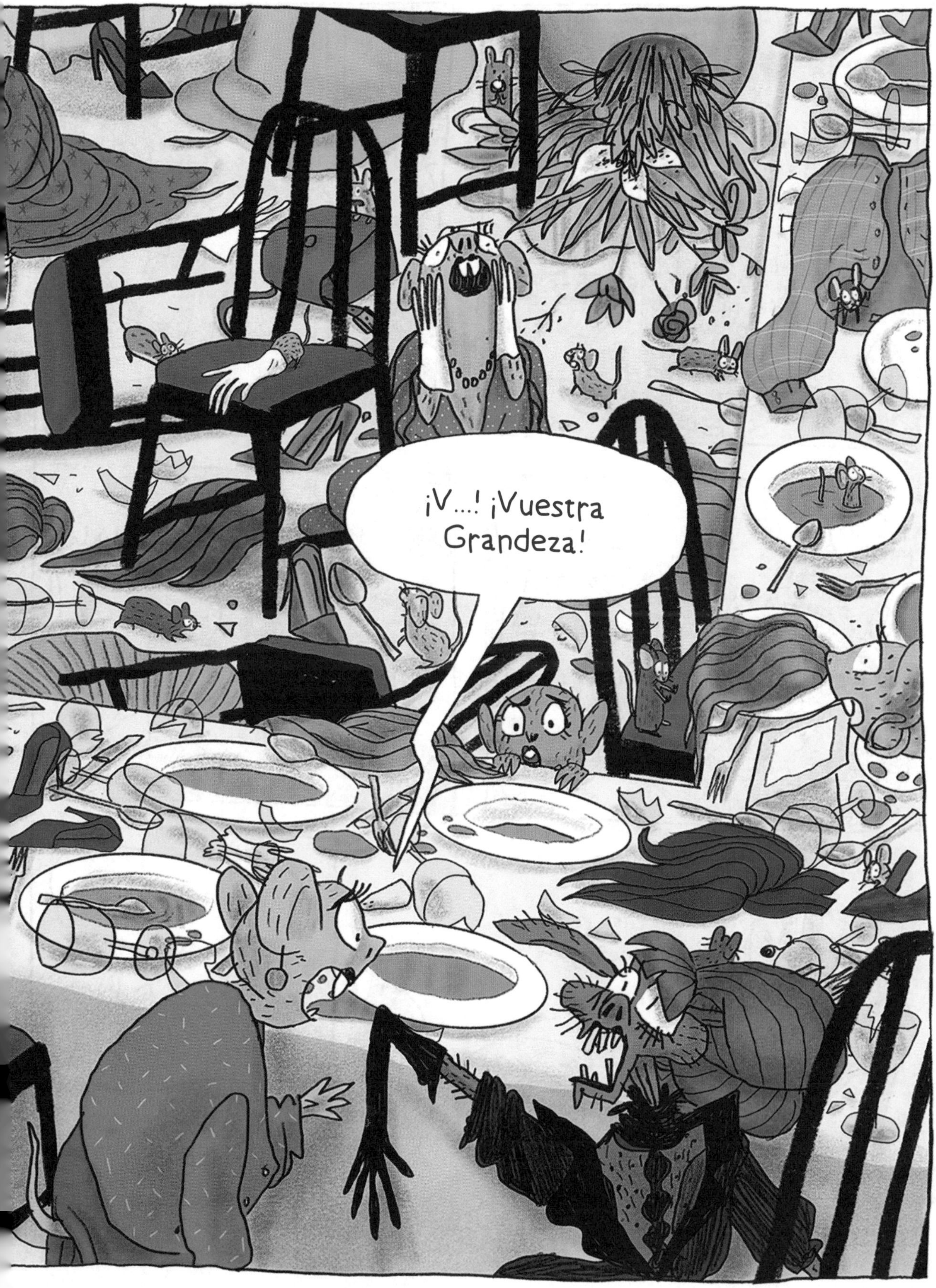
¡V...! ¡Vuestra Grandeza!

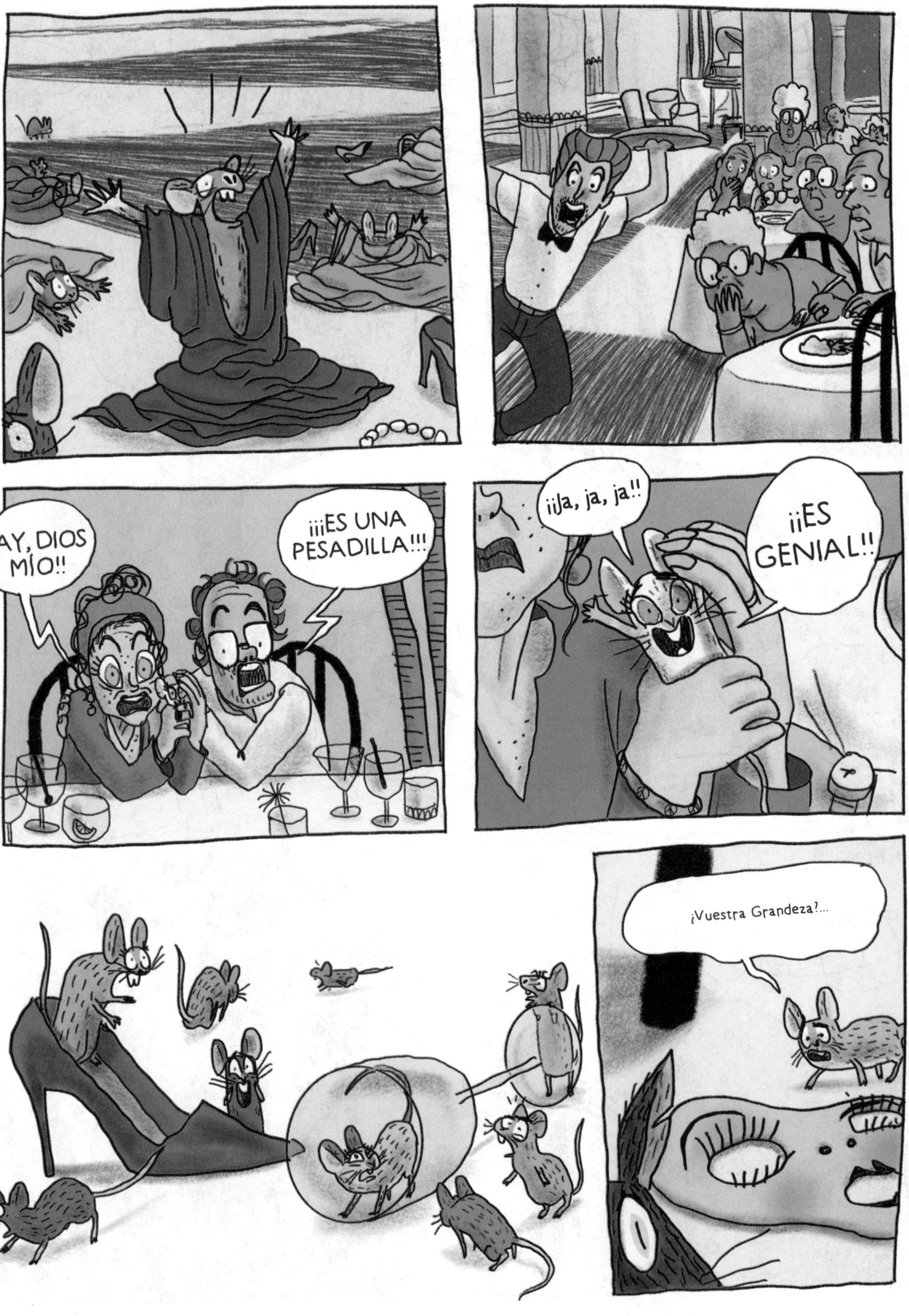
¡¡AY, DIOS MÍO!!
¡¡¡ES UNA PESADILLA!!!
¡¡Ja, ja, ja!!
¡¡ES GENIAL!!
¿Vuestra Grandeza?...

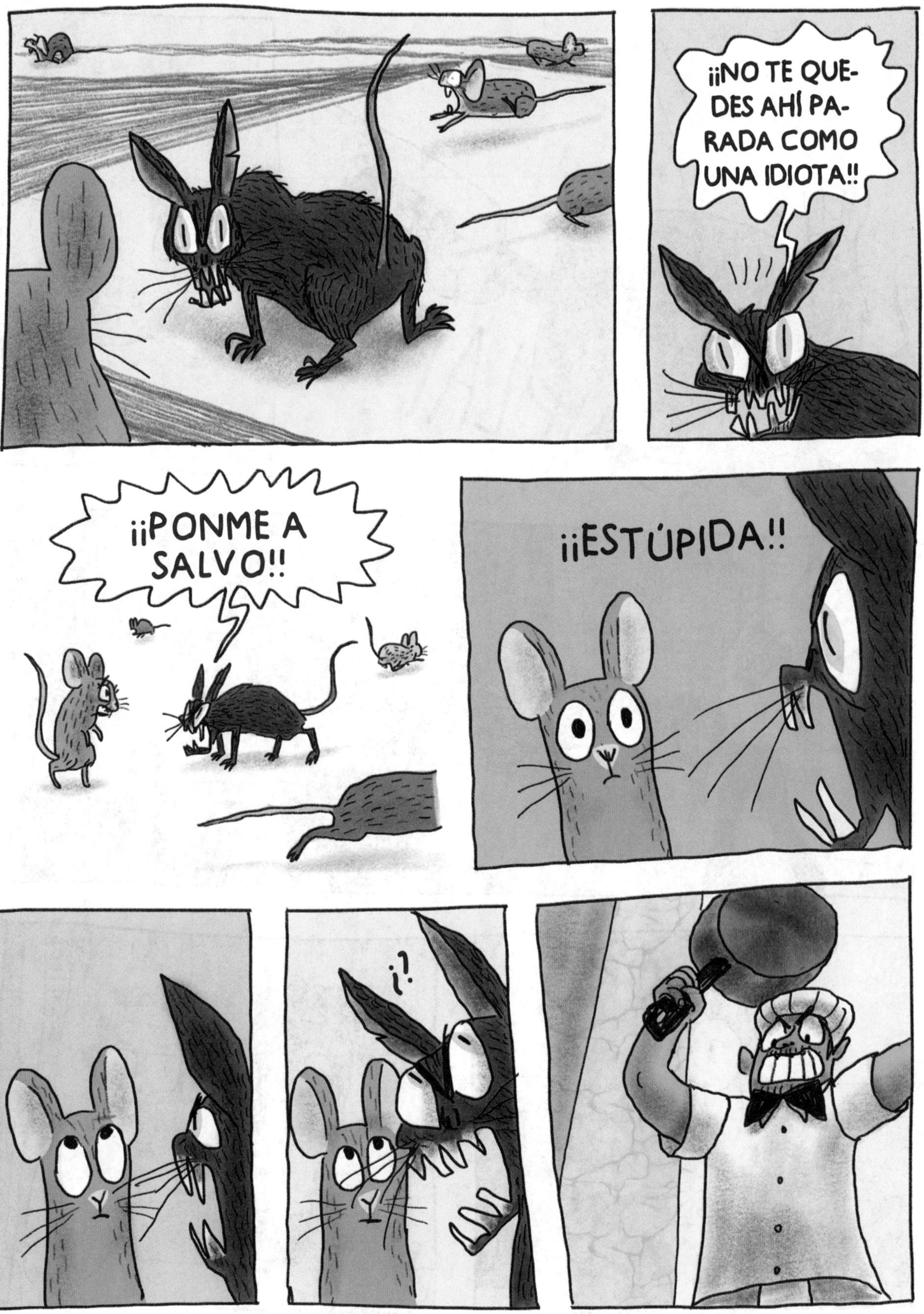
¡¡NO TE QUE-
DES AHÍ PA-
RADA COMO
UNA IDIOTA!!
¡¡PONME A
SALVO!!
¡¡ESTÚPIDA!!
¿?

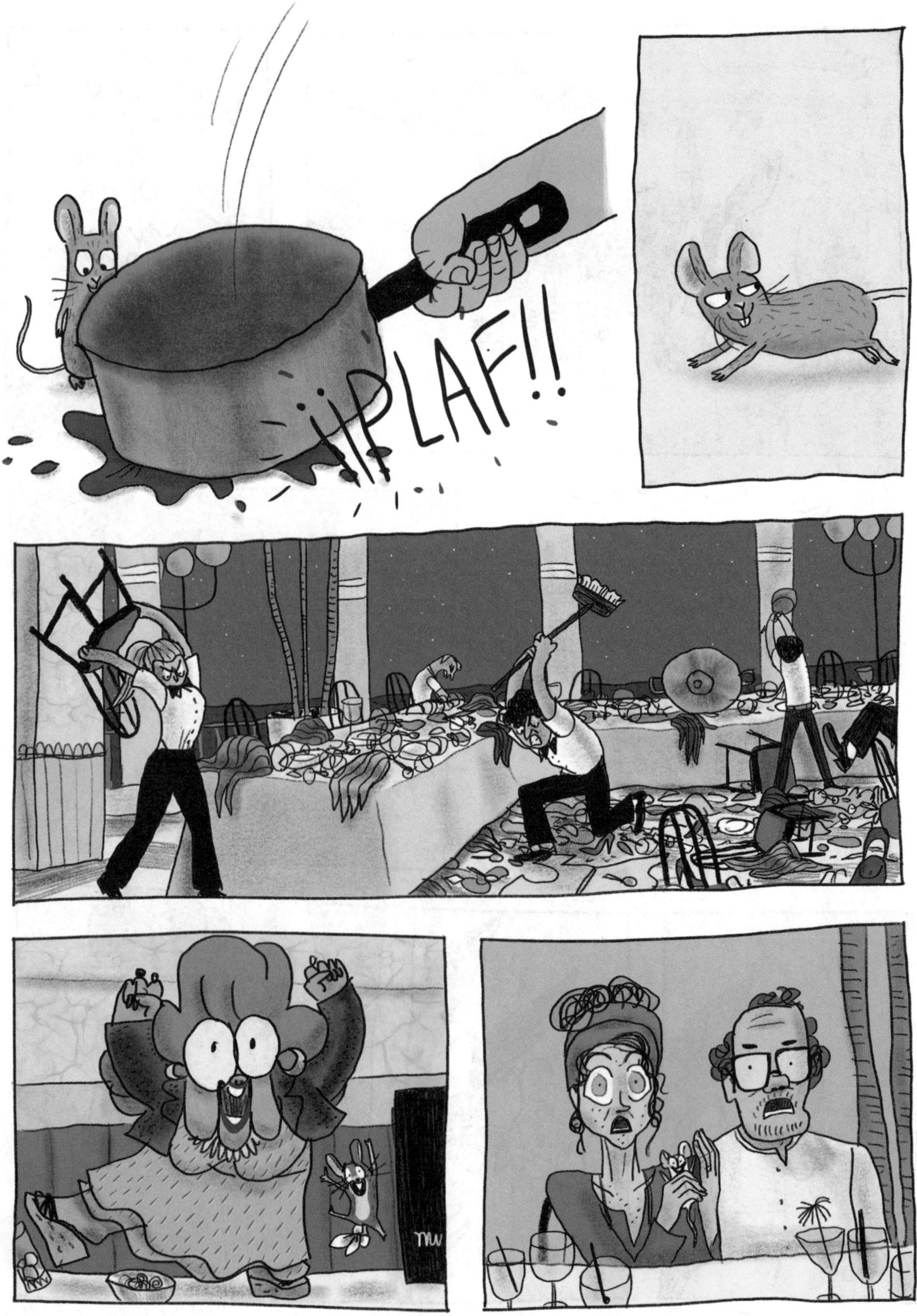
¡¡PLAF!!

¡¡DEJÁDMELAS A MÍ!!

¡PLAM!

Creo, cariño mío, que la velada se va a poner algo fea.

Sí.

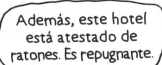

Además, este hotel está atestado de ratones. Es repugnante.

¿Volvemos a casa?

De acuerdo.

¡No!

¡Espera!

¡Sí?

Esto... Yo...

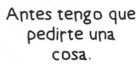

Antes tengo que pedirte una cosa.

¡¡OTRA!!

¡¡¡AH!!!

...

Ejem, ejem.

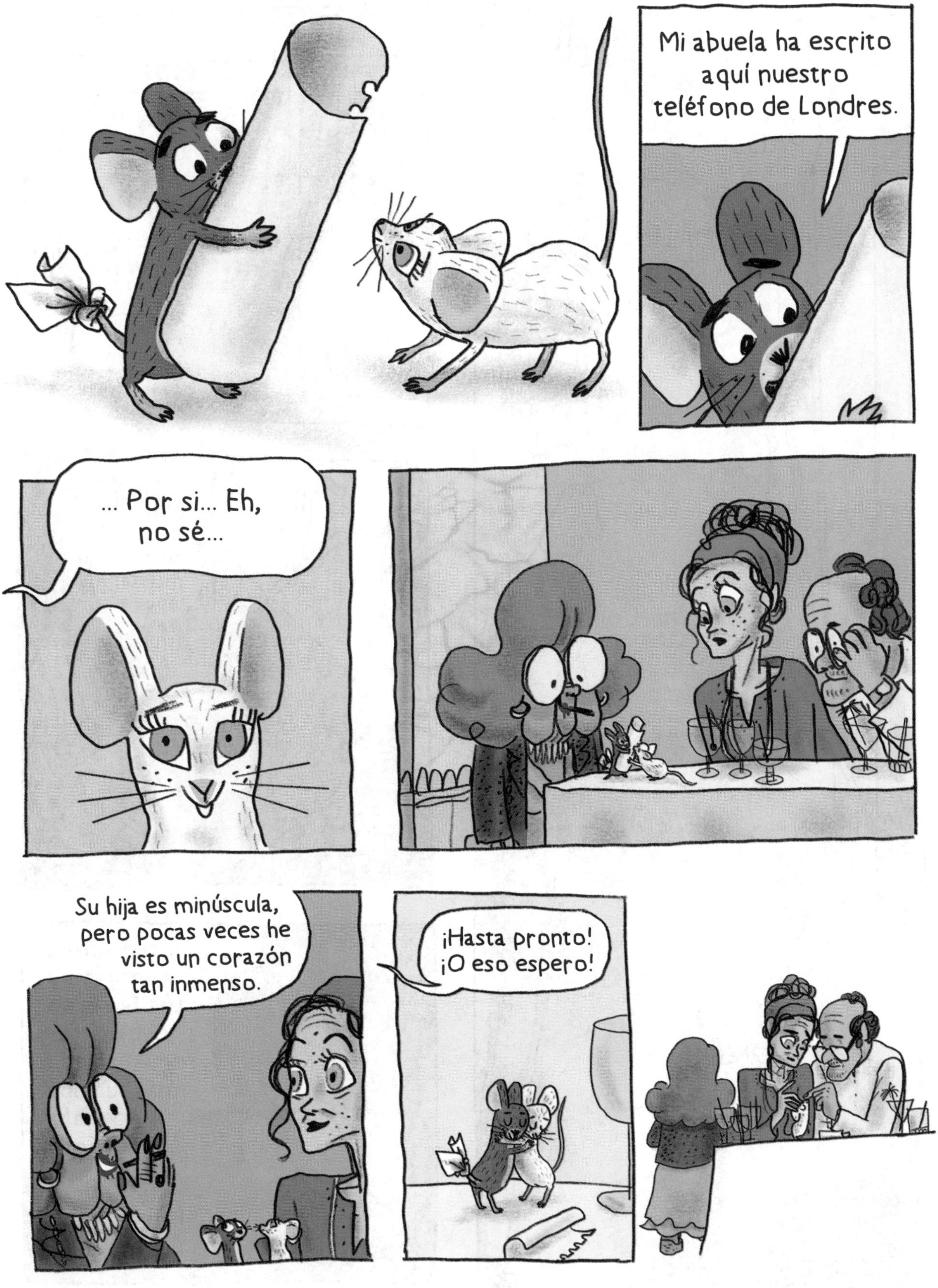
Mi abuela ha escrito aquí nuestro teléfono de Londres.
... Por si... Eh, no sé...
Su hija es minúscula, pero pocas veces he visto un corazón tan inmenso.
¡Hasta pronto! ¡O eso espero!

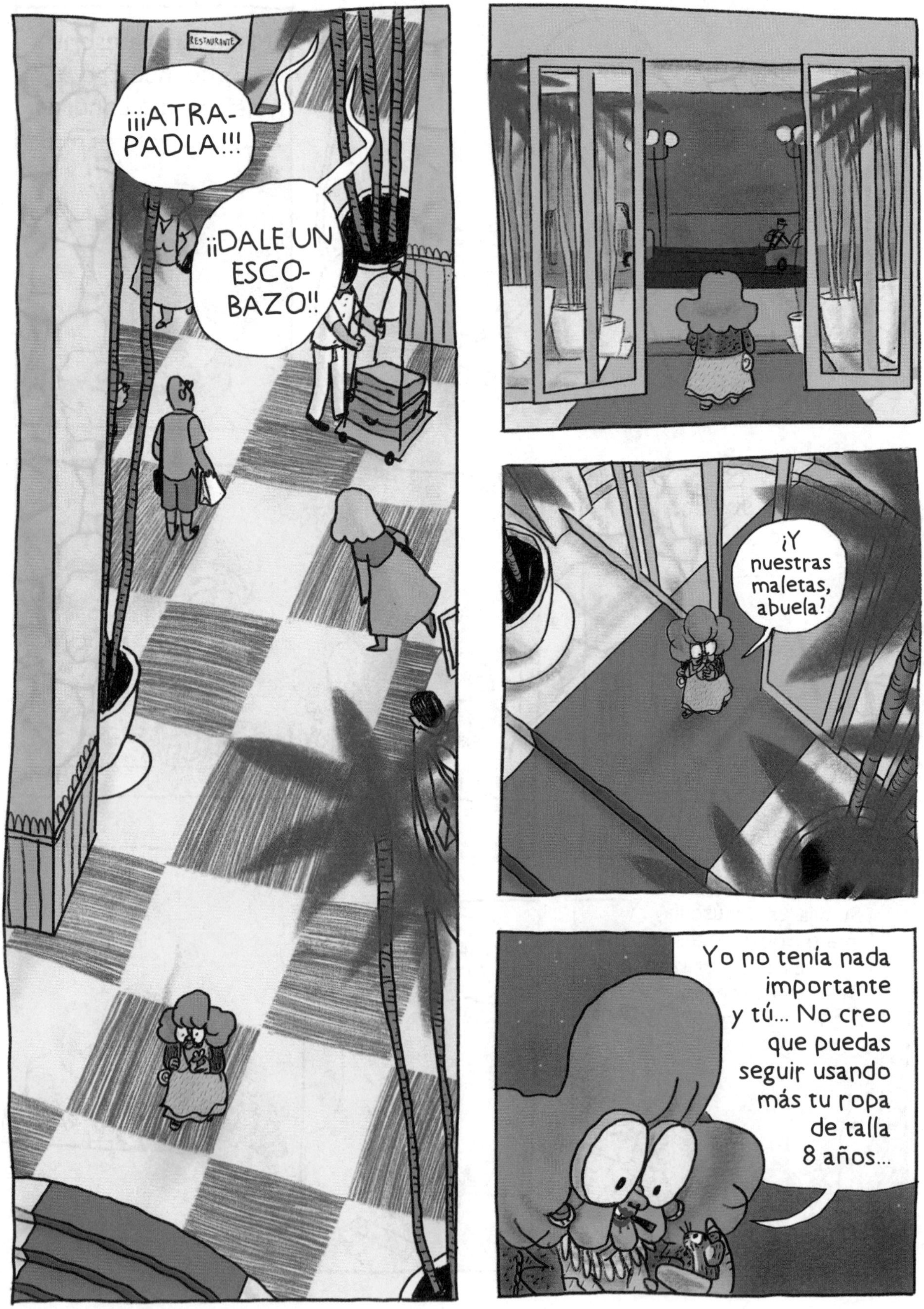

RESTAURANTE
¡¡¡ATRAPADLA!!!
¡¡DALE UN ESCOBAZO!!
¿Y nuestras maletas, abuela?
Yo no tenía nada importante y tú... No creo que puedas seguir usando más tu ropa de talla 8 años...

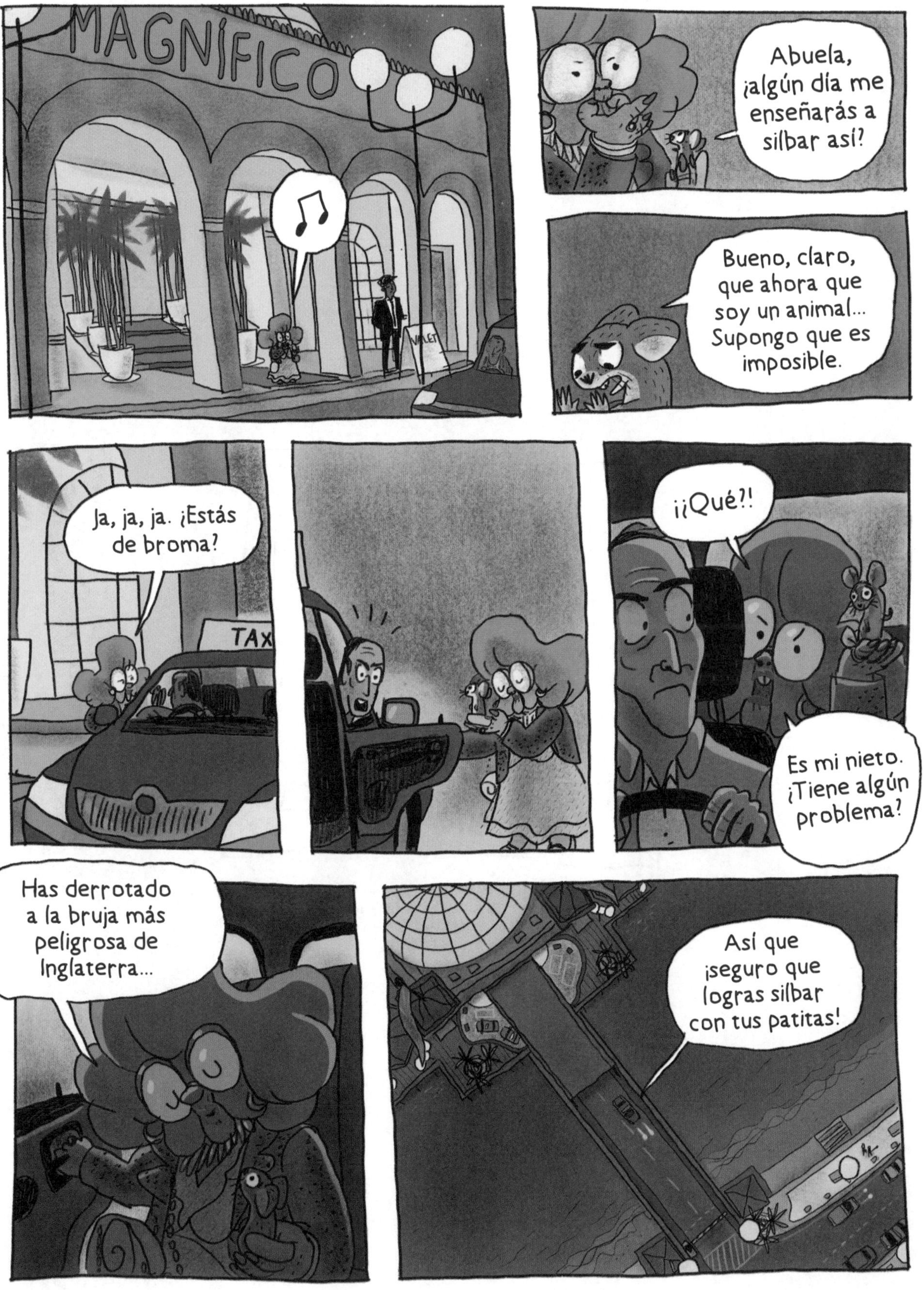
MAGNÍFICO
VALET
Abuela, ¡algún día me enseñarás a silbar así?
Bueno, claro, que ahora que soy un animal... Supongo que es imposible.
Ja, ja, ja. ¿Estás de broma?
TAX
¡¿Qué?!
Es mi nieto. ¿Tiene algún problema?
Has derrotado a la bruja más peligrosa de Inglaterra...
Así que ¡seguro que logras silbar con tus patitas!

Un mes después...

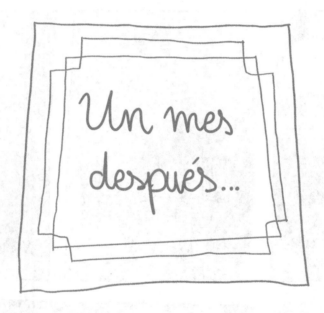

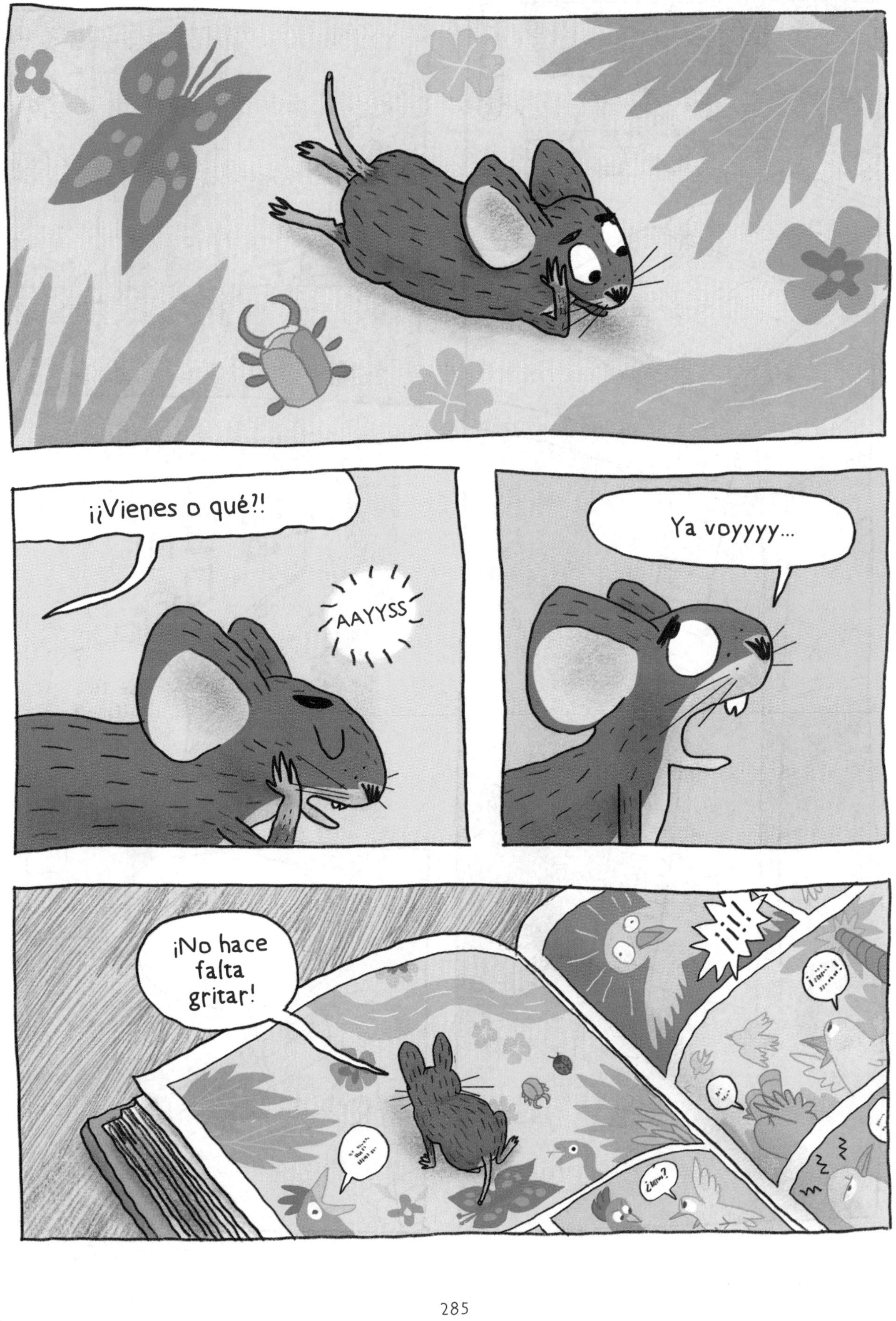
¡¿Vienes o qué?!
AAYYSS
Ya voyyyy...
¡No hace falta gritar!

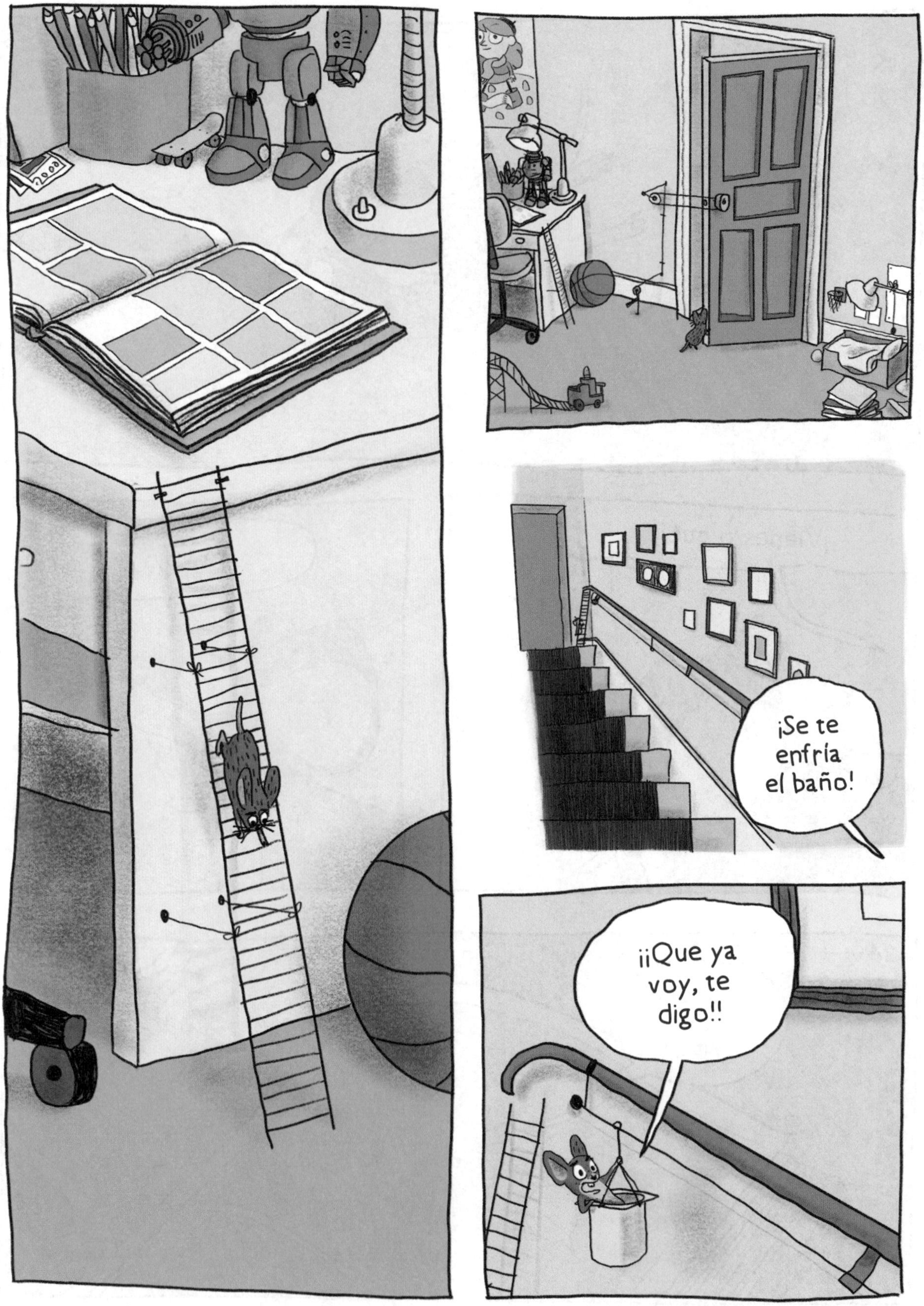

¡Se te enfría el baño!
¡¡Que ya voy, te digo!!

¡Por qué me tengo que lavar CONSTANTEMENTE?

¡Que seas un ratón no significa que tengas que oler a queso rancio!

No es justo.

Soy el ÚNICO ratón del mundo...

... ¡que se baña!

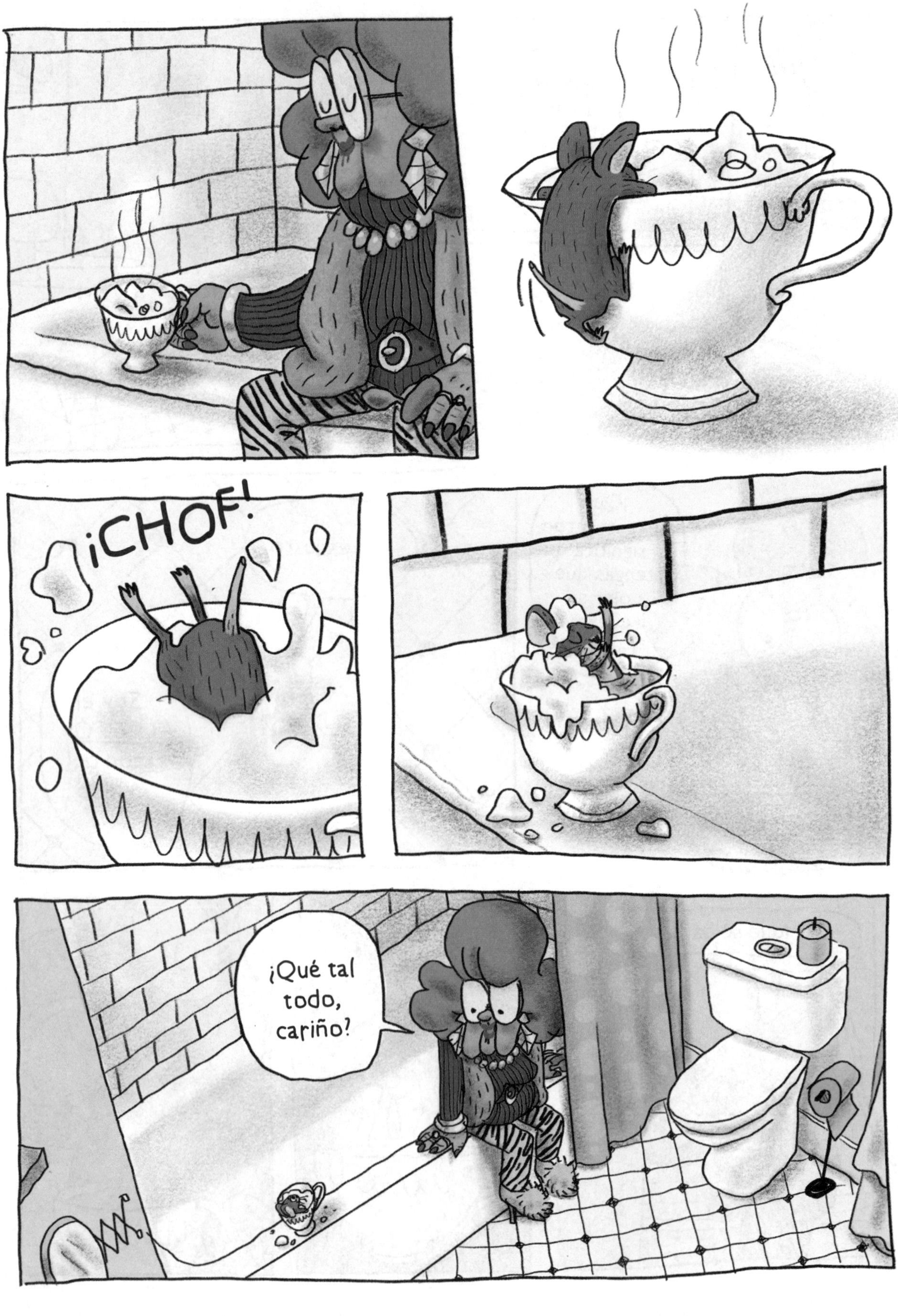
¡CHOF!
¿Qué tal todo, cariño?

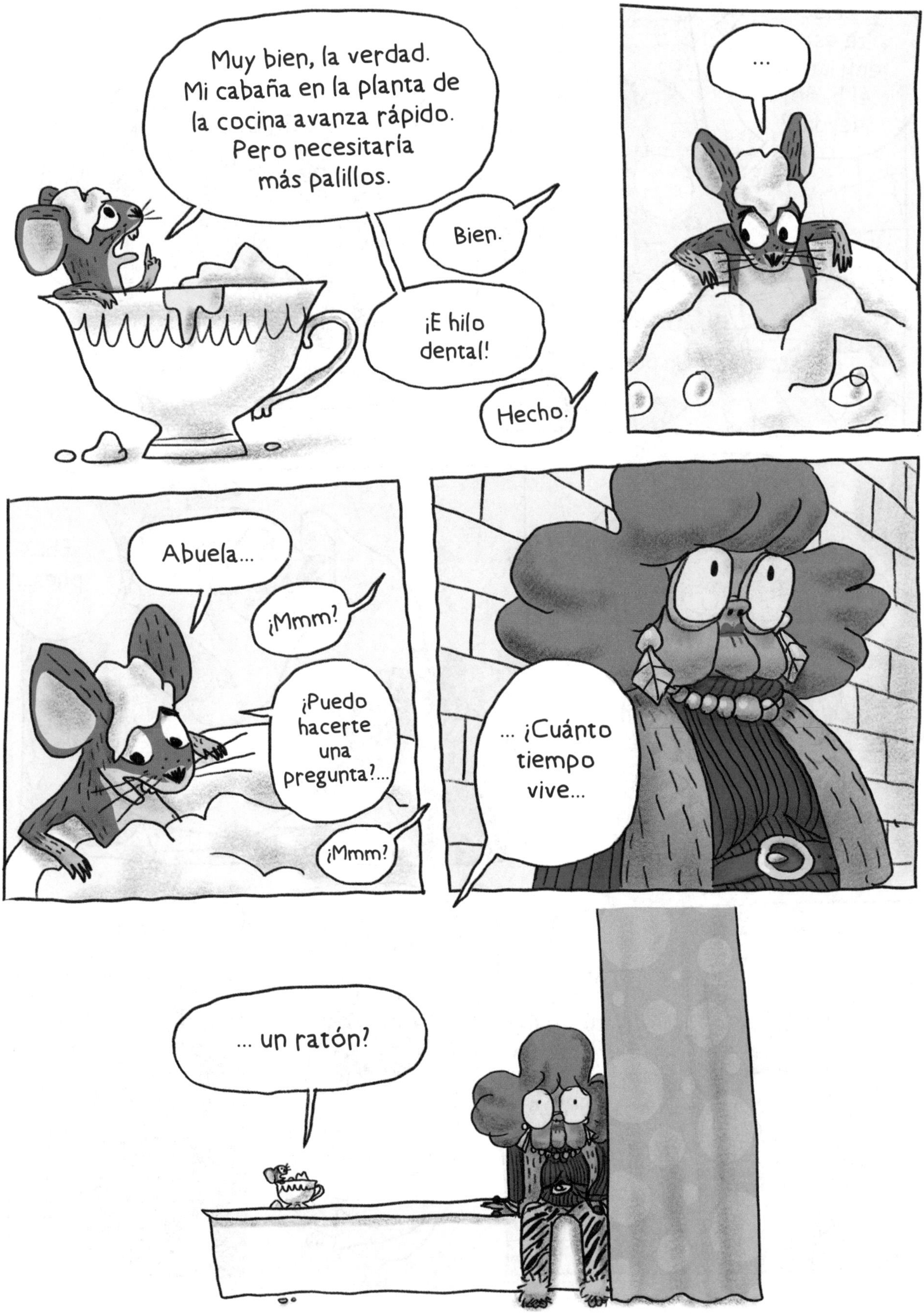
Muy bien, la verdad. Mi cabaña en la planta de la cocina avanza rápido. Pero necesitaría más palillos.
Bien.
¡E hilo dental!
Hecho.
...
Abuela...
¿Mmm?
¿Puedo hacerte una pregunta?...
¿Mmm?
... ¿Cuánto tiempo vive...
... un ratón?

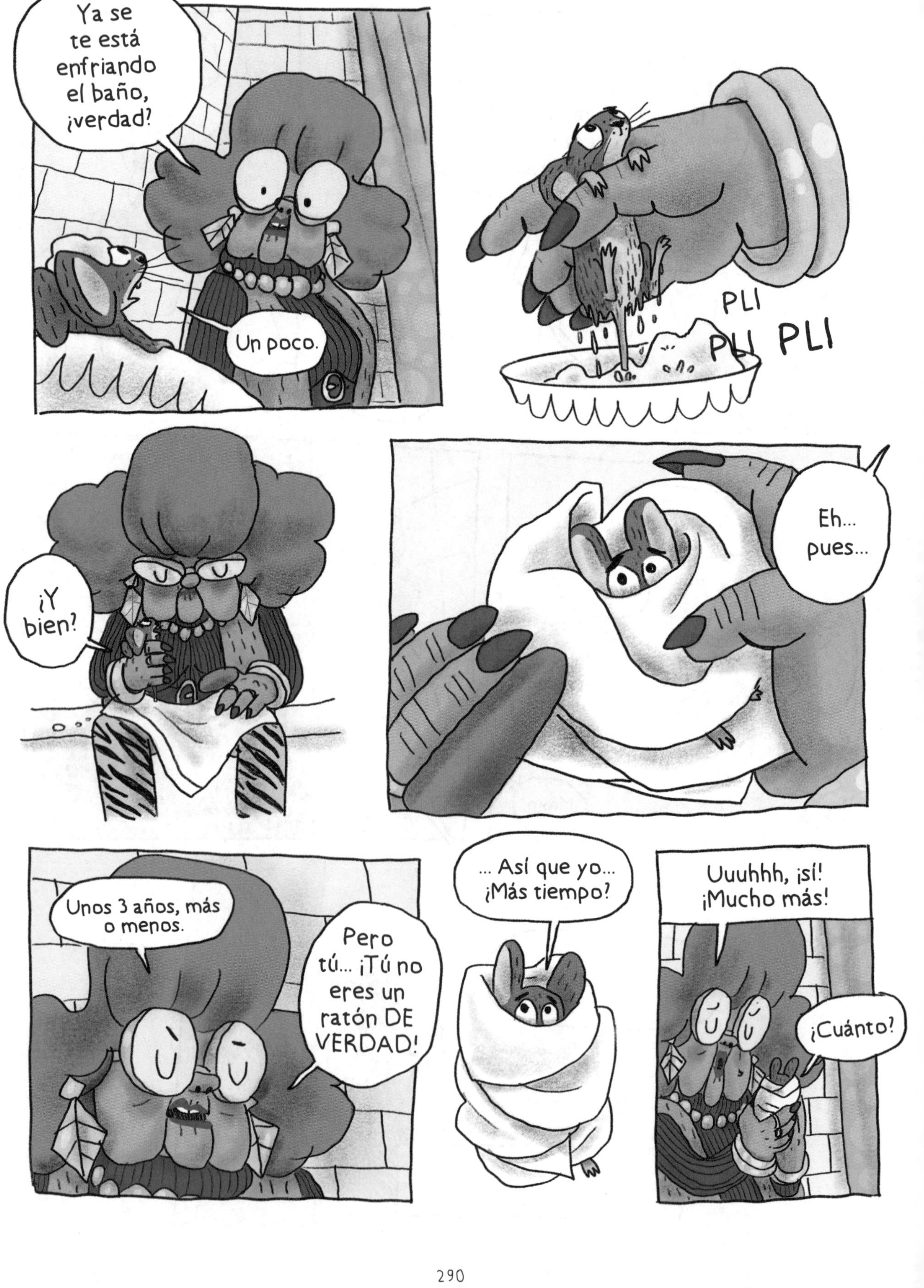
Ya se te está enfriando el baño, ¿verdad?
Un poco.
PLI
PLI PLI
¡Y bien?
Eh... pues...
Unos 3 años, más o menos.
Pero tú... ¡Tú no eres un ratón DE VERDAD!
... Así que yo... ¿Más tiempo?
Uuuhhh, ¡sí! ¡Mucho más!
¿Cuánto?

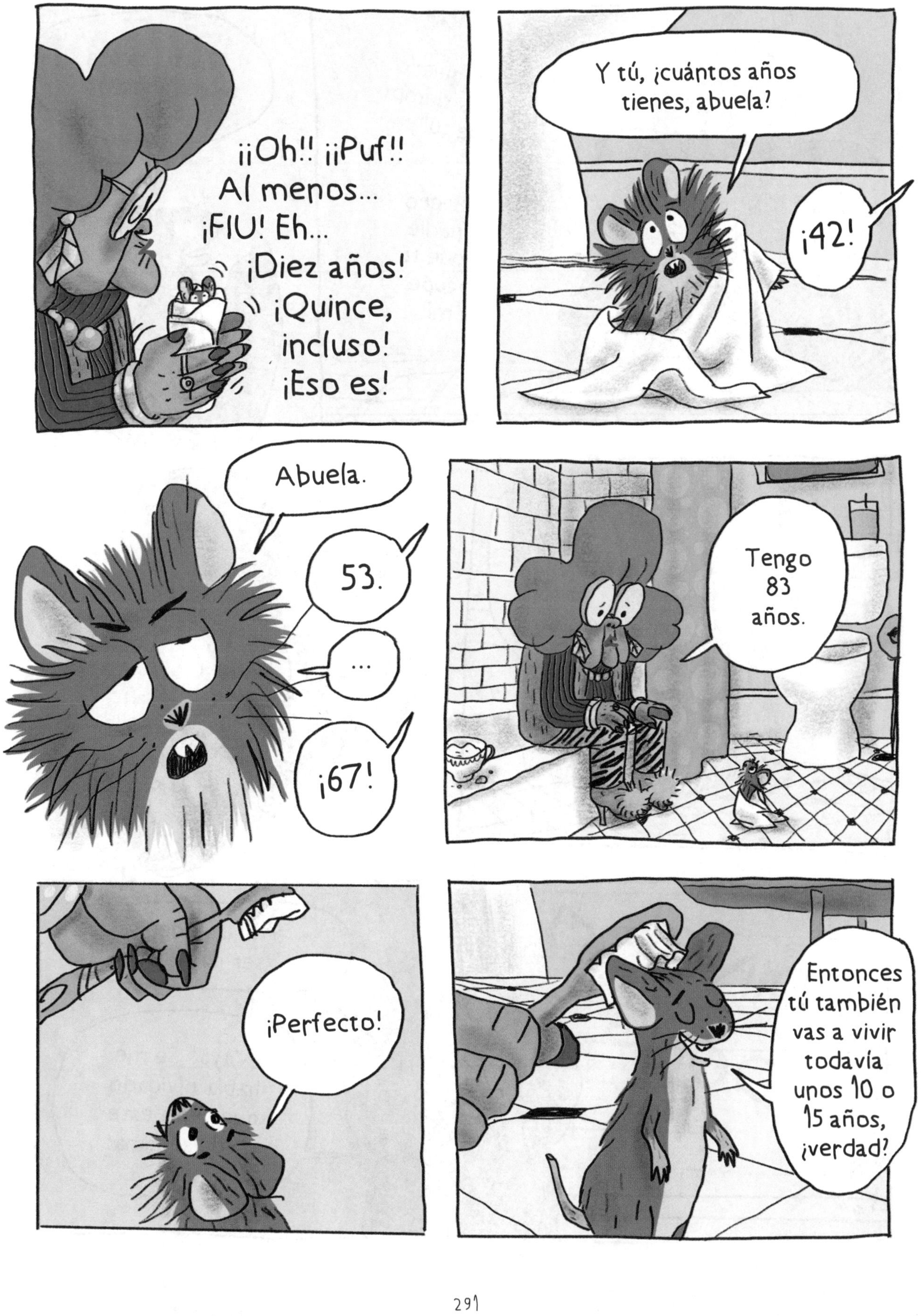
¡¡Oh!! ¡¡Puf!! Al menos... ¡FIU! Eh... ¡Diez años! ¡Quince, incluso! ¡Eso es!
Y tú, ¿cuántos años tienes, abuela?
¡42!
Abuela.
53.
...
¡67!
Tengo 83 años.
¡Perfecto!
Entonces tú también vas a vivir todavía unos 10 o 15 años, ¿verdad?

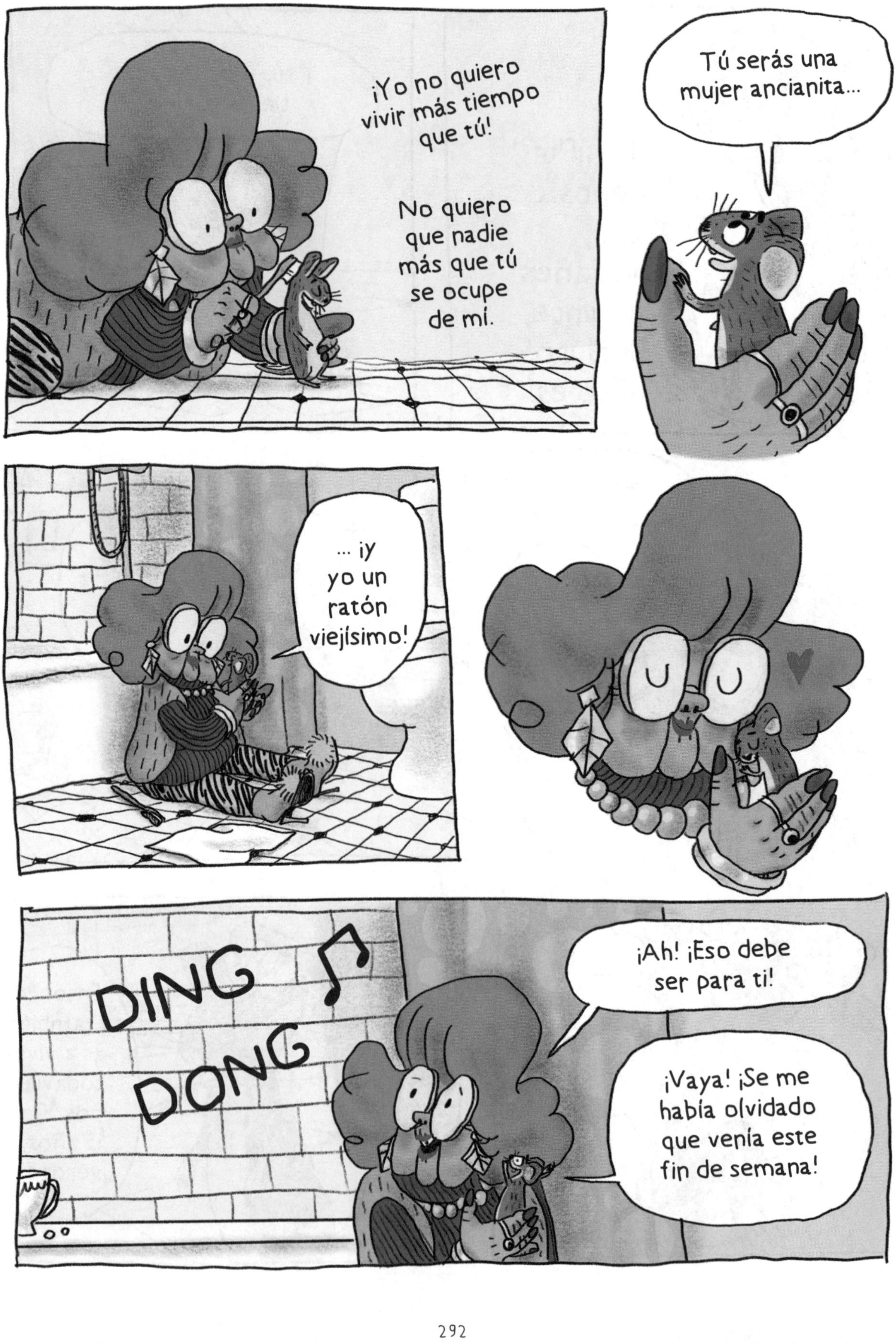
¡Yo no quiero vivir más tiempo que tú!
No quiero que nadie más que tú se ocupe de mí.
Tú serás una mujer ancianita...
... ¡y yo un ratón viejísimo!
DING DONG
¡Ah! ¡Eso debe ser para ti!
¡Vaya! ¡Se me había olvidado que venía este fin de semana!

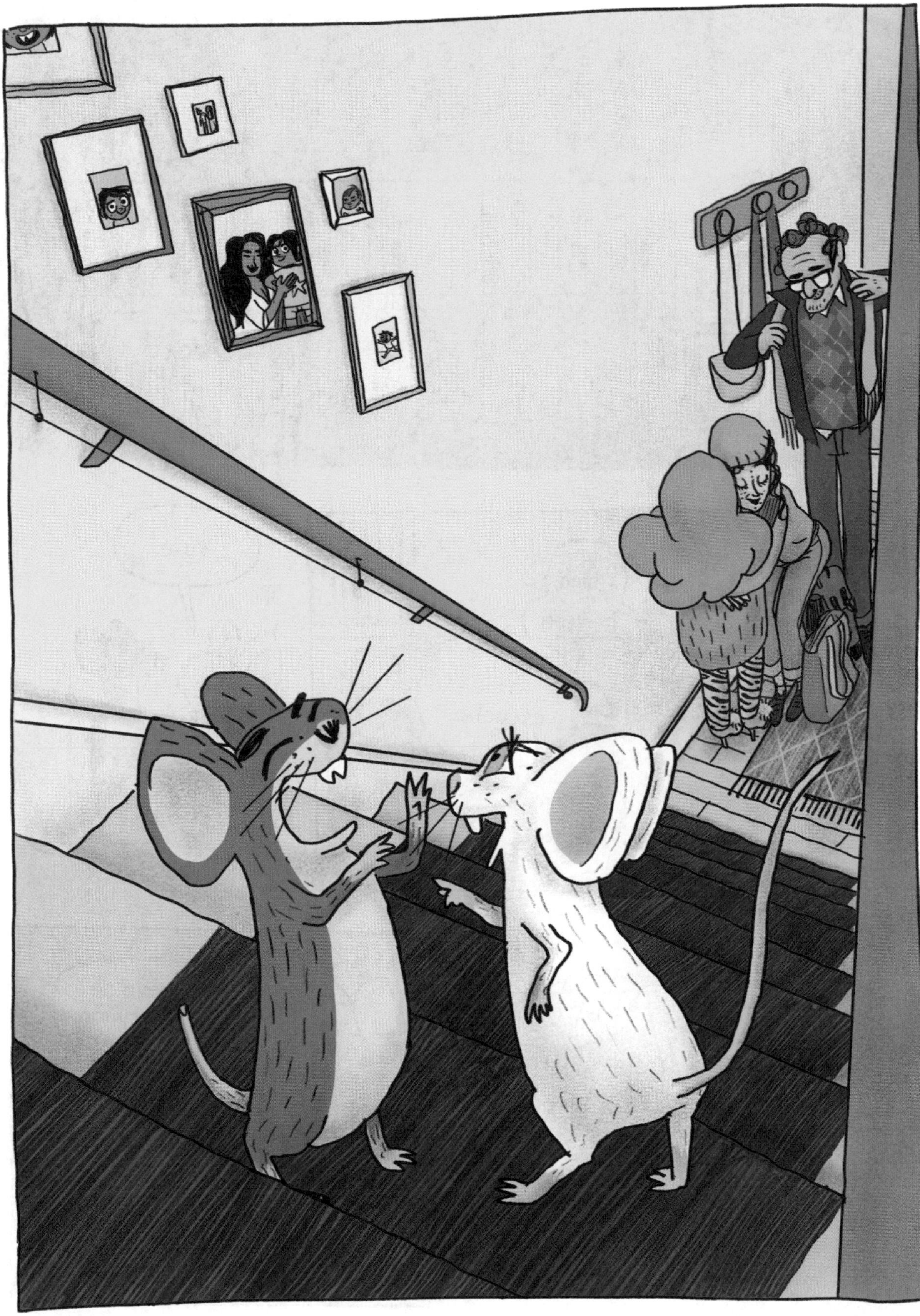

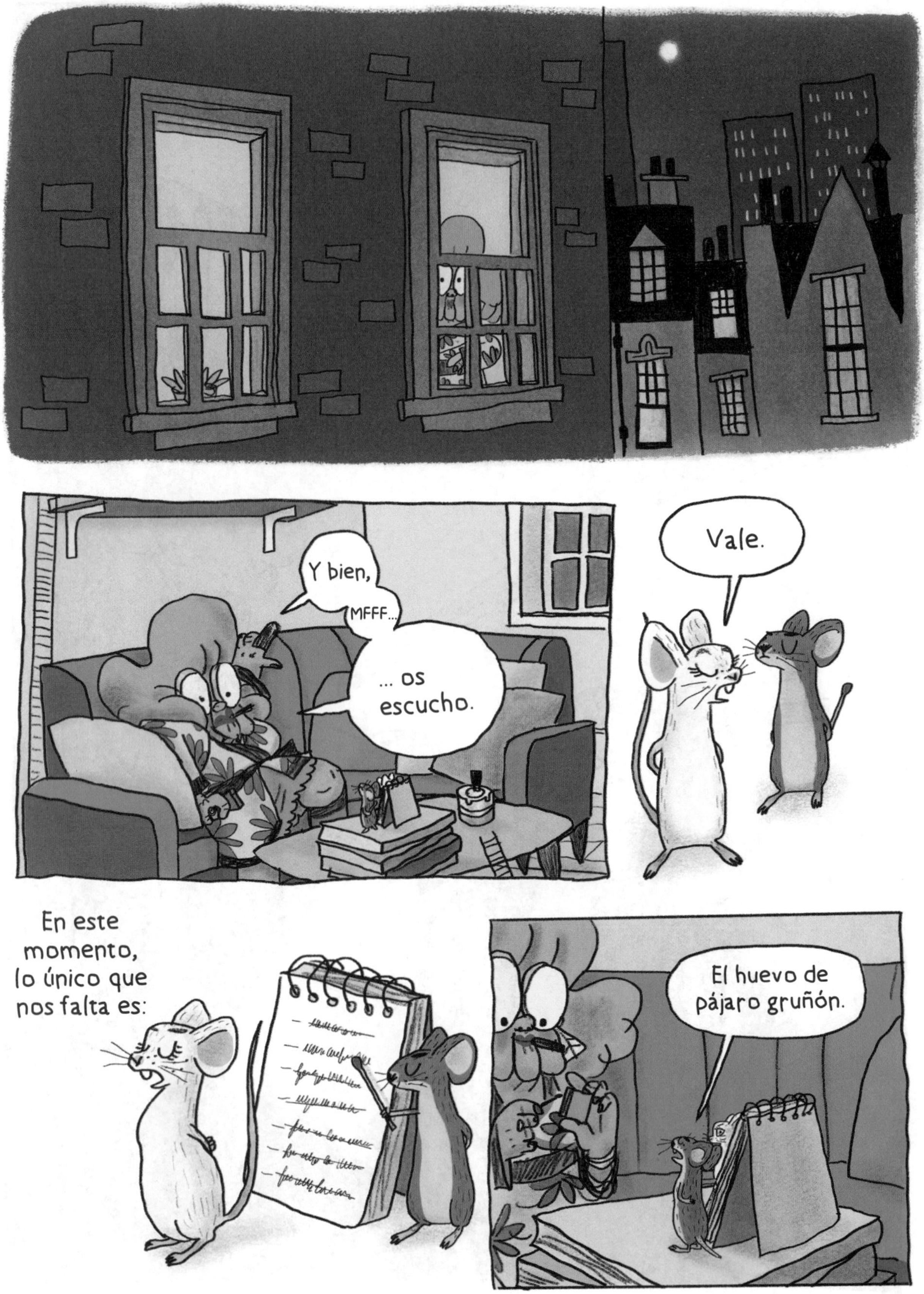
Y bien,
MFFF...
... os escucho.
Vale.
En este momento, lo único que nos falta es:
El huevo de pájaro gruñón.

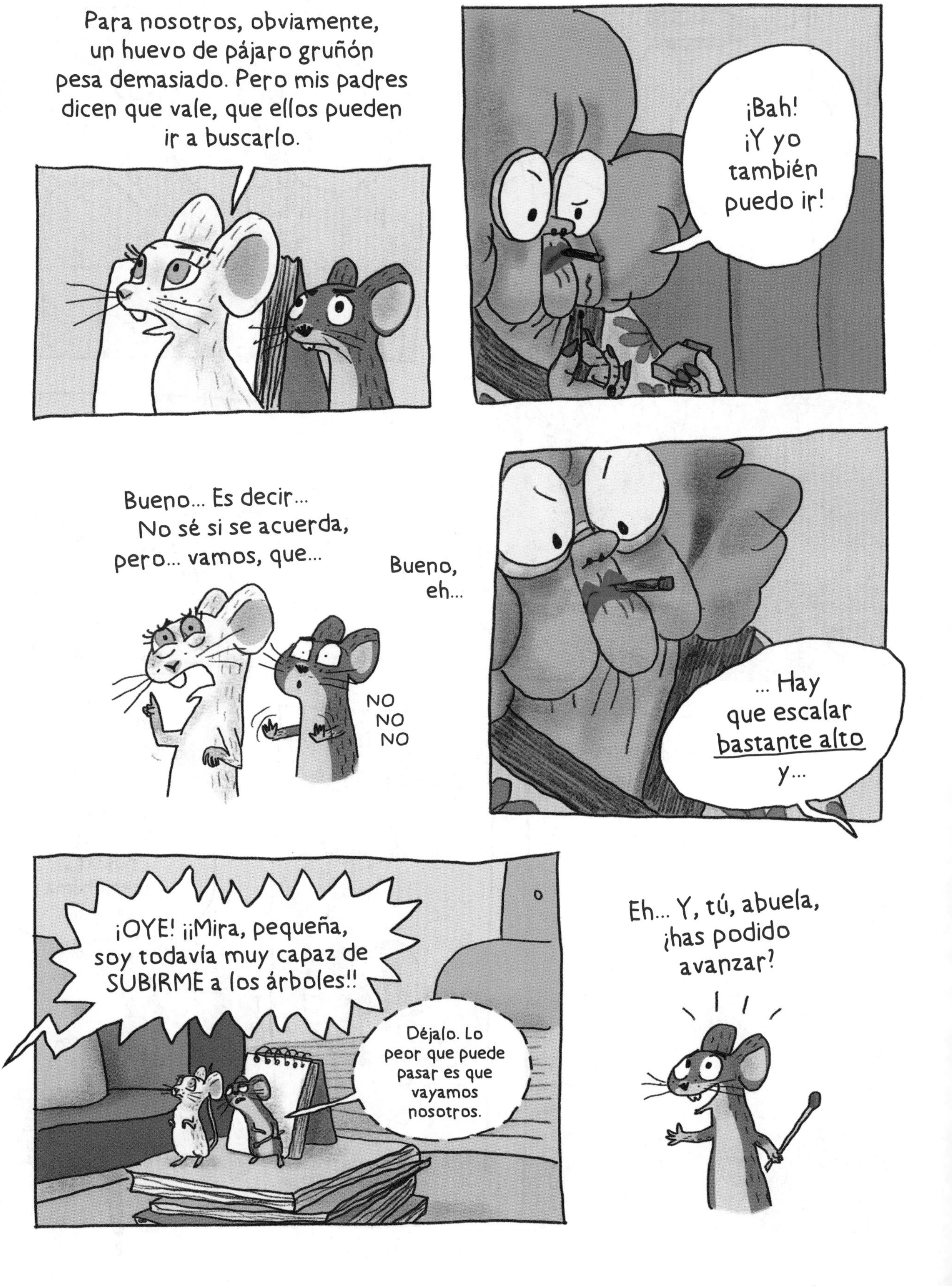

Para nosotros, obviamente, un huevo de pájaro gruñón pesa demasiado. Pero mis padres dicen que vale, que ellos pueden ir a buscarlo.
¡Bah! ¡Y yo también puedo ir!
Bueno... Es decir... No sé si se acuerda, pero... vamos, que...
Bueno, eh...
NO NO NO
... Hay que escalar bastante alto y...
¡OYE! ¡¡Mira, pequeña, soy todavía muy capaz de SUBIRME a los árboles!!
Déjalo. Lo peor que puede pasar es que vayamos nosotros.
Eh... Y, tú, abuela, ¿has podido avanzar?

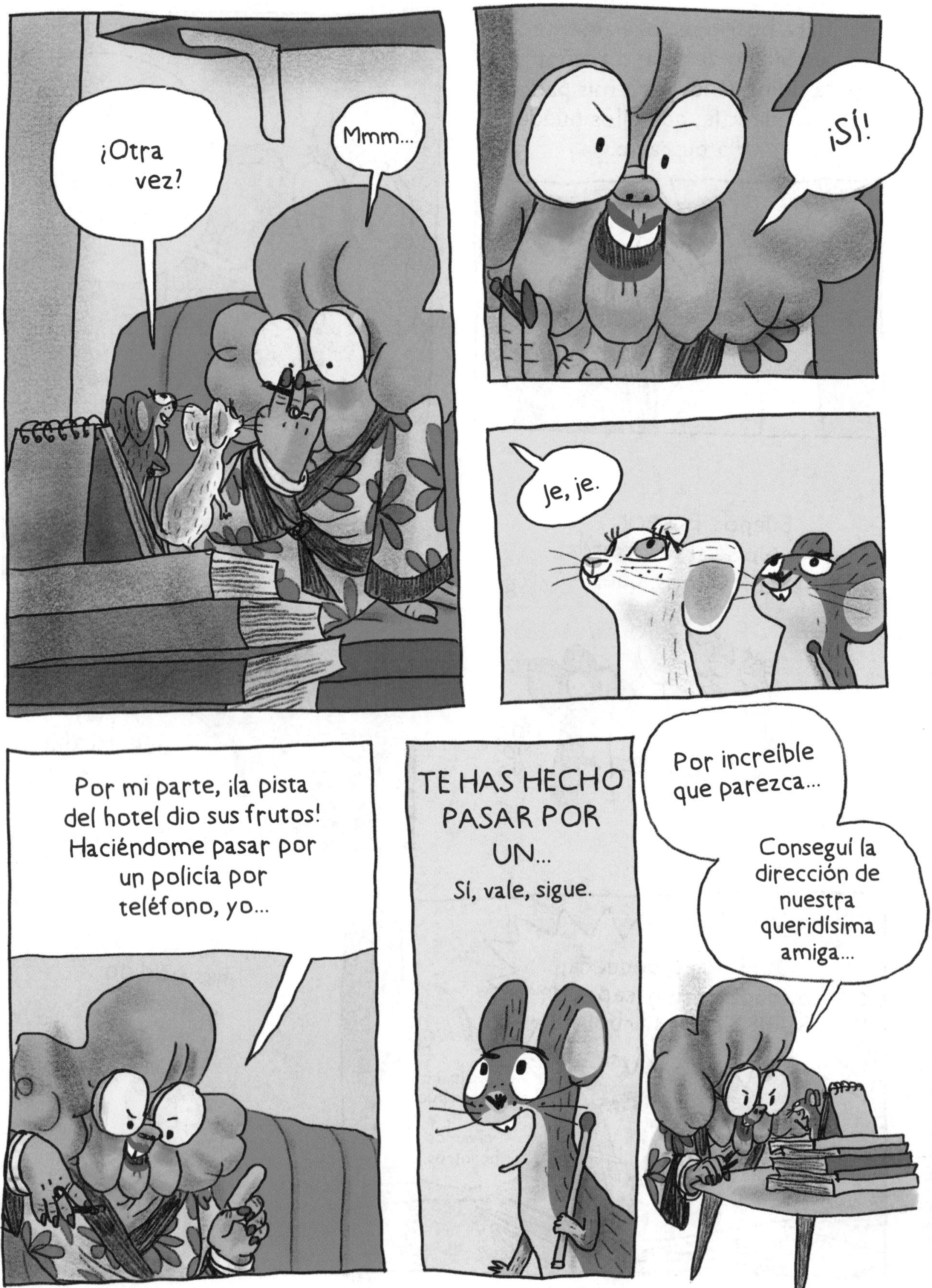
¿Otra vez?
Mmm...
¡SÍ!
Je, je.
Por mi parte, ¡la pista del hotel dio sus frutos! Haciéndome pasar por un policía por teléfono, yo...
TE HAS HECHO PASAR POR UN...
Sí, vale, sigue.
Por increíble que parezca...
Conseguí la dirección de nuestra queridísima amiga...

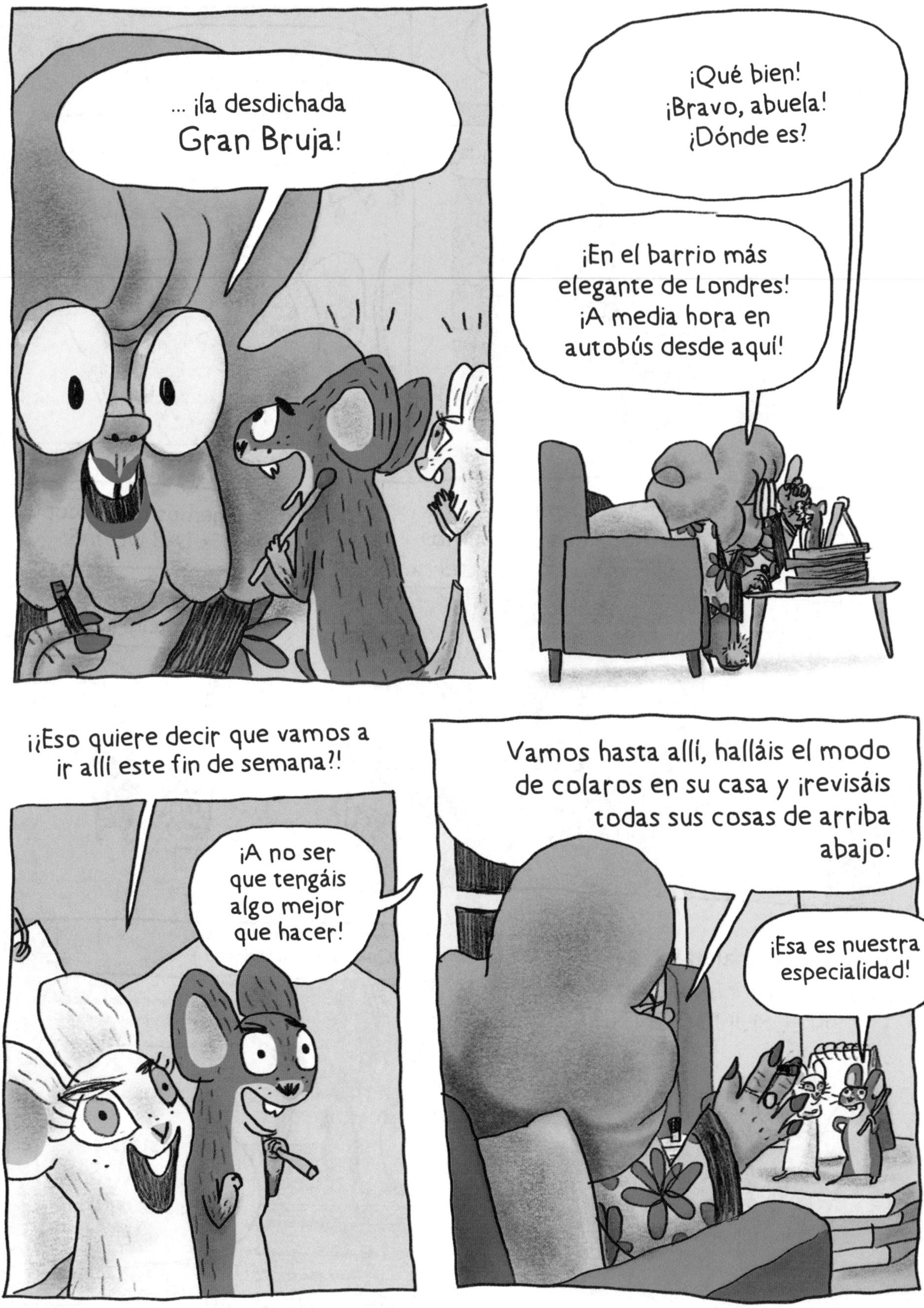
... ¡la desdichada Gran Bruja!
¡Qué bien! ¡Bravo, abuela! ¿Dónde es?
¡En el barrio más elegante de Londres! ¡A media hora en autobús desde aquí!
¡¿Eso quiere decir que vamos a ir allí este fin de semana?!
¡A no ser que tengáis algo mejor que hacer!
Vamos hasta allí, halláis el modo de colaros en su casa y ¡revisáis todas sus cosas de arriba abajo!
¡Esa es nuestra especialidad!

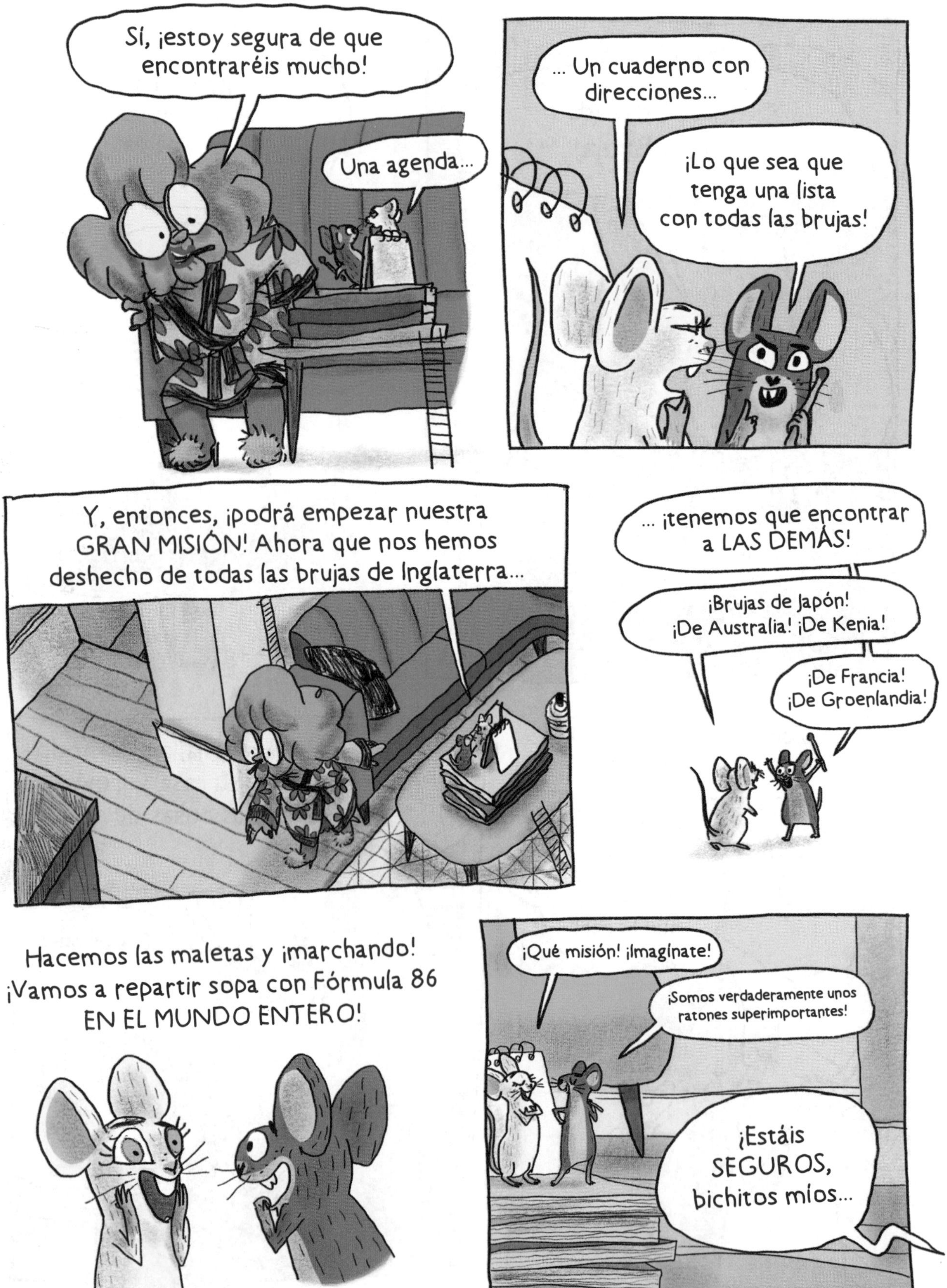
Sí, ¡estoy segura de que encontraréis mucho!
Una agenda...
... Un cuaderno con direcciones...
¡Lo que sea que tenga una lista con todas las brujas!
Y, entonces, ¡podrá empezar nuestra GRAN MISIÓN! Ahora que nos hemos deshecho de todas las brujas de Inglaterra...
... ¡tenemos que encontrar a LAS DEMÁS!
¡Brujas de Japón! ¡De Australia! ¡De Kenia!
¡De Francia! ¡De Groenlandia!
Hacemos las maletas y ¡marchando! ¡Vamos a repartir sopa con Fórmula 86 EN EL MUNDO ENTERO!
¡Qué misión! ¡Imagínate!
¡Somos verdaderamente unos ratones superimportantes!
¡Estáis SEGUROS, bichitos míos...

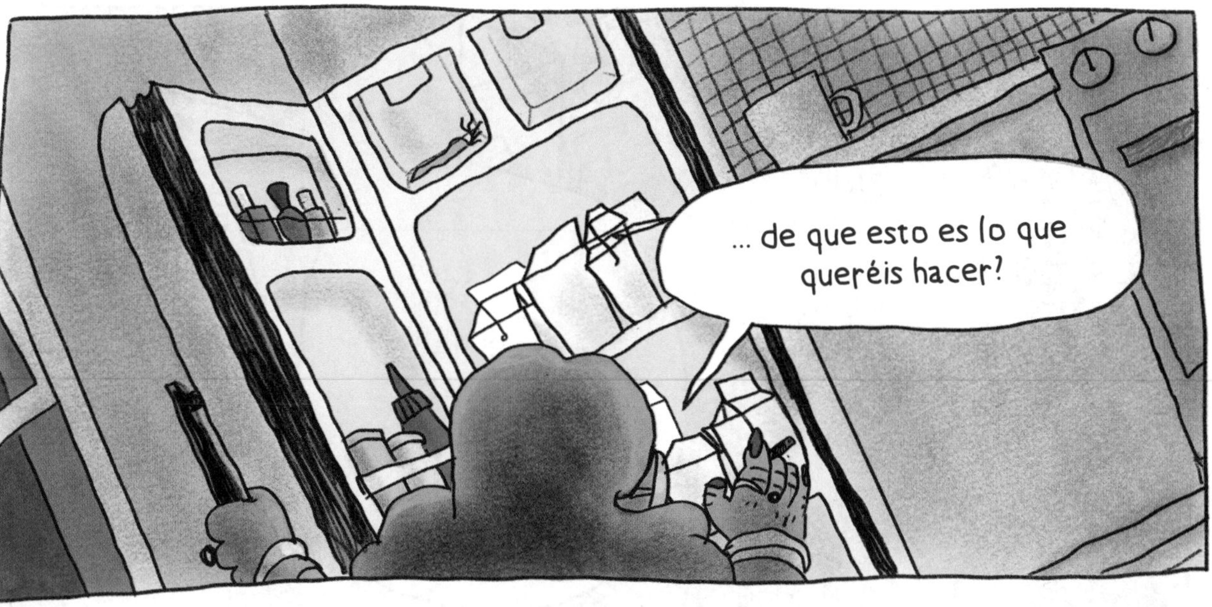
... de que esto es lo que queréis hacer?

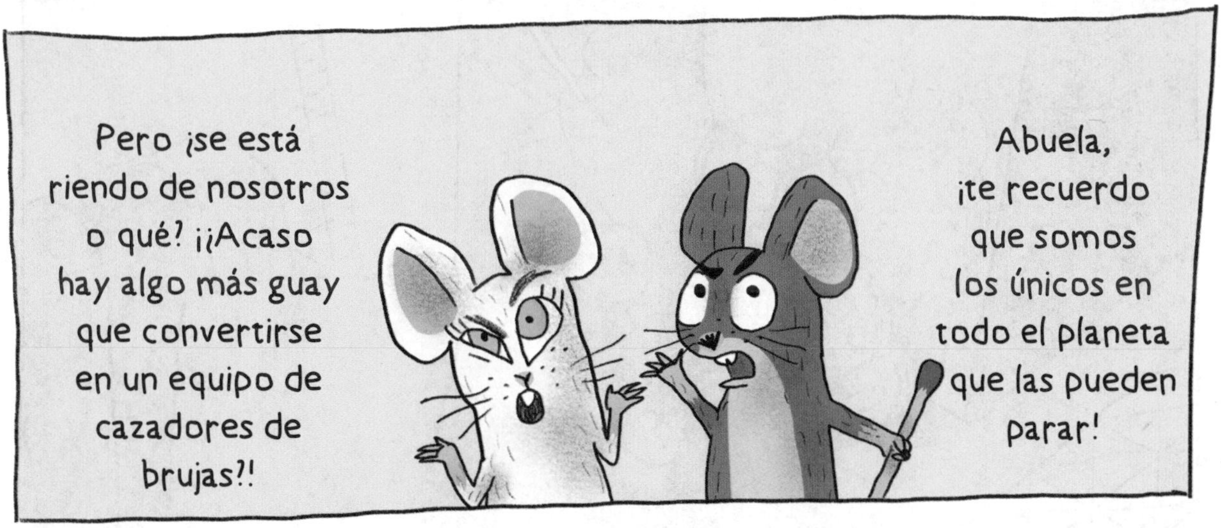
Pero ¿se está riendo de nosotros o qué? ¡¿Acaso hay algo más guay que convertirse en un equipo de cazadores de brujas?!
Abuela, ¡te recuerdo que somos los únicos en todo el planeta que las pueden parar!

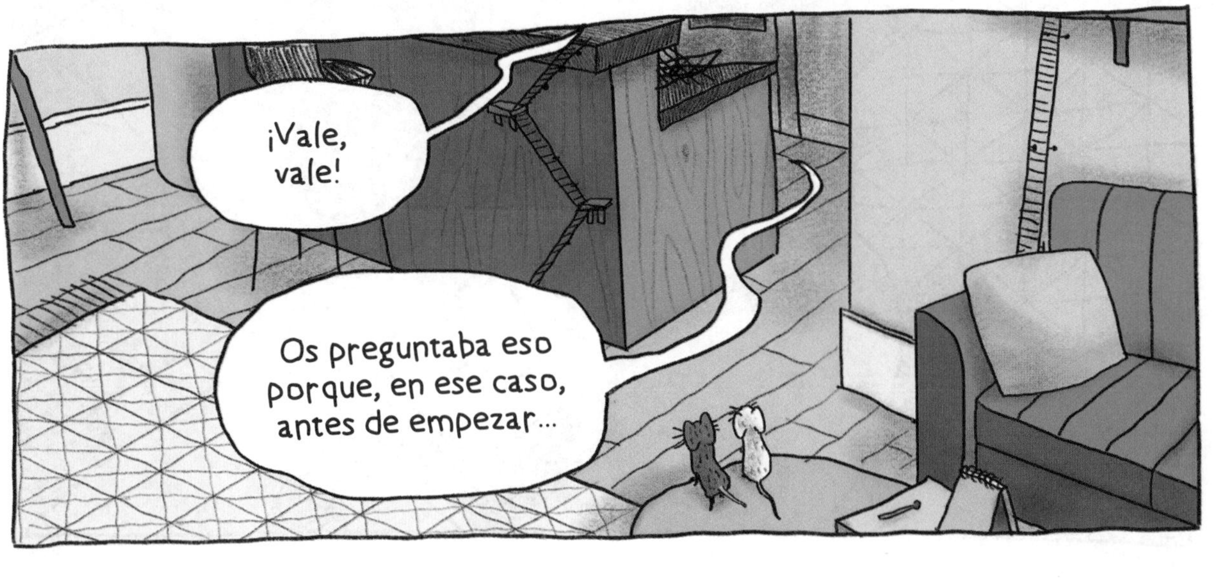
¡Vale, vale!
Os preguntaba eso porque, en ese caso, antes de empezar...

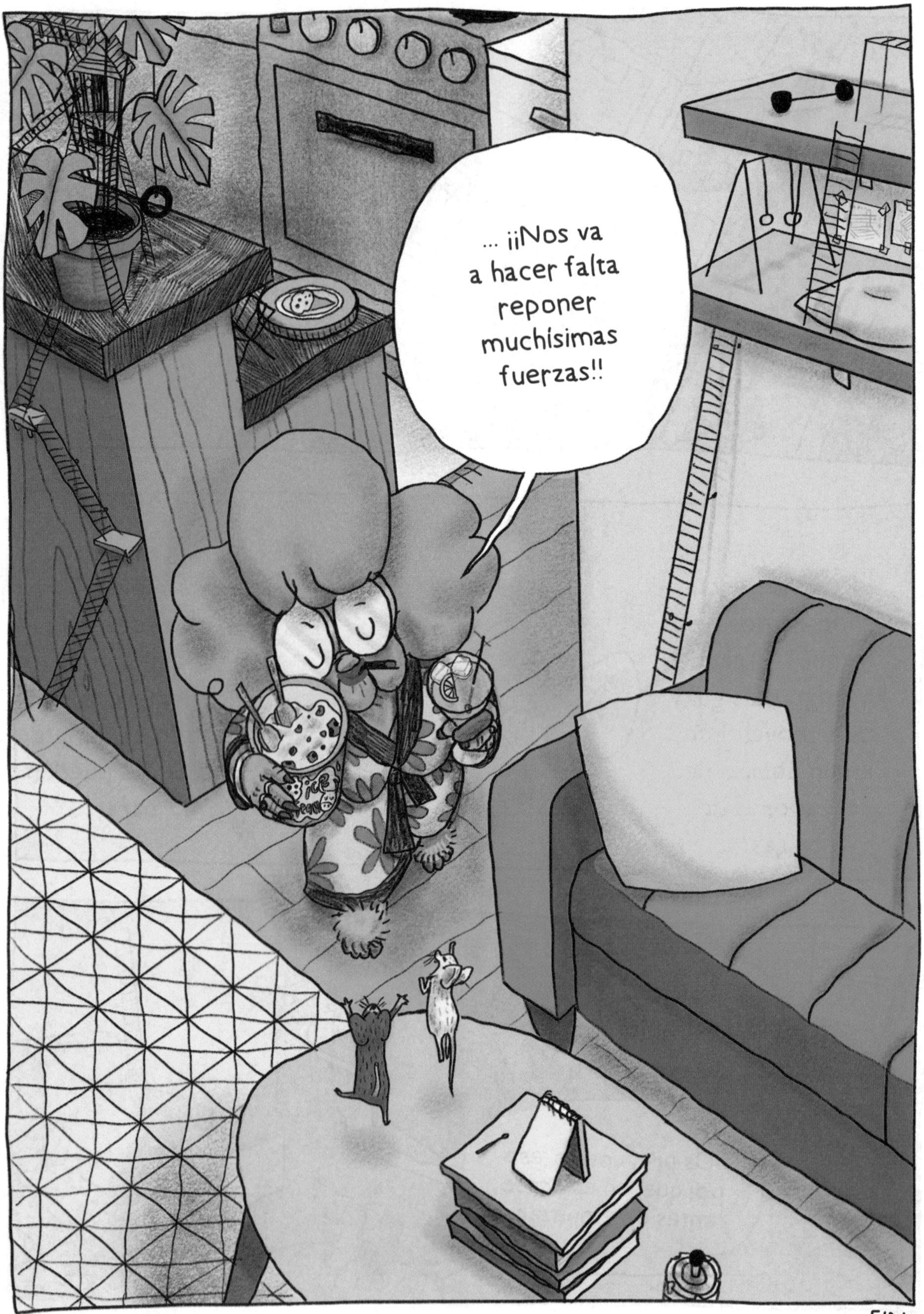
... ¡¡Nos va a hacer falta reponer muchísimas fuerzas!!

FIN

Este álbum no habría podido existir sin la ayuda
de Gallimard Jeunesse y, sobre todo, de Christine Baker,
Muriel Chabert, Sandrine Dutordoir, Thierry Laroche,
Nicolas Leroy, Olivier Merlin y Hedwige Pasquet.

Gracias a Luke Kelly y a todo el equipo
de la Roald Dahl Story Company.

Gracias por su revisión maravillosa a Mona Chollet, a Camille,
Salomé, Reiko, Zehra, Maureen, Robin, Elliot y Louna
por sus colores, y un agradecimiento especial a Drac.

Gracias a mis amigos y mi familia por su apoyo y sus consejos,
sobre todo a mi madre, Victoria y Sophie Thimonnier.

Y gracias infinitas a Benjamin.

P. B.

PÉNÉLOPE BAGIEU

Pénélope Bagieu nació en 1982 en París,
algunos meses antes de la publicación
original de *Las Brujas*.

Tras haber creado en 2007 «¡Mi vida es lo más!»,
un blog ilustrado cuyo éxito lo llevó a las librerías,
dibujó las aventuras de *Josefina* y creció
como ilustradora para editoriales y prensa.
En 2015, firmó *California dreamin'* (Harvey
Award, 2018) y consiguió un éxito rotundo con
Valerosas, ganadora del Eisner Award
al mejor libro extranjero en 2019.
Traducida a 17 idiomas, la serie se
adaptó para animación por France TV
(y se estrenó en marzo de 2020).
Pénélope vive actualmente en París.

ROALD DAHL

Roald Dahl fue espía, experto piloto
de combate, historiador del chocolate
e inventor médico.

También fue quien escribió *Charlie
y la fábrica de chocolate*, *Matilda*,
El Gran Gigante Bonachón y muchas
más historias geniales.

Continúa siendo el número 1 mundial de
los contadores de historias.

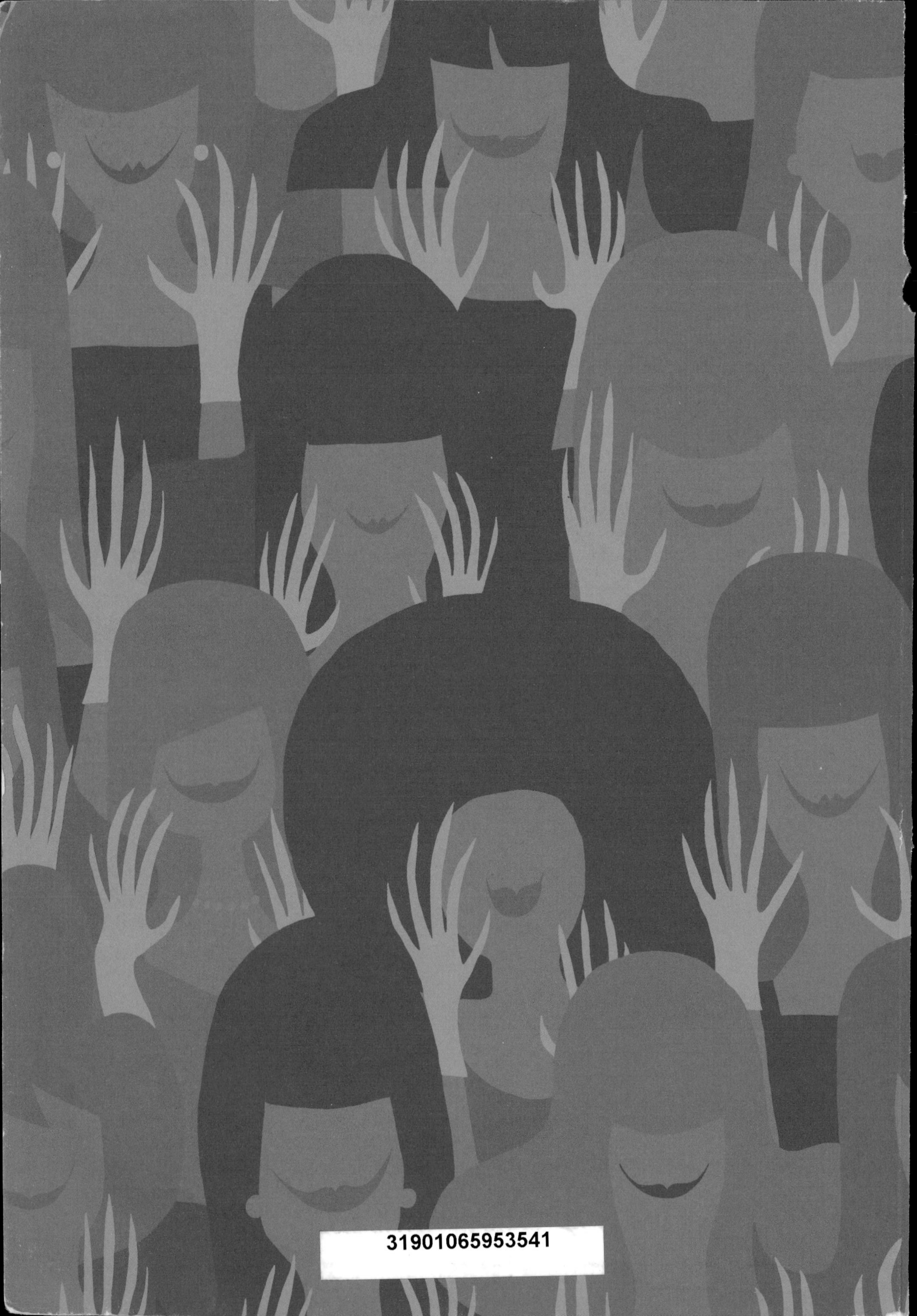

Dinner with Mr Darcy

Recipes inspired by the novels
and letters of Jane Austen

PEN VOGLER

CICO BOOKS
LONDON NEW YORK

For my Mum
For being much like
Mrs. Austen and nothing
like Mrs. Bennet

Published in 2013 by CICO Books

An imprint of Ryland Peters & Small Ltd
20–21 Jockey's Fields
London WC1R 4BW
519 Broadway, 5th Floor
New York, NY 10012

www.rylandpeters.com

10 9 8 7 6 5 4 3 2 1

Text © Pen Vogler 2013
Design and photography © CICO Books 2013

A CIP catalog record for this book is available from the Library of Congress and the British Library.

ISBN: 978-1-78249-056-2

Printed in China

Copy Editor: Lee Faber
Designer: Louise Leffler
Food Photographer: Stephen Conroy
Home Economist: Emma Jane Frost
Stylist: Luis Peral

NOTES:
All recipes serve four unless indicated otherwise.
All eggs are large (UK medium) unless indicated otherwise.

For digital editions, visit
www.cicobooks.com/apps.php

CONTENTS

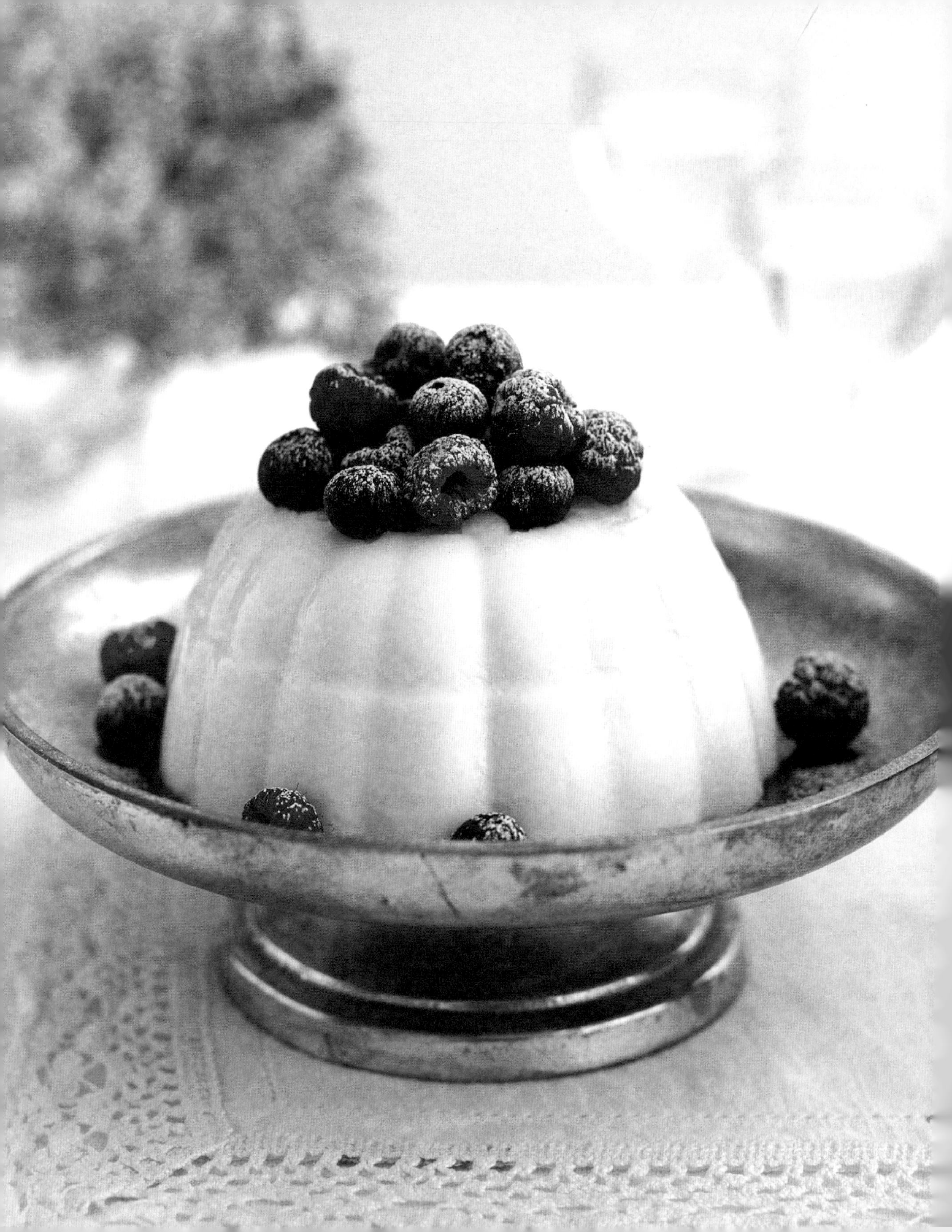

INTRODUCTION

The picnic at Box Hill in *Emma*: Mrs. Bennet preening herself over a fat haunch of venison, roasted to a turn; a gooseberry tart offered to a tired and homesick Fanny Price—Jane Austen's novels and letters are lightly sauced with dishes, dinners, and picnics, which tell us much about her characters' warmth, neighborliness, ambitions, and anxieties, and about the important role that food played in comfortable society in Georgian England. And, with a bit of help from contemporary recipe books, Jane's novels let us put together a wonderful idea of what life tasted like at the time.

In Jane's comic Juvenilia, she happily describes whole meals her characters enjoy, but in the mature novels, her least lovable characters are often those most preoccupied with what they eat. We are a little repelled by the indolent and greedy Dr. Grant in *Mansfield Park*, and a little scared by the active and punctilious—but equally greedy—General Tilney in *Northanger Abbey*. It is great fun to laugh at Mrs. Elton's social anxiety as she professes to be shocked at the quality of the rout cakes in Highbury, in *Emma*, or the ghastly Mrs. Norris as she "spunges" pheasants' eggs and cream cheese from Mr. Rushworth's housekeeper, or pilfers the remaining jellies after the Mansfield Park ball, but Jane's true heroines are unembarrassed by hunger or greed.

In her letters, however, Jane shows a lively interest in housekeeping and she describes meals she has enjoyed, or plans to have, and the many edible gifts that were made within her large family and circle of friends.

Her first home at Steventon Rectory in Hampshire offered marvelous training for what Mary Crawford archly describes as "the sweets of housekeeping in a country village". Mr. Austen was both rector and farmer, producing meat from his pigs, and dairy from five Alderney cows. He was particularly proud of his excellent mutton. Mrs. Austen ran the dairy, poultry yard, and a productive fruit and vegetable garden, besides having a family of six boys and two girls (Jane was the seventh baby.) They were self-sufficient in all, except some Georgian essentials such as coffee, tea, oranges, lemons, and spices.

When Jane was twenty-five, her father retired, and the family moved to Bath. Jane's letters started to mention prices and the problems of getting good meat and dairy, later reflected in Mrs. Grant's gentle rejoinder to Mary Crawford when she points out the "exorbitant charges and frauds," which were part of housekeeping in towns. Jane has a very funny passage on the price of fish:

"I am not without hopes of tempting Mrs. Lloyd to settle in Bath; meat is only 8d. per pound, butter 12d., and cheese 9½ d. You must carefully conceal from her, however, the exorbitant price of fish: a salmon has been sold at 2s. 9d. per pound the whole fish. The

Duchess of York's removal is expected to make that article more reasonable—and till it really appears so, say nothing about salmon." (Letter to Cassandra, May 5 1801.)

The widowed Mrs. Lloyd and her daughters, Martha, Eliza, and Mary, had become great friends with the Austen family when they lived in Mr. Austen's second parish of Deane in Hampshire. After the deaths of Mrs. Lloyd and Jane's father in 1805, Martha joined the Austen household, partly to combine resources, but also because Martha was the trusted "friend & sister under every circumstance" for the Austen sisters (letter to Cassandra, October 13 1808.) She moved with Mrs. Austen, Jane, and Cassandra to Southampton where, by 1807, they were in a town house in Castle Square; here at least they had access to fresh sea fish and their own garden. Their happiest domestic arrangements came with the cottage at Chawton in Hampshire, which became their home in the summer of 1809. It was the gift of Jane's brother Edward, who had been adopted by a childless couple, the Knights, and inherited the estates of Godmersham in Kent, and Chawton Manor in Hampshire. There were other wealthy friends and relatives, too: Mrs. Austen's cousin lived at Stoneleigh Abbey in Warwickshire; her son Henry, Jane's favorite brother, was a successful banker in Covent Garden. Jane, Cassandra, and Mrs. Austen all spent happy visits in these houses, writing light-heartedly to one another of their temporarily grand lifestyles and dinners.

It was at Chawton that Martha Lloyd compiled her Household Book of recipes, and gave us a wonderful record of dishes that Jane ate with her family and friends. Many of the recipes in Martha's book were given to her by her circle, but it is also easy to trace the influence of some of the key cookery writers of the day. Foremost of these was Hannah Glasse, whose *Art of Cookery Made Plain and Easy*, written in language "the lower Sort" could understand to "save the Ladies a great deal of Trouble," was a smash hit in the second part of the eighteenth century. The earliest source for the recipes in this book is John Nott's *The Cook's and Confectioner's Dictionary* of 1723. His recipes crystallized English food of an earlier generation, but which was still enjoyed eighty years later. The latest is one recipe from Mrs. Beeton from 1861 (because it makes me laugh). A few from Eliza Acton are also included; her *Modern Cookery for Private Families*, was published in 1845, a little after Jane Austen's lifetime, but Eliza's sensible take on fresh food and elegant recipes that work was learnt in the France of her youth, so we can assume that the French cooks of Jane Austen's world (the Monsieur Halavant employed by her brother Henry, or the "two or three French cooks at least" that Mrs. Bennet imagines Mr. Darcy to have) would have been producing similar dishes.

The aim of this book is to give some ideas to anybody who would like the fun of reconstructing dishes and dinners from Jane's life and novels, without having to struggle with a "peck of flour" or "one spoonful of good barm." I hope that many of these dishes are different enough from our own to be worth exploring; you will find sweetbreads, mutton rather than lamb, boiled rather than roasted meat. I hope also to revive some tastes that have become unjustly unfashionable (bring back caraway seeds!) and also some of the sense of fun in food that the Georgians had with their "hedgehogs" and "hen's nests". But there won't be any scary calf's heads or fish heads, delicacies for the Georgians, but the stuff of health and safety nightmares for us, on the menu.

So I hope you will enjoy rustling up some "rout cakes" for your card parties, or impressing your own Mr. Darcy with venison and roast partridges and, above all, that you will enjoy tasting your way into Jane Austen's England.

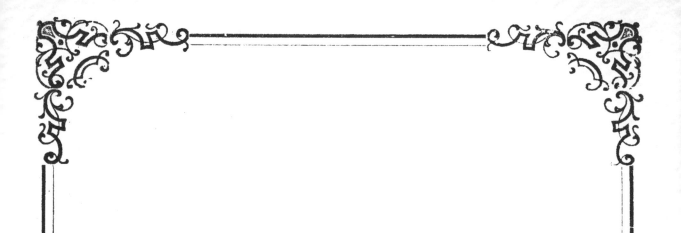

Breakfast with General Tilney

NORTHANGER ABBEY

General Tilney looms over the breakfasts of *Northanger Abbey* with his comic but uncomfortable mix of gastronomy and discipline. Catherine, breakfasting with the Tilneys in Bath, finds his attentiveness a trial, but he does put on a good spread: "never in her life before had she beheld half such variety on a breakfast-table." At Northanger Abbey he drinks cocoa and serves the richest of breads (rather like *brioche*) from a Staffordshire breakfast service. Mrs. Morland, thinking that her daughter was spoilt by grandeur, not love, worries that "I did not quite like, at breakfast, to hear you talk so much about the French bread at Northanger."

Mrs. Austen (Jane's mother) gives us an idea of the kind of elegant variety Catherine would have encountered; staying with her cousin at Stoneleigh Abbey in Warwickshire, she was offered a breakfast worth writing to her daughter-in-law about: "Chocolate, Coffee and Tea, Plumb Cake, Pound Cake, Hot Rolls, Cold Rolls, Bread and Butter, and dry toast for me."

Breakfast would be served at around 9 or 10 a.m., but workers or travelers might breakfast early on something hot or meaty; William Price has pork and mustard and Henry Crawford eats hard-boiled eggs before leaving Mansfield Park for London. The big cooked breakfasts of everything from kidneys to kedgeree were not part of the country-house weekend or visit until Victorian times, but visitors to Bath were spoiled with luscious, sugary Bath Buns and the local version of French bread, Sally Lunns.

BATH BUNS

Mrs. Raffald tells us to "send them in hot for breakfast," which sounds rather indigestible for these rich, buttery buns, and may have been why, when Jane was staying with a rather mean aunt, she joked to Cassandra that she would make herself an inexpensive guest by "disordering my Stomach with Bath bunns." (January 3 1801)

Makes 12 cakes

1 lb/450g all-purpose (plain) flour

1 tsp salt (optional — not in original, but we find yeast buns very bland without it)

⅔ cup/150g butter

¼ oz/7g sachet active dried yeast

2 tbsp sugar

1 tbsp caraway seeds

1 cup/225ml milk

For the glaze

2 tbsp superfine (caster) sugar

1 tbsp milk

Sugar nibs, or a few sugar cubes, roughly crushed and mixed with a few caraway seeds. These are in place of the caraway comfits— sugar-coated caraway seeds—that Mrs. Raffald would have used.

1 Add the salt, if using, to the flour, and rub the butter in until it is like coarse breadcrumbs; sprinkle in the yeast, sugar, and caraway seeds, and mix together well. Warm the milk, and stir it into the dry ingredients to give a soft dough; add a little milk if necessary.

2 Give it a good knead for about 10 minutes on a floured surface until it is smooth and pliable; return to the bowl, cover with a cloth, and let it rise in a warm place until double in size; it may take a good 2 or 3 hours because the butter in the dough impedes the rising action of the yeast.

3 Punch the air out of the dough and make up 12 cakes. Put them onto greased baking sheets, cover with a damp dish towel (tea towel) or plastic wrap (clingfilm) and leave to rise again for up to 1 hour.

4 Preheat the oven to 375°F/190°C/Gas Mark 5.

5 Bake for 12–15 minutes until they are golden brown.

6 Heat together the milk and sugar for the glaze, and brush it over the hot buns, then strew the crushed sugar cubes and caraway seeds over the top.

Bath Cakes

Rub half a pound of butter into a pound of flour, and one spoonful of good barm. Warm some cream and make it into a light paste, set it to the fire to rise. When you make them up take four ounces of caraway comfits, work part of them in and strew the rest on the top. Make them into round cakes the size of a French roll. Bake them on sheet tins and send them in hot for breakfast.

ELIZABETH RAFFALD, *THE EXPERIENCED ENGLISH HOUSEKEEPER*, 1769

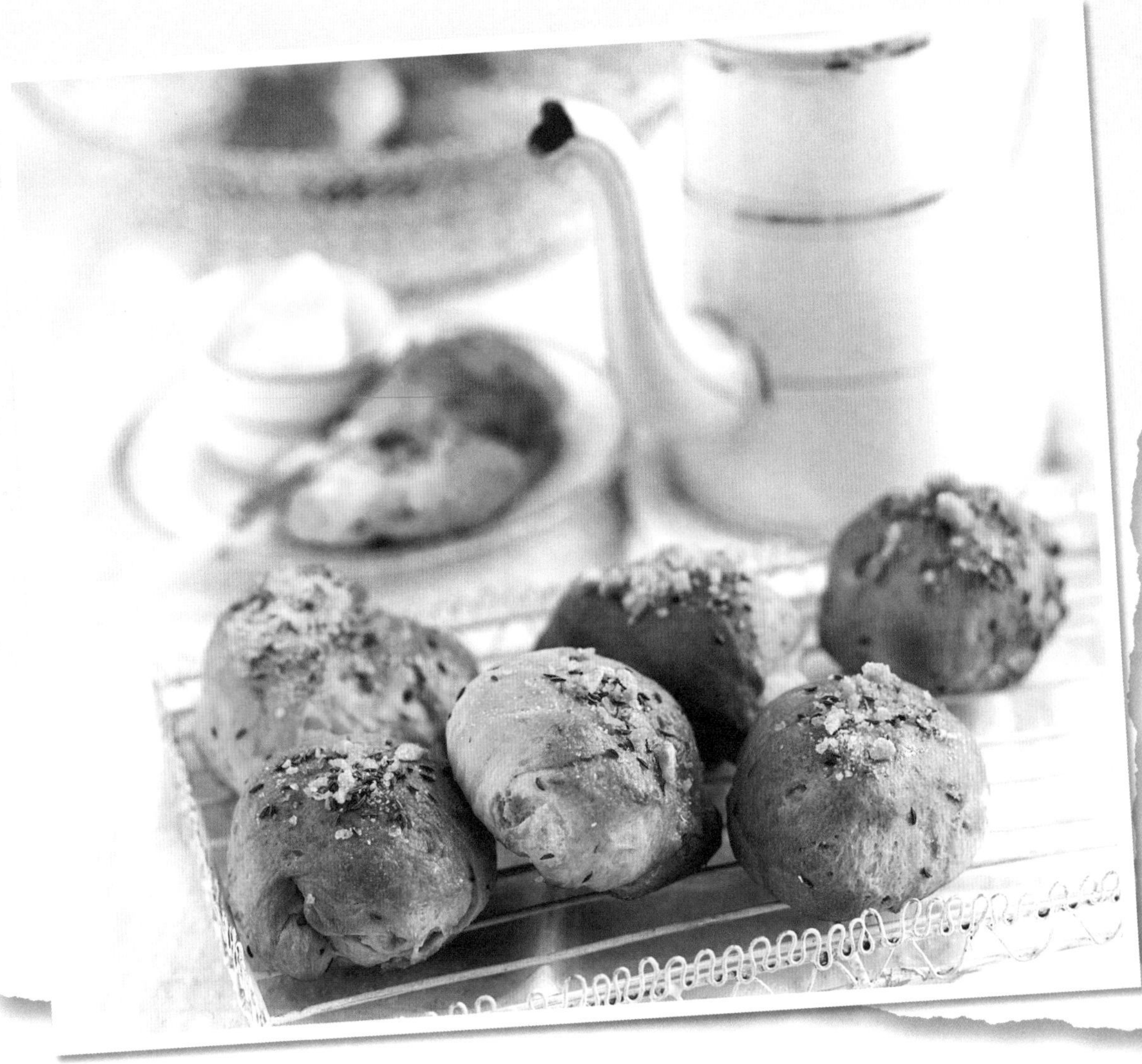

MEALTIMES

As the middle classes or "middling sort" began to grow more numerous in Georgian times, one of the ways that the gentry sought to distinguish themselves was by taking later meal times, particularly dinner.

People rose between 6 and 8 a.m., but breakfast for the leisured classes was taken at 9 or 10 a.m., or later. Jane wrote letters before breakfast or, in Bath, went shopping. In *Pride and Prejudice*, when the note is delivered with news of Jane's illness, Elizabeth walks three miles or so after her own breakfast, to find the Netherfield party still at theirs.

"Morning" was the time up to dinner when callers would be offered a little something, such as cold meat or cake. Miss Bates, always generous, hopes Emma and Harriet will have "sweet-cake from the beaufet" when they call on her. Lunch or luncheon (or "noonshine" as Jane and others sometimes called it) was generally a thing of the Victorian future when dinner had moved to the evening from the afternoon; but it might be taken by travelers. When Kitty and Lydia meet Elizabeth and Jane returning from London, at the George Inn, Lydia says "we treated the other three with the nicest cold luncheon in the world" (although the elder sisters paid.)

Ladies might take about an hour (or, in the case of Miss Bingley and Mrs. Hurst, an hour and a half) to change before dinner. The ridiculous Mr. Collins tells Elizabeth not to worry about dressing up for dinner with Lady Catherine: "I would advise you merely to put on whatever of your clothes is superior to the rest," as "She likes to have the distinction of rank preserved." Men would also dress for dinner, particularly if they had been out shooting or hunting. In *The Watsons*, Mrs. Robert Watson chides her husband for not putting fresh powder in his hair, nor making "some alteration in your dress before dinner when you are out visiting".

Your dinner time was a statement of how traditional or fashionable you saw yourself, although it grew later for everybody around the turn of the century. In December 1798, Jane wrote from Steventon to Cassandra at Godmersham: "We dine now at half after three, & have done dinner I suppose before you begin—We drink tea at half after six. —I am afraid you will despise us." But by 1805, she dined at four or five o'clock. Mrs. Dashwood dines at a comfortable four o'clock at Barton Cottage, whereas General Tilney prefers six o'clock and the Bingley-Hurst household, anxious to distance themselves from the "trade" source of their fortune, dine at 6:30 p.m.

Tea, coffee, and cake were taken an hour or so after dinner, once the gentlemen had joined the ladies from the dining room. A rural party would amuse itself with cards, music, or even dancing, whereas those in town might go to the theatre, before taking supper some time between 9 p.m. and midnight. Supper might be anything from bread and cheese, or some cold leftovers, such as apple tart, to a complete meal of a few freshly-cooked "made" dishes, such as those the old-fashioned Mr. Woodhouse liked to offer his guests. Jane's niece Anna "had a delightful Even' with the Miss Middletons—Syllabub, Tea, Coffee, Singing, Dancing, a Hot Supper, eleven o'clock, everything that can be imagined agreable." (Jane to Cassandra, Friday 31 May 1811). A ball supper would be even later: "We began at 10, supped at 1, & were at Deane before 5." (Jane to Cassandra, November 20 1800).

In *Persuasion*, Elizabeth Elliot knows she should ask Mrs. Musgrove's party to dine with them, "but she could not bear to have the difference of style, the reduction of servants, which a dinner must betray," and convinces herself that giving dinners was old-fashioned, country hospitality. And who can blame her? A hostess whose guests stayed the whole evening would have to provide not just a dinner of several dishes, and several servants to wait on them, but another two whole meals. Entertaining was a serious, and expensive, business.

ENGLISH MUFFINS

Mr. Woodhouse comments on Emma passing the muffins to her guests an overattentive (and indigestible) twice. Muffins were also served with after-dinner tea in *Pride and Prejudice* and in *The Watsons*. Traditionally they were toasted front and back (not in the middle) and pulled (not cut) apart around the waist and, of course, laden with butter.

Makes 12 muffins

1 lb/450g strong bread flour
¼ oz/7g sachet active dried yeast
1 tsp salt (optional—not in original, but we find yeast buns very bland without it)

2 tbsp/25g butter
Generous 1¼ cups/280ml milk
1 egg

1 Mix the yeast and salt, if using, into the flour and make a well in the center. Warm the butter in the milk until it melts. Beat the egg, and pour into the center of the flour; add the milk, and draw the flour in from the edges until you have a dough.

2 Knead it on a floured surface until it is smooth, then return the dough to the bowl, cover it with a clean dish (tea) towel and leave to rise in a warm place until double in size—about 45–60 minutes. Punch out the air and make the dough into a flat cake about ⅜ inch/1cm high on a floured board, and cut out circular cakes with a cookie (biscuit) cutter. Let them rise again in a warm place on a lightly floured baking sheet for half an hour. Heat a griddle or heavy-based frying pan with very little oil or lard, and griddle them for 8–10 minutes each side on low to medium heat.

Muffins Mix two pounds of flour with two eggs, two ounces of butter melted in a pint of milk, and four or five spoonfuls of yeast; beat it thoroughly, and set it to rise two or three hours. Bake on a hot hearth, in flat cakes. When done on one side turn them. Note: Muffins, rolls, or bread, if stale, may be made to taste new, by dipping in cold water, and toasting, or heating in an oven, or Dutch oven, till the outside be crisp.

MRS. RUNDELL, *A NEW SYSTEM OF DOMESTIC COOKERY*, 1806

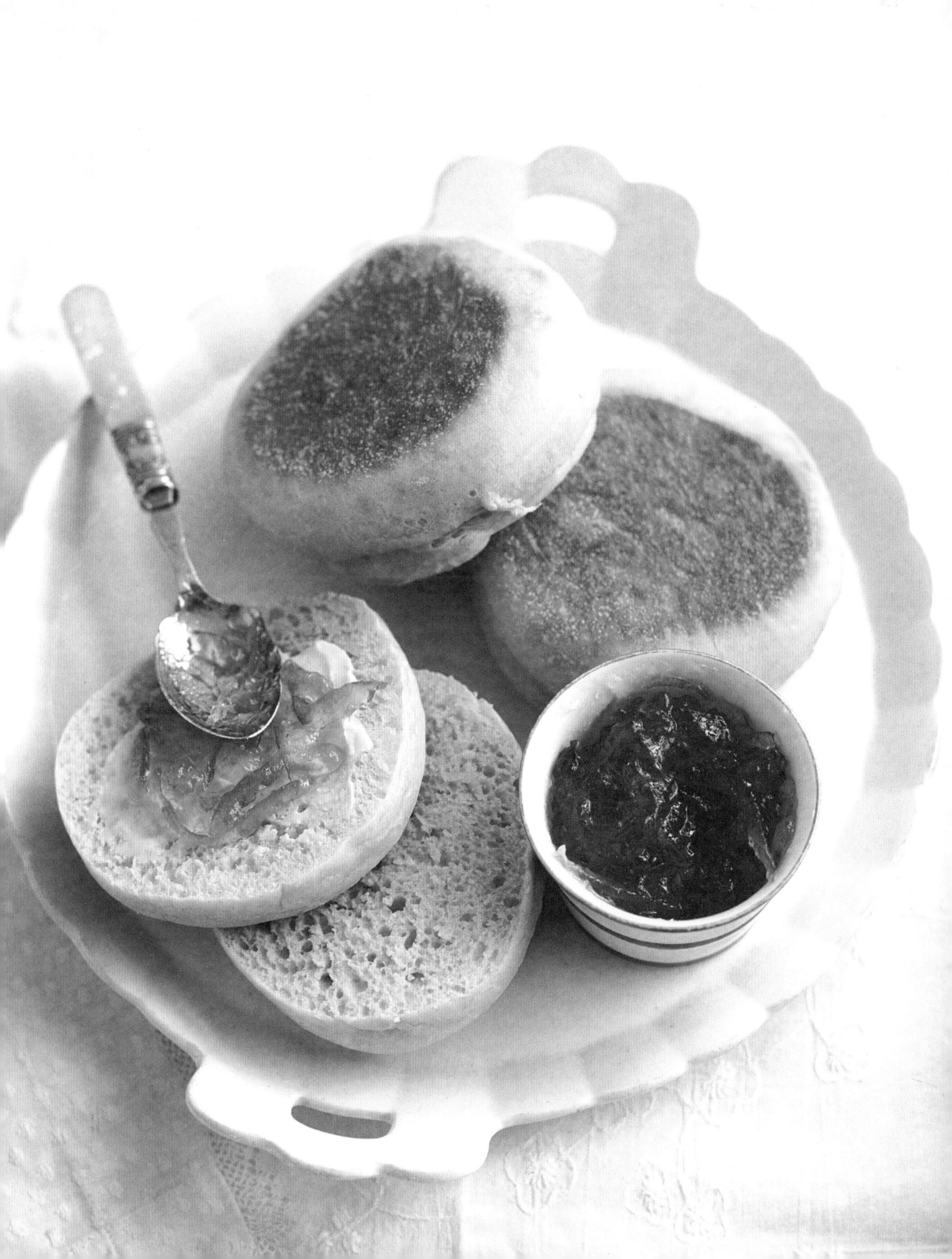

SALLY LUNNS

Sally Lunns were warm and golden bread cakes, eaten at breakfast with butter or clotted cream—even more extravagant than the rich French bread that General Tilney served. Legend has it that they were named after their inventor, Solange Luyon, a French Huguenot refugee who worked at a bakery in Bath.

Makes 6 cakes

¼ oz/7g sachet active dried yeast

2 tbsp superfine (caster) sugar

2 eggs plus optional extra egg white for glazing

Generous 1¼ cups/280ml cream or milk

1 lb/450g strong bread flour

1 tsp salt (optional — not in original, but we find yeast buns very bland without it)

Butter or clotted cream, to serve

1 Blend the yeast with the sugar and beat it thoroughly with the eggs and cream. Sift in the flour and salt, if using, to make a dough that is smooth, but not sticky (add a little milk if it feels too dry.)

2 Knead it on a floured surface for about 10 minutes until it feels elastic. Put it back in the bowl, cover with a clean dish towel (tea towel) and let it rise for 1½ hours.

3 Punch the air out of the dough and divide it into 6 cakes (you may find it helpful to flour your hands.) Lay the cakes on a greased baking sheet.

4 Cover and let them rise again until double in size—30 minutes to 1 hour.

5 Preheat the oven to 400°F/200°C/Gas Mark 6. Glaze them with egg white or milk if you fancy it, and bake for 12–15 minutes.

6 Serve with butter or clotted cream.

Note: Margaret Dods warms a little saffron in the milk or cream to improve the color, but organic eggs with good orangey yellow yolks should make them properly golden.

Sally Lunn Cakes *Make them as French bread, but dissolve some sugar in the hot milk. Mould into the form of cakes. A little saffron boiled in the milk enriches the colour of these or any other cakes.*

MARGARET DODS, *THE COOK AND HOUSEWIFE'S MANUAL*, 1826

Breakfast with General Tilney

CHOCOLATE TO DRINK

Chocolate wasn't yet eaten as a solid sweet, but, like cocoa, taken as a drink, luxurious enough to be served at a wedding breakfast Jane attended. It was grated from a solid block and gadget-lovers such as the General would have had a special chocolate mill to give it a fine froth—quite a palaver as the original recipe shows!

3½ oz/100g bittersweet (plain) good-quality
chocolate (70% cocoa solids)

1¾ cups/400ml milk or milk and light
(single) cream

1 Chop the chocolate into very small pieces or, even better, grate it into a mixing bowl.
2 Warm the milk or milk and cream to just below boiling point, then turn off the heat.
3 Whisk in the chocolate.
4 Serve in coffee cups or small teacups.

Chocolate Those who use much of this article, will find the following mode of preparing it both useful and economical:
Cut a cake of chocolate in very small bits; put a pint of water into the pot, and when it boils, put in the above; mill it off the fire until quite melted, then on a gentle fire till it boils; pour it in a basin, and it will keep in a cool place eight or ten days, or more. When wanted, put a spoonful or two into milk, boil it with sugar, and mill it well. This, if not made thick, is a very good breakfast or supper.

MRS. RUNDELL, *A NEW SYSTEM OF DOMESTIC COOKERY*, 1806

Scotch Orange Marmalade

Each 1 lb of oranges requires 1½ lbs of lump sugar. Quarter the oranges, then take off the rind and cut part of the white substances from it. Put the rinds into boiling water and boil them quickly for an hour and half or two hours. Slice them as thin as possible. Squeeze the pulp thro' a sieve adding a little water to the dregs. Break the sugar fine. Put it in the pan, pour the pulp on it—when dissolved, add the rinds, then boil the whole for twenty minutes—a little essence of lemon may be added before it is taken off the fire, in the proportion of a small teaspoonful to twelve oranges.

MARTHA LLOYD'S HOUSEHOLD BOOK

MISS DEBARY'S MARMALADE

Miss Debary was one of the "endless Debarys"; four sisters unloved by Jane who said they were "odious"' (letter to Cassandra, September 8 1816,) and had bad breath (letter to Cassandra, November 20 1800!) Marmalade was made from all kinds of fruit and eaten for dessert until the Scots made it from bitter Seville oranges and started serving it for breakfast at the end of the eighteenth century.

Makes 6 x 1 lb/450g jars
3¼ lb (1.5kg) Seville oranges
2 sweet oranges

About 6 lb/2.75 kg preserving sugar
1 scant gallon/3.5 liters water
Juice of 2 lemons

1 Weigh the fruit and for each 18 oz/500g of fruit weigh out 26 oz/750g sugar. Quarter the fruit and cut off the rind, taking off a little of the pith if you want a sweeter marmalade.
2 Boil the rind in water for 1½ –2 hours; there should be a third of the water left. When it is cool, cut the rind into thin slices about ⅜–¾ inch/1–2cm long; Georgian cooks called these "chips". Chop the pulp and pick out the seeds (pips) and pith, or push it through a sieve. Put the chips, pulp and lemon juice into the water used to boil the rind, and bring to a boil. Add the sugar and boil vigorously for 20 minutes, stirring to make sure it doesn't catch on the bottom. When you have put the marmalade on to boil, leave a saucer in the fridge and put your jars on baking sheets into the oven at 350°F/180°C/Gas Mark 4 and leave them to sterilize for 20 minutes.
3 After 20 minutes, put a little of the marmalade onto the cold plate. If it sets, it is ready; if not, test every 5 minutes until you get a set.
4 Let the marmalade cool a little before decanting it into the hot jars. When it is cold, put wax paper on the surface, before adding the lids.

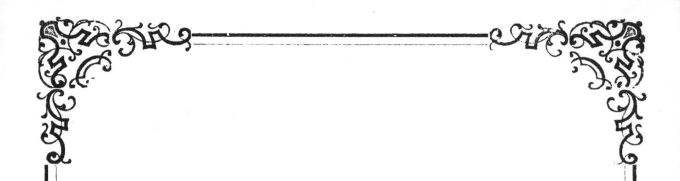

Mrs. Bennet's Dinner to Impress

PRIDE AND PREJUDICE

Only Jane Austen's most ridiculous characters fuss about food, but it is thanks to the Mrs. Bennets of the novels that we glean so much about what was served and what it all meant. Planning the dinner for fifteen at Longbourn, Mrs. Bennet, anxious that Bingley will marry Jane, decides that nothing less than two full courses would "satisfy the appetite and pride of one who had ten thousand a year." The September menu is suggested here, with some help from her self-congratulatory post-mortem.

"The venison was roasted to a turn—and every body said,
they never saw so fat a haunch. The soup was fifty times better
than what we had at the Lucas's last week; and even Mr. Darcy acknowledged,
that the partridges were remarkably well done; and I suppose he has
two or three French cooks at least."

This is an excellent summary of the burning issues for the Georgian hostess: how to better the neighbors; how to stake your claim on the social ladder with game, the food of landowners and aristocracy; and the combination of admiration and suspicion English country folk felt for French food and French chefs.

Mrs. Bennet knows who is worth impressing—not Charlotte Lucas who has to shift with the family: "I hope my dinners are good enough for her." But when Mr. Bennet announces that "a gentleman, and a stranger" is to come to dinner, her first thought is to summon Hill, the cook, and lament that there wouldn't be any fresh fish available to impress her mystery guest.

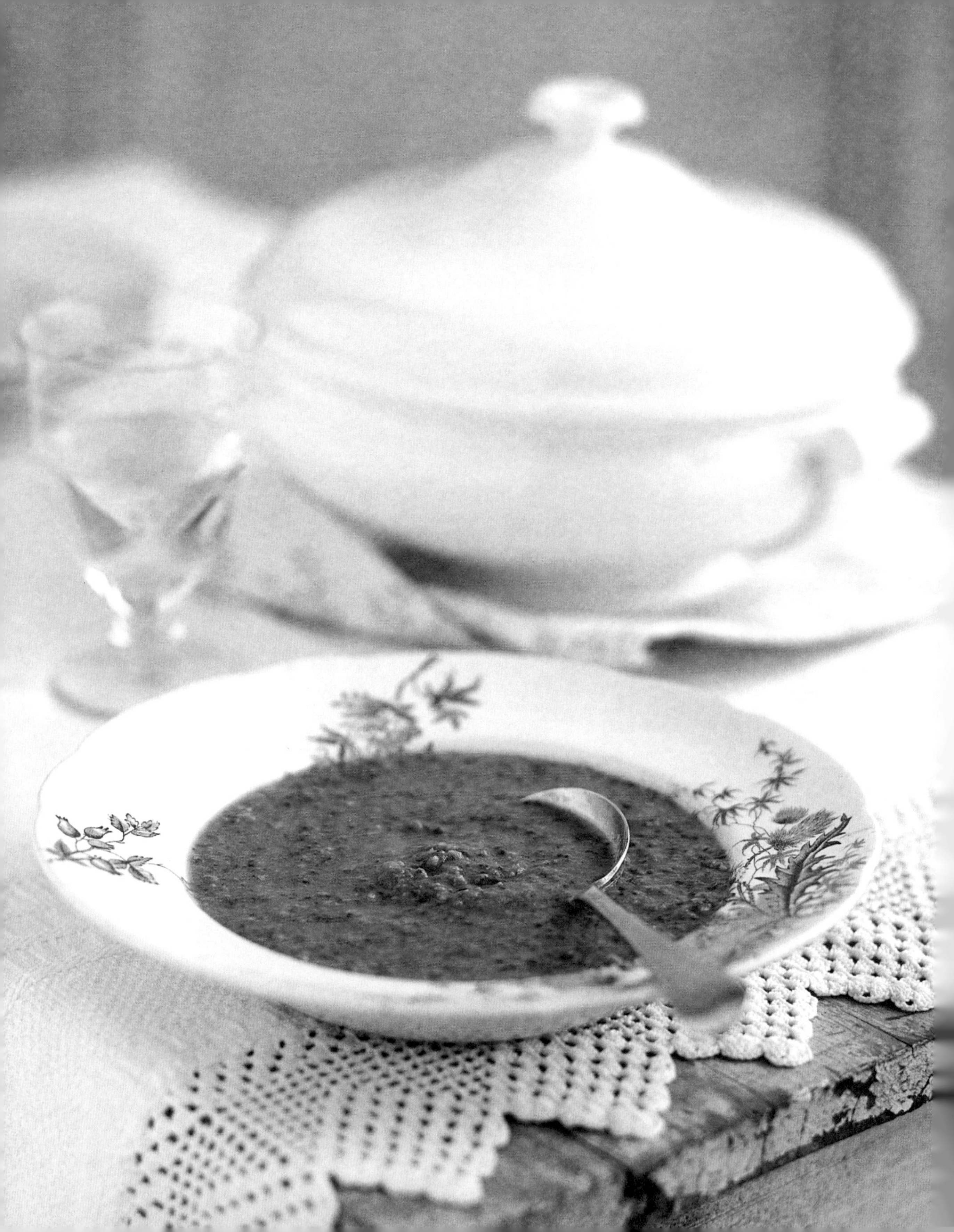

FRESH PEA SOUP

Pea soup was an Austen family favorite; Jane wrote that she was not ashamed to invite an unexpected guest to "our elegant entertainment" of "pease-soup, a spare rib and a pudding" (letter to Cassandra, December 1 1798.) This was a perfect way of using up the older peas from the garden to produce a fresh, vividly colored soup.

2 celery sticks, finely chopped
1 onion, finely chopped
Scant ½ stick/50g butter
Few sprigs of mint and parsley, chopped
3 anchovies or 6–8 anchovy fillets, chopped
Freshly ground white pepper
4 cups/500g frozen or fresh peas

Generous 1 quart/1 liter light vegetable or chicken stock
Pinch of sugar
4–5 good handfuls of spinach (you could use lettuce and/or chopped cucumber instead of the spinach)

1 Gently cook the celery and onion in butter until it is soft but not browned, then add the mint, parsley, and anchovy, grind in a little white pepper, and cook for a few minutes.
2 Stir the peas into the mixture, add the stock and a good pinch of sugar, and simmer for 10 minutes.
3 Add the spinach (or lettuce and/or cucumber) at the end of the cooking time, and cook for a few minutes more. Let it cool, then whizz with a blender. This gives a nice grainy texture, but push it through a sieve if you would like a smooth soup in the Georgian manner. Reheat gently to serve.

Pease Soup Take two quarts of pease. Boil them to a pulp. Strain them. Put ½ lb of butter into a stewpan, Celery, half an onion, and stew them til tender. Then put two anchovies, powdered pepper, salt, mint and parsley, (each a small handful) and spinach, and heat of each a small quantity. Half a spoonful of sugar. The soup be boiled as thick as you like it and the whole to be ground together, boiled up and dished.

Martha Lloyd's Household Book

NEWCASTLE PICKLED SALMON

I like to imagine that Mrs. Bennet chose this recipe from Newcastle because her favorite daughter, Lydia, had been dispatched there with Wickham shortly before the date of this dinner. Mrs. Raffald specified "strong beer alegar" which is close to vinegar, and "long-pepper," which is a little hotter than black pepper.

2¼ cups/550ml pale ale (Newcastle Brown Ale is good and appropriate, but will color the fish slightly)
1 tsp sea salt
4 salmon fillets
⅔ cup/150ml white wine vinegar

½ tsp ground mace
½ tsp ground cloves
½ tsp black peppercorns
Long pepper, if you can find it, or a pinch of dried chili flakes
1 inch/2.5cm fresh ginger, sliced

1 Bring the ale, 1¼ cups/300ml water and the salt to a boil, and take the scum off the top. Put the fish skin-side down in the mixture, and poach lightly for 7–8 minutes, then carefully remove each fillet onto a plate, reserving the poaching liquid in a container. Leave covered in the fridge overnight.

2 The next day heat the ale and salt liquor in a pan, and add the vinegar, mace, cloves, peppercorns, long pepper or chili flakes, and ginger slices. Bring to a boil and simmer for 5 minutes. Put the salmon in a glass dish, and pour the hot liquid over, making sure the fish is fully covered.

3 Once it has cooled, put an airtight lid or plastic wrap (clingfilm) over the dish, and keep in the fridge. It can be eaten after 3 days, and will keep for a week or more. Mrs. Raffald put hers in earthenware pots covered with strong brown paper, and says it will keep a whole year (but I wouldn't like to risk it.)

To pickle salmon Newcastle Way

Take a salmon about twelve pounds, gut it, then cut off the head, and cut it across in what pieces you please, but don't split it. Scrape the blood from the bone and wash it well out, then tie it across each way as you do sturgeon. Set on your fish pan with two quarts of water and three of strong beer, half a pound of bay salt and one pound of common salt. When it boils scum it well, then put in as much fish as your liquor will cover, and when it is enough take it carefully out lest you strip off the skin, and lay it on earthen dishes. When you have done all your fish, let is stand till the next day, put it into pots. Add to the liquor three quarts of strong beer alegar, half an ounce of mace, the same of cloves and black pepper, one ounce of long pepper, two ounces of white ginger sliced. Boil them well together half an hour, then pour it boiling hot upon your fish. When cold cover it well with strong brown paper. This will keep a whole year.

ELIZABETH RAFFALD, *THE EXPERIENCED ENGLISH HOUSEKEEPER*, 1769

PARTRIDGES WITH BREAD SAUCE

The partridges would have been placed before a guest to flatter him as being refined and manly, because shooting game was a noble and masculine pursuit. Mr. Darcy's praise unites him with these qualities in the reader's mind, if not Mrs. Bennet's. Partridge is not hung for long so it has a delicate flavor, which the mild-mannered bread sauce matches well.

4 partridges
Butter
4 partridge livers (or 1 chicken liver quartered)
A few sprigs of parsley or sage leaves, roughly chopped
8 thin rashers streaky unsmoked bacon

Gravy
2 tsp flour
1¼ cups/300ml hot game or chicken stock
Port wine (optional)

Bread sauce
2 cups/500ml milk
1 onion, peeled and halved
6 peppercorns or allspice berries and/or a blade of mace
5 slices/150g two-day-old bread, torn into small pieces (leave it to air-dry slightly if it is fresh)
Pinch of salt
2 tbsp/30g butter

1 For the bread sauce, bring the milk to simmering point with the onion, mace, and peppercorns or allspice, and leave it for an hour or two for the spices to flavor the milk.
2 Remove the onion and flavorings and add the bread to the milk. Leave it for half an hour to swell. Add more bread or milk to get the consistency you want, then throw in the salt and butter.
3 Preheat the oven to 425°F/220°C/Gas Mark 7.
4 Rub a little butter on the partridge breasts, put the livers and chopped herbs into the breast cavity, then wrap the bacon around the birds, making sure the breast is covered. Put in a roasting pan.
5 Roast for 15 minutes, then reduce the heat to 325°F/160°C/Gas Mark 3. Remove the bacon so the partridge breasts can brown, but leave it in the pan to crisp, and roast for another 10 minutes, basting with the pan juices.
6 Take the partridges and bacon out of the pan, and cover them with foil to rest for a few minutes.
7 Make the gravy by adding the flour to the juices in the roasting pan over a low heat, beating vigorously with a wooden spoon to remove the lumps. Slowly add the hot game or chicken stock, stirring all the time as it thickens. Add a dash of port if you have some.
8 Gently heat the bread sauce, mixing well.
9 To make the traditional liver toast, fry some bread cut into small squares or triangles to make "sippets", and add the mashed livers from the cavity. Serve separately.

Mrs. Bennet's Dinner to Impress

Partridges

Take three partridges, and make a forcemeat of the livers as before named, and put it into 'em, blanch 'em in a hot marinade, spit them across, and tie them upon another, put on some lards of bacon and paper, and roast them softly.

WILLIAM VERRAL, *A COMPLETE SYSTEM OF COOKERY*, 1759

Bread Sauce

Put a small tea-cupful of bread-crumbs into a stew-pan, pour on it as much milk as it will soak up, and a little more (or, instead of the milk, take the giblets, head, neck, and legs, &c. of the poultry, &c. and stew them, and moisten the bread with this liquor) put it on the fire with a middling-sized onion, and a dozen berries of pepper or allspice, or a little mace; let it boil, then stir it well, and let it simmer till it is quite stiff, and then put to it about two table-spoonfuls of cream or melted butter, or a little good broth; take out the onion and pepper, and it is ready.

WILLIAM KITCHINER,
THE COOK'S ORACLE, 1817

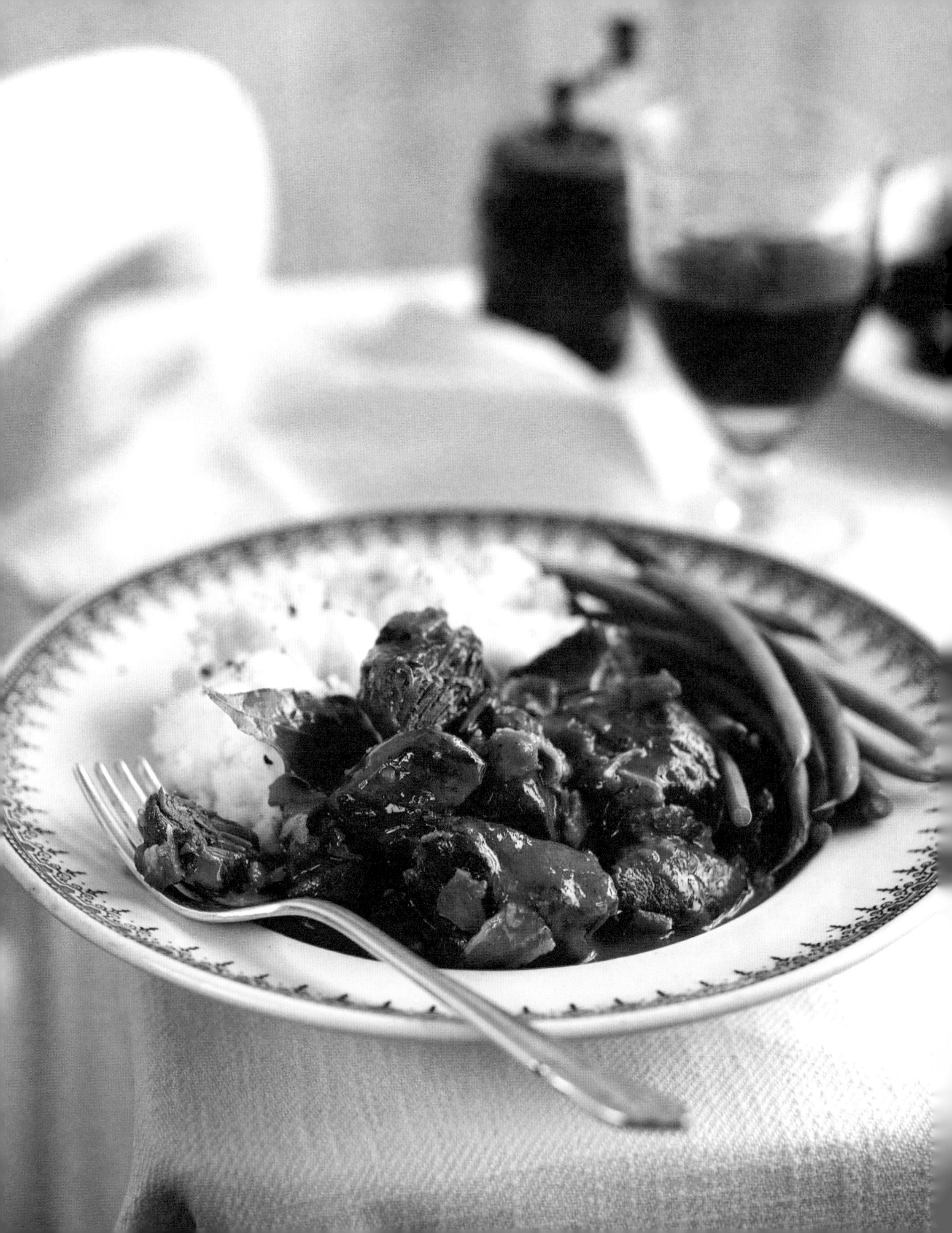

VENISON IN WHITE WINE

Mrs. Bennet's haunch of venison shows her guests that she has friends with a deer park and a good cook who knows the trick—a flour and water paste—to keep it moist as it roasted on the spit. Even without these advantages, we can enjoy this simple and deeply savory recipe for "a piece of Stag's Flesh."

1½ lb/700g cubed stewing venison (or use boned leg or shoulder and cut it into chunks)
Sea salt and freshly ground black pepper
6 thick rashers streaky bacon
½ bottle white wine
⅔ cup/150ml stock or water

½ tsp grated nutmeg
2–3 bay leaves
Bouquet garni
Couple of pieces of lemon zest, pith removed
Beurre manié: 1 tsp butter and 1 tsp flour blended to a paste
1 tbsp salted capers, rinsed

1 Season the meat with pepper and very little salt.
2 Chop the bacon into lardons and fry until the fat runs, then add the venison and brown all over (don't stir too much—let the surfaces get rich and sticky).
3 Add the white wine, stock or water, nutmeg, herbs, and the lemon zest, bring to a boil, cover it, and simmer for 1–1½ hours, adding a little more water if it's drying up.
4 If the sauce is too thin, thicken it with the butter and flour paste. Remove the lemon zest and herbs, add the capers and let it carry on cooking for a minute or two.
5 Serve with French beans, and the Spiced Mushrooms on page 36

To dress Venison in a Ragoo Take a piece of Stag's Flesh, or other Venison, lard it with large Lardons of Bacon, well seasoned with Salt and Pepper, fry it in Lard, or toss it up in a Sauce-pan with melted Bacon; then boil it for three or four Hours in an earthen Pan with Broth or Water, and some White-wine, seasoned with Salt, Nutmeg, two or three Bay-leaves, a Piece of green Lemon, and a Faggot of sweet Herbs: Thicken the Sauce with Flour, or bind it with a good Cullis, and when you serve it up to Table, add Lemon-peel and Capers.

JOHN NOTT, *THE COOK'S AND CONFECTIONER'S DICTIONARY*, 1723

BAKED SOLE

In Southampton, the Austens had the rare luxury of fresh fish. In February 1807 they were sent a fowl in a basket from friends in Berkshire. The winter cold meant Jane could return the basket with "four pair of small soals" (costing six shillings) with the reasonable hope that they would arrive still fresh. (Letter to Cassandra, February 8 1807.)

4 whole flat fish such as lemon sole, skinned and cleaned
Scant 1 stick/100g butter, warmed until it is just melted, plus extra for greasing

2 eggs, beaten
2 cups/150g dried white breadcrumbs, seasoned with salt, ¼ tsp ground mace, ¼ tsp grated nutmeg, and ⅛ tsp cayenne pepper

1 Preheat the oven to 400°F/200°C/Gas Mark 6.
2 Wash the fish and pat them completely dry with paper towels (kitchen paper).
3 Mix the melted butter and beaten egg together very well, and brush it over the fish, top and bottom. Have the seasoned breadcrumbs laid on a plate so you can press both sides of the fish into them.
4 Grease a large, well-buttered, flat ovenproof dish (or you may need two dishes if your fish are on the large side) with a teaspoonful or two of melted butter. Lay the fish top to tail so they fit snugly in the dish. Add the remaining breadcrumbs, pressing them onto the fish with a fish slice or palette knife.
5 Bake for 15–20 minutes.

To serve
Eliza Acton recommends shrimp, lemon juice, and minced parsley as accompaniments to sole.

Baked soles. (A simple but excellent receipt.)

Fresh large soles, dressed in the following manner, are remarkably tender and delicate eating; much more so than those which are fried. After the fish has been skinned and cleansed in the usual way, wipe it dry, and let it remain for an hour or more, if time will permit, closely folded in a clean cloth; then mix with a slightly beaten egg about an ounce of butter, just liquefied but not heated at the mouth of the oven, or before the fire; brush the fish in every part with this mixture, and cover it with very fine dry breadcrumbs, seasoned with a little salt, cayenne, pounded mace, and nutmeg. Pour a teaspoonful or two of liquid butter into a flat dish which will contain the fish well; lay it in, sprinkle it with a little more butter, press the bread-crumbs lightly on it with a broad-bladed knife, and bake it in a moderate oven for about twenty minutes.

ELIZA ACTON, *MODERN COOKERY FOR PRIVATE FAMILIES*, 1845

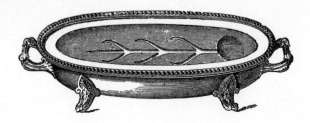

TABLE
ARRANGEMENTS

When the newly married Lydia returns to Longbourn, and the party are assembled in the
drawing room, ready to go in to dinner, she says, "Ah! Jane, I take your place now, and you
must go lower, because I am a married woman." Ladies processed into the dining room,
following the hostess, in a strict hierarchy, followed by the men, also in order of rank.
Earlier in the eighteenth century, the sexes had sat separately, but this gave way to the more
interesting sounding "promiscuous seating", by which gentlemen and ladies chose their
own places.

The party would find the table already covered with the first course; a great quantity of
symmetrically placed dishes. There would often be a soup or salmon "at top" balanced with
a roast meat or another soup "at bottom," plus a balanced number of savory roasts, ragouts,
and pies, with some sweet dishes such as blancmange or cheesecakes. Side dishes were
usually preserves and pickles from the household stores, and, as Hannah Glasse advises,

"your Sauce in Boats or Basons, to answer one another at the Corners. "The servants would take away the "removes," such as the fish and soup, after they had been served, and replace them with fresh roasts.

The seats at either end of the table were taken by host and hostess, so Mr. Collins is in raptures when Lady Catherine asks him to deputize for the host and take the position opposite her at Rosings. The host, or occasionally hostess, would serve guests from the dishes "at top;" Mr. Knightley advises Emma to invite Mr. Elton to dinner "and help him to the best of the fish and the chicken, but leave him to chuse his own wife". For the remainder of the meal, the gentlemen served the ladies next to them, but only from the dishes close at hand; Jane was amused by one inattentive neighbor who, far from courting "Miss P.T." as Cassandra supposed, had to be asked "to give her mutton twice without being attended to for some time." (Letter to Cassandra, January 24 1813.) Carving well was an essential skill for gentlemen; the Earl of Chesterfield advised his son: "Do you use yourself to carve adroitly and genteely, without hacking half an hour across a bone, without bespattering the company with the sauce, and without overturning the glasses into your neighbours pockets."

If there was a second course, the table would be completely cleared, cloth and all; at the Coleses' dinner, Emma Woodhouse and Frank Churchill have to pause in their flirting, during an awkwardly long interval between the courses, until "the table was again safely covered, when every corner dish was placed exactly right." This would be laid with similar symmetry, with fresh roasts and savory dishes, and a greater number of sweet ones such as pies, tarts, and jellies. Then would come "dessert" of sweetmeats, fruit, and nuts.

"You see your dinner" was an apologetic expression for there being no removes or further courses; in the modest dinner served by Elizabeth in *The Watsons*, the entrance of a roast turkey "formed the only exception to 'You see your dinner'."

The table was so entirely taken up with food, that there was little room for the flowers, crystal, candles (except in wintertime) of Victorian times, although Susan Price, returning to Mansfield Park with Fanny, has anxious visions of the silver forks, napkins, and finger glasses that will confound her.

At the end of the meal, the most senior lady would give the signal for the ladies to withdraw, and leave the gentlemen to their claret and port. Early in Jane Austen's lifetime, all the gentlemen would return to the drawing room at once, the host in the rear, but by about the turn of the century, each man could do so when he chose.

SPICED MUSHROOMS

Martha Lloyd has a recipe for drying mushrooms with spices which is adapted here, with the addition of a little wine, for big, fresh field mushrooms. These have an earthy, robust flavor that goes well with venison, and would have been in season for Mrs. Bennet's September dinner.

12 small whole shallots, peeled
2 tbsp/30g butter
1 lb/450g field mushrooms, quartered
Freshly ground white pepper
¼ tsp ground cloves

½ tsp ground mace
½ tsp grated nutmeg
Sea salt
2–3 bay leaves
Small glass of white or red wine (optional)

1 Gently cook the shallots in the butter until they are nearly soft – about 15 minutes. Add the mushrooms to the pan with a little more butter if needed, and cook for about 10 minutes until they are brown on all sides and oozing juice. Sprinkle over the spices and salt, add the bay leaves, cover with the wine, if using, and simmer for 10–15 minutes until there is just a little liquid remaining.

2 If you have a mushroom glut (or want an umami hit) and want to dry them, omit the wine, and leave the mushrooms somewhere very warm, such as the bottom of an Aga, or the top of a woodburner, for a few hours. The dried mushrooms can be powdered and added to stews, or left whole and reconstituted in water.

To Dry Mushrooms Take a peck of mushrooms without taking out the combs, peel the biggest and wash the others, then put them into a kettle with 12 onions, two handfuls of salt, a good quantity of pepper, cloves, mace, nutmegs and some bay leaves, then hang them on the fire and let them boil till almost all the liquor is consumed, often stirring them about, and when they can boil no longer for fear of burning, stir into them about half a pound of butter, and when they are cold pick them out and lay them singly on earthen platters, and set them into the oven as soon as you have drawn your bread, and so do as often as you like till they are thoroughly dry. Then beat them into a powder, and put it up close in a gallipot; a spoonful of this powder gives a rich taste to any made dish, and helps to thicken the same.

Martha Lloyd's Household Book

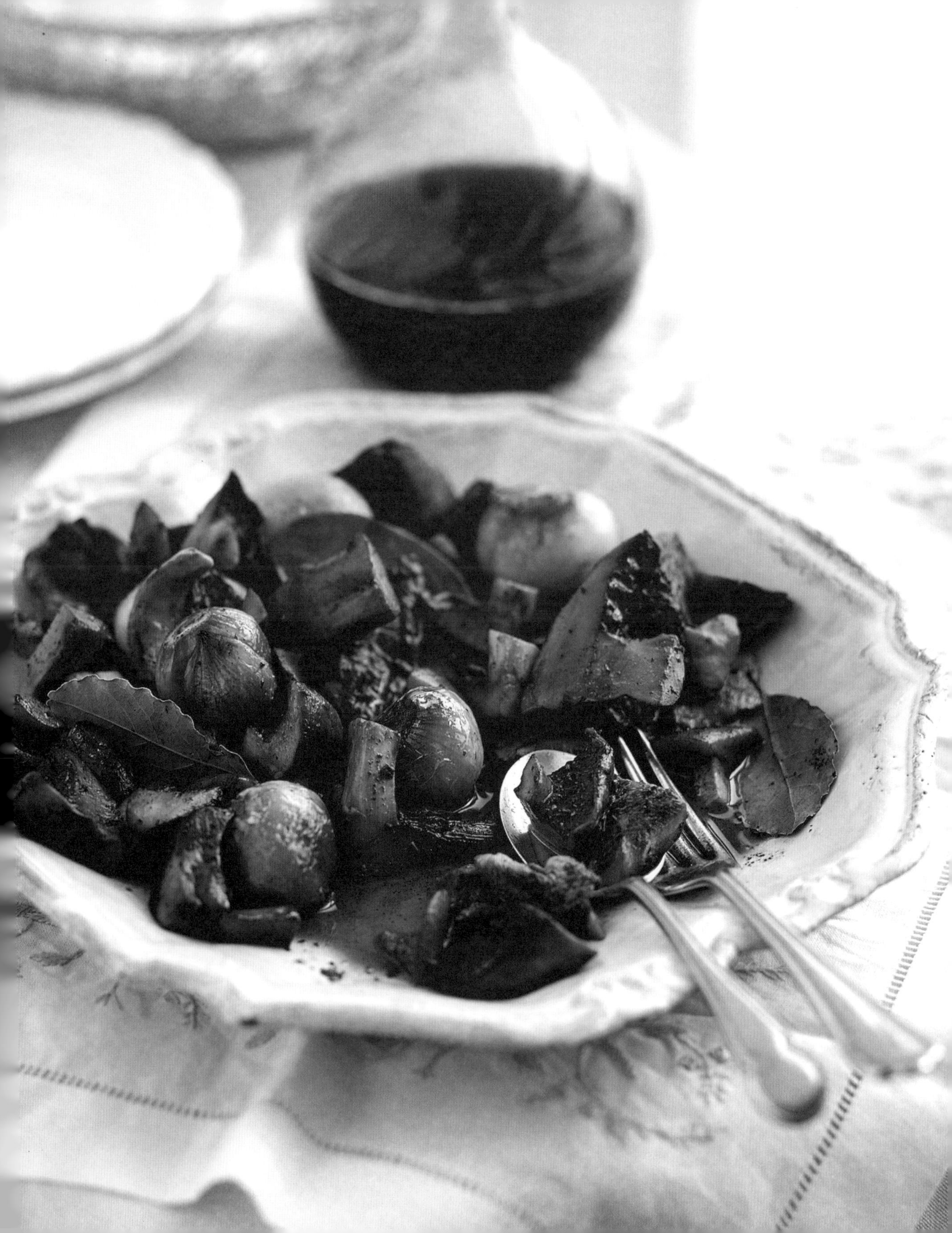

EVERLASTING SYLLABUB

In *Lesley Castle*, the food-obsessed Charlotte Lutterell says "my sister came running to me in the Store-room with her face as White as a Whipt syllabub." Hannah Glasse's version is whipped too, but the earliest versions were made in the dairy by squirting the milk directly from the cow into a bowl of cider or ale.

⅔ cup/150ml medium sherry or medium sweet white wine
Juice of 1 orange
Zest of 1 lemon

1¼ cups/150g confectioners' (icing) sugar
2¼ cups/560ml thick cream
1 tsp natural orange flower water (with no added alcohol)

1 Put the sherry, orange juice, lemon zest, and confectioners' sugar together in a bowl, and stir well until the sugar dissolves.

2 In another bowl, beat the cream until it is stiff (Hannah gives it half an hour!), and then fold in the prepared liquid and the orange flower water.

To serve
This could be used as a topping for the Calf's Foot Jelly (recipe on page 103), or served by itself in pretty wine glasses with a sprig of rosemary or a curl of lemon zest to decorate.

To Make Everlasting Syllabub Take five half pints of thick Cream, and half a Pint of Sack, the Juice of two Seville Oranges, or Lemons, grate in just the yellow Rind of three Lemons, and a Pound of double-refined Sugar well beat, and sifted. Mix all together with a Spoonful of Orange-flower Water, beat it well together with a Whisk half an Hour, then with a Spoon fill your Glasses.

HANNAH GLASSE, *THE ART OF COOKERY MADE PLAIN AND EASY*, 1747

Mrs. Bennet's Dinner to Impress

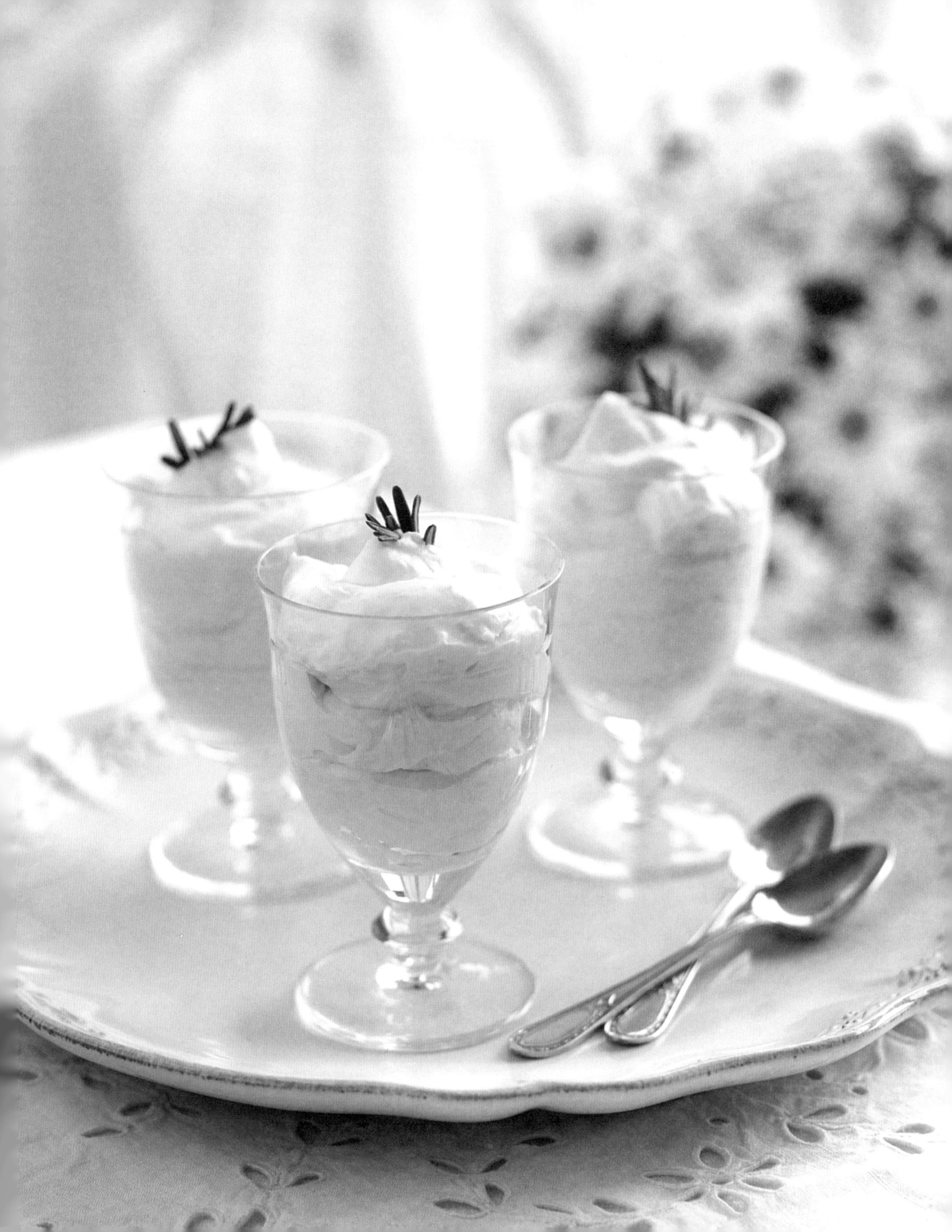

Pork and Apples: An Autumn Dinner with the Bateses

EMMA

Old Mrs. Bates and chatty Miss Bates, probably the poorest characters in the major novels, receive, cook, and share food with such gratitude and generosity that their love of eating is remarkably uncensored by their author. They are delighted by the Woodhouses' gift of a hind-quarter of a porker (a young pig raised for pork rather than ham and bacon) and grateful to Mr. Knightley for a sack of apples. They excitedly plan how to "dress" (cook) the pork and share it with a neighbor, and cook the apples to tempt Jane Fairfax's feeble appetite.

They would have a fire over which Patty, their maidservant, makes her excellent apple dumplings and roasts pork. These are hearty dishes for ladies whose warmth in winter must come mostly from their food intake. They could not afford an oven, so bread, cakes, and apples would be sent to Mrs. Wallis, the neighborly baker, who lets them bake apples in her brick oven as it cools overnight.

The Austens, although they had wealthy relatives, had their own domestic cares. At Steventon Rectory they had livestock, including pigs to be slaughtered and preserved. Jane writes that Mrs. Austen, having a pig salted for her seafaring son, "means to pay herself for the salt and the trouble of ordering it to be cured by the sparibs, the souse, and the lard."
(Letter to Cassandra, January 21 1799.)

Apples also featured highly in their menus; as Jane wrote to Cassandra, she was pleased to hear a good report of a new cook because, "Good apple pies are a considerable part of our domestic happiness."
(Letter, October 17 1815.)

DRIED PEA SOUP

Dried peas had been the stock food of the poor for centuries, either as a thick pease pottage or boiled in a cloth to make pease pudding. It was more genteel to have them in a soup and this would be the perfect way for the Bateses to get the most from the salted leg.

To boil a ham hock
1 ham hock
1 onion, halved

1 celery stick, roughly chopped
½ tsp black peppercorns
1 bay leaf

1 If it is salty, soak the ham in water overnight and rinse in a fresh change of water.
2 Cover it in cold water, add the rest of the ingredients, and bring it to a boil. Simmer on low heat for 2–2½ hours.
3 When it is cool, sieve the liquid into a measuring cup and make it up to 1 quart/1 litre if you don't have enough (a little over a quart/liter is fine.)
4 Shred the ham and reserve it for stirring into the soup at the end.

Soup
1 quart/1 liter water from the boiled ham
¾ cup/140g yellow or green split peas
2 carrots, finely chopped

1 turnip, finely chopped
1 leek, finely chopped
1 celery stick, finely chopped

1 Add the peas to the ham liquor, bring to a boil, and simmer with a lid on until the peas are mushy, about 50 minutes (or for about 30 minutes if you have soaked them overnight in water).
2 Add the chopped vegetables, and simmer for another 30 minutes, or until they are cooked through. Add a little more water if it is getting too thick. Let the pea mixture cook a little, then blend it.
3 Serve with the ham stirred through or on top.

Old Peas Soup

Save the water of boiled pork or beef; and if too salt, put as much fresh water to it; or use fresh water entirely with roast-beef bones, a ham or gammon bone, or an anchovy or two. Simmer these with some good whole or split peas: the smaller the quantity of water at first the better. Simmer till the peas will put through a colander; then set the pulp, and more of the liquor that boiled with peas, with two carrots, a turnip, a leek, and a stick of celery cut into bits, to stew till all is quite tender. The last requires less time: an hour will do for it.

MRS RUNDELL, *A NEW SYSTEM OF DOMESTIC COOKERY*, 1806

To dress a Loin of Pork with onions Take a Fore-Loin of Pork and roast it, as at another time, peel a Quarter of a Peck of Onions, and slice them thin, lay them in the Dripping pan, which must be very clean, under the Pork, let the Fat drop on them; when the Pork is nigh enough, put the Onions into the sauce-pan, let them simmer over the Fire a Quarter of an Hour, shaking them well, then pour out all the Fat as well as you can, shake in a very little Flour, a Spoonful of Vinegar, and three Tea Spoonfuls of Mustard, shake all well together and stir in the Mustard, set it over the Fire for four or five Minutes, lay the Pork in a Dish and the Onions in a Bason. This is an admirable Dish to those who love Onions.

HANNAH GLASSE, *THE ART OF COOKERY MADE PLAIN AND EASY*, 1747

ROAST LOIN OF PORK WITH ONIONS

Mr. Woodhouse hopes the Bateses don't roast their gift "for no stomach can bear roast pork." Minutes later, Miss Bates arrives to gossip about Mr. Elton's marriage, and to thank Mr. Woodhouse because, "My dear sir, if there is one thing my mother loves better than another, it is pork—a roast loin of pork."

3½ lb/1.5kg loin of pork
Sea salt and freshly ground black pepper
1 tsp vinegar
1–2 tsp olive oil

2¼ lb/1kg onions
1 tbsp good wine vinegar
2 tsp Dijon mustard or 1 tsp English mustard

1 Preheat the oven to 425°F/220°C/Gas Mark 7.

2 Score the skin of the pork, rub it with salt, pepper, and a little vinegar and olive oil, and roast in a large roasting pan in a hot oven for 20 minutes.

3 Meanwhile, peel and slice the onions into thin rings. After 20 minutes, reduce the heat to 325°F/160°C/Gas Mark 3. Take the pork out of the oven and transfer to a plate, add a little olive oil to the pan and put it back in the oven for 5 minutes to heat. Then add the onion rings, stirring them so they separate into rings and get coated in oil. Put the pork back into the pan and roast for an additional 25 minutes per each pound/450g.

4 The onions should cook very slowly and become deliciously sweet and sticky. Stir them from time to time, and add a tablespoon of water if they are starting to brown too early, or are looking dry.

5 When the pork is done, take it out of the oven, cover with foil, and let it rest for 10–15 minutes. Lift the onions into a saucepan, leaving the fat behind in the roasting pan for gravy. Put the saucepan over low heat and let the onions finish cooking for 10 minutes, then add the wine vinegar and mustard, and cook for another 3–4 minutes.

6 To serve, carve the pork into thick slices, and put the onions in a serving dish to let people help themselves.

BARBECUED LEG OF PORK

A luxurious way for the Bateses to enjoy their pork would be Elizabeth Raffald's suggestion of basting the leg with two bottles of red wine as it roasts on a spit. Here "barbecued" refers to the basting and the sauce, rather than the way of cooking.

3½–4¼ lb/1.5–2kg bone-in leg of pork
Sea salt
Vinegar
1 bottle red wine (something inexpensive will do)
2 salted anchovies or 6 anchovy fillets, rinsed and chopped
Sweet herbs, such as 2–3 sprigs thyme, 2 sprigs winter savory, and 1 bay leaf *or* a bouquet garni

⅛ pickled lemon, finely chopped (see recipe on page 148), or Dijon or English mustard
2 tsp mushroom ketchup or walnut ketchup
2 tsp tarragon vinegar or wine vinegar plus a little tarragon finely chopped.
1 tbsp brown sugar (optional)
Juice of ½ a lemon

1 Preheat the oven to 425°F/220°C/Gas Mark 7.
2 Score the skin of the pork and rub a little salt and vinegar into the pork skin and fat. Let it dry.
3 Put the pork leg directly into a heavy-based roasting pan. Roast for 30 minutes.
4 Take the pan out of the oven and reduce the heat to 350°F/180°C/Gas Mark 4. Baste with the fat in the pan, pour the red wine over, and add the other ingredients, except the lemon juice, to the pan, mashing the anchovies and lemon pickle with the back of a fork. Continue cooking for 25 minutes per each pound/450g, basting every 20–30 minutes.
5 Take the pork out of the oven and let it rest for 20 minutes. Pour the lemon juice into the gravy and discard the rind. Let the liquid cool a little in the pan, and skim off the fat. Strain it, or pick out the herbs, return it to the roasting tin, then reduce it over high heat. This gives an intensely flavored sauce, which you can either pour over the meat or serve separately.

To barbecue a Leg of Pork

Lay down your leg to a good fire, put into the dripping pan two bottles of red wine, baste your pork with it all the time it is roasting. When it is enough, take up what is left in the pan, put to it two anchovies, the yolks of three eggs boiled hard and pounded fine with a quarter of a pound of butter. Add half a lemon, a bunch of sweet herbs, a teaspoonful of lemon pickle, a spoonful of catchup, and one of tarragon vinegar or a little tarragon shred small, boil them a few minutes. Then draw your pork, and cut the skin down from the bottom of the shank in rows an inch broad, raise every other row and roll it to the shank. Strain your sauce and pour it on boiling hot. Lay oyster patties all round your pork and sprigs of green parsley.

ELIZABETH RAFFALD, THE EXPERIENCED ENGLISH HOUSEKEEPER, 1769

VEGETABLE PIES FOR WINTER AND SUMMER

The word "vegetable," as used by Martha Lloyd, was just beginning to replace "garden stuff," "herbs" for leaves, and "pot-herbs" for root vegetables. In the spirit of early cookery books, which often give several different recipes for the same dish (under the heading "another way"), I suggest Martha's veggie pie for winter and Mrs. Rundell's for summer.

Winter Vegetable Pie

2 parsnips

4 leeks

4 carrots

1 rutabaga (swede)

2 onions

¼ cabbage, about 11 oz/300g

Butter for frying

Sea salt and freshly ground black pepper or white pepper to taste

1 tsp chopped thyme and/or 2 tsp flat-leaf parsley (optional)

1 batch of shortcrust pastry (see recipe on page 153)

1 Preheat the oven to 375°F/190°C/Gas Mark 5.

2 Chop the vegetables and fry them in butter until soft, giving the onions a head start of a few minutes. It should take 20–25 minutes. Add salt and pepper and the herbs if using.

3 Put into a well-buttered pie dish and add a couple tablespoons of water. Cover with shortcrust pastry, make a couple of slashes in the top to let the steam out, and bake for 25–35 minutes.

4 Serve with a good veal, chicken, or onion gravy.

Summer Vegetable Pie

1 cup/100g shelled fava beans (broad beans) (Start with about 1 lb /450g beans in their pods)

⅔ cup/100g fresh peas

4 young carrots

2 baby turnips

2 artichoke bottoms

1½ cups/100g mushrooms

1 onion

1 crisp lettuce, such as romaine (cos) or Little Gem

4 sticks celery

1 tbsp chopped flat-leaf parsley

Sea salt and freshly ground black pepper or white pepper (optional)

1 batch of shortcrust pastry (see recipe on page 153)

1 Preheat the oven to 375°F/190°C/Gas Mark 5.

2 Blanch the fava beans and peas.

3 Cut the other vegetables into cubes and fry in a little butter for 20 minutes until soft. Add the fava beans, peas, and parsley toward the end, and season with a very little salt and pepper, if desired.

4 Put into a well-buttered pie dish and add a couple of tablespoons of water. Cover with shortcrust pastry, make a couple of slashes in the top to let the steam out, and bake for 25–35 minutes.

5 Serve with a good veal, chicken, or onion gravy.

Vegetable Pie Take as many vegetables as are in season, cabbage, turnips, carrots, cucumbers and onion. Fry them in butter. When well fry'd drain, and season them with pepper and salt and lay them in layers in your dish. Cover them with a crust, have ready some good gravy to put into the pie when baked. It must not be put into a very hot oven.

MARTHA LLOYD'S HOUSEHOLD BOOK

Vegetable Pie Scald and blanch some broadbeans; cut young carrots, turnips, artichoke bottoms, mushrooms, peas, onions, lettuce, parsley, celery, or any of them you have; make the whole into a nice stew, with some good veal gravy. Bake a crust over a dish, with a little lining round the edge, and a cup turned up to keep it from sinking. When baked, open the lid, and pour in the stew.

MRS. RUNDELL, *A NEW SYSTEM OF DOMESTIC COOKERY*, 1806

HERB PIE

Mrs. Rundell and her contemporaries did not distinguish between what we call leaves and herbs. The beauty of her herb pie is that you could use any combination of leaves and add any leafy herbs; even herbs that the Georgians wouldn't recognize, such as cilantro (fresh coriander) or arugula (rocket), would work here.

1¾ lb (about 16 packed cups)/800g of mixed seasonal herbs and greens. Mrs. Rundell uses parsley, spinach, lettuce, mustard and cress (easy to grow on a windowsill,) borage, and white beet leaves. You could use beet leaves, chard, kale, or spring greens, or add a little mint, dill, or chives.
Sea salt and freshly ground black pepper

Butter, to grease pie dish
2 eggs
1 scant cup/200ml milk
1 generous cup/250ml light (single) cream
2 tbsp flour
1 batch of shortcrust pastry (see recipe on page 153)

1 Preheat the oven to 375°F/190°C/Gas Mark 5.
2 Quickly blanch the tougher leaves—spinach, beet, kale, chard stalks—in boiling water, then immediately plunge into cold water. Using your hands, gently squeeze out the excess liquid and chop roughly. Mix with the more delicate leaves, season with salt and pepper, and put aside in a buttered pie dish.
3 Beat the eggs well, then add the milk and cream, continuing to beat. Thicken with the flour, whisking thoroughly to ensure that there are no lumps, and pour over the mixed greens.
4 Roll out the shortcrust pastry and cover the pie dish, making a couple of slashes to release moisture. Bake in the oven until the pastry is lightly golden and cooked through, about 30–40 minutes.

An Herb Pie Pick two handfuls of parsley from the stems, half the quantity of spinach, two lettuces, some mustard and cresses, a few leaves of borage, and white beet-leaves: wash and boil them a little; then drain, and press out the water: cut them small; mix, and lay them in a dish, sprinkle with some salt. Mix a batter of flour, two eggs well beaten, a pint of cream, and half a pint of milk, and pour it on the herbs; cover with a good crust, and bake.

MRS. RUNDELL, *A NEW SYSTEM OF DOMESTIC COOKERY*, 1806

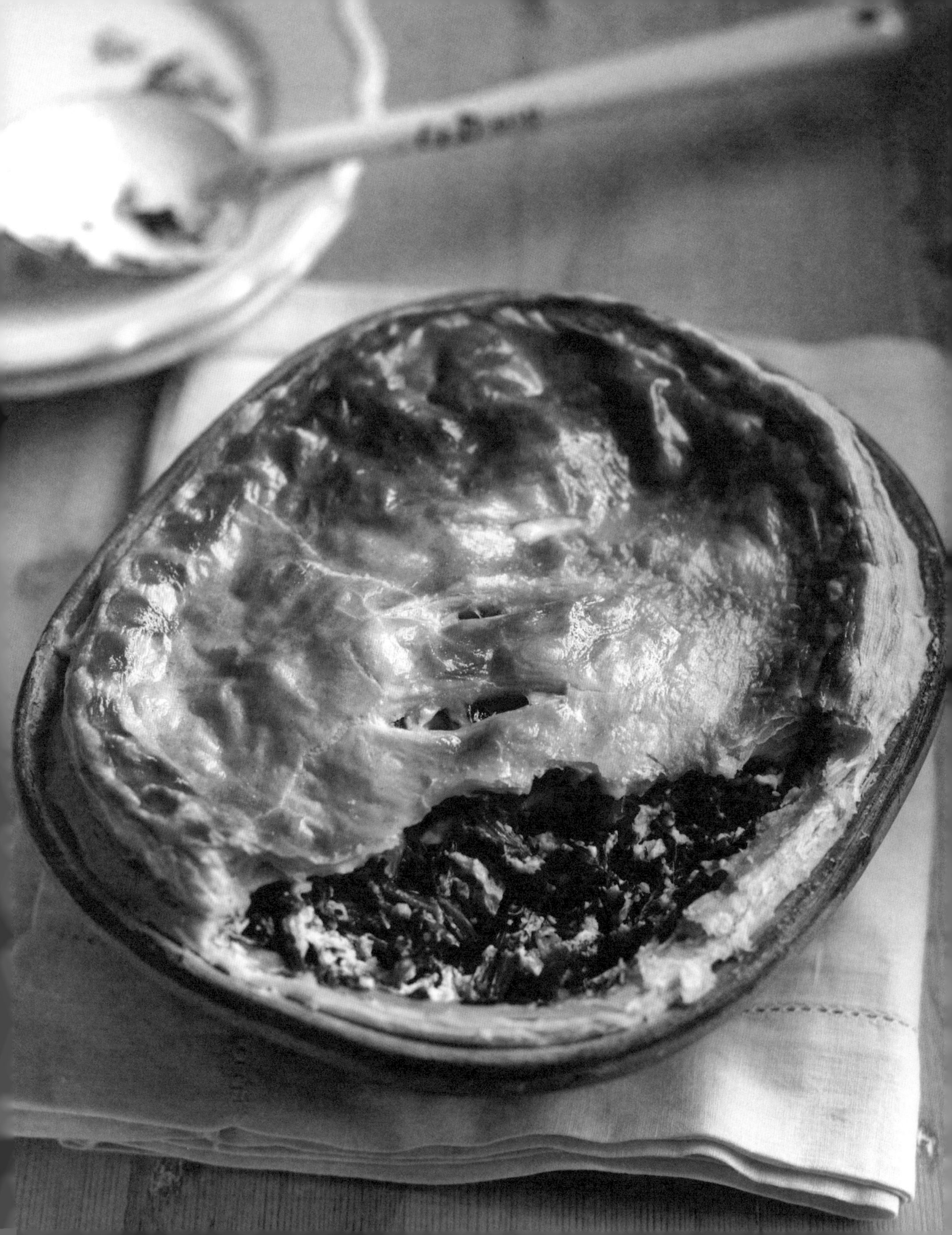

BAKED COMPOTE OF APPLES

The Bateses twice-baked apples would be whole, unpeeled apples left over two or three nights in the baker's cooling brick oven until they were, as Eliza Acton says in her recipe for Dried Norfolk Biffins, "the form of small cakes of less than an inch thick." This recipe can be made with a normal domestic oven.

6–8 McIntosh or Cox's orange pippin apples
2 tbsp soft light brown sugar

6–8 small pieces of thin lemon zest

1 Core the apples.
2 Pack them closely together in a casserole dish, and sprinkle with the sugar and lemon zest.
3 Cover tightly and leave them at 250°F/120°C/Gas Mark ½ or in the bottom of an Aga for 5–7 hours.
To serve Eliza Acton recommends serving them hot or cold with custard.

Baked Compote of Apples Put into a wide Nottingham jar, with a cover, two quarts of golden pippins, or of the small apple which resembles them in appearance, called the orange pippin (this is very plentiful in the county of Kent), pared and cored, but without being divided; strew amongst them some small strips of very thin fresh lemon-rind, throw on them, nearly at the top, half a pound of good Lisbon sugar, and set the jar, with the cover tied on, for some hours, or for a night, into a very slow oven. The apples will be extremely good, if not too quickly baked: they should remain entire, but be perfectly tender, and clear in appearance. Add a little lemon-juice when the season is far advanced.

These apples may be served hot as a second course dish; or cold, with a boiled custard poured round or over them.

Eliza Acton, *Modern Cookery for Private Families*, 1845

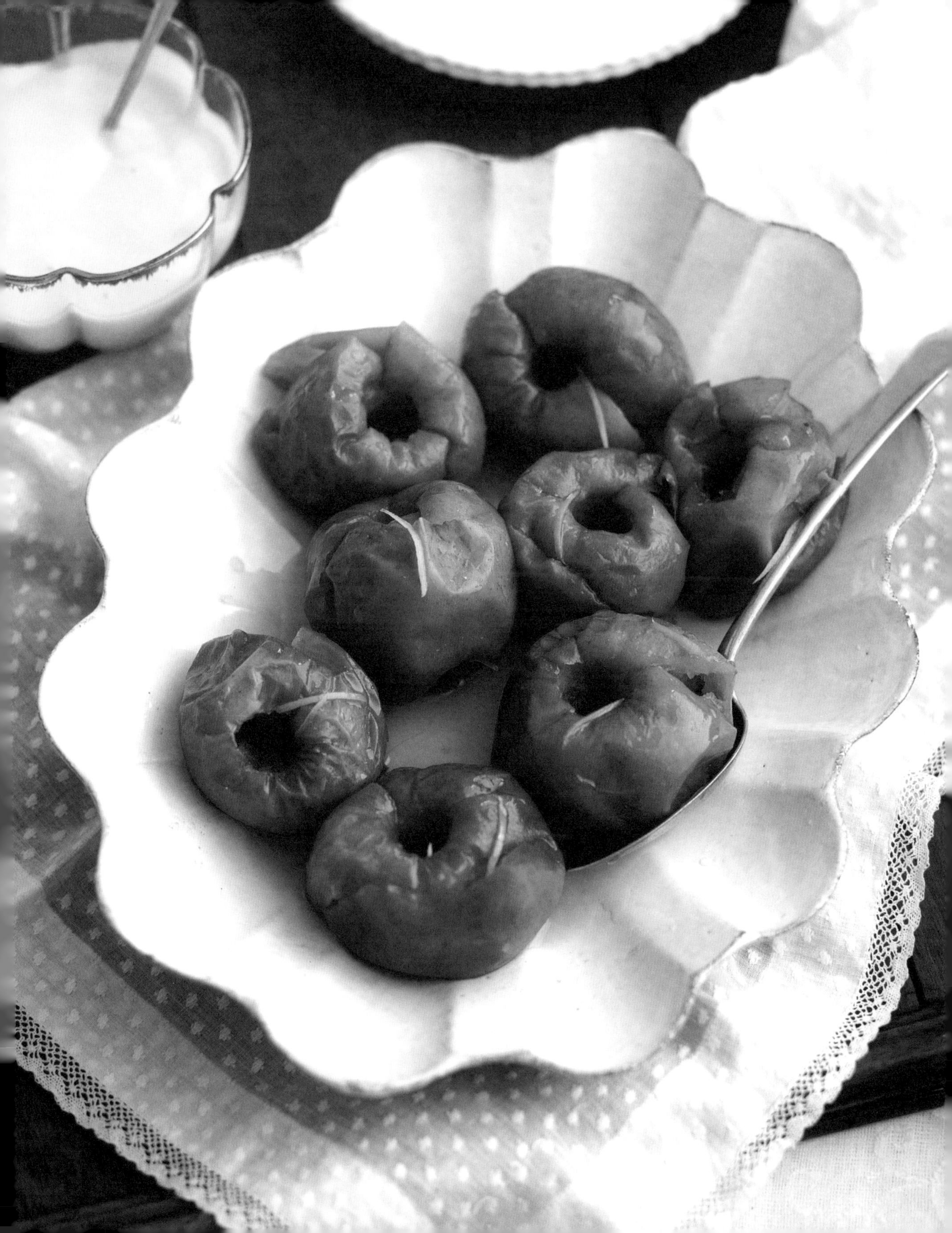

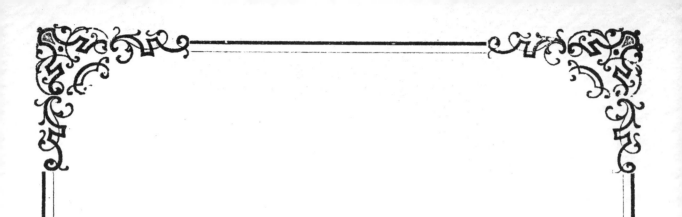

Jane's Family Favorites

LETTERS OF JANE AUSTEN

Mrs. Austen was clearly a knowledgeable housekeeper, who had a talent for making food a shared source of enjoyment and entertainment, which she passed on to her daughters and to Martha Lloyd. Some of the recipes in Martha's book are in Mrs. Austen's writing, including one in rhyme. She delegated to Cassandra when she was on visits or during her not infrequent illnesses, and to Jane when Cassandra was away. An early letter of Jane's to Cassandra, shows that Jane enjoyed her temporary elevation, and enjoyed mocking herself even more.

"My mother desires me to tell you that I am a very good housekeeper, which I have no reluctance in doing, because I really think it my peculiar excellence, and for this reason—I always take care to provide such things as please my own appetite, which I consider as the chief merit in housekeeping. I have had some ragout veal, and I mean to have some haricot mutton to-morrow." (Jane at Steventon to Cassandra at Godmersham, November 17 1798)

Jane clearly loved what we would call stews, as she mentions three different kinds (veal, mutton, and an ox-cheek) in the same letter.

Later in her life, though, when housekeeping was no longer a novelty, she confessed she was relieved when she no longer had to think about entertaining visitors, and could get on with her writing: "Composition seems to me Impossible, with a head full of Joints of Mutton and doses of rhubarb." (Letter to Cassandra, September 8 1816.)

HARICOT MUTTON

Jane's family were very proud of the quality of the meat they produced at Steventon. Jane wrote to Cassandra, "Mr. Lyford [a neighboring surgeon] gratified us very much yesterday by his praises of my father's mutton, which they all think the finest that was ever ate." (Jane at Steventon to Cassandra at Godmersham, December 1 1798.)

8–12 neck chops of mutton (a sheep older than 2 years) or hogget (a sheep of 1-2 years)
Vegetable oil for frying
2 small turnips, roughly chopped
3 large carrots, roughly chopped
2 tbsp/25g butter
1 large onion, finely chopped

4 tsp flour, plus extra for dusting, seasoned with salt and pepper
2 cups/500ml lamb stock
Bay leaf and 1 tsp chopped thyme (optional – not in original)
2 tsp mushroom ketchup or Worcestershire sauce

1 Trim the chops of excess fat and dust with seasoned flour.
2 Melt a little oil in a large frying pan and brown the chops lightly on both sides. Drain off any fat, then add the turnips and carrots and very lightly fry them for a minute or two.
3 In a separate pan, melt the butter and gently fry the onion for 5-8 minutes, until it is starting to go soft. Stir in the flour and let it cook for a minute or two. Slowly add the stock, stirring it vigorously into the flour mixture until you have a smooth gravy; bring it to a boil and let it simmer for a few minutes, adding the bay leaf, thyme, and mushroom ketchup or Worcestershire sauce at the end. Add the meat and vegetables to the stock, cover, and simmer on very low heat for a good hour. Add more stock if it is getting dry.
4 Let it cool, then remove the bay leaf and skim off the fat before reheating and serving.

A Harrico of Mutton Cut a neck of mutton into steaks. Flour them and fry them brown on each side. Put into your stewpan a piece of butter and 2 spoonfuls of flour, and let it simmer together until it is of a good light brown (keeping it stirring all the time). Add to it some good gravy and let it boil up, then put in your steaks, and turnips and carrots and let it stew one hour. Pepper and salt to your taste and 2 spoonfuls of catchup – when done if greasy mix some flour with cold water and put to it, but let it only boil up once afterwards.

MARTHA LLOYD'S HOUSEHOLD BOOK

RAGOUT VEAL

The name of this dish hints at the tug of love between good English meat and fancy French treatment. Jane relishes the contrast in *Pride and Prejudice* when she seats Elizabeth next to the unappealing Mr. Hurst, "who, when he found her prefer a plain dish to a ragout, had nothing to say to her."

½ stick/50g butter
About 3 lb/1.3kg veal knuckle or shin (sometimes called Osso Buco) cut into four slices with the bones in, each 1½–2 inches/ 4–5 cm thick
Flour to dust, seasoned with salt and pepper
1 onion, finely chopped
3 celery sticks, finely chopped
1 tsp thyme, finely chopped
1 tbsp flat-leaf parsley, chopped

1 large glass white wine or a small glass sherry or madeira
Pinch of cayenne pepper
Blade of mace
scant ½–⅔ cup/100–150ml veal or light beef stock or water
2 cups/225g fresh or frozen peas
2 tbsp chopped flat-leaf parsley, to serve (optional—not in original)

1 Melt half the butter in a saucepan, dust the veal slices in seasoned flour, and brown them all over, then remove them from the pan.

2 Melt the remaining butter in the pan and sauté the onion and celery until soft, adding the thyme and parsley at the end.

3 Return the veal to the pan, and cover with the wine, letting it bubble until it has nearly evaporated. Add the cayenne and mace, and enough stock or water to come level with the top of the veal. Cover firmly, and let it simmer very softly for 1½–2 hours, turning the meat once or twice so it doesn't dry out on top, and topping up the stock a little if necessary. You want to end up with meat falling away from the bone in a little thick gravy.

4 Stir in the peas 20 minutes before the end of cooking time (or serve them separately).

5 To serve, sprinkle with chopped flat-leaf parsley.

Knuckle of veal en ragout

Cut in small thick slices the flesh of a knuckle of veal, season it with a little fine salt and white pepper, flour it lightly, and fry it in butter to a pale brown, lay it into a very clean stewpan or saucepan, and just cover it with boiling water; skim it clean, and add to it a faggot of thyme and parsley, the white part of a head of celery, a small quantity of cayenne, and a blade or two of mace. Stew it very softly from an hour and three-quarters to two hours and a half. Thicken and enrich the gravy if needful with rice-flour and mushroom catsup or Harvey's sauce, or with a large teaspoonful of flour, mixed with a slice of butter, a little good store-sauce and a glass of sherry or Madeira. Fried forcemeat-balls may be added at pleasure. With an additional quantity of water, or of broth (made with the bones of the joint), a pint and a half of young green peas stewed with the veal for an hour will give an agreeable variety of this dish.

ELIZA ACTON, *MODERN COOKERY FOR PRIVATE FAMILIES*, 1845

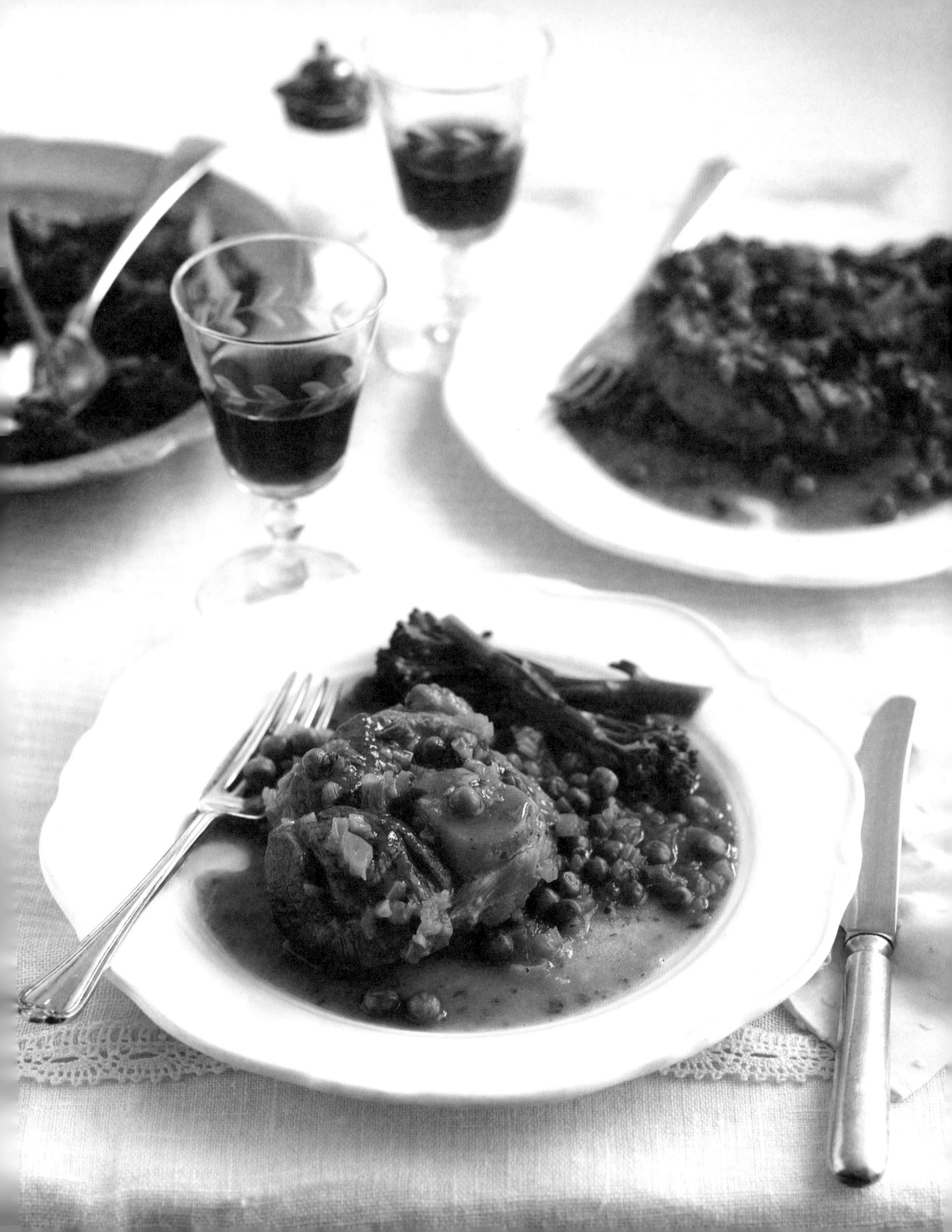

BRAISED BEEF CHEEK

Beef cheek (ox cheek), cooked long and slow, makes a meltingly tender and savory stew, which Jane was anticipating when she wrote, "I am very fond of experimental housekeeping, such as having an ox-cheek now and then; I shall have one next week, and I mean to have some little dumplings put into it, that I may fancy myself at Godmersham." (Jane at Steventon to Cassandra at Godmersham, November 17 1798.)

2 beef cheeks (ox cheeks)
Vegetable oil for frying
Flour seasoned with salt and pepper for dusting
2 onions, finely chopped
3 carrots, roughly chopped
3 leeks, roughly chopped
2 turnips, roughly chopped

2 cups/500ml beef stock or 1¼ cups/ 300ml ale and 1 scant cup/200 ml beef stock (optional—not in original)
Bay leaf
½ tsp peppercorns
1 tsp allspice
Boiled dumplings or mashed potato, to serve

1 Preheat the oven to 300°F/150°C/Gas Mark 2.
2 Cut the beef cheeks into cubes — you will need a very sharp knife and a bit of muscle power.
3 Heat the oil in an ovenproof casserole on the stove, roll the cubes in seasoned flour, and brown on all sides, then remove to a plate.
4 Cook the onions in the oil for 5–8 minutes until soft, then add the carrots, leeks, and turnips, and cook for a few minutes, stirring them around. Add the ale (if using), and bring it to boiling point, then add the stock, herbs, and spices. Make sure you scrape up all the flour from the bottom of the pot and stir it in. Let it reduce by about a third before you add the meat. Put into the oven and cook for 2–2½ hours until the cheeks are completely tender.
5 Serve with boiled dumplings. Georgian diners would not have expected mashed potato, but it does also go beautifully with this dish.

Stewed ox-cheek, plain

Soak and cleanse a fine cheek the day before it is to be eaten; put it into a stew-pot that will cover close, with three quarts of water; simmer it after it has first boiled up and been well skimmed. In two hours, put plenty of carrots, leeks, two or three turnips, a bunch of sweet herbs, some whole pepper, and four ounces of all-spice. Skim it often; when the meat is tender, take it out; let the soup get cold, take off the cake of fat, and serve the soup separate, or with the meat.

It should be of a fine brown; which might be done by burnt sugar; or by frying some onions quite brown with flour, and simmering them with it. This last way improves the flavour of all soups and gravies of the brown kind.

MRS. RUNDELL, *A NEW SYSTEM OF DOMESTIC COOKERY*, 1806

KITCHENS AND
KITCHEN GARDENS

Kitchens in the early Georgian period were hot places where cooking was done over an open fire with clockwork spits in front for meat, and hooks above for pots and pans. Big kitchens and bakeries, such as Mrs. Wallis's in *Emma*, had brick ovens next to the fireplace; others might have a Dutch oven such as the one Martha Lloyd mentions in her instructions to put a Breast of Mutton "in a Dutch oven before the fire to brown." This tin box was open on one side so food was cooked both by the fire and the heat from the polished tin on the other side.

By the 1770s and 1780s, however, kitchens began to change when cast-iron ranges, invented by "Count Rumford," were introduced. When Catherine Morland visits Northanger Abbey, she is disappointed to find, not the Gothic pile with echoing fireplaces she expected, but a thoroughly elegant and modern interior, and the drawing-room fireplace "contracted to a Rumford." Thanks to General Tilney we are offered a rare tour of a kitchen, to see the contemporary "stoves and hot closets… The general's improving hand had not loitered here: every modern invention to facilitate the labour of the cooks had been adopted."

In Jane's early life at Steventon, the family was almost entirely self-sufficient in meat from Parson Austen's farming, and in poultry, vegetables, and fruit from Mrs. Austen's yard and garden. Their moves to Bath and Southampton brought about some anxiety about the price and availability of meat, although Southampton had the advantage of a walled town garden, which they had turned into a productive place of currants, gooseberries, raspberries, and strawberries. When Mrs. Austen is offered Chawton Cottage by her third son Edward, who inherited the estates of Chawton and Godmersham from the wealthy but childless Mr. and Mrs. Thomas Knight (much as Mrs. Dashwood is offered Barton Cottage,) Jane's first question was, "What sort of a kitchen garden is there?" (Letter to Cassandra, October 24 1808). Chawton was fruitful in all senses: here she wrote *Mansfield Park*, *Persuasion*, and *Emma*, and saw her earlier books revised and published; and her letters from Chawton report crops of "Orleans plumbs" (but not many greengages), peas, strawberries, gooseberries, and currants, and honey from the bees.

Jane invites us to admire those characters in her novels associated with old-fashioned gardening, fruit, and fruitfulness. Mrs. Jennings recommends Colonel Brandon's Delaford to Marianne as a "nice, old fashioned place… quite shut in with great garden walls that are covered with the best fruit-trees in the country; and such a mulberry tree in one corner." Emma, too, becomes the happy wife of Mr. Knightley, who gives away apples from his famous orchards, and shares the fruits of his strawberry beds at Donwell Abbey. We can guess that Elizabeth and Georgiana Darcy will become friends when the latter receives their morning call at Pemberley, and the servants bring in "cold meat, cake, and a variety of all the finest fruits in season." Although Georgiana is too shy to talk much, it is promising that "the beautiful pyramids of grapes, nectarines, and peaches, soon collected them round the table." General Tilney, as if trying to align himself with this club of admirable Austen characters, shows off his modern kitchen gardens to Catherine, but undermines himself when he mentions that "he loved good fruit—or if he did not, his friends and children did."

Jane's admiration of gardening surely came from her beloved mother, who could be seen, well into her old age, working in the garden at Chawton and who wrote, in response to a jokey challenge to compose a poem whose lines all rhymed with "rose":

"My flesh is much warmer, my blood freer flows,
When I work in the garden with rakes and with hoes."

JANE'S SPONGE CAKE

The Oxford English Dictionary notes that the first recorded use of the word "sponge-cake" is by Jane, writing to Cassandra (June 15 1808): "You know how interesting the purchase of a sponge-cake is to me." Its other name, "pound cake," referred to the quantity of each ingredient, an easy way to remember the recipe when many cooks couldn't read. Mercifully, Martha's recipe has just half a pound of sugar.

2 sticks/225g butter

Heaping ½ cup/110g superfine (caster) sugar

4 eggs

1¾ cups/225g all-purpose (plain) flour

1 tsp baking powder (optional—not in original but it gives a lighter result)

Pinch of salt (optional—not in original but it helps bring out the flavors)

¼ cup/25g caraway seeds

Eliza Acton notes that a sponge cake may be flavored "with lemon rind, or with bitter almonds, vanilla, or confected orange-blossoms reduced to powder," so you could omit the caraway and use one of the flavorings below:

Zest of 1 lemon

½ tsp natural almond extract

½ tsp natural vanilla extract or use vanilla sugar instead of the superfine sugar

Zest of 1 orange, plus 1 tsp natural orange flower water (with no added alcohol)

1 Preheat the oven to 325°F/160°C/Gas Mark 3.

2 Cream the butter and sugar until pale and fluffy. Whisk the eggs well and add them a little at a time to the butter. If the mixture starts to curdle, add a spoonful of flour.

3 Sift the flour, baking powder, and salt together, and fold into the butter and egg mixture with the caraway seeds or other flavoring.

4 Grease and line an 8-inch/20cm round cake pan and spoon the mixture in. Tap the pan sharply on the work surface a couple of time to release the bubbles.

5 Bake for 50–60 minutes until a toothpick (skewer) inserted in the center comes out clean.

A Pound Cake Take a lb of fine flour well dried. Then take a lb of butter and work it very well with your hands till it is soft. Then work into it half a pound of sugar. Then take 12 eggs putting away half the whites, then work them also into your butter and sugar. Then strew your flour into your butter, sugar and eggs, by little and little, till all be in, then strew in 2 oz of caraway seeds. Butter your pan and bake it in a quick oven, - an hour and a half will bake it.

MARTHA LLOYD'S HOUSEHOLD BOOK

MRS. AUSTEN'S PUDDING

This rhyming recipe for a light bread pudding was probably contributed by Mrs. Austen to Martha's household book. The cookbook writers of the time, particularly women, were highly conscious of thrift and waste, and offered a number of recipes for puddings that reused old bread or cake, often with fresh or dried fruit.

2 cups/475ml milk

Piece of lemon zest (optional)

¾ stick/85g butter

4 cups/225g fresh breadcrumbs

Heaping ½ cup/110g superfine (caster) sugar, plus 2 tsp for sprinkling

1⅓ cups/170g currants

¼ tsp grated nutmeg or mace

5 eggs, well beaten

Cream, to serve

1 Preheat the oven to 350°F/180°C/Gas Mark 4.

2 Add the lemon zest to the milk, if using, and simmer for a few minutes to infuse. Discard the lemon zest and melt the butter in the milk.

3 Pour this over the breadcrumbs and let them stand for half an hour until the bread is soaked through.

4 Add the sugar, currants, nutmeg or mace, and beaten eggs to the breadcrumbs. Turn the mixture into a well-greased shallow dish and sprinkle the top with 2 tsp sugar.

5 Bake for 40–50 minutes.

6 Serve with cream.

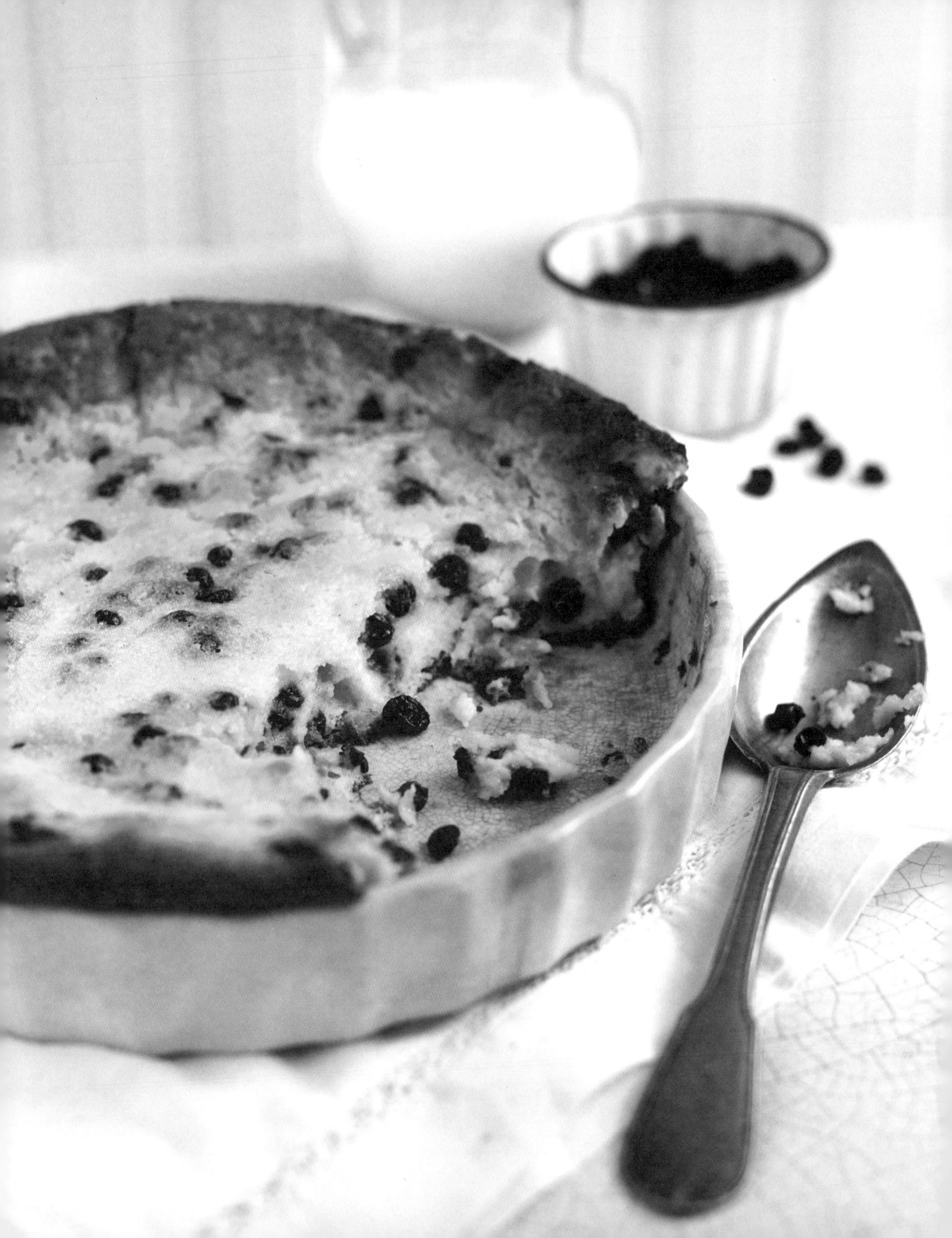

A Receipt for a Pudding

If the vicar you treat,
You must give him to eat,
A pudding to his affection,
And to make his repast,
By the canon of taste,
Be the present receipt your direction.

First take 2lbs of bread,
Be the crumb only weigh'd
For crust the good housewife refuses.
The proportions you'll guess
May be made more or less
To the size the family chuses.

Then its sweetness to make;
Some currants you take,
And sugar, of each half a pound
Be not butter forgot.
And the quantity sought
Must the same with your currants
be found.

Cloves and mace you will want,
With rose water I grant,
And more savoury things if well chosen.

Then to bind each ingredient,
You'll find it expedient,
Of eggs to put in half a dozen.

Some milk, don't refuse it,
But boil as you use it,
A proper hint for its maker.
And the whole when compleat,
With care recommend the baker.

In praise of this pudding,
I vouch it a good one,
Or should you suspect a fond word,
To every guest,
Perhaps it is best
Two puddings should smoke on the board.

Two puddings! - yet - no,
For if one will do
The other comes in out of season;
And these lines but obey,
Nor can anyone say,
That this pudding's without rhyme
or reason.

MARTHA LLOYD'S HOUSEHOLD BOOK

The Picnic Parade

EMMA

In Mrs. Elton, we have another of Jane Austen's most amusingly unattractive characters to thank for giving us a glimpse of Georgian ideals of food and entertainment, particularly for outdoor eating.

Trying to muscle in on Mr. Knightley's arrangements for the strawberry party at Donwell Abbey, Mrs. Elton proposes a table spread in the shade, in typical Georgian taste, by which much bustle and artifice goes into creating something "natural and simple." Although eating out of doors was "delightful," great care was taken to make it a world away from the bread and cheese lunches that farm laborers had in the fields; so although Emma hopes for an "unpretending" picnic at Box Hill, she also wants it to be "elegant," and infinitely superior to the "pic-nic parade of the Eltons."

In the end it is hijacked by Mrs. Elton with her plans for cold lamb and pigeon pies. The pigeon pies, made in pie dishes with gravy, were slightly awkward foods to have at a picnic, probably eaten on a rug on the ground (Jane Austen does not tell us) and certainly requiring knives, forks, and plates—and quite possibly a few gravy stains down the front. Cold lamb and other cold meats were standard picnic fare; in *Sense and Sensibility*, Sir John Middleton's exuberant hospitality means that, in summer, he was "for ever forming parties to eat cold ham and chicken out of doors."

Does Jane disapprove of eating out of doors? The picnic at Box Hill ends in ruffled tempers and hurt. Perhaps Mr. Knightley voices her opinions when he firmly tells Mrs. Elton, "My idea of the simple and the natural will be to have the table spread in the dining-room."

SOUSED LAMB

Jane remarked in a letter that she and her young nieces had been "devouring some cold souse, and it would be difficult to say which enjoyed it most." (Letter to Cassandra, January 14 1796.) Her "souse" was probably pickled brawn. Sousing—boiling with vinegar, lemon or wine—is a good way to make tender a tougher lamb joint, such as the shoulder.

3½ lb/1.5kg shoulder of lamb, boned
¾ tsp sea salt
½ tsp nutmeg, coarsely grated
½ tsp ground ginger
Few sprigs fresh parsley, chop the leaves and keep the stalks to add later
Grated zest of ½ lemon
2 tsp whole coriander seeds, lightly crushed

4–6 slices streaky unsmoked bacon
½ tsp salt
1 inch/2.5cm ginger root, peeled and sliced
Bulb of fennel, quartered and chopped
6 bay leaves
Half a bottle of white wine
½ lemon, sliced

1 Wash and dry the meat well and lay it flat on a board, skin-side down. Mix the salt, nutmeg, ground ginger, chopped parsley, lemon zest, and coriander seeds, and rub this into the lamb. Lay slices of bacon over it from top to bottom, roll it up tightly, and tie it with string.
2 Wrap the lamb in some cheesecloth or a white dish towel (tea towel), and tie the ends like a Christmas cracker, so it is tightly enclosed. Bring a pan of water to a boil, adding half a teaspoon of salt, the slices of ginger, chopped fennel and parsley stalks, 6 bay leaves, and the white wine. Cover the pan and boil for 30 minutes per pound/450g. Add the sliced lemon five minutes before the end. Take the lamb in its cloth out of the water, and unwrap carefully.
3 To serve, cut it in thick slices to show the spiral pattern. It can be eaten hot or cold. If serving it hot, it is a good idea to make it in advance and let it cool to allow the flavors to develop (keep it wrapped in the cloth, but take it out of the water.) Reheat by boiling it in the water for about 15 minutes.

To souce a side of lamb Bone it, soak it well from the blood, wipe it dry, and season it with salt, nutmeg, and ginger beaten, sweet herbs, and lemon-peel minc'd, and Coriander-seed whole. Lay broad slices of lard (or bacon, or miss this out) over the seasoning; then roll it into a collar, and bind it up in a linen cloth; put it into boiling liquor, scum it well, put in salt, nutmeg, and ginger slic'd, fennel and parsley roots; when it is almost boil'd put in a quart of white-wine; when it is enough, take it off; put in slices of lemon, the Peel of two whole ones, and a dozen bay leaves, and give it a boil close covered.

JOHN NOTT, *THE COOK'S AND CONFECTIONER'S DICTIONARY*, 1723

PIGEON PIE

It was the custom to put "nicely cleaned" pigeon feet in the crust to label the contents (although sensible Margaret Dods says, "we confess we see little use and no beauty in the practice.") Georgian recipes for pigeon pie called for whole birds, but I've suggested stewing the birds first, so your guests don't have to pick out the bones.

Serves 6–8 as part of a picnic spread
4 rashers of streaky bacon, chopped
Slice of lean ham, chopped
2 white onions, roughly chopped
4 pigeons with their livers tucked inside
(the livers are hard to come by, but worth
hunting out)
Flour, seasoned with salt and pepper
9 oz/250g steak, diced (original cooks would
have used rump steak, but you could use
something less expensive such as topside,
diced across the grain of the meat)
Butter

Olive oil
Finely chopped parsley
A bouquet garni of any of the following, tied
together: thyme, parsley, marjoram, winter
savory, a bay leaf
Beurre manié made with about 2 tsp butter
and 2 tsp flour
1 lb/450g ready-made rough puff pastry, chilled

Optional additions
1 onion, peeled and quartered
2 carrots, roughly chopped
1 celery stick, roughly chopped

1 Brown the bacon and then the ham in a frying pan, then add the onions, and cook until they are translucent. Transfer the mixture to a large saucepan.
2 Flour the pigeons well and brown them all over in butter and olive oil in a frying pan, then set them aside. Flour and brown the steak in the same way.
3 Put the pigeons in a saucepan, and push the steak, bacon, ham, onions, and herbs down all around them (choose a saucepan in which they will be quite tightly packed). Although the original recipe doesn't include them, you may want to add the other onion, carrots and celery stick to improve the stock. Add approximately 1¼ cups/300ml water, or enough just to cover the contents. Cover the pan, and simmer slowly until the meat comes off the pigeon bones—at lèast an hour. Do not allow the pan to come to a boil or the beef will toughen. Remove from the heat.
4 When it is cool enough to handle, discard the herbs, and remove the steak and pigeons with a slotted spoon Carefully pull the pigeon meat off the bones, keeping it as chunky as possible, and put it, with the livers from the cavity, with the steak. You should have a good thick sauce; if it is too thin, stir in the beurre manié a little at a time. Wait for it to cook the flour, and thicken before adding any more, until you have the right consistency.

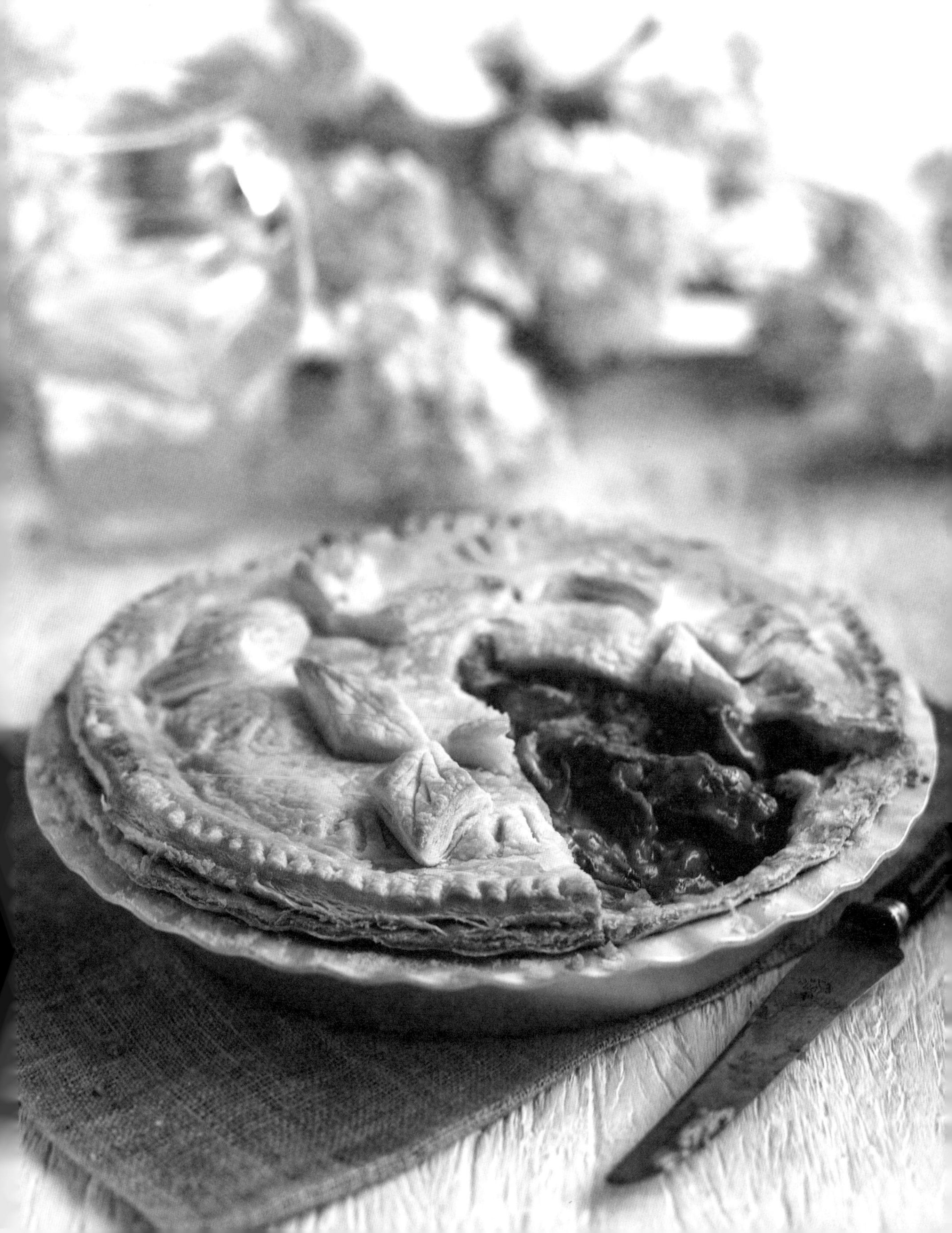

5 Preheat the oven to 375°F/190°C/Gas Mark 5.

6 Roll out two-thirds of the pastry and line a pie dish about 3 inches/8cm deep, keeping a good ¼ inch/5mm of pastry above the lip of the dish to allow for shrinkage.

7 Prick the bottom of the pastry and bake blind for 12 minutes. Add the meat mixture and pour in enough gravy to come to within an inch/2.5cm of the top. Roll out the remaining pastry to cover the top, crimping the edges together. Make a vent in the center, and use the trimmings to decorate. You may like to use the point of the knife to make small slash marks in the shape of pigeon footprints — a nod to the "nicely cleaned feet" of the original recipe. Bake for 25–30 minutes until the pastry is lightly golden, and cooked through.

Note: This is a juicier pie than we are used to for picnics, so to serve you will need plates, knives and forks, in the Georgian manner.

To stew pigeons brown Take a piece of fat and lean bacon, and a piece of butter, let this brown in the saucepan, and when you have stuffed four pigeons put them into the pan and brown them. When they are brown all over put to it an onion, a bundle of sweet herbs. Put to them warm water enough to cover them, with an anchovy, put the giblets in it, this will help the gravy. When it is cooked enough strain it and add a piece of butter and a little flour.

MARTHA LLOYD'S HOUSEHOLD BOOK

Pigeon Pie Clean and season the pigeons well in the inside with pepper and salt. Put into each bird a little chopped parsley mixed with the livers parboiled and minced, and some bits of butter. Cover the bottom of the dish with a beef-steak, a few cutlets of veal, or slices of bacon, which is more suitable. Lay in the birds; put the seasoned gizzards, and, if approved, a few hard-boiled yolks of egg into the dish. A thin slice of lean ham laid on the breast of each bird is an improvement to the flavour. Cover the pie with puff paste. A half-hour will bake it.

Observation — It is common to stick two or three feet of pigeons or moorfowl into the centre of the cover of pies as a label to the contents, though we confess we see little use and no beauty in the practice. Forcemeat-balls may be added to enrich the pie. Some cooks lay the steaks above the birds, which is sensible, if not seemly.

MARGARET DODS, *THE COOK AND HOUSEWIFE'S MANUAL*, 1826

VEAL CAKE

This veal cake is the less hefty forerunner of the veal and ham pie so loved by the Victorians. The recipe was given to Martha Lloyd by her great friend Mrs. Dundas of Barton Court, Berkshire, whose recipes for biscuits and cheese pudding also appear in Martha's household book.

3-4 slices breast of veal; *or* veal scallops (escalopes) plus three rashers unsmoked streaky bacon)
4 good slices of ham
3 hard-boiled eggs, chopped

Handful of parsley, finely chopped
Sea salt and freshly ground black pepper
1 lb/450g veal bones (or beef bones if veal not available)
Pickle to serve

1 Preheat the oven to 350°F/180°C/Gas Mark 4.
2 Choose a casserole dish that fits your slices of veal and oil it well. If your veal is lean, such as a scallop, you may be better off putting slices of bacon on the first layer, then putting in the veal, so it doesn't dry out. Season with a little salt and pepper, then sprinkle with parsley and the chopped eggs. Cover with a layer of ham, then layer with veal and so on, finishing with the thinnest piece of veal at the top.
3 Pour ¼ cup/60ml (Mrs. Dundas says "a coffee cup") of water over it. Put the bones on top; the jelly from the bones stops it drying out. Cook for an hour and remove the bones. Mrs. Dundas recommends covering it with a weighted-down plate as it cools, "so that the cake may be close and firm".
4 Serve with a good sharp pickle, such as India Pickle (see recipe on page 150.)

Bone a fat breast of veal, cut some slices of ham, the yolks of six eggs (boiled hard) and a handful of parsley chopped fine; cut your veal into three pieces, put the fat piece at the bottom of a cake tin, then season with pepper salt and parsley, (eggs and ham between each layer). Put the thinnest piece of veal at the top. Pour a coffee cup of water over it. Bake it three hours in a quick oven, with the bones over it - when done take them off, and lay a weight on your meat in a small plate, (as it cools the weight must be heavier that the cake may be close and firm). The brisket of the veal is the only part used.

MARTHA LLOYD'S HOUSEHOLD BOOK

LEMON CHEESECAKES

Jane wrote to Cassandra about "a good dinner" she had at Devizes while traveling: "amongst other things we had asparagus and a lobster, which made me wish for you, and some cheesecakes..." (Letter, May 17 1799.) Georgian recipes for cheesecakes often contained no cheese; these are little egg custards enriched with almonds.

Makes about 12 cakes

1 batch of shortcrust pastry or sweet rich shortcrust pastry (see recipes on page 153)
½ stick/50g butter
½ cup/100g superfine (caster) sugar
Zest of 1 large or 2 small lemons

2 whole eggs, plus 1 yolk
2 tsp natural orange flower water (without alcohol)
1 tbsp cream
1 cup/100g ground almonds

1 Preheat the oven to 375°F/190°C/Gas Mark 5.
2 Roll out the pastry, and cut it into circles to line tartlet pans of about ¾ inch/2cm depth.
3 Cream the butter and sugar with most of the lemon zest until pale and fluffy.
4 Whisk the eggs with the orange flower water and cream until frothy, then add them bit by bit to the butter and sugar mixture; if it starts to separate, add a few ground almonds. Stir in the ground almonds at the end.
5 Spoon the mixture into the pastry cases, leaving a little space at the top for it to rise slightly. Bake for 10–15 minutes until golden and firm on top.
6 Decorate the cakes with the remaining lemon zest.

Lemon Cheesecakes Take ½ lb of almonds, blanch'd in cold water, let stand all night, beat fine with orange flower water. Take ½lb of fine sugar. Then take the peel of two lemons, paired very thin, boil it in water till they are very tender and not bitter; then beat it very fine in a mortar with the sugar, then mix it with the almonds. Take eight eggs (leaving out half the whites); take ¼lb of butter, melted, and let it be cold, then mix altogether. Bake it in a fine paste in small patty pans, put some sugar to your paste.

MARTHA LLOYD'S HOUSEHOLD BOOK

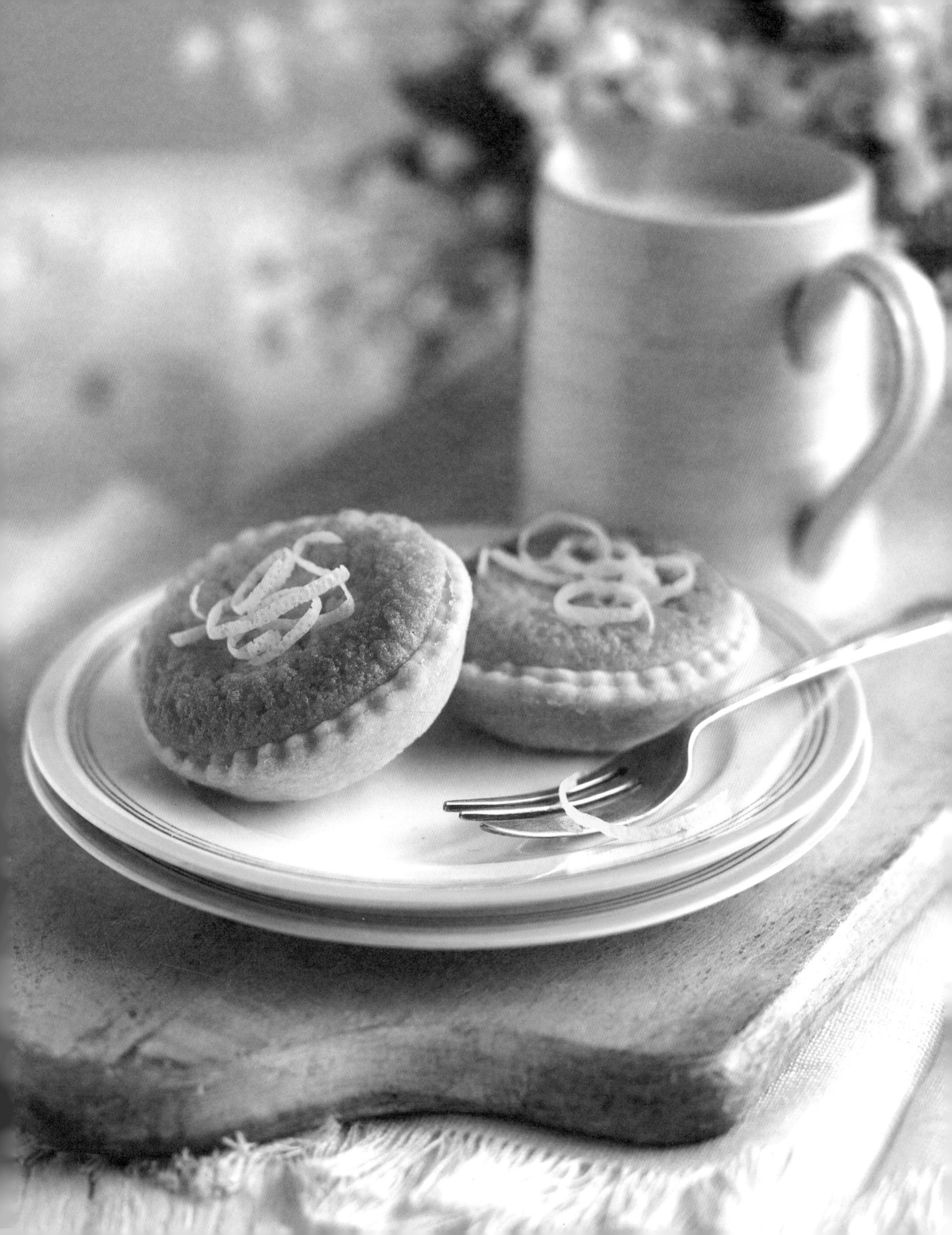

Strawberry tartlets Take a half-pint of freshly-gathered strawberries, without the stalks; first crush, and then mix them with two ounces and a half of powdered sugar; stir to them by degrees four well-whisked eggs, beat the mixture a little, and put it into patty-pans lined with fine paste: they should only be three parts filled. Bake the tartlets from ten to twelve minutes.

ELIZA ACTON, *MODERN COOKERY FOR PRIVATE FAMILIES*, 1845

STRAWBERRY TARTLETS

In one of the funniest passages in *Emma*, Mrs. Elton, picking strawberries at Donwell Abbey, gushes about "the best fruit in England", but downgrades them to "too rich... inferior to cherries" as she wearies in the sun. These summery tarts are filled with a strawberry fool; a lovely way to use up any squishy fruit. This combines Eliza Acton's recipes for "strawberry tartlets" which are too delicate to carry out on a picnic, with her more robust crème pâtissière, or pastry cream.

Makes 4 small tarts or 1 large tart
1 batch of shortcrust pastry or sweet rich shortcrust pastry (see recipes on page 153)
1 egg, beaten
1 pint/200g soft or damaged strawberries, hulled

3 egg yolks
¼ cup/50g superfine (caster) sugar
Heaping ¼ cup/40 g all-purpose (plain) flour
1¼ cups/300 ml milk
Extra berries to decorate

1 You will need 4 x 4-inch/10cm tartlet pans or one 9-inch/22cm pie pan.

2 Preheat the oven to 400°F/200°C/Gas Mark 6.

3 Roll out your shortcrust pastry to about ¼ inch/5mm thickness and use it to line four well-greased pans (or single pan, if using), leaving about ¼ inch/5mm pastry above the edge of the pans to allow for shrinkage. Paint the bottom of each with beaten egg, prick with a fork and bake blind for 10–12 minutes for the tartlets or 15–18 minutes for the large tart. Reduce the temperature to 375°F/190°C/Gas Mark 5.

4 Crush the strawberries in a dish, and set aside as the juice runs out.

5 Beat the egg yolks and sugar in a heavy bowl until the mixture is pale yellow, and the sugar has dissolved. Sift in the flour, a third at a time, beating vigorously after each addition. Boil the milk, then pour it gradually onto the flour mixture, beating it in as you go. Return the custard to the pan, and reheat it gently to boiling point, beating thoroughly, until it holds its shape. Take off the heat, stir in the crushed strawberries and pour into the pastry cases. Bake for 10–15 minutes.

6 When cool, decorate with half strawberries.

Tea and Cake

MANSFIELD PARK

Fanny Price is twice rescued by after-dinner cake in *Mansfield Park*. Too delicate to face "Rebecca's puddings and Rebecca's hashes" in Portsmouth, she is saved from hunger by sending her little brothers out for biscuits and buns after dinner. At Mansfield Park, "The solemn procession, headed by Baddeley, of tea-board, urn, and cake-bearers" liberates her from Henry Crawford's unwelcome attentions, so she can pour the tea for Lady Bertram. This office was often occupied by daughters; after Mrs. Bennet's dinner, Jane makes the tea, while Elizabeth pours the coffee and hopes that Mr. Darcy will come and talk to her.

Tea, coffee, and cake were served an hour after dinner, once the gentlemen had rejoined the ladies in the drawing room. Friends might come just for evening tea; the two unloved ladies who spoil Jane's evening in London by "offering themselves to drink tea," arrive at 8 p.m. (Letters to Cassandra, Friday November 24 and Sunday November 26 1815.) "Afternoon tea" wasn't really "invented" until 1840 when dinner became so late that the times for tea and dinner swapped places, and the Duchess of Bedford invited her lady friends to have a little something to help them last the afternoon.

Cakes and cookies, or biscuits, of the time were usually flavored with rosewater or orange flower water, caraway, dried fruit, and spices. They were denser than ours; there were no raising agents except yeast, and your cook's strength as she beat air into eggs. Hannah Glasse tells you to beat her Pound Cake mixture "for an Hour with your Hand, or a great wooden Spoon."

GINGERBREAD

Emma Woodhouse, waiting for Harriet Smith in Highbury, notices the homey details of the High Street, including "a string of dawdling children round the baker's little bow-window eyeing the gingerbread." In Martha's recipe, the caraway seeds work really well, but we would find using just molasses (black treacle,) as she does, quite intense.

Makes 24–30 cookies (biscuits)

2½ cups/340g all-purpose (plain) flour

1 tsp baking soda (bicarbonate of soda)

2 heaping tsp ground ginger (or 3 if you like a bit more fire)

½ tsp ground nutmeg

¼ tsp ground cloves (optional—not in Martha's recipe but an excellent ingredient in old gingerbread recipes)

½ cup/100g soft brown sugar

1 tbsp caraway seeds

4 tbsp light corn (golden) syrup

1 tbsp molasses (black treacle)

1 stick/125g butter

2 tsp brandy

1 egg, beaten

Candied orange peel (optional)

1 Preheat the oven to 350°F/180°C/Gas Mark 4.

2 Sift the flour, baking soda, and spices into a bowl and stir in the sugar and caraway seeds.

3 Put the syrups into a saucepan, using a heated spoon. Warm gently, add the butter, and when it is just melted, add the brandy, and then the beaten egg.

4 Make a well in the flour and gradually pour the treacle mixture in, gathering the flour from the edges of the bowl.

5 Leave it to cool in the fridge for 20–30 minutes. You should end up with a stiff dough; if it is cracking, add a little more brandy or water, or a little more flour if it is too sticky.

6 Roll it out to 1½–2-inch/4–5cm depth on a well-floured board and cut out round "cakes" with a cookie cutter. When you have put these on a greased baking sheet, as Martha says, "You may add what sweetmeats you please." Pieces of candied orange peel work especially well with the spices and caraway.

7 Bake for 8–10 minutes, but watch them like a hawk as they burn very easily.

To make Gingerbread Take four pints of flour rub into it 3 quarters of a pd of butter 2oz of Ginger a Nutmeg, one oz of Carraway seeds a quarter of a pint of Brandy, 2 pd of treacle, mix it altogether; & let it lay till it grows stiff then roll it out, & cut it into cakes, you may add what sweetmeats you please.

MARTHA LLOYD'S HOUSEHOLD BOOK

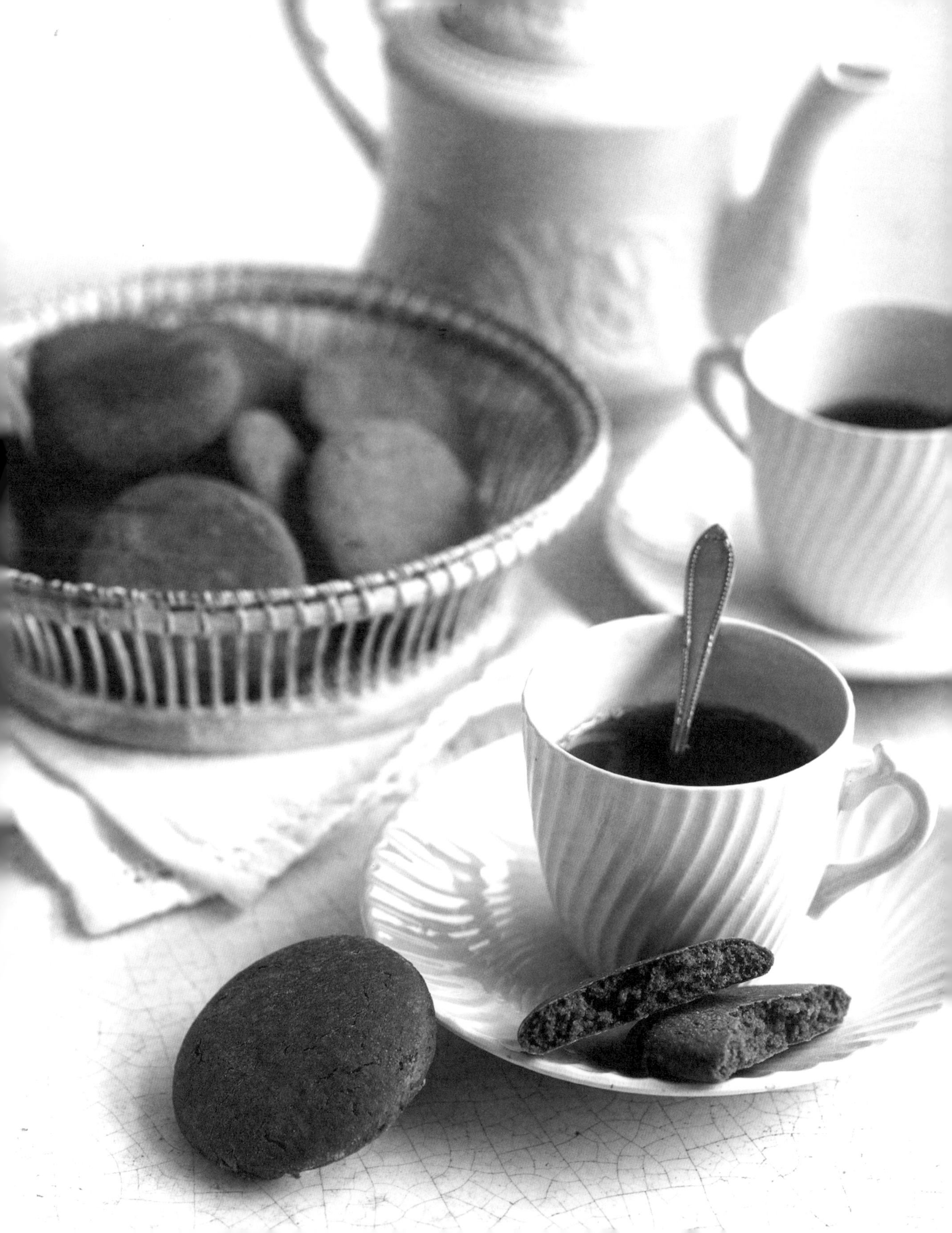

JUMBLES

Fanny enjoyed cookies (biscuits) after (or instead of) dinner and Mr. Woodhouse offered them to Mrs. Bates with tea (along with baked apples and wine.) These jumbles are old-fashioned cookies that were originally made from stiff dough and tied in knot shapes. By Georgian times they were simply dropped from a spoon and baked on cookie sheets.

Makes approx. 20 cookies (biscuits)
1⅓ cups/175g all-purpose (plain) flour
½ tsp baking powder
1 stick/125g butter

1 cup/150g light brown sugar
Zest of 1 lemon
1 egg, well beaten

1 Preheat the oven to 350°F/180°C/Gas Mark 4.

2 Sift the flour and baking powder into a bowl.

3 Gently melt the butter over low heat, add the sugar and lemon zest.

4 Whisk the egg into the butter mixture, then pour into the center of the flour, mixing well to combine the ingredients.

5 Drop the mixture in heaping teaspoonsful onto well-buttered or silicone baking sheets, giving them plenty of room to spread out.

6 Bake for 10–12 minutes.

Jumbles *Rasp on some good sugar the rinds of two lemons; dry, reduce it to powder, and sift it with as much more as will make up a pound in weight; mix with it one pound of flour, four well-beaten eggs, and six ounces of warm butter: drop the mixture on buttered tins, and bake the jumbles in a very slow oven from twenty to thirty minutes. They should be pale, but perfectly crisp.*

ELIZA ACTON, *MODERN COOKERY FOR PRIVATE FAMILIES*, 1845

BUTTER BUNS

For a cosy fireside tea, people would toast and lavish butter on these "butter buns", which we know as teacakes. Martha's recipe is quite plain, but the cookery writer Mrs. Rundell suggests flavoring them with nutmeg, Jamaica peppers (allspice), caraway, or rosewater.

Makes 12 teacakes
1 lb/450g strong white bread flour
¼ cup/50g sugar
¼ oz/7g sachet active dried yeast
1 tsp salt (optional – not in original but we find yeast buns very bland without it)
½ stick/50g butter, diced
Handful of currants

1¼ cups/ 285ml milk
2 egg yolks

Optional flavorings
1 tsp nutmeg and/or 1 tsp allspice
1 tbsp caraway seeds
2 tsp of natural rosewater (with no added alcohol)

1 Put the flour, sugar, yeast, and salt, if using, into a large bowl and mix well. If you are flavoring with the nutmeg and/or allspice, or the caraway seeds, mix them in at the same time.
2 Rub in the butter until the mixture resembles breadcrumbs, then stir in the currants. Warm the milk to blood heat and lightly beat in the 2 egg yolks, and the rosewater for flavoring, if using.
3 Make a well in the flour, pour in the milk mixture, and draw the flour into the liquid to make a soft dough. Knead on a floured board for 10 minutes; if it is too sticky, add a little flour, but keep it as supple and moist as possible.
4 Return it to the bowl; cover with a dish (tea) towel and let it rise in a warm place for an hour.
5 Punch out the air, and on a floured board, make into 12 buns and flatten each slightly; then put them on a large baking sheet greased with butter. Cover them again with a dish (tea) towel, lightly dampened, and let them rise again until double in size—about 45 minutes in a warm place or overnight in the fridge.
6 Preheat the oven to 400°F/200°C/Gas Mark 6 and bake the buns for 15 minutes until golden brown on top.

Butter Buns Put ¼ lb of butter into 2 lbs of flour, a ¼ lb of sugar, a handful of currants, two spoonfuls of good yeast. Set it to rise before the fire. Add the yokes of two eggs and about a pint of warm milk, mix into a limp paste and make it into forty buns.

MARTHA LLOYD'S HOUSEHOLD BOOK

SERVANTS

Daniel Defoe once mistook a maid for a mistress and was so mortified by his mistake he wrote an attack on maid-servants for their dishonesty, insolence, and extravagance, recommending a strict cut in wages in order to keep them in their place (Defoe, *Everybody's Business is Nobody's Business*, London, 1725). The rest of the eighteenth century saw the beginnings of a new fluidity in class structure, which made relations between demanding employers (particularly of the new "middling sort") and uppity servants increasingly fractious. Jonathan Swift also waded in to the attack with his *Directions for Servants*, in which his satirical recommendations include pilfering, loitering, wiping dirty shoes on the bottom of a curtain, blaming your mistress if the meal is late, or—my favorite—"If a Lump of Soot falls into the Soup, and you cannot conveniently get it out, stir it well, and it will give the Soup a high French Taste."

The servants' day was a very long one, starting long before their employers' leisurely 9 a.m. breakfast and ending only when the last scraps of their late evening dinner had been cleared away. The Austen ladies generally had a manservant and two maids, with additional help for washing and cooking, but finding and training good servants was never straightforward. Like Mrs. Price, plaintively asking Fanny whether her sister Lady Bertram was "as much plagued as herself to get tolerable servants," Jane reports problems with a manservant who drank, or being without a second maid or, more happily, a promising new maid, who although she knew nothing of dairying, "is to be taught it all."

Like Mrs. Bennett, tartly informing Mr. Collins that none of her daughters cooked the dinner, the ladies of the Austen household would not have done the physical work of brewing, preserving, dairying, baking, and cooking, but gave expert supervision to the servants. When she was unwell, Mrs. Austen handed over the housekeeping to Cassandra with Jane as deputy, which she enjoyed, writing, during Cassandra's absence, "I am very grand indeed... I carry the keys of the wine and closet, and twice since this letter began have had orders to give in the kitchen. Our dinner was very good yesterday, and the chicken boiled perfectly tender; therefore I shall not be obliged to dismiss Nanny on that account." (Letter, October 27 1798.)

Servants, particularly women, were paid very little; a housemaid received about £5 per annum, a cook about £8–10 per annum. Male servants had a higher status: a French (male) cook might be paid £50-60 per annum. Jane's favorite brother, Henry, had a French cook called Monsieur Halavant, and Jane asked Cassandra, on a visit to Henry in London in 1801 to describe "how many full courses of exquisite dishes" he makes from the turkey that was to be dispatched from Steventon. (Letter, January 25 1801).

Most servants in the novels slip namelessly in and out of the text as they deliver messages, announce callers, bring food, or are thought of in terms of expense, although a few are mentioned by name. Mr. Knightley clearly appreciates his estate manager, William Larkins; Baddeley, the Mansfield Park butler, heads the procession bearing tea, and Lady Bertram, when it is too late, sends Chapman, her maid, to help Fanny dress for the ball. Cooks are mentioned more than any; Mrs. Bennet wants to summon Hill immediately when she learns there will be a guest for dinner; Mr. Woodhouse believes "Serle understands boiling an egg better than anybody." Poorer families might have a maid of all work; even the impoverished Bates family have their maid and cook, Patty (who "makes an excellent apple-dumpling") and Mrs. Price has the "trollopy-looking" Rebecca, whose greasy bread and butter, puddings, and hashes make Fanny queasy.

Knowing your place as a servant in Jane Austen's world includes having a suitably diminutive name—Betty for the Dashwoods, Patty for the Bateses, and Jenny for the Austens themselves—whereas the terrible Rebecca dares to be seen with a flower in her hat, and Mrs. Musgrove tuts at Jemima, her daughter-in-law's nursemaid, who is "always upon the gad".

ROUT CAKES

Mrs. Elton, in *Emma*, professes herself a little shocked at her unsophisticated new neighbors, particularly the lack of ice at card parties, the want of two drawing rooms, and "the poor attempt at rout-cakes." These are a little like elegant rock buns, with the typical eighteenth-century taste of flowers and spirits.

Makes 12 little cakes
¾ cup/100g self-rising flour
½ stick/50g butter
¼ cup/50g sugar
⅓ cup/50g currants
1 egg

1 tsp natural orange flower water (with no added alcohol)
1 tsp natural rosewater (with no added alcohol)
1 tbsp brandy

1 Preheat the oven to 375°F/190°C/Gas Mark 5.

2 Rub the butter into the flour and add the sugar and currants. Whisk the egg with the orange flower water, rosewater and brandy.

3 Add the egg mixture to the flour a little at a time, mixing until you have a paste that is sticky, but holds its shape; you may not need all the liquid.

4 Put heaping teaspoonsful of the mixture onto greased baking sheets and bake for 10–12 minutes.

Rout Drop Cakes Mix two pounds of flour, one ditto butter, one ditto sugar, one ditto currants, clean and dry; then wet into a stiff paste with two eggs, a large spoonful of orange-flower water, ditto rose-water, ditto sweet wine, ditto brandy; drop on a tin-plate floured, a very short time bakes them.

Mrs. Rundell, *A New System of Domestic Cookery*, 1806

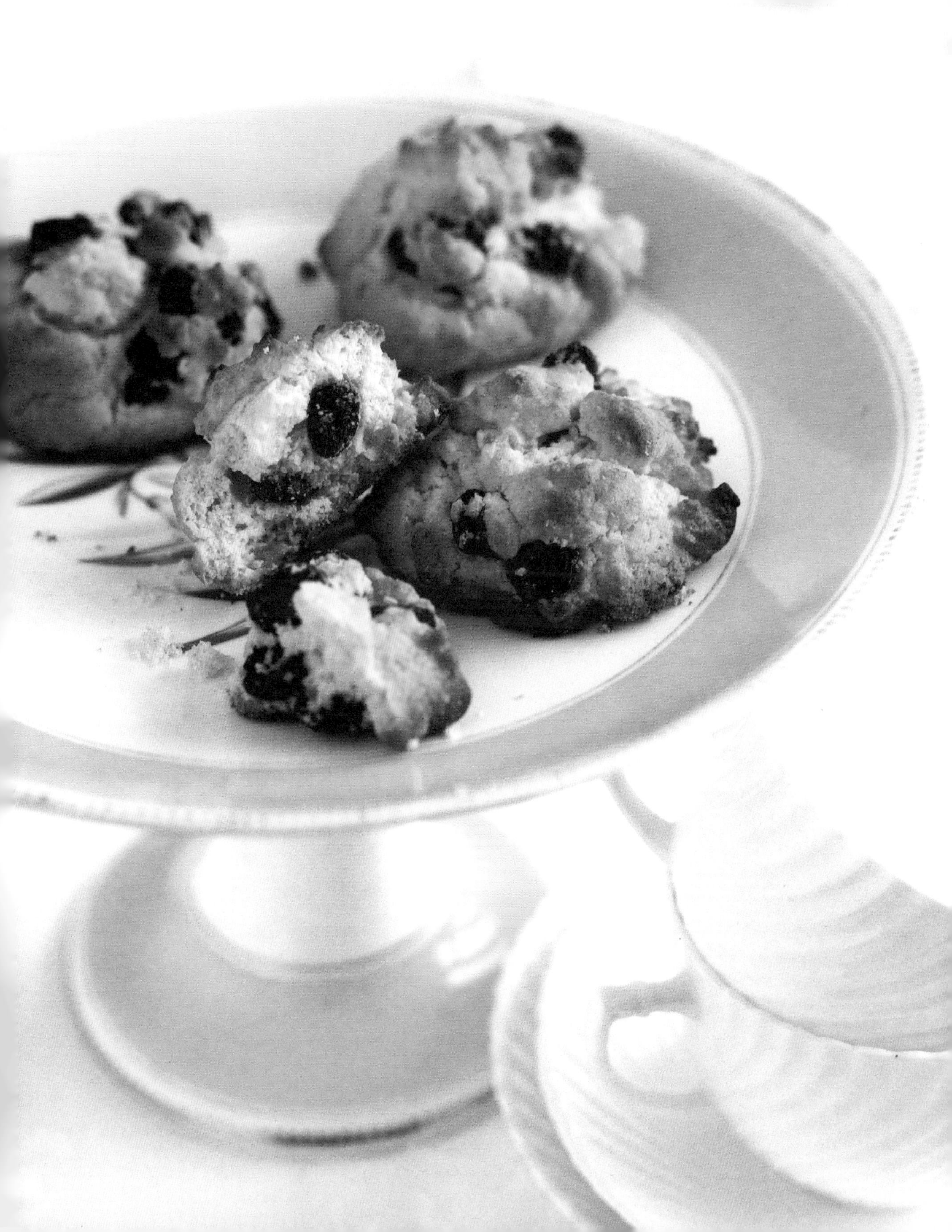

RATAFIA CAKES

Martha Lloyd suggests making these macaroon-like biscuits with apricot kernels or bitter almonds. Both have an excellent flavor but, less desirably, contain small amounts of cyanide (bitter almonds are banned, but apricot kernels are still available.) To get that distinctive nutty taste, use natural almond extract, which is made from bitter almonds with the cyanide removed.

Makes 25–30 small cookies
2¼ cups/225g ground almonds
1⅔ cups/225g confectioners' (icing) sugar
3 egg whites

2–3 drops natural almond extract *or* 1 tbsp Amaretto plus 1 extra tbsp ground almonds

1 Preheat the oven to 325°F/160°C/Gas Mark 3.
2 Put the ground almonds in a bowl, sift in the confectioners' sugar and mix well.
3 Whisk the egg whites until they form soft peaks, beating in the almond extract or Amaretto at the end; and then fold them into the almond mixture until you have a smooth paste. If you've used Amaretto, you may need to add a few more almonds to get the texture right.
4 Put heaping teaspoonsful onto baking parchment on baking sheets, and bake for 12–15 minutes until golden brown.

Take 8oz of apricot kernels, if they cannot be had bitter almonds will do as well. Blanch them and beat them very fine with a little orange flower water, mix them with the whites of three eggs well beaten and put to them 2lbs of single refined sugar finely beaten and sifted. Work all together and it will be like a paste, then lay it in little round bits on tin plates flour'd. Set them in an oven which is not very hot and they will puff up and soon be baked.

MARTHA LLOYD'S HOUSEHOLD BOOK

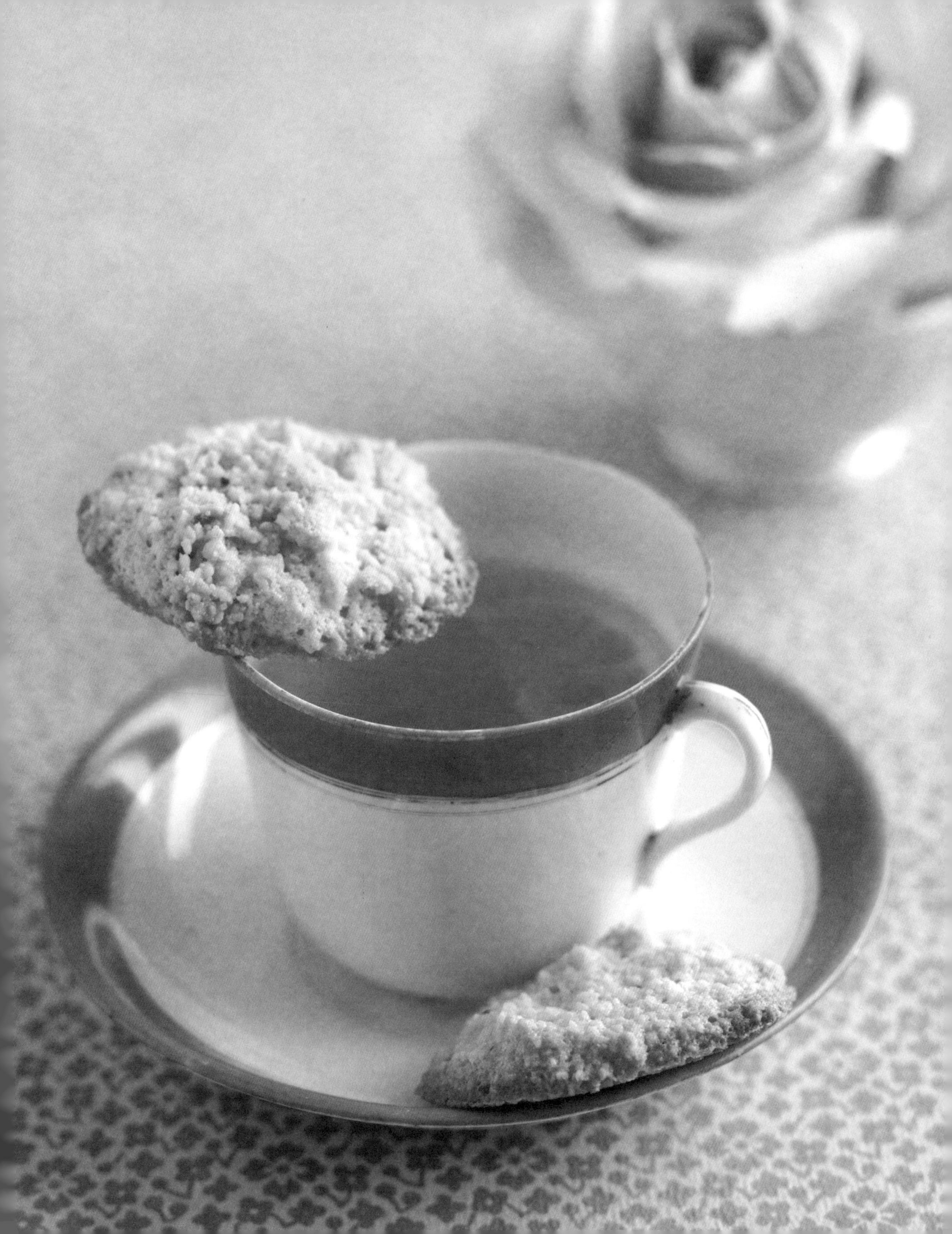

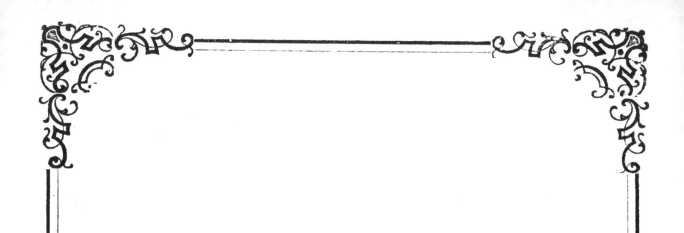

The Ball
at Netherfield

PRIDE AND PREJUDICE

"As for the ball, it is quite a settled thing; and as soon as Nicholls has made white soup enough, I shall send round my cards", Mr. Bingley tells his sister. White soup was a highlight of ball suppers; we know that there is soup at the ball supper at The Crown Inn in *Emma* because Miss Bates gasps at the range of dishes: "Dear Jane, how shall we ever recollect half the dishes for grandmamma? Soup too! Bless me!" Most of the rest of the food, such as chicken, ham, turkey, cheese, dessert, and fruit, would be served cold, but there would be Negus, a sort of mulled wine, served at the end of the evening, to warm people on their way. Fanny Price goes to bed after the Mansfield ball, "feverish with hope and fears, soup, and negus."

Suppers were served at midnight or later; the dance before supper was the one for a gentleman to engage his favorite partner, as he would take her into supper and sit beside her. Mrs. Weston's proposal for a supper of sandwiches for The Crown Inn ball is rejected as "wretched", because it gave no such opportunities for flirting. "A private dance, without sitting down to supper, was pronounced an infamous fraud upon the rights of men and women."

The table at a private ball would look magnificent with silver, crystal and candles, huge roasts, pyramids of fruit and sweetmeats, and playful dishes in the shape of fruits or animals, or glittering jellies with moons and stars.

WHITE SOUP

This highlight of the Ball Supper was a creamy chicken soup, enriched with veal and almonds. It was found on the most aristocratic tables from Medieval times onward, and earlier versions, known as Queen Soup, or *Potage à la Reine*, or blancmange, were decorated with pomegranate seeds and lemon slices.

2 lb/900g veal bones, chopped
A boiling fowl (with giblets)
6 oz/170g lean ham
Heaping ⅓ cup/55g rice
2 anchovy fillets, rinsed of salt
Black peppercorns
Bouquet garni (or a bundle of sweet herbs —
as many as possible of thyme, winter savory,
parsley, bay leaf, marjoram)
1 large onion, chopped

Half head of celery, chopped
(you might also want to add a couple of
roughly chopped carrots and leeks to the
stock, although author John Farley, doesn't)
2½ quarts/2.35 liters water

To finish
¾ cup/85g ground almonds
Sea salt
¼–½ cup/60–120ml cream (or to taste)

1 Put the veal bones into a large pan and rest the chicken, breast down, on top of them. Add the remaining stock ingredients (including the chicken giblets.)

2 Add the water and bring to a boil, skimming off the froth and scum. Simmer slowly for 2–3 hours. Take out the chicken and reserve.

3 When the soup has cooled, strain it through a sieve and let it stand a few hours or overnight. When it is quite cold, skim off the fat from the jelly, return the jelly to a saucepan, and warm it. Add the ground almonds and simmer for 20–30 minutes. Add salt to taste. Cool a little and strain again.

4 To serve: The original soup would be quite smooth and thin, in which case use the chicken meat for another meal, add the cream and heat to just below boiling. Alternatively, shred some or all of the chicken meat, and return it to the saucepan to heat through with the soup, adding the cream at the last minute. If you wanted a heartier (and less wasteful) version, discard the bones, giblets, and herbs, and blend rather than strain the white mixture.

The Ball at Netherfield

White Soup

Put a knuckle of veal into six quarts of water, with a large fowl, and a pound of lean bacon; half a pound of rice, two anchovies, a few pepper-corns, a bundle of sweet herbs, two or three onion, and three or four heads of celery cut in slices. Stew them all together, till the soup be as strong as you would have it, and strain it through a hair sieve into a clean earthen pot. Having let it stand all night, the next day take off the scum, and pour it clear off into a tossing-pan. Put in half a pound of Jordan almonds beat fine, boil it a little, and run it through a lawn sieve. Then put in a pint of cream, and the yolk of an egg, and send it up hot.

JOHN FARLEY, THE LONDON ART OF COOKERY, 1783

To Make Ollivers Biscuits Take 3llb of flour, ½ a pint of small beer barm. Take some milk and warm it a little put it to your barm and lay a spunge, let it lay for one hour. Then take a quarter of a pound of butter and warm up with some milk and mix your spunge and lay it to rise before the fire. Roll it out in thin cakes, bake it in a slow oven. (You must put a little salt in your flour, but not much, use them before the fire before you put them in the oven).

Martha Lloyd's Household Book

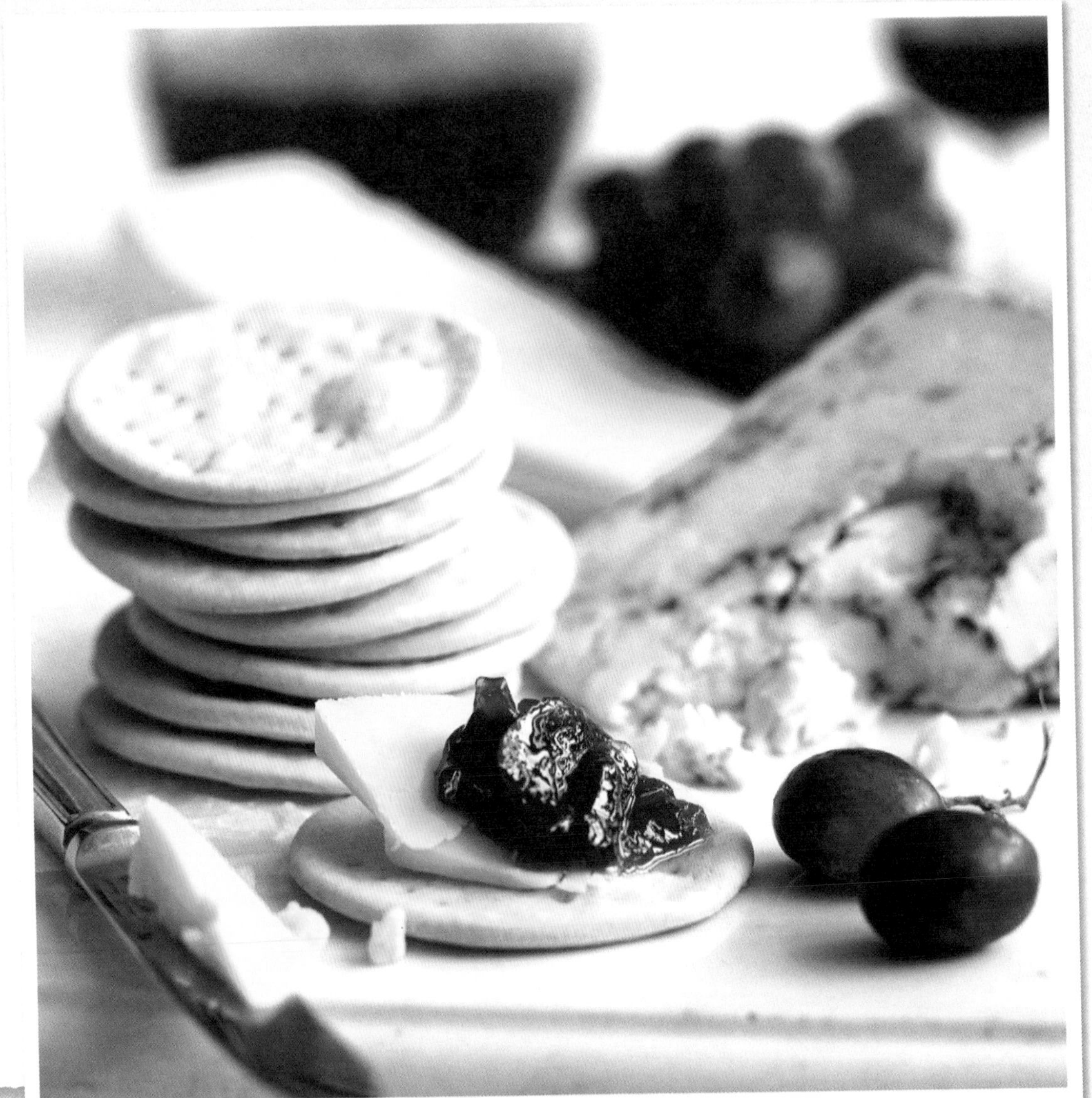

BATH OLIVERS

These savory crackers (biscuits) were devised by William Oliver, an eighteenth-century physician in Bath, after he realized the Bath Buns he had also created were making his fashionable patients even fatter. They are perfect served with the English cheeses that the Georgian "higher sort" were beginning to enjoy.

Makes 30–40 crackers

3¾ cups/500g all-purpose (plain) flour
¼ oz/7g sachet active dried yeast

Pinch of salt
2 tbsp/30g butter
⅔ cup/150ml milk

1 Preheat the oven to 325°F/160°C/Gas Mark 3.
2 Sift the flour into a bowl and add the dried yeast and salt. Warm the butter and milk together, make a well in the flour and slowly add the liquid, stirring the flour into the center until you have a dough. Add some warm water if necessary.
3 Knead the dough on a floured surface until smooth; put it back in the bowl, cover and let it rise in a warm place for 30 minutes.
4 Roll out well on a floured surface several times, folding the dough on itself, until it is very thin.
5 Cut out 30–40 crackers with a circular cookie cutter and prick the surface of each one with a fork.
6 Bake for 20–30 minutes until they are hard and bone-colored; if they are turning color, turn the oven down to 300°F/150°C/Gas Mark 2.

To serve: With a rich local dairy industry, Jane's circle and characters were likely to have often served local cheeses, including the famous Somerset Cheddar. Mr. Elton gives a clue to what a cheese course might consist of when he unromantically describes his whole dinner of the previous night to Harriet, when Emma overtakes them, and finds "that she was herself come in for the Stilton cheese, the north Wiltshire, the butter, the celery, the beet-root and all the dessert." Mrs. Norris happily gets both a receipt for and a sample of "a famous cream cheese" from the housekeeper at Sotherton. Mrs. Austen describes "good Warwickshire cheese" made in the "delightful dairy" at Stoneleigh Abbey.

SALMAGUNDY

This gorgeously presented salad should balance salt, sour, sweet, and savory flavors and offer an invigorating contrast of textures and colors. Hannah Glasse gives three different ways of making and serving it, with the helpful comment that "You may always make a Salamongundy of such things as you have, according to your Fancy". In fact, this salad can be made from almost any ingredients, all chopped small.

Herring

Anchovies (the whole fish, not just the fillets)

Roast chicken, duck, or pigeon meat

Parsley

Cucumber

Apples, peeled (a sprinkling of lemon juice will help keep them from going brown)

Onion, or small pickled onions

Hard-boiled eggs, whites and yolks chopped separately

Pickled gherkins

Celery

Pickled red cabbage

French beans, cooked and sliced

Grapes

Any combination of the following: spinach; sorrel leaves; nasturtium leaves and flowers; watercress

1 Layer contrasting ingredients on small saucers to form individual, cone-shaped portions, finishing off with a sprig of parsley, *or* make one big cone and "set an orange or lemon on the top," *or* put the different ingredients on individual saucers, with the central one raised. Put the saucers on a big plate or clean tray, and decorate around the saucers with watercress, nasturtiums (which Hannah calls "Station Flowers"), cooked French beans, or grapes.

To Make Salamongundy Take two or three Roman or Cabbage Lettice, and when you have washed them clean, swing them pretty dry in a Cloth; then beginning at the open End, cut them cross-ways, as fine as a good big Thread, and lay the Lettices so cut, about an Inch thick all over the Bottom of a Dish, take a Couple of cold roasted Pullets, or Chickens, and cut the Flesh off the Breasts and Wings into Slices, about three Inches long, a Quarter of an Inch broad, and as thin as a Shilling; lay them upon the Lettice round the End to the Middle of the dish, and the other towards the Brim; then having boned and cut six Anchovies, *each into eight Pieces, lay them all between each Slice of the Fowls, then cut the lean Meat off the Legs into Dice, and cut a Lemon into small Dice; then mince the Yolk of four Eggs, three or four Anchovies, and little Parsley, and make a round Heap of these in your Dish, piling it up in the Form of a Sugar-loaf, and garnish it with Onions, as big as the Yolk of Eggs, boiled in a good deal of Water very tender and white. Put the largest of the Onions in the Middle on the Top of the Salamongundy, and lay the rest all round the Brim of the Dish, as thick as you can lay them; then beat some Sallat-Oil up with Vinegar, Salt and Pepper, and pour over it all. Garnish with Grapes just scalded, or French Beans blanched, or Station Flowers, and serve it up for a first Course.*

HANNAH GLASSE, *THE ART OF COOKERY MADE PLAIN AND EASY*, 1747

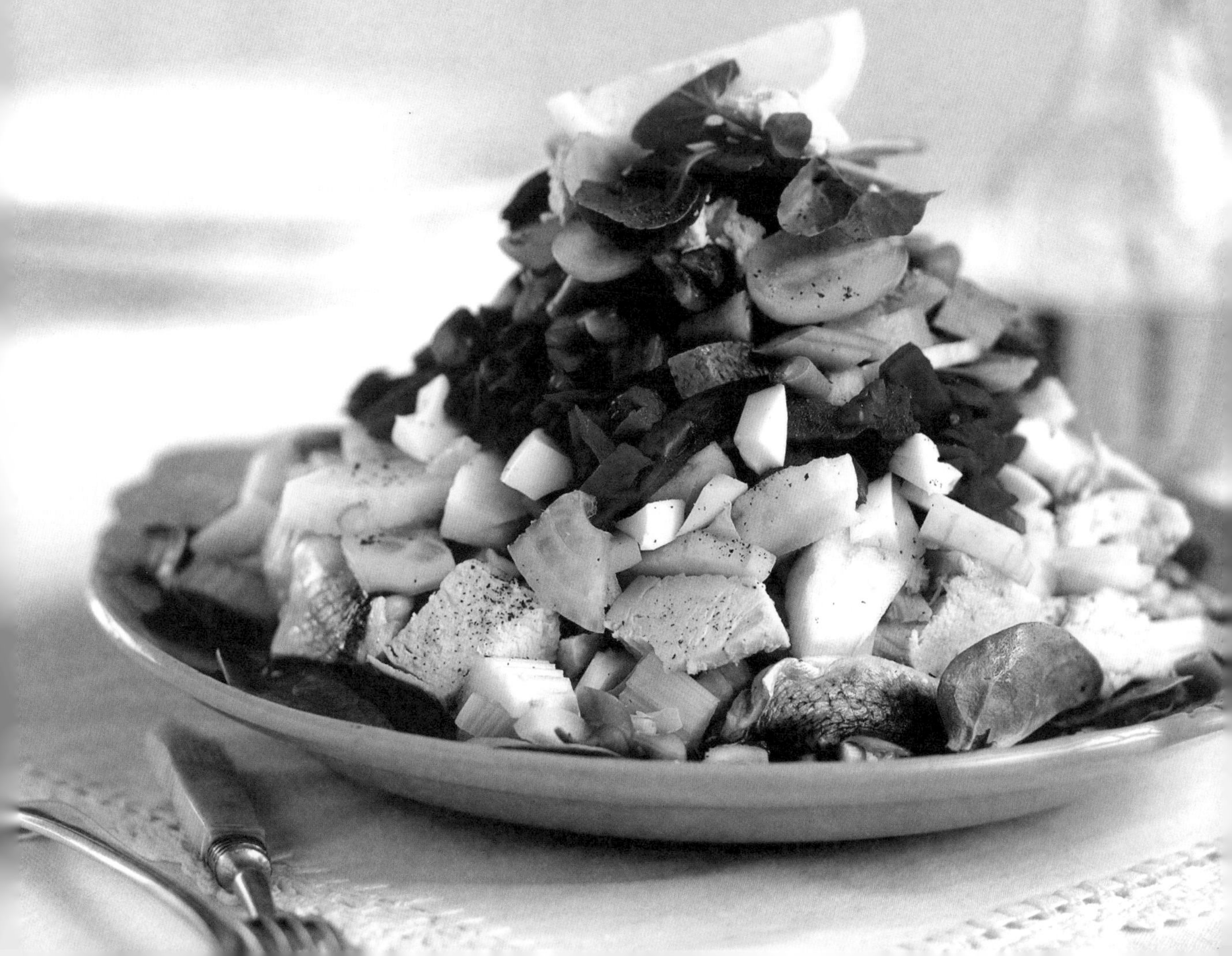

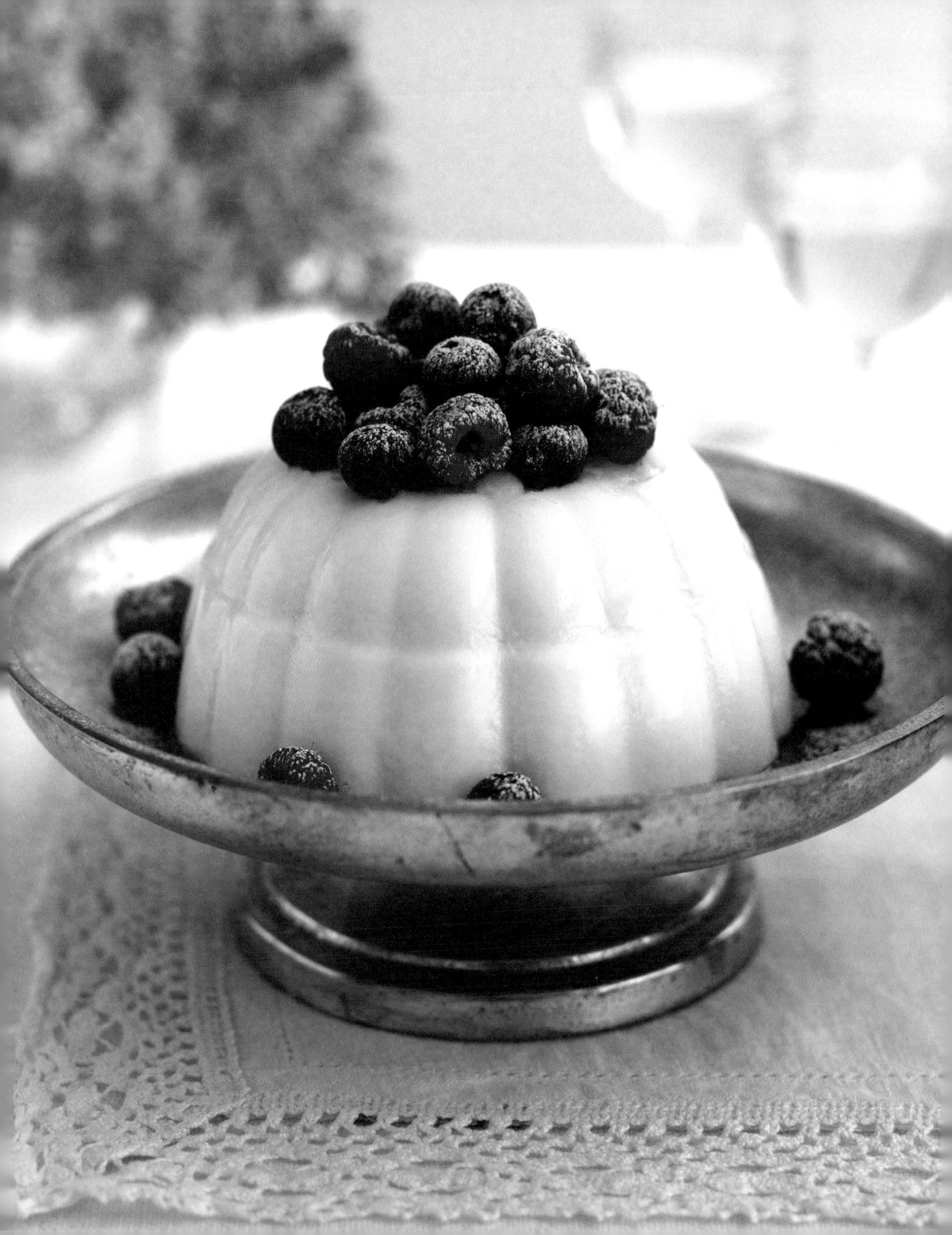

FLUMMERY

Flummery is a white jelly, which was set in elegant molds or as shapes within a clear jelly. Its delicate, creamy taste goes particularly well with rhubarb, strawberries, and raspberries. A modern version would be to add puréed fruit to the ingredients, omitting the same volume of fluid.

5 gelatin leaves
1¼ cups/300ml milk
½ cup/50g ground almonds
1–2 tbsp superfine (caster) sugar

1 tsp natural rosewater (with no added alcohol)
A drop of natural almond extract
1¼ cups/300ml heavy (double) cream

1 Put the gelatin in a bowl and cover with cold water; leave for 4–5 minutes.
2 Pour the milk, almonds, and sugar into a saucepan and heat slowly until just below boiling.
3 Squeeze out the excess water from the gelatin leaves and add them to the almond milk, along with the rosewater, and the almond extract. Simmer for a few minutes, keeping it below boiling point. Let it cool a little and strain it through cheesecloth, or a very fine sieve.
4 Whip the cream until thick, and then fold it into the tepid mixture. Wet your molds (essential, to make it turn out), put in the flummery (keeping some back for the hen's nest recipe on page 104 if you'd like) and leave to stand in the fridge overnight.
5 To serve: If you don't have a jelly mold with a removable lid, dip the mold briefly into boiling water before turning out the flummery.

To make Flummery Put one ounce of bitter and one of sweet almonds into a basin, pour over them some boiling water to make the skins come off, which is called blanching. Strip off the skins and throw the kernels into cold water. Then take them out and beat them in a marble mortar with a little rosewater to keep them from oiling. When they are beat, put them into a pint of calf's foot stock, set it over the fire and sweeten it to your taste with loaf sugar. As soon as it boils strain it through a piece of muslin or gauze. When a little cold put it into a pint of thick cream and keep stirring it often till it grows thick and cold. Wet your moulds in cold water and pour in the flummery, let it stand five or six hours at least before you turn them out. If you make the flummery stiff and wet the moulds, it will turn out without putting it into warm water, for water takes off the figures of the mould and makes the flummery look dull.

ELIZABETH RAFFALD, *THE EXPERIENCED ENGLISH HOUSEKEEPER*, 1769

To make Calf's Foot Jelly

Put a gang of calf's feet well cleaned into a pan with six quarts of water, and let them boil gently till reduced to two quarts. Then take out the feet, scum off the fat clean, and clear your jelly from the sediment. Beat the whites of five eggs to a froth, then add one pint of Lisbon, Madeira or any pale made wine if you choose it, then squeeze in the juice of three lemons. When your stock is boiling, take three spoonfuls of it and keep stirring it with your wine and eggs to keep it from curdling. Then add a little more stock and still keep stirring it, and then put it in the pan and sweeten it with loaf sugar to your taste. A glass of French brandy will keep the jelly from turning blue in frosty air. Put in the outer rind of two lemons and let it boil one minute all together, and pour it into a flannel bag and let it run into a basin, and keep pouring it back gently into the bag till it runs clear and bright. Then set your glasses under the bag and cover it lest dust gets in.

If you would have the jelly for a Fish Pond, Transparent Pudding, or Hen's Nest, to be turned out of the mould, boil half a pound of isinglass in a pint of water till reduced to one quarter, and put it into the stock before it is refined.

Elizabeth Raffald, *The Experienced English Housekeeper*, 1769

CALF'S FOOT JELLY (WITHOUT THE FEET)

Cooks would have to extract their own gelatin by boiling calves' feet to make this lovely wobbly jelly. It is ideal for showy puddings, or as a clean-tasting contrast to creams, syllabubs, or pastries. After the ball at Mansfield Park, Mrs. Norris snaffles the "supernumerary" jellies, supposedly "to nurse a sick maid."

10 gelatin leaves
2½ cups/600ml water
2½ cups/600ml white wine *or* elderflower cordial

1 tbsp dry sherry, brandy, or other spirits (optional)
Juice of 4 lemons
Zest of 2 lemons
6 tbsp sugar

1 Give yourself a good few hours before you want to serve the jelly. Gelatin takes longer to set than the commercial jellies we are used to, and the lemon juice also slows down its setting properties.

2 Soak the gelatin leaves in cold water for 4–5 minutes.

3 Put the water, wine, and other alcohol if using, the lemon juice and zest, and sugar in a saucepan and heat slowly. Squeeze the excess water from the gelatin leaves, add to the liquid, heating until the gelatin and sugar are dissolved, stirring all the time. Remove the lemon zest.

4 Pour into wetted molds, the fancier the better, or pretty glasses, and let it set overnight in the fridge (or speed it up in the freezer if necessary.)

5 To serve: If you don't have a jelly mold with a removable lid, dip the molds briefly into boiling water before turning them out.

6 Variation: For a light, non-alcoholic version, diluted elderflower cordial makes a perfect clear, sparkling jelly.

A HEN'S NEST

The hen's nest is one of the easiest of Mrs. Raffald's flummery and jelly designs; she also gives directions for making a fish pond, moon and stars, eggs and bacon, a Solomon's temple, and even cribbage cards.

3 medium (UK small) eggs (the smaller the better, to fit in the mold, with room for the jelly to go around them)
Flummery (see recipe page 101)
Calf's Foot Jelly (see recipe page 103)

For the candied lemon zest
3 unwaxed lemons
2½ cups/500g sugar
2 cups/500ml water
Or use a suitable colored "fruit string" for children

1 It's best to start the hen's eggs the day before, to give the flummery time to set.
2 Empty out the shells of the 3 eggs by tapping a little hole in the top of each egg and letting the white and yolk slide out (you may need to break the yolk); put the contents aside for another recipe. Carefully wash the egg shells out with hot water. Put the shells back into an egg box, hole uppermost, and fill each with the flummery mixture through a small funnel. Leave them in the fridge to set for several hours or overnight.
3 Pour a third of the cool jelly into a 2-pint/1 liter bowl and leave it to set for a few hours in the fridge (putting it in the freezer will help it along if you are short of time.) Keep the remainder in the saucepan.
4 Meanwhile, make the straw for your nest by peeling three lemons, keeping the strips of zest as long as possible and discarding any white pith (you can scrape it off with a small knife.) Make the sugar syrup by dissolving the sugar in the water in a small saucepan over low heat— don't let it boil. Put the lemon zest in a sieve and quickly blanch by pouring a kettle of boiling water over it. Then cut the zest into long, thin strips, add them to the simmering sugar syrup and leave for one hour, stirring as little as possible. Remove the candied zest from the remaining syrup and spread on a baking sheet to cool and dry.
5 When both the flummery eggs and the jelly have set, crack the shells around the eggs, peeling them carefully. Lay the eggs on top of the jelly in the bowl and pile the lemon-zest straw (or fruit string) around it like a nest. If the jelly in the saucepan has set, warm it up slightly to make it liquid and let it cool again. Fill the bowl nearly to its brim with the remaining cool jelly mixture and leave it to set in the fridge for several hours.
6 Turn it out very carefully, dipping the bowl into a pan of near boiling water for a few seconds to help loosen it.

The Ball at Netherfield

To make a Hen's Nest Take three or five of the smallest pullet eggs you can get, fill them with flummery, and when they are stiff and cold peel off the shells. Pare off the rinds of two lemons very thin and boil them in sugar and water to take off the bitterness, when they are cold, cut them in long shreds to imitate straws. Then fill a basin one third full of stiff calf's foot jelly and let it stand till cold. Then lay in the shreds of the lemons in a ring about two inches high in the middle of your basin, strew a few corns of sago to look like barley, fill the basin to the height of the peel and let it stand till cold. Then lay your eggs of flummery in the middle of the ring that the straw may be seen round. Fill the basin quite full of jelly and let it stand, and turn it out the same way as the Fish Pond.

Elizabeth Raffald, *The Experienced English Housekeeper*, 1769

A HEDGEHOG

This delicate marzipan is made into a hedgehog with almonds for the spines and dried currants for eyes. Although we might make it for a child's birthday, it would have been made to amuse adult guests, served on a pool of flavored cream or jelly.

2½ cups/250g ground almonds
¾–1 cup/120–140g confectioner's (icing) sugar
A little natural orange flower or rosewater
(with no added alcohol) or orange juice

Half almonds or slivered (flaked) almonds
Currants for the eyes (and nose, if you like)

1 Preheat the oven to 350°F/180°C/Gas Mark 4.
2 Mix the ground almonds and sugar well together; add the liquid, a teaspoonful at a time, until you have a thick, moldable paste that doesn't crack (like marzipan).
3 Hannah makes this paste into one big hedgehog, using almonds for the spines, and currants for the eyes. I think it is nicer to make it into little ones (or one bigger one and a few little ones,) and bake them for 10 minutes or so until the outsides are golden brown. This is the sweetmeat called "marchpane" in Tudor times; it has a lovely, chewy texture and is nicer than raw marzipan.
4 To serve: Hannah suggests surrounding it with a fine Hartshorn Jelly (not recommended) or a mixture of cream, wine, and orange juice. To make a green jelly in the traditional way, color the jelly recipe given on page 103 with a little spinach juice. Don't worry—you can't taste the spinach through the lemon and sugar in the recipe!

To make a hedgehog Take two Quarts of sweet blanched Almonds, beat them well in a Mortar, with a little Canary and Orange-flower Water, to keep them from oiling. Make them into a stiff Paste, then beat in Sugar, put in half a Pound of sweet Butter melted, set on a Furnace, or slow Fire, and keep it constantly stirring till is is stiff enough to be made into the Form of a Hedge-Hog, then put it into a Dish.

HANNAH GLASSE, *THE ART OF COOKERY MADE PLAIN AND EASY*, 1747

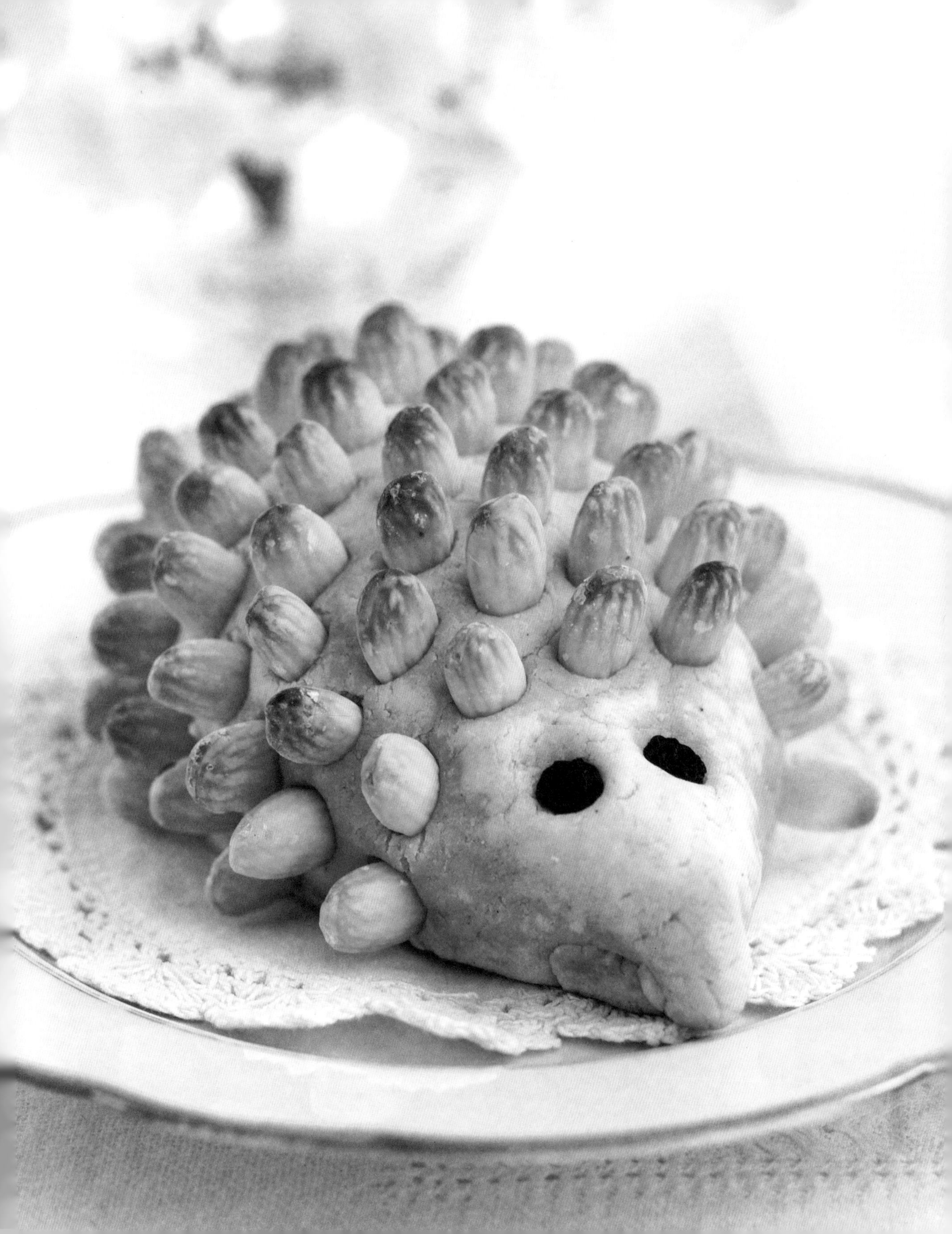

ICE CREAM

Grand country houses and specialist confectioners made this, the latest in luxury, in a special "freezing pot" with ice from the new ice-houses, mixed with salt. There must have been an ice-house at Godmersham, from where Jane wrote to Cassandra: "I shall eat Ice & drink French wine, & be above vulgar economy." (Letter to Cassandra, June 30 1808).

6 egg yolks
½ cup/100g superfine (caster) sugar
1¼ cups/300ml milk or light (single) cream
1¼ cups/300ml heavy (double) cream
Strip of lemon zest

Flavorings
1 cup/150g raspberry purée or pineapple pulp
or
⅓ cup/75ml strong Orange Pekoe tea or Gunpowder tea
or
1 tsp orange flower water (without alcohol)

1 Beat the egg yolks to a froth with the sugar and add to the milk and cream (or to the creams) and lemon peel in a double boiler or heavy-based saucepan.

2 Cook over low heat, without letting it boil. Stir it continuously until it becomes a smooth custard consistency (thick enough to coat the back of a spoon.) Take off the heat and add one of the flavorings suggested above. Hannah Glasse recommends raspberries (add the raspberry purée to the cream, but omit the lemon zest). Confectioner William Gunter adds a small cup of very strong Gunpowder or Pekoe tea to the cream, which makes an unusual, refreshing ice cream. G.A. Jarrin, author of *The Italian Confectioner*, suggests a little orange flower water, or "as much pineapple pulp as you like," strained into the mixture (in which case reduce the milk proportionately.) Beat in the flavoring well, then let the mixture cool completely.

3 Freeze in an ice-cream maker. Alternatively, pour into a freezer container, or ice-cream carton, and half-freeze, whisk it in a mixer or food processor to stop ice-crystals forming, then return to the freezer container. Repeat this two or three times.

Ice cream Take a pint of good fresh cream, and mix it slowly in a small copper pan with eight yolks of eggs, which must be quite fresh; cut a very thin slice of lemon peel, just the surface of the rind of a lemon, and put it in the cream; put your pan on a slow fire, and stir the cream constantly with a whisk, taking care not to let it boil, for it will turn to curds; this you will easily perceive as it then begins to form small lumps; you will know when it is done enough by the cream becoming of a thicker consistence, and instead of turning round the pan, it at once stops; then immediately take it from the fire, add to it half a pound of pounded sugar, more or less, according to taste, strain it through a sieve over a basin, and give it what flavour you choose. In case of necessity you may use half milk and half cream, by adding the yolks of two more eggs, but it is better with new cream and fewer eggs.

G.A. JARRIN, *THE ITALIAN CONFECTIONER*, 1820

NEGUS

This mulled wine, created by Colonel Francis Negus (d.1732) was served at the balls in *Mansfield Park* and *The Watsons*, and was often offered to guests before their chilly journey home. By Victorian times it was thought to be the thing for children's birthday parties! This version is safer served to adults.

Serves 16-20
1 x 25 fl oz/75cl bottle of port
3 cups/750ml water
1–2 tbsp brown sugar
Zest and juice of 1 lemon

About 1 tsp freshly grated nutmeg
1 cinnamon stick and/or 8 whole cloves
(optional)
Segments of orange and/or lemon, to serve

1 Put the water in a saucepan and add the lemon zest, a tablespoon of sugar and the spices. Bring it to a boil and let it simmer very gently for 10–15 minutes. Add the lemon juice.
2 Strain, return to the saucepan, and reheat. Pour in the port; taste it, and add a little more sugar if you like. Heat very gently to serving temperature. Put slices of lemon and/or orange into glasses before pouring in the Negus, or serve it from a pitcher (jug).

1 pint port wine
2 pints water
¼ lb sugar,
in lumps
1 lemon
grated nutmeg
to taste

As this beverage is more usually drunk at children's parties than at any other, the wine need not be very old or expensive for the purpose, a new fruity wine answering very well for it. Put the wine into a jug, rub some lumps of sugar (equal to ¼ lb) on the lemon-rind until all the yellow part of the skin is absorbed, then squeeze the juice, and strain it. Add the sugar and lemon-juice to the port wine, with the grated nutmeg; pour over it the boiling water, cover the jug, and, when the beverage has cooled a little, it will be fit for use.

Negus may also be made of sherry, or any other sweet white wine, but is more usually made of port than of any other beverage. Sufficient - Allow 1 pint of wine, with the other ingredients in proportion, for a party of 9 or 10 children.

MRS BEETON'S *BOOK OF HOUSEHOLD MANAGEMENT*, 1861

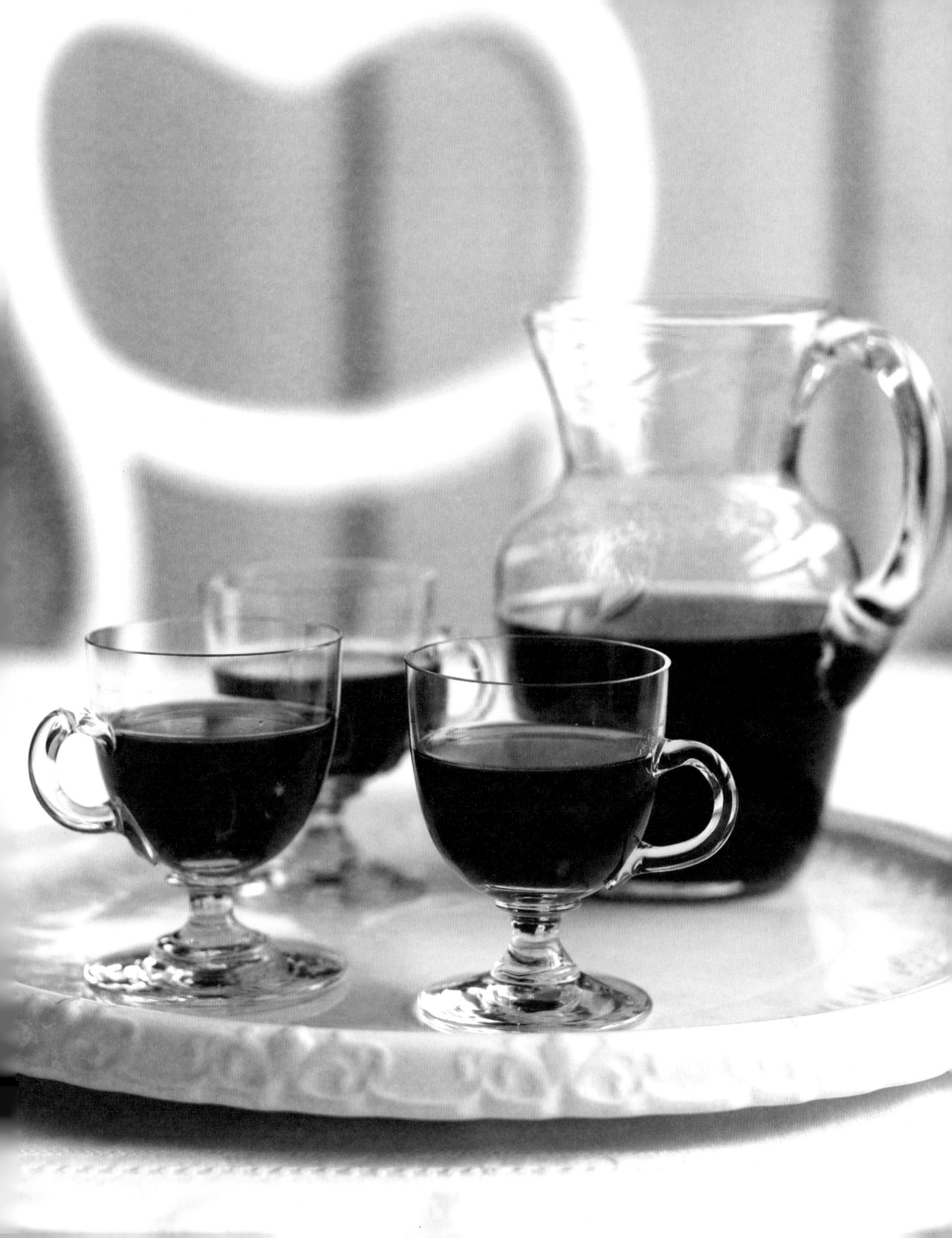

An Old Fashioned Supper for Mr. Woodhouse and his Guests

EMMA

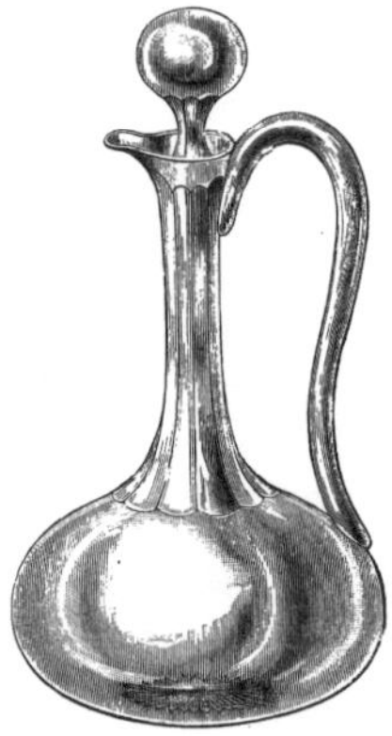

In Jane's early years, when dinner was usually taken in mid-afternoon, supper might be quite a substantial meal, served at nine or ten o'clock at night. By the time she wrote *Emma* (published in 1814–15), the fashionable dinner hour was so much later that a hot supper was outdated; Mr. Woodhouse "loved to have the cloth laid, because it had been the fashion of his youth."

Supper would be taken in the drawing room (or the supper room if the house is, like Northanger Abbey, large enough to have one) and eaten from small tables. It was served after the evening's entertainment, perhaps the theatre, if in town, or music or card games at home. The Bennet girls' aunt Philips invites them to join her party after dinner for a vulgar, but fun "nice comfortable noisy game of lottery tickets, and a little bit of hot supper afterwards."

Mr. Woodhouse enjoys inviting his elderly neighbors for a proper old-fashioned supper of "made" dishes, such as sweetbreads with asparagus, scalloped oysters, and minced chicken, and recommending foods that he considers "not unwholesome." He would surely have disapproved of the supper the Austens provided for guests in Southampton—a tray of wigeon and preserved ginger ("as delicious as one could wish") and black butter (a sort of apple preserve,) which was "not at all what it ought to be; it was neither solid nor entirely sweet." (Letter to Cassandra, December 27 1808.) Supper, often whatever one fancied, and eaten with intimate friends, was a cozy meal, such as the one Jane describes having with the family's benefactress, Mrs. Knight, when they shared tart and jelly in her dressing room.

FRICASSEE OF SWEETBREADS
WITH ASPARAGUS

Mrs. Bates is disappointed when that old fusspot Mr. Woodhouse fancies the asparagus undercooked, and sends it back. Perhaps his cook, Searle, had been reading William Verral's 1759 cookbook, as he recommends boiling the asparagus for this dish, "not so much as we boil them to eat with butter."

4 lamb sweetbreads (the stomach sweetbreads are the best ones to use; they are bigger and rounder than the thymus ones, which have a tendency to fall apart)
Flour, seasoned with salt, pepper, nutmeg
1½ cups/100g white button mushrooms, finely chopped
1 scallion (spring onion), chopped

Knob of butter
Bundle of asparagus (about 18 spears)
Small glass of white wine
1 tbsp parsley, finely chopped
Sea salt and freshly ground black pepper to taste
Squeeze of lemon juice to taste

1 To prepare the sweetbreads, soak them for 2–3 hours in cold water, changing the water 3 or more times until they are white.

2 Put them in a pan of fresh water, bring it to a boil and simmer for 3–4 minutes. Take them out and put them into iced water. Once they are thoroughly cooled, trim away any visible gristle and large veins from the exterior (easiest done using your fingers.) Do not try and remove all of the finer membranes, or the sweetbreads will fall apart completely.

3 Dry them thoroughly, then slice them, coat them in the seasoned flour, and fry until each side is golden and lightly crisped. Remove from the pan and keep warm. To the same (uncleaned) pan, add the mushrooms and scallion and a knob of butter, and cook over medium heat for a few minutes.

4 Meanwhile steam or boil the asparagus lightly. Add the white wine to the mushroom pan, let it boil, and reduce for a minute or two, then add the parsley, and salt and pepper to taste. Return the sweetbreads to the pan briefly, then serve the mixture with the asparagus on top and a squeeze of lemon.

An Old-Fashioned Supper for Mr. Woodhouse and his Guests

Lambs sweetbreads, with tops of asparagus

Blanch your sweetbreads, and put into cold water awhile, put them into a stewpan with a ladle of broth, with pepper, salt, a small bunch of green onions and parsley, and a blade of mace, stir in a bit of butter with flour, and stew all about half an hour; make ready a liaison of two or three eggs and cream, with a little minced parsley and nutmeg; put in your points of asparagus that I suppose to be boiled, and pour in your liaison, and take care it don't curdle add some juice of lemon or orange and send it to table. You may make use of pease, young gooseberries, or kidney-beans for this, and all make a pretty dish.

WILLIAM VERRAL, *A COMPLETE SYSTEM OF COOKERY*, 1759

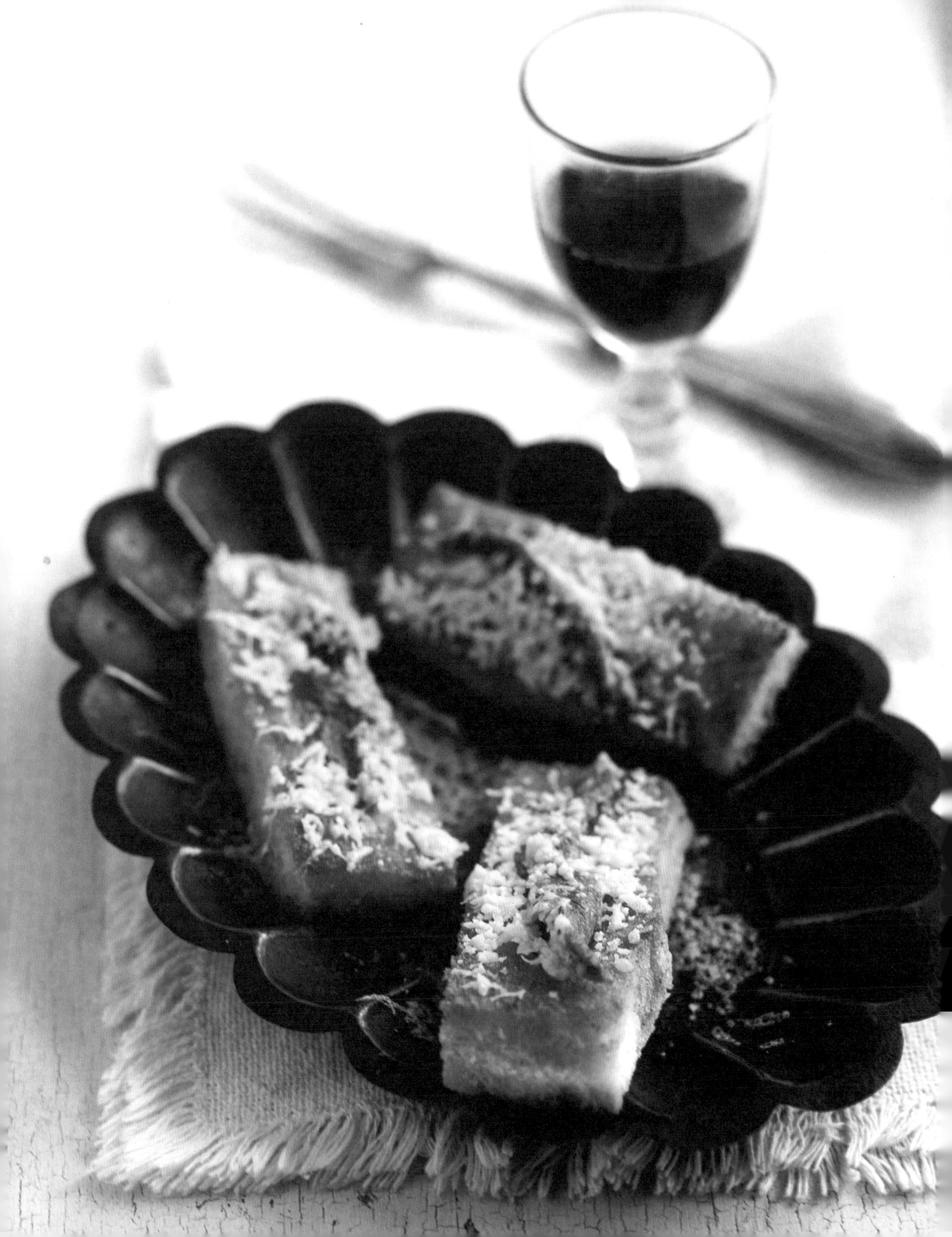

TOASTED CHEESE

When Fanny Price stays with her parents, she finds the house a maelstrom of people; her father calling for rum and water, her little brothers begging for toasted cheese for supper. Jane remarks to Cassandra on the hospitality of a gentleman who "made a point of ordering toasted cheese for supper entirely on my account." (Letter, August 27 1805.)

4 whole salted anchovies or 8–12 anchovy fillets

4 slices sourdough or Italian bread, such as ciabatta

A little olive oil

Garlic clove (optional)

7oz/200g Parmesan cheese or other strong cheese, such as mature Cheddar, grated

1 Put a baking tray in the oven and preheat to 400°F/200°C/Gas Mark 6.

2 Rinse the anchovies and pat them dry with paper towel. Drizzle a little olive oil on the breads and, if you like, rub them with the cut side of a garlic clove.

3 Cut the whole anchovies longways into two and lay them or the fillets on the bread. Put them on the hot baking tray, cover with the grated cheese, and bake for about 10–12 minutes until the cheese is melted and the edges are browned.

4 Alternatively, toast one side of the bread, lay the anchovies and cheese (with oil and optional garlic) on the untoasted side as before, and let it brown under the broiler (grill) for 5–6 minutes.

Anchovies, with Parmesan Cheese Fry some bits of bread about the length of an anchovy in good oil or butter, lay the half of an anchovy, with the bone upon each bit, and strew over them some Parmesan cheese grated fine, and colour them nicely in an oven, or with a salamander*, squeeze the juice of an orange or lemon, and pile them up in your dish and send them to table. This seems to be but a trifling thing, but I never saw it come whole from table.

WILLIAM VERRAL, *A COMPLETE SYSTEM OF COOKERY*, 1759

★ A salamander was an iron disc with a wooden handle, heated in the coals until it glowed red, and then held over dishes to grill them.

BUTTERED APPLE TART

Mr. Woodhouse reassures Miss Bates that he is offering her a tart made from fresh apples and "You need not be afraid of unwholesome preserves here. I do not advise the custard." I hope you disregard Mr. Woodhouse's views on custard and enjoy Hannah Glasse's unusual but happy marriage of egg custard and apple tart.

4–5 cooking apples
2 tbsp/30g butter
2–4 tbsp sugar
½ tsp grated nutmeg
½ tsp ground cinnamon (optional — not in original recipe)

Juice and zest of 1 orange
1 batch of Sweet Rich Shortcrust Pastry (see recipe page 153)
3 eggs, separated
Confectioners' (icing) sugar, to serve

1 Skin, core, and slice the apples and cook them in a tablespoon of water until just soft.
2 While the apples are hot, stir in the butter, sugar to taste, the nutmeg, and cinnamon if using, and the orange zest and juice.
3 While the mixture cools, preheat the oven to 375°F/190°C/Gas Mark 5, and line a 10-inch/25cm pie dish with the pastry.
4 Beat the egg yolks and stir them into the apple. Whisk the egg whites to stiff peaks and fold them into the mixture. Pour the mixture into the pastry case and bake for approximately 30 minutes until the eggs are set.
5 Serve with a dusting of confectioners' sugar over it.

A Buttered Tort Take eight or ten large Codlings and scald them, when cold skin them, take the Pulp and beat it as fine as you can with a Silver Spoon, then mix in the Yolks of six Eggs, and the Whites of four beat all well together, a Seville Orange squeez'd in the Juice, and shread the rind as fine as possible, some grated Nutmeg and Sugar to your Taste; melt some fresh butter, and beat up with it according as it wants, till it is all like a fine thick Cream, then make a fine Puff-paste, have a large Tin Patty, that will just hold it, cover the Patty with the Paste, and pour in the Ingredients, don't put any Cover on, bake it a quarter of an Hour, then flip it out of the Patty on to a Dish, and throw fine Sugar well beat all over it. It is a very pretty Side-dish for a second Course. You may make this of any large Apple you please.

HANNAH GLASSE, *THE ART OF COOKERY MADE PLAIN AND EASY*, 1747

DR KITCHINER'S RECEIPT
TO MAKE GRUEL

Mr. Woodhouse liked to serve generous suppers although he himself ate only a small basin of thin gruel. Some elderly people also had arrowroot (which Jane spells "arraroot",) considered easily digestible food for the infirm or elderly; Emma sends some to the ailing, probably anorexic, Jane Fairfax and is hurt to have it returned.

Gruel Ask those who are to eat it, if they like it thick or thin; if the latter, mix well together by degrees, in a pint basin, one table-spoonful of oatmeal, with three of cold water; if the former, use two spoonfuls.

Have ready in a stew-pan, a pint of boiling water or milk; pour this by degrees to the oatmeal you have mixed; return it into the stew-pan; set it on the fire, and let it boil for five minutes; stirring it all the time to prevent the oatmeal from burning at the bottom of the stew-pan; skim and strain it through a hair-sieve.

To convert this into caudle, add a little ale, wine, or brandy, with sugar; and if the bowels are disordered, a little nutmeg or ginger, grated.

WILLIAM KITCHINER, *THE COOK'S ORACLE*, 1830

CAUDLE

An eighteenth-century caudle was spiced ale thickened with oatmeal. The word "coddle" came from "caudle", both meaning to boil gently. Its first recorded use as meaning "to indulge" is in *Emma* when Mr. John Knightley tells his wife, "Be satisfied with doctoring and coddling yourself and the children, and let me look as I chuse."

2 cups/500ml ale
2 cups/500ml water
3 tbsp/25g fine oatmeal
A little grated nutmeg

Small lump of ginger root, peeled and bruised (use a rolling pin)
3 tbsp/25g sugar

1 Put all the ingredients except the sugar in a saucepan, bring to a boil and then simmer very gently for 10 minutes.
2 Stir in the sugar and take out the ginger root just before serving.

POOR KNIGHTS

This, or "Poor Knights of Windsor" — perfect for Sir Walter Elliot of Kellynch Hall — is the old name for the supper dish that Hannah Glasse calls "pain perdu" or "cream toasts" and which we know as French Toast or Eggy Bread. The toasts were also sometimes made with wine; a drop of rum or brandy makes them a fine dish for the end of the evening.

4 eggs

1 scant cup/200ml milk

2 tsp rum or brandy (optional)

A little grated nutmeg

½ cup/100g caster sugar

8 slices soft day-old bread or brioche, crusts removed and cut in half diagonally

1 stick/125g unsalted butter

1 Preheat the oven to 225°F/110°C/Gas Mark ¼.

2 Combine the eggs, milk, and nutmeg (and rum or brandy if using), and beat in the sugar until it is dissolved.

3 Pour the mixture into a flat dish so that you can lay the slices of bread flat. Let them soak up the mixture for a few minutes on each side.

4 Heat the butter in a frying pan until it is foaming, and fry the bread for a couple of minutes on each side until golden. You will need to do them in batches, wiping out the pan after each, and keeping them warm in the oven while you finish the remainder.

To serve

John Nott serves them with a mix of butter, sugar, and rosewater, warmed together and poured over the toasts. They are very good with sharp stewed fruit, such as rhubarb or berries.

Cut a couple of Penny Loaves into round Slices, and dip them in half a Pint of Cream or Water; then lay then spred in a Dish, and beat up three Eggs with Cream, Sugar and Nutmeg grated. Then melt Butter in a Frying-pan; wet the Sides of the Toasts, and lay them in the Frying-pan the wet Sides downwards, then pour the rest of the Cream, Eggs etc upon them and fry them; when they are done, serve them up with Butter, Sugar and Rose-water.

JOHN NOTT, THE COOK'S AND CONFECTIONER'S DICTIONARY, 1723

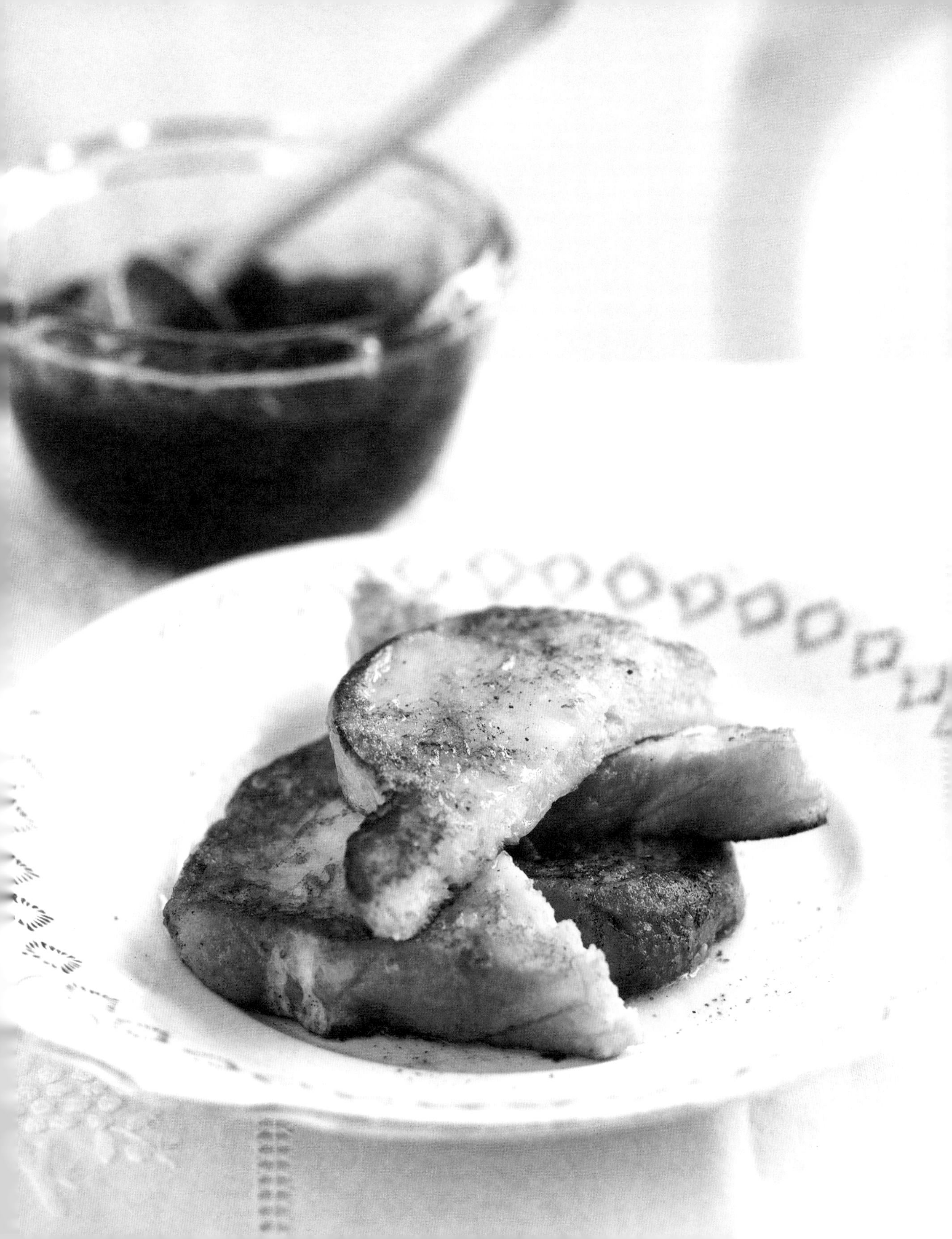

Christmas with the Musgroves and other Celebrations

PERSUASION

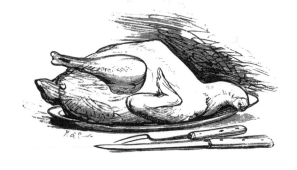

The old-fashioned warmth and hospitality of the elder Musgroves is a foil to the chilly self-consciousness of Bath society, never more so than at Christmas, one of the only times that food is mentioned in *Persuasion*. When Anne Elliot and Lady Russell call on the Musgroves in the Christmas holidays, they find a "fine family-piece" of chattering girls and riotous boys, with "tressels and trays, bending under the weight of brawn and cold pies."

Christmas pies could be huge affairs—Hannah Glasse's Yorkshire Christmas Pie has a pigeon, partridge, fowl, goose, and turkey boned and stuffed inside each other—or they might be mince pies, much loved since medieval times. Brawn, made from the face meats of a pig, set in jelly, is (to us) a strange special treat, but made when the pigs were slaughtered in November, it went with the time of year.

Roast beef was England's top celebratory dish, but turkeys had become popular since their introduction from America in the sixteenth century. Jane writes to Martha Lloyd about the "pleasant duties" at Christmas of giving to the poor and "eating Turkies" (November 29 1812.) Geese were fattened up throughout harvest time, and eaten at Michaelmas (September 29); Jane has a Michaelmas goose at Godmersham in 1813, and Harriet is entrusted with one as a seasonal gift in *Emma*.

Plum (meaning dried fruit) puddings would have been eaten throughout the season, but it took Dickens to make them synonymous with Christmas pudding. Lavish fruit cakes were eaten at Twelfth Night, rather than Christmas, in Georgian times, and also, as we know from the one that so alarms Mr. Woodhouse, at weddings.

ROAST LEG OF MUTTON
STUFFED WITH OYSTERS

On Christmas Eve, Emma meets Mr. John Knightley with his boys on their way home to eat roast mutton and rice pudding; that evening a saddle of mutton was served at the Westons' dinner party. Oysters and anchovies were often used to intensify the flavor of the mutton, which was the most commonly eaten meat in Georgian times.

Serves 6–8

A leg of mutton, part boned, 5½–6¾ lb/ 2.5–3kg (mutton is stronger and less fatty than lamb and is ideal for this dish, but if you cannot source it, use lamb, or hogget which is a sheep of between 1 and 2 years old)

For the stuffing

1 cup/50g fresh white breadcrumbs

3½ tbsp/50g suet

2–3 whole salted anchovies (or 8–12 fillets), well rinsed

3 hard-boiled egg yolks

1 shallot, finely chopped

1–2 tsp chopped thyme

1–2 tsp chopped winter savory

12 oysters (keep the liquor for the sauce)

¼ tsp grated nutmeg

1 egg, beaten

For the gravy

Oyster liquor

A wine glass of good dry red wine

1 salted anchovy, or 3-4 anchovy fillets, finely chopped

A little nutmeg

1 small onion

A few oysters (but not essential)

1 Preheat the oven to 425°F/220°C/Gas Mark 7.

2 Chop, but do not mash, all the ingredients for the stuffing very finely, except the oysters, which should be left whole. Bind with the raw egg. The leg of mutton should have the shank bone in, and a cavity at the top for your stuffing; push it down as far as it will go, fold the top flaps over the stuffing and tie it tightly with kitchen string.

3 Hannah advises roasting the meat and boiling the sauce separately, but I part-roast the meat in a preheated oven for 30 minutes, turn the oven down to 325°F/160°C/Gas Mark 3 and pour the ingredients for the gravy around the mutton. Roast for 15–20 minutes per lb/450g.

4 When the meat is done, put it on a separate plate, cover with foil and let it rest for 15–20 minutes while you skim the fat off the gravy.

To Stuff a Leg or Shoulder of Mutton

Take a little grated Bread, some Beef Sewet, the Yolks of hard Eggs, three Anchovies, a Bit of an Onion, some Pepper and Salt, a little Thyme and Winter Savoury, twelve Oysters, and some Nutmeg grated; mix all these together, shred them very fine, work them up with raw Eggs like a Paste, stuff your Mutton under the Skin in the thickest Place, or where you please, and roast it: For Sauce, take some of the oyster liquor, some claret, one Anchovy, a little Nutmeg, a Bit of an Onion and a few Oysters; stew all these together, then take out your Onion, pour your Sauce under your Mutton, and send it to Table. Garnish with Horse-raddish.

HANNAH GLASSE, *THE ART OF COOKERY MADE PLAIN AND EASY*, 1747

BRAISED TURKEY

Turkey was enjoyed all year round, as well as at Christmas—but only by the wealthy. As Mary Crawford says: "A large income is the best recipe for happiness I ever heard of. It certainly may secure all the myrtle and turkey part of it." This is an excellent way of keeping a turkey moist during cooking.

Serves 6–8
One turkey, 9 lb/4kg (this will also work for chicken)
6–8 rashers streaky bacon (in squares, plus a larding needle; or strips)
White pepper
1 tsp spices (such as mustard powder, ground nutmeg, cayenne pepper, or ground allspice)
Parsley, finely chopped

For the braise
4 small onions, roughly chopped
6 carrots, roughly chopped
1 turnip, roughly chopped
Head of celery, washed and roughly chopped
Bouquet garni or any of bay leaves, thyme, marjoram, parsley
½ lb/225g chestnuts
Turkey giblets (optional)
1 quart/liter light stock (chicken or vegetable)

For the salpicon
A salpicon is simply a mix of ingredients chopped small, sometimes bound with a liquid.
1 veal sweetbread (or liver), chopped small (See sweetbread recipe on page 114 for instructions for preparing sweetbreads)
3 mushrooms, diced
2 slices ham, cut small
2 gherkins, diced
A little gravy
Small glass of white wine
Beurre manié (butter and flour, blended in equal quantities)
Sea salt and white pepper
A little chopped parsley
Squeeze of lemon juice

1 Preheat the oven to 325°F/160°C/Gas Mark 3.
2 Try to get hold of a larding needle, which will allow you to sew the bacon onto the turkey. If not, use strips of bacon draped over the breast. Season your bacon squares with pepper, any of the spices you fancy, and parsley.
3 Put the turkey in a big pot or heavy-based roasting pan, surrounded by the vegetables, herbs, chestnuts, and giblets, if using, and cover the vegetables with light stock. Cook in the oven for

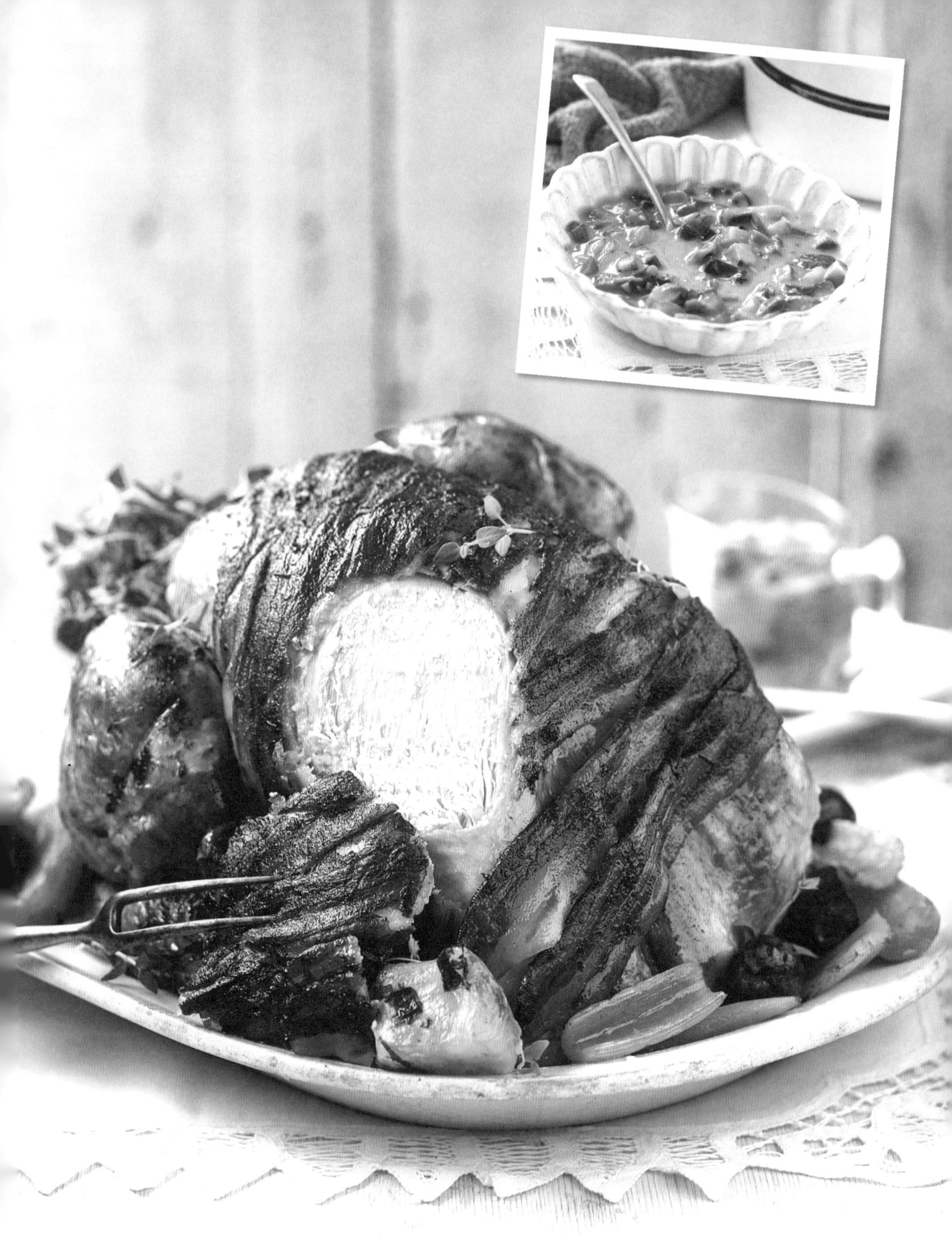

20 minutes per lb/450g, basting it now and again. It is ready when the juices run clear when you insert a metal skewer into the meat.

4 Take it out of the oven and let it rest out of the braising liquor for 20 minutes while you finish off the gravy.

5 Take the chestnuts out of the braise, to be served around the turkey; sieve the liquid, pushing some of the vegetables through the sieve to help thicken it, then reduce it in a saucepan over high heat. Serve this gravy separately.

6 For the salpicon, sauté the sweetbread or liver and the mushrooms in a little butter or oil, add the ham, gherkins, a little gravy (or stock taken from the turkey as it cooks,) and the white wine. Let it simmer for 5–10 minutes, and if necessary, thicken with the beurre manié and cook for a few minutes longer. Check for seasoning and add the parsley and a squeeze of lemon juice.

7 To serve: William Verral pours his salpicon over the turkey, but I imagine it would get rather lost, so suggest serving it up separately.

Turkey in a braize with chestnuts, with a salpicon sauce

Lard your turkey with a few large square pieces of bacon, seasoned with a little beaten spices, pepper and salt, and a little parsley; take a pot about its bigness, and line it with thin slices of bacon, and cover with the same; season pretty high, with onions, carrots, a turnip or two, such herbs as you like, a little spice and pepper, parsley, and a head or two of celery, fill up with a little broth and water mixt, cover it down close, and let it go gently on till every part of your turkey is very tender.

NB This braize will serve for any thing else the same day, or for four or five days following. I should first have spoke of preparing the chestnuts by blanching, peeling, and putting into the body of the turkey, with a little farce or force-meat in the crop, and skewer'd up; let your turkey lay in the braize till towards dinner-time; and now prepare your salpicon; take a thin slice or two of boiled ham, a veal sweetbread, the yolk or two of hard eggs, or a knot is better, a pickled cucumber or two, two or three mushrooms cut all into small dice, and put into as much cullis as is suitable for your dish, dash in a glass or Champagne, or other white wine; boil all a little while, throw in a little minc'd parsley, try if it is seasoned to your mind, squeeze in the juice of a lemon, and pour over your turkey well drained, and serve it up.

WILLIAM VERRAL, *A COMPLETE SYSTEM OF COOKERY*, 1759

PLUM CAKE

"Plum" means dried fruit, and rich plum cakes were made for Twelfth Night revels and weddings. Mr. Woodhouse tries to persuade Mr. Perry, the apothecary, that they are indigestible. "There was a strange rumour in Highbury of all the little Perrys being seen with a slice of Mrs. Weston's wedding-cake in their hands: but Mr. Woodhouse would never believe it."

1¼ cups/170g currants

1¼ cups/170g raisins

2 tbsp/30ml brandy

2 tbsp/30ml sweet wine

1¾ cups/225g self-rising flour

¾ tsp ground mace

¾ tsp grated nutmeg

½ tsp ground cloves

½ tsp ground allspice

2 sticks/225g butter

1 heaping cup/225g soft dark brown sugar

Grated zest of ½ lemon

4 eggs, beaten

Heaping ½ cup/60g ground almonds

¾ cup/60g slivered (flaked) almonds

¼ cup/60ml cream or milk

1 Leave the dried fruit to soak in the brandy and wine overnight.

2 Preheat the oven to 300°F/150°C/Gas Mark 2.

3 Sift the flour and spices together.

4 Cream the butter with the sugar and lemon zest until pale and fluffy. Beat in the eggs, a little at a time; if the mixture starts to curdle, throw in a little flour to stabilize it.

5 Fold in the remaining flour and then stir in the rest of the ingredients.

6 Butter a deep 8-inch/20cm cake pan with a removable base, and line it with 2 thicknesses of parchment paper. Line the outside with two thicknesses of foil or brown paper, tied with string.

7 Spoon the mixture into the pan and bake for 3 hours, or until a toothpick inserted into the center comes out clean. If it starts to brown too early, cover with layers of foil or parchment paper.

Plum cakes Mix thoroughly a quarter of a peck of fine flour, well dried, with a pound of dry and sifted loaf sugar, three pounds of currants washed and very dry, half a pound of raisins stoned and chopped, a quarter of an ounce of mace and cloves, twenty Jamaica peppers, a grated nutmeg, the peel of a lemon cut as fine as possible, and half a pound of almonds blanched and beaten with orange-flower water. Melt two pounds of butter in a pint and a quarter of cream, but not hot; put to it a pint of sweet wine, a glass of brandy, the whites and yolks of twelve eggs beaten apart, and half a pint of good yeast. Strain this liquid by degrees into the dry ingredients, beating them together a full hour, then butter the hoop, or pan, and bake it. As you put the batter into the hoop, or pan, throw in plenty of citron, lemon, and orange-candy.

If you ice the cake, take half a pound of double-refined sugar sifted, and put a little with the white of an egg, beat it well, and by degrees pour in the remainder. It must be whisked near an hour, with the addition of a little orange-flower water, but mind not to put much. When the cake is done, pour the iceing over, and return it to the oven for fifteen minutes; but if the oven be warm, keep it near the mouth, and the door open, lest the colour be spoiled.

MRS. RUNDELL, *A NEW SYSTEM OF DOMESTIC COOKERY*, 1806

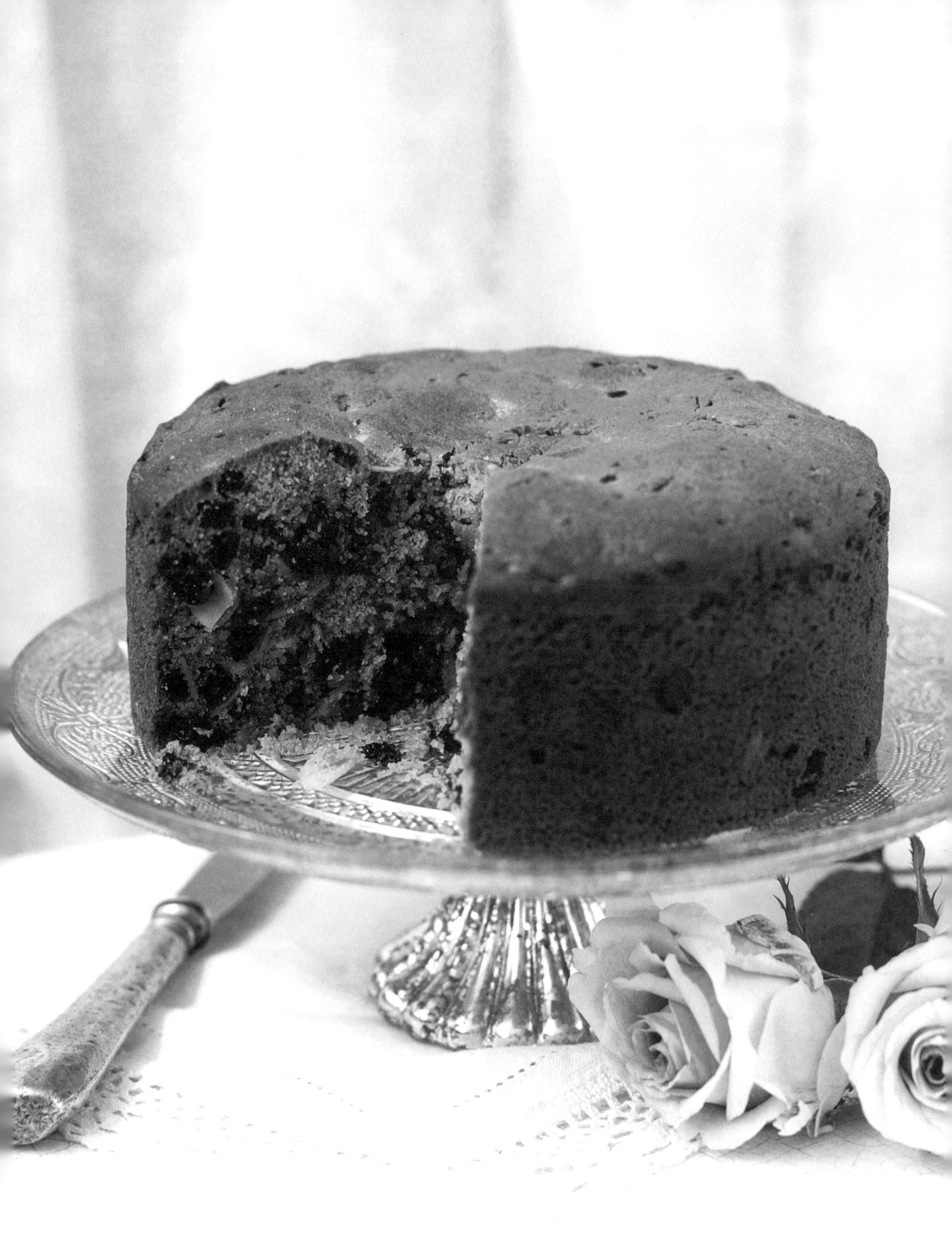

MINCE PIES

Mince pies were originally made with mutton, beef, or tongue, but this was becoming optional by the eighteenth century. "If you chuse Meat in your Pies, parboil a Neat's-Tongue, peel it, and chop the Meat as fine as possible, and mix with the rest," writes Hannah. Hers is quite a boozy mincemeat; delicious! She suggests making several small pies, as we do, or one slightly larger one.

For the mincemeat
Scant ½ cup/100g suet, shredded
7 oz/200g apples, cored and chopped
1 heaping cup/150g raisins
Heaping 1½ cups/160g currants
¼ cup/50g brown sugar
1 tsp ground mace
¼ tsp ground cloves
½ tsp nutmeg
3 tbsp/45ml brandy
3 tbsp/45ml sherry

For the pie
Double batch of shortcrust pastry (see recipe on page 153)
A neat's tongue (a beef [ox] tongue) or about 1¼ cups/200g boiled beef or tongue, chopped small (optional)
Scant ½ cup/50g candied peel
Zest of 1 orange
Juice of ½ lemon or ½ orange
2 tbsp/30ml red wine

1 Make the mincemeat by mixing together the suet, apples, dried fruit, sugar, spices, brandy, and sherry.
2 Preheat the oven to 400°F/200°C/Gas Mark 6.
3 Line a pie dish with shortcrust pastry, then add the following: a thin layer of meat (such as beef or tongue, chopped small); a thin layer of citron (candied peel will do); a good layer of mincemeat; a layer of thinly cut orange zest; finishing with a thin layer of meat.
4 Mix together the juice of half a lemon or half an orange with 2 tablespoons of red wine and sprinkle this over, before covering with a pastry lid.
5 Bake for 25–35 minutes.

Variation: Lemon mincemeat, a pleasant, light version, was popular for Christmas pies. It was made with the addition of a lemon boiled and mashed to a pulp. Martha Lloyd has a recipe for it, and so does Duncan MacDonald, the cook at the Bedford Tavern in London's Covent Garden and author of *The New London Family Cook*. Jane knew of the tavern; in *Northanger Abbey*, John Thorpe tries to impress Catherine by saying he knows General Tilney because "I have met him forever at the Bedford."

To make Mince-Pies the best Way

Take three Pounds of Suet shread very fine, and chopped as small as possible, two Pounds of raisings stoned, and chopped as fine as possible, two Pounds of Currans, nicely picked, washed, rubbed, and dried at the Fire, half a hundred of fine Pippins, pared, cored, and chopped small, half a Pound of fine Sugar pounded fine, a quarter of an Ounce of Mace, a quarter of an Ounce of Cloves, two large Nutmegs, all beat fine; put all together into a great Pan, and mix it well together with half a Pint of Brandy, and half a Pint of Sach; put it down close in a Stone-pot, and it will keep good four Months. When you make your Pies, take a little Dish, something bigger than a Soop-plate, lay a very thin Crust all over it, lay a thin Layer of Meat, AND THEN A THIN Layer of Citron cut vey thin, then a Layer of Mince meat, and a thin Layer of Orange-peel cut thin, over that a little Meat; squeeze half the Juice of a fine Sevile Orange, or Lemon, and pour in three Spoonfuls of Red Wine; lay on your Crust, and bake it nicely.

HANNAH GLASSE, *THE ART OF COOKERY MADE PLAIN AND EASY*, 1747

Lemon Mincemeat

Squeeze a lemon, boil the outside til tender enough to beat to a mash, add to it three apples chopped, four ounces of suet, half a pound of currants, four ounces of sugar, put the juice of a lemon and candied fruit as for other pies. Make a short-crust and fill the patty pans.

DUNCAN MACDONALD, *THE NEW LONDON FAMILY COOK*, 1808

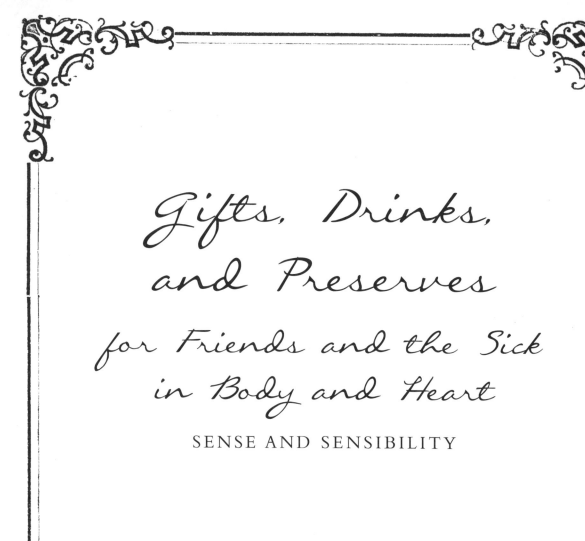

Gifts, Drinks, and Preserves

for Friends and the Sick in Body and Heart

SENSE AND SENSIBILITY

The gestures concerning food in *Sense and Sensibility* are tellingly balanced between the kind-hearted and the wrong-headed. John Dashwood understands that his obligation to his family is to care for the impoverished Mrs. Dashwood, and provide his half-sisters with three thousand pounds apiece, but allows his awful wife to whittle this down to the entirely insufficient "presents of fish and game, and so forth, whenever they are in season." With pleasing symmetry, Mrs. Dashwood's cousin, Sir John Middleton, welcomes her and the girls to the cottage he has provided for them with "a large basket full of garden stuff and fruit," followed shortly after by "a present of game."

Mrs. Jennings also shows her concern for the Dashwood girls by means of food, hoping to help mend Marianne's broken heart with dried cherries, olives, Constantia wine—and a good fire. This makes Mrs. Jennings a warm but faintly comic character, who doesn't see that the feelings of Jane Austen's heroines are too profound to be consoled by food. She would go down well with the spoilt Middleton child, though, who stops her tantrum at the mention of "apricot marmalade."

Jane's letters are full of mentions of practical and kindly made gifts of food: for example, she sends fish to friends in Berkshire from Southampton; Mrs. Austen sends her seafaring sons home-cured hams, and dispatches turkeys from her poultry yard to Henry in Covent Garden; and Jane asks her niece to pass on thanks for the "extreemly acceptable" gift of the asparagus-like seakale or "Seacale" as Jane spells it. (Letter to Caroline Austen, March 14 1817).

Orange Wine Take twelve pounds of the best powder-sugar, with the whites of eight or ten eggs well beaten, into six gallons of spring-water, and boil it three quarters of an hour. When it is cold, put it into six spoonfuls of yeast, and also the juice of twelve lemons, which being pared must stand with two pounds of white sugar in a tankard, and in the morning skim off the top, and then put it into the water. Then add the juice and rinds of fifty oranges, but not the white part of the rinds; and so let it work all together two days and two nights; then add two quarts of Renish or White Wine, and put it into your vessel.

HANNAH GLASSE, *THE ART OF COOKERY MADE PLAIN AND EASY*, 1747

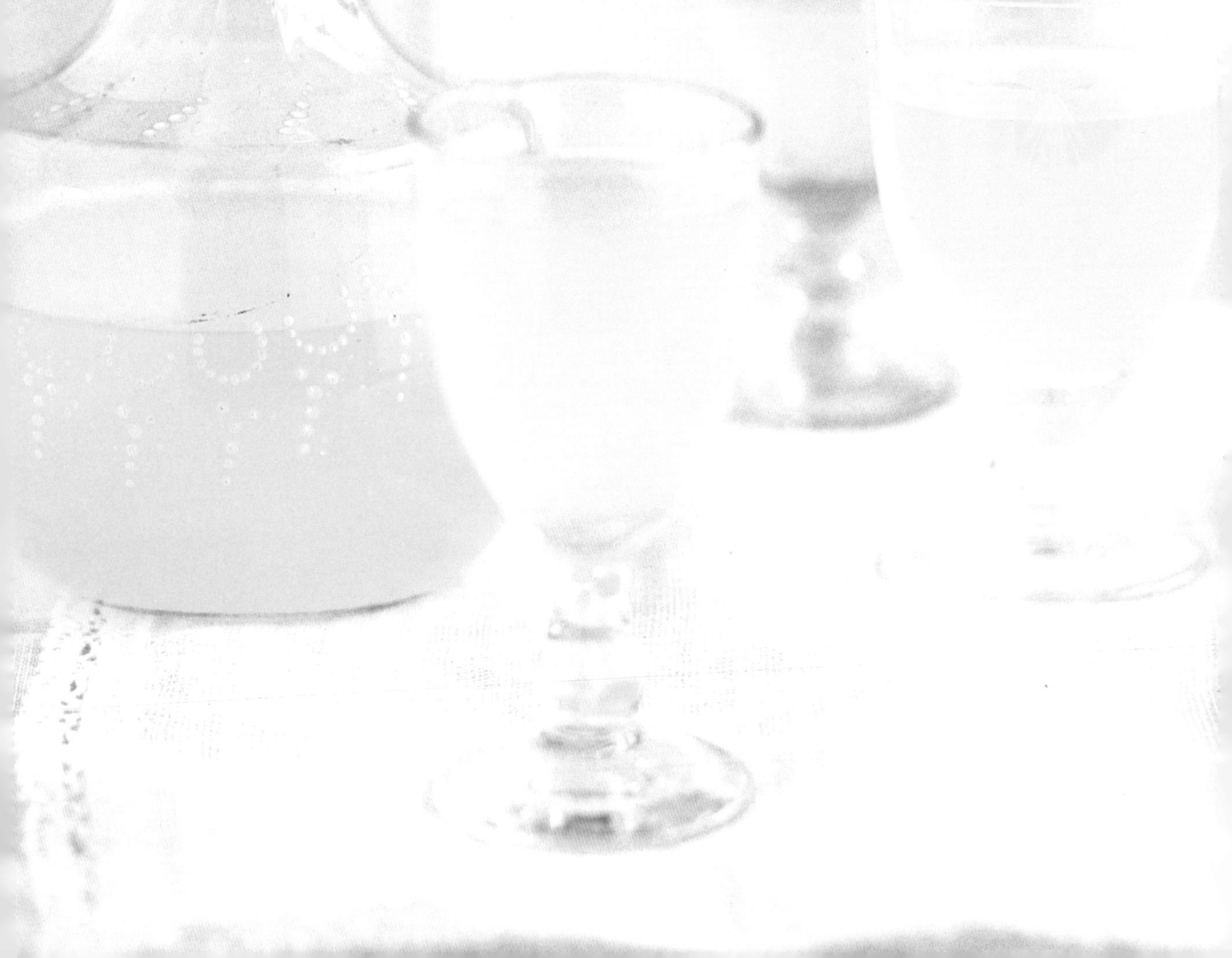

ORANGE WINE

Jane asked her friend Alethea Biggs for her receipt for orange wine made "from Seville oranges, entirely or chiefly." This version, really a sparkling orangeade, from Hannah Glasse, uses ordinary oranges, so it can be made at any time of year, plus it is ready in two days rather than the year allowed in Alethea's recipe, which is included in Martha Lloyd's Household Book.

Makes 2 quarts/2 liters
2¼ cups/450g granulated sugar
1½ quarts/1.5 liters spring water
Juice of 1 lemon

Juice and zest of 4–5 oranges, being careful not to include the pith
¼ teaspoon brewer's yeast (also known as ale yeast or wine yeast)

1 Boil the sugar and water together for a few minutes to make sure the sugar dissolves. Let it cool a little, and add the lemon juice, orange juice, and orange zest. When it has cooled to blood heat, sprinkle the yeast on the surface. Cover, and let it stand overnight at room temperature.

2 The next day, strain it through a fine sieve or cheesecloth. Using a funnel or jug, decant it into a 2 quart/2 liter (or two 1-quart/liter) clean plastic water bottles, leaving a couple of inches/5 centimetres of air at the top. (Don't use glass bottles, in case they explode.) It should be ready in two or three days, when the gas has expanded inside the bottles and they feel hard to the touch. If you don't intend to drink it immediately, let a little of the air out (so the bottles don't explode). Afterward, keep in the fridge to stop the yeast working.

To serve
This gives a light, sparkling orangeade to mix with a sweetish cold white wine. Hannah recommends "Renish" or Rhine wines. You could also add a little brandy.

APRICOT MARMALADE AND
APRICOT "CAKES"

Lady Middleton successfully deploys "apricot marmalade" (which we would now call jam) to stop her daughter's attention-seeking screams. The apricot cakes are made from a thick purée, which is dried in the oven to make delicious, chewy sweets.

Makes 2 quarts/2 litres
18 oz/500g fresh apricots or dried apricots, reconstituted overnight in apple juice (drained weight)

1¼ cups/250g preserving sugar for marmalade/1¾ cups/350g preserving sugar for cakes

1 Pit the fruit and boil it until tender — about 30 minutes. Then rub through a sieve or purée in a blender, stir in the sugar and bring back to a boil. Boil until the sugar has dissolved.
2 To make apricot cakes, spoon the mixture into oiled muffin cups and smooth down. Leave in a very low oven, 175°F/80°C/Gas Mark ¼ (or lower if possible) to dry out for 5–6 hours, turning them over halfway. If using Gas Mark ¼, check the cakes after a couple of hours.

To make Apricot Marmalade When you preserve your apricots, pick out all the bad ones and those that are too ripe for keeping. Boil them in the syrup until they will mash, then beat them in a mortar to a paste. Take half their weight of loaf sugar and put as much water to it as will dissolve it, boil it and skim it well. Boil them till they look clear and the syrup thick like a fine jelly, then put it into your sweetmeat glasses and keep them for use.

Apricot Paste Pare and stone your apricots, boil them in water till they will mash quite small. Put a pound of double-refined sugar in your preserving pan with as much water as will dissolve it, and boil it to sugar again. Take it off the stove and put in a pound of apricots, let it stand till the sugar is melted. Then make it scalding hot, but don't let it boil. Pour it into china dishes or cups, set them in a stove. When they are stiff enough to turn out put them on glass plates. Turn them as you see occasion till they are dry.

Elizabeth Raffald, *The Experienced English Housekeeper*, 1769

Gifts, Drinks and Preserves

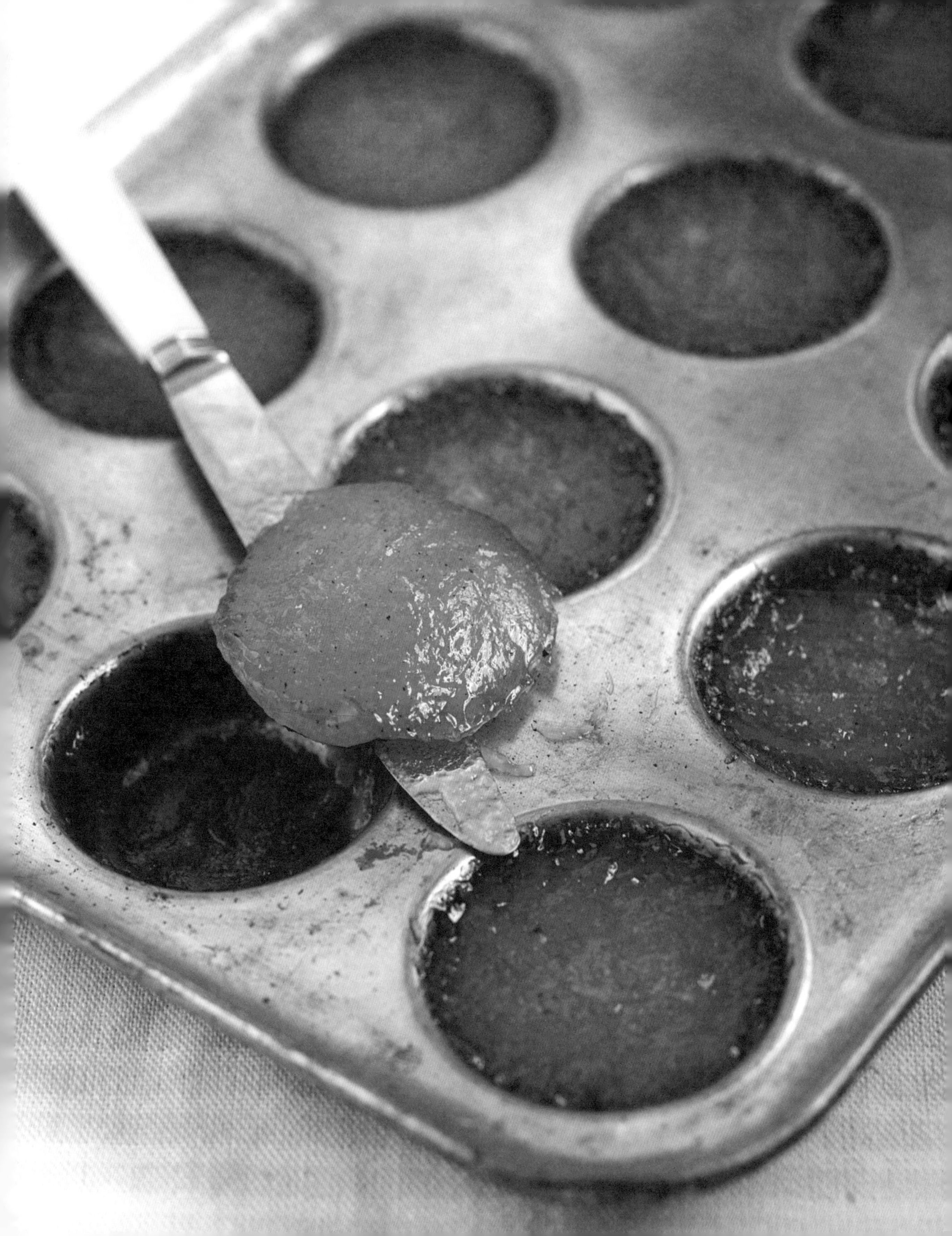

CHERRIES EN CHEMISE

When Willoughby has rejected Marianne in favor of the wealthy Miss Grey, well-meaning Mrs. Jennings seeks to cure her broken heart with olives and dried cherries. This recipe from Margaret Dods part-dries the cherries and makes an uplifting gift for a friend, whether broken hearted or not.

1⅔ cups/250g fresh ripe cherries with stems
1–2 egg whites
Confectioners' (icing) sugar or superfine (caster) sugar

For the meringue
2 egg whites
¼ cup/50g superfine (caster) sugar

1 Take large, ripe cherries and cut off the stems with scissors, leaving about 1 inch/2cm to each cherry.

2 Beat an egg white until it is frothy, and roll the cherries in the egg and then in confectioners' (icing) sugar.

3 Place them on parchment paper, and let them dry at room temperature until the "frosting" adheres. They should keep for about a week.

4 They are too delicate to transport, though, so for a gift that will go in a box, make meringues to surround them. Beat the egg whites until they are stiff, and fold in the superfine (caster) sugar. Pile teaspoonsful of the mixture onto parchment paper, and place half a pitted cherry on top. Leave some uncovered, and cover some with another blob of meringue. Turn the oven to 225°F/110°C/Gas Mark ¼. Give them 2½–3 hours to dry out in the oven.

Cherries en chemise, a very pretty little dish Take the largest ripe cherries you can get. Cut off the stalks with scissors, leaving about an inch to each cherry. Beat the white of an egg to a froth, and roll them in it one by one, and then roll them lightly in sifted sugar. Lay a sheet of paper on a sieve reversed, and laying them on this, set them on a stove till they are to be served. Obs the same may be done with bunches of currants, strawberries, hautboys, etc. Fruits en chemise look well and cost little.

MARGARET DODS, *THE COOK AND HOUSEWIFE'S MANUAL*, 1826

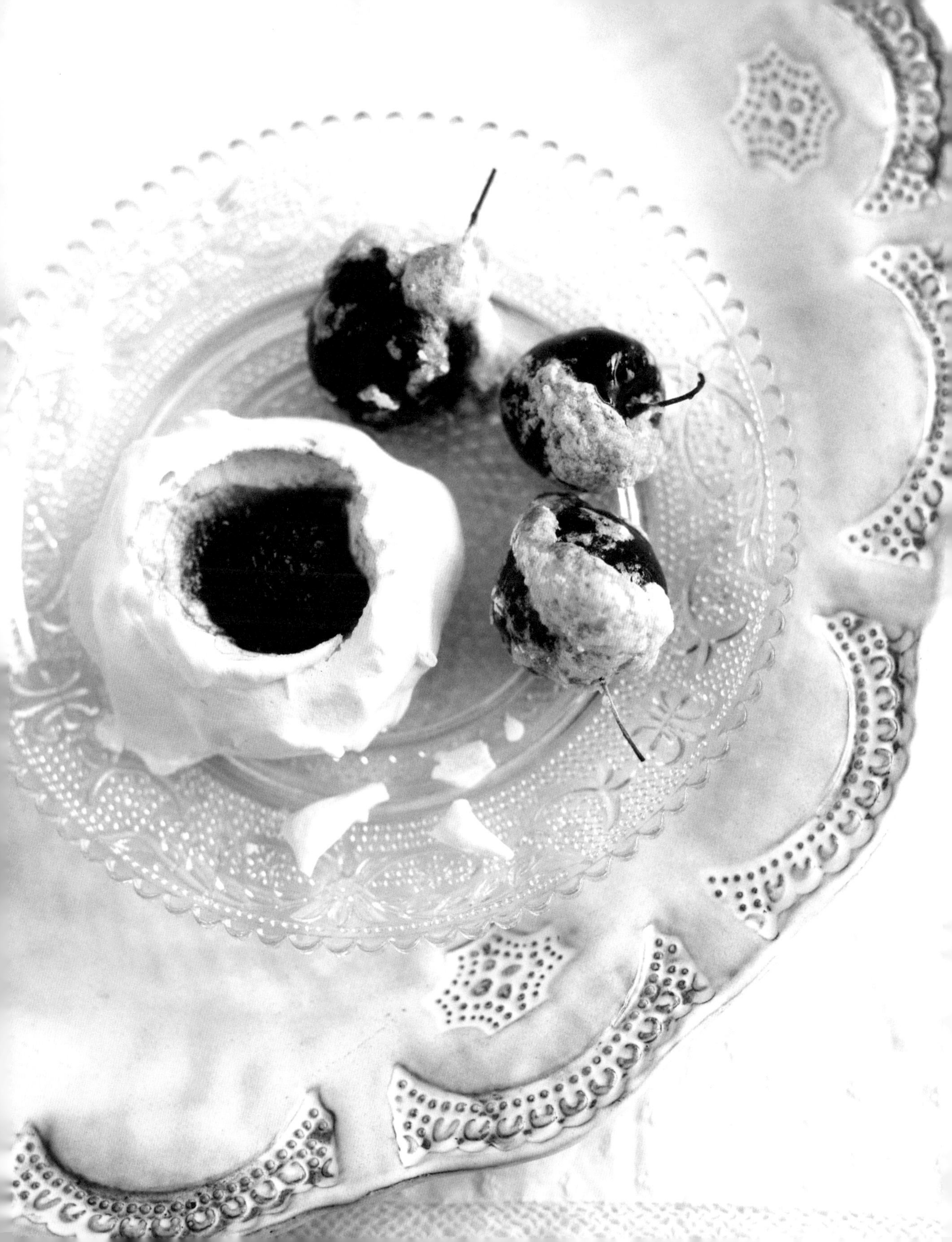

THE STILLROOM
OR PANTRY

The fruitful period of the kitchen garden was accompanied by a frenzy of preserving, so that there was something to eat all year round. Even out of season, fruit tarts could be made with the "unwholesome preserves" that Mr. Woodhouse warns his guests against. In Martha's Household Book, Mrs. Craven wrote "Good luck to your jamming" beneath her recipe for Gooseberry Cheese, and, as with all other recipe books of the time, the pages are filled with vinegars, pickles, syrups, candying, "catchups," marmalades, and preserves.

Meat and fish, too, had to be cured, salted, and pickled, particularly pork, which had poor keeping qualities. Jane writes to Cassandra (October 1 1808): "My mother has undertaken to cure six Hams for Frank; —at first it was a distress, but now it is a pleasure." Francis Austen, a naval officer, would have needed the preserved meat for his long voyages. Once meat started to go off, it had to be eaten; Mrs. Grant in *Mansfield Park* worries that the turkey she had wanted for her husband's Sunday dinner wouldn't keep that long, because of the unseasonably mild weather. Those lucky enough to have an ice-house would pack it with game; otherwise, people had to get used to it well-hung. In *The Watsons*, the gouty Mr. Watson was pleased to be treated as an invalid, partly because "the partridges were pretty high" and so sent to the other end of the table that they might not offend him. In their Southampton home, the Austens had the rare luxury of fresh fish, but salted anchovies were used extensively to give a depth of taste to fish and meat dishes.

Jane's wealthier brothers were lucky to have French wine to drink, and, in Mary Crawford's words, that "indolent, selfish bon vivant" Dr. Grant is pleased to use Henry Crawford's stay as "an excuse for drinking claret every day." The more homey Austen and Lloyd household brewed its own wine from oranges, green gooseberries, currants, cowslips, and elder. Cassandra had care of the bees and their honey was used for mead; after the poor summer of 1816 Jane wrote: "We hear now that there is to be no Honey this year. Bad news for us. —We must husband our present stock of Meads." Martha's recipe for mead includes honey, nutmeg, mace, cloves, race-ginger, and "a large handful of sweet briar" and the scary line: "Add a little balm to it, if it does not work turn it and let it stand a day or two." Brewing was a long-term project, needing knowledge of how to make the ingredients turn to drinkable alcohol without going off or exploding, how long to leave it in casks, and when to bottle and leave to age again. It was on Jane's mind when she wrote to Cassandra from Godmersham, that "The Orange Wine will want our Care soon" (June 30 1808,) and we know that the family also make spruce beer (which is served at Mr. Knightley's strawberry party at Donwell Abbey). Made from the fresh tips of spruce trees (although some recipes called for "Essence of Spruce") it was a favorite of Martha's, as Jane jokes it "is brewed in consequence" of her arrival at Southampton. (Letter to Cassandra, October 7 1808).

In addition, housewives would make their own physic—remedies for illnesses from the minor, such as sore eyes or chapped lips, to whooping cough, or consumption (tuberculosis). For this latter, perhaps knowing that somebody had gone to the trouble to take "Two ounces of the express juice of Hore-hound, mix'd with a pint of fawn's milk and sweetened with honey" (in Martha's recipe) would be as effective as the remedy itself. Cosmetics were more benign; here are lavender water and cold cream and, endearingly, a recipe from Captain Austen for Milk of Roses (rosewater, almond oil, and salt of tartar) to protect sailors' weather-beaten complexions.

GOOSEBERRY TART

Poor ten-year-old Fanny Price, arriving at Mansfield Park for the first time, is so exhausted and homesick that "vain was even the sight of a gooseberry tart towards giving her comfort." Recipes of the time were either for summer pies made with fresh gooseberries or all-year-round tarts made with jam.

1 lb/450g gooseberries
1–1½ cups/200–300g superfine (caster) sugar per 2 lb/1kg of gooseberries

Double batch of shortcrust pastry (see recipe on page 153)

1 Wash, then top and tail the gooseberries.
2 Put the gooseberries in a saucepan with a tablespoon of water and simmer very gently until the skins start to break—about 5–8 minutes. Then add sugar, starting with ½ cup/100g per 1 lb/450g of fruit and adding a little more if it needs it, and simmer for a couple of minutes more.
3 Preheat the oven to 375°F/190°C/Gas Mark 5.
4 Roll the pastry out and cut into two pieces, one twice as large as the other. Use the larger piece to line a 9–10-inch/22–25cm round metal pie pan with pastry. Roll the smaller piece out and cut into strips of about ¾-inch/2 cm wide. Pour in the fruit and make a lattice pattern on the top with the pastry strips.
5 Bake for 30 minutes until the pastry is golden.

Gooseberry Jam for Tarts Gather your gooseberries (the clear white or green sort) when ripe; top and tail, and weigh them; a pound to three quarters of a pound of fine sugar, add half a pint of water; boil and skim the sugar and water; then put the fruit, and boil gently till clear; then break and put into small pots.

MRS. RUNDELL, *A NEW SYSTEM OF DOMESTIC COOKERY*, 1806

GINGER BEER

Martha Lloyd has a recipe for refreshing and fizzy ginger beer, which a generation of Enid Blyton readers dream of having on picnics. The Georgians also had the spruce beer that Mr. Knightley serves at Donwell Abbey. Mr. Elton likes it so much he writes down the instructions for brewing it in his pocket book.

Makes about 2 quarts/liters

2 quarts/1.75 liters spring water
½ lb/225g sugar cubes
5 tbsp/40g ginger root, peeled and grated
1 lemon, sliced

1 tsp cream of tartar
2 tsp ground ginger (optional—to make a more fiery brew)
¼ tsp brewer's yeast (also known as ale yeast or wine yeast)

1 Boil the sugar in the water for a few minutes until it dissolves. Let it cool a little, then add the ginger, lemon, and cream of tartar (and extra ground ginger if using). Give it a mix and let it cool to blood temperature.

2 Then sprinkle on the yeast and let it cool completely. Cover and let it stand overnight.

3 The next day, strain it through a fine sieve or cheesecloth, and pour into clean plastic water bottles, leaving a couple of inches/5cm of air at the top. (Don't use glass bottles, in case they explode.) It should be ready after 2–3 days, when the gas has expanded inside the bottles and they feel hard to the touch. If you are planning to keep it for longer, put it in the fridge to stop the yeast working, and let some of the gas out gently, as even plastic bottles will go pop with enough pressure inside.

4 You can make this with baker's yeast, but it will leave a slightly "off" flavor in the ginger beer.

Ginger Beer Two gallons of water, two ozs of Cream of Tartar. Two lbs of lump sugar. Two lemons sliced, 2 ozs of ginger bruised. Pour the water boiling on the ingredients, then add two spoonfuls of good yeast; when cold bottle it in stone bottles, tie down the corks. It is fit to drink in 48 hours - a little more sugar is an improvement; glass bottles would not do.

MARTHA LLOYD'S HOUSEHOLD BOOK

LEMON PICKLE

This pickle was used to enhance meat and fish dishes much as preserved lemons are used in North African cuisine today. Mrs. Raffald says that she hasn't given a recipe for "cullis" (an expensive gravy) in her book as "lemon pickle and browning answers both for beauty and taste."

Makes 4 x 1 lb/450g jars

6 unwaxed lemons
½ cup/100g sea salt
¼ cup/50g fresh grated horseradish (leave this out if you can't find fresh)
6 cloves garlic
2 tsp whole cloves

2–3 blades mace
1 quart/1 liter white wine vinegar
2 tsp freshly grated nutmeg
2 tsp cayenne pepper or one whole chili, chopped finely
1 tbsp mustard powder

1 Cut the lemons into eighths, discarding the pips. Sprinkle them with the salt and leave them in a warm place in a non-metallic bowl for a day or two, or at least overnight, to soften.
2 Grate the horseradish and crush the garlic roughly and mix this up with the lemon pieces.
3 Toast the cloves and mace in a dry frying pan and crush them roughly in a pestle and mortar, then sprinkle these over the lemons.
4 Bring the vinegar to boil with the cayenne, nutmeg, and mustard powder and let it boil for 15 minutes, then pour the boiling liquid over the lemons. Pour it while still warm into warm jars that have been sterilized in the oven at 350°F/180°C/Gas Mark 4 for 20 minutes.
5 Keep for 4–6 weeks before using. It should keep for up to a year.

Receipt to make lemon pickle Take six large lemons, or a doz Lady Williams small ones, pare them thick and cut them into eight half quarters. One pound of salt, six large cloves of Garlic, two ozs of horse radish, nutmeg, mace, cloves and Cayenne pepper, of each a quarter of an oz; two ozs of the best flower of mustard, and let it boil a quarter of an hour, then set it by, and stir it once or twice a day for a fortnight, then strain it up and bottle it.

MARTHA LLOYD'S HOUSEHOLD BOOK

Gifts, Drinks, and Preserves

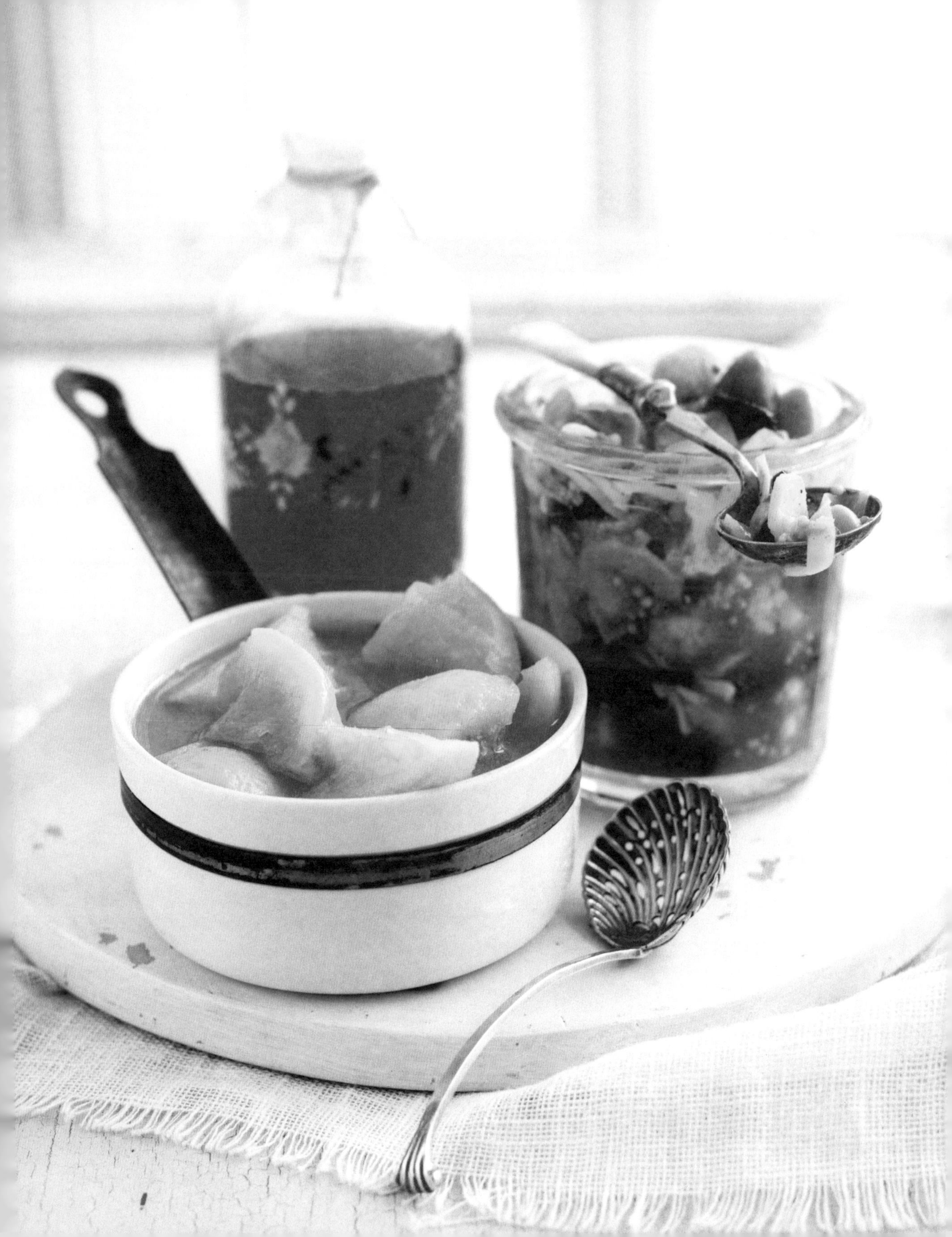

INDIA PICKLE

This gets its cheerful yellow color from turmeric and its distinctive taste from mustard which also helps to preserve the vegetables. Why we now call it "piccalilli" is something of a mystery; Hannah Glasse was the first to introduce India Pickle as Paco-Lilla; a decade later Mrs. Raffald was calling it Piccalillo.

Makes about 6–7 1 lb/450g jars

9 oz/250g fresh garlic

9 oz/250g fresh ginger root

Approximately 1½ lb/650g sea salt

4½ lb/2 kg vegetables including 1 large white cabbage and 2 medium cauliflowers. You could also add French beans, pickling onions, little cucumbers

scant ½ cup/60g mustard seeds

⅓ cup/40g dried long pepper or ⅓ cup/40g black peppercorns plus 1 tsp red pepper (chili) flakes

2 quarts/2 liters white wine vinegar or white malt vinegar

1 cup/250ml cider vinegar

4 tsp ground turmeric

4 tsp ground allspice

2 tsp mustard powder (optional—not in original recipe)

½ cup/50g cornstarch (cornflour) (optional—not in original recipe but it gives a thicker liquid, more like modern piccalilli)

1 tbsp sugar (optional—not in original recipe)

1 Peel the garlic and ginger and slice thinly. Scatter generously with salt and leave overnight in a cool place. Quarter and core the cabbage and trim the cauliflower into small florets.

2 Make a strong brine (10 oz/300g salt per quart/liter of water); you will probably need about 2 quarts/2 liters of water to immerse the vegetables entirely. Put the vegetables in a non-metallic container and completely cover with brine (weight them with an upturned plate if they keep bobbing to the surface). Leave to stand overnight.

3 The next day, remove the vegetables from the brine and rinse them briefly under cold running water.

4 Bring a large, deep saucepan of water to a rolling boil. Add the cabbage quarters. After 2 minutes, add the cauliflower florets, and other vegetables. After an additional 3 minutes, remove all the vegetables from the pan and rinse them with cold water. Leave to drain well, then shred the cabbage into strips with a large kitchen knife (as fine or as coarse as you like,) gently squeezing out as much excess water as you can as you go. Arrange the vegetables on baking sheets in single layers.

5 Rinse the garlic and ginger well to remove the excess salt, and dry well, then spread in a single layer on a baking sheet and place in your oven on its lowest temperature for 90 minutes, along with the sheets of vegetables.

6 Toast the mustard seeds in a dry frying pan. Place in a mortar along with the peppercorns and chili flakes and crush very lightly. You don't want to reduce anything to a powder, just to crack some of the seeds.

7 In a non-metallic or stainless preserving pan (large enough to hold all your veg,) combine the mustard seeds, pepper, garlic, ginger, and vinegars and bring to just under boiling point. Put into a cup the turmeric and allspice and, if you are using them, the mustard powder and cornstarch, and thicken first with a little vinegar to get a smooth paste, then add some of the hot vinegar to make a thin paste. Tip this back into the vinegar pan, simmer everything together gently for 3 minutes, then add the veg and bring to a boil. The moment the pan boils, remove from the heat and set aside to cool.

8 When cool enough to handle but still warm, spoon it into warm jars that have been sterilized in the oven at 350°F/180°C/Gas Mark 4 for 20 minutes and seal immediately; the heat of the pickle will help make the jar airtight.

9 Leave in a cool, dark place for 4–6 weeks before using. It should keep for a year.

Take White Cabbage and Cauliflower, cut them in quarters and boil them one minute. Put a little salt in the water then separate them leaf from leaf on a tin and dry them, put them into the following pickle. A gallon of vinegar, one oz of long pepper, a ¼ of a lb of ginger, an oz of Jamaica pepper, half a pint of mustard seed bruised, an oz of Termeric and a pound of garlic boiled salted and diced as the cabbage. Cover your pickle boiling and let it stand to be cold before you put in the cabbage. Anything else may be done in the same manner.

Martha Lloyd's Household Book

RASPBERRY VINEGAR

The Austens grew raspberries in their gardens in Southampton and Chawton; when Jane stayed with her brother Henry in Covent Garden she sent an SOS to Cassandra asking her to bring him some raspberry jam (letter to Cassandra, March 5 1814). Here is Martha Lloyd's raspberry vinegar for sore throats.

1 lb/450g raspberries (use up the mushy ones, but cut off any moldy bits)

2 cups/450ml white wine vinegar or cider vinegar
2 cups/400g sugar

1 Mash the raspberries, add the vinegar, and leave in covered bottles or jars for 5–10 days, giving it a shake or a stir every now and again.

2 Drain it thoroughly through cheesecloth for a few hours (but don't push the raspberry mush through as it will eventually discolor the vinegar.)

3 Put it into a non-metallic or stainless saucepan with the sugar and bring to a boil. Boil it for 10–15 minutes, removing any scum from the surface. When it is quite cold, put it into sterilized glass bottles with airtight lids. For a gift, tie "a piece of linnen or pricked paper," as Martha Lloyd suggests, over the tops.

4 To serve: Use a splash in salad dressings and gravies, as a sauce on ice cream, watered down as a refreshing cordial or, as Martha does, with brandy for a sore throat.

To make Raspberry Vinegar *Take ripe Raspberries pick'd when quite dry, fill a stone jar with them within 2 inches of the top, then pour upon them Vinegar sufficient to quite cover them. Tye the pot quite close with leather. Let it stand 12 days in a dry place then take the buff scum and pour off the ligor quite clear by drawing the dregs through a cullender. To a pint of juice add a lb of lump sugar, boil it to a syrup keeping it scum'd, when quite cold put it into bottles tying them with a piece of linnen or pricked paper.*

(Dr Molesworth rect. [receipt/recipe] for fevers, sore throats or any small beverage — in ulcerated sore throats two teaspoonsful of Brandy to one of Raspberry Syrup, taken three or four times a day.)

Martha Lloyd's Household Book

PASTRY

Before the days of dietary domination by potatoes, pasta, and rice, it is not surprising that menus featured many hefty pies and tarts. Every cookbook offered a huge range of recipes for pastry or "paste" with varying quantities of flour, butter, sugar, cream, eggs, suet, and even ground rice or potatoes. Mrs. Austen gave Martha Lloyd two recipes for pastry made from butter and lard. These two, from Mrs. Rundell, are a little lighter.

Shortcrust pastry

1¼ cups/170g all-purpose (plain) flour

Pinch of salt

Scant stick/115g unsalted butter (cold, from the fridge)

2–3 tbsp cold water

1 Put the flour and salt into a bowl.

2 Add the cold butter, then chop it with a knife until each piece of butter is as small as you can make it; along the way, make sure the butter pieces are thoroughly coated in flour. When you can chop no more, rub it in using just your fingertips; this keeps the mixture from becoming too warm, which may make it dense. Sprinkle in 2 tablespoons of cold water and mix it with a knife until it clumps together. Add a little more water if necessary. Bring it together with your hands to make a smooth dough, but don't knead it.

3 Cover it with plastic wrap (clingfilm) and let it rest in the fridge for 20 minutes before using.

4 When you are ready to use it, roll it out to an even thickness on a lightly floured surface.

Sweet rich shortcrust pastry

1¾ cups/225g all-purpose (plain) flour, plus extra for dusting

Pinch of salt

2 tsp superfine (caster) sugar

1 stick/125g unsalted butter (cold, from the fridge)

1 egg yolk

3 tbsp cold water

1 Mix the flour, sugar, and salt in a bowl. Add the butter and chop and rub it in as in the previous recipe. Stir the cold water and egg yolk together, and add it to the flour and butter mixture. Use a knife to stir it so the mixture forms nice big clumps, adding a little more water if necessary. Bring it together with your hands to make a smooth dough, but don't knead it.

2 Wrap it in plastic wrap (clingfilm) and let it rest in the fridge for 20 minutes before using.

3 When you are ready to use it, roll it out on a lightly floured surface, handling it as little as possible to keep it cool.

Excellent short crust

Make two ounces of white sugar, pounded and sifted, quite dry; then mix it with a pound of flour well dried: rub into it three ounces of butter, so fine as not to be seen; into some cream put the yolks of two eggs, beaten, and mix the above into a smooth paste; roll it thin, and bake it in a moderate oven.

Another, not sweet but rich

Rub six ounces of butter in eight ounces of fine flour; mix it into a stiffish paste, with as little water as possible; beat it well, and roll it thin. This, as well as the former, is proper for tarts of fresh or preserved fruits. Bake in a moderate oven.

Observations on pastry

An adept in pastry never leaves any part of it adhering to the board or dish, used in making. It is best when rolled on marble, or very large slate. In very hot weather, the butter should be put into cold water to make it as firm as possible; and if made early in the morning, and preserved from the air until it is to be baked, the cook will find it much better. A good hand at pastry will use much less butter, and produce lighter crust than others. Salt butter, if very good, and well washed, makes a fine flaky crust.

MRS RUNDELL, *A NEW SYSTEM OF DOMESTIC COOKERY*, 1806

Gifts, Drinks, and Preserves

BIBLIOGRAPHY

Primary sources

Acton, Eliza, *Modern Cookery for Private Families*, London, 1845

Austen, Jane, *Emma*, ed Fiona Stafford, Penguin, London, 2003

    Lady Susan, The Watsons, Sanditon, ed Margaret Drabble, Penguin, London, 2003

    Mansfield Park, ed Kathryn Sutherland, Penguin, London, 2003

    Northanger Abbey, ed Marilyn Butler, Penguin, London, 2003

    Persuasion, ed Gillian Beer, Penguin, London, 2003

    Pride and Prejudice, ed Vivien Jones, Penguin, London, 2003

    Sense and Sensibility, ed Ros Ballaster, second edition, Penguin, London, 2003

    Minor Works, ed. R.W. Chapman, Oxford, revised edition, 1963

    Jane Austen's Letters, ed. R.W. Chapman, second edition, Oxford, 1979

Beeton, Isabella, *Beeton's Book of Household Management*, London, 1861

Collingwood, Francis and Woollams, John, *The Universal Cook, and city and country housekeeper*, London, 1792

Dods, Mistress Margaret (pseud. Christine Isobel Johnstone), *The Cook and Housewife's Manual: A Practical System of Modern Domestic Cookery and Family Management*, Edinburgh, 1826 (fifth edition, 1833)

Farley, John, *The London Art of Cookery And Housekeeper's Complete Assistant On a New Plan*, (Principal Cook at the London Tavern), London, 1783

Frazer, Mrs, *The Practice of Cookery, Pastry, Pickling, Preserving &c*, Edinburgh, second edition, 1795

Glasse, Hannah, *The Art of Cookery Made Plain and Easy (by a Lady)*, London, 1747

Grigson, Jane, *English Food*, Ebury, London, 1974

Gunter, William, *The Confectioner's Oracle*, London, 1830

Hartley, Dorothy, *Food in England*, Macdonald, London, 1954

Jarrin, G.A., *The Italian Confectioner or Complete Economy of Desserts*, London, 1820

Kitchiner, Dr. William, *Apicius Redivivus or The Cook's Oracle*, London, 1817

MacDonald, Duncan, *The New London Family Cook or, Town and Country Housekeeper's Guide*, London, 1808

Nott, John, *The Cooks and Confectioners Dictionary or, The Accomplish'd Housewives Companion*, London, 1723

Raffald, Elizabeth, *The Experienced English Housekeeper*, Manchester, 1769

Rundell, Maria Eliza, *A New System of Domestic Cookery*, John Murray, London, 1806 (revised edition 1816)

Verral (also spelled Verrall), William, *A Complete System of Cookery*, London, 1759

White, Florence, *Good Things in England: A Practical Cookery Book for Everyday Use*, Jonathan Cape, London, 1932

Secondary sources

Black, Maggie and Le Faye, Deirdre, *The Jane Austen Cookbook*, British Museum Press, London, 1995

Black, Maggie, *A Taste of History: 10,000 Years of Food in Britain*, The British Museum Press, London, 1997

Brown, Peter, *Pyramids of Pleasure: Eating and Dining in 18th Century England, An exhibition at Fairfax House*, York, 1990

Davidson, Alan, *The Oxford Companion to Food*, Oxford, 1999

Hickman, Peggy, *A Jane Austen Household Book*, with Martha Lloyd's recipes, David and Charles, London, 1977

Lane, Maggie, *Jane Austen and Food*, Hambleton Press, London, 1995

Sanbourn, Vic, *Jane Austen's World*, http://janeaustensworld.wordpress.com/

Wilks, Brian, *Jane Austen*, Hamlyn, London 1978

The Republic of Pemberley, www.pemberley.com, website

Cookery

Collister, Linda, *The Great British Book of Baking*, Michael Joseph, London, 2010

Conran, Caroline; Conran, Terence; Hopkinson, Simon; *The Conran Cookbook*, Conran Octopus, London, 1997

David, Elizabeth, *English Bread and Yeast Cookery*, Allen Lane, London, 1977

Fearnley-Whittingstall, Hugh, *The River Cottage Meat Book*, Hodder and Stoughton, London, 2004

Note: in the text, the date of the first edition is given. Where a different edition has also been consulted, this is indicated in parentheses.

INDEX

ACKNOWLEDGMENTS

Thanks to David and Charles for their kind permission to reproduce the version of Martha Lloyd's recipes from *A Jane Austen Household Book*, which have been written out and rationalized by Peggy Hickman; and to Oxford University Press for their kind permission to quote from Jane Austen's letters from their edition edited by R.W. Chapman.

My greatest thanks go to those excellent cooks who generously gave their advice, expertise, and time testing recipes: Mariateresa Boffo-O'Kane, Isabelle de Cat, Sarah Christie, Simone Doctors, Ben Martin, Ruth Segal, Lesley Reynolds, Phoebe Taplin, James Urquhart, Shan Vahidy, Jill Vogler, Miranda Vogler-Koss, Hannah Vogler, Miriam Vogler, Emma Whiting. Thanks also to Cindy Richards, Penny Craig, and particularly Sally Powell at CICO Books, and to the ever-supportive Peta Nightingale at LAW. And, of course, Stewart McGillivray, chief tester of ideas and recipes.

PICTURE CREDITS

Additional images: page 14, © Lebrecht Authors/Lebrecht Music & Arts/Corbis; page 34, © Andreas von Einsiedel; pages 62, 86, 144, photography by Andreas von Einsiedel © CICO Books Limited.